W9-DDK-659

LIGHTS OUT

David Crawford

This is a work of fiction.
Any similarity to any person, living
or dead, is purely coincidental.

Halffast Publishing
Texas, USA
Copyright © 2010 David Crawford
All rights reserved.
ISBN: 0615427359
ISBN-13: 978-0615427355

Acknowledgements

I never knew how many people it took to get a book into print until I wrote this one. Literally, hundreds of people have helped me with suggestions, corrections, and encouragement. Without all of you who read, helped with, and encouraged others to read the online version, Lights Out would not have been finished. I feel this is not so much my story, as it is our story. Thank you all so much.

A few people need to be mentioned by name. John "Frugal" Maniatty for providing the first place for me to post this humble story, Steve "Desert Doc" Nichols for all the initial help and encouragement, Jim "Slipstick" Karenko for being my first editor without me even having to ask and for all of the technical info, Paul "Fight 4 Your Rights" Britton for pimping LO all over the Internet, James W. Rawles for recommending it to all his readers, Joe "Giltweasel" Devos for creating and hosting the PDF that went viral, Eric "Melbo" Melbardis for hosting the story and making it a household name in the survival/preparedness community, Elaine Scott-Culbertson for going through the story multiple times and catching all the errors no mere mortal could possibly see, Sherrie Carlson for editing while she read the story the first time, Robert "Acman" Jewell for kicking me in the ass when I needed it, Norman Comparini and Karisa Prestera for the help with the cover and the marketing, Fernando "Ferfal" Aguirre for encouraging me when I needed it, James Yeager of Tactical Response and John Willis of SOE Tactical Gear for making me believe the work has commercial value, and finally to my wife, Rosemary, and my daughter, Samantha, for being my first proofreaders, and to my son, Danny, for the artwork and being a sounding board.

Again, thanks to everyone who had a hand in getting the story to this point. You all are the best!

To my mother, Claudette, who always believed in me,
and to Masters Felix Lara and Nick Smith who
made me believe in myself.

Chapter 1

"Damn it!"

Mark Turner didn't curse often, but he was pissed. It wasn't the fact that the lights went out that upset him. They did that three or four times a year in this older, industrial section of town. What bothered him was the fact that the uninterrupted power supply hadn't kept his computer running, and he'd lost over an hour's worth of work. He needed tech support to send him a new UPS, so he picked up the phone and dialed their number with the help of the dim glow of the emergency lights. Nothing. He hung up the phone and picked it up again, putting it up to his ear this time. There was no dial tone.

"Crap!" he said to himself. "Whatever happened took the phone system down, too."

Mark stepped out into the hall. Some of the other accountants were already there.

"Hey, Mark."

"Hey, yourself, Jim."

Jim Davis was Mark's closest friend at work, but no one would have guessed it by looking at them. They were complete opposites. Jim was six-foot-three, 215 pounds, and had super jock written all over him. Mark was barely five-foot-nine and had an average build. Even though he held a black belt in karate, he looked like a computer nerd.

"What's the matter?" Jim asked.

"Oh, it's just that my UPS went bad, and I lost a bunch of work," Mark answered.

"That's strange; my UPS went down, too. Maybe they bought a bad lot of them. Well, hopefully we'll get to go home early with the power out, and we can worry about it tomorrow."

"Fat chance, buddy."

"Yeah, I guess you're right," Jim said, as his shoulders dropped.

After five or ten minutes of discussing the upcoming football season, Suzy Sullivan, the office worrywart, interrupted the guys.

"Something's really wrong!" she said.

"No joke," Jim replied with a wry grin. "The power went out again."

"No," she answered, oblivious to the sarcasm, "it's more than that. I went out to my car to listen to the news to see what happened, but the radio won't work, and the car won't start either. So, I pulled out my cell phone to call my husband, and it's dead, too."

"Probably your car battery is dead, and the power outage knocked out all the close cell sites," Jim said.

"I don't think so. The car will turn over…it just won't start, and my cell phone won't even come on. I charged it up last night, too."

Mark pulled his phone out of his pocket. It was off and wouldn't come on no matter how many times he pushed the power button. Jim's was the same.

"Let's go take a look at your car," Mark suggested.

When they got outside, Mark noticed that there wasn't a cloud in the sky, and it was already starting to get warm. He wondered how the power going out

1

could have kept their cell phones from coming on. He wasn't an electrical engineer, but it just didn't make sense.

When they got to Suzy's late model Mustang, Mark asked her to pop the hood.

"Now, try and start it."

Suzy turned the key, and the motor turned over but wouldn't start.

"See what I mean?" Suzy said, mostly to Jim.

Mark reached down and pulled a plug wire loose and held it close to the engine block.

"Try it one more time, Suzy."

Suzy engaged the starter again.

"OK, that's enough."

"What's wrong with it?" she asked.

"Well, I don't know exactly why, but you don't have any fire."

"What do you mean?"

"You see, you only need two things for an engine to run…fuel and fire. Gas and an electrical spark to ignite it, in other words, and you don't have any spark."

"Why not?"

"I don't know, Suzy. I'm just an accountant."

"Jim, why don't you go try your truck, and I'll try mine."

As Jim walked toward his truck, Suzy followed Mark to his old Jeep.

"I just don't know what could have caused all of this, but it's got to be bad. Oh, God, this is really bad. I have to get home. There are probably a hundred things that could cause this, and none of them are good. What if…"

"Suzy! Calm down. We don't know enough to even guess what's going on, and panicking isn't going to help, no matter what."

Mark tried the Jeep, but just like Suzy's car, it would turn over but not start. He had hoped that since it was a 1978 model and didn't have all the new electronics like the newer cars, it would be okay.

"My truck won't start either," Jim said as he walked up. "Do you hear that?"

"Hear what?" Suzy said nervously.

"Exactly. I don't hear any cars going up and down the street."

"Let's go look," Mark suggested.

"When they got to where they could see the street, Mark's eyebrows knitted and his back stiffened. All of the vehicles were stopped. Many had their hoods opened with the owners looking under them. What could have done this, Mark wondered, just as he caught some movement out of the corner of his eye. Coming down the road was an old city bus, slowly weaving its way between the stalled cars. People were trying to wave him down, but the driver just kept on going, a little puff of black smoke belching from the exhaust stack every time he mashed the throttle. As he passed, Mark could see that the bus was crammed full of people. It stopped at the bus stop less than a half block down from where Mark, Jim and Suzy were standing. There must have been at least twenty people waiting to get on. The driver opened the door but didn't allow anyone on. Mark heard him yell to the people on the curb that his bus was full but there would be another in about ten minutes. Mark wondered what the chances were that it would be full, too.

"Look at that!" Suzy yelled, snapping Mark out of his own thoughts. Suzy was pointing to the north.

There were four distinct columns of thick, black smoke rising into the air. Three were in the direction of the airport, and one was further to the east. One of the columns, the one that looked closest to the airport, was significantly bigger than the other three.

"I'm thinking Suzy's right. Something *is* really wrong!" Jim said.

"What do we do now?" Suzy asked.

"Let's go back inside and see if anyone has a radio that will work," Mark answered.

"I think Mr. Davis has an emergency radio in his office," Suzy said excitedly.

Mr. Davis was the owner of the company, and Suzy was his executive assistant. Mr. Davis hardly ever came in, and Mark never had been able to figure out why he needed an assistant, but Suzy was at least entertaining with all of her conspiracy theories and paranoia.

When they got to Mr. Davis's office, Suzy unlocked the door and walked in. Mark had never been inside, and he felt a little funny about entering, so he looked through the door. He could feel Jim stretching to see over him. Suzy walked to a metal storage cabinet and opened it. She pulled a green ammo can out and set it on the desk. The ammo can surprised Mark, and he wished he could see what else was in the cabinet. Suzy opened the can and pulled out a wind-up emergency radio. She walked over and gave it to Mark. He turned it on, but nothing happened.

"It doesn't work, either," he said.

"I think it's one of those wind-up ones," Jim said.

"Oh, yeah," Mark cranked the radio and static came from the speaker.

"Well at least it comes on," Jim said. "Try 1200, Mark."

Marked rolled the dial to 1200.

...is the Emergency Alert System. Please tune to 640 AM for further instructions. This is 1200 AM, broadcasting on reduced backup power. This is the Emergency Alert System. Please tune to 640 AM for further instructions. This is 1200 AM, broadcast...

Marked spun the dial to 640.

...five minutes. This is the Emergency Alert System. Please stand by for an important announcement in five minutes. This is the Emergency Al...

Mark turned the volume down.

"I guess we'll know what's going on in five minutes," he said.

As word got around that there was a working radio, the area outside Mr. Davis' office began to fill up with people asking all kinds of questions and telling everyone what they thought was going on. When the hallway could hold no one else, Mark suggested that they all go to the break room, where people kept pouring in. After five minutes, Mark turned the radio up.

...Ladies and Gentlemen, the Vice-President of the United States.

My fellow Americans, as you know, an hour and three minutes ago, the power went out. Also affected were most of the communication and

3

transportation systems in the continental United States, most of Canada, and parts of Mexico. We are receiving reports that parts of Europe have been affected, as well. This seems to be the effect of a large Electromagnetic Pulse. We are not sure at this time of the source of the high energy burst, and we do not know if it was accidental, an act of God, or a malicious attack. We do know that the EMP is not the result of a nuclear attack. I repeat, we have NOT been attacked with nuclear weapons. As many of you know, the President and most of his cabinet were on their way back to Washington. Air Force One was waiting to take off from Dallas when The Burst hit. Several planes that were taking off or landing crashed. We are not sure if one of them hit the President's plane, but we have not had any contact with him since The Burst.

"Oh my God! The President is dead!" someone in the room cried.

"SHHHHHHH!!!" others replied.

I am assuming command until we can contact the President. I am activating all of the reserve units of the military until we can determine the cause and source of the EMP burst. I am asking all of the state governors to call up the National Guard to help local authorities until we can get the power back on. All off-duty police, fire, and emergency personnel should report for duty as soon as possible. I am asking all other Americans to remain calm and to try to get to your homes. Most of your vehicles will not run until the electronics have been replaced. If you have a running vehicle, please help your friends and neighbors get to their families. FEMA will be setting up shelters in the major cities for those of you that cannot get home. You can get information on these shelters here on these EAS stations, as it becomes available.

Our first priority is to get the power, communications, and transportation systems back online as quickly as possible. However, it may take a day or two to get the power back in the major cities, and the rural areas may take a little longer than that. Please stay in your homes and follow the instructions of your local authorities. I am imposing a curfew for all Americans effective at dark.

This is an emergency we Americans have not had to face before. I know that if we all pull together just as we did on September 11th, we will emerge from this stronger and wiser as a nation. We will keep you as updated as possible. Thank you for your cooperation and God bless.

This is 640 AM. We will be back in a moment with a list of FEMA shelters for the city.

Mark turned the radio off.

"What are we going to do now?" someone yelled.

"Everybody, just simmer down now," Todd Rosenberg, the company CEO, instructed as he stepped up on a chair so everyone could hear him. "I would like to meet with all the department heads in the conference room in five minutes. Is Tom Baskins here?"

"Right here, Todd."

"Good. Tom will you go see how many of the delivery trucks will run and then come to the conference room?"

"On my way."

"OK, everybody else, please go out and see if your car will start. If it will, come back and give your name and where you live to Mark Turner here. If it won't, don't panic. We'll find a way to get you home. Come back to the break room or go wait in your office and just relax. Everything is going to be okay."

Almost everyone made a mass exit toward the parking lot.

"Mark, can you get a pad and write down where everyone lives who has a running car?"

"Sure thing."

"And do you think you can dig up a map of the city?"

"I have one in the Jeep."

"Great. Just try to keep everyone calm, okay?"

"Okay, Todd. Just one question."

"Yes."

"Who's supposed to keep me calm?"

Chapter 2

Mark was worried about his family. As he walked to his Jeep to get the map, he thought about how he was going to get them home. Jessica, his wife, and David, his thirteen-year-old, were at the junior high. He knew there was no way Jess's newer SUV was going to start. Samantha was at the high school, where she was a junior. The junior high was only about three miles from the house, but the high school was a lot further than that. Mark wasn't really sure, but he figured it was between ten and twelve miles…a long way to walk, but not nearly as long as the twenty-six miles he might have to walk just to get home. It was comforting to know that they should be safe at the schools until he could get there. As he was walking back into the building, he heard a car start. It was Joe Babcock's old Volkswagen Rabbit. He walked over to the car.

"Hey, Joe, looks like you're going to be Mr. Popular."

"Yeah, lucky me! I bought this diesel Rabbit for the gas mileage, not because it was EMP proof. Look, Mark, I've got to get home. I think I'm just going to bug out right now."

"Joe, I don't know how smart that would be. Everyone's going to hate you if you just leave, and they won't forget it when the power comes back on either. Why don't you stay long enough to hear what Mr. Rosenburg and the department heads come up with? Probably they just want you to give a ride to the people who live closest to you. If not and you don't like the plan, you can leave then."

"I guess you're right. This whole thing is just kind of freaking me out. I'm sorry."

"Don't worry about it. We all feel the same way, and if my Jeep would start, I'd think about leaving, too. Now, what part of town do you live in?"

When Mark got back to the break room, there were three people waiting for him. Two had diesel pickups, and one had a diesel Cadillac. Mark was encouraged that perhaps the old diesel pickup he had at home would run. He unfolded the map on one of the tables and started marking where the diesel owners lived. As he finished, Todd and the department heads came into the room.

"What have you got, Mark?" Todd asked.

"We have four running cars and trucks, all diesels by the way. Two live on the north side, one out just west of town, and the last one lives about twenty-five miles south of town, close to Poteet. What did you all come up with?"

"Well, best count, we have a hundred and sixty-eight people to get home. Two of the delivery trucks will run, both of the older ones; the new one won't start. Tom thinks he can get the old gasoline flatbed truck maintenance uses to run if he can get a new coil and points and something else. I can't remember what he called it."

"Condenser?" Mark asked.

"Yeah, that's it. Since it doesn't have a computer, he thinks that's all it will take. Anyway, maintenance is going to build some benches to put in the back of the delivery trucks, and we'll use them like busses. They can hold about thirty people each. While they work on one, Tom is going to take the other to see if he can find the parts for the flatbed. Anyway, we're going to get everyone out into the parking lot and figure out where they need to go."

"Todd, my old Jeep probably just needs the same parts the flatbed does. Do you think Tom could pick them up for me while he's out?"

"That's a good idea. We'll see if anyone else has an older car that he thinks we can get started, as well. You seem to know a little about cars; maybe you can help him?" Todd suggested.

"Well, I was kind of a gear head back in high school, but that was all older stuff. I don't know much about these new cars."

"It's not the new ones we're worried about, is it?"

"I guess you're right."

The two men walked out into the parking lot. While they were waiting for everyone to assemble, they listened to the radio again. The station was restating what the Vice President had said and giving the locations of the FEMA shelters. Mark thought to himself that things would have to be really bad for him to go to one of those shelters. When it looked like most everyone was there, Todd stepped up into the bed of his brand new pickup. It struck Mark as strange that, just the week before, he'd been envious of the truck. Now it was serving the most useful purpose it could…as a platform. Just as Todd was beginning to speak, Billy Newman, the head of maintenance, ran up and whispered something to him, then ran back off toward the maintenance building.

"OK, this is where we are. We have two delivery trucks that will run, and maintenance is going to build some benches for them. We can get you all home in them. It won't be comfortable, but it's better than walking. Tom and Mark are going to try to get some of the older vehicles fixed. If your car is older and doesn't have a computer, come see one of them, and they'll try to help you. We have four folks with personal vehicles that will run, and we're asking them to carpool some of you home if you live close to them. We have several hundred gallons each of gas and diesel for our trucks, and anyone who helps take people home is welcome to some. Billy just told me that the gasoline generator is working and that he can get the bobtails ready pretty quickly now that they can use the power tools. Tom was going to take one of the bobtails to get parts for the cars, but now that Billy can work on both of them quickly, would one of you who has a running car be willing to take Tom and Mark to the auto parts place?"

"I can take them," one of the men with a diesel pickup said.

"Thanks. That will help a lot. Okay, Mark has a map of the city, and Billy should be bringing us a board to tack it up on in a minute. Suzy has some pushpins, and I would like everyone to come up in an orderly fashion and put a pushpin where you live. If you don't live in town, then put a pin on the edge in the direction you live. I know you're all nervous to get home, and we're going to try to work it out so we can get the most people home the quickest. If you live close and want to walk, that's fine. Human Resources has list of everyone. If you decide to walk, please let them know, so that we can make sure we don't lose anyone. Make sure you drink plenty of water before you leave. It's going to be really hot today. I wish we had some canteens or something so you could carry some with you."

"Excuse me, Todd." It was James Houseman from Human Resources. "We have some of those promotional sports bottles left over from last year."

"Really? How many?"

"At least a couple of hundred, I would guess."

"That's great. Alright, if you're going to walk home, see James and get a sports bottle for water before you leave." Todd paused. "Here comes Billy with the board for the map. So, if you have an older car, see Tom and Mark. If you want to walk home see James and Mary from HR. Everyone else, get a pushpin from Suzy and put it on the map. As soon as we get the trucks ready, we'll get started. Any questions?"

A woman in the back raised her hand.

"Yes?"

"My mother lives with me, and she's on an electric oxygen pump. She can't go more than an hour or two without it, so I really need to get home to check on her."

"Good point. Does anyone else need to get home quick?"

About 40 hands went up.

"OK, I know we're all anxious, but does anyone else have a life or death situation?"

No one said anything.

"Where do you live, Sarah?"

Mark was always impressed by Todd's ability to remember everyone's name.

"Over close to the medical center."

"Mark, do any of the running car owners live close to there?"

"No," Mark answered, "but I bet Joe Babcock would be willing to take her."

"How about it Joe?" Todd asked.

"Sure thing!" Joe responded, giving Mark a grateful look. "Cindy and Bill live close to me, so I can take them, too."

"OK, then you guys check out with HR and get going. Joe, do you need any fuel?"

"No, I filled up last night."

"OK, everyone else knows what to do, right?"

About thirty people came over to where Tom and Mark were standing.

Mark asked the first one, "What kind of car do you have?"

"An '88 Taurus."

"OK, everyone listen," Tom began. "If you have a car with fuel injection, we can't help you. Everything since about '85 has fuel injection, and that means they have a computer. If you're not sure, we can go look."

Almost two-thirds of the group left with dejected looks. After looking at several of the other cars and eliminating them for having computers, they were left with four cars plus the Jeep and flatbed that they thought might be easily salvageable. Dave Thomson, the man who volunteered to take Tom and Mark, started up his truck, and they all loaded up. On the way, Mark thought about his family and hoped they were okay. A look at the other men told him they were thinking similar thoughts. It didn't seem like it had been a little over two hours since the lights had gone off. Things were happening fast. Mark still had the radio in his pocket, so the men listened to it and heard mostly the same news as before, except that the mayor had come on and asked all the police and fire personnel to report for duty. He said the new city busses that were propane powered to reduce pollution weren't working, but that about twenty percent of the fleet were still the old diesel engine busses and that they were still working. He said that they were working on a revised route schedule and would be passing it on as soon as it was ready.

When they got to the parts store, Mark noticed it was an independently owned store, much to his amazement. He thought they'd all been run out of business by the big chain stores. Tom knew the owner, and they had no problem getting the parts they needed and charging it to the company. Dave figured it would be a good idea to get a new serpentine belt for his truck, and when he didn't have quite enough cash, the owner just put it on an invoice and said that Dave could come back and pay for it when the lights came back on. On the way back, Tom commented on how he could have saved the company a little money by buying at one of the big chains, but that he and Todd thought it was a good idea to support local businesses when they could.

"It sure paid off for us right now," he added. "Just try getting a favor like that from Manny, Moe, and Jack! If their computers are down, they can't even sell a pack of gum."

When they got back to work, they decided that the flatbed was the priority, and in less than fifteen minutes, they had it running. There was a cheer from a group of onlookers who had come over to watch. Mark really wanted to work on the Jeep next, but he knew everyone else was just as anxious as he was. He told Tom he could wait until last, and Tom thanked him and asked him to drive the flatbed over to Billy. After he delivered the truck, he walked over to Todd and the map.

"Hey, Mark. How'd it go?"

"We got the flatbed running, and Billy's working on the benches for it right now. He said it should be done in about twenty minutes and should hold eighteen or twenty people. How's it going over here?"

"Good. We only have thirty-six to get home still. As soon as the flat bed is ready, we have a group of seventeen to take to the northeast side. How about the Jeep, is it running?"

"Not yet, I told Tom we could work on the others first. How are you going to get home?"

"Well, three others and I don't live that far from Dave, so I'm going to ask him to take us as soon as everyone else is gone," Todd said.

"That's good. Well, I'd better get back to helping Tom."

"OK, but make sure you come see me before you go home."

"Sure thing," Mark answered, wondering what Todd might want.

As he was walking over to where Tom was working on the next car, Jim caught up with him.

"Hey, old bestest buddy in the whole wide world, if you get the Jeep running, will you give me ride home?" Jim asked.

"Well, of course, under one condition."

"What's that?"

"If we don't get it running, you help me push it home," Mark said with a sadistic smile.

"OK, deal, smartass!"

"Well, since it's my Jeep, I think that's 'Mr. Smartass' to you."

Mark and Jim went over and helped Tom with the older cars. As they got them running, the owners would thank them and then drive over to see Todd, pick up some passengers and head out. Tom couldn't get the third car to start, even with the new parts. They worked on it for a while but finally had to give up. The dejected owner went to see Todd about getting a ride with someone else. When they got the new parts installed in the Jeep, Mark was nervous as he turned the key. When the CJ caught and fired, his apprehension faded away. The three men climbed into the Jeep and headed over to see Todd.

"Good! You got it running. You wouldn't want to trade even for a brand new truck would you?"

"Todd, last week I would have said 'yes' in a New York minute, but today, I think I'll just stick with my old rust bucket."

"I don't blame you. Do you need some gas?"

"Well, I don't really *need* it, but I wouldn't mind topping off the tank, if that's okay."

"Sure, why don't you let Tom do that while the three of us talk for a minute?"

Tom nodded at Todd and drove the Jeep over to the fuel storage tanks.

"Mark, Jim, I want you to come to a meeting here at the office in the morning."

"What's the meeting about, Todd?" Mark asked, wondering what could be so important to meet about when the power would probably still be off.

"You'll see in the morning, say 7:30."

"OK, Todd. Whatever you say," Jim said.

"Hey, where's Dave?" Mark asked. "Isn't he supposed to take you home?"

"I sent him on with the others. They were getting pretty antsy. Tom's going to take the flatbed and drop me off before he goes home."

About then, Tom drove back up in the Jeep.

"All gassed up and ready to go," he told Mark.

"Okay," Todd said before Mark could reply. "You guys get going, and I'll see you both in the morning."

"Bye," the two friends replied in unison. They climbed into the Jeep, Mark put it in gear, and they headed out the gate.

Chapter 3

Mark glanced at his watch. It had been almost four and a half hours since The Burst. "What do you think the meeting is going to be about?" Jim asked.

"I don't know," Mark answered. "Maybe about how much the power is going to affect the bottom line? But, if it's that, I don't know why it couldn't wait. I just can't imagine what could be so important."

"Hey, does the radio work?"

Mark reached over and turned on the Jeep's radio. He spun the dial, but there was nothing.

"Looks like it's fried, but I forgot to give Suzy back the wind up," he said, as he pulled it out of his pocket and handed it to his friend. "Turn it on."

...confirmation that a private jet crashed into Air Force One as it was waiting to take off. There is no word yet on survivors. We will update you as soon as we have any more information.

It appears that most commercial airliners were disabled by The Burst, and there are hundreds of crashes being reported. One plane inbound to Las Vegas was able to crash land on a highway in the desert. The passengers and crew sustained mostly minor injuries, but all are expected to recover fully. Most of the aircraft airborne at the time of The Burst were not so lucky. The dead, both from the air and on the ground, are expected to number in the tens of thousands. The devastation around the airports of major cities is indescribable.

The city of Cincinnati is awash in riots. The local police have been overwhelmed, and deaths are reported to be upwards of six hundred and rising. Between the fires from the jet crashes and those set by the rioters, the Cincinnati Fire Department has said they can only hope to keep the fires from spreading to other parts of the city. The governor of Ohio has called up the National Guard to put down the rioters and to protect the firefighters with 'whatever means necessary.' Riots have also been reported in Detroit and Seattle.

The Vice President has scheduled a press conference for 6 PM Eastern Time.

This is the CBS radio network. We now return you to your local programming.

This is KSTX in San Antonio, Texas. News 640 AM.

Six airliner crashes inside the city limits are pushing the San Antonio Fire Department to its limit. The three on the airport property are being allowed to burn, and an all effort is being put into the fires in residential areas. The drop in water pressure caused by the loss of electricity is seriously hampering their efforts. The Fire Marshall is asking all municipal and volunteer fire departments from the area with tanker trucks to please send them to help. Please report to the temporary fire command center at the corner of Broadway and Loop 410.

City Power and Light has stated that it may take several days to restore power throughout the city. A spokesperson stated that the first priority is medical centers and nursing homes with no back up power generators.

All local hospitals are closed to non-life threatening injuries and illnesses. They have been inundated by the burns and injuries sustained by victims of the airliner crashes.

FEMA shelters are now open at most area high schools. Generators are being delivered to Judson, Madison, and South San high schools. Only the infirm and elderly at risk from the severe summer heat are being admitted at these locations.

The sunset curfew put into place by the Vice President will go into effect in the San Antonio area at 8:11 PM. SAPD has stated that anyone found on the streets after that time without a legitimate emergency will be arrested.

This is KSTX, 640 AM. We'll be right back after this break.

Do you suffer from the embarrassing effects of dandruff? If so, then we invite you try our new and improved...

Jim turned off the radio. "Damn! It's like the end of the world, and they're playing commercials?"

Mark ignored the rhetorical question. "Jim, if we had rioting here, like they have in Cincinnati, what would you do?"

"Well, right now, I would just get behind you. After all, you're a bona fide Billy Bob badass black belt."

"No, I'm serious. What would you do?"

"Well, if we could get out of town, we would go stay with Lisa's parents in Uvalde. If not, then I'd batten down the hatches and hope for the best."

"Wouldn't you be scared?"

"Yes and no."

"How's that?"

"Well, 'yes' because I would be scared for Lisa and the girls if things went really bad, and 'no' because have you forgotten who lives next door?"

"You mean Gunny?"

"Yeah, before a mob could even get to me, they'd have to get past Gunny and that old Garand of his, and he loves the girls like they were his own grandchildren." Jim paused. "The other thing I might do is to stay at your place. I doubt rioters would get that far out."

"I agree. Why don't you guys come out and stay until this blows over? Besides, it would save me from having to come pick you up in the morning."

"When we get to the house, I'll ask Lisa."

When the guys pulled into Jim's driveway, Gunnery Sergeant Marcus T. Pickwell, USMC (Retired), was in his front yard, nailing a piece of plywood over a window.

"Hey, Gunny, what are you doing?" Jim called.

Gunny limped over to where Jim and Mark were standing as fast as his one artificial and other soon-to-be-replaced knees would allow.

"I don't trust these worthless sumbitches 'round here to not go riotin' like they're doing in the big cities up north," Gunny began. "I'm boardin' up the winders on the front of my place in case they come by and start some shit. 'Course I'm leaving a slot big enough at the bottom for Beulah. If'n I was you Jimbo, I'd do the same. I got some extra plywood and nails."

"Well, I hope it doesn't come to that, Gunny. Do you remember my friend, Mark, from work?"

"The karate man, right?" Gunny said, as he stuck out his hand. "That's a pretty nice horseless carriage you got there, Karate Man. Use to drive one kinda like it in Korea. How'd you get it to run? My old piece of shit truck won't start."

14

"We replaced all the ignition parts," Mark told him. "That's probably all yours needs, too."

"Well, we better get in and check on the girls, Gunny," Jim said.

"I been keepin' an eye on 'em for ya, Jimbo."

"Thanks, Gunny, I knew you would, and it made me feel better knowing you were next door."

"What's neighbors fer?" Gunny replied, as Jim and Mark went in through the garage door.

"Who's Beulah?" Mark asked.

"That's Gunny's 12 gauge riot gun. You wouldn't want to get into an argument with her!" Jim informed him. "Man, he sure likes your Jeep. The only thing of mine he ever admired that much, except for the girls, is my M1A."

When Jim's girls saw him, they both ran up and hugged a leg. Lindsey and Lacy were 8-year-old twins. Lisa was right behind them and grabbed Jim around the waist. She was almost as tall as Mark, thin with long, blonde hair and probably could have been a model if she hadn't married her college's star tight end. Before the twins were born, she had worked as an operating room RN. When their first child turned out to be two, she and Jim decided she should stay home to take care of them. Now she was home schooling them, as well.

"Oh, Honey," she said, "I was worried about you. I'm so glad you're home. Nothing's working, and even my car won't start. It's so hot in the house, but I was afraid to leave the front door open. Gunny told me that the President's dead and that all the planes crashed and that they were already rioting in some of the cities and ..."

"It's okay, baby," Jim said soothingly. "I'm here now, and nothing bad is going to happen to us."

"I know, but it's just that this is the worst thing I've ever...Oh, hi, Mark."

"Hi, Lisa."

"Baby, Mark wanted to know if we would like to go spend a night or two at his place."

"I don't know...I mean I'm sure he and Jessica have enough to worry about without having guests, and I don't know if it's a good idea to leave the house."

"I'll tell you what," Mark told her, "it's probably too hot to sleep in our house, too. How about we pull your pop-up camper over to our place, and you can set it up in the back. We're probably going to spend the night in ours. If the generator still works, we can use it to run the air conditioners in both campers. At least everybody will get some sleep that way."

"Well, if you're sure it's no trouble. I know I would probably feel better out in the country than in town."

"Okay, y'all pack all the stuff you want to bring over. Put the most important stuff in the camper. I've got to run and pick up my crew from their schools, and then I'll be back. If I can get the truck started, I'll bring it, and you'll have room for a lot of stuff. If not, I'll bring the Jeep back, and what you get in the camper will be about all there's room for. It's almost 2:30 now. I'll be back by, let's say, four o'clock."

"That sounds great, Mark," Lisa said. "Thank you so much."

"No problem. After all...what's neighbors fer?" Mark said, winking at Jim.

15

On his way home, Mark figured he should probably stop by the house to see if Jess or the kids had perhaps gotten a ride home. As he was driving through one of the poorer sections of town, he noticed a lot of people eyeing the Jeep. He reached under the seat, unzipped a case, and put his Colt Lightweight Commander under his thigh. If someone wanted to car jack him, he figured the .45 was way better than the little .32 he always carried in his back pocket. As he drove, he thought about what they might need. They had their own well and could run the pump with the gasoline generator. Mark was pretty sure that it would work since it was similar to the one Billy had been using at work. He could fill up the camper tanks, and he had a couple of plastic 55 gallon barrels he used to haul water down to the deer lease. That would take care of water. Food might be a problem. Jess was notoriously bad about waiting until there was nothing to eat before she went to the store. He knew the camper had some food in it, but he wasn't sure how much was there or how old it might be. Most of the deer he had killed last year was still in the freezer. They would have to do something with that anyway with the power out. Before he knew it, he was turning into his subdivision, Silver Hills. It was just over the Wilson county line and consisted of about 60 one to five acre lots, about 50 of which had homes on them. A medium-size farm on each side and a large ranch in the back bordered the development. Mark's four acres were toward the back, and when he pulled into the driveway, David was shooting a basketball at the goal over the garage.

"Hey, Dad!" David shouted, as he ran toward the Jeep.

"How did you get home?" Mark asked.

"Mom and I walked. It only took us about an hour."

"What about your sister?"

"The school bus brought her."

"That's great!" Mark said, as he headed toward the front door.

As he walked in, he noticed how hot the house was. It wasn't as hot as Jim's had been, though, since all the doors and windows were open.

"God, I'm glad you're home," Jess said, as she came around the corner. She was 5'3" with red hair and green eyes. Mark remembered that the first time he saw her, he thought she was the prettiest girl he had ever seen. She was still pretty, and had an Irish temper Mark had learned to avoid when possible. She had studied to become a marine biologist, but when there was no work in her field to be had, she'd gone back to school to get her teaching certificate and now taught 8th grade biology and 7th grade earth science.

"I'm so glad you're all home. I figured I would have to pick you all up."

"No. David and I walked home before it got too hot, and Samantha got a ride home on the bus."

"How did you get home?" Jess asked.

"We got some new parts for the Jeep. Are all of the school busses running?"

"No. Only about half. Just the old ones. Remember the school bond that got voted down last year and how mad I was about it?"

"Yeah."

"Well, some of that money was going to replace the old busses. Now I'm glad it didn't pass."

"Do you know everything that's going on?"

16

"Pretty much I think. We heard some at school and when I got home, I went out to your shed and got your short-wave radio. I had to get batteries out of some of the flashlights to get it to work, but I've been listening off and on for the last two hours."

"The short-wave works?" Mark said.

"Well, duh, it was in a metal cabinet in a metal building."

"Good maybe everything in the shed was protected."

"Maybe. But we don't have any water. We only flushed a couple of times and washed our hands, and then the pressure dropped to nothing."

"Well, duh back at you, Miss Science Whiz, the pressure tank is only seven gallons."

"That's stupid. It should be a lot bigger."

"Well, it's not, but I think I can use the generator to run the pump."

"Good. Can you do it now?"

"No. I have to go pick up Jim and Lisa, and I want to see if the truck will run. We're going to bring their camper over, and I figured we could stay in ours until the lights come back on, too. By the way, when was the last time you went to the store?"

"Day before yesterday, but I didn't buy that much."

"Is there enough to get us by for three or four days?"

"Yes, I think so."

"Okay, I'm going out to check the truck and camper out."

"Oh, before you go, Jon Olsen, you know that former Marine who runs by the house early every morning, came over earlier and said he and some of the other men were going to have a meeting at his house after the Vice President's speech. He said they were going to talk about putting some kind of guard at the entrance of the subdivision. He said he really wanted you to come."

"Not another meeting!" Mark explained to Jess that he and Jim had to go into work tomorrow for a meeting. He agreed with her that it seemed silly, but since his boss insisted, what could he do? "Besides," he added, "I've kind of gotten used to eating on a regular basis, and having a paycheck ensures I can keep doing it."

"Well, I guess you got me on that one, Mister. What do you think about what Mr. Olsen wants to do?"

"I think all of these old Marines are just a little more gung-ho than I like, and they need to cool their jets just a little bit."

"I agree."

With that, Mark saluted his commander, smartly turned around and headed out the back door. He walked along the side of the shed and climbed up into the 1991 Ford F-350. He turned the key on and the 'Wait to Start' light came on. Mark waited…and waited…and waited. When it wouldn't go off, he figured that the glow plug controller must have been burned out by The Burst. He started to crank the truck, and after several minutes of cranking, it started and ran rough until the engine warmed up. He figured if it was that hard to start when it was almost a hundred degrees outside, it would be next to impossible when it was cooler. He let the truck run and went back to the camper that sat in its bed. The slide in truck camper, or cabover camper as they were sometimes called, had served the Turner crew very well for a lot of years. He checked the water pump, the hot water heater, the propane refrigerator, and the built-in stereo. Everything seemed to work except the radio. The camper was equipped with four electric jacks to lift it off of the truck, but when Mark tried them, they didn't work.

"Damn," he said to himself. That was the second time he'd cursed that day. That meant he owed his 'swear box' two dollars. He couldn't remember the last time he'd had a two-dollar day.

Mark retrieved the emergency hand crank for the camper jacks and went to work. After cranking for about thirty minutes, he had the camper off the truck. It would need to be lowered closer to the ground for them to stay in it, but that could be done later. He would have to hurry if he was to get back to Jim's house by four. He put the tailgate back on the truck and drove it up next to the house.

Mark ran into the house, changed into a clean shirt, and headed back outside. He got his pistol out of the Jeep and put it into the truck. He climbed in the big red truck and headed back to town.

When he got to Jim and Lisa's a few minutes before four, Jim already had the pop-up pulled out of the garage and loaded. Lisa had the things she wanted to bring stacked up in the garage where the camper had been. There wasn't as much as Mark had expected. Mark backed up to the camper, and he and Jim hooked it up. Then they loaded up the back of the truck.

"Do you think I should bring some of my guns?" Jim asked.

"If it makes you feel better," Mark said, thinking it was unnecessary.

"I'm going to bring a couple for just in case."

Jim went over to the gun safe Lisa had made him put in the garage because it was too ugly to go in the house. He opened it and withdrew a .357 and a 12 gauge. He took out a holster for the revolver and some ammo and put everything except the shotgun into a small duffel bag. He put the shotgun in a soft case and then placed all of it behind the back seat of the four-door pick-up.

About that time Gunny came hobbling over. "Gonna get the hell out of Dodge, huh?"

"We're going out to stay with Mark until the power comes back on," Jim explained.

"Gonna be gone a while, then. I'll keep an eye on your place."

"Thanks, Gunny, but we should just be gone a day or two until the power comes back on."

"You really believe what you hear on the radio?" the old man asked.

"Why wouldn't we?" Jim replied.

"Them sumbiches in Washington are lying through their teeth. No way the lights are coming back on in less than a month, or maybe forever!" Gunny said.

"Well, I hope you're wrong this time, Gunny, but thanks for watching the house. If you need anything, you know where the key is. We've got to get going. Mark wants to be back home for the Vice President's press conference."

Mark pulled the truck and camper into the street, then he helped Jim push Lisa's car into the garage. Jim locked the house, and they all loaded up into the truck and took off with the girls waving at Gunny. When they got back to the house, Jim set up his camper, and Mark lowered his with some help from David. They almost had the campers ready when it was five o'clock and time for the press conference. They headed up to the deck where Jess had a pitcher of lemonade. Mark turned on the radio and sank into one of the lawn chairs.

Chapter 4

When the Vice President came on, he really had no news to report. He confirmed that Air Force One had been destroyed, but there was still no definite word on the President. Condolences were offered to those who had lost loved ones and promises of help were made to those who had lost their homes. He reported that the experts were still working on the source of The Burst. He encouraged everyone to work with FEMA and their local authorities, and he rebuked those who would start riots and make a bad situation worse. He assured everyone that most of the power would be back on in two or three days at the most. He promised he would be speaking to the nation every day at this time until the situation was back to normal. Afterwards, one of the network's 'talking heads' came on to micro-analyze what the VP had said.

"I guess we don't need to listen to this," Mark said as he turned off the radio. "Jim, would you walk down to this meeting with me? Maybe your experiences in dealing with Gunny will come in handy."

The two men walked down the road and discussed what they had to get done before dark. Finishing setting up the campers was the first priority, and pumping some water was next. The women could fix dinner as soon as the campers were set up. Mark wanted to plug the deep freeze into the generator for a while, too. Everything else could wait until tomorrow. When they got to Jon Olsen's house, there were a several men already there. Mark introduced Jim to the ones he knew. They were all cordial, but none were very friendly. By the time Jon called the meeting to order, a few more had shown up.

"I think the first thing we need to do is to put a 24-hour guard at the entrance to the subdivision. I think it should be two men at a time for four hour shifts," Jon began. "That means we need twelve men each day. If we have twenty-four volunteers, then everyone will just have to do one shift every other day. We can alternate the shifts every week between day and night. That way, nobody gets stuck on a bad shift forever."

Mark was watching most of the other men nodding their heads. "Excuse me, Jon, but even if we needed guards, why would we need them for weeks? The power's going to be back on in two or three days, or maybe a little longer than that out here, but it isn't going to be weeks."

"I know that's what they're saying, Mark, but we don't think it's true. Tell them, Scott."

"OK," one of the men said to Jon. He turned to face everyone. "My name is Scott Simmons. Most of you don't know me, but those who do know I work for City Power and Light. I do repair work, and today we were not too far from our office when The Burst hit. We walked back to the office, and they told us to get home however we could and that they would announce on the radio when they needed us to come back in."

"I don't see what that proves," Mark stated flatly.

"Let me finish. You see, we heard they also sent home the crews from the two coal-powered generating plants. Supposedly, the control systems and most of the spare parts were fried by The Burst. Some of those parts have a six-month lead-time when things are normal. The factory that makes our control circuits supplies almost all of them for most of North America, anu runs on electricity, which it doesn't have. Even if they get it running on backup power, there's no telling how long it's going to take to make replacements for all of the generating stations in just the major cities. It's kind of funny if you think about it. They can't make electricity without the circuit boards, and they can't make the circuit boards without electricity."

"The good news is that our auxiliary natural gas powered generators were not online that early in the day. They only kick them in during the peak demand, which is usually late afternoon when it's the hottest. They said they might be able to get them running again in a few days, BUT they can only supply about ten percent of the city's normal power demand, *and* they run on natural gas that has to be pumped by, you guessed it…electric pumps.

Then there's the job of replacing every transformer in town. I work for CPL, and I don't even know how many there are, but they have to number in the tens of thousands. We have crews to replace a hundred and fifty to maybe two hundred in a 24-hour period. The worst thunderstorm we've had in the last ten years took out just over three hundred transformers. Think about it. Sometimes after a bad storm, some areas don't have power for two days, and that's just to replace two to three hundred transformers. Now we have to replace maybe a hundred thousand? All of the spares we had were on the ground outside behind the offices. One of the engineers told me that the EMP cooked them, even though they weren't connected to the grid. You see, The Burst charged them, and they grounded out through the ground. Now I don't know how long it's going to take the transformer companies to produce enough transformers to replace every single one in America, but you can bet your sweet ass that it's going to take more than three days!"

"Did the engineers tell you all of that?" Mark asked.

"Parts of it. The rest is just common sense," Scott replied defensively.

"OK, let's assume Scott's right, and it's going to be months or maybe even years before we have power again. What do you think placing two guards at the entry is going to accomplish?" Mark argued.

"They can make sure nobody gets in if they don't live here," someone in the group answered.

"How are they going to do that? Shoot anybody they don't know?"

"They could shoot out their tires," a man Mark didn't recognize said.

Mark rubbed his chin for a moment. "Well, about 99% of the cars aren't running, and even if some kids did come out here in a running car, what are you going to do after you shoot out their tires? Now they're stuck here. Who's going to put them up and feed them? Or were you going to reinstitute the firing squad?"

No one answered for a long moment.

"Well, some of us would just feel better having a couple of guys with rifles at the entrance, just to, if nothing else, discourage the riff-raff," Jon said.

"Is it even legal for us to put armed guards on the road?" Ted Petrie, a professor at San Antonio College, asked.

"It's a private road. We can do whatever we damn well please!" the tire shooter said with a smug look.

"If they were having riots in San Antonio, then I might agree to the guards, but until then, I think it's silly." Mark really wanted to use the word 'stupid,' but thought better of it. He looked around and only saw three or four people nodding in agreement with him.

"Let's take a vote. I think that only subdivision homeowners should vote, though," Jon said looking at Jim. "Anyone disagree?"

No one said anything.

"All those who think we should post some guards and would be willing to volunteer, raise your hand."

Almost all the hands went up.

"Looks like the ayes have it. I'll make the schedule for the first week," Jon said.

It was quiet for a long moment.

"OK, then, I think that's enough for now. If there's nothing else?"

"Jon, can I say one more thing?" Mark asked.

"Who could stop you?" Jon said, rolling his eyes.

Mark ignored the sarcasm. "I may disagree about the guards, but we're still all neighbors. Jim and I are going home and hooking up a gasoline generator to my well. If any of you needs water, just bring up something to put it in. Heck, if you don't have anything to put it in, just come down, and we'll figure out how to get it back to your place."

The expression on almost everyone's face changed.

The two friends had hardly gotten home when Scott showed up with a red wagon that had two five gallon buckets on it. He also had some electrical tools and offered to help wire up the pump.

"Hey, Scott," Mark said, "did the engineer tell you anything about what caused the EMP?"

"He just said it was most likely from nukes being detonated in space, but he also said it could have come from the sun or even from space outside our solar system."

"If it was nukes, who launched them?"

"I asked the same question, but he didn't have a clue," Scott said.

Mark wondered if they would ever know the truth.

Scott said they could pull the 220-volt receptacle off of the generator and wire it directly to the pump, but Mark told him he wanted to be able to easily move the generator around. Scott asked him if he had any 220 plugs around. Mark didn't, and the only one he knew of was on the clothes dryer. After making him promise over and over to buy a new plug as soon as possible, Jess reluctantly agreed to let them cut the plug off of the dryer. Ten minutes later, it was spliced onto the pump, and when Mark pulled the starter cord the second time, the generator roared to life. They let it warm up for a moment and then plugged in the pump. The pressure gauge began to rise, and Mark felt the same way he had when the Jeep started. By this time, there were almost thirty-five people at Mark's house with everything from empty two liter soda bottles to a huge wheelbarrow with a visqueen liner in it. Everyone thanked Mark profusely, and some even offered to pay. Mark thanked them but declined, saying it was only the neighborly thing to do. After a while, when some were showing up for their third or fourth trip, and others who had just gotten the word were showing up for the first time, Mark put Samantha and David in charge of the hose with strict orders not to accept any money. Then he went to the back to finish setting up the camper.

When he got to the back, Jim's pop-up was all set up, and Jim was standing next to Mark's charcoal barbeque pit cooking burgers.

"Man, that smells good," Mark said, realizing he hadn't eaten anything since breakfast.

"They do, don't they?" Jim said.

Mark leveled the camper, opened all the windows and vents, and turned on the refrigerator and the hot water heater. The camper ready, he helped Jim finish the burgers.

When they were done and all of the water borrowers had gotten what they needed, the two families sat down at the picnic table on the deck to eat. Mark said grace and asked for the Lord to protect them and give them wisdom in the midst of this crisis. Jess had only bought one package of buns, which was usually more than enough for four, so anyone who ate a second burger had to eat it on plain, white bread. When Mark and Jim were on their second burger, and David was on his third, a small older lady came around the corner of the house with an empty half-gallon milk jug in her hand.

"Excuse me, but are you the ones giving away the water?"

"Yes, ma'am," Mark said, as he stood up.

"Could I bother you for some?"

"It's no bother, but don't you need more than just a half of a gallon?"

"I could use more, but this was the only clean container I had," she explained.

Mark walked over to the woman. "Hi, my name's Mark Turner."

"Hello, I'm Abigail Petersen," she said, as she extended her hand to Mark.

"It's nice to meet you," Mark said, as he shook her hand. "I have several five gallon jugs already full. Would you like to borrow one?"

"I would never be able to carry that much," the woman, who looked to be around seventy, answered.

"Mrs. Petersen, that's why God put teenagers on the earth, just so we adults don't have to carry the heavy stuff."

"David!" Mark called.

"Yes, Dad," David answered, with his mouth half-full of hamburger.

"Go to the shed and get the water jug with the spigot on it and take it over to Mrs. Petersen's house."

"Yes, sir!" the boy answered, swallowing the last bite of his burger and running toward the shed.

"He doesn't have to do that," Mrs. Petersen objected.

"Mrs. Petersen, the boy just ate half a cow. You're doing him a favor by letting him get some exercise."

A moment later, David appeared with a wagon with the water jug in it. Mrs. Petersen thanked Mark, then she and David started out to her house. In just a few minutes, David was back with a 'Risk' board game in the wagon.

"Where did you get that?" his mother asked.

"Mrs. Petersen gave it to me. She said that she used to play it with her grandchildren, but they're all grown up now," David said.

22

"I thought I told you not to take anything for the water," Mark chastised.

"You said not to take any money."

"Is that what I said?"

"It is, Dad," Samantha came to the defense of her brother, which was something that didn't happen often.

"Well, okay then, but I think you should consider it a loan, not a gift."

"Okay, Dad. Man, you should have seen the den in her house. It was full of animal heads. Most were from Africa, but she had some of the biggest whitetail deer I've ever seen. She told me her husband was a big time hunter, but he died about two years ago. Her house was so cool."

"I'm glad you like it because you're probably going to be hauling water over there on a regular basis until the power comes back on," Mark told his son.

Mark looked at his watch. The curfew took effect in four minutes. Mark and Jim moved the generator to where they could plug both campers into it. They cranked it up, turned on the A/C units in the RV's, and then ran an extension cord from it to the deep freeze. Jess, with Lisa's help, moved as much of the contents of the refrigerator in the house to the ones in the campers as they could, but there were some things that wouldn't fit. Mark got his large ice chest and put four of his 'ice bottles' in it. He had found that if he took a two-liter plastic soda bottle and filled it full of water and then put it in the freezer, it would freeze at colder than 32 degrees since the pressure caused by the expanding water would lower the freezing point. He wasn't sure how cold they actually got, but he'd found on his fishing trips to the coast that they would last a long time. He then placed the remainder of the food from the refrigerator in the ice chest.

With all of the work that had to be done finished and all of the children occupied, the four adults sat down at the picnic table and discussed the events of the day. They spoke mostly of what Scott Simmons had told the men. Jess and Lisa felt that, although Scott was a nice fellow, he was just a repairman at the power company, and he didn't know what he was talking about. After all, why would the Vice President lie about how long it was going to take to restore the power? They wondered what the meeting with Todd was about for a while, and then the discussion drifted to how it must have been to have lived before there was electricity. After what seemed like a short while, Mark looked at his watch again. It now read 10:33. He announced that he was going to take a quick shower in the camper and go to bed. Jim said he was going to do the same. The women decided to talk a while longer and said they'd round up the kids and come to bed in a little while and that they'd shut off the generator before they did. Before he headed to the camper, Mark went into his bedroom and with a flashlight found the black box on his dresser. He pulled two one-dollar bills out of his wallet and put them in the box. After his shower, Mark wound up and set the alarm clock that stayed in the camper and climbed up into the bed. The last thing he remembered thinking was that so much had happened in the last fourteen hours.

Chapter 5

When the alarm went off at 6:00, it startled Mark out of a deep sleep. He reached for the alarm, but couldn't find it. It took him a moment to remember he was in the camper. He found the alarm clock, turned it off, and looked at his watch. He was calculating if he could get a few more minutes of sleep when Jess rolled over.

"What time is it?" she asked.

"Six o'clock, go back to sleep."

"Okay." She rolled back over and pulled the sheet up around her neck.

Mark remembered that last night he'd figured that he better get up at 6 if he was to make Todd's meeting at 7:30. He usually gave himself forty-five minutes to make the normally thirty-five minute trip to work, but with all of the stalled cars, it might take an hour to get there. Most of the cars had been pushed to the side, but there were a few still in the roads. He pulled on a clean pair of jeans and a polo shirt, put on his socks and shoes, and headed over to Jim's camper to see if his friend was awake yet. There was a light on inside.

"Jim," Mark whispered.

"Be right out," he heard Jim whisper back. A moment later, the door opened and Jim stepped out of the pop-up. He was dressed the same way Mark was.

"Which vehicle are we going to take?" he asked.

"Let's try to get the truck started. I'd rather take it, but if it won't start pretty quick, we'll take the Jeep," Mark answered.

They walked over to the truck, and Mark cranked on it for five minutes or so with no luck. He was ready to give up when Jim asked if he had any starting fluid. Jim said he remembered hearing an old truck driver talking about using ether to start semis before they had glow plugs. Mark found an old can of starting fluid in the shed and gave it to Jim. When he engaged the starter, Jim sprayed the fluid into the air cleaner intake. The truck started almost immediately but ran roughly for the first couple of minutes. While they were waiting for the engine to warm up, Mark got five jerry cans out of the shed and put them in the back of the truck. He hoped Todd would let him borrow some gas for the generator. When the idle smoothed out, both men climbed in, and Mark eased the truck into gear and slowly let his foot off of the clutch. When they approached the entrance to Silver Hills, it was just getting light enough to make out the two armed guards. Mark stopped the truck, and Manuel Hernandez stepped up to the window. Mark didn't know the other man, but he recognized him from the meeting at Jon's house and from the water line. Manuel was holding an old Winchester .30-30, and it looked like the other man had a shotgun.

"Good morning, Manny," Mark said. "Everything go alright last night?"

"Good morning to you, gentlemen," Manny replied. "No problems so far. Where are you off to so early?"

"Our boss told us to come in to work today." Mark paused. "Hey, will you do me a favor?"

"Sure."

"I don't know how long we're going to be gone, but will you tell the guards to expect us back? I wouldn't want my tires shot out," he said with a wink.

"No problem. We'll keep an eye out for you," Manny promised. "Listen." He was whispering now. "The chickens have been laying pretty good. I usually give the extra eggs away at work, but since I won't be going in for a while, Rosa and I want you all to have them."

"Thanks, Manny. We'll come get them when we get home. That's very kind of you."

"It was very kind of you to give all of us water, especially when you disagreed with us."

"It was the right thing to do, and you would've done the same," Mark said.

"Maybe. But I don't think some people would have."

"Perhaps not." Mark patted Manny on the hand as he eased the truck forward and onto the road.

Jim and Mark again discussed what could be so important that Todd would have them come in. They came to the conclusion that Todd probably wanted to know how much money the company could spare to help its employees, since they would be missing at least three or four days' work. The company was always very generous to its workers, especially during hard times.

They didn't see another running car until they were well into town. Even then, it was only a couple of cars and a few of the city busses. At least on the major roads, someone had moved all the cars that hadn't already been pushed to the side. They were making better time than they thought they would. Jim commented that they were lucky The Burst hadn't come at rush hour.

"Think about the west coast," he told Mark. "The Burst hit them at about 7:30, their time. The way their highway system is always packed, they'll never be able to get the roads cleared."

When they pulled up to the gate at work, Tom was there and opened it. Mark pulled the truck through, and Tom closed and locked the gate. He then climbed into the bed of the big Ford and patted on the roof to signal that he was ready to go. Mark parked in front of the main office building, and the three men got out of the truck and headed to the conference room. Todd was already in there, and they all took seats, Jim and Mark on one side and Todd and Tom across from them.

"Good morning. You both have probably been wondering why I wanted you here today," Todd started.

Both Jim and Mark nodded their heads.

"First off, how are you and your families doing so far?"

"Pretty good," Jim answered first. "Mark pulled my pop-up camper over to his place, and Lisa and the girls and I stayed over there last night."

"You're not on city water are you, Mark?"

Mark shook his head.

"What was it like with no power and no water?"

The two friends looked at each other and grinned sheepishly.

"What? Did I miss something?"

"I have a gasoline generator we use for camping and at the deer lease. One of the neighbors helped us wire up the pump on my well, so we could plug it in to the generator. Almost the whole neighborhood came over and got water last night. Then we plugged our campers up and ran the A/C's long enough so we could sleep comfortably."

Todd and Tom looked at each other. Mark couldn't tell if the look they were giving each other was one of amazement or humor, or perhaps a little of both.

"Tell me, guys," Todd said, turning his attention back across the table, "what would you do if the power was off for several months to a year?"

"Why are you asking that?" Mark said. "You're the third person in twenty-four hours to suggest to us that the lights aren't going to be back on in a few days. Do you really know something, or are you just speculating? And do you have any idea what caused the EMP?"

"For now, let's just play 'what if.' I'll answer your other questions later."

"Okay," Jim said. "The first things to worry about would be water, food, and shelter."

"That's a good start. Let's take those one at a time," Todd said. "It looks like you guys have water covered, as long as you have gas for the generator. What about food?"

"We probably only have enough at our house for the eight of us for another week at most. We'd need to buy some, and if you were talking about closer to a year, I'd try to put in a garden and raise some small livestock like chickens and rabbits," Mark answered.

"We have enough food at my house for probably another two or three weeks," Jim added. "Since Lisa doesn't work, she buys a lot of stuff in bulk to save money, and if something goes on sale, she buys a lot of it. Lisa knows quite a bit about gardening and small livestock since she grew up in the country."

"Then for shelter," Mark took back over. "We obviously have our houses, but they aren't meant to be lived in without power. Even with all the doors and windows open, it was really hot in our house yesterday afternoon. If you had an old house built before they had central air and heat, you could get by pretty well. We'd probably stay in our RV's. At least we would until it cooled off enough to stay in the house."

"That all sounds pretty good," Todd said. "What else would you be concerned about?"

Mark answered first. "The next thing I'd be worried about would be medical care and then the education of my children and our personal safety."

"I'd be worried about our families and friends," Jim added. "Lisa's already worried about her parents. What's the point to all these questions, Todd?"

"What do you all know about the founder and chairman of the board of our company?" Todd asked.

"You mean Mr. Davis?"

Todd nodded his head.

"They say he's crazy as a loon, kind of a modern day Howard Hughes," Mark answered.

"Crazy like a fox, maybe. That would be closer to the truth," Tom spoke for the first time since the meeting started.

"You see, Mr. Davis has been concerned for some time that something might happen to disrupt our way of life. He'd even planned for this exact EMP scenario, which he thinks is the result of some terrorist nation getting some nukes and finding a way to get them above the atmosphere. He bought a big

27

ranch down where they built Choke Canyon Reservoir," Todd explained. "He has about twenty-five hundred acres on the upper portion of the lake. It's good farmland and is game rich. The lake is one of the better fishing lakes in the state."

"We've fished and duck hunted on Choke. In fact, our deer lease isn't too far from there," Jim offered.

"We know," Tom continued. "We have a group of people, nineteen families right now, who have been hand-selected to move down there in case of, shall we say, a worst case scenario. We have very reliable information that the power cannot be totally restored in less than eighteen to twenty-four months. In that amount of time, who knows what's going to happen? We know for sure that there will be more riots like they've had up north. It would be silly to think, when people can't get food and water, that they won't go ballistic. We expect full scale rioting in every major city in the United States in the next few weeks."

"So, you're a group of those crazy survivalists?" Tact had never been one of Mark's strong points.

"Well, I don't think we're crazy, especially if what we think is going to happen comes to pass, but yes, I guess you could say we're survivalists."

"Even if you're right about the power, what does that have to do with us?" Jim asked.

"I think in a few days, we'll all know if I'm right or not," Todd said. "But to answer your question, we've been watching the two of you for quite some time. You both have qualities and skills we're looking for. We probably would have been talking to you anyway in the next few months and trying to slowly incorporate you both into the group, but the lights going out has forced us to accelerate our plans."

"What do you mean you've been watching us?" Mark was slightly indignant.

"Exactly what it sounds like," Todd explained, not the least bit apologetic. "We know a lot about you and your wives. We're very selective about who we bring into the group. We don't want any surprises, so we research our prospective members thoroughly."

"I don't like the fact that you have been spying on us, but what is it that makes you think you want us in your group?"

"You both have outdoors skills. You know how to hunt and fish, and we don't have anyone who has real skills in those areas. Mark, we were impressed by the fact that you're a black belt and teach a karate class. We want the whole group to learn karate for both fitness and defense. Your wife is a schoolteacher, and we have a lot of children who are going to need educating. Jim, we know you're an accomplished marksman. You shoot long range rifle matches, and you almost always come in first, second, or third in those pistol matches you go to…what do you call them?" Todd asked Tom.

"IDPA," Tom informed him.

"Yeah, that's it," Todd continued. "We want someone who can teach our people to shoot. Plus, your wife is a real treasure trove of skills. She has skill with livestock, knows how to home school, and is an RN. We have a doctor in the group, but we could really use a nurse, especially one who has experience in the operating room. We know you both go to Protestant churches regularly, and

28

that you're both fairly conservative politically. Your family values fit in with our philosophy, and you would be welcomed members to our group."

"So, why would we want to join?" Jim inquired.

"Well, we're totally set up logistically. We have enough food stored for everyone for three full years. Plus, we have a tractor and seed to plant and grow our own food. We have cattle, chickens, and rabbits. We have a good well and a diesel generator for the pump with enough fuel to last ten years. We have running vehicles and gas. We not only have a doctor, but we have medical supplies and a good supply of medicine. Each family has their own cabin to live in that's set up for no or little power like you were talking about, Mark. The location is very remote and secure. Just in case, we have weapons and security measures for the possibility of someone attacking us. We have the means to make it through almost any crisis. Your families would be fed, sheltered, and protected with us. It is an ideal situation to be in if 'the shit hits the fan.'"

"It sounds like you've thought of everything," Jim said.

"We've tried to," Todd responded. "And Mr. Davis has spared no expense to make sure we have everything we might need."

"You mentioned that we fit in with your philosophy. Can you tell us exactly what your philosophy is?" Mark asked.

"We are conservative and believe in the Constitution. We want to protect and maintain the ideas that created this great nation. That is, the belief in God, hard work, and the right to life, liberty, and the pursuit of happiness. I'm starting to sound a little corny. Basically, we're all Protestant, we...."

"Excuse me. Todd, you're Protestant?" Mark asked in disbelief.

"Yes."

"I always thought you were Jewish."

"The Rosenberg threw you, huh?" Todd smiled. "My great-grandfather was a Jew from Russia. He came to America in 1896 and converted to Christianity. I go to a Baptist church. In fact, that's where I first met Mr. Davis."

"I'm sorry, I just assumed..." Mark started to apologize.

"That's okay, you're not the first to make that assumption, and you probably won't be the last. Anyway, back to our philosophy. We believe that charity is the Church's job, not the government's. We believe if a man wants to eat, he has to work, and that the destruction of the family unit has become the downfall of our nation. Mr. Davis feels that a national tragedy just might bring our country back to our core values and morality."

"Well, I can't really argue with any of that," Jim said.

"I can't either," Mark agreed. "So, what's next?"

"We want you and your families to come out and see the ranch whenever you'd like. It's best if you can stay two or three days. Here's a map of how to get there. We think once you see it, it'll be easy to decide, but no matter what you decide, we want you and your families to be safe and secure. With the power out, the ATM's won't work, and no one is going to take a check or credit card. Cash is king, at least until everyone figures out that it's worthless. It's not quite the end of the month, but we're paying you this month's salary in cash. We're also giving you $100 in quarters that were made before 1965. These are 90% silver coins. Yesterday morning, they were worth about $1,000. Today, who knows? Use the cash until people won't take it anymore, and then use the silver."

"I don't know what to say, Todd," Mark said with his mouth half open.

"Me, either. I'm speechless," stammered Jim.

"We're doing this to show you how serious we are and how well we've planned for just this sort of emergency," Todd said, handing each man a briefcase.

"Thank you," they both said in unison.

"Is there anything else we could do for you?" Todd asked.

"I was wondering if I could fill up my truck with diesel and take some gas for my generator," Mark said.

"Take all you need. Tom and I are moving our families down to the ranch this afternoon, and we're not coming back until this all blows over."

"Shoot! I was hoping to fix my truck and get it out of here in the next day or two," Jim said.

"Here, take my keys to the gate and to the fuel tanks," Tom offered. "That way, you can get your truck whenever you want. If you need more fuel, take it. We'll get squared up once, or maybe I should say *if*, things get back to normal."

"Anything else?" Todd asked.

"Yes, I need to return this wind-up radio Suzy got out of Mr. Davis's office," Mark said, as he pulled it out of his pocket.

"You keep it," Todd said. "We have plenty of them at the ranch."

"I don't know how to thank you guys for all of this," Mark said.

"Me, too," Jim added.

"Well, we hope you do it by joining us at the ranch. In fact, we're sure you will," Tom answered.

"Just two more things," Todd said, as everyone was shaking hands. "First, when you come out to visit, tie this yellow bandana on the antenna of your truck. That way, we'll know it's you. Second, and this may be the tough one, the offer to join with us and stay at the ranch is only for you and your wives and children. No relatives or friends. We just don't have the resources to take in everyone."

"We understand. We'll talk it over with the girls, and then I'm sure we'll be out to visit," Mark promised.

Chapter 6

The two men were still in shock as they walked back to the truck.

"What do we do now?" Mark asked Jim.

"Let's talk about it while we're getting the fuel," Jim suggested.

Mark drove the truck over to the fuel tanks, and he filled up the truck while Jim worked on the jerry cans. They thanked Todd and Tom again when the pair stopped in the flatbed to say goodbye and remind the friends to lock the gate. Jim really wanted to see if he could get his truck fixed, so they decided to go back to the auto parts store to try to get the parts. After they locked the gate, Mark drove to the parts store he'd gone to yesterday with Tom. They noticed that most of the small Mom and Pop stores were open, and that most of the big chain stores were closed. When they got to the auto parts place, Mark thought it best for him to stay in the truck with the money. He gave Jim a list of parts he wanted for the truck and the Jeep. Jim was in the store for about twenty minutes. When he came out, the shop owner was helping him carry out some bags. The owner shook Mark's hand and then handed him a small box.

"This is the glow plug controller for your truck, but I don't know if The Burst got to it or not. If you'll just sign this invoice for it, you can pay me later or bring it back if it's no good," he told Mark.

"Let me pay for it," Mark argued. "I don't like to owe people."

"No, I insist," the parts man said. "I owe Tom and your company so much. If it wasn't for people like y'all, I might not be in business. Your friend paid me for everything else, but I won't take money for a part that might not be good."

"Thank you," Mark said, as he signed the invoice.

"No problem. You fellas just come back if you need anything else."

Jim climbed back into the truck and thanked the parts man one more time. They backed out of the parking lot and headed back to Jim's truck. Jim explained to Mark that the parts store owner had told him that the computer on the '91 Chevy only controlled the spark advance and the fuel mixture for the throttle body. He said Chevrolet had been making basically the same small block motor since 1955 and that lots of the parts were interchangeable over most of those years. He sold Jim an aftermarket performance intake manifold and carburetor, and a vacuum advanced distributor with everything he needed to convert his truck. He told Jim how to install the parts and told him it should only take two or three hours. Jim figured the money for the new parts was wasted if the lights came back on, but if they didn't, it was a good investment. It was a worth the gamble to make sure he had transportation, he figured. When they got back to work, they pushed Jim's truck into the shade, pulled the toolbox out of Mark's truck, and started to work.

"Do you think Todd's right about the power?" Mark asked.

"I don't know. Like you said, he's the third one to say it. Gunny's kind of a conspiracy theorist, so I take everything he tells me about that kind of stuff with a big grain of salt, but sometimes, he's right. I thought Scott was a complete nut job at first, but he seemed pretty normal when he came over and helped us last night, and now, Todd tells us the same thing. We know he's intelligent, and I've never known him to lie. Heck, I can't ever remember him being wrong," Jim rambled.

"What do you think about joining their group?"

"Well, Lisa's not going to like it if we can't have her parents out, but we have to at least go see the ranch."

"I agree. The way I see it, we have three ways to go. First, if Todd's wrong, then we just go back to the way things were. But if he's right, then we could go to the ranch or we could stay right where we are. You and Lisa are welcome to stay with us as long as you like, and it wouldn't be a problem for her parents to stay either. Heck, if we have to start raising our own food, I'd kill to have her dad's expertise."

"Thanks, Mark. If the power stays off, I don't think we'd want to be in town. I agree with Todd and Tom on that at least. If things go back to normal or if we go stay at the ranch, we don't really need anything, but if things go bad and we stay at your place, what do we need?"

"Man, a ton of stuff. Fuel, gardening stuff, canned food, building materials, fencing, animals, ammo, medical supplies…I can't even imagine what all we might need."

"When we get back to your house, we can sit down with the girls and make a list. They're about twice as smart as we are anyway," Jim said with a grin.

"They're not that smart!" Mark retorted. "After all, they married us!"

After two and a half hours, Jim tried the starter. The Chevy seemed like it wanted to start but just wouldn't quite fire. Mark got a wrench and loosened the new distributor. He turned it counter clockwise about 20 degrees.

"Try it now, Jim."

Jim hit the starter, and the engine roared to life.

"Hot damn! It runs! What did you do?"

"I just retarded the timing a little. It sounds like the idle circuit on the carb needs adjusting. Hand me a regular screwdriver."

Mark made a few adjustments to the carburetor and the new distributor, then replaced the air cleaner. Jim pulled the truck over to the gas storage tank, and they topped off his tank. Mark was glad they'd gotten Jim's truck running. It was lifted and had 35-inch tires on it. It would go almost anywhere the Jeep would, but, unlike the Jeep, had the capacity to carry a decent load. It also had a winch on the front that was useful for many chores. It would make their lives easier having two running trucks.

"What now?" Mark asked.

"Feel like working on another truck? I bought the parts for Gunny's truck. Plus, I think I want to get the rest of my guns and clean out our cupboard."

"Okay. His should be easy to fix next to this one. While I'm working on it, you can get what you want out of the house."

Jim led the way, and he went through the bad neighborhood. Mark wished he'd gone the long way. He wondered if Jim remembered how much money he had in the truck. He reached down and made sure the Colt was in a position where he could get to it with the seat belt on. Mark noticed that there were more people out, and in larger groups, than the last time he drove through here. He was nervous. No one tried anything, although the two running vehicles received a hard look from more than one of the groups. When they got to Jim's house,

32

Jim backed his truck into the driveway, and Mark backed in right beside him. He figured Jim might have more than his truck would hold. About the time Mark got out of his truck, Gunny came limping out of his house.

"Hey, Jimbo!" He called. "You got that sissy wagon running, huh?"

"Yeah, Gunny," Jim answered. "Mark helped me fix it."

"Ah, Karate Man. You good with a wrench, too?"

"You better hope so, Gunny," Jim said. "I bought some parts for your old truck, and Mark's going to try to fix it for you."

"Really?"

"Yes, Gunny," Mark said as he pulled his toolbox out of the bed of his truck. "Should we get started before it gets too hot?"

"Whatever you say, Karate Man."

Mark worked on the old Dodge while Gunny paced and fretted like an expectant father. Thirty minutes later, the engine was resurrected, and Mark topped off Gunny's gas tank. Gunny was so happy he shook Mark's hand until his shoulder joint was almost worn out. Then Mark went to see how far along Jim was. When he got into the house, Jim just about had all of the canned and dry food in boxes, so Mark started carrying them out to the trucks. When all the food was loaded, Jim opened his safe and put all of his long guns in cases and placed them in the extended cab of his truck. Then he got all of the pistols and revolvers, already in cases or boxes, and stacked them on top of the rifles and shotguns. His ammunition was all in metal GI ammo cans that were clearly labeled as to what was in them. These he placed in the bed of Mark's truck, as the back of his was quite full. When they were getting into the trucks, Gunny came out of his house with a box of his own.

"Here are some books you guys might find useful," Gunny offered.

Mark looked down in the box and saw a series of books called "Foxfire" and a large book named "Back to Basics." Mark didn't really want to take the books, but he didn't want to hurt the old man's feelings.

"Thank you, Gunny," Mark said as he took the box. "Listen, yesterday you said the lights won't be back on for quite a while. Why do you think that?"

"That EMP is some bad shit," Gunny started. "We studied it in the Marines. It cooks everything electrical unless it's protected. All our trucks and radios and stuff had special parts that were supposed to be EMP proof...I just don't see how there's any way they can fix all the damage that The Burst did in two or three days. It'll take months, at least."

"But, the Vice President is saying that they can do it," Jim argued.

"Jimbo, you have a tendency to hear what you want to hear. You remember the President who said 'Read my lips...'? I believed that President, but that didn't make what he said true, now did it? Most folks around here think bread, milk, and eggs come from the grocery store. They have no idea how, or even the means, to provide for themselves. When the grocery store shelves are empty and the faucets won't run, the shit is really gonna hit the fan. The VP's just trying to postpone the inevitable, I suppose. Now you boys get going, you hear."

"Gunny, here's a map to my house. If things get bad, you come on out, okay?"

Gunny took the map, looked at it, and then handed it back to Mark.

"I appreciate that, Karate Man, but you boys don't need a broken down old geezer like me to worry about. Now scoot before I put a boot up your ass." With that, he did an about face and marched into his house.

Chapter 7

The two men just stared at the door that slammed behind Gunny.

"That's the closest I've ever seen him come to being emotional," Jim said in disbelief. "Oh well, first time for a lot of things in the last two days. What do you want to do now, Bud?"

"I need to run by the hardware store, and I wouldn't mind getting a little more ammo from the gun store, but with all this stuff in the trucks, I'm as nervous as a long-tailed cat in a room full of rocking chairs. Let's go home. I'll feel a lot better when all this money is in the safe."

"Hey, do you think we should move my safe over to your house?"

"If the power isn't back in a couple of days, then that's probably a good idea. We'll need a couple more guys to help put it in the truck though."

The two men got into their trucks and slowly worked their way out of the subdivision. When they approached the entrance to Silver Hills, it was almost two o'clock. Mark slowed his truck way down and stuck his hand out of the window to wave at the guards. They waved back, and he made the turn into the subdivision. Jon and Scott were on duty.

"Hey, Jon, Scott."

Jon was holding an AR-15, and Scott had a scoped, bolt-action, hunting rifle slung over his shoulder. Jon also had a pistol in a military holster on his side.

"Hey, Mark," Jon returned. "Are you going to pump water again today?"

"I can. What time do you think is good for everyone?"

"We're going to get together at my house after the Vice President's speech again today, just to discuss what's going on. How about right after that, just like last night?" Jon suggested.

"Sounds good. See you at the meeting."

Mark and Jim drove to the back of the subdivision and parked their trucks behind the house. The girls were on the deck, under the awning. Lisa was going over some math with the twins, and Jess was reading a book. Samantha and David were nowhere to be seen.

"Jim, you got your truck running?" Lisa shouted, as he got out.

"Yes, ma'am," he answered.

"How did the meeting go?" Jess asked, as the men stepped onto the deck with the briefcases.

"Pretty good," Mark said with a big smile. "Wouldn't you say it went pretty good, Jim?"

"As a matter of fact, I would," Jim said, with a huge smile of his own.

"You guys look like the cat that just swallowed the canary," Lisa said. "What's up?"

"Oh, just this!" Jim stated, as both men set the briefcases down and opened them for the women to see.

Both women's mouths fell open.

"Where did you get that?" Jess stammered.

"Todd gave it to us," Mark answered, as Jess reach out to touch the money, like she wanted to make sure it was real.

35

"How much is it?" Lisa inquired.

"It's this month's pay," Jim answered.

"What's with the rolls of coins?" Jess wanted to know.

"That's a gift," Mark responded to even more quizzical looks on the wives' faces. "You see these are pre-1965 quarters. That means they're 90% silver."

"But I don't understand. Why would Todd pay you when you'll be back at work next week?"

"He doesn't think we'll be back at work any time soon," Mark said.

Lisa shooed the twins away to go play, and the adults all sat down at the picnic table. Mark and Jim explained what they'd been told at the meeting and about the offer to stay at the ranch. Jess was a little skeptical, but Lisa didn't like it at all. The four of them debated the pros and cons of Todd's offer. After discussing it for a while, they agreed they had to at least go look at the group's setup at the ranch, but the women wanted to wait and see if the power would come back on first. They decided that if the lights weren't back on in the city by day after tomorrow at noon, they'd make their visit. They also discussed what to do with the money in case they decided to stay where they were. Lisa suggested that they each work on a list independently and compare them later.

"After all, it's not like we need to spend it if the lights come on," she said.

Everyone agreed that this was a reasonable course of action. The men carried the cases into the study, and Mark opened his large gun safe. They put the cases on the top shelf of the safe and then carried in Jim's guns. The handguns all fit easily, but there wasn't room for all of the long guns. They decided to remove some of the less expensive long guns and place them in a locking closet. Then they carried the food into the house and put Jim's ammo in the shed next to Mark's. Mark put Gunny's box of books in a cabinet in the shed. While they were doing that, Jess was warming up some soup and making grilled cheese sandwiches for the men. The gas stove would at least work until the propane ran out.

While Mark and Jim were eating, the women sat down with them, and they all discussed what might happen if the power didn't come back on pretty soon. They all agreed that things could get ugly. When it came to food, most people could get by for a week or maybe two without having to buy much. Some couldn't, but even they could probably borrow enough for a while. Then there was water. As soon as there wasn't enough water pressure in town for drinking and flushing, people would panic. None of them knew how long the City Water Board could keep pressure if the lights didn't come back on. The women thought maybe it would be a good idea to go ahead and buy some food if the grocery store was open. After all, they needed to eat whether they had lights or not, so the food wouldn't go to waste, and it might be too late if they waited.

While they were talking about groceries, Mark remembered that Manny had promised him some eggs. He asked where David was so he could send him over to the Hernandez house but was told that he was over at his friend's house. Sam, he learned, was in the camper listening to her mp3 player and generally feeling sorry for herself. Mark called her out of the camper to see what was wrong. It seemed that no one could be expected to live without a cell phone, especially a 16-year-old. Mark instructed her that people had lived for centuries without telephones and that they walked to other people's houses to visit. Just so that she could see how it was done, she could walk over to the Hernandez's and get the eggs Manny had offered.

"But, Dad, do I have to?" she whined.

"Yes. You have to!" Mark whined back in a sarcastic voice. "Now get going and just be glad he's not giving us a side of beef."

Samantha rolled her eyes at her father as her mother handed her an empty egg carton. She turned and walked off, slightly stomping her feet, knowing exactly how far she could push it and not get into trouble.

That girl, Mark thought to himself. Why does she always have to be so moody? Jess isn't like that. I wonder where she gets it from? If I had told David to go get the eggs, he would have just said 'Yes, Sir,' and been back in less time than I spent arguing with her.

Mark sat back down at the picnic table with the rest of the adults and listened to the news on the radio.

The city of Cincinnati has been almost totally burned to the ground. Fire crews were unable to successfully battle the hundreds of fires set by the rioters, and the National Guard was not able to squash the riots in time to save the city. Most of the citizens were able to evacuate, many on foot, as burning cars blocked most of the streets in the city. However, it is estimated that fifty to sixty thousand were trapped by the fires and unable to escape.

The situation in Detroit is much the same. Over half the city has been lost. Fire crews are gallantly trying to save the area where most of the automotive plants are located. The Mayor of Detroit asked the Governor of Michigan to send National Guard troops in to put down the rioters and to seize firefighting equipment from other cities to help fight the fires in his city. The Governor has called up the National Guard, but as of now, there is no word from the capitol on seizing the property of other municipalities.

The riots in Seattle were quieted quickly once the Mayor of that city ordered police to shoot arsonists on sight. Police report over four hundred arrests connected with the riots and twelve deaths. Fire crews in Seattle were helped by the rain that has been falling there since yesterday.

Sources inside the Pentagon have hinted that The Burst was the result of several nuclear explosions in space. Our CBS experts have theorized that such explosions would pose little or no risk of radioactive fallout to the United States but would cause the kind of widespread system disruptions we have seen. There was no word on who may have caused the explosion or how.

It is rumored that in his speech to the nation tonight, the Vice President will confirm that the body of the President has been recovered and identified.

In state news, the Texas Governor has called up all of the National Guard troops in the state. The Governor is quoted as saying, "We need them ready, just in case."

In Houston, the once proud Exxon Building was burned to the ground today. Fire crews in Houston, still busy fighting fires in residential areas, could spare only enough manpower to ensure that the fire did not spread to other buildings in the downtown area.

Locally, the San Antonio Police Department is reporting a city record twenty-three murders last night. Most appear to be drug or gang related. However, a spokesman for the department said, with the communication interruptions, there may be more that we don't know about yet. The Mayor has asked for all residents to stay in their homes after dark. The sunset curfew goes into effect at 8:10 PM today.

Now for the weather. It will be hot and dry today, with highs reaching near one hundred degrees. The low tonight will be in the mid-seventies, with a slight chance of rain after dark. For tomorrow, you can expect more of the same.

This is KSTX, 640 AM. We'll be back after this break.

Mark turned off the radio.

"Thank God we don't live in Cincinnati!" Lisa exclaimed.

"You can say that again," Jess agreed, as the men nodded their heads.

Mark looked at Jim. "You want to help me with that glow plug controller on my truck?"

"Sure thing, buddy."

"Yes, you boys go play while Lisa and I work on a grocery list," Jess dictated.

"Yes, ma'am!"

Jim and Mark started working on the Ford. Mark noticed that Sam had come back and given the eggs to her mother and then returned to the camper and probably her sulking. Just after they removed the old controller, Jim noticed it was time for the Vice President's speech. Mark called Lisa and Jess to bring the radio over to the truck, so they could keep working.

The local newscast from earlier was correct; the President's body had been found. The VP said he had taken the oath of office, and as the new President, he would be submitting his nominee for Vice President to the Congress as his first order of business. The new President asked for all Americans to pray for the country during these troubling times. He indicated that they were very close to restoring limited power to some of the major cities on the East Coast. He encouraged everyone to help and watch out for his or her neighbors, and he assured the country, and the world, that the United States would emerge from this crisis stronger and more resilient. He warned those who would try to take advantage of this situation, both domestic and foreign, that punishment would be swift and sure.

When the speech was over, Jess turned off the radio. No one said anything for a while.

"Let's all go down to Jon's and see what's going on," Mark suggested somberly.

"Good idea," Jess agreed. "I'll get Sam to watch the girls for you, Lisa."

The four of them walked to the corner where Jon's house was. Several of the men brought their wives this afternoon. Everyone milled around and met the neighbors that they didn't already know. The main subjects of interest were the former President's death, and whether or not the new President was telling the truth about the power. Opinions were split. Generally, the women believed the President, and the men did not. There were exceptions of course, but not many. Mark and Jim talked it over and agreed that they should help stand watch at the gate. They spoke to Jon about taking a shift.

"What made you change your minds about needing guards?" Jon asked.

"Oh, we still don't think it's really needed, but we want to do our fair share," Mark explained.

"I see," said Jon. "Listen, I already have the schedule made up and posted for the next week. Could I use you two for alternates until I make the new schedule and then work you in to the rotation?"

"That would be fine with us, Jon."

Before he left, Mark announced that he'd be running the water pump as soon as he got home. Once there, he and Jim moved the generator and plugged in the pump. Mark put Sam and David in charge from the start today. Back at the truck, they finished hooking up the new controller, and Mark climbed in to try it. The engine had cooled completely off, so this would be a good test. He turned the key on, and the 'Wait to Start' light illuminated. After about fifteen seconds, it went off, and Mark engaged the starter. The big diesel turned over, caught, and idled like a sewing machine. He turned the truck off, whispering a prayer of thanks.

When everyone had gotten water, Mark and Jim moved the generator back by the campers. Mrs. Petersen had brought back the five-gallon container, and David had refilled it and carried it back to her house. Mark plugged in the campers and the deep freeze. They wouldn't be able to waste the gas to run the A/C's every day if the power didn't come back on, but Mark thought it was best to acclimate everyone slowly, so they could use it for a week or so. He checked the freezer, and it wasn't as cold as he thought it should be. He may need to run the generator for a while each morning to keep everything frozen, at least until the weather cooled off some. He took out four fresh ice bottles and replaced the four in the ice chest. The food in the cooler was still cold. Then he put the four from last night back in the freezer. The bottles he took out of the ice chest were still frozen in the very center. It wouldn't take too long to freeze them back solid.

Mark heard Jess calling him. He walked back to the deck and saw the Risk game Mrs. Petersen had given them on the picnic table. They all sat down and played until almost eleven o'clock. When they were done, Mark went into the house and put a dollar in the box for a word that had slipped out when he busted a knuckle working on the truck. Then he turned off the generator and went to the camper to go to bed. He tried to go to sleep, but his mind was racing. It was a long time before he finally dozed off.

Chapter 8

When the alarm went off at 6:30, Mark was already awake. He had slept fitfully. He lay in bed and looked through the vent in the roof of the camper for a moment. The sky was just starting to turn pink. What day was it? The Burst hit on Tuesday, so today was Thursday. It was hard to believe how much had transpired in less than forty-eight hours. He got out of bed, pulled on his jeans, and went into the house. He found a pair of running shorts, a t-shirt, and his running shoes with the help of a flashlight. He dressed and then headed out the door. After stretching his back and calves, he began to run.

He thought about what they would need if they decided not to go stay at the ranch. He didn't see a way they could amass the resources they'd need to survive here if the power didn't come back on quickly. Even with Jim's help, there was no way to buy and do even the minimum. If the lights weren't on in a few days, the only logical choice would be to join Mr. Davis's group.

Mark really wanted to believe that the power would be back on, but he was finding it more and more difficult. There was something in what the President said last night that didn't seem quite right. Mark didn't know exactly what it was, but something was telling him the lights wouldn't be back on any time soon. Maybe he was just getting paranoid. He glanced over his shoulder and then laughed to himself. His thoughts turned to other things.

His karate class was supposed to have been last night. Of course they didn't have it. The lights were out, and the school was locked up. Mark missed it. The best part of the martial arts to him was teaching. Seeing a kid who thought he couldn't suddenly begin to think 'I can' was so rewarding.

He was approaching the half-mile mark, and if he wanted to run just a mile, he would turn around here and run back home, but, he thought, I don't have to go to work, just a little further. A tenth of a mile further, he was at the entrance to Silver Hills.

"Good morning, Adam," he said to one of the guards.

"Good morning, Mark. Nice morning for a run, huh?"

"I think so." He had met the other guard last night, but couldn't remember his name. "How's it going for you this morning?"

"Pretty good," the man answered.

Mark wondered whether to turn east or west for about a half a second. He turned east to be able to see the sun rise. Too bad they didn't have some solar panels. With them and a battery bank, they could at least have some light in the house. Maybe they could find some twelve-volt ceiling fans. Did they even make such a thing? If they did, he would bet they had them at the ranch. The more he thought about it, the more he knew they had to go. But how would he convince the women? Wait, he didn't have to; the lists would. They would see that it was hopeless to stay here.

By the time he realized it, he must have been over two miles from the house. Even on his long runs, he didn't usually go over three miles, and he had missed the sunrise. He was sure he'd seen it, but he couldn't remember. He turned around and started running back. What was he going to do about Sam? David seemed to be taking it all in stride, but he could care less about going to school, and many of his friends lived in the subdivision. Sam was a social animal. She had lots of friends, and they lived all over. He needed to get her involved in something, but what? He would talk to Jess about it. What of the rest of his family? His parents, brother and one of his sisters and their families lived in Waco. Would they be safe where they were? What about Jess's sister in California? What about Lisa's folks, and Jim's Mom, and his brother? Mark shook his head. Running was supposed to make things clearer for him. This time he ended up with more questions than answers.

Mark could just make out the Silver Hills sign ahead. He quickened his pace a little. When he turned into the subdivision, he waved at the guards as he passed. It was slightly uphill to his house from here. His calves were burning, but he put his head down and picked up his pace a little more. Perhaps the answers could be found in pushing himself harder. When he turned the corner, he broke into a sprint. Harder, he thought, but no answers came as he pushed himself. When he reached the front of the house, he looked at his watch. It said 7:34. He walked to the corner and back to cool down. He must have run close to five miles. Surprisingly, he didn't feel that tired. He stretched some more to cool down.

Mark got some clean clothes out of the house and went back out to the camper to shower. When he got out, Jess was frying up the eggs Manny had given them. Jim and Lisa were up, but all of the kids except for Sam were still asleep. They all sat down at the picnic table to eat breakfast. Mark noticed that the yolks on these eggs were much darker than the eggs they bought at Kroger. They also tasted better. As they ate, they talked about what they each wanted to get accomplished for the day. Jess wanted to start working on a curriculum for Sam and David. She said they would need it whether they stayed here or went to the ranch. Lisa wanted to get to the grocery store with the list she and Jess had made the night before. Sam asked if she could go with Lisa, who said she would be glad to have the company. Lisa asked Jim if he'd work with the twins on their math this morning. She told the others that Jim always had more success with the girls on math than she did because their brains worked the same way. Mark wanted to go pay for the glow plug controller, go to the hardware store for the plug to the dryer, and maybe run by the gun store for some ammo. It was decided that Mark, Lisa, and Sam would go to town, and Jim and Jess would 'hold down the fort.'

The three shoppers loaded up in Mark's truck and headed to town. They first stopped at the hardware store. It was a small, independently owned store that had been run by the same family for almost sixty years, and the store looked like hadn't changed much in that time. Mark found the plug he needed to replace the one he had stolen from the dryer. The girls wandered off to look through the store. Sam found Mark and pulled him over to where Lisa was looking at some kerosene lamps.

"Look, Mark," Lisa said. "They have kerosene lamps and lanterns. They also have big tubs and wash boards. If the power doesn't come back on, and we stay at your place, we're going to have to come back here."

"Boy, I hope it doesn't come down to washing our clothes with wash boards," Samantha said. "That would be cruel and unusual punishment, and the

Constitution prohibits that, doesn't it? Besides, we have the generator that'll run the washer, right Dad?"

"Yes, it will, but I don't think we'll be able to spare the gas to wash clothes for very long."

Mark paid for the plug, and they headed to the gun store. When they got there, Mark was a little surprised that it was closed. The Watson family ran the store, and it wasn't like them to close. The Mom and Dad had started the business in the early 1960's, and both sons now worked at the store. Jerry ran the front, and Tony was an excellent gunsmith. He'd been taught by his father and now ran the back of the store. Perhaps Mark would run by Jerry's house later and see if everything was okay.

When they got to the Kroger, there was a line to get into the store. All three in the truck wondered what was going on. Mark parked the truck out in the parking lot a ways, as was his custom. It could be very difficult to get the long truck out of a parking space if people parked too close. They got out and walked up to the entrance. When they got to the door, there was a table with one of the managers sitting behind it. Standing next to him was a San Antonio police officer. The manager explained that they'd had a run on the store when the lights went out and that since they didn't know when they would be resupplied, they were limiting each family to fifty dollars worth of groceries. He told them the store was only accepting cash or public assistance cards. He asked for one of their ID's. Mark handed the man his driver license. The manager looked at it and opened a notebook to the T's. He looked for Turner, and at each one he found, he compared the address to the one on Mark's license. When he didn't find a match, he wrote Mark's name and address down in the book. He gave Mark a number and told him that when his number was called, a sales associate would take them through the store with a flashlight and add up their items on a calculator. Mark informed the manager that he'd also brought Lisa to the store, and she had her own family. He checked and recorded Lisa's license and gave her a number, too. Then they went and stood in line. Lisa pulled out the list and started numbering the items on it by importance. When she got to the point where she knew she was over a hundred dollars, she got a piece of paper out of her purse and wrote some of the items on a new list. She then scratched them off of the original. She gave the new list to Mark and told him to get as far down it as he could. It took almost forty-five minutes before their numbers were called. Mark went with his assigned associate, and Sam elected to wait and go with Lisa. It didn't take Mark too long to reach fifty dollars. He was able to get most everything Lisa had put on his list. The associate took him to the front of the store, and he paid in cash as they bagged his groceries. It was only a minute or two until Lisa and Sam were done paying for their food. They put all the bags into one basket and pushed it toward the truck. When they got there, Mark opened the back door, and they started stacking the groceries in the floorboard of the back seat. As they were unloading the basket, Mark noticed three scruffy looking guys walking past the truck toward the store. His radar went up a little, but once the men passed the truck, Mark felt better. He realized that he, too, probably looked a little scruffy. After all, it had been two days since he'd shaved. Once all the groceries were loaded, the girls got into the truck, and Mark pushed the basket over to the cart corral. When he turned to go back, the three men were between the truck and him. Mark's senses went into overdrive. He looked at the truck. The girls had the doors closed and, he hoped, locked. His .45 was also in the truck. He looked side to side, but there was no one else this far out in the parking lot. He felt trapped with the corral right behind him, so he stepped to the left enough so he could back up if he needed to. He looked at the three men. The one on the left was tall and muscular. The middle one was average height and skinny, and the one to the right was moderately overweight.

The middle one spoke to Mark. "Hey, mister, what's the deal with the long line to get into the store?"

Mark tried to answer in a natural voice. "They're only letting everyone have fifty dollars worth of groceries. The employees take you through the store with flashlights."

Mark was waiting for some kind of reply when he saw the knife in Skinny's hand. He took half a step back. They were too close for him to get his little pistol out of his back pocket. He figured his best option if he had to fight was to use his hands and try to create enough space to bring his gun to bear.

When Skinny saw that Mark had seen the knife, he extended it toward Mark's midsection. "Listen up, asshole. Give us the keys to the truck, and no one gets hurt." Tubby stuck his hand out toward Mark for the keys.

Mark thought that the truck and the groceries weren't worth getting killed for, but he also knew that if these guys had a gun, they'd be using it. He had no intention of providing them with one by letting them have his Colt that was in the truck. Most importantly, what might these criminals do to Lisa and Sam?

Mark reached into his left front pocket and pulled out his office keys. He figured that if he dropped them, Tubby might bend over to pick them up, and he could kick him into Knife Boy. Mark reached his hand out toward the carjackers, praying they wouldn't notice that the keys weren't car keys. He dropped the keys right in front of the man with the knife. At that instant, everything seemed to go to slow motion.

The man's eyes got wide with anger, and he lunged at Mark's stomach with the knife. "You motherfu…" he started to scream, but wasn't able to finish. When he lunged, Mark thrust his hands forward and grabbed the man's knife hand around the wrist. At the same time, he pulled his hips back to get his midsection as far away as possible from the knife. Mark stepped to his left and jerked the man's arm past him. The knife wielder, with his weight going forward from his own thrust, went flying by with the assistance of Mark pulling him, and he landed face first on the asphalt. The big man to Mark's left stepped in and badly telegraphed a right-handed haymaker. Mark stepped inside the punch and brought his arms up to intercept the man's arm. When the punch was stopped, Mark ducked under and slid his right hand down to the man's wrist and grabbed. The palm heel of his left hand slammed into the back of the attacker's elbow. The arm bent back the wrong way, and the man howled. Mark then side kicked to the man's knee. With the adrenaline pumping, he kicked too high, and it landed in the man's thigh, knocking him down.

Mark looked back, and Knife Boy was still down on all fours groaning. He changed his focus to the last man. Tubby was standing wide-eyed and frozen. When Mark looked at him, a dark stain appeared in the crotch of his jeans. Mark backed up toward the truck and pulled the Kel-Tec out of his pocket and pointed it in the direction of the three men. Tubby, seeing this, took off running at a pace that could have set a world record. The other two looked at Tubby and then, seeing why he was running, did their best to catch up with him.

Mark was still pointing the pistol at the men, even after they were well out of range. Even though he'd been in karate for six years and had his Concealed Handgun License for four, this was the first time he'd ever had to defend himself. He stood there shaking from the adrenaline dump. Sam rolled down the window of the truck.

"Dad...Dad...DAD!"

"Yes?" Mark finally answered. Time sped back up to a normal pace.

"Are you OK?"

"Yes, I think so."

"Dad, you were so awesome. I was so scared, but you kicked butt! I know we practice that stuff in karate, but seeing you go full speed, I never thought it would be that effective."

"Honey, I never thought it would be either, but thank God it is."

"Let me check you to make sure you're not injured," Lisa said. She looked Mark over and could not find any injuries. "Did you even get hit?"

"I don't think so."

"What do we do now?" Lisa asked.

"I guess I should go make a report with that policeman at the entrance." Mark said, as he put the .32 back into his pocket.

The trio got into the truck, and Mark drove up to the entrance. He pulled the truck up to the curb and got out.

"Hey, buddy, you can't park there," the policeman admonished.

"I was just attacked out in the parking lot," Mark informed him.

"Are you OK? What did they get?"

"Yes, I'm all right, and they didn't get anything." Mark finished telling the policeman what had happened.

"Did you shoot them?" the policeman asked.

"No. I didn't even fire a shot, but I dislocated one guy's elbow, and the other guy could have fallen on his knife."

"Can I see your CHL?" the officer requested.

Mark started to reach for his wallet in his left hip pocket and paused. "I'm just getting my wallet." He wanted to make sure the policeman was at ease.

"I understand."

The policeman took out a little notebook from his breast pocket and wrote down Mark's name and CHL number. He then gave Mark back his license.

"OK, I wrote down your name and address in case we have any questions."

"Aren't you going to take a formal report?"

"Mr. Turner, if these were normal times, yes, I would take a formal report. Under the circumstances though, I won't. The PD is swamped. You didn't get hurt, nothing was stolen, and the three guys who tried to attack you only got what was coming to them. You should be thanking God and your training that things went so well for you. I have your information if anything comes up. Go home and next time, watch your six better!"

"Thank you, Officer, I will." With that, Mark got back into his truck. His hands were shaking so badly that he could barely find first gear.

Chapter 9

Mark drove back over to the cart corral. He asked Sam if she would pick up the keys that were still on the ground. She hopped out and got them. When she got back in, Mark eased out on the clutch and turned the truck toward home.

"I thought you wanted to go by Jerry Watson's house," Sam said.

"Not now, Honey. I just want to go home."

"Mark, would you like me to drive?" Lisa asked, noticing that his hands weren't very steady.

"No. I think I'll be okay," Mark said.

The ride home was quiet and uneventful. When Mark parked the truck, they carried the groceries in. Sam was talking a mile a minute, relating the Kroger parking lot incident. Jess was shocked, Jim was impressed, and David just said it was 'COOL.'

"It was not cool! Someone could have gotten killed. Maybe even me, or your sister, or Mrs. Davis. Would you still think it was 'COOL' then?"

Mark saw the hurt in his son's eyes at the same time that Jess put her hand on his arm. "I'm sorry, David. I didn't mean to yell at you. I'm not mad at you; it's just that I'm still kind of freaked out by what happened. Will you forgive me?"

David nodded his head. Mark pulled him and hugged him. That was something David rarely let him do in front of other people. When they released the embrace, David had tears in his eyes.

"I'm going out to the shed to check the freezer," Mark announced, just wanting to get away from everybody for a minute.

When Mark walked outside, Jim followed him, seeing that his friend was still shaking, even though it had been almost an hour since the incident.

"Want to talk?" Jim asked.

"NO...Yes...I don't know."

"Are you upset that you hurt those guys?"

"Hell, no. They got off lucky, as far as I'm concerned. Once I got my gun out, I would have shot them in a heartbeat if they had kept attacking. It's just that I was scared shitless." There went a dollar. "If I didn't know how to defend myself, or if I hadn't had my .32, no telling what might have happened. I was mostly scared of what those assholes would have done to Lisa and Sam given half a chance." Two dollars. "I can tell you this. That .32 probably saved my life, but it felt like a peashooter in my hand. I was cursing myself for not having the .45. I will never leave the house to go anywhere without it and a couple of extra magazines on my hip from now on. The .32 is okay for a backup, but I can tell you if you really need a gun, you want the biggest fucking gun you can hold." There was a word Mark almost never used. Well, if he was going to owe three dollars in less than a minute, he might as well get his money's worth.

"You learned something from this, then. Maybe it wasn't totally a bad thing," Jim said.

"Yeah, I learned how vulnerable we all are. I'm careful Jim, but if those guys had a brain between them, they probably would have killed me. If all three would have attacked at the same time, I'd be dead right now, and things are only going to get worse if the power doesn't come back on. We're not safe here. We have to go stay at the ranch. It's the only way to be sure nothing will happen to the girls and the kids. Besides, there's no way we can buy everything we'd need to live here. There's just too much that we need to make it if the power's off more than a month or two. I know the girls don't like the idea of moving out there, but hopefully with what happened today and when we look at the lists of what we need, they'll see that there really isn't a choice."

"Mark, I think you might be overreacting a little. We might all agree to move to the ranch with Todd. I mean, we still need to go look it over, but I don't think you should let one incident influence you so much."

"Well, I can see how you might think I'm overreacting," Mark snapped, "but when it's you in that moment, knowing that all that stands between your daughter and your best friend's wife getting assaulted and maybe killed is just you, you might think differently."

"Maybe so, but when you start ranting like this, there's no sense in arguing with you. If you want to talk instead of argue, come get me." Jim turned and left.

Mark checked the freezer. It was still pretty cold. He poked at a big piece of venison wrapped in butcher paper. It was still hard as a rock. He had run the generator longer last night, maybe that was enough, he thought. He was glad Jim had come out with him but was glad that he'd left, too. Mark was exhausted. The adrenaline had done its job and turned him into a mama grizzly defending her cubs, but now that it had worn off, he was as tired as he could ever remember being.

He went back into the house. When he walked in, everyone got quiet. Mark knew they'd been talking about him. He didn't care. He told Jess that he was going to rest in the camper for a while. When he got into the camper, taking his shoes off seemed to take all of the energy he had. He climbed up onto the bed and just lay down on top of the blanket.

When Mark woke up, he felt like he'd slept for days. Was it dusk or dawn? He couldn't tell. He looked at his watch. It was almost curfew. Mark got up and put on his shoes. He walked out of the camper and could see everyone else up on the deck with the Coleman lantern burning close enough to light the Monopoly game they were playing. He stepped up onto the deck, and Jess was the first one to see him.

"Hey, Stranger, how was your nap?"

"I don't remember," he said, as he rubbed the back of his head.

"Man, you were really out of it," Jess informed him. "I tried to get you up to help Jim with the generator, but you were dead to the world."

"You ran the generator?"

Everyone nodded their heads.

"I got Jon to help me," Jim said.

"Wow…I never heard it. Listen, I want to apologize to everyone for how I acted, especially to David and Jim."

"Don't worry about it," Jim replied.

"It's okay, Dad. You must have been pretty stressed," David said.

"That's no excuse for the way I acted. I'm really sorry." Mark then changed the subject. "Did you guys listen to the news and the President?"

48

"Yes, we did," Jim told him. "It was pretty much the same old news. Rioting in a few more cities. Baltimore and Chicago, I think. The Pres said they weren't moving quite as fast as they thought on the power, but that it should only be another day or two before the lights would be back on in some cities."

"Hmmm," was all Mark had to say.

"Then we all went down to Jon's," Lisa continued to fill him in. "There were a lot more people there tonight. Everyone was talking about one of three things. The third most popular topic of conversation was the power. Less people believe the power is going to be back on in a couple of days. Now there's a group in the middle who believe it may be several weeks to a month or two before the power is restored. The second favorite topic was the $50 limit at Kroger. And the most talked about item at the Silver Hills community meeting for today was..." her voice crescendoed. "Drum roll, please." She paused again. Jim beat his hands on the picnic table. "The amazing Kung-fu feats of one Mister Mark Turner!"

"You didn't," Mark protested.

"It seems that your son told one of his friends," Jess explained, "and by the time the meeting rolled around, everyone knew."

"Of course, the rumor mill had upped the opponents to eight, and they all had knives, but that was okay because you just jumped into a phone booth and came out with tights, a cape, and a big red 'S' on your chest," Lisa kidded.

Mark groaned.

"Seriously though, some people came up and asked me if you might be willing to teach a self defense course for the neighborhood," Jim said.

"Well, I would, if we were going to stay here," Mark informed them.

"Don't we all get a say in that?" Jess inquired.

"Of course you do, but I think you'll come to the same conclusion I have. There just isn't any other choice. We don't have what we need to live here for an extended period, and even if we did, it's not safe."

"What do you mean 'it's not safe?' You don't even think Jon's guards are necessary," Jess said.

"My thinking has changed since this morning. The guards may be able to stop a carload of teenagers from toilet papering houses, but there is no way they're going to stop a hungry and determined bunch of rioters and looters."

"We could always beef up the guards," Jim said.

"So you think we shouldn't go, too?" Mark said accusingly.

"I didn't say that. I'm still leaning toward staying at the ranch, but I haven't made my mind up yet. I think we have to see it first and then weigh all of our options," Jim retorted.

"You all just can't see that we have no options. You are clinging to the fantasy that civilization still exists. I got a hard lesson today in reality, and I can see what's coming. I thought it would be obvious to all of you, as well. I guess it doesn't matter though. When we sit down with our lists, it's going to be apparent that we have to go," Mark said.

"That may be true, Mark," Jess shot back, "but we need to see the ranch and review our lists first. I won't be forced into making a decision based on one occurrence. I know it must have been scary. I was scared just hearing about it.

But this is too important of a decision not to look at everything and everyone involved."

"Well, we leave for the ranch at noon tomorrow. In the meantime, I'm going to work on my list." Mark wheeled around and marched off much the same as Sam had the day before.

"When you're ready, we have our lists done," Jess called after him.

*   *   *

Mark woke up at 6:30 again. When he climbed out of bed, he noticed that he was a little stiff. He went into the house to find his running clothes and get dressed. He spent some extra time this morning stretching. When he started running, he could really feel the five miles he'd done yesterday. He set a pace that was a little slower than usual and figured a mile or two would work out the soreness. He started thinking about the ranch and how to convince the others to go. When he passed the guards, they razzed him.

"There he is," said the first. "The famous Silver Hill's Kung-fu master, himself. Be careful, one look from him will make you wet your pants."

"I heard he could catch a bullet in his teeth," the second guard teased.

"You guys go back to sleep," Mark waved them off. "Besides, everybody knows that real Kung-fu masters don't have any teeth."

The two men laughed.

As Mark turned east, the sun was just peeking over the horizon. He made a conscious effort to watch it come up this morning. When he was about a mile from his house, he turned around and picked up his pace just a tad. His legs were beginning to feel better. When he got back home, he found some clean clothes and showered. When he got out, Jess was just waking up.

"Are you doing anything this morning, or are we just getting ready to go to the ranch?" she asked.

"I still need to pay for the truck part, and I want to go see Jerry Watson to get some ammo, but I guess that can wait until we get back. Let's eat and then go over our lists. Then we can get ready and head out to visit the ranch."

Jess and Mark cooked breakfast together. There was still tension about the disagreement from the day before, so they both steered clear of that subject. Just before the pancakes were ready, Mark woke everyone up. They all ate, and then the adults got their lists and went through them. Mark had more on his than anyone else did. They discussed them for a couple of hours but were making little progress. Jim suggested they table the discussion until they got back from the ranch. After they loaded the trucks, Mark walked down to ask Jon to pump water for the neighbors until they got back. He asked Jon to please remember to take water to Mrs. Petersen and to plug up his freezer for three or four hours each day.

When the two trucks pulled out of the subdivision, Jim was in the lead. Mark looked in his rearview mirror and saw the Silver Hills sign. His hand reached down and felt the Colt Commander on his hip, as the sign got smaller.

Chapter 10

They were almost halfway to the ranch when Mark's watch read noon. Jim was slowing down every time they topped a hill, as there were still a few cars stalled on the highway. Mark asked Jess to turn on the portable radio.

This is KSTX, 640 AM. It's 93 degrees with sunny skies at straight up twelve o'clock. Now, for the news.

The presidential funeral is scheduled for three o'clock eastern time. The proceedings will be carried live on this CBS radio station.

The Pacific Rim markets were down for the third straight day. The Nikkei is now down over twenty percent since The Burst, and other world markets are not far behind. Japanese officials are talking about suspending trading until the New York and European markets are back online. It is expected that all of the markets will follow the Japanese lead.

The riots in Chicago have been halted by the Illinois National Guard. Before they could be brought in, however, the Mayor's house was burned to the ground. The rioters in Baltimore are still marching through the streets, destroying everything in their path. Even though the Governor has dispatched the Maryland National Guard, they have been unable to contain the lawlessness. There is an unconfirmed report that less than half of the state's guardsmen have reported for duty. The city of Cincinnati is now considered to be a total loss. Damage estimates are in the billions. The Detroit Fire Department was able to save almost a quarter of the city's automotive production facilities. The Mayor of Detroit has squared off against the Governor for not acting to save his city. So far, there has been no response from the Michigan capitol.

In local news, gunfire tore through a housing development last night in apparent gang warfare. Eleven people were killed, and twenty-three were wounded. Many of the victims were reported to be innocent bystanders, including several children.

Kroger stores have instituted a fifty-dollar limit per family on groceries. This has worked well throughout most of the city. However, a large number of people were arrested at the store at 281 and Thousand Oaks. An unidentified man, insisting that he should be allowed to buy as much as he wanted, incited a crowd to riot. There are also several reports of people being mugged for their groceries.

The City Water Board is asking all residents to be very conservative with their water usage. A spokesman reported that the backup generators are unable to keep up with the current demand for water pressure. He assured the media that with strict conservation, there is plenty of water for everyone. He asked that citizens not fill up their bathtubs or other containers, and for those who had already done so, to please use that water before running their faucets.

City Power and Light is reporting that they should have power to medical facilities that do not have their own backup power by the end of the weekend, or Monday morning at the latest. When asked about restoration of power to the whole city, the spokesman would not give a definitive answer but said it should not be too much longer.

Now, for the weather. Today's high will be in the mid....

Jess turned the radio off. "Nothing but more bad news. Looks more and more like Todd and Scott are right about the power."

Mark didn't say anything.

When Jim turned off of the county road to go through the first gate to the ranch, he tied the yellow bandana to his antenna. They had to pass though several ranches and gates to get to the group's ranch. When they were going through the last ranch before they reached their destination, Mark noticed that the power lines that had followed the road they were on had stopped. At the gate, they were met by two men, who were carrying black rifles and wearing a camouflage uniform in a pattern Mark hadn't seen before.

Mark noted that the gate was made of heavy pipe and had long, heavy spikes extending from it. If someone tried to crash through it with a pickup or SUV, they would at least ruin their radiator. The gate was hung on huge, twelve-inch, steel pipe fence posts cemented into the ground. In addition to the no-climb fencing, called that because the wire mesh was too closely woven to get a foothold in, and three strands of barbed wire across the top of the eight foot high fence, a heavy cable ran from metal fence post to metal fence post about twenty-four inches above the ground and back into the brush as far as Mark could see. There would be no way for anything less than a tank to make an unfriendly entrance to the ranch. Mark felt that if the rest of the ranch security was anywhere close to as good as the gate and fence, they would be very safe here.

The two guards spoke into a radio and then opened the gate. They told the families to follow the road until they reached the main complex. The nicely graded road wound through the mesquite trees and scrub bush. When they reached the complex, there was an eight-foot tall chain link fence around it, but the gate was open this time. Todd was standing just inside it. He pointed to where they should park. When they got out of the trucks, Todd shook everyone's hands.

"It's so good to see you all. Welcome to the New Age Ranch. Let me show you to your quarters, and then I'll give you the nickel tour."

Todd showed each family to their cabin. They were actual log cabins with three bedrooms and a large bath. Downstairs, there was a large living area with a big fireplace and the master bedroom and bathroom. The ceiling in the living area was vaulted and over twenty feet high in the center. The upstairs loft, which only covered the area over the master bedroom and the bath, was divided into two, smaller bedrooms. All three bedrooms had small, wood-burning stoves in them, as well as propane heaters. The furniture was modest but of high quality. Jess asked why there was no kitchen, and Todd told her that the group always ate together in the community dining room. Todd showed the families that each cabin had a bank of batteries to run the twelve-volt lights and ceiling fans in each room. Mark mentally patted himself on the back for knowing the ranch would have the battery-powered fans.

There were solar panels on the roof to keep the batteries charged, and the bathrooms had running water, supplied by an RV-type pump and propane water heater. There was no air conditioning, but the cabins were designed to stay tolerable without it. It was mid-afternoon in the middle of August and must have been in the mid-90s outside; however, it was very comfortable in the cabin with the ceiling fan on. Todd said that one reason they did all the cooking in one place was to keep from heating up the cabins. When both of the families had carried their clothes into their cabins and got settled in a bit, they met Todd at the community dining and meeting room. Todd showed them the huge kitchen and the food storage area. He told them they had enough canned food to last a hundred people for three years without adding anything by farming, ranching, hunting, or fishing. There were enough of some staples, like flour, sugar, and salt, for ten years if they were careful. They had a large room just for skinning and quartering game and livestock, with a walk in cooler attached. In the dining room, there were about thirty tables. Todd told them that not only did they eat in here, but they also used the room for meetings and church services. He asked Mark if it was big enough for a karate class, and Mark told him they could probably train about twenty-five people if they moved the tables to one side. Todd mentioned that they also used it for entertainment. They had a piano for music, many board, card, and domino games to play, and a big screen TV and DVD player that had been protected from The Burst.

Todd took them outside to the garden. It was over an acre in size. Only a small portion of it was planted, and Todd told them they would be planting all of it with fall crops, as soon as it cooled off just a little. They had chickens, rabbits, and two milk cows in the barn. There was a lot of hay and a medium-sized John Deere tractor stored in the barn as well. Todd told them they had about a hundred head of beef cattle on the ranch, too. He explained that their goal was to produce everything they needed and not have to deplete their stored food. He explained that everyone had several jobs. Most everyone had one primary job and then helped out in two or three other areas. He told them that even the small children had to help with some things like feeding the livestock, gathering eggs, and milking the cows. Mark noticed that Sam wrinkled her nose at the last one.

Next, Todd took them by the clinic where they met Dr. Sullivan. He was Suzy the Worrywart's husband. Lisa was very impressed with how well equipped and stocked the clinic was. Then, they went to the laundry. There were several commercial washers and gas dryers. Jim asked how they were powered, and Todd told them that they had several generators. The biggest was a diesel-powered, 30,000-watt model. They also had a couple of smaller generators, one diesel and one propane. They had lots of diesel stored in an underground tank, and there were separate, buried, thousand-gallon, propane tanks for each of the cabins and more for the kitchen and laundry. Estimates were that there was enough fuel for three years without any resupply. He told them each family was assigned one of the washers, one day a week, and that they hung the clothes to dry unless the weather wouldn't permit it.

The next building they visited was the combination library and school. There were several small classrooms and a modest library. Todd told them that they had schoolbooks for all grades and subjects and that they would start teaching school in a few days. For now, they were giving everyone a chance to settle in. They already had two teachers; one was an English major and the other was a math major. He told Jess they were really looking forward to having her for the science classes. The last building in the complex was a combination garage and armory. The garage was huge, and they had a couple of new jeeps and about a dozen Polaris ATV's inside. David was very taken with the ATV's. Todd said they would take some out to look over the ranch, but since it was so close to dinnertime, they would have to wait until tomorrow morning. There were tools, mechanic and carpentry, air compressors, welders, and much more in the shop. On one end, there were stacks of lumber reaching almost to the ceiling. Along one wall, there were parts bins filled with many things you'd find at a hardware or auto supply store.

The other end of the building held the armory. The racks held a number of battle rifles Mr. Davis had bought in the event they needed to defend the ranch. There were even two Barrett M82A1's. Jim whistled when he saw the Barretts. He'd always wanted a .50 BMG rifle but couldn't afford it.

"You like the big boy toys?" Todd asked him.

"Man. Those are sweet, Todd."

"We also have a complete reloading room over there. We can reload most of the major calibers in handgun and rifle, and we have 12 and 20 gauge shotgun reloaders." Todd pointed to a door, and the men looked at the equipment. Mark had never reloaded, but Jim did, and Mark had looked at some of the catalogs that were on Jim's reloading bench. He noticed that the presses were all high-dollar Dillons. When they finished looking the armory over, Todd asked the women and children if they'd like to go back to their cabins and get cleaned up for dinner while he took the men to meet Mr. Davis. They agreed, although Jess and Lisa didn't seem to like being dismissed.

When everyone else left, the men started walking toward Mr. Davis's cabin.

"Hey, Mark, I bet one of those .50's wouldn't have felt like a peashooter when those three dirtbags attacked you," Jim observed.

"You're right about that."

"What are you talking about?" Todd asked.

The two friends filled Todd in about Mark's encounter at the grocery store. Mark gave the bare facts, and Jim filled in the juicier parts. Todd was very impressed by the story. When they got to the leader's cabin, Mark noticed that it was significantly bigger than the others. Todd knocked on the door, and an older woman answered it.

"Yes, Todd," she said.

"Hi, Millie. I have Mark Turner and Jim Davis here. He wanted to meet them."

"Of course. Please follow me."

The three men followed the woman into a large sitting room. She then disappeared.

"Is that Mrs. Davis?" Mark asked.

Todd chuckled. "No, Mr. Davis isn't married. That's his personal assistant, Millie."

A moment later, a man came into the room. He was about five foot seven or eight, trim, and bald. He held out his hand to Jim and introduced himself.

"Nice to meet you...Reginald Davis," he said.

"It's nice to meet you, Mr. Davis. I'm Jim Davis."

"You have any relatives from Pennsylvania?"

"No. As far back as I know, we're all from Texas."

"Then I guess we're not related," the gentleman said with a smile.

The man turned his attention to Mark and reached his hand out.

"You must be Mark Turner."

"Yes, sir, Mr. Davis," Mark said while shaking his hand. "It's so nice to meet you."

"The pleasure is all mine. I've heard a lot of good things about each of you. Please, gentlemen, have a seat. I assume Todd has shown you around."

"I showed them around the complex. We're going to look over the ranch in the morning."

"Good. I know Todd has probably told you quite a bit about what we are trying to do here, but let me tell you a little about why we're doing this."

"We believe America has been on the wrong path for quite some time now. The hard workers, such as yourselves, are no longer rewarded for their efforts but instead are punished with high taxes and restrictions on their God-given rights. Conversely, the lazy are rewarded by a system that becomes more and more socialistic every year. Entitlement programs, funny name…somehow people who refuse to work are entitled to food, housing, education…everything that you work so hard to provide for your families. Anyway, entitlement programs are bankrupting this country both financially and morally. Our government had become the problem instead of the solution. We knew that, sooner or later, something would happen that would throw this country into turmoil. We want to make sure that people come out on the other side who can put America back on the right track. People who share the philosophy that a man who doesn't work shouldn't eat. People who feel like government should serve the people, not the other way around."

"I agree with you, Mr. Davis, but do you think that twenty or twenty-five families will be enough to turn the tide?" Mark asked.

"No. Twenty to twenty-five families are not enough, but what if you had over one hundred locations with twenty to fifty families in each location? People who, after a crisis, have the knowledge and desire to reshape America into the nation she was meant to be. People who are leaders, teachers, and hard working professionals, who want America to hold a future for their children. People who are not afraid to make some hard choices to insure that this once great nation becomes what the founding fathers intended it to be."

"Depending on how bad the crisis was, that number of people could make a huge impact," Jim answered. "Do you really have that many locations?"

"No, I only have this one, but we're part of a network of many groups. I don't even know where all the groups are or even how many there are for sure, but I can assure you that there are well over a hundred. Some have been in existence for over twenty years. Some are newer, like us, but we all share the same goals."

"Are the groups under the control of a central headquarters or something?" Jim asked.

"No. Each group is independent and autonomous. There is no central command. We just have an alliance with the other groups," Mr. Davis explained. "Any other questions?"

Mark had lots of questions, but something in Mr. Davis's tone told him that 'Any other questions?' meant 'That's all for now.' Jim must have gotten the same message because he was just shaking his head and saying no. Mark copied his friend.

"Okay, then. It's almost dinnertime. You'll excuse me if I don't join you tonight, but I have a lot of work to do. We hope you'll decide to stay with us. We really need hardworking team players to turn our goals into reality. I believe both of you would be assets to the group. I can see why Todd speaks so highly of you. Have a good dinner, and after you look over the ranch in the morning, come back to see me, and we'll chat again," Mr. Davis instructed.

The men stood up and shook hands. Todd led them outside and advised them to go back to their cabins and clean up a little if they wanted. Dinner would be at five o'clock sharp, he informed them. Mark looked at his watch. They had about fifteen minutes. When he walked into their cabin, Jess was waiting for him.

"How did it go? What's he like?" she asked.

"He's not at all what I expected, but I guess it went okay."

"So what's the drill? How does all of this work?" she fired in rapid succession.

"We have to meet with him tomorrow after we tour the ranch. I'm sure he'll tell us more then. However, he said that there were over a hundred different groups like this one throughout the country. They're all run separately but have common goals."

"What are the goals?"

"To put America back like it is supposed to be."

"How is it supposed to be?"

Mark explained to her exactly what Mr. Davis had said.

"I see," she said. "And who gets to decide what the 'hard choices' are?"

"I don't know, but I'll try to find out tomorrow," he answered. He tried to use the same tone Mr. Davis had used when he didn't want to answer any more questions.

He went into the bathroom and washed his face and hands, and then combed his hair. When he came out, Jess and the kids were ready to go. They stepped outside, met Jim and his family, and headed to the dining room. When they got into the room, everyone was chatting. Todd asked for everyone's attention and then introduced the families to everyone. Todd asked Dr. Sullivan to say grace, and they all lined up to eat. The food was served cafeteria-style. The Davises and Turners were invited to go through the line first with Todd's family. Then they sat down at a long table to eat. Todd, Jim, and Mark sat at one end, and their wives sat at the other, with the kids in the middle.

"So, what did you think about the meeting with Mr. Davis?" Todd asked the men.

"He wasn't what I expected," Mark answered.

"Me, either," Jim agreed, "but I agree with what he was saying."

The men talked more about what Mr. Davis had said, and then conversation turned to security around the ranch.

"We have the two guards at the entrance, two more are on patrol on the four wheelers, mostly around the fence line, and at night, we have two on duty inside the complex. Guard shifts are six hours long. and we use MURS radios for communications," Todd said.

"Hey, Todd, what's that camo pattern the gate guards were wearing?" Mark asked.

"It's called Multicam. It is made to blend into just about any environment. It costs more than the older camouflage patterns, but it's a good example of how Mr. Davis has spared no expense here at the ranch."

Mark looked down to the other end of the table and saw that Jess and Lisa were talking with Todd's wife, Andrea. Mark thought they were probably gossiping about who had the nicest cabin. The men's talk drifted to the ranch's water supply. Todd explained that there were several wells already on the ranch when Mr. Davis bought it. They were for the cattle and were pumped by windmill. The closest one to the camp had been fitted with a solar jack pump that used solar panels and a DC current pump. The brighter the sun shone, the more water it would pump. It filled a three thousand gallon tank that gravity fed an identical tank in the complex. Each cabin was hooked into that tank. When both tanks were full, the overflow was piped to a freshwater pond on the ranch. Mark and Jim both thought it was an ingenious system.

When dinner was over, the women who had been serving cleared the tables. Some of the children got board games and played quietly on one side of the room. Most of the younger children went outside to play, and a couple of the mothers went out to watch them. The rest of the adults and some of the teenagers gathered to listen to the President's speech.

The President said that some power should be on any time now, but that it may take a little while to totally restore power. He assured the world that the US would get the power back on to Wall Street as soon as possible and that they should remain bullish on America. He ended by saying what a great loss the country had already endured and that everyone needed to concentrate their efforts to rebuilding America, not rioting and looting.

After the speech, everyone talked about it, much like the talk at Jon's house every night. The big difference that Mark noticed was that everyone here pretty much agreed. They all believed the President was covering up the truth. The only difference of opinion here was the degree to which he was lying.

After a while, some of the adults excused themselves to do some of the chores that needed to be finished before dark. Others started getting games out and playing. Many of the women were playing Scrabble. Jess and Lisa joined them. Some of the men were playing dominoes. Todd asked Jim and Mark if they knew how to play 42. When they said yes, he asked if they'd like to play him and Tom. When Mark and Jim had won three games in a row, Todd commented good naturedly that he should have known better than to challenge two number crunchers. By that time, it was about 8:30 and dark. Everyone started drifting off to their cabins. Jim decided it was time to do the same and said good night to everyone. Mark and his family were right behind them. Before they left, Todd told them that breakfast was at 7:00 AM and that they'd tour the rest of the ranch right after.

When they got back to their cabin, Mark asked everyone what they thought so far. David thought it would be great to live here. Sam said she hated it, which was no big surprise. Jess told Mark she thought it was a great setup, but that she was holding her opinion until she saw a little more. Mark was pleased that she was being so open-minded. Perhaps there was a chance she would see the logic of moving here. Everyone took their turn at the shower and then went to bed.

Mark woke up a little after six. It had been the best night's sleep he'd had since The Burst. The cabin was pretty comfortable with the ceiling fan, and the fact that the complex had security didn't hurt either. He got out of bed and thought about running. Since he didn't know exactly what the security routine was, he decided to take the day off. Instead, he did some stretching and some pushups and sit-ups. After that, he got dressed and woke everyone up. A few minutes before seven o'clock, they headed over to the dining room.

Todd was already there, talking with a few of the men about some things they needed to get accomplished. A couple of minutes later, Jim and his family came in. When they were done eating, Todd invited both families to go on the tour. He said that he would drive the women in a Jeep, and the guys could ride the ATV's. Jess, Lisa, and Sam asked if it would be OK for them to just hang around the complex. Todd told them that was fine, and the three men, with David in tow, headed to the garage. The ATV's were all new Polaris four-by-four quads. Todd asked David if he'd ever ridden one, and David told him that one of his friends had one and he rode it all the time. The men climbed on the four closest to the door and took off. When they left the complex, they headed toward the lake, single file.

At the lake, they stopped the ATV's and got off. Todd showed them the boats they had. There were two 16-foot Jon boats with 25 HP engines, and a 17-foot canoe. They also had an 18-foot fiberglass boat with a center console and a 90-horse motor. All were tied to a floating dock with a walkway out to it from the bank, except the canoe was turned upside down on the dock.

"Nice boats," David said.

"Do you think these are what we need?" Todd asked the men.

"The Jon boats are great for duck hunting and running trot lines. The skiff will be nice to fish out of. I don't know how much you'll use the canoe, unless you run out of gas for the motors," Jim answered.

Mark smiled. "I don't know how comfortable I'd be in a canoe with the size of some of the gators I've seen in this lake."

"What's the biggest you've seen?" Todd inquired.

"Maybe twelve feet long, but I didn't put a tape measure on him, if you know what I mean." Mark winked.

The men climbed back onto the four wheelers and rode around the perimeter of the ranch. They saw deer, turkeys, and signs of feral hogs. The ranch was loaded with rabbits and had lots of dove and some quail. When they rode up to the pond that the solar jack pump overflowed into, they scared ten or twelve ducks off of the surface.

"It looks like there's lots of game," Mark observed. "You just need to manage it a little, and it should supplement the food supply nicely."

"That's one of the things we want you guys for," Todd stated. "What do you say we head back for some lunch? Then we can talk to Mr. Davis again."

They made the short trip back to the complex just as lunch was being served. Todd excused himself to report to Mr. Davis. He told the men he'd come get them when the meal was over. Mark and Jim found their wives and headed over to eat. The couples sat together, and the men told the women about what they had seen on the tour. When they were done filling in the women, Jess and Lisa had some things to tell the guys.

"We visited with a lot of the women here while you were on the tour," Jess began, "and they're not treated as equals here. They have little say in what goes on and how the work is split up. In fact, Mr. Davis makes the work assignments, and he makes it clear that it's his way or the highway."

"That's not all we noticed," Lisa continued. "What percentage of the population of South Texas would you say Hispanics represent?"

"At least half," Jim answered, as Mark nodded his head in agreement.

"Well, I don't know the exact number, but you're probably close. However, there's not one Hispanic or Black family here."

"That's interesting," Jim said.

"None of that means anything, necessarily," Mark stated. "The women probably aren't used to having to work under crisis conditions, and maybe they just haven't found any Mexican families who fit what they need yet."

"Mark Turner, where there's smoke there's probably fire. You need look at this whole thing objectively."

"I am looking at things objectively," Mark whispered, rather than raise his voice and cause a scene. "Maybe things aren't perfect here, but they don't look that bad to me. At least here we know we'll be fed and protected. That's something we don't have any assurances of at home."

"Well, I'm not real comfortable discussing this here. Why don't you go have your meeting with Mr. Davis, and then let's go home, so we can make a decision with no outside pressure," Jess suggested.

"I want to stay another day," Mark blurted.

"I don't," Jess shot back. "Let's take a vote."

"I'm with Jess on this one," Lisa said meekly.

"I think I am, too, Mark," Jim told him.

"I thought you were my friend!" Mark said.

"I am your friend, even when it's hard to be your friend, like right now," Jim told him. "Look, we've seen what we needed to see. Let's see what Mr. Davis has to say, and then go home and make a decision."

"Damn you all!" Mark was so mad he saw red. "I think you're conspiring against me sometimes. But since I'm 'outvoted,' I guess we'll go home this afternoon." He got up and walked outside.

Why did he get so mad so fast lately, he wondered to himself? He should be able to control his temper better than that, but the others wouldn't look at the reality of how serious this could be. What was more important, equal rights or survival? He'd have to find a way to convince them. He just had to stay cool and logical if he was going to have a chance of doing it. He turned around and walked back into the dining room.

"I'm sorry I lost my temper. I still disagree with you all, but that was no reason to act like that," he said.

"That's okay, buddy." Jim squeezed Mark's shoulder and shook him a little. Lisa smiled weakly, but the look on Jess's face told Mark he'd have to stay in the dog house for a while longer.

A minute later, Todd came in and asked the men if they were ready. They walked over to Mr. Davis's cabin and knocked on the door. Millie showed them to the same room as last night. Mr. Davis was already there.

"So what did you think of the ranch?" he asked.

"It's beautiful," Jim answered.

Mr. Davis beamed. "We think we have a good setup here, with everything we need to weather this thing through. The biggest challenge is getting the right people to make it work. We believe you two and your families are the right people, but there are some things that we want to go over with you."

"First, we can only take in the eight of you, no extended family or friends. We just don't have the resources to feed or house a lot more people."

"Todd made that clear to us before," Jim told the older man.

"Good. The second thing is that this is not a democracy. We will listen to input from everyone, but in the end, there can only be one leader. Right now, that leader is me. If something were to happen to me, Todd would take over."

"We understand," Mark said.

"Lastly, once you come, there will be a verbal contract between us. If you decide to leave, or in the unlikely event that we ask you to leave, you will never be allowed back."

"What would cause you to ask someone to leave?" Jim asked.

"Not pulling their weight, refusing to follow orders, stealing, or some major infraction. We haven't had to do that, and we don't expect to ever have to, but it's best if everyone knows all the rules up front."

"That only sounds reasonable," Mark said.

"Okay, now that we have that out of the way, I want to tell you what we want you and your wives to be responsible for. Both of you will be in charge of supplementing our stored food by hunting and fishing. We'll assign men to help you, as you need them and as their schedules permit. Mark, we want you to be in charge of the group's physical fitness and to start a martial arts and self defense class. Let us know how many times per week you think people should train, and we'll work it into everyone's schedules. Jim, you'll be responsible to teach the men and boys to shoot. We were thinking about a comprehensive course for everyone and then regular refreshers, but it'll be up to you to present us with what you think we should do. Both of you will also have to pull some guard duty. Jim, Lisa will be assigned to the clinic, and Mark, Jessica will be in charge of teaching science at the school. The women will also have to help in the kitchen on a regular basis. The children will be given responsibilities in line with their ages and abilities. Everyone will be expected to help with the gardening and the animals from time to time. That is what we want from you. In return, you will be full members of the group with all the benefits that living here provides…food, shelter, security, and a sense of community, plus a chance to be a real force in the rebuilding of this country when we get through this thing."

"That sounds really good to me," Mark said.

"But we need to talk it over with our wives and make sure that we're doing the best thing for our families," Jim interjected.

"Of course," Mr. Davis said. "You're welcome to stay here as long as you wish, or if you want to go home to make up your mind, that's fine. We will expect your answer within a week."

"The women want to go home to talk about it, so we'll be leaving this afternoon, but we'll have an answer in a week," Mark explained.

"That's fine," Todd said, speaking for the first time.

"I have a couple of questions," Jim stated.

60

Mr. Davis looked at Jim.

"I noticed that the men and women don't often share the same responsibilities. Some might consider that the women aren't seen as equal to the men on the ranch." Jim was being unusually tactful, and Mark wondered if Lisa had coached him on what to say.

"'Equal' and 'the same' are two different things. The women are treated equally, but they do not always do the same jobs the men do. Everyone is expected to help out where they are the most useful. It would do us little good to put you in the clinic to help Dr. Sullivan, right?"

"I see your point," Jim answered. "I also noticed that there were no minority families here. Is there a reason for that?"

"We aren't prejudiced, if that's what you are asking," Mr. Davis answered flatly. "We have a certain profile we look for in prospective members. They must be hard working, conservative in their politics, have family values and be moral. We also require them to be of a Protestant religion, and most of all, they must bring skills that we need to the table. Most Hispanics are Catholic, and the majority of Blacks were raised in urban areas and have no skills that would be useful to the group. If we could have found someone who was a minority who fit the profile, I'm sure we would have made them the same offer we are making you."

"I figured it was something like that," Mark said looking at Jim with a 'So there!' look.

"Gentlemen, if there's nothing else, I must excuse myself. I look forward to hearing from you in the next week." Mr. Davis shook each man's hand and walked out of the room.

Todd, Jim, and Mark walked outside. Todd shook the hands of the two guests and explained that he had to go check on some work to make sure it was getting done. He told the two friends how much they would be appreciated at the ranch and expressed his hope that they'd decide to move here. He told them to use the yellow bandana again when they came back. Jim and Mark thanked him for the group's hospitality and told him they would see him in about a week.

When the men got back to the cabins, the women and children had already loaded the trucks. The families loaded up and headed for home. Mark wondered if they would ever be back.

Chapter 11

The trip home was uneventful. On the way, Mark told Jess about what all Mr. Davis had said. She was still very skeptical. Mark knew she'd be a hard sell, and he'd have to be at the top of his game if he was going to have any chance of convincing her. He wondered why his wife and friends couldn't see that the ranch was their best chance to make it through this mess. It seemed like politics was more important to them than survival. The only legitimate reason he could see for not going to the ranch was the fact that they couldn't bring their extended families. Mark felt that the obligation to his immediate family outweighed his responsibilities to his extended family. He owed it to his children to see that they got the best chance not only to survive, but to prosper after this crisis had passed.

When they got to the Silver Hills entrance, one of the men on guard duty, whose name Mark couldn't remember, waved them down.

"Hi, Mark. How was your trip?" the man asked.

"Pretty good," Mark answered, wondering how he knew they were on a trip. "How did things go around here?"

"It's been quiet. Listen, Jon wanted to know if you could go see him as soon as you got home?"

"Sure thing."

"Thanks," the man said.

When the families got back to the Turner house, Mark told the Davis's what the guard had asked. Lisa and Jess told Mark and Jim to go see what he wanted while they got unloaded and started supper. When the men got to Jon's house, they knocked on the door. Jon answered wearing his Beretta on his hip. A few days ago, Mark would have thought it was ridiculous to wear a pistol around the house. Now he thought it might be a good idea.

"Hi, guys," Jon greeted them. "I was hoping you'd be back today." Jon invited them inside. The house was hot, but with all the windows open, it was bearable. The three men sat down in the living room.

"There are a couple of things I want to talk to you about, guys," Jon started. "First of all, we picked up on the fact that you and Jim were going to look at a place to move to until things settled down."

"Where did you hear that?" Mark wanted to know where the leak was.

"Your wives mentioned it to my wife the night that you didn't come to the meeting."

Mark started getting red in the face.

"Please don't be mad. I'm glad we found out. It made me look at how much we need you around here. I know you and I are two ends of the spectrum and that we rarely agree, but you're respected by a lot of people in the neighborhood, me included. You make me look at the other side of the problem. If you move off, we lose that. Plus, if you move, a lot of other people are going to start feeling insecure around here. I guess what I'm saying is that I don't want you to leave. We talked about it some at the meeting last night, and just about everyone else feels the same way."

"That's nice to hear, Jon. To be honest with you, we haven't decided what we're going to do, but it's mostly going to come down to what's best for our families."

"I understand. Just please give a little thought to what's best for your neighbors, too."

"We will," Mark promised. "What was the other thing you wanted me for?"

"Some of us are getting a little low on groceries. We were wondering if you would run us to the store to get our fifty dollars' worth since no one else has a running car?"

Mark couldn't help but wonder if this was the real reason they didn't want him to leave. He and Jim had the only running vehicles in Silver Hills, and he was the only one who had a generator to pump water. "Sure, Jon, we'd be happy to. How many people want to go?"

"Everybody," Jon said sheepishly.

"Oh, I see." Mark was a little overwhelmed. Did they really expect him to take everyone to the store?

"We know we can't all go in one trip. We made a list of who needs to go the most, and they can go first. The rest can go as you can take us," Jon explained.

"When did the first ones want to go?" Mark asked.

"About ten families are real short on food. Do you think there's any way you could go today?"

"Sure," Mark answered cheerfully. He wasn't so cheerful on the inside though. "Why don't you get them over to my house as soon as possible. As long as some don't mind riding in the back of my truck, we can take ten people easily."

"Thanks, Mark. I'll have them over to your place within thirty minutes."

While Jim and Mark were walking back to the house, Jim suggested that they run by the office and get more gas for the generator, as long as they were making a trip to town. Mark thought that was a good idea. They could go get the gas while the others were waiting to get into the store. When they got home, they told the women what Jon had said and about the request he had made.

"Why do you have to take them?" Jess questioned.

"Who else can?" Mark answered, seeing an opportunity to make a point. "It must be thirty miles round trip, and nobody else has any running vehicles. If we stay here, we're going to have to be doing this kind of thing all the time."

Jess didn't say anything. Mark and Jim went to the shed to get the jerry cans. Two were completely empty, and the third was only about half full. They poured the two and a half cans of gas into Jim's truck and then loaded all five cans into the bed of Mark's. While they were doing this, they talked about what they might need in case they got attacked again. Then they went back into the house and got their rifles. Both men also got their pistols and put them and some extra magazines on where they could be concealed under an untucked shirt. They carried the long gun cases out to the truck and put them behind the back seat. About that time, the first of Jon's shoppers showed up. Within five minutes, all ten had arrived at Mark's. Eight were men, and only two were women. They were thanking Mark incessantly. The two women and one of the men climbed into the back seat of the big Ford. The other men got into the bed and sat down. Mark and Jim sat in the front seat, and Mark started the truck. On the way to the store, Mark, Jim, and the three in the back seat chatted. Mark told them that he and Jim were going to drop them off and go get some fuel for the generator. Hopefully, they'd be back about the time the shoppers were through. If not, Mark advised, they should stay close to the store and wait. The two friends dropped off the shoppers and headed to the office. When they got there, Jim opened the gate, and Mark pulled through. Jim locked the gate behind them and walked over to where the fuel tanks were. Mark filled the truck with diesel while Jim filled the jerry cans with gas.

With the gas in the back and the Ford's two tanks full, the men headed back to the store. When they arrived, their passengers were still in the store. After about twenty minutes, the first came out and got into the truck. Ten minutes after that, the last was loaded up and ready to go. On the way home, the main topic of conversation was what the store was out of.

"They were out of canned meat, beef stew, and candles," Sherri Henderson reported.

"I couldn't get any canned meat, either. I never thought Kroger would run out of Spam! They were out of some canned fruits and vegetables, as well, and they didn't have any matches. I did get the last bag of dog food. It's not Ricky's and Lucy's regular brand, but it'll beat nothing. I hope they get some more," the other woman said.

Scott Simmons was sitting inside for the trip home. "They were also out of AA, C, and D batteries. All they had were AAA, 9-volt, and those big, 6-volt, lantern batteries. I noticed they were pretty low on Coleman lantern fuel, too. I guess some people don't know you can use unleaded gas in the lanterns and stoves."

"The man at the table said they are supposed to get resupplied sometime next week, even if the power's still out. He said they'll allow every family another $50 worth if that's the case," Sherri said.

"That's encouraging," Jim said.

"Sure is," Mark agreed.

By the time they got home, the President's speech was over. Jess and Lisa filled the men in on what he'd said, as they walked to Jon's for the daily gathering.

"Mostly, he said they'd run into a few unexpected snags on the power, but that it shouldn't take more than another two or three days to get it back on," Jess said.

"I'm starting to agree with everyone who thinks it's going to be a while before we have power. It's been what? Five days. They said two or three days when The Burst hit on Tuesday. Now it's still going to be two or three days? It's starting to sound like a broken record," Lisa admitted.

Mark thought that might be a sign that the women were softening their position. Maybe he did have a chance to convince them to move. When they got to Jon's, Mark noticed that just about everyone from the neighborhood was at the meeting. He also noticed that the mood was a little gloomy. The shoppers filled everyone in about what they were and were not able to buy at Kroger. Mark and Jim announced that they'd make two trips to Kroger the next day. They would take both trucks, so they could handle twenty shoppers per trip as long as some didn't mind sitting in the back again. They said they would make the first trip about 8:00 and the second probably around 2:00 in the afternoon. The list of shoppers was brought out, and the next twenty were told to be at Mark's by 7:45. Jon asked Mark and Jim if they would mind filling in on guard duty from midnight to four o'clock. He said that he hated to ask since they were taking everyone to the store the next morning, but one of the men who was scheduled for the shift was sick and the other had filled in the night before for someone else. The men agreed to do it since everyone else had taken their turn.

Mark really wanted to talk over going to the ranch with Jim and the women, but if he was going to be on guard duty for four hours, he knew he'd better get some sleep. Maybe this was good, he thought. He and Jim would have plenty of time to talk tonight, and if he could convince Jim, then he'd have an ally in trying to convince the women. The old divide and conquer might just work. When the meeting was winding down, Jon asked if anyone had anything else to bring up. Abigail Petersen raised her hand.

"Yes, Mrs. Petersen?"

"I was thinking we might have a street dance one of these nights. It would help to take everyone's minds off of their problems at least for a little while."

Jon's brow knitted at the word 'dance,' but when a murmur of approval went through the crowd, he seemed to relax a bit.

"I have a big boom box with fresh batteries that will play CD's and cassettes," someone volunteered.

"What about lights?" someone else shouted.

"We could push a couple of cars over and use the headlights," a third person suggested. "At least we could get some use from the worthless pieces of junk that way."

"Well, I guess that would be all right," Jon said. "Does anyone see a problem with it?"

Mark did. Didn't they have more important things to deal with? However, when everyone else seemed to be on board with the idea, Mark decided not to object.

"Alright, Mrs. Petersen, you thought of it, so I guess you're in charge," Jon said. "If you want to help, see Mrs. Petersen. When you have everything set, just let us know."

Everyone left Jon's house in a pretty good mood. Mark was surprised how quickly everyone's spirit picked up at the mention of a dance. It was funny how little things could make a big difference in people's attitudes. Jess and Lisa were talking about how they could make some cake or cookies to take to the dance. Mark just shook his head. If they didn't go to the ranch, he had no idea how they were going to eat next month, and the girls are talking about baking cookies. They just didn't get it.

Chapter 12

When the alarm went off at 11:30, Mark got out of bed. He pulled on his clothes, put his Colt on his hip, and grabbed the daypack he'd loaded before he went to bed. It contained a big flashlight, his camouflaged rain jacket, a couple of bags of peanuts, a canteen of water, and the magazines for his Marlin Camp .45. He had chosen the .45 carbine for night time guard duty mostly because it had a red dot scope on it. It wasn't a night vision scope, but if you could make out the silhouette of the target, you could put the lighted dot on it and shoot. Mark had killed a couple of feral hogs in the dark on his deer lease with it, and he had a lot of confidence in this carbine. It had an effective range of only about seventy-five yards, but it made a big hole and was light and handy. When he stepped out of the camper, he noticed the cool front that the weatherman had predicted had arrived. It was in the low seventies, and a light wind was blowing out of the north.

Jim stepped out of his pop-up with his Glock on his hip. He was carrying his Mossberg shotgun and a daypack similar to Mark's. The two men walked down to the entrance of the subdivision. They chatted with the two men they were relieving for a couple of minutes and then took their post by the Silver Hills sign. Jim loaded the magazine on his shotgun, and Mark inserted a magazine into his carbine. Neither man chambered a round. Someone had left a couple of lawn chairs, and the two men put their packs on the ground and then sat in the chairs, holding their long guns across their laps.

"I guess this makes everyone feel better, but I still think it's a waste of time," Mark said.

"Why do you say that?" Jim asked.

"Because the two of us alone couldn't stop a gang of mutant zombie bikers from just driving into the subdivision. We might slow them down a little or give them something to think about, but we couldn't stop them from driving through the field or even running over us. If we had security like they have at the ranch, we could do some good, but not like this."

"You think the ranch security was good?"

"Heck, yeah," Mark said. 'Heck' wasn't a dollar word. "Didn't you?"

"Well, the gate and fence were impressive," Jim said.

"Impressive, hell!" 'Hell' was a dollar word. "Nothing less than a tank is going to get through that gate."

"I'm not sure they're any better off in some respects than we are. I was thinking maybe we should run by Gunny's house tomorrow and see what he thinks about the ranch's security."

"They have those guys at the gate, two roving guards, and two guards in the complex after dark. Plus they have real weapons, not Grandpa's old deer rifle. How could you not think they're light years ahead of us?" Mark asked.

"In some ways, they are, but I think they may have some holes, too. If we talk to Gunny, we'll know for sure. What could that hurt?"

"It won't hurt anything, but I think he'll be pretty impressed when we tell him about their setup."

"Maybe. What do you think about the rest of the setup they have?" Jim asked his friend.

"I thought it was great. Didn't you?"

"Yes, but Lisa pointed out a couple of things that concern me some."

"You mean the women and minority issue?" Mark stated more than asked.

"Well, that, too, but some other things, as well."

"Like what?"

"Like some of the seeds they had for the garden were hybrids," Jim said.

"So?"

"You see, hybrid seeds are engineered to produce better fruit, but they can't produce viable seed to replant. So after you run out of store bought seeds, you're out of luck."

"I didn't know that."

"Neither did I. And that's not all she pointed out to me."

"What else?" Mark asked.

"Well, she noticed that they had a lot of hay in the barn, but they didn't have any equipment to cut or bale their own once they run out. She said that if it didn't rain for several months, the cattle could go through all of their hay pretty quickly."

"Maybe they have the equipment, and we just didn't see it."

"That's what I said, but she asked around while we were touring the ranch. Some of the men told her that all of the equipment was in the barn."

"Hmmm."

"Another thing she asked about was canning equipment. There isn't any, so they don't have any way to store what they get from the garden except to freeze it. That's okay, but what if they run out of fuel for the generator and can't use the freezer?"

"I guess that could be a problem down the road," Mark admitted.

"I noticed a couple of things, too. You saw all the reloading equipment, right?"

"Yes. It all looked like top of the line stuff."

"It is, but it's all brand new."

"What's wrong with that?"

"Nothing in and of itself. It's just that I don't think they know how to use it. They've bought a lot of the things they need, but if you don't know how to use it, what good is it?" Jim asked. "It's like those Barretts they have. They look impressive, but if you don't have someone who really knows how to use one, they aren't any better than grandpa's old deer rifle."

"At least they have the stuff," Mark said emphatically. "And they can learn to use it, can't they?"

"Maybe so, but what if their survival depends on something they haven't figured out yet? There's little room for error in a survival situation. If this thing goes for a long time and gets as bad as they think it might, they can't afford many mistakes. If the cattle die because they can't make hay, where will they get more? If they can't grow food next year, because they grew hybrid strains of vegetables, who's going to give them more seeds? If they need to reload ammo for the fifty calibers, and no one in the group knew that they needed a particular powder, where are they going to buy it? Knowledge is the one thing you can't just go out and buy. You say all the time that the mind is the ultimate weapon. Well, in a survival situation, knowledge and experience are your best tools. Plus, what if they did get attacked by a gang of 'mutant zombie bikers,' as you called them? Do they have enough manpower to really defend against a large group? I just don't know…that's why I want to talk to Gunny. The other thing that really concerns me about the ranch is Mr. Davis."

"How so?" Mark asked.

"It's his attitude. How did Jess put it? My way or the highway. It just rubs me the wrong way that he just stays in his cabin while everyone else carries out his wishes. It's his ranch, so he can do what he wants, but I'd like to have some say in things that affect me and mine."

The two men sat quietly for a while.

"Well then, if we decide not to go to the ranch, what are we going to do?" Mark said.

"I think we have several options. We could haul the campers down to the deer lease and stay there. It's far enough from any large city and far enough off of the paved road that we should be safe there, but we'd also be isolated from help if we needed it, and while we could eat deer, hogs, and turkey for a while, what are we going to do for fruits and vegetables? Not to mention the other things we'd need. We could go to Lisa's parents in Uvalde. Her dad stopped farming after his stroke, and sold off his land. He still does some gardening, though. There's plenty of room for all of us at their new place, but it's pretty close to town. Uvalde is fairly small, but if there was rioting there, I don't know how safe it would be. But I think you're sitting against the best answer."

Mark looked over his shoulder at the sign. "What? Plywood?"

"No, Mr. Literal. Silver Hills."

"How do you figure that? It's still just our two families."

"It's not just us. You have good neighbors. That's obvious from the meetings at Jon's house. With the right leadership, this subdivision could evolve into a real community. There's room for gardening, and we could raise some small animals here. We have room here for all of our families, too. There are enough people here to do a lot of work, and you have a pretty diverse group. I don't know if we could hold off a big group of mutant zombie bikers any better than they could at the ranch, but we have a lot more manpower. Jon should be able to come up with some kind of defense plan since he was in the Marines."

"I guess if everyone worked together, it could be a viable option," Mark admitted. "So you've made up your mind against going to the ranch?"

"No. I still think the ranch has a lot going for it, and it might be our best option, despite all of the negatives, but I believe we really need to look closely at all our options. Once we choose, we might not be in a position to change our minds."

"I guess I've been really narrow-minded the last few days," Mark said.

"As a matter of fact, you have, but we all knew you were just overreacting to what happened at Kroger and we also knew you'd calm down eventually. You always do."

"Am I that easy to read?"

"Mark, why do you think the guys at work always invite you to play poker?"

"Maybe it's because of my sparkling personality," Mark said with a big grin.

"Yeah, that's it," Jim said rolling his eyes.

The two friends spent most of the remainder of their time on guard duty talking about what might happen in San Antonio if the power didn't come back on. They also spent some time just looking at the stars. The lights from town usually blocked out all but the brightest stars, but with all of the lights out and the clear sky that the cool front had brought, you couldn't have counted all of them in a lifetime. When their shift was over, they walked back up the hill and went back to their beds.

Chapter 13

When Mark's alarm clock went off, it seemed like he had just fallen asleep. He'd spent most of the early morning hours laying in bed and thinking about what he and Jim had talked about on guard duty. Maybe staying here wasn't such a bad idea. They didn't have everything they needed, but maybe it could work with what the neighbors had and what they could buy, beg, or borrow. He got out of bed, dressed, and exited as quietly as possible.

Jim was already outside and was loading his shotgun into his truck. The early shoppers started arriving at 7:30, and by 7:40 all twenty were present. They climbed into the trucks and headed to town.

When they dropped the riders off, the line was longer than Mark had seen it on the two previous times he'd been there. Mark and Jim parked the trucks next to each other, out a ways from the other cars. The two men kept a watchful eye for trouble while they waited. Once the shoppers were done, they headed home. Jon was sitting in the front seat with Mark for the ride home.

"Man, my wife made a list of what we needed, but I was only able to get a little over half of it before I was at my limit," Jon explained.

"I know what you mean," Manny Hernandez said. "My list only had very basic items on it, but I couldn't get to the bottom of it. I hope they get a truck in, so we can buy another $50 worth."

"Little good it would do me," the man who was standing guard duty with Manny the other day said. "We only have another thirteen dollars in cash at home. If the banks don't open, we won't be able to buy any more anyway."

"I'm sure we could lend you some cash," Manny offered.

"I appreciate that, Manny. Hopefully, this will blow over quickly, and things will get back to normal," the man replied.

"Did y'all see the fight?" Jon asked.

"No. I just heard about it," Manny answered.

"What happened?" Mark wanted to know.

"Some guy tried to keep putting items in his basket after the clerk told him he was at his limit. The clerk tried to take one of the items out of the basket, and the guy decked him. Then he tried to run out of the store with the basket. He ran toward the front door, but the policeman who was inside stopped him and arrested him," Jon explained.

"How badly did the clerk get hurt?" Mark asked.

"It was mostly just his pride, but he'll still have a nice shiner to show for it. Who ever thought you should get combat pay for working at Kroger?"

"Hey, Jon, speaking of combat pay, do you think we should upgrade the security for the neighborhood?" Mark inquired.

"I don't know. What did you have in mind?"

"I didn't have anything in mind. I was just wondering if we need more guards or something."

"I don't understand, Mark. You don't think we need the guards we have now, and you're asking me about more?"

"I didn't think we needed them, but that was when I thought the power would be back on in a couple of days. I believe it's going to be considerably longer now, and I was just thinking we might need more security."

"Well, I'll look at it and let you know."

On the way home, not far from the subdivision, they passed a small Baptist church with its doors open. Mark noticed several bicycles parked in front and a few people walking down the road towards it, as well. Mark looked at his watch. It was almost ten o'clock. Time for Sunday school, Mark thought. Maybe next week, he and his family would go. They were Methodist, but Baptist was close enough. Besides, Jim was Baptist, and they could go together. When they got back to the house, several of the men offered Jim and Mark a can of this or that for taking them to the store. They politely refused.

When Mark and Jim walked into the house, a big breakfast was cooking, and everybody was up. Sam was reading a book to the twins, and David was working on a big 500-piece puzzle. The men went into the kitchen and got out the dishes and silverware to set the table. They told their wives about the fight at Kroger. Mark mentioned going to the church down the road, and they agreed that it was a good idea. When they sat down to eat, Mark found that he was as relaxed as he had been since The Burst. He knew they still needed to make a decision, but he was comfortable that they would make the right one. After breakfast, Jim and Mark worked on a map of the ranch to show Gunny. David walked by and pointed out a couple of things they missed. Mark thought that a teenager's memory was a strange thing. They could remember the most minor detail of some place they'd been to once, but they couldn't remember they'd been told to clean their room.

When they were through with the map, Mark got out his list of the things they would need if they stayed at home. As he reviewed it, he found some things he no longer considered necessities and others that he added. He went down the list and prioritized them. He put the number one next to anything they absolutely had to have, twos went next to the items that would be difficult to live without, and anything that would be nice to have received a three.

As he looked at the list, he felt like they could achieve most of the ones and many of the twos. The biggest problem he felt they faced was how to pump water if and when there was no fuel for the generator. Hopefully, they could sit down this afternoon or tonight and make a master list from their four separate lists. Mark's thoughts drifted to other things. He was sitting in his favorite chair in front of the TV. It was Sunday afternoon, and if things were normal, he might be watching a football game right now. The next thing he knew, Jim was shaking his shoulder and telling him to wake up. Jim told him that it was almost two o'clock, and the second group of shoppers was starting to arrive. Mark asked how long he'd been asleep, and Jim said he'd started snoring about forty-five minutes ago.

When they got to Kroger, the line was even longer than it had been in the morning. Mark figured it would take at least two hours to just get into the store. The shoppers delivered, Mark and Jim headed for Gunny's. They parked their trucks in Jim's driveway, and Gunny was outside before they could get out.

"Hey, Jimbo, I was wonderin' when you was gonna come by and check on your stuff."

"Hi, Gunny. How are you doing?" Jim answered.

"'Cept for this damn knee, I'm doing fine. This change in the weather's got it achin' like a sumbitch…Say, how are my favorite girls doin'?"

"They're fine, Gunny, but they sure do miss you."

"You're prob'ly jus' sayin' that to make me feel good, but damn if it don't."

"Listen, Gunny," Jim said. "We didn't come here to check on the house. We came to see you. We need your expertise."

"Expertise on what? How to stay regular?"

"No, Gunny. We want you to look at the security arrangements at this place we're thinking about moving to."

"OK, let's go inside," Gunny invited.

When they went in Gunny's house, Mark noticed that it was very warm inside. Since Gunny had boarded up the windows on the front of the house, there wasn't much air movement. The men sat at the table, and Jim pulled out the map they had drawn. Mark and Jim filled him in on the gate, the fences, and how the guards were deployed. Gunny looked the map over and asked a few questions.

"Do the guards check in with someone on a regular basis?"

"Not that we saw," Jim answered, as Mark shrugged his shoulders.

"Do they have any hidden guard posts or lookouts who can see someone coming from a ways off?"

"If they did, they didn't tell us, and at meals I only noticed four families each time who didn't have the husband at the table. I don't think there are more than four guards during the day and six at night."

"Do the men in the compound carry their weapons on them?"

"Not unless they're carrying concealed," Mark answered this time. "They have all of the weapons stored in the armory."

"Well, if there's nothing else y'all don't know about, I could take the whole place with about a half a troop of drunken girl scouts."

"How are you going to do that, Gunny? How are you even going to get through that gate?" Mark asked incredulously.

"Ahh, Karate Man," Gunny said, faking a bad accent, "ancient Chinese proverb say you no attack a man's strength, but where he is weakest."

"Okay, I hear what you're saying, and I see how that applies to the gate, but how are you going to take the ranch with just a few attackers? I though the defender's advantage was three to one. Even if you just count the twenty-five men at the ranch, you would need seventy-five to defeat them. Right?"

"The defender's advantage only applies when the defenders are dug in and expectin' an attack. This is how I would do it. I wouldn't try to crash that gate. It sounds pretty bulletproof. I reckon I'd cut a hole in the fence before daylight and then sneak up behind the guards at the gate. I'd wait until the shift change at oh six hundred and take all four out at one time. Since the compound is about a mile away, they shouldn't be able to hear the shots. The rovers won't hear it over those fancy four wheelers they ride. Then I'd move back to where I came through the fence and set up on the rovers 'fore they found the hole I made and take them out the same way as the other four. After that, I would march me and my girl scouts into the compound after daybreak when the night guards are off duty. Secure the armory, and all they got left to shoot at you is the finger."

"Damn," Mark said. "I had no idea it would be that easy."

"Well, we do have inside info, and that helps a lot. A random attack without any intel might or mightn't work. That gate and fence would prob'ly intimidate most civilians, but it presents almost as many problems as it solves. There's just too much of it to watch to catch a halfway motivated and organized force before they breach it. They need to put a standing guard of at least five or six men in the compound twenty-four/seven, and they need a lookout who can see the shit before it hits the fan and set off an early warning system. It would be best to have some fox holes just inside the compound fence here, here, here, and here," Gunny said as he pointed at the map, "and I would teach the women to shoot. Twenty-five men ain't a lot. Plus they all should at least wear a pistol when they're not on guard duty and keep rifles in their cabins. I could prob'ly suggest some other stuff if'n I saw the place, but just those things would make it a lot more secure."

"Thanks, Gunny," Mark said. "Say, would you be willing to come out to my neighborhood and tell us what you think we could do to secure our places?"

"Sure thing, Karate Man. That's the least I can do for you fixin' my truck. When do you want me to come?"

"Day after tomorrow about lunch time? I can come pick you up."

"Naw. Just draw me another map, and I'll drive myself."

"Okay, Gunny. By the way, how are you set for groceries?"

"Don't worry 'bout that, Karate Man. I got lots, plus I went to the store yesterday and bought some more."

"Thanks for your help, Gunny. We'll see you on Tuesday," Mark said.

"Yes. Thanks, Gunny. The girls will be excited to see you," Jim said, as he and Mark went out the door.

The two friends checked Jim's house quickly and then headed back to Kroger. The shoppers were waiting by the front of the store. They all loaded up and headed home. When they got back to Mark's house, it was a little after five, and dinner was ready. They ate and then listened to the President. He had nothing different to say than yesterday. They headed down to Jon's, and Mark saw his neighbors a little differently than he had before. If they decided to stay here, he would be depending on these people, and they him. Mrs. Petersen reported that they had planned the dance for Tuesday night, after the meeting was over. She said they had everything they needed, except for ice. Jess suggested that everyone bring their ice trays to Mark when they came to get water and that they would fill them and put them in the deep freeze. When the meeting was over, the four friends went home, and after the guys had pumped water for the neighbors and put about a hundred ice trays in the deep freeze, they pulled out their lists. All four were remarkably similar. Sometimes one would have something that the others missed, but for the most part, they all had the same items. Once they had the master list complete, they split the list into categories. Each item was placed under food, water, shelter, clothing, security, power, or transportation. Everyone liked Mark's idea of prioritizing the items and did it to the new list. They discussed where they could buy the things on it and how much they would cost. When it started getting late, they decided to work on it some more tomorrow. Mark went into his bedroom and put two dollars in his black box. Then he and Jess walked to the camper and went to bed.

74

Chapter 14

Mark woke up a little later than usual. Jess was already up, and so was David. Sam was still asleep, so Mark got dressed quietly and went outside to run. He had a lot that he wanted to do today, so he only ran a mile and knocked out a few pushups and sit-ups and then hit the shower. By the time he got out, everyone was awake and breakfast was almost ready. They all sat down and ate. Everyone discussed what they wanted to get done for the day. Lisa and Jess wanted to go back to the hardware store and look at some of the things they needed. Mark wanted to go pay the man at the auto parts store and go check on Jerry Watson and his family. Jim wanted to get all of his reloading equipment and supplies from his house. Sam wanted to go with Jess and Lisa, and David wanted to go over to his friend's house and play football.

They decided that David would go with Mark and that Jim would escort all of the girls. Since there were six in Jim's group, he would take the Ford, and Mark and David would take the Jeep. They all left at the same time, and Mark headed for Jerry's house. Jerry lived closer to town than Mark did, but it was still fairly rural. He and his brother lived next door to each other, and his parents lived across the road. When Mark pulled up to Jerry's, the gate was locked. Mark honked the horn, and Jerry looked out the door and, after a second or two, waved at Mark. He pulled his head back inside and then a minute later came back out carrying a rifle. He jogged the hundred yards or so down to the gate and opened it. Mark pulled through while Jerry relocked the gate. Jerry jumped in the back of the Jeep, and Mark drove up to the house.

"Hey, Mark. Hi, David. What are you two doing here?" Jerry asked.

"Hi, Mr. Watson," David said.

"We came by to check on you all. I was a little worried when the store was all locked up. I didn't think you guys would close just for no lights," Mark said.

"That's nice of you to think of us. We're all doing fine. We normally wouldn't close, but none of our trucks are running, and even if they were, we wouldn't be able to sell any guns since we can't call them in for the background check. The only people who can buy guns right now are ones like you with a concealed handgun license. By the way, how did you get the Jeep to run?"

"I just had to change out the parts that The Burst fried. Since it's a '78, it doesn't have a computer."

"Man, I wish we could get one of our vehicles to run. Tony and I had to hike into town the other day to buy groceries and check on the store. You take for granted how far something is when you're used to driving."

"We might be able to get one of your trucks running. What is the oldest vehicle you have?"

"Dad's truck is an '04. Everything else is a 2008 or newer," Jerry reported.

"Hmm, I don't think we could get any of those running. Jim got his '91 to run by replacing a lot of parts, but anything newer than '92 or '93 is probably not going to be fixed without a new computer."

"We have an old Jeep that stays down at our ranch. Do you think it would run? It's not much, but it would sure beat nothing."

"Yes, I think it could be fixed. I'm going to an auto parts store after this. If you want to go, we can see if he has the parts," Mark offered.

"That sounds good."

"You said that you and Tony went to the grocery store. Did your folks get some groceries?"

"No. It's just too far for Dad to walk. We took Dad's driver's license with us, but they wouldn't let us buy his groceries. They didn't need much. Mom buys food like Tony and I still live there, so they can get by for a while. We actually were going to use his allotment to buy more for Tony's family."

"Well, if you get the Jeep running, then you can take him. Say, is that an AK you had when you opened the gate?"

"Almost," Jerry replied. "It's a Galil. It's an Israeli built .308 on the Kalashnikov design. They're great weapons. I had this one in the store for $3000, but when The Burst hit, I decided to bring it home for safekeeping."

"You keeping it safe, or it keeping you safe?" Mark asked with a grin.

"Both!"

"That's cool. How many magazines do you have for it?" David asked.

"I only have three. I wish I had more, but that was all the guy who traded it to me had."

"Dad's been carrying his FAL and five mags with him since those guys tried to steal his truck," David said.

"What happened?" Jerry asked.

Mark wasn't pleased that David had spilled the beans about the Kroger incident, but he wasn't mad. It was hard for thirteen-year-olds to keep anything to themselves. He told Jerry about what had happened.

"The fortunate thing about it was that, other than dislocating one of their elbows, no one really got hurt," Mark finished.

"You left out the best part, Dad."

Jerry was amused, as he could see that Mark was embarrassed to talk about his heroics. "And what part was that, David?"

"When Dad pulled his Kel-Tec out, one of the guys peed his pants!"

"You're right, David, that is the best part!" Jerry said laughing.

"Are you ready to go?" Mark asked, trying to change the subject.

"Sure."

Jerry told his wife that he was going to go with Mark to the auto parts store. Then they loaded up into the Jeep and drove down to the elder Mr. Watson's house. Jerry asked his dad exactly what year, model, and engine size the Jeep was. The older man was excited to learn that they might get a vehicle to run. Mark offered to drop him off at Kroger if he wanted to buy some groceries. He accepted, and they all left in the Jeep. Jerry told his Dad the story of Mark's encounter at Kroger, and they all had a little fun with Mark about it. Mark still felt a little bad about hurting the guy, but he was starting to get over it. He couldn't imagine how he would have felt if he had been forced to shoot one of them. He prayed he would never have to find out. When they got to Kroger, and dropped the elder Watson off, the line was about the same as it had been the day before. Mark figured they had about three hours. They drove to the auto parts store, and once there, the two men and David went inside.

"Hello, Mr. Turner. How are you today?"

"I'm fine, thanks. And you?" Mark was embarrassed that he couldn't remember the man's name.

"I'm doing well, thank you. Man, I like your Jeep."

"Well, thanks to you, it runs. I want to introduce you to my friend, Jerry. Jerry this is…I'm sorry, I'm horrible with names."

"Rodney." The man stuck out his hand. "Rodney Roberts."

"Nice to meet you, Rodney," Jerry shook Rodney's hand. "Jerry Watson."

"Mr. Turner, did that glow plug controller work?" Rodney asked.

"Please, just call me Mark. The controller worked perfectly. That's why I'm here, to pay for it."

"Okay, Mark, I'm glad it worked," Rodney said, as he took Mark's money and made change.

"Rodney, is there any way to get a '04 Chevy truck running?" Mark asked.

"Not without replacing the computer and a lot of the electronics. I don't carry but a few of the parts you would need. I know a couple of guys who went to the dealer, but every new computer they checked was fried. They were just too sensitive to the EMP."

"How about parts for a '74 Jeep?" Jerry asked.

"There I can help you," Rodney smiled.

Rodney asked Jerry for the particulars on the Jeep and then went in the back and brought out the parts. Jerry paid for the parts as Mark was looking at the empty, small battery rack. Mark asked Rodney if he had any more and was disappointed to learn that he was sold out. Mark then asked if he had any 12-volt deep cycle batteries. Rodney replied that he only had few car and truck starting batteries. He suggested that Mark try to find some 6-volt golf cart batteries. He could wire two of them up in a series to make 12-volts. Rodney said he had all of the cables Mark would need to wire up a bunch if he wanted. The golf cart batteries were larger deep cycle batteries, and they would last a long time and take more charging and discharging cycles than a standard boat or RV 12-volt would. Mark thanked him for his suggestion and said he might be back to buy some cables. Rodney replied that he didn't know how much longer he would be keeping the store open. The first couple of days, he had been pretty busy, but it was slowing down, and he was out of a lot of the parts that people wanted. He wrote his home address on the back of a business card and gave it to Mark.

"If I'm not here, just come by the house, and I'll open up for you."

Mark and Jerry thanked him and left. Jerry asked Mark if he would mind taking him by the gun store, so he could check on it. Mark didn't mind at all since he wanted to buy some ammo. When they got to the store, Jerry had Mark park in the back. He then unlocked the back door, and the trio walked in. Jerry grabbed a flashlight and then locked the door behind them. The store was dark, as there were heavy curtains over the front windows that the Watsons closed at night to keep people from seeing in when the store was closed.

"Do you want me to open the curtains?" Mark asked.

"No. I'd just as soon no one knows we're here," Jerry replied.

He looked around the store. Satisfied that everything was okay, he turned to Mark. "What do you need?"

"It's a pretty big list," Mark told him.

"Let's see it."

Mark handed the list to Jerry.

"Let's see....45 auto, 5 boxes...9 millimeter, 10 boxes....30-06 soft points, 5 boxes..." Jerry read down the list and pulled double what the list said and set it on the counter.

"Jerry, I only have half that much on my list."

"I know, but don't worry; I'm going to make you a good deal." He continued down the list pulling double. ".243, 5 boxes....22 magnums, 10 boxes....22 long rifles, 5 bricks...AR-15 mags...You don't have an AR do you?"

"No, but Jim has a couple. He said that if you had some mags to buy them for him."

"Let me go look in the back and see what I have."

A couple of minutes later, Jerry came back out with six magazines.

"Alright, the ammo is half price today, and the magazines are a gift from me to you and Jim," he said.

"Jerry, I can't accept that."

"Before you say no, listen to what I have to say. I need a favor. If you can't do it, I understand. It does not affect this deal at all."

"Just name it, and if there is any way I can do it, I will," Mark promised.

"Our Jeep is at our ranch in Cotulla. It's almost a hundred miles from here. I need a ride and some help to fix the Jeep."

"I couldn't go until Wednesday. Is that alright?"

"That's more than alright; it's wonderful. Thank you."

"I don't know what to say, Jerry. Thanks."

"That's all you need to say."

Mark paid cash for the ammo, and they loaded everything into the Jeep. Jerry locked the store, and they drove back to Kroger. When they got there, Mr. Watson was still in line. He was very close to the front, so it wouldn't be too long, Mark figured. The line behind Mr. Watson had grown to what looked like a five-hour wait. It also looked like the natives were growing restless. As they were waiting, Mark noticed a city bus pull up and drop two city police officers off and pick up the two they were replacing. Mark and Jerry discussed how long it would be before San Antonio would see riots if the power didn't come back on. Mark thought it would take a while before any riots happened here, and they would most likely be small. Jerry wasn't so optimistic. He felt they had a week, or maybe two at the most, and when the riots started, they would be bad. Hopefully not as bad as the Cincinnati riots had been, but still pretty severe. Jerry mentioned one of the things they wanted a vehicle for was to transfer as much of their stock as possible to his dad's place. They would have to make lots of trips in the Jeep, but it was better than nothing. Mark offered Jerry the use of his truck, and Jerry said he would probably take Mark up on the offer. About that time, Mr. Watson walked out of the store with his groceries.

"I never thought it would take over three hours to buy a couple of bags of food," Mr. Watson said, as he climbed into the back of the Jeep with David. "I'm glad we came when we did. Look at how long the line is now. The man who signs you in and gives you your number said they're supposed to get a couple of trucks in tomorrow. If that happens, they'll let everyone have another fifty dollars' worth."

"That's good news," Mark stated.

"I asked the man what would keep someone from going to the other Krogers in town and buying more if they didn't get the trucks in. He said they had no way to control that for cash customers...they're keeping the Lone Star food cards of the people on public assistance to control them...and that he was sure some people had already gone to more than one store. However, he thought the fact that most people were walking was keeping them from doing that too much," Mr. Watson explained.

"I know when Tony and I came, we wouldn't have wanted to walk any further to go to a second Kroger," Jerry said. "But if we were hungry enough, I guess we would have walked as far as we needed."

"I'm just thankful we have a vehicle," Mark added, as he started the Jeep. "It's at least thirty miles, round trip, from our house."

"Well, Mark, thank you for bringing me. I couldn't have made the walk."

"That's not all we need to thank him for, Dad. Mark's going to take us to the ranch on Wednesday and help us fix our Jeep, and he's offered us use of his pickup if we want to move some stuff out of the shop," Jerry told his father.

"Well, then, double...no, triple thanks."

"Jerry has thanked me enough that it's I who owe you thanks," Mark said. Mr. Watson looked at his son with a quizzical expression.

"I just made him a good deal on some ammo," Jerry explained.

"I hope you made him a real good deal, seeing everything he's doing for us," Mr. Watson said.

"Don't worry, Mr. Watson. It was a great deal."

When he dropped the Watsons off, he made arrangements to pick them up at 7:00 on Wednesday. David climbed into the front seat next to his father, and they headed for home. Jim and the girls were already there, and they filled Mark and David in on their day.

"When we got to the store, they were out of a lot of the stuff that we went to look at. The kerosene lamps you looked at the other day were all gone. We asked if they had any more, and they said no and that they didn't know how or when they would get any more. We decided we better go ahead and buy some of the stuff we'd need if we stayed here. I hope you're not upset," Jess said.

"Of course not. The auto parts store was already out of batteries. Some things are going to get harder and harder to find," Mark answered. "What all did you buy?"

"The most important things we bought are the seeds. They had a lot of them, and we bought what we figured were two years' worth of the non-hybrid seeds. Some of the vegetables were only available as hybrids, so we bought four years' worth of those. Hopefully they'll stay good for that long. If not, they were only about a dollar a pack, so we didn't waste much. We'll have to keep our eyes out for some non-hybrids," Lisa informed him.

"We also bought a bunch of gardening tools. Spades, rakes, and hoes. Hopefully we can find a garden tiller to buy or borrow, but we bought the hand tools just in case. I hate to think about doing it all by hand, but if we have to, we have to," Jim added.

"We got a bunch of galvanized buckets and tubs, and Mom bought two washboards. I hope we never need them. Washing clothes by hand is gonna bite." Sam actually smiled as she told her dad about it.

"We bought several rolls of chicken wire and some hardware cloth and wire we can use to make rabbit cages. We were afraid we might not be able to find any of this stuff if we waited too long. Jim paid, so we owe him half," Jess said.

"You don't owe me anything. It wasn't that much, and it's the least I can do for you guys letting us stay here. Anyway, after we left the hardware store, we went by the house and picked up my reloading equipment. I had it all packed up and stored in the attic, so it was already in boxes. Tomorrow, I want to inventory my supplies and see if we think we need any. Gunny was happy to see the girls. He said he'd rather come early in the morning, so I told him we'd meet him about 8:00. I hope that's okay. Hey, did you find Jerry?" Jim said.

"Yes, we did," Mark said. "He sold me the ammo two for one, so I got double what we had as a minimum." Mark went on to tell about the Watsons' Jeep and how he would be taking them to get it.

After they put away the ammo, they started fixing dinner. While they were eating, they discussed the decision they had to make about where to stay. They quickly came to the conclusion that the only two viable options were the ranch or staying where they were. They discussed the pros and cons objectively. Even Mark was leaning toward staying in Silver Hills. Gunny's assessment of the ranch security made him feel that they stood just as good of a chance here as there. In the end, they decided to wait until Thursday to make a final decision, but in the meantime, to proceed and prepare as if they would stay here. If they decided to go to the ranch, some of the things they bought might be for nothing, but that might not be as bad as if they couldn't get something later.

After dinner, they listened to the news and the President's speech. The news reported massive rioting in Los Angeles. Mark and Jim were both surprised that LA had held out this long. New riots were also reported in Atlanta, Miami, and Cleveland. The world markets had taken another beating, and there was more talk of shutting them down until the American markets were back online. The local news reported that the San Antonio city council had passed an ordinance making all outdoor water use illegal until the power came back on. When the President came on, he said the same things that he had said for the last several nights. Lisa was right about it sounding like a broken record, Mark thought.

Both families headed down to Jon's for what was becoming the social highlight of their day. There was more talk of the dance than there was of the bad news. Mark started thinking that maybe the dance wasn't such a bad idea after all. At least it took people's minds off things a little. He mentioned to Jon that he'd invited Gunny to look around tomorrow and asked if he'd like to join them. Jon didn't think they needed any outside advice on security.

"If you guys want to waste your time with some old has-been, that's your business, but don't expect me to implement anything just on his say-so."

Mark was a little taken back by Jon's attitude.

When the meeting was over they went back home, pumped water, played a few games with the kids, and got ready for bed. It was the first day since The Burst that Mark didn't have to put money into his black box. Maybe that was a good sign.

Chapter 15

Gunny showed up at the house at 7:30. Mark had already run and was knocking out the rest of his PT when he heard the knock on the door.

"Hey, Gunny. I wasn't expecting you until 8:00. Did you have any trouble finding the place?"

"Twasn't no trouble at all, Karate Man. I jus' didn't know fer sure how long it would take to get here, so I left early."

"Let me see if Jim's up. I want to take a quick shower, and then we can get started."

Mark finished his shower, got dressed and was back outside with Jim and Gunny in less than five minutes. They got into the Jeep to save the wear and tear on Gunny's bad knees. Jon waved them down as they passed his house.

"I decided maybe I'd better go with you all," he said as he climbed into the Jeep. Mark introduced the two Marines to each other. The two men talked a little and found that they'd served on some of the same bases, although at different times and in different capacities. Gunny had always been a combat Marine, and Jon had spent his four-year enlistment in supply. As they drove toward the gate, Gunny told them that the first thing they needed to work on was some training for the guards.

"Hell," he said, "I jus' drove up here and told them boys I had me an appointment with the Karate Man. They jus' waved me through, and they didn't know me from Adam. They didn't even get out of the chairs they had on the shady side of the sign. I know I'm jus' a broken down, old man, but no strangers should get in without someone who knows 'em comes to the gate and gets 'em."

"Excuse me, Sergeant Pickwell, but we don't have a gate," Jon pointed out.

"Then you damn well better get one! I coulda jus' run them boys over, sittin' in them lawn chairs like they was on a picnic or something.' By the time they woulda figured out they was in deep shit, I'da been in, and they'da been dead. Pickets should be where they can see threats from all directions, not sittin' on their asses in the shade shootin' the shit. You shoulda known that, Marine, just from basic training."

"But these men aren't Marines," Jon said, in a voice bordering on whining.

Mark could see that Jon was getting a little ruffled by Gunny's candor. He suggested they look at everything and then sit down and talk about what they could do to fortify their defenses. They spent the next hour driving around the subdivision and up and down the county road each way for a mile or so. Gunny asked several questions about how many people lived in the subdivision and how many houses there were. Jon knew there were 62 lots and 47 houses, but no one knew exactly how many people were living or staying in the neighborhood. When Gunny had seen the whole subdivision, he told Mark to head back to the house. He asked for some paper and a pencil. Then the men sat down at the picnic table. Gunny started drawing a map of the area as he spoke. Mark was amazed at the accuracy.

"Most of your threats will come from the road, and that's where I would concentrate my efforts first. You have one lane into the subdivision, and one out, with the 'Silver Hills' sign 'tween them. I'd tear down the sign so that it don't obstruct the guards' view neither way. Then I'd barricade off one of the lanes and put a badass gate 'cross the other, kinda like the one you told me about at that ranch," Gunny said nodding at Mark. "I'd dig a good fox hole about thirty, maybe forty yards from the gate for the guards. Close 'nough to be able to talk to someone, but not so close that they could get the jump on ya. Then, if'n someone needs to be let in, one guard opens the gate, while the other covers him. The sub-division is about six hundred yards wide, and the main road through it runs pert' much right up the middle. There's a fifty or sixty yard buffer between the county road and the closest properties. That contains the ditch, the front fence and then some empty field. The perimeter is fenced by a good five-strand barbwire fence on the back and the sides, but the front only has that little decorative wood fence on this side of the ditch. I'd dig out the ditch so it has a four-foot vertical wall on this side. That'll keep anything on wheels from being able to just drive through the ditch and into the field. I'd also try to find me some wire and put a barbwire fence across the front about ten feet this side of the little fence too. That'll slow down anybody trying to get in on foot. Then, you should dig two more foxholes, one on each side of the road, half to two-thirds of the way to the side fences. If someone attacks from the front, you can get some men in those holes and have over lapping fields of fire. You might even want to put two on each side. You also need to come up with some kind of comm system for the guards to get reinforcements if they need them. That should pert' much cover the front. Now, for the sides and back. To guard them effec....."

"You mean we need to guard the sides and back, too?" Jon asked.

"Yes, sir," Gunny said flatly. "The east side is pretty easy because it's all pasture. Anyone tryin' to get across it is gonna be easy to see. Most of the west side is farmland. As long as the crops aren't tall, it'll be easy, too. But, if'n it gets planted in corn or something, it'll be hard to see anyone 'til they're right on the fence. The back and some of the west are gonna be a real bear. Most of that is brush, and anyone with any kind of woodcraft at all is gonna be able to get over the fence before you could stop them. Fortunately, it's also the least likely place for neophytes to try to bust in or attack from. But you get any shadow warrior types, that's where they'll come from, and they're gonna ruin your day if'n you're not ready. We need to look at the back and sides some more and figure out exactly how we want to guard and defend 'em. Fer now, I would get started on the front, and when that's finished, we'll get on the sides and then the back. The last thing I would work on is an observation post to see people coming up and down the road."

"Don't you think all that's kind of overkill?" Jon aked.

"Depends how much your ass is worth to you. Karate Man asked me to tell you what I think, and that's what I think. Whether you do it or not is up to you."

Jon looked like he had just bitten into a turd. "I've got to go. We'll talk this over later," he said to Mark as he walked out.

"Wait up, Jon. I'll walk with you," Mark said. "Thanks, Gunny. Lisa and Jess are fixing lunch. We'd be pleased if you would stay and eat with us," Mark offered.

"Thanks, Karate Man. Don't mind if I do. Now, where's my girls, Jimbo?"

The four men got up from the table. Jim and Gunny went to find the twins, and Mark walked with Jon back to his house.

"I don't think we need to do all of that stuff," Jon said. "Nobody is going to try to attack us in force like that or try to sneak in the back. It's just a waste of resources and manpower."

"That may be, Jon, but I think we should consider it. We don't know what is going to happen, and wouldn't it be better to be safe than sorry?"

"Maybe, but I just don't think it's necessary," Jon said emphatically.

When they reached Jon's house, he and Mark spoke for a few more minutes. Jon reluctantly promised to think about what Gunny had suggested. As Mark walked home, he found it curious that Jon had first wanted to put guards at the entrance and he was opposed to it. Now the roles had effectively reversed. When he got home, lunch was on the table. Gunny sat down, and one twin sat on each side of him. Mark imagined that the old Marine had never looked happier.

During lunch, they discussed the events of the last week. Gunny wasn't bashful about adding his two cents' worth. When he heard about Mark's encounter at Kroger, he really laid it on thick, teasing Mark about making that poor, little, defenseless boy piss his pants. Everyone else joined in the fun. Mark was getting used to it. When the topic turned back to the serious side, everyone agreed that so much had happened, it seemed more like a month than a week since The Burst. When they were almost done with lunch, Mrs. Petersen dropped by.

"Hi, Mrs. Petersen. How are you?" Jess, the first to see her, said.

"I'm doing fine. I was just wondering if I could get some ice to chill some of the things I've fixed for the party," she answered.

"Sure. How much do you need?" Mark said.

"I think ten pounds should be enough."

"A lot of the trays were already frozen last night, so I emptied them into some plastic shopping bags and refilled them. David, would you go get one of the bags and bring it out to Mrs. Petersen."

"Yes, sir," David answered his dad.

"Mrs. Petersen. I'd like to introduce you to my neighbor. This is Gunnery Sergeant Marcus Pickwell," Jim said, and then looked at Gunny. "This is Mark and Jess's neighbor, Abigail Petersen."

Gunny stood up and walked over to Mrs. Petersen. He shook her outstretched hand. "Everyone just calls me 'Gunny.' It's a pleasure to meet you, ma'am."

"The pleasure is all mine, Marcus," Mrs. Petersen smiled and then spoke again. "Marcus, would you help me with this ice?"

"Yes, ma'am," Gunny snapped out his answer and then smiled back.

Everyone just stared in disbelief as Mrs. Petersen walked back toward her house with Gunny in tow, carrying the ice. When they were safely out of earshot, Jim cracked up. The others followed suit.

"Did you see the way he snapped to?" Jim asked, barely able to catch his breath. "I thought he was going to salute when he said, 'Yes, ma'am.'"

"Did you hear the way she called him 'Marcus' after he said to call him 'Gunny'?" Lisa added.

Gunny was gone for the better part of an hour. When he came back, Mark and Jim were readjusting the new carburetor on Jim's truck. He had a big smile on his face, bigger than the one Mark had noticed at lunch, and he seemed in a hurry to leave.

"What's your hurry, Gunny? You sure took your time over at Abigail's," Mark said with a big grin, seeking revenge for the ribbing he had gotten earlier.

"We was jus' talkin'!"

"Talking, huh?" Jim jumped on Mark's bandwagon this time. "Is that what they used to call it?"

"Boy, you watch the tone you take with me," Gunny was using his best Drill Instructor voice, "or I'll stick my foot so far up your ass that the next time you go to the doctor, he'll ask you how you got them boot tracks on your tonsils."

"Okay, Gunny. We were just teasing. Why don't you stay for dinner?" Mark offered.

"Abby invited me to the dance tonight. I figured you boys could do with some watchin' to make sure you don't get out of hand. I'm going home to get cleaned up, and then I'll be back," Gunny explained.

"I guess we could use a chaperone," Jim said.

"Chaperone, hell. What you two boys need is a warden, but until we can find one, I guess I'll just have to do the best I can," he said, as he climbed up into his truck. "I'll be back before dark."

"Alright, Gunny. We'll see you then," Jim said.

Everyone ate dinner and then got ready for the dance. After the President's speech, they all walked down to Jon's. Mark had all of the ice in a big cooler that he'd put in the wagon. Even though the dance wasn't supposed to start until dark, the festivities had already begun. Music was playing, and everybody was visiting. Mark noticed that almost everyone was smiling for a change. This is a good idea, he thought. For the second time today, he found himself on the other side of the fence from where he started out.

"Ironic," he mumbled to himself.

Mark pulled the wagon over by the punch bowl, and Jess set down a big plate of chocolate chip cookies on a table that was already half full of cupcakes, brownies, and other treats. Many people had brought lawn chairs to sit in, and Mark asked Jim to go back to the house with him to bring some for the two families. When they got back, the dance was in full swing. Gunny had arrived and was talking with Mrs. Petersen, and she was introducing him to some of the neighbors. A George Strait song started playing.

"Hey, Cowboy, wanna dance?" Jess asked her husband.

"Sorry, ma'am, but I'm married to a mean, old hag who might just castrate me if she found me dancing with a pretty, young filly like you."

Jess punched him in the arm. "Get your sorry ass out here and dance with me, you bum."

"Oh, baby, I love it when you talk dirty to me," Mark said as he led Jess out to the street turned dance floor.

The dance was a huge success. Everyone got to know each other a little better. Mark spent some time with neighbors he'd previously only known as names and faces. He also filled in some of the men on Gunny's suggestions for security. Some thought they should implement them as soon as possible, and others, like Jon, thought they were unnecessary. He talked with Professor Petrie for quite a long time. He'd also changed his position on security and thought Gunny's proposal was a good idea. Security wasn't all they talked about. Ted Petrie was in charge of the history department at the local junior college, and he and Mark discussed at length the growth in power and size of the federal government since the Civil War. They also spent a little time talking about how much Samantha was dancing with Ted's son, Alex. After a while, Jess came back over and made him dance with her some more. In fact, no one escaped having to dance. David was forced to dance with the twins some, and even Gunny, protesting that his knee hurt, had to take a couple of turns around the floor with Abby.

At about ten o'clock, the dance started winding down, and by 10:30, everyone had headed home. As the two families walked toward their house, they noticed a cool breeze out of the north.

"Must be another little cool front coming in," Jim observed.

"It sure won't hurt my feelings any," Mark added. "Did Gunny leave in time for curfew?"

"Yes, but he didn't look too happy having to leave the party before it was over," Jim said. "It kind of reminded me of Cinderella, but with combat boots instead of glass slippers."

Everybody laughed. When they were almost to the house, David asked a question.

"Dad, do you think it's good the power went out?"

"No, son. Do you?"

"In some ways. I know a lot of people have died, and I know that some people don't have a lot of food, but if it hadn't happened, we wouldn't have gotten to know the neighbors like we have."

"I see your point. I guess there's always some good that comes out of everything. It shouldn't take something like The Burst to make us get to know the people who live around us, but for some reason, it did. Hopefully, we'll learn from this. If the lights don't come back on soon, we may learn a lot of things."

Chapter 16

Once the twins had been put to bed, the adults and teenagers talked about what they wanted to do the next day. Mark was going to take Jerry to get his Jeep, and Sam and David both wanted to go with him. Lisa wanted to go check on her parents. Mark thought he should try to get to Waco to check on his family, too. Jess said she needed to review their master list and see if Kroger had received the shipment they were expecting.

"Does this mean we're going to stay here? We never have made a definite decision," Mark said.

"What does everyone think?" Jess asked.

"I vote for here," Lisa stated. "I don't like the politics at the ranch."

"If we could get this place secured like Gunny suggested, I think we stand a better chance here. The ranch location is better than here, but they have too few people to really secure it. I think the larger group here gives us the best chance," Jim gave his opinion.

"I liked the ranch, but I'd rather stay here at our house," David said, which surprised Mark a little.

"I want to stay here, too," Jess implored. "I think everybody knows my reasons."

"I may have different reasons than everybody else, but I want to stay, too," Sam added.

"Well, I guess I'll make it unanimous," Mark said. "I'm still very concerned about some things, though."

"What's your biggest concern?" Jess asked.

"Water."

"We have water."

"Only as long as we have fuel for the generator. Once that runs out, and I don't know when that'll be, we can't run the pump," Mark explained.

"There's tons of gas in the cars that don't run," Lisa said.

"Yeah, but gas doesn't last forever," Jim said, "It can go bad in as little as three months."

"What about a hand pump like they used in the old days?" David asked.

"I don't think those pumps will pull water up from very far. Our well is almost two hundred feet deep."

"What would do it?" Jim asked.

"A Solarjack pump, like they have at the ranch, would do it or a windmill. We'd have to figure out how much water the neighborhood would need per day, then see how many gallons per hour a windmill can pump."

"Dad, remember at the ranch. They said they took out an old windmill to put in the solar pump. Maybe we could get that windmill," David suggested.

"That's good thinking, Dave," Mark said, as David beamed.

"Maybe we could work out a trade with them," Jim added. "Hunting, fishing, shooting, and karate lessons for the windmill and some of the other stuff we might need."

"I guess we need to go talk to them before Saturday," Mark said. "Man, we have so much to do and so little time."

"We have plenty of time, don't we?" Jess asked.

"Not really. According to the news, the riots are getting worse in the big cities. It's only a matter of time before they start here, and when they do, I don't know how much we're going to be able to go into town, or go anywhere for that matter."

"He's right," Jim said. "Todd and Mr. Davis figured about two weeks before riots started here. I think we may have a little longer, but they studied it at least some. To be on the safe side, we should try to get the most important stuff done by Sunday. Why don't we make a list of everything we need to do and get and prioritize it?"

Everyone agreed that Jim's idea was a good one. They worked on the list for more than an hour. They couldn't agree on some of the priorities, but they were able to put to bed what everyone needed to do the next day. Mark and Lisa would take the Jeep and drive the Watsons to their ranch. Then they'd come home through Uvalde and check on Lisa's parents. Jim and Jess would take the trucks to town and buy more groceries if Kroger would let them. Then they'd try to buy some jerry cans and get as much gas as they could from cars in the neighborhood. Mark said they could no longer afford the gas to keep the deep freeze going, so Sam would start cutting the deer meat in the freezer into strips for jerky while she watched the twins. David was given the job he least wanted. Someone needed to poll all of the neighbors and find out how many people each house contained, what skills everyone possessed, how they were fixed for food, if they had any medical needs, and what supplies and equipment they might have that the whole neighborhood could use. Mark explained to David to ask specifically about gardening equipment. He suggested that Jess ask Mrs. Petersen if she'd go with David. He assured David that he trusted him to do the job and told him that some adults might be more comfortable answering questions if an adult was accompanying him.

With the assignments for the next day done, everyone headed for bed except for Mark and Sam. They first went to the freezer and took the meat to the kitchen to thaw out.

"Dad, do you think the lights will ever come back on?" Sam asked.

"Of course they will, sweetheart."

"When?"

"That's the big question, isn't it?" Mark answered. "It could be two days, two weeks, or two years. I just don't know, but I think we're doing the smart thing. We're preparing like it's going to be two years."

"Can we make it for two years without power?"

"I think we can, but I'm not going to lie to you. It's going to be tough. There's a lot of work to do and a lot of stuff we need. The work we can do, but I don't know where we're going to get some of the stuff. But we'll find a way to get by."

"I know we will, Dad. Just promise me one thing."

"What's that?"

"I love the twins, but promise me I'm not going to be the one to watch them all the time."

"Sweetheart, I can promise you that, but you probably will have to watch them more than you're going to want. We aren't going to have the luxury of making sure all of the work is evenly divided. Everyone's going to have to pitch in where they can do the most good and where they're needed most. It's not a punishment; it's just part of being a responsible adult."

"I know, Dad. It's just I want to do some of the exciting stuff, too."

"Be careful what you ask for, Sweetie. You may find that the exciting stuff isn't as exciting as you think." Mark kissed his daughter on the head. "Now, get your butt to bed. You've got a lot of meat to cut tomorrow."

"Alright, Dad. I love you."

"I love you, too."

Sam headed out the door for the camper. Mark looked around. He thought that if it would just cool off a little more, they could sleep in the house. He wondered if there was anything they could do to get more circulation in the bedrooms. He'd have to give that some thought. After he locked the doors, he headed to the camper and climbed into bed. He knew he had a big day tomorrow and needed to get some sleep, but his mind was racing. The last time he remembered looking at his watch it said 2:30.

When the alarm went off, Mark wished he'd slept more. He got up, showered, dressed, and headed outside. It was almost chilly. He checked the thermometer on the side of the camper. It said 64 degrees. Not exactly a blue northern, but pretty cool for September in Texas. He went to the shed and set three of the full jerry cans and one of the five-gallon water jugs next to the Jeep. Two of the jerry cans went onto a carrier on the tailgate that also held the spare tire and a hi-lift jack. The third gas can and the water jug went behind the back seat with the toolbox and first aid kit. There was also a 12-volt air compressor, an extra quart of oil, and a tow strap back there. Mark then topped off the Jeep's gas tank with another gas can and checked the oil.

About that time, Lisa and Jim came out of their camper.

"Need any help?" Jim asked.

"No, I think the Jeep's ready. I was just going in the house to get a rifle. Is Lisa going to take a gun?"

"She didn't really want to, but I told her she had to take at least a handgun. I'm giving her my .357. She likes shooting it, and she's pretty good with it."

Mark, Jim, and Lisa walked into the house. Jess was in the kitchen.

"What are you doing in here?" Mark asked.

"I live here, remember?" she shot back with a wink.

"I know; I mean I didn't see you get up."

"I got up when you were in the shower. I wanted to fix you and Lisa a good breakfast before you left."

"Thank you."

"You're welcome. Now sit down and eat, all of you."

While they were eating, Jess was fixing sandwiches and putting them into a small cooler. They all discussed again what they had to get done that day.

"You guys be careful," Jess admonished, as Mark and Lisa got into the Jeep. She handed the cooler to Lisa.

"We will," Mark promised.

"Tell your folks I'm sorry the girls and I couldn't come this time and that we love them," Jim told Lisa.

"I will," Lisa answered. "We'll see you all tonight."

Mark started the Jeep and headed out of the subdivision. As he turned onto the main road, the sun was just peeking over the horizon. When he and Lisa got to Jerry's house, the brothers were waiting outside. They each had a rifle case and a small duffel bag. Mark helped them load the bags behind the back seat on top of the other stuff. They climbed into the back as they said hello to Lisa and put their rifle cases on the floor. As Mark pulled out onto the road, Jerry handed him a map with a route highlighted.

"We figured it might be best to stay off the interstate," Jerry explained. "This is the way we go on holiday weekends to beat the traffic. It's a little longer, but we shouldn't have to dodge as many stalled cars."

"That sounds good," Mark replied. "After we get your Jeep running, Lisa and I are going to drive up to Uvalde to check on her parents."

"I was wondering why she came with you," Tony smiled. "I thought maybe she got elected to make sure we didn't get into any trouble today."

"Jess told me to watch you Watson boys real good. She said if Mark came home with another gun, all of you would be in big trouble," Lisa teased back.

The men all laughed. The trip to Cotulla went quickly. The foursome chatted about the events of the last eight days and how much longer it could go until it really got ugly in the city. Jerry had been right about there not being too many stalled cars on this route. However, any time Mark came to a hill or blind curve, he slowed way down, just in case. When they got to the Watsons' ranch, Jerry unlocked the gate, and they drove up to the camp house. It only took Mark about twenty minutes to get the parts replaced on the Jeep. When they tried to start it, the battery wouldn't turn the engine over fast enough to start. They hooked up the jumper cables from Mark's vehicle, and the old CJ sprang to life on the next turn of the key. As Mark was taking the cables off of the battery on the Watsons' Jeep, he was distracted for a moment when Lisa said something about eating. When he glanced away, the unshrouded fan hit the outside edge of his right hand.

"Shit!" Mark yelled, as he realized that this was the first time he had cursed in a couple of days. He dropped the cables on the ground and clutched the hand to his chest.

"What happened?" Lisa asked.

"The fan hit my hand," he responded, as he looked at the injury. There was a small cut that didn't seem to be bleeding. "But I think it's okay."

Mark had spoken too soon. The fan strike had initially mashed the capillaries closed, but they opened back up, and the blood started to flow freely.

Lisa looked at it and had Mark move his fingers. She informed him that it would be okay, but it was going to throb for several days. She got the first aid kit out of the Jeep and cleaned and bandaged Mark's hand.

"You know, if you really got hurt, it might be hard to find proper medical care, even if we weren't in the middle of nowhere," she warned him.

"I know," he said sheepishly. "We all need to make sure we're extra careful."

The men washed up with some of the water Mark had brought, and then Lisa pulled out the cooler and handed out sandwiches to everyone. After they'd eaten, Jerry and Tony went to a storage building and retrieved some gas cans and filled the Jeep's tank. They loaded the remaining two full cans along with their bags and rifles into their Jeep.

"How long are you two going to stay in Uvalde?" Jerry asked.

"Probably only about an hour," Lisa answered. "I just want to check on my folks."

"We were thinking about going with you, if that's okay." Tony inquired. "We'd feel better if we all stuck together, just in case one of these old rust buckets broke down or something."

"We appreciate that," Mark responded. "Are we ready to go?"

Everyone nodded their heads, loaded into the Jeeps, and headed out.

As they approached the area where Lisa's parents lived, some of the houses were burned to the ground. A few of them were still smoldering. The closer they got to the subdivision, the worse the devastation was. When they reached the entrance, it was apparent that none of the houses had escaped destruction. Lisa was in tears.

"I'm sure they got out," Mark said, as he brought the Jeep to a stop.

"What could have happened?" she asked.

"I don't know. Let's go back to town and find out."

Mark turned the Jeep around, and Jerry followed him. They drove to the courthouse and parked near the entrance to the Sheriff's department. Mark noticed that the vehicles parked in the spaces reserved for patrol cars didn't look quite right. Each had a light bar, antennas, and a sheriff's emblem on the door, but they were all different colors and makes. There was a maroon 1970's LTD, an old Dodge pickup that still had some blue paint on it, and a beautiful late 60's GTO in candy apple red. Tony whistled as they passed the muscle car.

"Man, what I wouldn't give to have one of these," he said longingly.

The other two men nodded agreement, but Lisa, if she even heard him, ignored the comment and marched directly for the entrance. When they got inside the door, there was a dispatcher and two deputies behind the counter. One of the deputies saw them and came to the counter.

"Can I help y'all?"

"I'm looking for my parents," Lisa blurted. "My name is Lisa Davis. They lived in the subdivision north of town on Highway 83. The whole neighborhood is burned. What happened? Do you know where they are? Their names are George and Alice Garrett. I have to find them."

"Ma'am, just calm down," the deputy drawled. "A small airplane crashed into the subdivision when The Burst hit. It started a fire, and the volunteer fire department wasn't able to stop it. Most of the residents were able to get out. Why don't y'all come back to my desk, and we'll see what information we have on your folks."

They followed the deputy, and he motioned for Lisa to sit in the chair next to his desk. The men stood behind her. The deputy dug through a pile of papers and finally found the ones he was looking for. He ran his finger down the first page and then flipped the page. When he had looked at all three pages, he flipped back to the first page and went through them again. He then set the report down and looked at Lisa.

"I have good news and bad news," he began. "The good news is that there are no Garretts on the lists of fatalities or injuries from the fire."

"Thank God!" Lisa exclaimed. "What's the bad news?"

"Well, all of the survivors went to stay with friends or relatives or are at the shelter set up at the high school. We got all of the names we could of who went where, but your parents aren't on any of the lists."

"What does that mean?"

"It means one of two things. First, and most likely, the records we have of survivors are very inaccurate. They may be staying with someone, and we just don't have it recorded. Or...now this is just a possibility...we have a few bodies we haven't been able to ID."

"Oh my God!" Lisa cried, putting her head in her hands.

Mark patted her on the shoulder, and the deputy took hold of her hands.

"Now look here, Mrs. Davis, there's no sense getting yourself all worked up until you know for sure what happened. This is what you need to do. First, go to the hospital and make sure they aren't there. Then go to the high school and see if they have any record of your folks. Finally, go to every friend or relative you can think of and see if they know anything. If you still can't find them, come back, and we'll test to see if any of the unidentified are your parents."

"What do you mean, test?" Mark asked.

The deputy blew a long breath out before he answered.

"The people we haven't ID'd yet were burned quite badly. Unfortunately, they're unrecognizable. The only way we can be sure of who they are is through a DNA test comparing them to a known relative. The bad part is we don't know how long it'll take to get the results once the power comes back on because there are going to be thousands of cases like this."

Lisa was shaking but had managed to stop crying.

"Well, I guess we'd better get busy," she said. "Thanks for your help, Deputy."

They walked back outside and headed for the Jeeps. Jerry whispered to Mark that he and Tony would stick with them for a while but would have to head for home before too long. Mark told him that he understood. They loaded up and headed out for the hospital. Mark could see Lisa was on the verge of crying again.

"Don't worry, Lisa. We'll find them," Mark promised, praying they would.

Chapter 17

The hospital didn't have any record of the Garretts. The drive to the high school was only about two miles, but it seemed like it took forever to Mark. He thought it must seem even longer to Lisa. At the high school, they found the Red Cross in charge in the gym. There were over three hundred people living there. Mark was thankful his family wasn't reduced to this option. He explained the situation to one of the ladies from the Red Cross, and she pulled out a long list of names. She flipped back through some pages and started reading down the list.

"I'm sorry," she said. "We don't have any Garretts listed with the people from the fire. Maybe they're staying with someone in town."

Lisa started to shake and then to cry.

"I don't know where else to look," she sobbed. "All of their friends I know of lived in the same neighborhood."

She started crying and Mark reached out to pat her on the back. She turned and wrapped her arms around his neck, burying her head into his shoulder. She was crying so loudly and squeezing him so tightly that it was hard for him to breathe. He patted her back and told her they would look until they found them. Mark had never seen Lisa be anything but cool and collected. Jim had told him she was extremely close to her parents, but Mark hadn't imagined she could lose it like this. He felt awkward and didn't know what to do or say. Jess was just the opposite of Lisa when something like this happened, and Mark had never had to deal with a situation like this. He wished Jim or Jess were here. They would know what to do.

"Lisa!" a voice called out. "Lisa, is that you?"

Lisa pulled her head out of Mark's shoulder. "Mom?...Oh, God!...Mom! It's really you! They said you weren't here. Where's Dad?"

"He's on the other side of the gym, playing cards. I was going to the ladies' room when I heard someone crying, and when I came closer to see what was going on, it was you," Mrs. Garrett said.

"I don't understand," Lisa explained. "They said that you weren't on the list of people from the fire?"

The Red Cross lady franticly looked through her list again.

"Here they are," she explained. "They're on the list of people stranded in town."

"That's because we were at the grocery store when The Burst hit, and we couldn't get home in our car," Alice stated. "We finally found a ride back home, but by the time we got there, the whole neighborhood was engulfed in flames. We had nowhere to go and nothing to wear, so we came here."

"I'm so glad we found you. I was afraid you'd been killed," Lisa cried with tears of joy now.

"You always jump to the worst conclusion. How many times have I told you to be more positive?" Alice scolded. "Why don't we go see your father?"

"Sorry about the mix up," the Red Cross lady apologized.

"It's okay," Lisa responded, as she, her mother, and the three men headed to the other side of the gym.

When they found Lisa's dad, she hugged him hard enough to make an anaconda proud. She reintroduced them to Mark, whom they vaguely remembered. Then she introduced them to the Watson brothers. While Lisa and her parents were catching up, Tony told Mark they needed to head home. Mark asked them to wait just a couple of minutes. He then interrupted the Garrett's visit with their only child.

"Lisa, I'm sorry to interrupt, but the Watsons need to get home, and so do we."

"But, Mark, can't we stay just a few more minutes?"

"What for?"

"So I can visit with my parents," she answered him indignantly.

"You can't visit with them on the way back?"

"You mean they can come with us?"

"Of course."

"Young man, we wouldn't want to be a burden," George Garrett said emphatically.

"Mr. Garrett, any family of Jim's and Lisa's is family of ours. Plus, I can already think of about a dozen things I can use your help on."

"I appreciate that, son, but I can't do that much work since my stroke. I won't be much help I'm afraid."

"I have plenty of strong backs, Mr. Garrett. It's knowledge I need. So, if you don't mind, why don't we get your stuff and hit the road."

"Young man, you drive a hard bargain. I'll accept under one condition, and that's for you to call me George." The older gentleman extended his hand.

"Well then, George, I think we've got a deal." Mark grabbed his hand and shook it.

Lisa was as happy as Mark had seen her since The Burst. It only took the Garretts a minute to gather the few possessions they'd bought or been given since the fire destroyed their home. They thanked the Red Cross people for their hospitality and headed for the Jeeps. The trip seemed short with everyone filling each other in on the events of the last week. Before long, Mark was pulling into his driveway. Gunny's truck was there. When the twins saw their grandparents, they ran up and launched themselves into the waiting arms of George and Alice. Jim came running up and hugged his in-laws, as well. They all went over to the picnic table and started catching up. Jess came out of the house with Sam and David. Mark hugged the kids and kissed his wife.

"What happened to your hand?" she asked.

"Oh, I just got stupid for a minute and cut it. Lisa bandaged it up and said it'll be okay...Where's Gunny?"

"I'll give you three guesses, but you'll only need one," Jess answered with a wink. "I invited them both for supper, so they should be along shortly."

Jim asked Mark to come look at what they had in the shed. When Mark walked in, he saw some 55-gallon metal drums.

"What are these for?" he asked, pretty sure he already knew the answer.

"They're for the fuel. Gunny knows this guy who sells barrels for a living. We bought ten of them. We can put the gas we get out of the nonworking cars into them. He also sells those blue water barrels. I figured if everyone in the

94

neighborhood bought one or two, we could cut back on how often we have to pump water. He even has some large water tanks, but they're pretty expensive."

"This is awesome. Did you get any groceries?"

"Yes, the Kroger got a shipment in, and we each got another $50 worth. The manager said they felt they could keep this up until the lights came back on. He also told me they were issuing credit to anyone who didn't have cash. I asked him if that was a corporate decision, and he told me it was, but rumor had it the government had strongly suggested they do it, and they'd reimburse Kroger for any losses. I figure we'll need to ferry everybody into town again. David has some good news, too."

"Yes, Dave, what'd you find out?"

"Well, most of the people here worked at things that won't help us much, but there's one exception. You know Mr. Hernandez's friend, Mr. Vasquez? He's really Dr. Vasquez."

"A doctor?" Mark was surprised.

"Not a people doctor, a vet. He said he has a lot of stuff at his office and was thinking about asking you if you could help him bring it to his house," David said smiling.

"That's great, son. I'm sure we can do that. Did you find any gardening equipment?"

"Yes, sir, three roto-tillers and lots of hand tools."

"Excellent. Anything else?"

"Quite a few people have hobbies that might be useful. Mrs. Petersen was really excited by one of the ladies who has a lot of jars for canning. I think the best thing was one of the men has a big welding shop. He said he can weld most anything. He's really a plumber, but he learned to weld in the Army. One of the other guys said he used to be into CB's a lot. He said he has several radios in storage and that maybe he could get some of them to work. There were some other things Mrs. Petersen thought might be useful, and she wrote them down."

"Son, that's wonderful. You did an excellent job."

David's face lit up. "Thanks, Dad."

Mark went back to the house to check on how Sam did with the venison. She'd cut it all up and was marinating it. Mark bragged on her and thanked her for watching the girls. Supper was ready, and Gunny and Abby showed up just in time. Introductions were made all around, and then they sat down to eat. As they ate, George and Alice filled everyone in on how it was to live in a shelter for a week.

"There was no privacy whatsoever. That was the hardest part for me," Alice said.

"I wouldn't wish it on my worst enemy," George agreed. "We lost our house and all of our belongings, but the thing I missed most was being able to have a private conversation with my wife."

After supper, it was time for the President's speech. They all gathered around the radio.

"My fellow Americans, I come to you tonight with some great news. Limited power has been restored to Washington, D.C., and some of the other major east coast cities. Most of this power is being allocated to hospitals and other

essential service providers. While we may still be a few days away from total power restoration, this is a promising first step."

"In spite of this wonderful news, I have some disturbing news, as well. I am very concerned with the rioting and lawlessness that continue to plague some of our major cities. Most of the citizens in the majority of the cities and towns in our great nation have worked together for the common good. I would hope that everyone would follow the example set by most of the country. If the rioting is not stopped in the few trouble spots by tomorrow, I will have no choice but to declare limited martial law in those areas. This is a measure I hope not to be forced into undertaking, but we will not tolerate the murder and mayhem that has been infecting these areas."

"I pray that you and your families are safe, and I ask you to pray for our country and its leadership in this crisis. Help your neighbors and your community. Thank you for your time. I will talk with you tomorrow. God bless."

"Please stay tuned to KSTX for the news and an important announcement."

The major items in the news were the announcement that the Kroger stores had resupplied and that people could buy more groceries and that the water was going to be off in the city for twelve hours starting at 7 PM tonight. Citizens were forbidden to store any more water than they needed for drinking and cooking for those twelve hours. The City Water Board said it was to do some maintenance on the pumps, but Mark thought it was to let them get enough water pumped up into the tanks to maintain the water pressure. The weatherman said they should enjoy the cooler weather for another day or two, but then it would be warming back up.

Just before the news ended, the announcer explained that the radio station had been running off an old back-up system powered by a diesel generator. They only stored enough fuel to run for a week, as they never expected it to take longer than that to get the power back on. He went on to say they'd been resupplied a couple of days ago, but they were unsure of when any more fuel could be counted on. Beginning tonight, the station would cut back their broadcast to five hours a day until the crisis was resolved. They would broadcast two hours in the morning, an hour at noon, and two hours in the evening. Mark wasn't sure, but he thought he heard the newsman's voice crack.

The whole group headed down to Jon's house for the meeting. The discussions were as spirited as Mark had seen them since the day the lights went out. Some people were encouraged by the news of some power being restored. Others thought it was nothing more than a ruse to buy the government a few more days. Most were skeptical at best. Another argument was over the wisdom of declaring martial law. Some said it was necessary to save the embattled cities from ruin. Others felt it was an overextension of the President's power and that it would set a dangerous precedent. Mark listened to the arguments for both sides. Each made good points, but Mark didn't know which side was right. Once that discussion died down, Mark spoke to the group.

"I have something I want to present to all of you. I'd first like to introduce you to George and Alice Garrett. They are Lisa Davis' parents. Their home in Uvalde was burned to the ground by a small airplane that crashed in their neighborhood when The Burst hit. They were living in the Uvalde high school gym, but now they'll be staying with us. George and Alice, until they retired, were farmers and did some ranching. None of us knows how long the power is going to be out, but it seems we all think it's prudent to assume it's not coming back on in the near future. We don't know how much longer Kroger's going to be able to sell food, so I think we need to try to start growing our own. Everybody here has at least an acre of land, and there are fifteen empty lots that could be turned into gardens. If we work together, we could get in some fall gardens and probably be able to get some food out of them in six to eight weeks." Mark stopped to let what he'd said sink in.

"I don't have time to take care of that," Jon said flatly. "Just taking care of security is becoming a full time job."

"Maybe someone else could help us out," Mark suggested.

"So, what do we need to do?" someone in the crowd asked after a minute.

"I think the first thing we ought to do is to form a committee to study and plan what the best course of action is. We know we have some gardening equipment in the neighborhood, and between George and some of the others, we have the knowledge. We have lots of labor available, so all we need is the raw material. I would suggest a four- or five-person committee be selected to present us with a plan in two or three days."

There were murmurs of approval from the crowd. "I nominate you, Mark, to head up the committee," someone shouted.

"Thanks, but this isn't my strong suit. I may be a 'Bean Counter,' but I never counted the kind of beans we're talking about now. I think George would be the logical candidate to head the committee."

"He doesn't even live here!" Jon shouted. "He doesn't have as much at stake as the rest of us."

"Jon, he does live here. He's staying with me and has just as much at stake as the rest of us. We're all trying to get our families through this mess. George is the only one here I know of who's made a living off of the land. Unless there's someone else more qualified, I believe he's the best man for the job."

It was quiet for a long moment. "I second the nomination of George Garrett to head the gardening committee," Professor Petrie said.

Mark smiled gratefully at the professor. "All those in favor…"

"I'll take care of that!" Jon said. "All in favor…"

A hearty 'Aye' arose from the crowd.

"All those opposed…"

Not a sound was heard. Mark looked at Jon and saw that he was standing with his arms folded. "Well, I guess the 'ayes' have it," he spat.

"Now, we need some people to help," Mark said. "Does anyone have any gardening experience who would like to help?"

Four hands went up, two women and two men. "Please give your names to George, and y'all set a time for your meeting. Today is Wednesday. Could you have a plan to present to us at the meeting Friday evening?" Mark asked. He was greeted by hearty nods of the head.

It got really quiet for minute.

"Are you going to be able to take us to the Kroger again, Mark?" Sherri Henderson asked.

"I'm busy for the next few days, but I know how badly everyone needs to get to the store. So, if it's okay with him, I'd like to lend my truck to Jon. He's

97

done a great job of organizing the food runs, and if it's alright with him, he can arrange to ferry you all back and forth tomorrow."

Jon looked shocked at first, and then the iceman attitude he'd been displaying melted. "Uh, yeah, sure. I can do that. But if the lines are long, we can probably only get two groups done tomorrow."

"Actually, Jon, if you don't mind the suggestion, I was thinking you could use the truck like a bus. Make a round trip every hour or so and drop off and pick up as people are ready. That way, everybody could go in one day."

"Yeah, that would work, I guess. Is there anything else?"

"Yes." The man David had pointed out to Mark earlier as the man with the welding shop raised his hand. Mark didn't remember seeing him at a meeting before. He was huge.

"Yes, sir," Jon said.

"Please don't call me sir. My name is Daniel Lopez, but my friends call me Chaparo." Mark noticed that all of the Hispanics at the meeting chuckled at the man's nickname. Mark would have to ask Manny about it.

"OK then, Chaparo, what's on your mind?"

"I heard that some of you got a Marine to give you a security evaluation, and that he made some recommendations of things we should do. Where do we stand on that, and could he brief the whole group?"

"I'm not finished evaluating everything Sergeant Pickwell suggested," Jon said.

"Well, can we at least hear what he had to say?"

"I guess so."

"If you'd like to hear it straight from the horse's mouth, Gunny's here," Mark said enthusiastically.

Jon shot him a drop-dead look. "Gunny, would you come up and briefly go over what you said to us yesterday?" Jon's shoulders were slumped.

Gunny got up in front of the group and laid out what he'd told Mark, Jim, and Jon the day before. Mark could see Jon visibly stiffen as Gunny spoke. When he was done, Chaparo asked his question again.

"So, where do we stand on all that?"

"Like I said, I haven't had time to review everything," Jon answered impatiently.

"Don't you think we should get started on it?" Chaparo suggested.

"I will as soon as I can."

"Maybe we should form another committee to study the plans," Professor Petrie suggested.

"That's a good idea," someone else shouted.

"Now wait a min…" Jon began.

A chorus of people supporting the formation of a security committee drowned out the rest of what Jon said. He folded his arms and plopped down in a chair.

"We could do that," Mark said loudly enough to quiet the crowd. "Who do we want to head up the committee?" Mark saw Dr. Vasquez's hand go up.

"I think you should do it, Mark," he stated.

"I don't think I'm the right person for this committee, either. I don't have any military experience."

"Then get Gunny to do it!" Mark didn't recognize the voice.

Jon jumped out of his chair like it was hot all of a sudden. "Now wait a minute! Gunny DOESN'T live here! I think that excludes him from being on a committee."

Jon's comments started the crowd murmuring again. After a moment, Mark asked the crowd to quiet down.

"I think Jon has a good point. Anyone on a committee probably should live here, but that doesn't stop the committee from bringing in any special advisors they deem fit. Does that seem okay to everyone?"

There was a chorus of affirmative answers.

"Does anyone have any combat experience?"

No hands went up. Most of the residents of Silver Hills were too young to have served in Vietnam, and too old for Desert Storm or Enduring Freedom.

"Does anyone have any military experience?"

Only two hands went up, Jon's and Chaparo's.

"Most of you know that Jon spent four years with the Marines in logistics and supply. Chaparo, what did you do?"

"I was in the Army for twelve years doing heavy equipment maintenance. I never saw combat, but I was close a couple of times."

Mark thought that he'd rather have this guy chair the committee. It seemed he had the same sense of urgency about security as Mark. Jon seemed to be threatened by Gunny, and that might get in his way of doing what was best for the community. He thought about asking the group to vote, but that would cause a problem, no matter the outcome. If Chaparo won, Jon would be very bitter, and if Jon won, then who knows what might happen with security. Suddenly, the solution came to Mark.

"Since we have two, well-qualified veterans, does anyone see a problem with them co-chairing the security committee?"

No one said anything.

"Well, since there are no objections, I guess you guys have the job. Who would like to help these fellows out?"

"We still want you to be on the committee, Mark," Professor Petrie said. "You may not be a military man, but you do know about self defense."

Mark thought for a moment. "I'll tell you what Professor; I'll do it if you'll do it."

"Well, okay."

"Anyone else?"

One of the women's hands went up. "I think it might be a good idea if you had a female on the committee. After all, we care about security as much as you men do. Plus, we can make sure you boys don't turn this into some kind of G. I. Joe fantasy."

The murmur of female agreement was unmistakable. "How about you, ma'am?" Mark asked the woman.

"Me?" the woman stammered. "Oh, no. I'm just a single mom concerned about my kids. I don't know anything about security. I just think a woman might think of some things you men might overlook. I'm sure one of the women here must have some experience that would be useful to the committee."

Mark looked around. "How about it? Any of you women want to help us out?"

No one said anything. "Well, ma'am," Mark looked at the single mom, "looks to me like you're the one. If you don't do it, who will?"

"Okay, I will. I guess that's what I get for opening my big mouth," she answered.

"Thanks," Mark said with a smile. "Jon, Chaparo, when do you want to get together?"

"Tomorrow after the meeting?" Chaparo asked, looking at Jon.

"I guess so."

"Is that okay with everyone else?" Chaparo said.

All of the other security committee members nodded their heads.

Mark looked at Jon. "Anything else?"

Jon shook his head. "I guess we'll see everybody tomorrow. If you need to go to the grocery store in the morning, come see me, and we'll figure out the bus schedule."

George got with the members of his committee for a moment, and then Mark's group walked back to his house. Gunny excused himself to go say goodbye to Abby before he had to leave. She came back with him and brought some clothes for Alice. George, who was close to the same size as Mark, was given two pairs of jeans and half a dozen shirts out of Mark's closet. Everyone was fairly tired from the long day, and shortly after dark, they headed to bed. George and Alice slept in the bed that the twins had been using in the pop-up, and the dining table and benches in the camper were converted into a bed for the girls. Mark, before going to bed, went into his bedroom and put a dollar in his black box. He wondered what tomorrow would bring.

Chapter 18

The next morning, Mark got up to exercise. As he ran, he felt weighed down by how much there was to do and how little time there was to do it. He needed to go back to the ranch and work out a deal with Mr. Davis for the windmill. He'd promised the Watsons that he'd lend them a truck to haul inventory to their house. They needed to go back to Jim's to get his gun safe and some other stuff. He wanted to see if he could find some golf cart batteries like Rodney had told him about. He needed to get the security committee moving, and they needed to train the guards. He wanted to figure out a way to keep the house cool enough, so they could sleep inside. He needed to help Dr. Vasquez get the medicine and supplies from his office. They needed to try to get all the gas they could from the stalled cars. Jess needed to get the kids going on their schoolwork. He wanted to go to Waco to check on his family. He knew they'd be okay for food. His brother, Mike, had stored a bunch of food and supplies for Y2K, and Mark knew he still had most of it put away. Heck, they were probably in better shape than he was, as far as food went. That was his number one concern…food. They could get by on the $50 worth a week from Kroger. It didn't provide a very diverse diet, but at least it kept their bellies full, but what if that was no longer available? If rioting started in town, Kroger may have to shut down, or worse, be destroyed. What would they do then? They were going to start growing some food, but how long would it take to get anything out of a garden? He could go down to his deer lease in a couple of months and get lots of game, as long as he had fuel to drive, that is, but hunting season was still over two months away. He felt that if they could get by for the next couple of months, then they could grow and hunt enough to stay fed. He'd have to talk this over with the others and see if they had any ideas.

When he was done, he showered and dressed. He filled his truck with fuel and then drove it down to Jon's house for use as the grocery shuttle. That was another problem, he was getting low on diesel for the truck. When he got back home, breakfast was ready, and all of the adults sat down to eat. As they spoke of what they needed to accomplish for the day, Mark filled the others in on some of his concerns. Jim suggested that they see if anyone else had a car or truck that they could get to run. Maybe then they could get some of the other families to run some errands. George asked if anyone in the neighborhood had a trailer. David said he thought he saw one at Chaparo's when he and Mrs. Petersen did their survey. Mark wondered how he hadn't thought of those things. What else had they not thought of? Well, Mark thought, better just concentrate on the things I have to get done today. He zoned back into the conversation that the others were having.

"…are going to look at the gardening equipment on David's list and then look at the empty lots. Then we should be able to come up with a plan to present to the group," George stated.

"That sounds like a good plan to me," Jim said, as the others nodded. "What do you think, Mark?"

"Yeah. That sounds real good," Mark agreed, not wanting anyone to know that he wasn't paying attention. "Jim, I'm going to walk over to Chaparo's house and see if he has a trailer. We'll need something to bring the windmill back from the ranch on. It might also be easier to load your safe on it than into the back of your truck. I figured we might go get it and whatever else you need from your house today. Want to come with me?"

"Sure thing."

When the two men got to the big man's house, they found him in the large garage behind his home.

"Mark, Jim, welcome to Casa de Chaparo," he said with a big smile as he shook their hands.

"Thanks. Hey, I wanted to ask what 'Chaparo' means," Mark said.

"It means 'Shorty,'" the huge man said with a big smile.

They all laughed for a minute.

"David told me you had a nice workshop, but I had no idea it was this nice." Mark said, as he noticed not only the welding equipment but also a big drill press, a metal lathe, and several other machines he didn't recognize.

"I was a machinist in the Army. I worked in the motor pool for most of my stint. We mostly fixed trucks and humvees, but sometimes we got to work on tanks and stuff, too. Now I just do this stuff as a hobby."

"It sounds like you enjoy it," Jim observed. "Why did you get out?"

"My *suegro*, my father-in-law, got sick, and he needed someone to take over his plumbing business," the big man said sadly. "But I can't complain. It has provided a good living for my family."

"I see," said Mark. "Hey, David mentioned that you might have a trailer."

"Yeah, let me show you."

The men walked behind the garage and saw the trailer. It was a 16-foot utility trailer with dual axles. Mark told Chaparo what he wanted to borrow it for, and the big man was happy to see it put to use.

"You guys need some help?" he offered.

"That would be great," Jim said. "The safe is really heavy, and we could use another strong back. We'll go get my truck and be back in a little while."

"I'll walk with you guys if that's alright. I'm just killing time out here, anyway."

The three men walked back toward Mark's house.

"Do you think we could go in your truck, Mark?" Jim asked. "Since mine's jacked up so high, the trailer would pull more level with yours. I could lend mine to Jon for the store runs."

"I'm sure we can. Let's go see him."

They didn't have to wait long before Jon drove up.

"Hey, Jon!" Jim said, as Jon climbed out from behind the wheel.

"Hello," Jon responded, a little more coolly than Mark liked.

"How's it going?" Mark asked.

"The lines are really long. I guess word is getting around about Kroger giving credit. The people I took at eight weren't quite halfway through the line by the time I made the eleven o'clock run. I think the twelve o'clock group is the last one that stands a chance of getting through the line by six."

"I agree. I guess we'd better take the rest tomorrow…early. We can use both trucks for a couple of runs in the morning."

"We won't need to. This next group makes fifty-one, and we only have twelve more that I scheduled for the one o'clock run. We can take them at eight in the morning."

"We only have forty-seven families who live here, and some of them went to the store yesterday," Mark observed. "How did we get sixty-three people that need to go to the store today?"

Jon's face screwed up, as if the words tasted bad. "A lot of people are inviting friends and relatives to move in with them." Mark could hear 'Like you!' even though Jon didn't say it. "I think we need to talk about this at the meeting tonight before we have so many people living in Silver Hills that we can't control them."

Mark didn't like the way Jon said 'control,' but he didn't want to get into an argument with him out here in the middle of the road. Probably better just to change the subject. "OK, Jon. Could we trade out trucks with you? We need to get some stuff from Jim's house, and we're going to pull Chaparo's trailer. It'll pull better behind mine."

"No problem, I guess."

"We'll go get Jim's truck and be right back."

Jon didn't say anything. The men walked up the road to Mark's.

"Who does he think needs to be controlled?" Chaparo asked sharply.

"I don't know, but I didn't like it either," Mark answered.

"Me either, but since I'm one of the ones he's talking about, my position's obvious," Jim said.

It wasn't long before the trailer was hitched up and the men were heading to Jim's house. As they drove, they passed the little Baptist church. There was a man mowing the grass in front of the stone building. Mark figured it was the pastor. On seeing the truck, the man waved. The three men waved back.

It didn't take long to load the safe onto the trailer with Chaparo's help. Gunny came out to help, as well, but he mostly just supervised. The men chatted as they helped Jim. Their discussion focused mainly around the meeting of the Security Committee. Chaparo agreed with everything Gunny had proposed. The biggest problem he saw was communication.

"If the guards need to call for backup, how are we going to do that?" he asked.

"David told me one of the men has some CB radios that he thinks he might get to work," Mark suggested.

"How many does he have?"

"I don't know...three or four maybe. I have a couple in the shed that may be okay. How many do we need?"

"One in every house and one for each guard position," Chaparo answered.

"That many?" Jim asked.

"Chaparo's right. Without good com, you can't effectively repel a group of MZB's. You need a way for the guards to call for reinforcements," Gunny interjected.

"MZB's?"

"Another term for Tangos that these two pencil pushers came up with. I kinda like it, though. It stands for 'Mutant Zombie Bikers,'" Gunny explained with a toothy grin.

"I see!" Chaparo laughed. "I kinda like it, too."

"We can see if anybody else has any radios at the meeting tonigh, that is, if Jon doesn't piss them off so badly that everybody leaves," Mark observed.

"I don't think too many people are going to like him suggesting they can't invite family to stay with them. I know the Mexican families won't," Chaparo said.

"Well, I guess we'll find out soon enough," Mark stated, as Jim put the last box from his house on the trailer.

The men stood around the trailer and talked for a few more minutes. Mark and Jim described the gate that was at the ranch to Chaparo, and he told them he could easily build one out of materials he already had.

Soon, they were headed back to Silver Hills. Gunny followed in his truck, with Jim riding shotgun in the old Dodge.

As they approached the church where the preacher had been mowing, Chaparo noticed something.

"What's going on there?" he asked.

Mark noticed a group of men standing in front of the church. They seemed to be working feverishly at something. As they drew closer, he could make out one man on the ground and six or seven others kicking and hitting him. Mark slowed the truck down and noticed it was the pastor on the ground, and the men who were kicking him looked like gang members. Mark slammed on the brakes, but before he could get the truck to a complete stop, Chaparo was out of the truck and running toward the brawl. Mark tried to get out of the truck, but as soon as he swung his feet out of the door, the truck lurched forward. He realized it was still running and in gear, and as soon as he had taken his foot off of the clutch, the truck had started moving. Fortunately, he'd also forgotten to take off his seatbelt, and it allowed him to remain in the truck and get it stopped and shut off. Mark's mind flashed back to the incident at the Kroger. However, instead of everything happening in slow motion, it seemed that time had sped up. Mark had his Colt Commander this time, but he couldn't use it with Chaparo between him and the gang bangers. He tried calling out to the big man, but Chaparo must have been so intent on his mission, he didn't hear Mark. The men kicking the preacher were so wrapped up in their mayhem, they didn't see Chaparo bearing down on them. When he reached the bangers, it looked like a tornado going through an RV park. Bodies went flying everywhere.

Chaparo bent over to pick up the preacher and started carrying him back toward the trucks. The bangers picked themselves up and started giving chase. Mark got out of the truck, but the bad guys were still too close to Chaparo and the preacher to bring his gun to bear. As Chaparo approached the truck, the bangers noticed the trucks and the three other men standing next to them. A couple of them stopped, but there were still four or five hot on the trail. Mark moved toward the goons and side-kicked the first one in the stomach just as Chaparo passed him with the preacher. The combination of Mark's foot moving toward the man as he was charging in folded him in half like a closing pocket knife. The impact also knocked Mark over, but he, unlike the man he'd just kicked, could still breathe. As he was getting back up, he noticed that Chaparo had practically thrown the preacher into the front seat of his truck. Once Mark was on his feet, he saw Chaparo on his right side and Jim on his left. There were still four assailants moving toward them. Mark snapped out a front kick and caught one of the men square in the testicles. He dropped like a rock, holding his jewels and moaning. Jim punched another one as he ran in, and Chaparo ducked a punch from one of the others and flipped him over his back as he stood back up. Mark was stepping toward the last man.

BOOM!

Everyone's head swiveled to see Gunny pointing Beulah up in the air. There was smoke pouring out of the muzzle of the big 12 gauge as he shucked out the spent shell for a fresh one and dropped her down so that she pointed at one of the bangers.

"You bastards better haul your asses outta here, or I'll fill 'em so full of holes you'll think you're Swiss!" Gunny yelled.

Mark didn't know if it was what Gunny said, or just the fact that his tone assured the gang members that he wouldn't put up with any shit, or just the big, black, business end of Beulah that scared them off. The ones who weren't too hurt picked up the ones who were, and they all ran toward an old pickup that Mark hadn't noticed before. The truck was running, and as soon as all seven men had jumped into the bed, the driver roared off toward town. The four men looked at each other, and when they realized they were all okay, they turned to check on the minister. He was lying across the seat and only seemed to be about half conscious. Chaparo reached in and gently pulled him out, which was a big contrast from the way he'd put the preacher into the truck. His head was bleeding profusely, but other than that, he didn't have any other obvious injuries. Mark reached behind the back seat of his truck and pulled out his first aid kit. Lying there was the FAL in its case. A lot of good it would have done me there, he thought. I have to start carrying it where I can get it into action quickly if I need it. He pulled out a large dressing, placed it on the preacher's head, and applied pressure.

"Gunny, can you take your truck and go get Lisa?" Jim asked.

"Roger that. Take this in case they come back," Gunny handed Beulah to Jim and headed for his truck. As he raced toward Silver Hills, the preacher started coming to.

"Did you see him?" the preacher asked.

"See who?" Jim said.

"Did you see the angel?"

"What angel?"

"When those men were kicking and hitting me, I asked God to send me an angel. He did, and the angel picked me up and carried me off. At first, I thought he was taking me to Heaven, but I guess he just took me away from those men." The preacher looked blankly toward the sky.

Mark, Jim, and Chaparo just looked at each other.

"Yeah, Preacher," Mark smiled, "we saw the angel. His name's Chaparo, and God sent him just in time."

Chapter 19

Within a couple of minutes, a small crowd had appeared, and they were asking questions about what happened. A woman came running up.

"Bob! Bob! Are you OK?" she cried.

"Cathy, it's okay. I'm going to be fine," the preacher said, seeming to regain his faculties.

"What happened?" she asked.

"I was working on the yard in front of the church when these hoodlums drove up and demanded I give them all the wine in the church. I tried to explain that we were Baptist and use grape juice for communion, but I guess they didn't like my answer, and they started beating me. Thank God these men came along and saved me."

"Thank you so much," she said to the three men with tears in her eyes. "Could you help me get him home? It's just a little ways down the road."

"We'd be happy to, ma'am, but my wife's on her way, and she's a nurse. Why don't we wait for her to get here before we move him?" Jim advised.

A couple of minutes later, Gunny came roaring up. He and Lisa got out of the truck, and she examined the pastor. Once she'd checked to see if he had any neck or back injuries, she gave the okay to move him carefully. They put him and his wife in the back seat of Mark's truck and drove them to their house. Once inside, Lisa bandaged his head and checked to see if he had a concussion. She determined that he did but said it was probably very mild. She then taped his ribs, as she figured they were at least cracked by looking at the bruising. Lisa instructed the preacher to take it easy for a while. She told his wife to wake him up every couple of hours during the night and to come get her if he wouldn't wake up, started having trouble breathing, developed a severe headache, or if anything else seemed to be bothering him. The pastor, who seemed to be getting better by the minute, introduced himself and his wife. He said their names were Bob and Cathy Jones. He thanked the men and Lisa over and over and insisted that they and their families come to church on Sunday.

"Mark's family and ours had already planned on coming this Sunday," Lisa said.

"That's great," Bob responded.

"I'll hafta to see if I kin make it," Gunny said.

"I hope you can."

"I haven't been to church in a long time," Chaparo explained, "and besides that, we're Catholic."

"Brother Chaparo, please don't let that keep you from coming. We had several Catholic families come worship with us last Sunday. It was just too far for them to walk to their church, and we were glad to have them visit. Plus, God is always happy to see His children in His house, no matter how long it's been."

"Well then, I guess we'll be there."

"Excellent."

"Pastor?" Mark asked. "I noticed the temperature in your house is very comfortable compared to ours. Is it because the house is all rock?"

"That may be part of it, but the main reason, I think, is the windows. You see, this parsonage was built in the late '40's, before they had air conditioning. The windows go almost all the way up to the ten-foot ceilings, and they open from the top, as well as from the bottom. That lets the hot air out. They put central air in the house eight or ten years ago, but we don't have to use it unless it gets really hot outside. The church is built the same way."

"I see. Too bad they don't build them like this anymore," Mark observed. "By the way, do you two need anything?"

"No, thanks, we're OK on food, and there isn't really anything else that we need," Cathy answered.

"How about water?"

"We're just inside the city water service line," Bob explained.

"OK then, I guess we'd better be going."

"Thanks again, and we'll see y'all Sunday."

"Make sure you come get me if he has any problems," Lisa told Cathy again as she showed them out. "Just send someone to the entrance of the subdivision, and the guards will tell them where Mark's house is."

"OK, I will," Cathy promised.

When the group got home, dinner was ready, and it was time for the President's speech. They listened to him talk as they ate. He made good on his threat from the day before. Los Angeles, Atlanta, Cleveland, and Detroit were placed under Martial Law. The President said that some Army Reserve troops were already in place, and reinforcements on the way, to take control of these cities. No one was allowed out of his or her home between 8:00 PM and 6:00 AM. Also, anyone seen looting or vandalizing would be shot on sight. The President said he regretted having to do this, but that there was no other choice.

When the local news came on, there were a couple of items everyone found interesting. The first was that City Water Board was shutting off the water again tonight. They said they weren't able to finish the pump maintenance last night and that they'd be working on it again. Mark didn't know much about how the city water system worked, but he didn't see how doing maintenance on a pump could shut the whole system down. He was thankful they had their own well. He just needed to get that windmill from the ranch. George had some experience with windmills, and he was confident they could get it to work. The second item of interest was that the Police Department was asking that property crimes not be reported to them unless the loss was over $50,000. They explained they didn't have the resources to record or investigate these crimes. They asked the citizens to document as much information as they could and to report it once the power was back on, so it could be logged into the computer.

When the news was over, everyone walked down to the Olsen house. George had a stack of papers he and his committee had worked on. When they got to the meeting, Mark noticed that there were more people here than he'd seen before. Jon was right about how many new people there were. Several people introduced members of their extended family who had come to stay in the subdivision. Mark also noticed that just about everyone was talking about the President's address. Some were outraged that he'd actually put the military in charge of some cities and suspended the rights of the people in them. Others argued that he'd done the right thing to make those cities safe, and, they said, what good are rights if you're afraid to go outside? A few people had heard about the attack on the Baptist preacher and came up to ask Mark about it.

Scott Simmons made an observation to Mark about the speech that he hadn't noticed before.

"Did you notice that he didn't make any promises tonight about when the power would be back on?" Scott asked. "I think he's been trying to forestall the inevitable, and now he's going to break the truth to the country real slow and hope things don't come crashing down around his ears."

Mark thought that Scott was probably right. If the country got used to the idea of the power not coming back on a little at a time, maybe things would be okay. On the other hand, if it came as a shock to a large part of the country, who knows how bad things could get? One thing was for sure, this was the first time Mark could remember the President not making a prediction about when the power would be back on. The more Mark thought about it, the more he felt a sense of urgency about getting all of their preparations done.

After a few minutes, Jon called the meeting to order.

"I know we're all anxious to hear what the gardening committee has to present," Jon started, "but there's an issue I feel we need to discuss first. It is apparent that many of us are moving our friends and family into the subdivision. I'm concerned that if this doesn't stop, we won't be able to grow enough food to support all of these people. We only have so much land to grow things on. I know each family that moves in can go to Kroger, but what if they shut down or cut back on what they let us get? What if we can't drive everybody anymore? Plus, we're all getting water from Mark. He runs his generator to pump us water. The more people we have here, the more water we need, and the more gas he uses. What are we going to do if we run out of gas?"

Jon paused for effect. Many in the crowd just looked around. Some nodded their heads in agreement. A few turned red in the face.

"So what are you suggesting, Jon?" someone in the crowd called out.

"I would suggest that we limit the number of people who can live on any one property to ten."

"You can't do that. Some of us are already over that number," another person shouted.

"We could grandfather anybody who already has more than ten to the number they now have," Jon explained.

"Let me make sure I understand what you're suggesting, Jon," Professor Petrie said. "You want us to limit the number of people who can live on my property?"

"Yes." Jon said.

"The property I paid for? The property brave service men and women have gone to war and died for so that I could own it and use it as I see fit?" The professor paused. "What are you going to suggest next? That we adopt the policy of Red China and limit every couple to one child?"

Mark looked around. The heads that had been looking around a moment ago were now nodding, and those who were nodding were looking around like guilty schoolboys.

"Well, it's something I think we're going to have to make some hard decisions about," Jon stammered. "Mark, how long can you keep pumping water?"

Yeah, Jon, drag me into it when you get your back against the wall, Mark thought, but he knew he needed to try to stay on Jon's good side since the security meeting was right after this one. "I don't really know, Jon. That's a valid concern, but it should make you all feel better to know that I have a plan to get a windmill. That should give us all the water we need."

"That's good to know, but we still have the food situation to deal with." It didn't seem like Jon wanted to let this go.

"Maybe we should hear what George and his committee have to say about growing our own food. Then maybe we can all think about it for a day or two. How does that sound to everyone?" Mark asked, hoping it would cool the crowd off without stepping on Jon's toes. Everyone seemed to be in agreement.

"Okay, then, I guess we'll hear from the committee now and talk about this more tomorrow," Jon said in a matter-of-fact tone.

George and the other committee members walked up to where the driveway met the garage. This had become the de facto speaking platform. The members conferred with each other for a second, and George cleared his throat to speak.

"We have a lot of good news. Some of it's preliminary, as we still need to find more seed and check out a few items. However, the soil here appears to be quite fertile, and we have enough land between the empty lots and everybody's backyards to grow a lot of food. What we've tentatively come up with is to use some of the empty lots to grow things we'll need a lot of, like corn, beans, and potatoes. Then, everybody who wants to can put in a garden for their family to use. We can also raise some livestock. Some of you already have chickens, and one family has some rabbits. We could even raise a milk cow or two if we could find someone to sell us one. The bad news is that we have a lot of work to do. We have three tillers, but one of them is pretty small. There are only three gardens in the subdivision right now, and only one of them is of any size. We need to get started tilling the soil that we want to plant immediately. A lot of the items we want to grow need to be planted in the next three weeks."

"How quickly can we get any food out of the gardens?" someone asked.

"Well, a few things you can start harvesting about two weeks after planting, but most real food stuff takes six to eight weeks to make. The committee thinks we should start tilling some of the empty lots tomorrow and try to get them planted as soon as possible. Some of the committee members are going to try to get seed tomorrow, and some of us are going to coordinate the tilling. We need volunteers to help with the work, and we're asking for donations for the seed."

Lots of hands went up. "Yes," George pointed at a gentleman in the front.

"Going back to what Jon was talking about, if we can get everything planted and going good, how many people can we feed?"

"That's a hard question to answer. It depends on a lot of things, but assuming we couldn't get any food except what we could grow…let's see, we have about forty-five acres in empty lots. If we use all of that for planting and keep any animals on the private lots, we could grow vegetables for about ten to twelve people per acre, conservatively. So that comes out to…say five hundred people, give or take."

"That's why I'm saying ten per household. We have forty-seven houses, and ten each would be four hundred and seventy." Jon interjected.

"Remember, that doesn't include any private gardens, or the possibility of bartering with a local farmer," George added. "Plus, the numbers I gave you are really rough. We could work on it some more and probably give you all a better answer in a few days."

The crowd seemed satisfied with that. A few hands went up, and George pointed at a man with his hand up. "Yes?"

"I can help plow."

"Thank you. Yes." He pointed to another man.

"If we want to donate, who do we need to give the money to?"

"You can give it to Mary Patterson. She's going for the seed tomorrow if we can get a truck," he answered, "and if you would like to help with the tilling or planting, meet us at Mark's house at seven o'clock in the morning." All of the other hands dropped. "Does anyone else have any questions?"

When no one said anything, George turned the meeting back over to Jon. Jon asked if anyone had anything else, and Mark raised his hand.

"Yes, Mark."

"I was wondering if anyone has an older car or a trailer we could use. We can probably get anything made before 1980 to run and maybe even some that are a little newer than that. Also, if anyone has any kind of trailer, it could be used to let us haul more stuff per trip."

Four hands went up. Dr. Vasquez had a two-horse trailer at his office. Another man had a small motorcycle trailer. Manny Hernandez had a 1988 Suburban. Mark told him they might be able to get it running and he'd talk with him about it later. The last man with his hand up was Professor Petrie. Mark called on him.

"I have a 1977 Trans Am in the garage. I tried to start it the day of The Burst, but it would only turn over. If you can get it running, we can use it for whatever, but I have to warn you, it drinks a lot of gas."

"We have plenty of gas sitting in the cars that won't run. Maybe tomorrow we can try to get the parts." Mark looked back at Jon. "That's all I have."

"Anyone else?" Jon asked looking around. "Well then, I guess we're adjourned. If you need to go to the store in the morning, be here at 7:30. Members of the security committee, we'll meet now."

Everyone except the committee members and Gunny headed home. Mark and Chaparo had asked him to stay for the meeting. Mark also had the map that Gunny had drawn for them the other day. Jon pulled a card table and some folding chairs out of his garage, and everyone sat down. Introductions were made all around. All the men knew each other, but they introduced themselves for the benefit of Susan Banks, the only woman on the committee. Susan was a vice president down at Wilson County State Bank. She had two boys, ages seven and ten. She told them she'd been divorced for almost three years.

Chaparo started the meeting by asking Gunny to go over the suggestions he'd made a few days ago. Gunny got the map from Mark, spread it out on the table, and explained what he thought they should do. He suggested they start with the front, as that would be where most people would try to get in from, at least at first. Then, he explained, they could work on the sides and the back.

"I would also get to trainin' the guards right away. I noticed they weren't sittin' down anymore, but they still ain't payin' 'tention like they should."

"Gunny, do you really think that's necessary?" Jon asked.

"Yes, sir, I do. Them boys you got up front prob'ly couldn't stop those assho...'scuse me, ma'am...those 'gentlemen' who attacked the preacher earlier. I counted eight of 'em. If'n they came armed, you'd be in heck of a jackpot."

"But that was just a bunch of gang members or druggies looking for some wine," Jon argued.

"Yeah, you're right, and it's only been what, nine days since the lights went out? And everyone still pretty much has food 'n' water. In a coupla weeks, when the food runs out or the water quits running, how big and how desperate do you think the groups are gonna be then?"

Jon didn't say anything. He just sat back in his chair with his arms folded. Several of the committee members, especially Susan, asked questions, and Gunny answered them as thoroughly as he could. Mark was surprised that all of the questions Susan asked were very insightful. When Gunny had answered all their questions, he excused himself to go tell Abby goodbye and drive himself home before sundown. Mark asked him if he could come over first thing in the morning and help run some errands. Gunny responded affirmatively and disappeared down the street.

"Well," Professor Petrie said, "what do we want to present to the group?"

"I think the gate might be a good idea, but doing the rest of that stuff is probably a waste of time," Jon stated flatly.

"I don't know, Jon. I think everything Gunny said made pretty good sense," Chaparo said, as the others nodded their heads in agreement. "I think we should suggest that we start on the gate, ditch, foxholes, and barbed-wire fence for the front and get a training program going for the guards. Once that's done, we can look at what the next priority should be."

"Who are you gonna get to train the guards?" Jon spewed.

"I was thinking you should do it. I pulled a lot of guard duty during my stint with the Army, but I understand you Marines are the best of the best. Isn't that why you devil dogs are in charge of security for all our foreign embassies?" Chaparo asked.

Jon's demeanor immediately softened. "That's true. I guess I could work out a training program." Mark was shocked that a guy as big and gruff as Chaparo could be such a diplomat.

"Alright, that sounds good," Professor Petrie said. "I second the motion that we present the work for the front of the subdivision to the group tomorrow."

"All in favor?" Chaparo asked.

Everyone, including Jon, raised their hands.

"Okay, then," Chaparo said. "Pending approval, I suggest we all take a part of the plan to head up. Jon's going to work on training the guards. I can be in charge of the gate and blocking off one of the driveways. Professor, can you take the fence?"

The professor nodded.

"That leaves the digging the ditch and the foxholes. Since that's the most labor intensive job, would you two take it?" Chaparo asked, looking at Mark and Susan.

Susan nodded as Mark answered, "That'll be fine."

"Alright, I guess we'll see if we get a 'go' tomorrow night."

Everyone got up, shook hands and said good night. They all headed home except for Mark, who went with Professor Petrie to look at his Trans Am.

When they were out of earshot from Jon's, Professor Petrie spoke. "Man, that Chaparo really handled that well, don't you think?"

"Yes, he did. It surprised me that he was so diplomatic."

"Me, too. I hope he can keep it up. I probably would have lost my temper with Jon, and I'm usually a pretty calm guy."

"I know I would have lost my temper, but Chaparo just acted like nothing was the matter. I'm glad we picked him to co-chair the committee."

"Me, too," the professor agreed.

When they reached the Petrie house, Mark looked at the car. He whistled. "Man, Professor, this is sweet. T-tops, four on the floor, and it's just like the one they used in 'Smokey and the Bandit.'"

"Please call me Ted. It was mine when I was in graduate school. I put it up after my son was born, so he could have it when he got his license. Do you think we can get it to run?"

"Yes, Ted, I do, and since it has a trailer hitch, it'll be a lot of help."

The two men made plans to go to the parts store in the morning, and then Mark headed home.

Chapter 20

Mark's alarm went off at six o'clock as usual, but today instead of getting up and running, he turned it off and rolled over to try to catch a few more Z's. He'd laid awake most of the night thinking about what might happen and what all he needed to get done before it did. The fact that the little cool front they'd enjoyed for the past couple of days had disappeared and the humidity South Texas was famous for had returned with a vengeance hadn't helped matters either. The next thing he knew, a truck was starting. He looked at the clock and it read 7:18. He looked out the window of the camper and saw Jon driving off in Jim's truck to take the last group of what was now a rapidly increasing population from Silver Hills to Kroger. He got up, showered quickly, and made his way to the kitchen in the house.

"Hey, Sleepyhead," Jess greeted him, as he noticed all of the other adults were sitting around the table. "What happened?"

"I just didn't feel like running this morning. I didn't sleep much last night."

"Yeah, I know. You tossed and turned all night."

"I'm sorry."

"That's okay. You only woke me up a couple of times, and I went right back to sleep. Alice fixed scrambled eggs and biscuits and gravy. You hungry?"

"You bet I am."

"So, how did the security meeting go last night, Mark?" Jim asked.

"Pretty good. Jon's being difficult at times, but Chaparo was able to get him into the boat with us. He agreed to start training the guards, if we get approval tonight at the meeting."

"Yeah, he told me he was looking at that. He said most of what y'all are going to suggest is probably a waste of time, but he figures it won't hurt anything, so he went along."

"Big of him. What did you think about his idea to limit our population?"

"Well, obviously I didn't like it. I mean, we already have ten living here. What if you or Jess wanted to bring your parents? It's your property, and if you want to have a hundred people living here, that's your business."

"Yeah, that's kind of the way I feel. I do see his point, though, about not being able to support too many people, but like Ted pointed out last night, I don't think we can tell people what or what not to do in their own homes. Hopefully, we can find a solution before we hit a population of a million or so," Mark said with half a grin.

"What do you have planned for today?" Jess asked her husband.

"I'm going to take Ted and maybe Manny to the parts store. We can probably fix Manny's Suburban the same way Jim fixed his truck, but I don't know if he has the $600 for the parts. Then I'm going to stop by Jerry's house and pick him up, so he can use my truck today."

"Manny has always been so good to us. Maybe we should help him pay for the parts," Jess suggested.

"You think so? I guess we could, but that's a lot of money, and I don't know how much use we'd be able to get out of it. If the stuff really hits the fan in the next week or so, I don't even know if we're going to be able to drive anywhere. I just don't think it would be a wise investment."

"I see what you mean, but if you change your mind, it's okay with me." She paused. "By the way, can I use the Jeep today?"

"I promised Dr. Vasquez we'd help him get his vet supplies moved. I was going to ask Jim to help him."

"Can we fit everything in the Jeep?" Jim asked.

"No, but remember, he has a horse trailer at his office. You can fill it up and pull it with the Jeep."

"Okay, I can do that."

"Take a rifle with you and leave it out where you can get to it. You might even want to take someone with you to stand guard while you and the Doc load the trailer." Mark didn't have to say why.

"Well then, since the Jeep is promised out, do you think Gunny could take us to the flea market?" Jess asked.

"What do you need from there?" Mark asked incredulously.

"Lisa, Alice, Abby, and I wanted to see if we could find anything we might be able to use." Jess had a look in her eye that told Mark he was in trouble, but he wasn't sure how.

"It's probably not even going to be open," he countered.

"Some of the women heard at Kroger that it's going to be open today and tomorrow."

"Well, maybe tomorrow someone can take you. I promised George and the gardening committee that someone would take them to get seed, and I already asked Gunny to do it."

"Too bad we don't have another vehicle."

Mark realized too late what was happening. "We just can't waste money on a vehicle that's not ours. We have too many other things we need," he argued.

"I see, and what good is that money going to do us if we can't even go to buy the things we need because we don't have enough running vehicles in the neighborhood to go where we need to?" Jess said, showing a little emotion.

Mark knew he couldn't win this without it costing him much more than it was worth, but his pride wouldn't let him give up. "But, Babe, that's a LOT of money!" Just then Mark saw Jim jump and look over at Lisa. He wasn't sure if she'd kicked his friend under the table, but he figured her legs were just long enough to reach. All she did was tilt her head slightly toward Mark once she had Jim's attention.

"Mark, I think Lisa and I would be willing to pitch in some on Manny's truck if that would help," Jim said.

"Yes, Jim. That would help. Thank you both. I guess I'll go talk to Manny." Mark wondered if the girls had set this up the night before, or if it was a spur of the moment thing. If it were spontaneous, they sure were on the same frequency. All he knew was, whether it had been a well-rehearsed plan or an impromptu one, he'd fallen into it head first.

As Mark went outside, he saw Gunny pull into the driveway. George had already gone out to coordinate the tilling. George told him they were going to start with the five-acre lot directly across the street from Mark's house. They planned to plant corn in it. Mark asked George who Gunny needed to take for

116

the seed. George called Mary Patterson and Dwight Rittiman over and introduced them to Mark and Gunny as the seed buyers. Gunny needed some gas, so Mark instructed him to the back where the fuel was stored. As they filled up the truck, Mark asked him if he had his shotgun where he could get to it quickly. Gunny assured him that he didn't need to worry, and once the truck was filled, he loaded up his passengers and headed down the road. Jim left in the Jeep to get Dr. Vasquez about the time Ted came walking up. Mark pulled his FAL and its magazines out from behind the back seat and put a loaded mag into the rifle. He didn't chamber a round, as that would only take a second, if needed. He put the big rifle in the front seat with the muzzle pointed down at the floor. Mark and Ted got in Mark's truck and drove down to Manny's house. Ted sat in the truck while Mark went up and knocked on the door. Manny answered, and the two men looked under the hood of the Suburban. It was fuel injected and looked like it would need the same parts Jim had used for his truck. Mark explained that the parts would be expensive, but he was sure they could get it to run. When Manny asked how expensive and Mark told him, Manny whistled.

"My friend, I don't have that kind of cash. In fact we've spent almost all of the money we had in the house. Will this parts man take a check or a credit card?"

"I doubt it, Manny, not with the power out, but Jim and I can cover you."

"I can't ask you to do that."

"You didn't ask; we offered. We need more working vehicles in the subdivision. This will benefit everyone. And besides that…our wives insisted."

Manny got a twinkle in his eye. "I see. It's that way at my house at times, as well. I wear the pants…but she picks them out."

"You got that right, buddy," Mark agreed, laughing.

When Manny climbed into the truck, he noticed Mark's FAL sitting on the front seat. "Do you think I should bring my rifle, too?" he asked Mark.

"It couldn't hurt," Mark answered, and Manny hopped out of the truck and ran back into the house. "Ted, we can stop by your house if you'd like to pick up a weapon."

"I don't own any guns. I had a .22 when I was growing up, but my wife doesn't like guns, and I never really saw the need to own any," Ted explained.

When Manny came out of the house with his old .30-30 and climbed into the back seat, the three men headed to town. When they got to the parts store, it was closed, as Mark had suspected it would be. He pulled out the card with Rodney's address on it and eased the truck back onto the road. As he made his way through the back streets to Rodney's house, he noticed that people seemed to have a different look about them. He couldn't put his finger on what it was, but something just felt different. When he got to the house, he left the truck running with Ted and Manny inside. As he walked up to the front door, it opened, and Rodney was holding an old, long-barreled shotgun.

"Hey, Mark. You need some more parts?"

"Yeah, Rodney, I do. How's it going?"

"Okay, I guess. Someone tried to steal my car the other night, but I scared them off with my scattergun."

"Really? Is everyone okay?"

"Yeah. I just fired a round into the air, and they ran off, but we've been keeping a close eye on things since then. Give me a minute, and I'll follow you back to the store."

"Thanks."

Mark climbed back into the truck, and a moment later, the garage door opened. Mark backed out of the way, and Rodney pulled a beautiful black Charger out of the garage. Mark followed him to the store, and when they got out, he asked Rodney about it.

"It's a '69," Rodney told him. "I put a 440 in it that I balanced and blueprinted. Plus, I spent a lot of money restoring her. She's a real sweet ride…quick, too. That's why I didn't want some scumbag stealing her."

The men went into the store and bought what they needed. Manny's parts weren't quite as expensive as Jim's had been because they didn't need to change the intake manifold on the Suburban. Rodney sold them a two-barrel carburetor that would just bolt on in place of the throttle body. Mark paid, and they all thanked Rodney. Mark asked if there was anything that they could do for him. He thanked them for the offer and told them he was doing fine.

They loaded up and headed for Jerry's. When they arrived, Mark honked the horn, and Jerry ran down to open the gate. Mark asked if he wanted to borrow the truck for the rest of the day. Jerry was elated but said they were about to run his mother to the doctor. He asked if he and Tony could come out to Silver Hills in an hour or so and pick it up. Mark told him that would be fine but that he needed the truck back by this evening because he planned to pick up a windmill tomorrow. Jerry told him that wouldn't be a problem. He said they'd already brought quite a few of the guns home in their Jeep. Mark reminded him how to get out to his house, and the three men headed home.

On the way home, the men talked of the things they needed to do. Mark filled the other two men in on his plans for the windmill and how he hoped they could run water down to the front of the subdivision, so people who lived there didn't have to carry water all the way from his house. Manny and Ted both spoke of their plans to put in gardens on their properties, as well as help with the community ones. Manny's five kids and three grandkids, plus his father-in-law and his son's girlfriend, meant that he planned to devote about an acre, or maybe a little more, of his property to gardening. Three of Manny's kids had already moved out. Two were married and had kids of their own. He told Mark and Ted how his kids had walked to his house. One of the married couples lived in La Vernia, so it was only a ten or twelve-mile walk for them, but the son and his girlfriend had backpacked in from San Antonio. It had taken them two days. Manny still had a daughter, son-in-law, and grandchild in Austin that he wanted to check on, but he was glad the rest of his family was safe and that he had enough room to put them all up, even if some of them were sleeping in the den and the dining room. Ted, on the other hand, only had his wife and son to feed and didn't plan to plant more than about a quarter of an acre. Mark hadn't really spent much time thinking about how much of his property he should plant…just what he needed, something else to get done.

As the conversation turned lighter, the men talked about what they missed the most. Mark really missed watching sports on TV and going to karate class. Ted said he missed doing research on the Internet and visiting with his fellow professors. Manny said what he missed the most so far was air conditioning. Mark thought about how lucky they were to have the campers to sleep in. It would really be miserable to have to sleep in the house. He asked Manny and Ted about it, and they both said that, while the first several days had been miserable, they'd started to get used to it. In fact, Ted said, until all of the humidity last night, it had almost been bearable for the last several days. If today was any indication, though, tonight wouldn't be a good one. It was only about eleven, and it had to be over 90 degrees already.

Mark was thinking about the preacher's house and how it was cooler when the cab of the truck seemed to explode. All of a sudden, there was a big hole in the middle of the windshield where the rearview mirror had been. Mark slammed on the brakes only to be greeted by a hammering jolt from the rear. What in the hell was going on? He tried to look in the mirror, but it was no longer there. He looked in the side mirror, but couldn't see anything. He turned his head to look out the back and noticed that the back window was gone, and most of it seemed to be on Manny. As he looked out the back, it was obvious that another truck had hit him. Okay, he thought, but what knocked a hole in my windshield? The reality of what was going on hit him like a semi squashing an armadillo on a lonely, Texas highway. The truck behind him was the same one that the men beating up the preacher had used to escape, and the hole had been caused by a gunshot. Mark's only thought was to get away. He down shifted the truck and put his foot on the floor. It was the first time in years he wished he had a gas motor instead of the diesel. The big oil burner would push the truck to over a hundred miles per hour. Mark had done it once, just to see, but it took forever to accelerate up to that. Mark looked out his side mirror and saw that the truck that had hit him was just starting to move. Maybe the head start would give him some time. He was in second gear now and approaching 40 mph.

"Are you guys okay?" he screamed, as he shifted the big truck into third.

"What happened?" Ted had a confused look on his face.

"I'm okay," Manny said. He was brushing the glass from the back window off of him. The look on his face told Mark that he knew what was going on.

"It's the guys who beat the preacher up yesterday," Mark explained. "I guess they want some payback." Mark kicked himself for chatting away like a schoolgirl and not paying attention to what was going on around him.

"You…you mean they're shooting at us?" Ted stammered.

Mark didn't answer. He was up to 65 now and shifting into fourth. He checked the mirror, and while the old International Harvester wasn't gaining on him, the Ford didn't seem to be acquiring the kind of distance he would've liked for it to, either. Mark's mind raced for a solution. They were probably four or five miles from home, but he couldn't just turn into the subdivision with this scum in tow. Even if they did stop when he got to the entrance, they would know where he lived. No, there had to be a better solution than that. Think, damn it, THINK, he rebuked himself. He could stop here and fight it out, but there had been eight yesterday, maybe more today, and he only had three, two really, because Ted probably wouldn't be very useful in a gunfight, and he didn't have a rifle anyway. Hell, he'd never been in a gunfight, either. How useful would he be? Well, the best odds he could hope for were two and a half; assuming Ted could shoot his .45, to eight. Not too promising. He needed help.

119

If only Gunny and Jim were here. Should haves, would haves, and could haves would do him little good now, he reasoned. Focus on the problem, he told himself. He looked out the side mirror again. The other truck was starting to gain. They were maybe seventy-five or a hundred yards behind him. Mark saw a man pop up out of the bed of the truck and lean over the cab with some kind of long gun. He saw a muzzle flash and instinctively ducked his head. The shot missed, he guessed, but the closer they got, the easier it would be to hit the big, red, rolling target he was driving. Mark looked at his passengers. Ted was scrunching down in his seat, and Manny was cautiously looking out the back.

"Manny, can you give them something to think about?"

"Will do!" Manny picked up his old Marlin and jacked a round into the chamber. He turned around in his seat and stuck the rifle out of the shattered back window. The sound of the bullet exiting the barrel barely registered on Mark's brain. Manny jacked the lever and fired again.

Mark was coming up on a curve, and he had to slow down a little. Once back on the straightaway, he put his foot back on the floor. He looked back in the mirror again and saw that the IH had almost lost control in the curve and had to slow down considerably. There was a big curve up the road about a mile. Mark could stop the truck, and they could open up on these MZB's as they came around the curve, but the chance of stopping them all was slim. Plus, they'd have to use the truck for cover, and Mark didn't want to have his truck all shot up if he could help it. Besides, probably only the engine would really stop a bullet. He looked, and they were gaining again. Now there were two men leaning across the cab. Mark could see one of them had a pistol. It wouldn't be very effective at this range. He was doing almost 75, and the diesel was accelerating very slowly at this speed. Just as he started to slow for the sharp curve, he decided not to stop. There had to be a better solution. The sign on the road said to take the curve at 35, but Mark figured he could push it up to maybe 50. He told Manny and Ted to hold on as he braked hard down to 45, put the truck back into third and hit the accelerator. The big truck took the curve like an elephant on a tightrope, but it stayed on the road. The driver of the other truck, not wanting to make the same mistake as before, slowed down, made the curve, and started closing the distance again. Mark heard something hit the truck.

"Manny, what was that?" Mark yelled.

"They shot the tailgate! It looks like buckshot. Five or six holes. It punctured the tailgate but not the cab, Gracias a Dios, else I'd be a dead man."

"Shoot some more and get them to back off!"

"Okay, Mark."

Manny shot at the truck two times, and it seemed to have the desired effect. The other truck dropped back to about a hundred yards. That would keep the shotgun and pistol from doing much harm unless the MZB's got real lucky, but if they had a rifle, it wouldn't keep him and his passengers safe. Manny had stopped shooting again.

"Manny keep shooting!"

"I only brought the bullets in the gun! I don't want to waste them."

Great, Mark thought. He knew the Marlin would hold six or seven rounds, which meant Manny had two or three shots left. The MZB's were starting to close the gap again. Work the problem, damn it, he thought. Maybe two miles to

120

the subdivision now, he figured. He could stop right in front of the entrance, and then he'd have the guards. Plus, maybe someone would hear the shooting and come to help. That might even the odds a little. He had to keep the other truck back far enough to make it though, and he needed Manny to have a functioning weapon when they stopped.

"Ted," Mark said. No answer. He looked at the scholar. Ted looked like he was in some kind of trance. "TED!!!"

"What?"

"Hand my rifle to Manny!"

Ted handed the rifle to Manny, and he stuck it out the back window.

"Where's the safety?" Manny cried.

"It's under your right thumb...push it down!"

"Got it," Manny said.

A second later Mark heard his rifle, but it wasn't the boom he had expected. It was the metallic sound of the hammer falling on an empty chamber.

"Manny! On the left side of the receiver...there's a round, black handle. Pull it all the way back and let it go."

Manny did as he was told and then put the muzzle of the rifle out of the window.

Mark felt more than heard the three booms of his weapon. He figured Manny must have hit the International Harvester because it slammed on the brakes. A second later, it was accelerating again. Half a mile to go, Mark thought. He could see the subdivision sign and the guards. He wondered who they were. He hoped they were good shots and wouldn't panic. This was turning into what Gunny had called a real jackpot. Mark heard a bullet hit the truck.

Manny fired a couple of shots back.

Mark's brain raced. If he stopped right by the guards, would they figure out what was going on quickly enough to help him? Or would they just get shot before they could think? No, he couldn't just stop right in front of them, but he needed their help.

"Please, tell me what to do!" Mark prayed out loud.

Mark didn't know if was truly divine inspiration, or the fact that he let his brain switch gears for a second, but suddenly he knew what to do. He would drive past the guards and stop once the MZB's were about a hundred yards past, too. That way, the guards could put them in a cross fire. He checked his mirror. The truck was about a hundred and fifty yards behind him.

"Get ready guys! I'm going to stop once we pass the Silver Hills sign!"

Mark roared past the entrance, blaring his horn. He recognized the two men on guard duty. One of them was Scott Simmons, but he couldn't remember the other's name. When they were almost even with the eastern edge of the subdivision, Mark slammed on the brakes and eased the truck into the shallow ditch. Once the truck had come to almost a complete stop, Manny began rapid firing at the quickly approaching old truck. Mark undid his seatbelt, turned around, and leaned out of the side window with his .45 in his hand. Ted had sunk down to the floor. Just as Mark lined up his sights on the MZB truck, its windshield exploded from a .308 round out of the FAL. The truck skidded to a halt, sideways in the road, about seventy-five yards from Mark, Manny, and Ted. Mark saw that most of the men in the old truck had pistols and a couple of shotguns. At this range, the pistols would be of little use unless somebody was really good or really lucky. He knew he wasn't that good and prayed none of the MZB's were, either. Luck could go either way. Then he saw an AK stick out of the driver's window. That's big trouble, he thought. Mark concentrated his fire on the driver's window. Manny was yelling something, but Mark couldn't make it out. It only took a few seconds for him to empty his magazine, and the way he was leaning out of the window, he couldn't reach the spares on his left hip. He pulled his upper body back into the truck to reload. Manny was struggling with a fresh magazine for the FAL that he must have reached over the front seat to get. Rounds were beginning to hit the truck with some regularity. Mark sank down in his seat and yelled at Manny to rock the magazine into the rifle front to back. A second later, he heard the big rifle bark. With a fresh mag in his Colt, he looked out the window again. The FAL had made the MZB's duck their heads, and they were firing blindly, so the impacts to the truck became almost nonexistent. The muzzle of the AK was sending out its deadly projectiles with flashes that looked like a Morse code message. Mark again opened up on the driver's window. This time, he tried to use a little more fire discipline, and when he saw a puff of dust just below the door, he raised his point of aim about three feet. As he was squeezing the trigger, he saw the AK fall out of the truck. Then he heard the smack. It was the same sound he heard when he knew he'd made a good shot on a deer. A microsecond after that, he heard the supersonic crack of a hunting rifle. It was the guards. The firing from the MZB's slowed, as they tried to figure out what had happened. Then the MZB's turned all of their attention to the new threat. Mark looked around and saw a mound of dirt about three feet high just inside the decorative fence to the subdivision. If he, Manny, and Ted could get behind it, it would give them some real cover. Mark yelled at Manny and Ted to get ready to bail out the passenger side and run for the mound. They both answered affirmatively, and Manny told Ted to take his .30-30 as it came over the seat. Mark looked out the window, and the MZB's were still looking back at the guards.

"GO!"

Both passenger side doors flew open, and Manny and Ted were running for the mound. Mark holstered his pistol, grabbed the three remaining FAL mags, and slid across the seat and out the door. Manny and Ted both ran to the short wooden fence, slowed to step over it, and then dove behind the dirt pile. As Mark was almost there, one of the MZB's saw him running and turned his pistol toward them, and the others followed suit. Mark jumped the fence in stride and slid feet first like he was trying to beat a short throw to third base. Bullets began to hit the dirt in front of them with sickening thumps. Mark heard the crack of one of the guards' rifles again, and an MZB fell out of the back of the truck like a rag doll that had been tossed out of a high rise. The others jumped out of the bed and hid behind it on Mark's side, looking and firing back at the guards. Manny pushed the big black rifle at Mark, and when he took it, Manny grabbed his rifle from Ted. Mark didn't know how many rounds the FAL had in it, so he pulled out the old mag and inserted a fresh one.

"Ready?" Manny asked.

"Let's rock!" Mark answered.

They popped up and fired. Manny shot once, and Mark shot twice. Mark saw two men fall, as he was ducking back down. The MZB's who were still on their feet all dropped their weapons and put their hands in the air at the same time, as if they had a collective consciousness. When Mark saw this, he popped up and covered them. The guards must have seen it, too, because they stopped firing. Mark looked, and Manny was standing right beside him.

"You all take five steps toward me and then lay down on the road," Mark called to the MZB's. The six men did as they were told, just like they had been practicing that particular move all of their lives. Mark and Manny came around the dirt pile and slowly approached the truck. Mark could see that the guards were cautiously closing in as well. A few men were now running down the main road of the neighborhood toward the entrance with rifles. When they got to the truck, Mark told Manny to cover the men who were lying down while he checked the truck. Two men were obviously dead next to the truck, and the third was holding his calf and rocking back and forth. Mark slung his rifle over his shoulder and pulled out his pistol to cover the man. He looked in the bed of the truck, and, seeing that it was empty, he picked all of the MZB weapons off of the asphalt and threw them into the back. He then looked in the cab. It looked like a five-gallon can of red paint had exploded. The driver was lying over in the seat, and most of the left side of his head was gone. The passenger was holding the right side of his stomach, and a dark red oozed out from between his fingers. Mark could see a sawed off, double barrel shotgun lying on the floorboard next to the bleeding man. He slowly walked around the truck, careful to cover the unfortunate attacker with his .45, opened the door and retrieved the gun that was covered in a sticky goo. Mark just stared at the man and started to shake. By then, the guards had gotten to the truck.

"Are you okay?" Scott asked.

"Yeah...I think so. Can you help Manny cover the guys on the other side of the truck?"

Scott nodded, and the other guard put his hand on Mark's shoulder and gently pulled him back from the truck. Mark looked at the man and still couldn't remember his name. He did recognize that the man's rifle was a Weatherby, though. Probably a .300 Weatherby magnum, Mark thought. That would explain the hamburger that the dead men had been turned into.

"Can you cover this guy?" Mark asked the guard.

"Sure thing, Mark."

Mark could see more and more residents being drawn to the MZB truck, as if it were a black hole and they were meteors passing through its gravitational pull. The closer they got, the faster they moved. Mark walked toward the ditch. When he got there, what seemed like a year's worth of biscuits and gravy was expelled from his stomach with the force of an Apollo rocket.

Chapter 21

When Mark had sufficiently recovered from heaving his breakfast into the ditch, he stood up. Quite a crowd had formed around the old International Harvester truck. They were mostly listening to Ted recount his version of what had happened, looking inside the gory cab, or over by Manny and Scott looking at and taunting the live MZB's. This was turning into a zoo. Mark saw Jon and called him over.

"Are you okay?" Jon asked, with eyes that looked like they'd just seen a UFO.

"Yeah, Jon. I'll be all right."

"It looks like a war zone here."

"Look Jon, I need you to take charge of this situation."

"What do I need to do?"

"First, you need to get all of these people back. Second, tell Ted to keep his mouth shut until we talk to the police. This will probably be treated as a crime scene, and we don't want to mess it up and be accused of having something to hide. Next, get those bastards who tried to kill us separated, so they can't collaborate on a story. Put some men on each one. Get Lisa to look after the wounded ones. Someone needs to go get the sheriff, and if anyone knows a lawyer who lives around here, get him, too."

"Okay, Mark."

Jon turned and started barking orders at the residents. He called for his guards who were already there to carry out what Mark had suggested or to go get more guards. Mark climbed back over the short, wood fence and sat on the ground. People were still running down the road to the battle site. Mark saw his family coming, and he waved them over to him before they could get to the shot up truck.

After he reassured them that he was fine, he sent the kids back to the house. He asked Jess to have Jon get Manny, Ted, Scott, and the other guard who was involved away from everyone else and to sit separately until the sheriff arrived. Mark saw Jim's truck turn the corner, weave around the IH and head toward Floresville. He wasn't sure who was driving. Jess talked to Jon, and Mark saw him grimly nod his head. She came back over to Mark.

"Did you shoot any of them?" she asked.

"Yes."

"Are you really okay?"

"No, but for the situation, I'm doing pretty well. I need you to try to get as many of these gawkers as you can back to work. Tell them we'll fill them in completely at the meeting tonight."

"Okay, Honey. Can I do anything else for you?"

"Yeah. Have David bring me a Diet Coke."

"They aren't cold."

"I don't care. I just have to get this taste out of my mouth."

"Okay," she said.

Once Jon had separated all of the Silver Hills men who'd been involved in the shootout, he came back over to Mark. "Anything else, Mark?"

"Did you find a lawyer?"

"Nobody knows any who live around here. They're all in San Antonio."

"Damn." There was a dollar word. Mark wondered how many he'd used during the shootout. He didn't remember any, but that didn't mean he didn't say a bunch in the heat of the battle. "Ask around again, Jon. I'd sure like to have one when the sheriff gets here."

"But you guys didn't do anything wrong. Why do you need a lawyer?"

"Jon, in these kinds of cases, it's not always about right or wrong. That's why we need a lawyer."

"I'll ask around again."

Mark could see that Jess had gotten most of the onlookers to head back up the hill. That girl was nothing, if not persuasive. As he was looking at Jess herd her group, he saw the Watsons' Jeep approaching the subdivision. The Jeep slowed and stopped when it got even with Jess. She pointed toward Mark, and then it continued down the road. Jerry stopped the CJ-5, and he and Tony hopped out and walked up to Mark.

"Are you okay?" Jerry asked.

"Yeah." Mark wondered how many more times he would have to answer that question. "But I don't think you'll be able to use the truck today."

"No shit!" Tony answered without a trace of sarcasm.

"Do you need anything?" Jerry inquired.

"Yeah. You know any lawyers around here?"

"I know one...good customer of ours...but he's just a tax attorney."

"At this point, I'll take what I can get."

"His name's Ralph Jones. We just delivered a safe to his house a couple of months ago, and he only lives a little ways from here. Tony, you want to go get him?"

"Sure." Tony wasn't one to waste words. He headed for the Jeep.

"Anything else you want me to do?" Jerry asked.

"Yes," Mark answered and held up a finger to ask Jerry to wait a second. "Jon...JON!" Jon turned and saw Mark waving him over. He jogged over.

"Jon, this is my friend Jerry Watson from Watson's Guns." The two men shook hands. "He taught my concealed handgun class, and he knows a lot about what needs to be done before the cops get here. Can you tell him where we're at and see if he thinks we need to do something else?"

"Roger that," Jon responded. "I couldn't find a lawyer."

"That's okay. Jerry knows one, and his brother went to get him."

"Good deal." Jon and Jerry walked off, as Jon was telling him what he had done so far.

A few minutes later, David and Sam returned with Mark's soft drink. Sam explained to her dad that she wanted to make sure he was alright. She told him she'd overheard some of the men say he'd probably be taken in to the sheriff's office. He could see she'd been crying, and he assured her everything would be okay. He told David, who had a very somber look on his face, as well, to tell his mother he was fine and not to worry. He sent the kids back up to the house with a big hug and then opened the Coke. He took a big mouthful, swished it around in his mouth, and then spit it out. He took a big swallow and wished it was cold.

Mark looked around. Jerry was pointing things out to Jon. There were guards on the MZB's, whose hands were tied behind their backs with big, black, wire ties. Lisa was looking at the one with the leg wound, while a guard watched his every move. The one who'd been inside the cab was just lying in the grass. Either Lisa had fixed him up as well as she could, or he was dead. Probably the latter, judging from how badly he had been bleeding. So that would make four dead, one wounded, and six captured. It was fortunate that these guys had just been a bunch of gang bangers with no real skills. If they'd had better weapons or skills, this could have turned out differently.

It didn't take Tony very long to get back with the lawyer. Mark was a little surprised to see a big, black man get out of the Jeep. When Jerry had said 'tax attorney,' Mark had pictured Casper Milquetoast. This guy looked like the Bears might have cut him because he scared Ditka. They walked over to Mark.

"Mark, this Ralph Jones," Tony said. "Ralph, this is Mark Turner."

"It's nice to meet you," Mark said, as he shook the man's paw.

"Looks like they bit off more than they could chew," Ralph commented. "What happened?"

Mark gave a brief account.

"Mr. Turner, I'm just a property tax attorney. Normally, I'd recommend another attorney and have you call him, but since the phones don't work, and things aren't exactly normal, I'll represent you while the authorities investigate this thing, if you'd like. I do have a little experience from years ago with criminal law," he said, as Mark was trying to figure out why this man looked so familiar. "But if you get charged or sued," Ralph continued, "we'll have to look for someone more qualified to handle that."

"Mr. Jones, that's wonderful. How much do you charge?"

"Call me Ralph. Any friend of the Watsons is a friend of mine, and since this isn't really my cup of tea anymore, I'll do it pro bono for now. Now who else was involved in this thing?"

"Manny Hernandez and Ted Petrie were in the truck with me," Mark informed the lawyer, as he pointed out Manny and Ted. "Manny and I did all the shooting from the truck." Then Mark swung his hand around to point in the other direction. "Scott Simmons and the other guard...I can't remember his name...were here on guard duty, and they helped us pin them down in a cross fire once we got here."

"How long until the sheriff gets here?" the big attorney asked.

"Someone left to get him about twenty-five minutes ago. I'm sure they probably had to go all the way to Floresville to find him. I figure he'll be here in fifteen or twenty minutes."

The big man nodded. "You sit tight and let me see if these other fellows want counsel. When the sheriff gets here, you don't say anything other than your name and address unless I'm with you."

Mark sat back down and took another drink of his Coke. Ralph talked with the other men involved. Just before the sheriff roared up with an ambulance and two other squad cars not far behind, Ralph came back over to Mark.

"Everybody's on the same page. Just tell the sheriff exactly what happened, and I don't think you'll have any problems. If I don't want you to answer something, I'll jump in."

"Okay, Ralph. Thanks for helping us."

"That's my job. Now here we go."

The sheriff got out of his car and took a cursory look around. He had his deputies take over the guarding of the MZB's, then he talked to the paramedics who'd taken over for Lisa. After that, he walked over where Mark and Ralph were standing. He moved like a big cat. Mark noticed a big, black pistol on his hip.

"Ralph," the sheriff said, as he nodded his head at the attorney.

"Curt," Ralph responded, "this is my client, Mark Turner."

"This ain't no property tax assessment case, Ralph," the sheriff said.

"Yeah, I know. It's a little out of my current field, but I was the only one available, and I guess these guys figured I was better than nothing."

"See your point," the sheriff said. "Mr. Turner, I'm Sheriff Curt Thompson. You wanna tell me what happened here?"

Mark told the narrative as best he could remember. When he was done, the sheriff asked to see his ID. Mark produced both his driver license and concealed handgun license.

"That your rifle?" The sheriff pointed to the ground where Mark had unloaded and set down his FAL.

"Yes, sir."

"And do you have your pistol on you?"

"Yes. It's on my right hip, and there's a .32 in my back pocket," Mark answered, knowing not to reach for them.

"Did you shoot the .32?"

"No, sir."

"Good, just leave it there, but I'm going to have to take your big pistol." The sheriff reached under Mark's outer shirt and removed his Colt from its holster.

"It's loaded," Mark warned the lawman.

"What good would it be if it weren't?" The sheriff pointed the pistol in a safe direction, removed the magazine, disengaged the safety, and removed the live round from the chamber. Mark was impressed. He'd seen city cops struggle with weapons they weren't familiar with. The sheriff looked the pistol over. "Nice weapons, Mr. Turner. They probably saved your life. Unfortunately, I'm going to have to take them in."

"I understand," Mark answered. "Do I have to go in, too?"

"I'll decide that after I talk with everyone else." The sheriff looked over his shoulder. "Buddy!"

A deputy ran up. "Yes, Sheriff?"

"Take this pistol and that rifle, tag and bag them, and then put them in the trunk of my car."

"Yes, sir."

The deputy did as he was told, and the sheriff, with Ralph right behind him, walked over to talk with Manny. While this was going on, Jim and Doc Vasquez pulled up in Mark's Jeep with the Doc's trailer attached. Jim, the Doc, and a young man Mark guessed was the doctor's son, got out of the Jeep. They walked up to Mark.

"Isn't that the truck those guys who were kicking the crap out of the preacher drove off in?" Jim asked.

"Yeah."

"What happened?"

Mark quickly explained the situation to Jim.

"I don't believe it!" Jim said. "Are you okay?"

That question again. Shit no, I'm not okay, Mark thought. "Yeah, I'll be OK," he said. Mark looked over, and the sheriff was taking Manny's .30-30. He then walked over to talk with Ted.

"I guess we'll go unhook the trailer at Doc's," Jim said, "unless you need me to do something else."

"No. That's fine. You may want to check with Jon and see what time he's supposed to go back to Kroger. We don't want our people waiting too long. They used your truck to go get the sheriff, but I saw it come back a few minutes ago. It probably needs gas now, and you may want to check on your father-in-law to see if he has enough help. Lisa could be shaken up, too. She came down to help with the wounded, and I think one died on her."

"Alright, Mark. Don't worry about that stuff. I'll check on everyone and make sure the Kroger crew gets picked up on time. You just take it easy."

"Thanks, Jim."

Mark sat back down and tried to relax. After the sheriff talked to Ted and the guards, he talked with the MZB's. Most didn't seem too talkative, but one bent his ear for ten or fifteen minutes. After that, the tall, lanky lawman walked over and talked to the giant of an attorney. They came over and talked to all five of the Silver Hills men who'd been involved in the shootout.

"Gentlemen, your attorney will fill you in more, but we're not going to take you all in. That doesn't mean we're out of the woods on this thing, but you should consider that to be really good news. Your weapons will be returned to you, barring any unforeseen revelations. However, I can't say how long it'll take. It could be a month, or it could be a year or more. Mr. Turner, I'm not going to tow your truck in. I'll be sending a police photographer back out later today to take detailed pictures of bullet holes in it and the other truck. Once he's done, you're free to move it. Until then, I'm leaving a deputy here to make sure no one bothers anything. He'll let you know when the photographer is done. Any questions?"

"What's going to happen to the guys who shot at us?" Ted asked.

"They're being arrested. Your attorney can fill you in. If there's nothing else, I have work to do."

The sheriff turned, and in a matter of minutes, he and his deputies had loaded the living MZB's into their cars and left. The ambulance had bagged the dead ones and left thirty minutes before. The remaining deputy's face looked like he'd just sucked a whole bag of lemons, as he sat down on the fence and folded his arms.

"Is there someplace we can go talk?" Ralph asked.

"Let's go to my house," Mark volunteered.

Jerry and Tony excused themselves to go home. Mark told them to come back Sunday or Monday if they still wanted to borrow a truck. He also said that he'd see that Ralph got home.

When the men got to Mark's, they sat around the picnic table, and Ralph filled them in. "One of the gang members in the truck confirmed your story, which is really good news. He's looking for a deal since they'll all be tried for murder."

"I don't understand. You mean attempted murder, right?" Manny asked. "None of us died."

"No. They'll be charged with murder. If you and Mark went into a store to rob it, and the owner shot and killed Mark during the robbery, then you'd be charged with Mark's murder, just as if you'd pulled the trigger yourself." Manny nodded his head, and Ralph continued. "The sheriff is handling this a little differently than normal since these aren't exactly normal times. Otherwise, he would have hauled you all in just to get your statements, if nothing else. He told me that he's had a couple of one-on-one shootouts, but this is the first big battle he's had. He said they've had a lot of these in San Antonio, though."

"Why aren't we hearing about them in the news?" Ted asked.

"I asked that same question, and the sheriff told me the FCC asked the media to 'cooperate,' and he said they were mostly rival gangs shooting it out and that no bystanders had been hurt yet, so no one really cares that much anyway. Anyway, you all told the same story, own homes, have jobs and families, so it was fairly obvious that y'all were just defending yourselves from a bunch of guys with needle tracks and wearing gang colors. I have to tell you, the sheriff was pretty impressed with the way you boys handled yourselves with eleven to five odds. If he needs anything else, he'll contact you through me. So, just relax and try to get back to normal, whatever that means these days. Any questions?"

"You don't think we'll be charged with anything?" the guard with the Weatherby asked.

"No, Charley, I don't. In fact, the sheriff told me he thought it was a 99% chance you wouldn't," Ralph answered. That was his name, Mark thought, Charley. Charley Henderson.

"What about a civil suit?" Mark asked.

"That's a horse of a different color," the lawyer said. "I'd say, when the lights come back on, chances are you'll all be sued. I don't think they could win, but it'll still cost you quite a bit to defend yourselves."

All five men's faces fell. "I wouldn't let that bother you right now. You're all alive and unharmed, and that's what counts. Plus, it may never happen, and if it does, I know a guy who's one of the best litigators in the country."

The men all stood up and shook hands and thanked the lawyer. Then Mark drove Ralph home in the Jeep. On the way there, Mark was racking his brain to remember how he knew this guy.

"You look familiar to me, but I can't put my finger on where I've seen you before. I don't think it was in the gun shop, but I'm not sure."

"It probably wasn't in the shop unless you go early on weekday mornings."
Mark shook his head. He usually went after work.

"Do you like football?"

"Yes," Mark answered, wondering what that had to do with anything.

"College?"

"Mostly pro, except at Thanksgiving. I almost always watch the UT – Aggie game with my dad."

"I used to be the starting right defensive end for the Longhorns," Ralph said with a smile.

Mark slapped his knee. "Now I remember! You got drafted by the pros, right?"

"Yeah, third round by the Seahawks."

"What happened?"

"Blew out my left knee in rookie camp."

"Man, I'm sorry."

"I'm not. I got to keep my signing bonus, so I used it to go back to school and get my law degree. Then I moved back home. Now I have a beautiful wife and daughter, a nice house, and a job I love. You know what the funny part is?"

"What?" Mark asked.

"I never really liked football. I was good at it, but I didn't love it. Now, baseball…there's a game! It's just too bad I could never hit a fast ball."

When the men pulled up in front of Ralph's house, he got out. Mark stuck his hand out to shake the big bear paw of the former defensive All-American. "Thanks for all of your help, Ralph. I don't know how I can ever repay you."

"You're more than welcome, Mark, and don't worry, I'll think of something because you owe me big time!" he said with a giant grin.

Chapter 22

As Mark drove home, he thought about what Ralph said the sheriff told him. If they were having a lot of shootouts in town like the one he'd just been involved in, then things must be worse than anyone was letting on. San Antonio was really a pretty laid back city for its size. If it was that bad here, it must be considerably worse in Houston and Dallas. He couldn't even imagine how bad it must be in the cities where martial law had been declared. Combined with the fact he believed the City Water Board was having trouble delivering pressure to its customers, they were sitting on a real time bomb. If the water went out for good in town, then things would go downhill in a hurry. He looked at his watch. Where had the five hours since the shootout gone?

As he passed the deputy watching the trucks, he waved. He barely received an acknowledgement. Mark turned into the subdivision, said hello to the guards, who looked at him strangely, and then drove up to his house. It was getting hot. If it wasn't a hundred degrees yet, it would be soon. He looked across the street at the men working on the five-acre lot to prepare it for planting. Most of the brush had already been cut down, and several men were working on some of the larger mesquite trees. There were two men running the bigger tillers, and several others standing in the shade under a makeshift awning. Mark walked over.

George saw him first. "Hey, are you doing okay?"

God, I'm sick of answering that question, Mark thought, as all the men turned to face him. "Yes. I'm fine. How are you all doing on this first lot?"

"Not too good," George answered. "We're getting the brush cleared alright, but with only two tillers, it's taking forever to turn the soil over."

"I thought we had three tillers."

"One of them is like a flower bed tiller. We may be able to use it some once the ground is worked, but it's pretty much useless right now. At the rate we're going, we'll be lucky to get an acre a day ready to plant."

"That's all?"

"This ground probably hasn't been plowed in fifteen or twenty years, and the dirt's hard as a rock. Tillers are made for family gardening, not the kind of stuff we're trying to do. Plus, it's gotten so hot that I'm only letting the guys work for fifteen to twenty minutes at a time, then switch with one of the guys cooling off under here. I already had to send two home with heat exhaustion. What we really need is a tractor. If I had my old John Deere, I could have had half the neighborhood plowed by now."

"Maybe Jim and I can work out a deal with the ranch to borrow their tractor when we go get the windmill. I don't know if they'll go for that, though. It's not like the windmill that's just sitting there and not needed. If something happened to it, they don't have another one, but we can ask. All they can do is say 'no.' In the meantime, we'll just have to do the best we can with the tillers. Did Gunny get back with your people and the seed?"

"Yes, just a few minutes ago. They had to go to a lot of places, but they found almost everything we had on the list."

"Great. At least we have some good news today," Mark smiled. "Do you know where Gunny is now?"

"I think he's still at your place."

"Good. Do you think you could break away from here for a few minutes?"

"Sure. I'm just here for moral support. These guys all know what to do," George answered.

The two men walked across the street. Mark wanted to have a meeting with everyone who lived at his place, plus Gunny and Abby. Jim was down at Manny's working on his Suburban; he'd already fixed Ted's Trans Am. Mark sent his kids to round everybody up.

Gunny wanted to know all about the firefight. Mark gave him a synopsis of what had happened while they waited for everyone. He said the only mistake he could see that Mark had made was not covering Manny and Ted, as they went to the dirt mound, and then them not covering him as he exited the truck.

"I'm not gonna ask you if'n you're okay, Karate Man, but when you're ready to talk, come'n find me."

Finally someone understood, Mark thought. "Thanks, Gunny."

"Sheriff took your weapons, huh?" Gunny asked.

"Yeah. He said it may be a while before I get them back," Mark said sadly. "Hey, I heard y'all did good on the seed."

"At first I didn't think we'd ever find even a fraction of what was on the list, but one ol' boy told us to try the feed store in Poth, an' they had jus' about everything. I noticed they had lotsa T-posts and bob-wire, too, if'n we want to put that fence in the front."

In just a few minutes, Jim and Abby were back with the teenagers, and they all sat around the picnic table. Mark explained what the sheriff had said about all of the violence in town and how he suspected that the city water wouldn't be flowing much longer.

"If that happens, I think things are going to get real bad in a hurry. What I want us to do is start going to a different Kroger each day and stock up on food and supplies as best we can until then. We have five qualifying addresses between us. That gives us $250.00 worth a day. That sounds like a lot, but for twelve people, it's not that much, especially if we only have two or three days to shop. The ladies can figure out what we need. Sam, I want you to work out an inventory system for the food and other consumables. That way, we know exactly where we stand. Food for the next two to three months would be the highest priority, I would think. After that, hopefully the gardens can keep us going. Don't worry about meat. We can get all we want from the deer lease pretty soon. The Krogers are pretty safe since the police are there, but if we go somewhere else, security has to be a major consideration. Jim and I have to go down to the ranch and work out the trade for the windmill and hopefully the use of their tractor. I'd like for the four women and Gunny to go to the next closest Kroger while we're gone. David, that means you'll need to watch the twins tomorrow. George, I know you want to keep an eye on the tilling, but when we get back, we're going to need help with the windmill. Does that make sense to everyone?"

All of the men and Abby nodded their heads. Jess and Lisa looked like they weren't so sure.

"I don't think it's right for us to get food other people can't get," Jess argued. "Going to a different store every day isn't in the spirit of what Kroger

134

intends. Most people are walking or riding bicycles to the store, so they couldn't do that even if they wanted."

"And what about the people who live here?" Lisa picked up where Jess had stopped. "What are they going to think of us if we're going to the store every day, and they can't?"

"At first, I felt the same way both of you do, and I realize that what I want to do isn't fair, but these aren't normal circumstances. I was in a gunfight today, and four men were killed, one or two of them by me. If you'd told me that was going to happen two weeks ago, I'd have thought you were crazy and probably would've called the men with white coats myself." Mark paused to let that sink in. He looked at each person to try to see if it had the desired effect. When he looked at Gunny, the old Marine gave him a little nod that told Mark to keep going. "Things have changed and will continue to change, and we better change, too, or we might not make it. This group right here is my family, some by blood, some by choice, and we have to worry about our family first. Then we can worry about the others. If things go down the crapper in the next few days, we're screwed. We don't have enough food to last until the crops come in. If someone else wasn't going to get their fifty dollars' worth of groceries because we bought them, then I wouldn't suggest this, but I haven't seen anyone turned away at the store. Have you?"

Everyone shook his or her head.

"If we were charging the groceries, I wouldn't want to do it, but we're paying cash. As soon as Manny's truck is fixed, we'll have six running vehicles in the neighborhood. That's if you count Gunny's truck and if the Ford isn't too shot up. Four of those belong to us. I don't think it's wrong for us to use at least one of our vehicles for our benefit. It was our choice to drive older vehicles and not get caught up in the trap of having to have a new car every couple of years, and I don't think we should be punished because we chose to be frugal. If we get to where we have plenty, then we'll stop going and let others use the vehicles we don't need. I don't want to horde food and supplies. I just want to make sure we can stay safe and healthy. As far as the neighborhood goes, I'd suggest we make at least one vehicle available to them each day, and they can take as many people to the store as they can. If it's all right with everyone here, I was going to tell the crowd tonight that we plan to start going to the store more than once a week, offer them one of the trucks, and suggest they do the same."

Everyone looked at each other and nodded.

"Is there anything else we need to think about?" Mark asked.

"Yes," Jess answered. "I want Gunny to move into our guest room. He's part of our family now, and it's silly for him to drive back and forth every day."

"Great idea. What do you say, Gunny?" Mark didn't think he would go for it, and that was why he'd never suggested it. Maybe the idea coming from one of the women would make a difference.

"I 'preciate the offer, but I'm gonna hafta decline," Gunny said as he looked at Abby. "Ya see, me an' Abby went to check on the preacher yesterday afternoon, an' he's gonna marry us after church on Sunday, so I'll be movin' into her place."

Mark thought the sound of the hammer falling on the empty chamber of his FAL earlier that day was the loudest silence he'd ever heard. It was dwarfed by the hush that followed Gunny's announcement.

After what seemed an eternity, Alice broke the quiet. "Congratulations to both of you."

"Thank you," Abby said with a smile.

The other women quickly added their felicitations. Abby blushed under all of the attention.

Jim was the first male to speak. "You old dog, you."

Gunny gave him a look that said that comment was all that would be tolerated, and the next one would be acknowledged by a visit from Gunny's boot to the speaker's nether regions.

The group ate dinner and listened to the radio. There was no significant news from either the President or any place else. Mark thought perhaps, just maybe, the news of their shootout would be reported. When it wasn't, it confirmed to him what the sheriff had said about the government controlling the news. When they got to Jon's, everyone just wanted to know about the shootout. Mark spent several minutes telling them the story, with Manny and Ted filling in some of the details. When Mark was telling the story, he noticed that the crowd was as quiet as church mice, and they all had glassy stares. He thought it might be shock because of what had happened. Once he finished, Jon asked the two guards to tell the story from their perspective. Scott and Charley moved to the front, and Scott started.

"We were just standing up there, bored and chit-chatting, as usual, when Charley saw Mark's truck coming up the road. He asked me if it looked like Mark was going real fast, and I told him, 'Yeah, it did.' About then, we noticed the old truck behind him. When Mark passed us, he honked, and we saw the rifle sticking out the back window. We knew something was wrong, but we just kind of stood there in shock."

Charley took over. "We must have just watched for the first fifteen seconds or so. The big rifle sticking out of the back of Mark's truck was shooting, as Mark pulled down into the ditch. Then I saw Mark stick his head out of the driver's window and start shooting his pistol. The truck with the gang bangers skidded to a halt about a hundred and fifty yards past us. All of this happened so fast, but when the bangers starting really shooting at our guys, we woke up. We jumped down behind the little masonry wall that the Silver Hills sign sits on. The rifle Manny was shooting must have gone dry about the time Mark started shooting. Mark emptied his pistol in less than five seconds, he was shooting so fast. I saw him go back into the truck, and with no one shooting at them, the attackers started really hammering the truck. I could hear the bullets hitting it pretty regularly. Manny started shooting again, and about that time, Scott yelled at me to shoot. All that time, we'd just been watching. I felt like an idiot. I could see the driver was shooting a rifle really fast, and I figured he was the most dangerous. I could make him out pretty good in my scope since there was no windshield in his truck, so I squeezed off a round and must have hit him because the rifle fell out of the truck. When we started shooting, the gang members all turned and started shooting at us. We ducked down, and they went back to shooting at Mark and the others. They were still in the back of the truck and were pretty easy targets. I dropped one out of the bed. Scott shot the one in the cab with the sawed off."

"Then they jumped out of the truck to use it for cover," Scott resumed. "They started shooting at us again. You can see the bullet holes in the sign, if you go look. I guess they forgot all about Mark and Manny. I didn't know they had moved behind the dirt pile until they jumped up and shot. It must have broken the spirit of the gang when they realized there was nowhere to hide. They gave up, and that was that." Scott paused. "I just want to say one thing to Mark, Manny, and Ted. I'm sorry we didn't react as fast as we should have. I was just in shock. I promise it won't happen again."

"That goes for me, too," Charley concurred. "I'm just thankful our mental lapse didn't get any of you killed."

"You guys have nothing to be sorry for," Mark said. "I don't know if I would have reacted as well as you did. You both saved our bacon. If you hadn't helped us, our wives would have all been planning funerals. I know I speak for Manny and Ted, as well, when I say thank you."

Jon then started talking to the crowd about the recommendations the security committee wanted to make. Mark felt that the events of the day must have given the former Marine a change of heart. Jon sounded like he firmly advocated each and every recommended security measure. It even sounded a little bit like everything was his idea. The vote was unanimous to start on the front defenses. Jon asked that people who would like to help to report to Susan Banks for assignment. He asked if anyone had anything else to talk about, and Mark raised his hand. Jon yielded him the floor.

Mark explained his thinking about what had happened today, what the sheriff had said, and how he felt that things could worsen in a short time where they might not be able to get into town again. The crowd listened to what Mark said as if he'd hypnotized them. He told them his family group was going to start going into town more than once a week to get groceries. Everyone just nodded their heads as though the thought had never occurred to them. He explained that he and his group would provide at least one vehicle per day for the neighborhood to share to do the same if they wished. The crowd just murmured their thanks, as Mark went back to his family. Ted offered to drive his car, and take as many as he could as well. Manny said that as soon as his truck was running, he would do the same. Mark was a little shocked that no one mentioned any of the concerns that his family had. Jon asked if Manny would take over being in charge of the grocery transportation, as he would be busy developing his training program for the guards.

When the meeting was dismissed, Mark and Jim walked down to the road to check on the Ford. Everyone else headed home. When they got to the truck, the police photographer was about halfway finished with his work. They chatted with the deputy and asked him what was to become of the other truck. He told them that since it had three flat tires, and since they didn't have access to a tow truck, the sheriff had told him to push it off of the road. Jim asked the deputy if he thought someone might come by and put good tires on it and drive it off. The deputy just shrugged his shoulders like it didn't matter. When the photographer, who was really just another deputy with some photography experience, finished, he and the deputy who had been on watch used the squad car to push the MZB truck into the ditch across the road from the subdivision.

Mark and Jim looked at his truck. Of course the back window was gone, and now there were several holes in the windshield, not just one. The tailgate looked like a strainer, and the heavy back bumper had several big dents in it. One of the tail light lenses was shattered, and the bed had two holes through the side. The worst body damage was to the roof, where a bullet had just skimmed the sheet metal, and it looked like the Jolly Green Giant had used a can opener on the truck. Mark groaned when he saw that. Everything else could be fixed up easily or didn't really hurt the usability of the truck. That big gouge would be a problem to fix, though. The good news was that, since Mark had pulled the truck down into the ditch, all of the tires and running gear had been protected. Mark started it, and they drove it back up to the house. Once there, Jim pulled a roll of duct tape out of his toolbox and started patching the holes, including the gouge in the roof. Mark found some heavy plastic sheeting and taped some in place of the back glass. The only bad hole in the windshield was from the shotgun blast that had started the incident. However, the cracks that it and the other holes had created made it almost impossible to see through. Mark had seen a regular cab half-ton truck, the same body style as his, toward the front of the subdivision. He went into the safe and took $200 from the money Todd had given him. He and Jim then drove down to the house where the two-tone little sister of his big truck was parked. Mark knocked on the door. After a moment, a man answered. Mark had met him before, but as was usual for him, he couldn't remember his name.

"Mark," the man said. "Honey, it's Mark Turner!" the man excitedly called over his shoulder.

"Well, Hank," his wife said, as she stepped into the entryway, "don't make him stand outside. Invite him and Mr. Davis in."

"Please, come in, both of you."

"I don't want to be any trouble, but I wanted to talk to you about your truck," Mark said, as he and Jim stepped in through the door.

"That piece of junk won't run. I tried to get the parts to fix it the day of The Burst, but no one had the computer," Hank said, as his wife elbowed him lightly in the ribs. "I'm sorry, Mark. This is my wife Jean. Jean, this is Mark Turner and Jim Davis."

The woman shook Mark's hand and looked at him as though he might have been a movie star. "It's so nice to meet you, Mr. Turner. Can I get you something to drink? I have some nice, sun-brewed, sweet tea. We obviously don't have ice, but it's still pretty good." She smiled like a star-struck teenager.

"Thank you, ma'am, but I just wanted to see if I could buy the windshield out of y'all's truck. You see, the one in mine got pretty shot up, and we have to go pick up the windmill tomorrow."

"Just give him the windshield, Hank," Jean said.

"Yes, please, just take it. That's the least we can do for all you've done for us," Hank insisted.

"I couldn't just take it. I need to give you something for it," Mark argued.

"We won't hear of it." Jean was emphatic. "It's not doing us any good, so if it'll help you, you just take it."

"Okay, but I insist that you let me replace it as soon as possible," Mark said.

"That's fine," Hank agreed. "Let me help you."

The three men went out, and in about an hour had removed the shot up windshield and replaced it with the one from Hank's truck. Jim sealed it with some clear silicone, and once they'd replaced the trim, it was impossible to tell that it hadn't been professionally done. They helped Hank push his truck into the garage, thanked him and Jean again, and then drove to Chaparo's to borrow the trailer. On the way there, Mark asked Jim if everyone was acting a little weird.

"You don't know why?" Jim grinned like the cat that had swallowed the canary.

"Know why, what?"

"You're a hero, man. These people think you hung the moon."

"You're full of shit!" Up to two dollars for the day, Mark thought.

"No, I've heard them talking today. Between you providing water, lending them your truck, the fight at Kroger, topped off by what you did today, you're like a god to these people."

"Well, there's only one God, and I ain't even close," Mark said emphatically.

"Maybe so, but they still worship the ground you walk on."

"I doubt that!" Mark said, hoping that statement plus the fact they were at Chaparo's would end this uncomfortable conversation.

Chaparo helped them hook up the trailer. He had already started on the gate and was excited to show Mark the work he'd accomplished. He had most of the metal cut and laid out on the floor of his shop. Even though Mark knew nothing about metal work, he told the machinist how impressed he was. Chaparo beamed at Mark's approval.

When the men got back home, Gunny and Abby were waiting. Abby handed him a box.

"Mark, I want you have this. It belonged to my late husband, and I know he would be proud to know that you have it."

"Thank you, Abby," Mark said, as he opened the box. Inside the plain brown corrugated box was another box that said 'Colt' on the top. Inside that box was a Series 70 Gold Cup .45 in Colt royal blue finish. Jim whistled when he saw it. Many of the experts considered this model to be the finest 1911 ever made. The pistol was obviously unfired.

"Abby, I can't take this. It's worth…well I don't know what it's worth, but I can't accept such a valuable gift."

"Nonsense. It just sat in the safe for years. Alfred never shot it; he just took it out once in a while to look at it and polish it. Gunny told me that the sheriff took your pistol, and I insist that you take this one. It's the least I can do for all that you and your family have done for me. In fact, you've made me part of your family, so you can't refuse."

"But, Abby…"

Before Mark could finish his thought, Gunny interrupted. "Look here, Karate Man, if'n Abby says she wants you to take the pistol, then you better take the pistol. Otherwise you might hurt her feelings, and if'n you hurt my girl's feelings, then, black belt or no black belt, I'll hafta take you behind the woodshed. Do you read me?"

"Loud and clear, Gunny. Thank you so much, Abby. I only hope I can live up to how much this old Colt must mean to you."

"You already have, Mark," the woman smiled.

Gunny and Abby excused themselves to spend a few minutes alone before Gunny had to leave. Jim just smiled at his friend.

"See what I mean?" he asked.

"I still say you're full of it."

"The way Chaparo acted when you said his gate looked good. The windshield. The Gold Cup. What more proof do you need?"

"Tell you what, smartass, when they erect a statue of me at the courthouse, then I'll start to think you might be right," Mark said. "We're leaving early, you better get some sleep."

"Yes, Kimosabe. Tanto proud to ride tomorrow with Lone Ranger." Jim did his best impression, which wasn't saying much. However, he must have struck the nerve he was looking for, because all he received in reply was the middle digit on Mark's right hand. That gesture would cost him dollar, Mark thought, but it was cheaper than saying what he was thinking.

Once it got dark, Jess sent the kids to bed. Jim, Lisa, and her parents excused themselves, as well. Jess reached across the kitchen table and took her husband's hand. "You know, it wasn't until you and the other men talked at the meeting about what happened today that I really understood how serious this could be." She squeezed his hand hard. "You could have been killed. Thank God you knew what to do and that He was watching over you. I don't know what I would have done if you'd been hurt."

Mark looked in Jess's eyes and saw they were filled with tears. He pulled her around the table and into his lap. She buried her head into his shoulder and began to sob. "It's alright, baby," he cooed. "We're going to be fine."

"I know you're right," she said, as she tried to catch her breath, "but I'm just so scared." She started crying harder.

Mark hugged her to him as hard as he could without hurting her. After several minutes, she started to regain her composure. Mark stood up, and the two of them went to their bedroom.

Chapter 23

Man, was it hot, Mark thought. He walked into the living room and turned the thermostat down. The air conditioner kicked on. He walked into his study, sat down, and hit the Internet Explorer icon on his computer monitor. He really needed to check the stock market and the value of his 401k. As he saw the graphs of his investments appear on the screen, he opened a can of Diet Coke and poured it over a tall glass of ice.

"Mark," he heard someone call.

"I'm in here," he answered over his shoulder. When he looked back, he now held a bottle of Shiner Bock, his favorite beer, and was pouring it into a frosty mug.

"Mark, are you in here?" the voice called again.

Who was bothering him when he just wanted to taste the cold beer? He heard the voice again and realized that he didn't have a beer. Reality slowly and callously crept up on him. Where was he? Oh yeah, he was in the house. He and Jess must have fallen asleep in here. As he continued to depart the heavy fog clouding his brain, he could see that it was already getting light. There was a light tap on the door.

"Mark, are you in there?" Jim whispered.

"Yeah, Jim, I'll be out in a minute."

Mark gently pulled his arm out from underneath Jess's head. He got up and pulled his jeans on. His arm was stiff where his wife had slept on it. She stirred, opened one eye, and looked at him.

"What time is it?" she asked sleepily.

Mark looked at his watch. "Crap. It's 7:45. I told Jim we'd leave by 7:30."

"Tell him I said it was okay if you're late. You earned a few minutes of extra sleep." She smiled at him.

"Thanks. You earned more than that in my book, but I have to get ready." He winked at her as he slipped out of the room.

Jim was in the kitchen fishing some Pop-Tarts out of the pantry. "Slept in the house, huh?" He grinned.

"Yeah. Sorry I overslept."

"That's okay. I mean, who can blame Jess for wanting to have a little hero time for herself?"

"Can we just drop the hero crap? I'm not a hero. I only did what anybody else would've done and was lucky to boot. Besides that, it's going to be a long day."

"Okay. Get dressed while I get the truck loaded and filled up."

"Thanks."

Mark ran to the camper, got out some clean clothes, and took a quick shower. He thought about how lucky they were to have hot running water in the camper. Everyone else in the neighborhood was probably reduced to taking hobo baths. Once he was clean and dressed, he headed out to the truck. Jim was waiting. He'd filled up the tanks and had two jerry cans of diesel in the bed, along with some rope and ratcheting straps for tying the windmill down. He also had his M1A across the front seat.

Mark wanted to take his new Gold Cup that Abby had given him, but it had never been fired. He went to the gun safe and removed the revolver he'd bought for Jess. He needed a long gun, too. He looked in the safe and tried to figure out what to take. He reached all the way in the back of the safe and pulled out his old Ruger Mini-14. He grabbed five magazines and two hundred rounds of ammo for it. As he walked out to the truck, he stopped in the kitchen where Jess was cooking breakfast to kiss her goodbye.

"What time do you think you'll be home?" she asked.

"If everything goes well, an hour to get there, two or three hours to work out the deal and load the windmill, and then an hour home. I'd say two o'clock at the latest."

"Good." That was all she said, but Mark knew there was something else.

"Is there a reason you asked?" He didn't want to wonder for half a day what was on her mind.

"I was thinking maybe you men could spend a little time with us women and teach us how to shoot a rifle."

Yesterday must have made a bigger impression on her than he'd thought. She'd never wanted to shoot a rifle before. He'd had enough trouble getting her to shoot her revolver once or twice a year. If she wanted to do it, though, he'd make the time. "It's a date," he smiled, as he headed out the door.

Mark started the truck and headed out. He told Jim about Jess's request to learn to shoot a rifle. Jim told him the girls must have talked about it some yesterday because Lisa and her mom had asked him the same thing last night.

Once the men hit the interstate and picked up speed, it became obvious that the plastic on the back window wasn't going to work. The wind shook it so badly that it made too much noise for the two friends to hear each other talk. Plus, Mark couldn't really see through it. After the MZB's snuck up on him the day before, he was watching much more carefully, and it made him nervous not to have a clear line of sight out of the back. They pulled over and removed the plastic. After that, although there was a little wind noise, the travelers had no trouble conversing. They spoke of the preparations they still needed to make, what was the highest priority, and how long they felt they had to get them done. While Mark thought they could have as little as a day or two, Jim's estimate was between five days and a week. Mark prayed they had a week, but he wasn't holding his breath.

His thoughts drifted to their living conditions. Their camper was getting really cramped, and it must be worse for Jim and his family, now that George and Alice were sleeping in there, as well. He'd really like to be able to move back into the house. Also, until last night, he didn't realize how much he missed the privacy of his own bedroom. Mark started thinking about the preacher's house with the tall windows and wondered if there was a way to do the same thing in his house. That was the same thing he was thinking yesterday when the shooting started, he thought, as he checked the rearview mirror. There was nothing there, though what Jim suggested next surprised him as much as the shotgun blast had yesterday.

"When we get home, I think we should pull that old International Harvester up to your house, clean it out, and try to get it running."

Mark looked at his friend like he'd lost his mind. "You're joking, right?"

142

"No. Why would you think that?"

"Oh…I don't know…let me see…because it's shot to pieces, because it's full of blood, brains, and guts, and…mostly because it doesn't belong to us."

"Didn't you see how the deputy reacted when you asked him about it? They don't care what happens to it. If we don't take it, someone else will," Jim reasoned.

"Well, that may be, but I don't like it, and I'm not going to have anything to do with it," Mark said emphatically.

"Last night, you said that things have changed and will keep changing, and we better change, too, or we might not make it. When you said that, I thought it was real wisdom. We're going to have to look at every situation differently than we used to. I'll need you to remind me just like I'm reminding you right now. Besides, I'm not talking about hitting someone over the head and stealing their car. I'm talking about using an abandoned vehicle. Those gang bangers are never coming back for it. We might as well get some use out of it. You could think of it as us keeping it safe until the lights come back on, if that makes you feel any better."

"You make a good argument, Jim, especially when you use my own words to make your point." Mark gave his friend a wry smile. "Let me think about it a while, and we'll talk about it again when we get home. Is that okay?"

"You've got a deal." Jim changed the subject. "You think they're going to let us borrow the tractor?"

"I'm not betting on it. I know I wouldn't lend it out if it was mine."

"That's what I thought, too. I wonder if we can find one."

"There have to be tractors that The Burst fried all over the place. I just don't know where to look, who to ask, or even where to get the parts to fix one. If we could find one, Rodney might be able to help us with the parts, but I don't know if he carries any tractor parts, or if they're interchangeable with car parts. Worst case, he could point us in the right direction."

"Maybe one of the farmers in our area has an old diesel one that'll still run, and we could make a deal with him to borrow it," Jim rationalized. "One thing's for sure, if we don't find one, George doesn't know how he and his gang are going to get all of the empty lots ready to plant, let alone the gardens everyone wants to put in at their houses. George told me he's worried about the tillers, too. They really weren't built to be used this hard, and if one of them breaks, he doesn't know if we can find the parts to fix it."

"I guess we better see if we can find a tractor. After we get the windmill set up, I guess that's our next priority," Mark stated.

To Mark, the trip seemed to take longer than it did last time. Part of it may have been that he was constantly checking his mirrors to make sure no one snuck up on them. He watched the front with the same vigilance. Any time there was a vehicle in sight, Mark subconsciously put a death grip on the steering wheel and watched the potential threat like a hawk. They passed several eighteen wheelers, most of which looked to be food transports, but the two friends only saw one other private car and a pair of motorcycles on the Interstate. Once they turned on the farm to market road, they found that they had it all to themselves.

When they turned onto the ranch road, Mark stopped the truck, and Jim tied the yellow bandana to the antenna. When they got to the gate, the guard opened the gate and waved them through. Todd was waiting at the compound for them. As they got out of the truck, he noticed the taped up bullet holes.

"What happened to your truck?" he asked, as he walked around to the back. When he saw the tailgate he reached out and touched one of the holes. "Holy shit!"

"A couple of my neighbors and I got into a shootout with a bunch of gang members yesterday," Mark answered sheepishly.

"Is everybody okay?" Todd was wide-eyed.

"Everybody on our side was."

"What happened...no, wait. I want Mr. Davis to hear this, too. Let's go." Todd wheeled around and led the way to Mr. Davis's cabin. He knocked on the door, and Millie answered it. She showed them in and then went to go get Mr. Davis. A moment later, the older man came into the room, and his guests rose to shake his hand.

"We were starting to get worried about you. How are you?" the leader asked.

"We were right to be worried," Todd interjected before anyone else could say anything. "Mark was in a big shootout yesterday, and his truck's shot to hell."

"Really? Are your families okay?"

"Yes," Mark replied. "It was me and two of my neighbors in the truck."

"What happened?"

Mark spent six or seven minutes giving Mr. Davis and Todd a detailed run down on the events of the day before. The two men stared at him in disbelief as he told the story. When he finished, neither one said anything for a few moments.

"I don't know what to say. Eleven to five odds, and you and your friends weren't even scratched." Mr. Davis finally said. "I guess we were right about you. You are levelheaded under fire. You'll be a great asset to us here. I'm sure after that encounter, you're both anxious to move here."

The two friends looked at each other. Jim spoke first. "Mr. Davis, we want you to know how much we appreciate your invitation to move here. We spent a lot of time thinking and talking about it, but, mainly because we can't bring our extended families, which we completely understand the reasoning for, we've decided to stay at Mark's place."

"We've taken a page from your book here," Mark continued. "We're not as well set up as you all, but all of the neighbors are working together, and I think we can make a go of it. I know you were counting on Jim and I to do some training for you, and we'd like to work out a deal where we can do that training in exchange for some of the things that we need."

Mr. Davis and Todd just looked at each other blankly. Neither said a word, so Mark continued to talk. "We noticed the windmill that you replaced with the solar-jack pump was just lying on the ground. That's the first thing we'd like to trade for." Mark noticed that Mr. Davis was turning red. "Whatever you think is fair would be fine with us."

The silence was deafening.

"What do you mean? You don't want to move here?" Mr. Davis's voice was thin and squeaky.

"It's not that we don't want to," Mark explained. "It's just that we have our parents and siblings to worry about."

"But...but...when the shit really hits the fan, your little shootout is going to look like a day at the beach. There is NO way you're going to survive in the city!" He was turning purple now, Mark thought. What color would Jess call that? Lavender? No, he was a darker shade than that. Too bad the girls weren't here. They would know exactly what shade that was. Heck, Jess would probably want to take him down to Sherwin-Williams and get his color duplicated to paint the guest room.

"We're not in the city, remember?" Jim was starting to reflect some of the hostility he was receiving. "And we think we can survive just fine."

Mark put his hand on his friend's arm. When he spoke, his voice was cool and even. "I'm sorry if we've upset you, Mr. Davis, but we've made up our minds. We'd really like to work out a deal with you that would be mutually beneficial."

"I don't think you realize what you're turning down!" He was almost royal blue and screaming now. "I'll give you one more chance to change your minds!"

"We don't need to think about it anymore." Mark was as calm as a lazy river. "We know what we're doing. Now about coming to an agreement on..."

"There will be NO agreement." The man's head looked like it might explode. "You are no longer welcome here. You can get off of my property right now. When your world turns to shit, and it will, don't come crawling back here, begging me to take you in, either. I give you an opportunity like this, and you throw it my face? Goodbye and good riddance, I say!"

With that, the man spun around and stomped out of the room. Mark hoped he was going to take his blood pressure medicine or a Valium or something. Todd showed them out. While he wasn't going ballistic, he was rather cold toward the two friends. They shook his hand and wished him good luck. His only response was to ask them for the key to the gate at work. Jim took it off of his key ring and put it in the outstretched hand. The now unwanted guests climbed into the truck and made their way off of the ranch.

They didn't speak for a long time. Mark was sorting though his feelings of disappointment, anger, and even some fear. After they were back on the interstate headed north, Jim finally spoke.

"You forgot to ask him if we could borrow the tractor!" he said with a straight face.

A second later, the friends were laughing so hard Mark could barely keep the truck on the road.

Chapter 24

When the men got home, they noticed the security committee had already started on the preparations that had been approved. The Silver Hills sign had been taken down, and Susan Banks was supervising a group of men digging a foxhole for the guards where Gunny had suggested. About ten other men were working on the ditch. Ted and a couple of other men were driving t-posts into the ground for the barbed wire fence, and another man was working with a posthole digger. Chaparo was putting a big pipe in the ground to hang the gate from. Mark stopped the truck to check on everyone's progress. Chaparo told him the gate was almost ready. It just needed a few finishing touches, and as soon as he had the pipes set, they could hang it. He'd found a bag of concrete to set the poles. Susan said she had quite a few volunteers to dig the foxholes and to dig out the ditch. She'd checked with Gunny, and he told her they needed to talk a little bit about where the other holes would go but that she could start on this one for the guard post. Ted came over and told Mark that he'd taken his Trans Am with the little motorcycle trailer to Poth to buy the T-posts. He said he didn't have enough money to buy all of the posts and barbed wire but that he was able to get enough to get them started. They were setting the posts every ten feet. Every fifth one was going to be a three-inch steel pipe that Chaparo had promised to make as soon as the gate was finished. Ted suggested they might want to ask for donations toward the rest of the materials, like the gardening committee had.

Chaparo finally noticed that Mark and Jim didn't have anything on the trailer. He asked them how it had gone, and they told him, Ted, and Susan what had happened.

"So what are we going to do about water?" Ted asked.

"We can keep using the generator for a while. There's plenty of gas in the cars that won't run to last several months if we're careful. We'll just keep looking; there has to be a windmill we can buy or borrow somewhere," Mark answered.

The two friends excused themselves and drove up to the house. Gunny and the four women were still at the store. George was supervising the tilling across the street and walked over when he saw the red truck pull into the driveway. Jim explained that their trip hadn't been successful. When they went into the house, Sam had emptied the pantry out onto the kitchen table and floor and was writing everything into a large, spiral notebook. David was reading a book to the twins. It was almost lunchtime, so the men fixed lunch for everyone. Afterwards, Jim headed back over to Manny's to finish fixing his Suburban. Mark looked in the shed, found a shovel and headed down to help with the digging. It was hard work. Gunny had told them that the near side of the ditch needed to be a four-foot vertical wall. The ditch was already three feet deep, so digging down another foot wasn't that hard. The hard part was digging to make the back wall perpendicular to the ground. As it warmed up, Susan made the men take more breaks to cool off. She also made sure everyone drank plenty of water.

Gunny and his crew pulled back into the subdivision at 1:15. They must not have recognized Mark, since he was down in the ditch and covered with dirt. He thought about how much he was going to enjoy a shower later and felt bad about the men who were as covered in dirt as he was and had no way to really get clean. The foxhole had been completed, and the men who had worked on it were now working on the ditch. Susan had a shovel and was down in the ditch working alongside the men. By a little after two o'clock, it had become so hot that she sent them all home for the day. They'd finished almost a quarter of the ditch and one of the foxholes.

When Mark got home, Jim had filled the shoppers in on the trip to the ranch. He told Mark that Manny's truck was now running. Mark asked Jess and Lisa about their trip to Kroger. They had some interesting and disturbing news, and Lisa told Mark and Jim what had happened.

"This Kroger wasn't nearly as busy as the closer one. We were thankful that we didn't have to wait as long, but then we found out why. Two days ago, they had a riot there over the busses. It seems a lot of people in that part of town were counting on riding the bus home instead of having to walk with their groceries. It was getting late, and people were waiting in line for their turn when a bus pulled up, and the driver announced that he was the last bus for the day. We were told there were over two hundred and fifty people waiting and only room for seventy, if people stood in the aisles. As many as could squeezed into the bus, but the ones who couldn't get on went crazy and started attacking the bus. The mob actually turned the bus over. Lots of people were hurt, and two were killed. The police at the store tried to quiet the mob, but the crowd turned on the officers. It got real ugly, and the two cops shot thirteen rioters before the mob overtook and killed them. The manager at the Kroger said only about half as many people had been coming to the store since then."

"That's awful," Mark gasped. "And we didn't hear about that on the news, either."

"The good news is that we bought enough staples to last us at least eight weeks. Even if we can't get any more food, we won't go hungry. It may get a little monotonous at meal times, but we'll make it," Jess said with a smile.

"That is good news," Mark agreed. "Which store are we going to tomorrow?"

Jess gave him a look that he didn't see often, but he knew what it meant. "Mark, tomorrow we're going to church and then to Gunny's and Abby's wedding. No one is going shopping. We can go first thing Monday."

Mark didn't argue. "Okay, I just hope we can go Monday. I guess we better go see about that old truck, Jim."

"What old truck?" Lisa asked.

Jim explained to Lisa that they were going to see if they could get the truck, left behind by the sheriff, running so that the neighborhood could use it. The two friends unhooked Chaparo's trailer and drove down to the MZB truck. It had three flats, but they could only find one tire with a bullet hole in it. Mark thought that the other two might have gone flat when the truck skidded sideways. If that was the case, then the tires could still be good. They tied a tow strap to the front of the truck and pulled it up onto the road. Jim took Mark's truck up to the house to get the air compressor, the generator, and a jack. While he was gone, Mark looked the truck over. Of course, the windshield was gone, and there were a few holes in the body, mostly in the doors, but it wasn't shot up as badly as his truck was. That was probably because he, Manny, and the guards had been more selective with their shots. He opened the hood, and there were two big holes in the radiator that Manny had probably made with the .308. The good news was that, since the engine was a straight six, it was long and skinny, and the bullets hadn't hit the engine block. One had totaled the alternator, though, and the other appeared to have passed through without creating further damage.

Mark looked inside. The keys were still in the ignition. The truck was full of blood and some small fragments of bone. Mark started to experience the sick feeling he'd felt the day before. Jim came back, and they used the jack to lift the back of the truck. Jim aired one tire up while Mark took the spare out of the bed and replaced the tire with the hole. With that done, they jacked up the front and used the compressor to re-inflate the other flat. Jim reached in and turned the key, and the engine roared to life. He turned it off and asked Mark if he wanted to drive it or pull it up to the house. Mark informed him about the ventilated radiator and suggested they tow it back to the house. Jim looked in the cab where two of the MZB's had met their fate and wrinkled his nose.

"Somebody has to get in there to steer," he stated, making it clear that he didn't want to be the one.

"This was your idea!"

Jim's shoulders slumped, and he walked over to Mark's truck and got the plastic that had been over the back window. He placed it over the seat of the International Harvester and climbed in. Mark reattached the tow strap to his truck and pulled the lame truck to his house. The men hooked the generator up to the well, so that the truck could be cleaned out with a garden hose. Mark explained that he had something else that he needed to work on. Jim, looking like he was beginning to regret his idea, unrolled the garden hose and pulled it over to the truck to get started cleaning. Mark went into the house to find the girls working on a cake for Abby and Gunny's wedding.

"I thought you girls wanted some shooting lessons," Mark reminded them.

"We do, but can't we do it after the meeting, when it's cooled off a little?" Jess asked.

"I don't see why not. When you're ready, just get Jim to help you. He's the expert," Mark instructed. "Where's David?"

"He's across the street taking water to the guys working the field."

Mark walked out of the house to find David just coming back with the empty pitcher. "Do you need to take more over?"

"No, sir. This was the third trip, and they're okay for now."

"Good. I need you to do something for me. Get the lawnmower and set it as low as it will go. Then mow the grass right behind the shed. I'm going to Chaparo's house, and when I get back, I'm going to need you to help me some more."

"Yes, sir." David took off to the shed.

Mark walked down to Chaparo's house and talked to the big man for a few minutes.

"Sure, Mark. We can do that. I was finishing the gate, but the concrete has to dry for at least twenty-four hours before I can hang it, anyway. Let me get the stuff we need, and I'll be down in a few minutes," Chaparo told him.

Mark walked back and found that David was finished with the grass and was waiting for him. Mark asked him to help him get out his table saw, and they ran an extension cord over to the generator. Chaparo showed up, and the three of them worked as quickly as possible on Mark's project. They finished just before time for the news and the President's speech. They borrowed the water hose from Jim and then tested their invention.

"What do you think?" Mark asked Chaparo.

"Not bad. Wish it had a little more pressure, but it should do. If you could find some flat black spray paint for the barrels, it would probably get hotter."

"That's a good idea. What do you think, Dave?"

"It's cool. Can I use it tonight?"

"If you want, but not until the men who plowed and dug today are done."

Mark shook Chaparo's hand, and the plumber headed home. Mark checked on Jim, and he'd done a good job on the interior of the old truck and was just cleaning the last of the blood out of the bed of the pickup. He, Mark, and David went into the camper, washed up, and then walked up to the house for dinner. Both the news and the President's speech were just the same old thing. The President did mention tonight that they were still working diligently on the power and that it should start coming back on soon. He didn't mention a definite time frame, though. He added Miami and Baltimore to the list of those under martial law. Mark wondered how many cities could be controlled by the military before the troops got spread so thin they became ineffective. The only other thing of interest on the radio was the fact that a tropical storm in the Gulf was expected to bring rain to South Texas in the next two to three days.

The group walked down to Jon's for the meeting. Nothing was new except for some of the faces. Their little community was growing by leaps and bounds. Mark reported on his failed attempt to get the windmill but told the residents not to worry. They had enough gas to last until they could find one. He noticed that the stares he got tonight weren't quite as bad as the night before, but it still made him uncomfortable. George and his committee reported on how it was going with the first lot. They were less than half completed with the ground breaking. Some of the men were going to work on it tomorrow and Monday. Then they hoped to row it up. George asked everyone to be on the lookout for a tractor they could beg, borrow, or steal.

Next, the security committee reported to the group. Each member told where they were with the preparations. Ted asked for donations to go toward the barbed wire and posts they needed to finish the job. Chaparo said he was waiting for the concrete to cure to hang the gate. He'd come up with the idea to place posts made out of six-inch pipe and filled with concrete about every three feet across the other drive to stop anyone from driving in that way. The fence crew could then string their barbed wire across the posts to stop anyone on foot. Everyone thought that was a good idea and voted for Chaparo to proceed. Jon reported that he'd start his guard training program on Monday and that half of the guards would be trained next week and the other half the week after. That meant the guards who weren't in training each week would have to take two shifts that week instead of one. Mark thought Jon was going to present his plan for training to the committee before he implemented it, but he didn't feel like fighting with Jon in front of everyone. At least he was taking it seriously enough to spend a week with each group.

When Jon was wrapping up the meeting, he asked if anyone had anything else. Abby raised her hand, as did Mark. Jon called on Abby, and she asked if Mark could go first. Mark knew what she was going to announce, and he didn't want to steal her thunder by going last, so he made his announcement.

"Chaparo, David, and I have rigged up a makeshift shower behind my shed. We put two 55-gallon water barrels up on the roof, and Chaparo plumbed them together and ran a showerhead off of them. We built a wood slat floor and hung a tarp around it. The sun should heat the water nicely during the day, I think. We could use some flat black spray paint to help the barrels absorb the heat, if anyone has any. I'd like to give the men who worked on ground breaking, post driving, and ditch digging the first shot at trying it out tonight. I don't know how warm the water will be since we just finished and filled it an hour ago, but if you're willing, just come on down around dark. If this works, we can see about building some more." When he finished, the whole crowd applauded. "Don't get too excited," he warned. "We don't even know how well it's going to work yet."

When the applause died down, Jon called on Abby. She told the crowd about her wedding and invited the whole neighborhood to the ceremony and simple reception in the church hall afterward. If they were happy about what Mark had announced, they were ecstatic about Abby's news. Everyone was clapping and shouting congratulations. Abby turned red at the attention, but if Gunny was embarrassed, no one could tell. He just stood as straight and stiff as a PFC reporting for his first assignment.

When the meeting was over, Mark's group walked back to his house. The women were reviewing the preparations they'd made for tomorrow with the same kind of vigor Mark wished they would put into preparing for what could be facing them in the next few months. When they got to the house, they all went back to look at the shower. The women were a little skeptical, but the men assured them it could be improved upon. Mark tested the water, and while it wasn't warm, at least the chill had been knocked off of it. There was still about an hour of daylight left, and maybe it would warm up just a little more.

The girls still wanted their shooting lessons. With the limited time before dark, Jim went over the basics with them and told them they could shoot tomorrow afternoon when they got back from the wedding. All four of the women plus Sam listened intently as Jim went over the four rules of gun safety, explained the different types of rifle actions and how they worked, and gave them a primer on lining up the sights and squeezing the trigger.

Just after sunset, the men who had worked at the dirty jobs started showing up to try out the shower. The first man to use it, John Greene, yelled when the water hit him. Mark thought something was wrong and asked if he was okay. He reported that nothing was wrong and that this was the best shower he'd ever taken. The men were considerate of each other and hurried as much as they could and used as little water as possible. Each of them thanked Mark continuously for providing them with the means to get really clean. Mark thanked each of them for their hard work and told them it was the least he could do. When he asked the men about the water temperature, they replied that, while it could have been warmer, it wasn't cold. He was just happy that there was some reward, if only small, for their dedication to the survival of this community.

Manny showed up just before the showers were finished. He'd brought some eggs down to thank Mark and his group for fixing his truck. He admired the makeshift shower.

"I may have to volunteer to dig out the ditch one day just so I can try it out."

"Manny, your new job coordinating the grocery trips is more important than digging the ditch. You'll get to try it soon, don't worry."

"Mark, you're always thinking of others, like helping me fix my truck. I wanted to bring you some more eggs as a small token of thanks."

"Thank you, Manny, but I was wondering if I could get you to invest these eggs for me?"

"Invest them? In what?"

"Let the chickens sit on them. I want some chickens of my own."

"Oh, I see." Manny's eyes twinkled. "Just take these to eat, and I have some special 'investment' eggs at home that I'll put into your account."

"Thanks, Manny."

"You're welcome. The way I see it, we all owe you."

*　　*　　*

The morning brought a flurry of activity. Mark got up and ran. He pushed himself hard to make up for the two days he'd missed. When everyone was awake, they all sat down to a big breakfast. Mark passed on the biscuits, but he ate plenty of eggs. After breakfast, everyone dressed up for church, and the women made sure that the food they'd made for the reception was ready to go. George headed across the street to make sure the men who had volunteered to work on the lot were sure of what was to be done. Everyone loaded up into the two trucks and made the short drive to the Baptist church. Manny pulled into the parking lot right behind them with his crew, including Chaparo and his family. Brother Bob was glad to see all of them. He shook everyone's hand as they entered the church. They found a seat toward the middle. A few minutes later, Gunny and Abby showed up and sat with the families from Silver Hills. Gunny was wearing his uniform. Mark had never seen the old man in anything except jeans and work shirts. Although he looked strange at first, Mark thought he was very distinguished looking in his dress blues.

Mark looked around. The church was filling up quickly. He wondered how many people had come here on an average Sunday before The Burst. Probably not that many, he thought. The church was rock, just like the parsonage, and the windows were tall and thin. They were opened on both the top and the bottom and, although it couldn't be called cool, it was comfortable. By the time the service started, the little church was packed, and some people were standing in the back. They sang a few hymns, and then the preacher asked anyone who was there for the first time to stand up and introduce themselves. There were quite a few first timers. The men from Silver Hills all took their turns and introduced their families. The preacher's sermon was short, but to the point. He read from Luke, Chapter 10, and then preached on the Good Samaritan. He related how he'd been saved by a Good Samaritan, just as the man in Christ's parable had.

152

The man who saved him, he explained, had never met him before and wasn't even of the same religion. However, he placed himself in danger to rescue a man he didn't know. Mark noticed Chaparo squirming a little. He thought Chaparo was probably afraid that Brother Bob was going to single him out, but the pastor didn't. He encouraged everyone to be a good neighbor and to help anyone they saw in need. When the service was concluded, he invited everyone to stay for the wedding.

The ceremony was a pleasant affair. Many of the congregation stayed, and some of the other residents from Silver Hills showed up to fill the few empty seats. When the preacher told 'Marcus' that he could kiss his bride, he gave her a little peck. Most of the men from the subdivision, including Mark and Jim, whooped it up when that happened. Abby blushed at all of the hollering, but Gunny just stared out into the crowd, his eyes like diamond-tipped drill bits.

The reception was enjoyable, with everyone eating cake and drinking punch. Mark visited with some church members he didn't know. Most of them had heard about his shootout with the men who had attacked their preacher. They were all grateful to Mark and his friends for saving Brother Bob, and some were even curious to hear firsthand of the battle that took place on Friday. Mark was polite and gave them an abbreviated version of the story. One of the men told him that he used to be an insurance salesman. He was gabby enough to be an insurance salesman, Mark thought. The man, whose name was Will Henson, had retired last year and bought a Christmas tree farm. It was just a few miles south of the church and was about a hundred acres. Now, he said, if the lights don't come back on soon, there'd be no way to sell the trees. He said that instead of selling life insurance all those years, he should've sold light insurance.

Christmas tree farm, Mark thought. "You don't have a tractor, do you?"

"Yes, it came with the farm," Will replied.

"Will it run?" Mark asked optimistically.

"No. If it would, I'd be driving it instead of riding my bicycle," the salesman grinned.

"How old is it? Do you think we might be able to find the parts in town to fix it?" Mark rapid fired the questions. He then explained their problem at the subdivision.

"You should be able to find the parts. It's only a few years old. I'm just not mechanically inclined. If you want to look at it and try to fix it, just come on by. If you can get it running, you're welcome to borrow it."

Mark asked the man if first thing tomorrow would be okay. He said yes, and Mark shook his hand enthusiastically.

About three o'clock, the celebration started winding down. A little later, everyone headed home, including Gunny and Abby.

This marriage had a benefit Mark hadn't realized until just now. Gunny was now a resident of Silver Hills.

153

Chapter 25

On the way home, Jess mentioned to Mark and Jim that some of the other neighborhood women had heard them talk about the shooting lessons they were to have after the meeting. She said that a couple of them were also interested, and that she and Lisa had invited them to come over. Jim said that was no problem, as teaching six or seven wasn't much more work than teaching four.

When they got home, Mark went out to check the water temperature on his shower. Since the water had been heating all day in the sun, it was very warm. Mark figured it was a good thing he hadn't painted the barrels black, or the water may have been too hot to bathe in. He could paint them later in the season if the days shortened up enough that it became necessary.

George had gone across the street to check on the guys who were finishing the tilling, and Mark walked over to see how it was going. When he got across the street, he could see that only one tiller was running. George and some other men were bent over the other one.

"What happened?" Mark asked.

George looked up, and the look on his face wasn't good. "Looks like we broke the drive chain."

"Can we fix it?"

"Maybe, but it chewed up the gears pretty good when it broke. We really need new parts."

"We can try to find some, but I wouldn't hold my breath," Mark warned. "If we can't, where does that leave us?"

"Well, it blows our plans to be finished with this lot by day after tomorrow. We were planning on starting the next lot after this, but it'll take at least a full week with only one tiller. We may want to get the individual gardens going first. I just hope you can get that tractor from the Christmas tree farm running. That'll solve all of our problems."

"I hope so, too, George."

"We're going to take this thing down to Chaparo's and see what he thinks about fixing it. I'll be back at the house after that."

When they went down to Jon's for the meeting that evening, there must have been at least three hundred people at the meeting. He wondered what the population of Silver Hills was up to. George reported the bad news about the tiller, and Chaparo said that he might be able to fix it. Mark told the group that he was going to look at a tractor tomorrow and see if he could get it to run. Mark was thinking he could use some help with the mechanics. Maybe one of the newcomers had some experience that could help them. He asked the question, and a man held up his hand and introduced himself.

His name was Bill Evans. He was Scott Simmons' brother-in-law, and he'd worked as a mechanic in a garage when he was younger. Mark asked him if he'd be willing to go look at the tractor tomorrow. He agreed, and Mark told him to be at his house at eight o'clock.

Jon then brought up the topic of limiting the amount of people in the subdivision again. Although some people agreed with him, the majority did not. Jon became visibly hostile.

"So what are we going to do? Let people move in here until we have no room to move or to grow enough crops? How many do you all think we can support? A thousand? Ten thousand?"

Mark stepped up to the front and spoke. "Jon, I think we all understand your concern, and you're right in that we cannot support an unlimited number of people, but shouldn't it be up to each family to decide how many people they want to be responsible for? Besides that, the more people we have, the more work we can get done, and there's a larger pool of skills to benefit from."

"Hear! Hear!" someone in the crowd shouted.

"You tell 'em, Mark!" someone else said.

"Well, I think we need to come to a decision on this. George said we can only feed five hundred, and with one of the tillers broken, maybe we can't even do that," Jon said angrily.

"Jon, that was an estimate. He based that off of only the empty lots. George, do you have any better info for us?"

"We put a pencil to it, and the best that the committee can figure, with the long growing season and good soil we have here, each acre planted should conservatively support fifteen people. We might even stretch that to twenty, but fifteen is a safe number, and the tiller, if we can't fix it, will slow us down, but a tractor puts us back ahead of the game."

"But you don't have a tractor yet! You, of all people, George, know you shouldn't count your chickens before they hatch."

If Jon was trying to get a rise out of George, it didn't seem to work. "That's true, Jon, but we'll turn all of the ground over by hand with spades, if that's what it takes."

"Maybe so, but who knows how long that would take? I think we need to at least put a temporary hold on our population growth until we have a better handle on the food situation. Plus it's getting harder and harder to get everyone to the store. Right, Manny?"

Mark could tell from the look on Manny's face that he didn't like being pulled into this. "Well, it is getting a little more difficult to work out the schedule, but with more trucks now, especially if Mark can get that old International Harvester going, we should be able to take everyone to at least two stores a week."

"Even so, we need to get an idea of what we can do before things get out of hand. I make a motion that we temporarily limit each house to ten people, or if it's already over ten, to its current number."

Everyone just looked around to see if anyone would confirm the motion. "I second it," a voice finally called out from the back.

"All those in favor?" A few meek 'ayes' were heard.

"All those opposed?" The no's were strong enough to knock a truck over.

"Wait a minute, only the people who live here can vote," Jon challenged.

"We all live here," someone angrily called out and was acknowledged with some hostile 'yeah's.'

"I mean, only the people who actually own a home here."

"That's not fair. If we're living here and working here, we should get a vote too," one of Manny's relatives yelled.

This was going downhill in a hurry, Mark thought. "I tell you what. How about we let just the homeowners vote and see if the results are any different. If they are, then we can talk about it some more; if not, then all of the arguing is for naught."

The crowd seemed agreeable to trying Mark's solution.

"Okay, then," Mark said. "All homeowners in favor of Jon's motion?"

There were a few scattered 'Ayes' that were perhaps not quite as meek as before.

"All those opposed?"

Even though the vote was closer, it was still obvious the motion hadn't passed. Mark could see that Jon and a few of the others weren't happy.

"Perhaps, there's a compromise we can come to." Mark wanted peace. "George told me that he and the gardening committee are going to talk about getting started on the individual gardens next. I think that's a reasonable approach. Does everyone agree?"

The response was unanimously 'yes.'

"How about we ask them to present us with a plan to do that tomorrow night? But until we know how much of the empty lots we're going to be able to use, we don't count on them. Every homeowner agrees to house only the number of people he can support on his own land. Remember that we may be down to turning the soil by hand if things don't go well, so don't plan on the tractor or even a tiller. In other words, if you invite people to live at your place, you're responsible for them, not the community. Can I make that a motion?"

"I second it," several people called out at the same time.

"All in favor?" The response was deafening.

"All opposed?" No one made a sound.

"Alright, then, does anyone have anything else?" Mark asked.

Everyone was either shaking their heads or shrugging their shoulders. "Then, I guess we're done. David and Sam will pump water for you in a few minutes. The shower water is really warm today. I'd like to give the guys who tilled today first shot at it. After that, I guess it's first come, first served, and one last thing, I'd like for the security committee to meet for a few minutes if that's okay with them." Mark didn't even notice he'd taken control of the meeting.

Everyone headed off in different directions except for the five security committee members. Mark told them that he knew they were going to resume work in the morning, but he asked that they allow him to go check the tractor. They all agreed that the tractor was a priority and told him not to worry about it. He told them he felt bad that he wasn't contributing more and that he especially wanted to apologize to Susan for leaving her to supervise the digging by herself.

"Don't be silly, Mark," she said. "We need that tractor worse than we need another shoveler tomorrow."

Ted agreed. "She's right Mark. We have to get our errands run as soon as possible. Like you said the other day, who knows how long we have until the world blows up. Right now, materials are more important than the work. I'm going back to Poth to get the rest of what we need for the fence in the morning. I got enough donations to get everything we need," he informed the group. Mark appreciated the professor not saying that most of the money had come from him.

"I have a question for Jon," Susan said.

"What?" Jon asked, as though he shouldn't be bothered.

"I was wondering if you'd mind running your guard training program by us." Mark was thankful that someone besides him had asked.

"Why?"

"Because we're a committee. We've run what we're planning by everyone else on the committee. Why shouldn't you let us in on your plans?" she asked sincerely.

"Well, if you must know, we're going to spend the first day doing PT. I need to get these guys into fighting shape. The second day we're going to learn the M-16 weapon system. The third day will be how to stand a post. Then some hand to hand training and some small unit tactics. The last day will be review."

"You're going to do PT all day the first day?" Mark asked with his eyebrows raised.

"Yes. What's wrong with that?"

Jon had just a little more attitude than Mark liked, but he ignored the sarcasm. "Don't you think that's a little excessive?"

"They ran our asses off the first day in the Corps."

"Yeah, Jon, but you were what? Eighteen or twenty? These guys are all middle-aged, and most of them have beer bellies. They won't last thirty minutes," Mark reasoned.

"I know I can't get them into shape in a day. God, I'm not stupid. But they need to be ready to fight if we have another incident. This will be a wake-up call for them. Then I'll get them on a daily work out."

Mark just rubbed his chin. How was he going to get through to this guy? Chaparo had a question too.

"Jon, you said you're going to teach them to use the M-16?"

"Yes."

"But these guys don't have M-16's. Don't you think it would be better to work with them on their own weapons?"

"Do you want me to do the training or not?" It was obvious that Jon was threatened now. "First, you all just let anybody move in here, even if we can't feed them. Then, Mark just takes over my meeting, and now you don't like the way I'm training the guards. Maybe I should just let you all do everything!"

"Jon, that's not what we want. We'd just like to have some input into anything having to do with security, just like you do with what we're working on," Ted pleaded.

"Well, if you want me to do the training, then I'm going to do it the Marine way, because that's the only way I know how!"

The rest of the group just looked at Mark. He knew they would go along with him. He also knew that Jon might learn a lesson if he let him have enough rope to hang himself. "Okay, Jon. You do it the way you think is right. If you need any help, just let us know."

Jon sat back in his chair smugly. Mark figured that he thought he'd won. Maybe his way would work, but Mark estimated his program would self-destruct within two hours of its launch.

"Anything else we need to discuss?" Chaparo asked.

Everyone just shook their heads. "See you all in the morning then."

Everyone headed home. When Mark got there, the kids were in the middle of pumping water. Mark checked the shower line. The line was longer than the water would hold out, he figured. After the guys who'd worked that day, the line consisted mostly of women. Maybe he should try to buy some more barrels tomorrow to make another shower or two. He asked the man who'd just come out how the water temperature was, and the answer was a resounding 'Perfect!' Mark told the women in the line to watch the water level in the barrels. He said that if it got down too low not to risk a shower. He smiled evilly as he explained that if one of them ran out of water in the middle of her shower, there would be no choice but to have one of the other women rinse her off with the cold water out of the hose. There was a collective shiver from all the women, and they nodded their heads as if they had just been told the meaning of life.

Mark could hear the .22's firing, so he decided to go see how the lessons were going. He wanted to check out his Gold Cup anyway. He walked down to the empty lot and was shocked when he saw Jim teaching twelve or fifteen women to shoot. Two women were on the line firing the rifles, and the rest were standing behind watching intently. Jim was standing between the two shooters, coaching them. When they were done firing their strings, two new shooters came up and took their turns. Mark watched in amazement at how quickly the women caught on. When everyone was done, Jim spoke to the whole group.

"I'm sorry that I wasn't really prepared for so many of you. We can pick up again tomorrow night. If you don't remember anything else, remember the four rules of firearm safety."

The women all came up to Jim to thank him and then made their way home. Jess, after thanking Jim, walked up to her husband and told him they wanted him to start a self-defense class for them. He told her that they'd talk about it. Mark walked up to his friend when all of the women had left.

"I thought you were going to have six or seven."

"Me, too. It probably would have been more, but some of the women said their friends wanted a shower just a little more than shooting lessons."

"How many did you have?"

"Fourteen."

"They all seemed to shoot really well."

"Women usually do," Jim told his friend. "They listen better than men do, and they don't have anything to prove. A man's ego usually gets in his way when it comes to shooting instructions. He wants to prove he already knows all there is to know, and that keeps him from learning."

"I've noticed the same thing in teaching karate."

"Funny you should mention that. They were talking about wanting to learn some karate after we finish shooting lessons."

"Yeah. Jess already warned me. Once we get caught up on some of the work, it shouldn't be a problem."

"That'll make them happy," Jim observed.

"And that's the main thing, isn't it? You know what I say…If mama's not happy…then nobody's happy."

"Bubba, you said a mouthful. Now, how 'bout we put that fancy new pistol through its paces?"

"You got it!" The two friends took turns shooting the gun. The Colt had a few hiccups at first, but after fifty or sixty rounds to break it in, it performed well. It was the most accurate .45 Mark had ever seen.

While they were shooting, Mark filled Jim in on the security meeting and Jon's plan for training the guards.

"Why did you give in to him?" Jim asked.

"Because he would have quit if we hadn't. This way, the guards will probably mutiny on him in the morning, and he'll have to change his plan. Maybe it'll teach him to consult us a little more."

"I wouldn't bet on it. I just thank God we're not in his first group."

"Now who said a mouthful?" Mark grinned.

The two men walked back to the house when they finished shooting. Mark noticed that the shower line was noticeably shorter. Sam told him that some of the women toward the back had left when it was obvious there wasn't going to be enough water for them. They all swore to be first behind the men tomorrow, she said. Mark laughed, and then, as he was walking into the house, he saw the other security committee members, less Jon, walking up to his home. They walked up to him, and before he could say hello, Susan spoke.

"Why did you agree to let Jon do the training the way he wants to? You know that dog won't hunt."

Mark smiled big, and she asked another question. "What's so funny?" She didn't seem amused.

"I've just never heard a woman use that phrase before."

"My daddy used to say that all the time. I guess it rubbed off on me," she said with a sheepish smile.

"That explains it," Mark acknowledged. "About Jon, I let him do what he wants because he's not going to listen to us until he fails. Even then he may not, but I'm hopeful he will."

"I see your point, Mark, but I'm getting tired of his shit. I think you should have let him quit." Chaparo was as upset as Mark had ever seen him.

"I was tempted to, but if this thing's going to work, we need everyone."

"We may see that, but Jon doesn't. Why should we do for him what he's not willing to do for others?" Ted argued.

"I know it's hard, but we need to try. If he doesn't come around on his own soon, we'll find a way to get through to him."

"Okay, Mark, you're right. He's just such an ass sometimes," Susan sighed. "By the way, I heard Jim's giving the women shooting lessons. Can I sign up?"

"I'm sure you can. I think he has all he can handle right now, but he's going to do another class after this one. Why don't you go inside and talk to him?"

"Will do." The only woman on the Silver Hills security committee turned and headed into the house.

"You know, Mark, I'd like some lessons, too, but not with the girls," Ted admitted.

"I'm sure we can work something out," Mark answered with a wink.

The three men chatted for a few minutes, and then Susan came back out. The visitors excused themselves, and Mark went into the house. David came up to his father.

"Hey, Dad, guess what today was?"

"What?"

"September first, opening day of dove season."

"Really? I haven't been keeping track of the date too well since The Burst."

"Do you think we can go try to get some birds?"

"David, I know how much you like to go bird hunting, but I don't know how much we're going to be able to do this year. First of all, we have a ton of work to do around here, and second, I don't think we can waste shotgun shells on doves. There just isn't enough meat for the number of shells you have to shoot to make a meal."

"That may be true for you, Dad, but if I shoot like I did last year, then it's worth it, right?" David had finally beaten his old man on the last day of dove season last year. He had limited out, twelve birds, with just seventeen shots. Mark, on the other hand, had shot almost a box and a half of shells, and had only killed seven birds. It was a fact David reminded his father of every time he got a chance.

"Maybe so."

"Then can we at least try to go?"

"We'll see."

David's shoulders slumped at the answer. 'We'll see' almost always meant 'no,' he and his sister often complained. Mark had to admit that they were right. In fact, about the only time that answer ended up meaning 'yes' was when Mark felt guilty about using it too often, as he did now.

Maybe, Mark thought, if they got caught up on the work a little, they could sneak away for a day of hunting.

Chapter 26

Mark ran and did his PT early. He was eating his oatmeal when Bill Evans showed up. Mark offered him some breakfast, and he graciously accepted. Bill told everyone at the Turner house that he'd worked for the phone company for the last twenty-two years. He, his wife, and two teenage children had lived in a small subdivision just inside the city limits. It had been very quiet for the first week. They were within easy walking distance of the neighborhood Kroger, and the neighbors were all watching out for each other. Then, he told them, things had gotten bad in a hurry. A gang was coming through the subdivision everyday and extorting one can of food from each house for 'protection.' A couple of the families refused to pay, and their houses mysteriously caught fire. Another family's seventeen-year-old daughter was 'invited' to join the gang. When her father declined the invitation for her with his shotgun, the gang left, only to return later, kill the father, and force the girl to go with them by threatening to kill the rest of the family. One of the neighbors went to get the cops, but they weren't able to do much. He said that was what made him decide to leave. They packed as much stuff as they could onto their mountain bikes and into some back packs and rode the twenty-odd miles out here early the next morning. Mark wondered how much of that kind of stuff was going on.

Gunny announced that he was going to make two or three runs to his house to finish moving his stuff. Abby, Jess, Alice, and Jim were going to the store. The men had agreed that it was getting too dangerous for the women to go by themselves. Since Jim was going, Lisa was staying home with the twins. Sam asked if she could go to the store with her mom. Mark asked how she was doing on the inventory, and she reported that she was almost done. Mark knew she'd been stuck at home, so he agreed to let her go. David then asked if he could go with his dad and was given permission. Mark, Bill, and David loaded into the Jeep. They first headed to Manny's house to give him the keys to the red truck. When they were heading out, they saw Jon with the first group of twenty guards doing the training in his yard. They were doing pushups.

"Scott was looking forward to his guard training. He said that hopefully it would prepare him in case he was involved in another incident like last week," Bill said.

"I hope he's not disappointed," Mark said.

When the men got to the Christmas tree farm, they were met by Will Henson, who showed them to the barn. The tractor was a Mahindra, which was a brand Mark had never heard of. Will explained that it was made in India. For implements, he had a brush hog, a plow, and a disc parked in the barn beside it. Bill and Mark looked at the tractor and noticed it had a solid-state ignition system. They checked it and found that it was definitely burned out. Bill figured their best shot at the parts was from the dealer, and Will told them that the dealer was in China Grove. They loaded into the Jeep and headed that way. When the four of them got to the tractor dealer, they were elated to see that he was open. They went in, and a large man in shorts and a sweat-stained t-shirt was behind the parts counter.

"He'p ya?" he asked.

Bill stepped forward. "We need all of the solid state ignition parts for a 2006 Mahindra E-350."

The fat man just laughed. "Yeah, right! If things were normal, I could call India and have them here in six, maybe eight weeks. Now, who knows?"

"Is there anyone else in the area who might have them?"

"No. I'm the only Mahindra dealer in South Texas. You boys, along with hundreds of other Mahindra owners, are what I would call shit out o' luck."

"Do you have any tractors that will run?" Mark asked.

"Yeah, I got two. A 1988 John Deere 850 and a 1991 Massey-Ferguson 231."

"Would you rent us one of them?"

The man laughed so hard this time Mark was afraid he might choke. "Son, the only way those tractors are leaving this yard is with a bill of sale. Before long, they're going to be worth their weight in gold. If I rented one out, how do I know I'd get it back?"

"You could come out with it. We'd even pay you to do the plowing for us." Mark suggested.

The fat man found each comment funnier than the last. "Do I look like I want to sit on a tractor all day? If you want a tractor from me, you're going to have to buy it!"

"I'm sure we can't afford it, but how much?" Mark asked.

"Two weeks ago, the John Deere was $6000, and the Massey-Ferguson was $9000, cash. Now I want $2000 and $3000 respectively."

"Two thousand cash for the John Deere?" Mark asked hopefully. They could possibly do that.

"No. Pretty soon cash is only going to be good for kindling fires or wiping your butt. I want $2000 in pre '65 silver coins. Or I'll take twenty ounces of gold. Or I could work out a trade with you. That Jeep, for example, I'll take it and $750 in silver. If you have any guns or ammo to trade, we can work on that, too."

Mark didn't know how those prices related to dollars, but he figured it was way more than they could hope to come up with. "We'll think about it."

"Those prices are only good for today," the fat man called to them as they headed out the door. They climbed into the Jeep, and Mark pulled out of the parking lot.

"I'm sorry. I should have told you the guy was kind of a jerk," Will said.

"You're right; he is a jerk, but he's also right. Our money's worthless, and I'd probably do the same thing if I was him," Mark said.

"What do you mean our money's worthless?" Will asked.

Mark explained that Federal Reserve Notes, the proper name for dollar bills, were not backed by anything but faith in the United States government. They were only worth something because people believed they were. When that faith was gone, then they were only worth the paper they were printed on.

"I thought our money was backed by the gold in Ft. Knox," Bill stated.

"That used to be true, but no longer. Our coins used to be real silver too, but in the 60's they changed them to mostly copper."

"I see. Well, what are we going to do about tractor parts now?" Bill asked.

"I know an auto parts man who might be able to help us. We're going to see him. Say, Bill, do you think there's any way we could convert the ignition over to an old distributor type?"

"Probably not. The engine would have to have a place for the distributor and gears on the camshaft to turn it. Even if it did, and I didn't see it, we'd have to find the exact distributor. I think we'd have better luck finding replacement parts."

"I see what you mean. Well, maybe Rodney can help us."

When the men got to Rodney's neighborhood, it looked deserted. Mark pulled up into the driveway and honked the horn once. He remembered how nervous Rodney was last time, and he didn't want to alarm him unnecessarily. Mark saw the door crack open, and he stepped out of the Jeep with his hands in plain view and waved. Rodney opened the door the rest of the way. Mark noticed that he was carrying a rifle today instead of his shotgun.

"Hey, Mark. What are you doing here? Were the parts you bought Friday okay?" the parts man asked.

"The parts were fine, Rodney. I came because I need some help with a tractor," Mark explained. "That's a pretty serious looking rifle."

"Yeah, well, things are getting pretty serious around here. There have been some shootings, and all the neighbors are pretty much staying in their houses or moving to a relative's house."

"Are you going to move?"

"All mine and my wife's relatives live on the east coast. I presume that it's probably worse where they are than it is here. So we have no choice but to stay put. You said you need tractor help?"

"Yes. We need the ignition parts for a tractor. Think you might have any?"

"What kind and what year?"

"It's a Mahindra, a 2006 model."

"I can't help you. Those Mahindras are made in India on old International Harvester equipment, but the parts aren't interchangeable. In fact, Mahindra parts are difficult to get in the best of times."

"You have any idea where we might find some?"

"Did you try the dealer?"

"Yeah, but he just laughed at us."

"I'm sorry; I just don't know anyone else."

"Thanks. Say, you wouldn't have an alternator and radiator for an IH truck, would you?"

"Sorry, again. I could order those if the phones were working, but those aren't parts I usually keep in stock." Rodney then told Mark they could probably fit an alternator and a radiator out of another vehicle that wasn't running into the old truck. He said to try a GM alternator because it had a built-in voltage regulator. "Those IH trucks are relics. Good solid trucks, but they're getting harder to find parts for. Whose is it?"

"We kind of acquired it after we left here Friday." Mark then went on to tell Rodney about the shootout.

The parts man said that he wasn't surprised. Some of the shootings he'd heard about in town had been pretty severe. Mark thanked the man and shook his hand. Mark asked him if he needed anything and was told no.

"Hey, why don't you and your family come out and stay at our place? We live way outside the city limits, so it's got to be safer than here. We're staying in our RV in the back yard, so there's plenty of room for y'all in the house. Or if you have any camping equipment, you can camp out in the yard."

"Thanks, Mark. I appreciate the offer, but this is our home, and I'm not going to let a bunch of lowlifes run me out of it."

"I understand, but if you change your mind, you're welcome to come out anytime."

Mark explained to his passengers what Rodney had said about the parts for the tractor. It was quiet for several minutes, and then David had an idea.

"Hey, Dad. Remember when we went to that Jeep Camp for vacation a few years ago?"

"Yes, Dave."

"Remember they told us that the first civilian Jeeps had been sold for farm use? And we saw some of the old ones they had there with that hookup thing like are on the tractors. Maybe we could put one of those on our Jeep and plow with it."

"What 'hookup thing' is he talking about?" Bill asked Mark.

"He's talking about a three-point hitch, and he's right. The old Jeep Willys was first marketed to be a multi-purpose farm implement. They came with the three-point hitch and a power takeoff. Maybe Chaparo could build us a hitch, and we could hook up a plow to the Jeep. Will, could we borrow your plow and disc?"

"Sure, they're not doing me any good, and I would assume I could use the Jeep from time to time if I needed to plow?"

"Absolutely."

"Then, I reckon we got ourselves a deal," the retired salesman said with a million-dollar smile.

Mark drove to where Jim had told him the barrel man had his business. When they got there, a high, chain link fence surrounded the large lot. Mark could see all types of barrels stacked through the fence and a trailer like they use for an office at construction sites. The heavy gate to the lot was closed, but it had a sign that said 'Honk for Service' on it. Mark tapped his horn. What happened next would have caused him to leave as fast as possible two weeks ago, but now it intrigued him. The door on the office trailer opened a crack.

"Are you here to buy some barrels?" a voice called out from inside.

"Yes," Mark called back.

"Good. In a minute, I'm going to come out to open the gate. You are going to be covered by rifles. Any funny business, and they'll shoot first and ask questions later. Do you understand?"

"Yes," Mark answered, as he saw rifles appear in two of the widows of the trailer.

A short man came out of the door and nervously jogged to the gate, his eyes glancing from side to side. Mark could see a big revolver on his hip. He unlocked the gate, opened it, and waved them in. Then he closed and re-locked the gate, while keeping one eye on the Jeep.

Mark slowly got out. The short man walked up to him and asked what he needed. Mark noticed that the man was a little shorter than he was and that his revolver had a very long barrel. It hung down almost to the man's knee and looked a little comical. Mark thought that it probably wouldn't seem too comical if you were staring down the business end of the monster gun.

"I need four 55-gallon water barrels," Mark told him.

"How are you going to carry four in a Jeep?"

"We're going to put the top down and tie them to the roll bars."

"OK. They are $40 each. Cash only or trade."

"I was told they were $20 each last week," Mark said.

"That was last week. Now they're $40."

Mark didn't want to pay that much. He knew that this guy knew Gunny. Maybe dropping a name would get him a little discount.

"Well, Gunny Pickwell told me to come see you if I needed any barrels, but I don't know if I can afford $40."

"You know Gunny?" The man's attitude changed completely at the mention of the old soldier's name.

"Yes, he's a friend of mine." This was working, Mark thought. "In fact, he lives down the road from me now."

"How is that old shrapnel magnet doing?"

"He's good. He got married yesterday."

"Married? I'll be damned. I thought that ol' boy would never be married to anything but the Corps."

"How do you know Gunny?" Mark asked.

"He was my platoon sergeant for my first tour in 'Nam. Saved my ass more times than I can remember. I was just a kid in '67 and didn't know squat about nothing. He was an old man, even back then, and what he taught us kept us alive. Even the LT did what Gunny said. I got reassigned for my second tour, and we lost track of each other. I ran into him at a unit reunion in D.C. a few years ago, and we found out we'd been living in the same town for years." The man stuck out his hand. "Breezy. Breezy Cunningham's my name."

Mark grabbed and shook it, as he wondered where the man had gotten that nickname. "Mark Turner."

"Pleased to meet you, Mark. Any friend of Gunny's is a friend of mine. That'll be $15 each for the barrels."

"Thanks, Breezy," Mark said, as he counted out sixty dollars. "I'll tell Gunny you said hello."

"You do that. If you need anything else, just come on back."

"Will do," Mark said, as he and his passengers lowered the soft-top and tied the barrels to the Jeep.

The trip home was uneventful. They dropped Will off at his house and told him that they'd be by with a trailer to pick up the plow and disc when they had the Jeep ready. They were back to Silver Hills by eleven o'clock. When they pulled in, they saw that work on the security arrangements was progressing nicely. Ted was back with his fencing supplies, and Susan was down in the ditch with her guys, digging. The gate was hung, and the guards on duty had opened it when they saw the Jeep coming. Mark, David, and Bill waved as they passed, and then they dropped by Chaparo's to talk to him about the three-point hitch. He thought he could rig something up without too much work. He asked Mark if that should come before the repair to the tiller or after. Mark asked how long each would take.

"I think I can fix the tiller in four or five hours. I'll need to go look at the hitch on the tractor to get the measurements, but I could probably have it done in two days, three tops. I need to borrow your generator for both projects, though," the big man said.

"No problem, just come and get it. I'd try to fix the tiller first. After that, you can take the Jeep to go over to the tree farm. One of us will show you where it is and introduce you to Will."

"Sounds good."

Mark also asked Chaparo if he had any more showerheads and pipe to make two more showers. He did, and he told Mark just to let him know when to come by and plumb them. As Mark was ready to leave, four men came up to the Jeep.

"Mark, you have to do something about Jon," Scott Simmons said grimly.

"He's trying to kill us," Charley Henderson added.

Mark and Chaparo just looked at each other.

"I want to be a guard and help out, but I didn't sign up for this shit!" another man said.

"What happened?" Mark asked. He already knew the answer, but he needed to let the men vent.

"When we got to Jon's house this morning, he said we were going to do some PT first. I thought that was a good idea. We could all probably stand to be in a little better shape. He had us do some jumping jacks, push-ups, and sit-ups. A hundred of each. It was hard, but we all did our best. Then, we started running through the neighborhood. Up and down every street. If someone fell behind, he started yelling at them, telling them they were a no good piece of shit and stuff like that. Joe Bagwell was the first one to get fed up. You know Joe; he's the real chunky guy who lives in the front? Well, he got tired of Jon yelling at the top of his lungs, mostly at him since he was having the most trouble keeping up, and he told Jon to go…" Scott's eyes glanced David's way. "…well, to go and, you know, to have knowledge of himself…in the biblical sense…you know?"

"I see," Mark said. "Then what?"

"Then he started on the next slowest guy. Asking him if he was going to effin quit like Baby Joe did. After two or three guys had enough, we all just told him to get lost, so to speak. He went back to his house hollering how we all better get our attitudes right and show back up tomorrow morning, or we'd be kicked out of the guard program."

"Don't worry about it. We'll talk to him and get it straightened out," Mark promised.

The four men thanked Mark and Chaparo and walked off.

"You want to talk to him now?" Chaparo asked.

"I was thinking maybe we should wait until Gunny's back and take him with us. He's the only one Jon even comes close to listening to."

"Sounds like a good idea to me."

Mark drove Bill back to Scott's house and asked him if he'd try to fit a radiator and alternator into the IH truck. Bill said he'd be glad to work on it. He asked about a windshield, and Mark suggested that, when it was running, he could take to a junkyard and try to find one for it. When Bill was getting out of the Jeep, he asked Mark a question.

"This morning when I told you Scott was looking forward to his guard training you said something like 'I hope he's not disappointed.' You knew this was going to happen, didn't you?"

"Let's just say I had a hunch. I hoped I was wrong, but we had to give Jon a chance. Don't worry; we'll get it fixed somehow."

"I'm glad it's you and not me."

"Why do you say that?"

"Because he's been acting like a big shot since I got here. Scott was his friend, but he told me he can't stand Jon anymore, and that was before what happened today. Somebody needs to feed that boy some humble pie. I know if I was in your shoes, I'd kick his ass up between his shoulders."

"Well, let's hope it doesn't come to that," Mark said, laughing, as he put the Jeep in gear and eased out on the clutch.

Mark and David pulled into the house and went in to check on Lisa and the twins. The shoppers weren't back, but Mark didn't expect them this early. They ate lunch, and then Mark asked David if he wanted to come help dig the ditch. David was excited to be asked to help, and the two of them changed clothes and headed down to the front. As Mark dug, his mind raced from subject to subject. He thought about what they might say to Jon to get his attention. The men and Susan finished the ditch to the west of the entrance and started working on the east side. They were making good progress. The hard work was a welcome relief to Mark, even if it was hot and humid.

A minute later, he saw Gunny and Abby drive in. He'd already spoken with Susan and Ted about what had happened, and they agreed that Chaparo, Mark, and Gunny should handle it. They thought that any more than three on one would probably upset Jon even more. Mark excused himself and headed up to Abby's house. When he got there, he spoke with Gunny about the problem. They headed to Jon's and picked up Chaparo on the way. Mark asked Gunny if he was through moving, and the old Marine said he needed to make one more trip. Mark told him that he'd met Breezy.

Gunny laughed. "That boy saved my whole squad's bacon one time," the old Marine said, as they reached Jon's house. "Remind me to tell you the story some time."

"I knew you guys would be coming to see me," Jon said, opening the door before they knocked.

"How'd you know that?" Chaparo asked.

"Because the guys all quit today, and I knew you'd come over to gloat, but I told them to be back tomorrow to continue training. I think I got their attention now, so they know what I expect. They'll do better tomorrow."

"Jon, we're not here to gloat, and the only way they're going to do better is if you do better," Mark said.

"What does that mean?"

"It means you can't treat them boys like raw Marine recruits," Gunny said. "You were treated that way when you joined up because you were a wet-behind-the-ears wannabe bad ass. The DI's had to tear you down 'n' teach you some respect 'fore you would learn. These men have all had families and

169

responsibilities for years. They already know about respect, and they deserve yours. If'n you don't treat them with the respect they deserve, they won't respect you or learn nothin' from you."

"They don't have to respect me to learn from me. They just have to listen to me and do what I say," Jon argued. "We can't afford to have soft guards if we get attacked. I'm going to tell them that tomorrow and make them understand. I'll back off a little on the PT until they get up to speed, but they're going to have to commit themselves to train hard."

"Jon, did you hear a word Gunny said? You have to change your method. We've talked about this, and we agree that what you're doing is going to drive these guys off. We need them more than they need us," Chaparo pleaded.

"What do you mean, you've all talked about this?" Jon demanded.

"The committee discussed what to do after several of the men came and talked to us about today," Chaparo answered.

"I knew you all were talking about me behind my back, and I knew you'd stab me in the back, too." Jon was really red in the face now. "Well, if you don't like the way I'm doing it, then I quit your little committee. You can find someone else to do your training, and while you're at it, you can find somewhere else to have the daily meetings, too."

"Jon, that's not what we want. We just want…" Mark was interrupted.

"I don't give a rat's ass what you want. You stabbed me in the back. Well, I'm not going to play your little games, Mr. Black Belt. Now if you'll excuse me, I have things to do."

Mark was shocked that Jon had blown up so quickly. Chaparo looked like this had taken him by surprise, too. Mark couldn't tell about Gunny; he had too much of a poker face. Mark decided to try one more time.

"Jon, I'm sorry we've upset you. That was not our intention. Remember when you asked me not to move away? You said we balanced each other out and that you needed me to stay here to help you. Did you mean that?"

"Yes," Jon answered shortly. Mark still thought it was just because of his truck, but he wasn't going to call the man a liar.

"Well, you may not know it, but we all need each other to balance the group and help each other. That's what we're trying to do here." The little that he seemed to be getting through to Jon stopped abruptly with the last sentence.

"No. You're not trying to help me. You just want me to do things your way. Well, I say, screw you and the horse you rode in on. I do the training my way, or I don't do it. It's as simple as that."

It was pointless to argue any more. First of all, Jon wasn't going to listen. Second, Mark knew he wouldn't be able to hold his own temper. "Alright, Jon. I'm sorry you feel that way. We'll see you later." Mark stood up and walked out the door. Gunny and Chaparo followed.

Gunny was the first to break the silence. "That boy is what we use to refer to as a popsicle. 'Course we us'lly used it for officers who thought their shit didn't stink."

"A popsicle, Gunny? How do you get that?" Chaparo asked.

"He's as cold as ice and got a stick up his ass."

Chaparo and Mark snickered quietly, as they were still close to Jon's house.

170

"Well, what do we do now?" Mark asked the other two men. It was mostly a rhetorical question.

"Let's get Susan and Ted and talk about it," Chaparo suggested.

The three of them walked down to where the work was going on. The four remaining committee members nominated Gunny to take Jon's place. Gunny said he'd be glad to help however he could. They asked if he could take over the training of the guards. He said he'd be glad to coordinate the training, and while he would do a lot of the teaching, he'd need help with some of the training. He said that he wanted Jim to head up the firearms training and Mark to do the hand to hand training and the PT. Mark asked if Gunny intended to run the guys like Jon did. He said no, but that the guards did need to improve their conditioning, just not all in one day. Mark agreed to hold the evening meetings at his house, at least temporarily. Everyone was used to coming there for water anyway, he said.

The group broke up, and everyone returned to their duties. Mark climbed back down into the ditch and started digging again. Susan came up and told him that David was working as hard as any of the men. Mark looked over at his son. He was digging hard. David always could work hard, and he seldom complained. That is, until it came to his schoolwork. Mark laughed to himself. He'd have to find a special reward for David. He turned his attention back to his digging. With each shovelful, he felt his frustration with Jon slipping away.

Chapter 27

By the time the meeting in Mark's front yard rolled around, most everyone had heard about what happened with Jon. The news hadn't brought them any new subjects to discuss, just a couple more east coast cities under martial law, so the main topics were the tiller and the guard training program. Mark asked George and his committee to present their plan for tilling the private gardens.

George started out with some good news. Chaparo had fixed the broken tiller. He'd used a motorcycle chain and machined new drive gears. Chaparo had warned them they needed to be careful, as he didn't think the new chain and gears were quite as strong as the old ones. George announced they had over half of the five acre field ready and that they'd begin planting it in corn soon. He then broke the bad news that they had been unable to get the tractor at the tree farm to run. He did tell them Chaparo was working on a hitch, so that perhaps plowing could be done with Mark's Jeep, but it would be a few days before they knew if that would work. He then went on to explain they had moved the working tiller to till the private gardens of the three people who had lent their tillers to the neighborhood. He explained that it only seemed fair to take care of these people first. The committee's plan for the other forty-four households was to hold a lottery. Each homeowner would, if the group accepted this plan, select a number from one to forty-four. Then they would till about a quarter acre for each in the order of their numbers. George figured they could have everyone's first plot tilled in ten or twelve days. Then when they got done with the forty-fourth person, they would start over with number forty-four and work their way back down to one doing another quarter acre, and keep going like this until everyone had the land they wanted tilled. Then they'd move back to work on the empty lots. The community voted on and accepted the gardening committee's plan. George announced that they already had numbers in a hat, and that the homeowners could pull them as soon as the meeting was adjourned.

Mark then spent a few minutes explaining that Jon had decided not to run the guard training program. Gunny would be taking over that, along with the scheduling, and would all the guards please report to him after the meeting for instructions. When Mark announced that he'd be working on two more barrel showers tomorrow, a huge cheer went up. No one had anything else, so the meeting was adjourned.

Mark asked Jess to pull their number, and she drew twenty-eight. Gunny asked Mark to meet the trainees at eight o'clock at Abby's to stretch them out and give them a very light workout. When all of the chores were done, everyone played games for a while and then went to bed.

When Mark woke up the next morning, he found that it was drizzling. He skipped his run since he'd be working out with the guards in a while. Gunny and Abby came over for breakfast and made an offer to George and Alice. They asked the displaced couple to move into the guestroom in their house. The Garretts graciously accepted, and since all of their possessions had burned, they moved with one quick trip after breakfast. Mark thought it was very generous of the newlyweds to offer to share their home. It would also help Jim and Lisa to have a little more room and privacy in their camper.

Gunny, Mark, and George all had duties that prevented them from going to the store today, so Jim was elected to lead the same group to the store as yesterday. Sam decided to stay home and finish her food inventory. Chaparo came by to pick up the Jeep. He and Bill were going to look at the tractor, and then he was going to work on the three-point hitch. Manny also came by to pick up a truck to take the shoppers to town. George headed out to start on private garden number one, and Gunny and Mark went to meet the guards.

Mark did a long, slow, stretch out with them. Most were quite sore from the day before, and Mark could smell the Ben-Gay when the breeze blew in the right direction. Then he had the men do a few pushups and sit-ups. They also slowly ran half a mile and then walked about half a mile. Most of the men said they were feeling better by the time they were done, and they thanked him.

Mark then went back to the house to work on the other two showers. He decided to put them right beside the first one. He and David got the barrels up on the roof and then started improving the shower stalls and building a bench inside each one. When that was done, they went by Chaparo's and told him that the showers were ready to be plumbed and asked him to please fill the barrels before he got the generator. He told Mark he would. He said Will had agreed to let him take the hitch off of the tractor to use on the Jeep. All he had to do was machine the mounts and figure out a way to raise and lower it. He said he might have it ready by Wednesday. Mark bragged on him but reminded him that the fence crew was depending on him for some metal posts to finish the fence and the big pipes to block the drive. Chaparo said he'd get those done first and then get back on the hitch.

Mark and David walked on down to the entrance and helped dig some more. The ditch was almost done, and Susan, with Gunny's help, had marked where the other foxholes should go. When the men had finished the ditch and had gone back over the few spots Gunny thought needed attention, they started on the foxholes. While Mark was digging, one of the guards came up to him.

"Mark, there are some people at the gate asking if we could give them some food," the guard said.

Mark put his shovel down and walked to the gate with the guard. When he got there, he saw two young couples with five children ranging in age from about three to ten. All of the adults and the three older children had backpacks. The two men were also carrying a large duffel bag each. The two smaller children were being pulled in a small wagon by one of the women. The other woman was pulling a larger wagon that was full. Mark introduced himself and asked where they were going. One of the men told Mark they had a friend with about forty acres in Gonzales. He went on to explain that they were neighbors in an apartment complex and that it was getting too dangerous to stay there. They'd decided to walk to their friend's place, hoping to cover the seventy-odd miles in three days. They'd only made about twelve miles yesterday and were going even slower today, as everyone was sore. The group had brought enough food for four days, one more than they thought they'd need, but now it looked like it might take six or even seven days to get there. He asked if anyone could spare any food to help them. Mark called David over and asked him to run up to the house and get three pounds each of beans and rice and six large cans of fruit. While David was gone, Mark and the guards chatted with the travelers about conditions in town. They told the same types of stories that Mark had been hearing from others. David was back in a few minutes with a grocery bag in each hand. He handed the food to the man who had done most of the talking, and they all thanked Mark and the others and started moving slowly east.

Mark and David went back to the foxholes. There were four to be dug, and they were big enough for six or seven men each. With the amount of men who were working, they had them finished in just a few hours. Mark looked at his watch. It was a little after four. It had stopped drizzling around lunchtime, but the sky was still cloudy. It wasn't as hot as it had been, but it was extremely humid, and all of the diggers were covered in dirt and sweat. Susan told the men that they were done for the day. She told them she might have some more work for them tomorrow. Mark told the men that the old shower should be hot enough that if they wanted to use it now, they were welcome to it.

Mark and his son walked back to their house. On the way, they stopped by the house where George was supervising the tilling. Mark asked him how it was going and his answer was 'Not bad.' He explained that the tiller Chaparo had fixed had a tendency to throw the chain if they got it going too fast, so they had to keep it under half speed. George told him it looked like they'd get two plots done with the good tiller, and one or one and a half done with the repaired one, not the five he'd hoped. He explained to Mark that he needed more men. A couple of his guys had been working all day with only the breaks he made them take. Mark told him they were through with the ditch and the foxholes, so they could probably send some men to help with these jobs tomorrow. George also expressed concern that most of the residents didn't have any seeds to plant. They needed to go back to the feed store and get what everyone wanted, if possible.

When Mark got back home, the shoppers were back, and the women were fixing dinner. Sam was adding what they'd bought into her inventory. Mark asked her how they were looking as far as food went. She said her figures showed that they could eat pretty well for eleven weeks. After that, it would be mostly beans and rice every day for another five weeks before they were completely out of food. Mark thought that was good. He felt they needed to talk about whether to buy more beans, rice, and other staples for a longer period, or to buy more variety for another few weeks. He wished now that they'd kept a few months' worth of food stored, or even a year as he'd heard Mormon families did. He certainly could see the wisdom in that now.

Jess asked if they could use the generator to wash and dry couple of loads of clothes. Mark told her that Chaparo was using it, but when he brought it back they were more than welcome. He asked if they could hang the clothes out to dry, instead of using the generator for that. She said they could, but they would need to wash early in the morning, so the clothes would hang long enough to dry. Jim suggested that some of the less dirty clothes could be washed and rinsed in the tub they'd bought to further save on fuel for the generator. The girls reluctantly agreed to try a load or two that way tomorrow.

Mark wanted to check on the showers. He found that Chaparo had plumbed and then filled the two new ones. Mark checked the water temperature in all three. The old one was lukewarm. The other two were just warm enough that the water wasn't chilly. Without the sun shining directly on them, the barrels seemed to heat up only a little more than air temperature. Well, he'd have no problem with anyone staying in too long today, he thought. A few of the men were walking up to use the shower, and he suggested that they use the middle one.

He walked over to the camper and prepared to take a shower himself. He turned on the water heater and heard the welcome 'woosh' of it igniting. It would take twenty minutes or so for the water to warm up. He wondered how much gas was left in the camper's tanks. He went outside to check, but he saw Gunny and Abby holding hands and walking up. He went over to talk to the old Marine about how the training went. Gunny told him it had gone well. He had covered all of the SOP's for standing watch at a gate. He then walked the men through several scenarios and had them role play. He said he let them come up with some of their own scenarios and work out the best solutions. Gunny said that Scott was the best student in the class and that he wanted to talk to the security committee about changing the guard schedule and appointing some captains. He felt they were going to need more than two men on duty if things got worse in town. He'd heard about the refugees that had passed today and told Mark that they would be only the first of many, and they wouldn't all be as polite as the ones today were. Mark said they needed to meet anyway to discuss the next phase of their security arrangements. He asked Gunny what he had planned for the men tomorrow and was told that Jim was going to work with the men on their shooting skills in the morning. He thought he might give them the afternoon off, since he needed to see what other arrangements they planned to make in order to tailor his program properly.

Mark excused himself to take his shower, and Gunny headed up to the house to talk to Jim about what he wanted him to do tomorrow. Mark was glad they had Gunny. Without him, they wouldn't have had any idea of what to do for security. Thank God for George, too, and where would they be without Chaparo? Mark was thankful for so many people, even Todd and Mr. Davis. Without them, he wouldn't have had the means to buy some of the things they so desperately needed. When he got out of the shower, he dressed and headed into the house. Jess came up and kissed him, now that he was clean. Maybe, he thought, that was a hint they should spend the night inside the house again. She then chased David out to take a shower before dinner. The teenager argued for a brief moment that he didn't need one, but when his mother put her hands on her hips and cocked her head to one side as she gave him 'the look,' he dropped his head and headed for the camper.

Dinner was the last of the deer meat from the freezer. The news came on and reported that three people in town had been arrested for watering their lawns. The radio said they faced a $5000 fine and sixty days in jail. 'Great,' Mark thought. There were murderers, rapists, and thieves running loose all over town, and the police were arresting water wasters. A thought flashed through his mind that the report might not be true. It could be just a scare tactic to stop people from wasting water. Either way, it probably would get people's attention. Several more cities were named off as now being under martial law. The list was getting so long that Mark didn't really even pay attention to the names of the cities anymore. The water board announced that they needed to do more maintenance, so the 7 to 7 no water rule was in effect again tonight. When the President came on, the only real news he had was that he was cutting back on his daily broadcasts. Now, unless there was something urgent, he would only have his little chats with the country on Tuesdays and Saturdays. He signed off without even mentioning the power. Five minutes later, people started showing up for the meeting.

Mark started the meeting by asking the gardening committee to give a report. The five-member committee moved to the front and asked George to speak.

"We finished planting corn in the part of the back lot that's ready. We could use some more volunteers for tomorrow. We also finished tilling the first three private plots today and have about a half of another one done. We'll pick up again tomorrow. We really need more help with the tilling, especially in the afternoon when it gets hot. I don't like for the guys to work more than twenty minutes at a time when it's really hot. If you can help, even for just a twenty-minute shift, it would be appreciated. We also need to buy the seeds for the private gardens. If you're not sure what you need to plant, please come see one of the committee members after the meeting, and we'll help you plan what you need. We want to make a run to the feed store tomorrow and pick up all the seeds everyone needs, so please get your order in with us tonight."

A hand went up, and George pointed at the woman. "What if we don't have enough money to buy the seeds we need?"

"Go ahead and order what you need. We're asking everyone who can to pitch in a little extra to help those who don't have the cash. If we don't have enough money, then we'll get as much as we can," George explained.

"So, if you can't buy everything, are you going to take some of my seeds that I paid for and give them to someone else?" a man in the back asked.

"No. If you pay for seed, you'll get it, but remember, we're all in this together," Mark interjected. "It behooves us all to make sure that everyone here has enough food. So, if you can spare anything, please help out your neighbors."

"Any other questions?" George asked.

When no one had any other questions, Mark asked for a report from the security committee. Chaparo got up and told everyone where they were with the preparations for the front of the subdivision. The ditch was dug, and so were the foxholes. The gate was hung, and the fence was coming along. He told the residents that the security committee was meeting tonight to discuss what they should do next.

When Chaparo was finished, Mark asked if anyone had anything else. Two people raised their hands. One was Bill, the mechanic, and the other was Sherry Henderson. Mark called on Sherry first.

"I'm becoming concerned about how much school my kids are missing. I was thinking maybe we could get another committee formed to look at how we can educate our children if the lights do stay off for an extended period."

A murmur of approval spread through the crowd. Someone seconded the motion. Mark asked for a vote, and it was almost unanimous. Then he asked for nominations to the education committee. Someone nominated Jess right off the bat. Then Ted was nominated. He tried to get out of it, since he was already on another committee, but the crowd wouldn't let him out. Someone said they'd heard that Lisa homeschooled her girls, and she was nominated also. Mark asked if anyone else wanted to help and two other women, one of them Sherry, raised

177

their hands. Mark asked them when they wanted to meet, and they agreed on the following day since Ted had his security committee meeting tonight.

Mark asked Bill what he had, and the former mechanic reported that the IH truck was now in running order. Mark asked if he'd found a windshield, and he said that while he couldn't find the exact windshield, he'd found a piece of Lexan and made one that covered all of the opening except for just a little on each side where the old windshield curved. He'd screwed the clear plastic down and duct taped the ends where needed. He warned everyone that no abrasive cleaners were to be used on it, and said that even the windshield wipers would scratch the plastic windscreen. Everyone seemed pleased to have another truck in Manny's fleet of grocery getters.

When the meeting was adjourned, everyone stayed around and chatted and then got their water. Mark noticed that while Jon and his family were absent from the meeting, his wife did come by to get some water.

The security meeting took quite a while. Gunny explained that the next things he thought needed to be done were to frame in the foxholes with wood and to put sandbags around them. He had some old canvas sandbags, but they would need to make or find a lot more. Susan suggested that perhaps they could use some pillowcases and fill them with sand, and everyone agreed that was a good idea. Gunny said there was no need to buy sand; they could use the dirt they'd dug up to fill the bags. He also felt they needed to try to finish the fence as quickly as possible. Then he explained how he felt they needed more guards on duty. Ted asked him how many they needed, and he said it depended on what they came up with for watching the sides and back of the property. He said he felt they really needed three at the front, starting tomorrow. In fact, he wanted to put three guys from the class he taught today up front as soon as Jim finished with them. Then he'd train the other twenty for gate duty on Thursday and Friday. He shared his thoughts with the group about the refugees and the danger they posed. The biggest obstacle they needed to overcome was how to call for more guards if the situation demanded it. Not only how, but who, and how they would know where to go. They knew they had a few working CB radios, but that was nowhere near enough to put one in every house. They discussed several options, but none of them seemed like they'd work as quickly as may be necessary, so they agreed to think about it some more. When they discussed how to watch the sides and back of the subdivision, Mark came up with the idea of building towers for the guards similar to elevated deer blinds. He said that a person could make out a deer five hundred yards away from one if they had a clear line of sight. Gunny and the others thought this suggestion had merit. He pulled out the map and put X's where they could put the watch stands. One on each back corner would cover the back and five hundred yards of the sides. One more on each side fence line about four hundred and fifty yards back from the county road would cover the rest of the sides. With two people in each tower and three on the gate, eleven people could cover the entire perimeter fairly well. Everyone started trying to figure out how many men they would need to cover eleven spots, twenty-four hours a day.

Gunny interrupted them. "We'll need more than 'leven people a shift if'n we really want to secure things."

"Why would we need more?" Ted asked.

"At night, nobody's gonna be able to see as far. We oughta have one or two roving teams after dark. That'll give anyone trying to sneak in something to worry about. You'll need two or three men for each team."

The committee members sat silently as they took in what Gunny was saying.

"We also need a way to watch the road in both directions. We shouldn't be finding out that we've got visitors when they get to the gate. A truckload or two of MZB's could be on the guards at the gate before they knew what was happening or had time to call for backup. I walked over to the hill on the other side of the road today and you can see at least a mile in both directions from there. We should put an observation post up on top and man it twenty-four hours a day. Maybe in the mornin', we can all go take a look."

Everyone nodded their head.

"So how many do we need on duty at one time, Gunny?" Ted asked.

"The 'leven perimeter guards, one or two in the OP, and two teams of three rovers…that's up to nineteen men," Gunny answered. "'Course it'll be less in the daytime."

"How are we going to do that?" Mark asked. "Even if we went with eight hour shifts and no days off, that's over fifty men, and if we go with the four hour shifts that Gunny likes, it's more like a hundred. We don't have that many men."

Susan cleared her throat. "Excuse me, Mister Macho, but why do all of the guards have to be men?"

Mark swallowed. "Well, I guess they don't have to be."

"Fuckin' A," she answered. Mark knew she'd used the 'F' word to make a point, a point that was all too clear to the men in the meeting. Mark shifted in his chair during the silence that seemed to last a long time.

"So, Mark, how do you make those towers?" Chaparo asked.

Mark was doubly thankful for Chaparo right now. He knew that Chaparo already knew how to do it, but he drew the welder a picture anyway. Then they talked about where the building of the towers should fit in priority-wise. They all agreed that the fence was first and then the hitch for the Jeep. These could come after that, if nothing happened. Chaparo said he had enough material to build one, but they'd need to buy some more to build the others. He also mentioned that he could use some help. Even if no one knew how to weld, just a go-fer could increase his production. Mark promised to ask for volunteers tomorrow at the meeting.

"Hey, Gunny," Ted asked, "Could we train some of the dogs in the neighborhood to help with the patrolling?"

"That's not a bad idea," Gunny said. "Do you know anyone who has any experience trainin' dogs?"

"No, I don't, but why can't we just put them on a leash, and have them walk around with us? Maybe we could have one at the gate, too."

"Without trainin', they might be more of a li'bility than an asset. What if one of them barks at the wrong time, or gets scared and tries to bolt? The dogs they use in the military go through some very intense trainin' 'fore they get used for any kind of duty."

"We could ask Doc Vasquez if he knows anyone," Susan said.

Everyone agreed that if they could find a dog trainer, and he could successfully train some animals, they would try to incorporate them into their plans. They arranged to meet at the gate to check out the hill at eight o'clock in the morning, and the meeting was adjourned.

Mark and Gunny walked back into the house to have a little meeting with their families about food. After talking it over some, they agreed to try to get up to a year's worth of staples like flour, sugar, and salt. Then they'd try to stock up on things they couldn't grow, like rice and some canned fruits. If they could get to the store enough, then they'd worry about providing variety for their diet. Mark asked if there was anything else they might need to buy before their money ran out. George suggested that they buy a grain mill to grind corn. He said they might even try to grow some wheat, and they could make flour if they had a mill. Gunny was concerned with having enough weapons for all of the guards. Most were using their deer rifles, and while better than nothing, they were too slow to fire and reload. Mark said he could check with Jerry and see if he had anything they could buy. Jess said she'd like to see if they could buy some clothes. Lisa wanted paper and pencils for the girls' schoolwork. Jim said that they could use some AA and D size batteries. Sam wanted to make sure they had plenty of her favorite shampoo, and David was worried if they had enough toilet paper. Everyone agreed that toilet paper was a necessity, and the women put it on their grocery lists for the next day. Since Jim was teaching the guards tomorrow, Mark was going to take the crew to Kroger.

At this point, the family meeting kind of dissolved into multiple conversations going on at the same time. Mark told the other men that they needed someone to help Chaparo with his work. Jim asked if they were looking for any particular skills, and Mark told him that Chaparo would take anyone with welding skills, but he could also just use a go-fer. David, overhearing this, told his father that he'd like to work with Chaparo. Mark told his son he'd talk to Chaparo about it in the morning, but he warned the young man that even if Chaparo said yes, this was not to get in the way of his schoolwork and that he better take his duties seriously. David promised he would.

Mark went to bed that night, in the house no less, feeling pretty good about the plans they'd made but wondering how they would pay for everything they needed.

Chapter 28

The next morning at eight o'clock, the security committee was at the gate. They walked across and down the road a few yards and then stepped over the old fence. The hill was only twenty or twenty-five feet tall and had been cut through about halfway up one side to allow for the road. They walked up to the top and looked both directions. You could see quite a long way in both directions. It would be easy to spot a car from at least a mile up here. The gate was about seventy-five yards away, and this spot gave a commanding view of the entrance to the subdivision. Susan asked Gunny if he wanted a foxhole on top for the lookout. He told her it would be better to move it off of the top and toward the road a little. He explained that it would be too easy to spot someone on the top, but if the Observation Post was moved down so there was something behind the lookouts, it made them much less visible. He explained to her that they wanted to camouflage the OP as much as possible.

The committee members all saw the wisdom in this, and Mark saw how having a guard or two in this position could not only give them some advanced warning of danger, but also give them a tactical asset in case of an attack on the gate. Ted raised the concern that this property didn't belong to them. The members considered that for a moment, but, as far as anyone knew, no one had lived here for at least twenty years. If the owners showed up, they could work out a deal with them then. Until that happened, no one really saw a reason not to build the OP. All of the volunteers had been assigned to George for the day, but Susan said they could get started in the morning. She asked Gunny if he wanted supervise the digging of this hole himself, and he agreed to do it.

On the way back, Mark talked to Chaparo about David, and he agreed to give him a try. Mark mentioned that he and Gunny were going to the grocery store today, and Susan asked if she could go with them. Mark told her to be at the house by 9:30. When he got home, he told David to go on over to Chaparo's and see what he could do to help the big man. Mark and Gunny walked down to see how Jim was coming with the guards. He was going over the basic mechanics of shooting with them. Each guard had brought his own weapon to practice with, and the rifles were all lined up on a folding table while the trainees listened to Jim's lecture. Mark noticed that there were a couple of Mini-14's, an SKS, and a Remington 742 in .30-06. Those were all of the semi-autos. There were seven lever actions, mostly .30-30's, and eight bolt actions. Mark could see what Gunny was concerned about. This was probably a good sampling of the weapons in the neighborhood. While the hunting rifles were powerful and accurate, they couldn't sustain any rate of fire. Once Gunny was satisfied that the class was going like he wanted, the two men walked back to Mark's to go to the store. Mark, Gunny, Abby, Alice, Lisa, and Susan loaded into Mark's truck and headed off to town.

The line at the store was very long. They got there at a little after 10:00, and by the time they all got out of the store it was almost 3:30 in the afternoon. It was funny, Mark thought, to see people standing in line with sack lunches. By two o'clock, when his stomach was growling, he thought it was pretty smart. At least they'd brought some folding chairs to sit in while they waited. People in the line were talking mostly about how the water hadn't come back on until 8:30 instead of 7:00, like the radio had promised. That raised a red flag for Mark. When they had their groceries, they loaded them in the bed of the truck and headed over to Jerry Watson's house.

When they arrived, Jerry asked Mark how he was doing after his shootout. Mark answered that he'd been so busy that he hadn't had time to think about it. Then he introduced the women to Jerry. The gun dealer already knew Gunny. Mark explained they were looking for some defensive rifles for the neighborhood that could be bought on a budget. He asked how many they needed. Mark looked at Gunny, and he said that they could use twenty or more, but if they could get at least ten, that would suffice. Jerry had them drive him across the street to his father's house. He went into the house, and he and his father came back out and led their visitors to the back yard. The older Watson had a large, metal storage building, and he unlocked the huge padlock on the door. Jerry slid the door back, and they went in. Along one wall was a twenty-foot shipping container. Its doors were locked with the same kind of lock as was on the outside door. Mr. Watson unlocked it and then stepped back to let Jerry open them. Jerry took a flashlight and went inside. He brought out two rifles. One was an AK-47, and the other was an SKS. They were both covered in some kind of smelly grease. He explained about the rifles.

"We bought a bunch of these when they were cheap. The AK type is Romanian, and the SKS was made in China. They both shoot the same cartridge. The AK takes removable magazines; I have 30's and a few 40's, and the SKS has a 10-round fixed mag and uses stripper clips. I've seen guys that were good with the SKS reload one faster than you can change a mag in the AK. Both of these designs are reliable and easy to learn. A lot of people don't care for the ergonomics on the AK, but it's a good weapon. The mags are cheap, and so is the ammo."

Mark looked at Gunny. "What do you think?"

"I been shot at wit' both," the old Marine grinned. "I don't really like shootin' either one of 'em. They just feel clunky to me, but I can tell ya, they'll get the job done."

"How much?" Mark asked Jerry.

"The SKS's are $250 each. The AK's are $450, and they come with one 30-round mag. Extras are $10 each. Ammo is $250 for 1000 rounds. It's steel cased, so you can't reload it. I also have some AR-15's, but they're going to be a lot more money."

Mark would have preferred to buy the AK's. He and Jim had looked at the cash they had left last night. They each had just over half the money Todd had given them. They had discussed it with the women and felt they should only spend $5000 on weapons and save the rest for food and other things. If he bought ten AK's and just two extra mags for each one, that wouldn't leave enough money for ammo. He would have to go with the SKS's. He could buy ten of them and a thousand rounds for each rifle and still have some money left. He asked Jerry about the stripper clips.

"They come in packs of twenty. Each rifle comes with one pack, after that, they're three dollars a pack." Jerry answered.

"How many SKS's do you have?" Mark asked.

"Lots!" Jerry answered with a grin.

"Give us ten of them, plus ten extra packs of stripper clips and ten cases of ammo," Mark said.

"Say, Jerry, how would you trade with us for pre-65 silver coins?" Gunny asked.

Jerry looked at his father. "Dad?"

"90% U.S. silver coins were going for $10 to $11 per dollar face value before The Burst," the gentleman explained. "I don't know how much it would be worth now, maybe more, maybe less. I'd bet more, though. I think we could take it at $12 per dollar face."

"If you want to do it that way, let's see...$2500 for the rifles, $2500 for the ammo, and $30 for the stripper clips would be $5030. Divided by 12 would be...call it $419."

"Where are you going to get silver coins from, Gunny?" Mark said.

"Don't you worry 'bout that, Karate Man. Jerry let Mark pay cash for the SKS's. I want to buy a few AK's with silver."

"How many?"

"Three, plus fifteen extra mags and another three cases of ammo."

"Then that would be..." Jerry paused for a second. "...$187.50 in silver."

"That sounds good, but I'll have to go home and get the silver," Gunny said.

"We have to go to the shop for you to fill out the yellow forms on these. Why don't we load them up in your truck, go by the shop, and then I'll go with you to your house to get the money, and you can bring me back. That'll save you a trip."

"Alright," Mark replied.

"I'd like to buy a rifle, too," Susan stated.

Jerry looked at her. "Do you have a Concealed Handgun License?"

"No, but I don't want to buy a handgun. I want a rifle."

"I'm sorry. I can't sell you one because I can't call you in to the National Instant Check system. Mark and Gunny can buy these because they have CHL's and are exempt from the NIC's check," Jerry explained to her.

"Can Mark buy it for me?"

"No, that's called a straw purchase, and it's illegal."

"Well, what can I do?"

"As far as a gun, nothing, but I can sell you all the ammo you want."

"Why would I need ammo if I can't..." A light turned on in Susan's eyes. "If I could buy a rifle, what would you suggest?"

"How much would you want to spend?" the dealer asked.

"No more than I have to, but I want a good one, something easy to learn."

Jerry went back into the container and came out with a hard case. He opened it up and pulled out a brand new AR-15. "This is what I think you would be happy with." He went on to explain the benefits of the rifle.

Susan looked over at Gunny and Mark. They each gave her a nod. "How much?" she asked.

"If Mark wanted it, I would sell it to him for $1000. Extra 30-round magazines would be $20, and ammo is $350 per case of a thousand rounds."

"Can I buy the magazines?"

"Yes."

"Well, then. I want five magazines and two thousand rounds of ammo for an AR. I also want to buy four cases of SKS ammo." She looked at Mark.

"Susan, do you have the cash for that?" he whispered.

"Did you forget where I work? When the lights went out, I withdrew every penny I had in the bank. I have plenty of cash." She smiled at Mark.

"You know, Jerry, I think I would like to have an AR. Could I buy that one and just buy 6 cases of ammo?"

"I don't see why not."

They loaded all of the rifles and ammo into the Ford and headed to the gun shop. Gunny watched the truck while Mark filled out the paperwork, and Jerry went in the back of the shop. He brought out a few old used M-16 magazines that he gave to Susan. He then went back again and brought out a rifle to show to Mark. It was a Century L1A1. "It's basically a cheap FAL assembled from surplus parts. Some people called these 'Franken-FALs,'" Jerry explained, as Mark looked it over. "I know it isn't the quality of the one you lost, but the old boy I got it from said it shot okay. You still have all your mags, right?" Jerry received a nod from Mark. "They'll all work in this one, plus it comes with three. If you want it, I'll sell it to you for $400."

"I'll take it. Thanks."

Finished at the shop, they went home and paid Jerry. Mark asked him if he'd mind sticking around while they had their meeting. He explained to Jerry that he wanted to talk to him but had to be here for a while. Jerry agreed to wait.

The news had been on when they got home, but Mark had missed it. Jess had listened, and Mark asked her if they'd said anything about the water not coming back on at 7 AM. She shook her head and said that the Water Board was turning off the water from 6 tonight until 8 in the morning. She told Mark that the radio had reported more cities under martial law. One of them was the Dallas/Ft. Worth metroplex. That got Mark's attention. The local news was mostly about the people who had been arrested today for either wasting or hoarding water. She stated people were arriving for the meeting, and Mark got them started.

He told everyone about the water not coming back on in town until late today and the extended hours of 'pump maintenance' tonight. He suggested that if anyone really needed any groceries, they get them in the next day or two. Manny said he'd be going to the closest Kroger tomorrow, and with the vehicles he had available, he should be able to take anyone who wanted to go. Mark introduced Jerry to everyone and reported that they'd bought ten rifles for the guards who didn't have any to use. Chaparo reported the posts for the fence and for blocking off the entrance opposite the gate were all set and that the men had started running the barbed wire. They expected to finish tomorrow. He then briefly outlined the security arrangements that had been discussed by the committee. The neighborhood voted on them, and they passed. George informed everyone that the repaired tiller had broken again and that they'd only finished two of the gardens today. He told the group that, in talking with Chaparo, they had decided not to spend any time fixing it so he could concentrate on the hitch for Mark's Jeep. The good news was that they did finish planting the corn in the plowed field and that the committee had been able to get almost all of the seed that had been ordered, thanks to some generous donations. One of the guards reported there had been three groups of people either walking or riding bicycles past the gate today. All had been loaded down, but only one couple had stopped to ask for food. They'd been given a little and sent on their way. Gunny announced that he'd have a short meeting with all of the guards after this one was done. No one had anything else to announce, so the meeting was adjourned.

Mark told his family that he had to take Jerry home, but he wanted to have a meeting with everyone when he got back. Mark and Jerry talked about what had been happening in town. Their stories were similar, but each had a few things the other hadn't heard. Mark asked Jerry if they were having any problems in their neighborhood. He said they really hadn't seen anyone. Even though they lived closer to town than Mark, the road they were on didn't go anywhere. Mark asked Jerry what he thought of the setup they had at Silver Hills. Jerry said it looked like they could handle just about any situation. Mark smiled and then asked what his plans were if things got dicey. Jerry said they were all going to move into his father's house. Mark told his friend they were all welcome to come out and stay with him if they'd like. He told Jerry he didn't think three families would be able to stand up to a big group of outlaws, even with the firepower they had. Jerry laughed.

"When I said we all were going to move to my dad's, I didn't mean just me and Tony. All of my aunts, uncles, and cousins are coming over, too. That would make twenty-nine adults and fourteen kids."

"Will all of you fit in your dad's house?"

"Better than we will in yours. Plus a couple of my uncles have travel trailers we could pull over with the Jeep. We also have some tents and stuff. We'll be fine. It'll be like a big family reunion."

Mark nodded his head as he thought about his family in Waco. "Well, if you need to, the offer stands, for all forty-three of you."

"That's very kind, Mark. Thank you."

"You're welcome, and thank you for helping us out. I know you could have made a lot more on those rifles if you wanted to. You've really been a good friend to us."

"As you have to us."

Once Jerry was dropped off, Mark's trip home went quickly. He passed a few people walking away from town on the county road. He wondered how safe that was. Once the MZB's figured out people were leaving town, it would be really easy to set up an ambush point and rob them.

When he got home, Ted was outside waiting for him. The professor asked if Mark could buy him a rifle like he did for Susan. He said he knew he could use one of the SKS's when he was on guard duty, but he wanted a rifle of his own. Mark told him that just an SKS and a thousand rounds of ammo would be $500 in cash. Mark knew Ted didn't have any cash because he'd had to loan him the money for the parts to get the Trans Am running.

"I know Susan paid $1850 for her rifle and ammo. How much would one of those AK rifles cost?"

"For a rifle and five extra magazines it would be $500, and the ammo is $250 for a thousand rounds."

"So for an AK and two thousand bullets, it would be $1000?" the professor asked.

"Yes."

"And the parts you bought to fix my car, they were around $100, right?"

"That's right." Mark answered, wondering where this was going. He didn't have to wait long for an answer. Ted reached into his pocket and started peeling twenty-dollar bills off of a big wad of money. When he'd counted to $1100, he handed the bills to Mark.

"That's for the car parts, an AK, five extra mags, and two thousand bullets."

Mark was dumbfounded. The words that came out of his mouth were more instinct than a result of conscious thought. "They're not bullets. They're called cartridges or rounds of ammunition. The bullets are the projectiles that are part of the cartridge and that are propelled from the rifle."

"Okay, then, I want two thousand cartridges with my rifle."

"Ted, I thought you didn't have any money!"

"I didn't, but Susan and I came to an arrangement. I sold her half of my car."

"I see," Mark said, even though he didn't. "Either Jim or I will get it for you tomorrow."

"Thanks, and can we get on those shooting lessons ASAP?"

"That's Jim's department, but I'm sure he'll be able to accommodate you."

"Good. Well then, I'll see you tomorrow." Ted left with a spring in his step.

When Mark went into the house, Susan was there, and Jim was showing her how to operate the AR. She must have sensed she was interrupting something now that Mark was back because she made Jim promise to help her sight it in tomorrow and left.

Mark told his family that he wanted them to try and get everything they had to have tomorrow. He said he hoped they still had a few days, but he felt the water situation in town was getting worse and that they couldn't afford to gamble on having more than another day. He asked Sam to give them all an update on their inventory of food. Sam reported that they had eleven weeks' worth of everything they needed. Beyond that, they had enough staples to last another fourteen weeks now. If five people went to the store tomorrow, that should get the staples up to about nine months' worth. Mark thanked Sam for doing such a fine job on the inventory. Then he asked Gunny if there was any way he could go to the store tomorrow. Gunny said he'd given the guards the day off tomorrow after what Mark had said at the meeting. He'd also assigned guards to the gate who'd gone through the gate training already. He also made sure the ones he assigned had wives who could go to the grocery store tomorrow. He told the group that he made a list of the rifles the guards were using and a list of the ammunition each man had. Many of the men had only twenty or thirty rounds for their rifles.

"Some of 'em had a little cash and asked if'n we could pick 'em up some ammo. I tol' 'em we would. However, lots of them boys are tapped out, and if'n we could hep 'em out a little, it'd let 'em use their rifles more, and we can use the ones we bought tonight fer ones who don't have any," Gunny said.

"What do we need Gunny?" Mark asked.

"Here's a list of tha boys who had some money and what they wants, and here's the list of boys that don't have no money and what caliber they's shooting. The number next to the caliber is how many rounds they got now. It'd be nice if we could get upta a thousand fer the boys with the semi-autos and three hundred fer the others. I know that's a lot of ammo, but whatever we can do would be good. I still got some silver I can pitch in."

Mark looked at the lists for a minute. The list of the ones with no money was over twice as long as the list of those who did. He handed them back to Gunny. "Well, you'll probably be going to the Watson's tomorrow after the store, so I'll leave it up to you. I can pitch in a little cash and maybe we can get a little if Jerry's got enough. I also got some money from Ted, and he wants us to pick him up an AK, five mags, and a couple of thousand rounds of ammo." Mark went on to tell the family about Ted selling Susan half interest in his car.

It was agreed that Gunny, Abby, Jess, Alice, and Jim would go to one of the Kroger stores in the morning. Lisa and Mark would try to get the other items they had discussed the night before.

With that settled, Mark asked Jess and Sam how the clothes washing had gone. They were able to get several loads done before David and Chaparo had come for the generator. They ended up washing three loads by hand. Sam asked her father if he remembered what she had said to him when they bought the washtubs. He didn't and asked her to remind him.

"I said it was going to 'bite,' and boy was I right!" she said, as she showed her father her scraped knuckles.

George asked David how it was going with helping Chaparo. David said they'd finished with the pipes for the fence before lunch, and then they'd started on the tractor hitch for the Jeep. He relayed that Chaparo thought they might be done with it by tomorrow night, if all went well. He said he'd learned a lot and really enjoyed the work.

The formal part of the family meeting over, everyone chatted for a while before they headed home or to bed. On their way out to the camper, Mark asked Jess how much she thought they could donate toward ammo for the guards. She felt they'd already gone above and beyond generosity by buying the SKS rifles and ammo. Mark agreed but felt they had to help at least a little. In the end, she agreed to them pitching in $300.

This night, when he went to bed, he didn't feel quite as good about their preparations as he did the night before, and he was even more worried about how long the money would hold out. They were further along than they had been, but something he couldn't put his finger on was bothering him. Whatever it was, it didn't keep him awake for long.

When the alarm went off, Mark decided to sleep a little longer instead of running. He turned the windup alarm clock off and went back to sleep. The next thing he knew, David was waking him up to come eat breakfast, and the clock said 7:45. Everyone ate and then headed off to do their jobs for the day. Sam was watching the twins today, and Mark could tell she wasn't thrilled about it, but there was no one else to do it. He would have to find a way to make it up to her. Mark and Lisa took the Jeep. Chaparo had taken all the measurements he needed, and he wouldn't be ready to start welding on it until late this afternoon at the earliest.

Mark and Lisa had no trouble buying the school supplies and most of the clothing on their list. They bought socks, underwear, jeans, and other sturdy clothing for everyone. They had to look quite a few places to find a grain mill, though. They finally found it at a specialty store that mostly catered to what Mark would call 'health food nuts.' It was expensive, almost $400 cash, but the clerk had said it was one of the best made. It was called 'The Country Living Grain Mill,' and it was built like a tank. The search for batteries, though, was not successful. Mark did find three bottles of the shampoo Sam liked, and he bought them for her. Mark and Lisa got home around two, and after they'd unloaded the Jeep, Mark drove it over to Chaparo's. He told Chaparo and his young apprentice about the people he'd seen walking and biking out of town today. It wasn't a mass exodus, but there were definitely more people leaving than they had seen before. Most were on the highways, and some had tried to thumb a ride with him, but he hadn't stopped. They chatted for a while, and Chaparo showed him the hitch. It was operated with a mechanical high lift jack instead of a hydraulic pump like the tractor had. When Mark saw Jim's Chevy drive by, he excused himself and went to the house.

Gunny and Jim were unloading the ammo, and they filled Mark in on the events of the day. The water in town had come back on later than it did the day before, even though it had been turned off earlier. Jim said the people in town were getting really spooked about not only the water, but the lawlessness that was getting worse. The big story at Kroger was how the police had tried to arrest one of the big gangs that was terrorizing a high-dollar neighborhood. The police had brought the SWAT team in case they had trouble, but they hadn't expected the gang would have over fifty members with guns. The firefight was terrible, but the police, with their training and better weapons were winning, until they ran out of ammunition. Then the gang members who were still alive cut them to pieces. That story made them really think about how much ammo they should buy, Gunny said. Even Jess had told the men to spend whatever they thought was prudent, Jim told his friend. They explained they hadn't been able to get much ammo for the hunting rifles chambered in non-military calibers. They needed .30-30 the most but were only able to get three hundred and sixty rounds. That was all that the Watsons had. They'd gotten two boxes for each rifle in a common caliber, but that was all they could afford of the commercial ammo.

Military surplus calibers were a different matter, though. Jerry had lots of it, and he offered the community a discount since they'd bought so much from him lately. Jim and Gunny took advantage of that. Jim and Mark were carrying the ammo into the shed, and Gunny was separating it into stacks. When they had carried the last of the heavy cases into the shed and the old Marine had told them where to stack them, Jim went back to his truck for a minute. He carried in two AK's and set them on the counter.

"This one is for Ted," Jim explained, "and I got another one." Mark noticed that Jim had a used Glock pistol, too. Jim saw him looking at it.

"It's for George. He lost his guns in the fire, and Lisa asked me to get him a couple. George was too proud to ask. Lisa's mom told her he felt bad he didn't have any guns, and Lisa told me."

"That was nice of you."

"Yeah, I guess. Neither of you can tell him how I found out, though, else I'll have Lisa and her Mom mad at me. I just did it on my own, understand?"

Gunny just grinned as he mimed turning a key on a lock on his mouth. Mark said that his lips were sealed, as well.

"Now, let's just hope we never need any of this stuff," Jim exclaimed.

"You got that right," Mark agreed.

The men went inside and were given the clothing that had been bought for them. Everyone looked at the grain mill. The women were all anxious to try it. Mark wondered how long that would last. No one was really surprised about the shortage of batteries. Mark gave the shampoo to Sam, and she almost had tears in her eyes as she hugged her father. Soon it was time to eat dinner and listen to the news. The national news was mostly about the progress, or lack thereof, toward getting the power back on. It seemed they were working to get one of the largest transformer manufacturers up and running, and the first transformers they produced would go toward getting other plants working. When it came time to announce the newest cities under federal control, the list was longer than it previously had been, and it contained the city of Houston. That meant the two biggest metropolitan areas in Texas were now under martial law. Mark knew San Antonio was the third largest. The biggest local item on the radio was about the water. The newsman reported the big pump the Water Board had been trying to fix at night for several days was still not working like it should. They had announced they were taking it out of service to get it fixed properly. It was going to be off-line for about three days. That meant for those three days, water would be supplied to the city for only four hours a day. Everyone would have pressure from 8 AM to noon. Each household was allowed to store one gallon of water for each person, plus five gallons to use to flush the toilet. The Water Board assured everyone this was temporary, and as soon as the big pump was repaired there would be water pressure twenty-four hours a day.

Jess asked what everyone thought the real deal was on the water. Gunny answered that the Water Board was just looking for some way to keep the water flowing in a reduced capacity without coming right out and saying they can't meet demand. That, he estimated, would start rioting like they had in Cincinnati. The other adults concurred.

The meeting was fairly short. George reported that they finished three gardens today. Chaparo told everyone he had hoped to be finished with the Jeep tonight, but that it was probably going to be closer to lunchtime tomorrow. Ted reported that the barbed wire was all strung on the west side of the gate and the east side was almost halfway finished. Gunny asked the guards who'd been on duty earlier how many groups had come by today. They said there were only two. One large group of twelve to fifteen people on bicycles went by and just waved. A couple on foot had come by, and the man got a little testy with the guards. He was insisting that they be allowed to stay. The guard told him they had to have a sponsor to move in with, and the woman tried to get the man to leave. He started screaming about it being a free country and demanding they be admitted. When the guards in the foxhole pulled their rifles up, the man decided to leave, but he cursed them for a good half mile at the top of his lungs, the guard reported. Gunny wanted to meet with the guards again for a few minutes tonight. Ted reminded the education group they were meeting again tonight, and then the meeting adjourned.

Mark and Jim went to the guard meeting, and Gunny assigned the shifts for tomorrow. He then took all the men to the shed and handed the ammunition each had bought or been given. After they were gone, Mark asked Gunny a question.

"What did you teach the guards to do if someone tried to climb the gate?"

"Shoot 'em," the old Marine said without emotion.

"Shoot them?" Mark must have looked even more shocked than he felt.

"Yes. If'n someone wit' a weapon is coming at cha, you'd shoot 'em, wouldn't cha?"

"But what if they don't have a weapon?"

"Don't matter. If you let them get over the gate and get in scuffle wit' 'em, then they might get your weapon. Then you'd be in a real jackpot, Karate Man."

"I see what you mean, Gunny, but there has to be better solution than shooting an unarmed man."

"Well, Karate Man, maybe you can train the guards in some of that Kung-Fu shit, and we might could 'corporate it into our gate training, but I say a guy who'll climb over a gate when he's got a couple of rifles trained on him has got nuttin' to lose, an' you don't want to get in no fight with a guy who's got nuttin' to lose."

"Well, maybe we can find a solution somewhere in the middle," Mark suggested.

"Maybe so, Karate Man, maybe so."

Chapter 29

In the morning, Mark, Jim, Alice, and Abby left to go to one of the Krogers. When they got to the store, the line was quite short. Mark figured they'd be done in a couple of hours. The people in front of them said that the water wasn't back on when they left their houses. Mark figured most people were waiting at home until the water came on, so they could store the water they were allowed before coming to get groceries. The main subject of conversation in the line was the big shootout between the SWAT team and the gang. Just before they went in, word worked its way up the line that the water had come on at 10:15. Mark looked back and saw a lot of people walking and riding their bikes to the store. Bicycle theft had become such a problem that people took their bikes in with them. They had the clerk push the basket for them while they pushed the bike.

When Mark's crew got out of the store, in a record two hours and twenty-five minutes, Jim suggested they try to find some batteries. Look as they may, there were none to be found. Mark wanted to buy some more barrels. They went to see Breezy and got four more of the blue water barrels. Frustrated by their inability to find small batteries, Mark thought about what Rodney had told him about golf cart batteries. He decided to see if they could find any. They wouldn't help much with flashlights, but they would let him go longer between recharging the campers' batteries. The golf courses they went to were all closed. At the last one he tried, he saw someone over by the office and called to him. The man came over and started to tell Mark the course was closed until the lights came back on. Mark explained they didn't want to play golf. He asked the man if they had any cart batteries they'd be willing to sell. The man opened the gate and let them in. He told them that all the batteries were discharged and that they had no way to recharge them at the course without any power. He said he'd be willing to sell some extras that he had. When Mark asked how much, the man replied $100 each. Mark thanked the man for his time but told him he couldn't afford that. As he and Jim turned to get back in the truck, the man said $75. Mark half turned and told him that was still more than he was willing to pay. The man asked Mark to make him an offer. Mark could see that this guy wasn't going to take the first offer, so Mark made his first price as ridiculous as the golf man's had been.

"$15 each."

"$15? They cost $65 new when the power was on. They're worth more than that now."

"Maybe, if they were still new and fully charged," Mark countered.

"Well, they have to be worth $50 each."

"That would be a fair price if I could just run down to the ATM and get some cash, but I can't, and no one else can either. I'll give you $20."

"I couldn't sell them for that little," the man stated.

"Okay, then, sorry to have troubled you."

"Wait…would you give $35?"

"I don't know," Mark rubbed his chin, as if he was deep in thought. "No, I think I'll go try Republic Golf Course down the street first and see how much they want."

"How about $30?" The man was starting to look anxious.

"I'd do $25 each." Mark was matter-of-fact.

"Could you give me $27?"

"I can do that," the bean counter said, holding out his hand. Mark shook it.

They went into the cart garage, and the man showed them the batteries. He asked Mark how many he wanted. Mark told him eight and paid him. The man helped Mark set the batteries by the door, as Jim backed his truck up. They loaded the big, six-volt batteries, and the man let them out of the gate smiling and waving.

"That was a good deal," Jim said, as he pulled back onto the road.

"It sure was. I would have paid $50 each if he had started out there. Of course, I would have only bought four instead of eight," Mark grinned.

This was a section of town they didn't frequent often. Mark noticed the houses were older and further apart and further from the road than in newer sections of town. As they drove down the street, they heard gunshots. The men instantly went on high alert. Mark grabbed his rifle, and Jim slowed the truck down. As they slowly rounded a bend in the road, they could see two men who had been pulling a wagon full of groceries crouched down behind a stalled car. The men each had a pistol, but most of the firing was coming from a barricade of several cars that completely blocked the road. There were six or seven guns firing from behind the cars. Mark couldn't see who was behind the cars, but it was pretty obvious what was going on. Unless the two with the wagon had a death wish, they clearly hadn't attacked the prepared position. Jim backed the truck out of the line of fire and stopped.

"What do you want to do?" Mark asked.

"We have to help those guys," Jim answered.

"Agreed." Mark made sure he had his rifle and the mag carrier that held his magazines for the Mini-14. He pulled his Kel-Tec out of his back pocket and handed it to Abby. "Just in case. You two stay here."

Abby reached into her purse and pulled a small revolver out. "Give it to Alice."

Mark handed the .32 to Alice. Jim had grabbed some web gear and his M1A. Mark and Jim ducked down behind the line of cars on the side of the road and ran as best they could in a crouched position until they got to where the two men were. They had been so intent on the barricade that they hadn't noticed the two men closing on their position. They startled when the friends reached them.

"Where did you come from?" one of the men asked.

"From around the bend," Jim answered. "Our truck is around the corner. We'll cover you as you fall back with your wagon. Then we'll take you home."

"But that is our home just on the other side of where the cars are parked," the other man stated.

Mark and Jim looked at each other. The bullets were thumping into the car they were behind, but they would have to pass through at least two engine blocks to reach them, and none of the shots sounded like they were coming from high power rifles. Mark looked at the men. One of them was quite a bit older than the other, and Mark thought they might be father and son. The older one had a 1911, and the younger one held a Beretta. He spoke to the younger one.

"You and I are going to cross the road and get behind the cars over there while the other two give us some covering fire. Then we'll cover them while they move up a couple of cars. We'll go back and forth a couple of times until we get around this curve some and have a better angle on them. Then we'll punch some holes in the cars they're hiding behind with our rifles. Ready?"

"I'm ready," the young man said, as he nodded his head.

Mark counted. "One, two, three, GO!"

Jim and the older man popped up and opened fire on the barricade. As Mark ran across the street, he heard the people behind the cars cursing as they ducked down behind their barricade. When Mark and the younger man were on the other side and in position, they heard Jim yell.

"Ready...GO!"

Mark and his companion opened up on the ambushers. When they saw that the men across the street had reached their next position, they dropped back down. Mark could see the young man struggling to change a magazine in his pistol.

"Just relax," Mark said, not believing these words were coming out of his mouth. "Take a deep breath and take your time." The man did and the magazine was changed and the empty one was put into his pocket. "How are you on ammo?"

"I have two more clips and an extra box in my pocket," the young man answered.

"Good. Are you ready to move?"

The man nodded his head, and Mark yelled for Jim and his new partner to cover them. When Mark was moving, he heard someone behind the cars yell.

"Shit! I'm hit."

"Let's get the fuck out of here!" another one yelled.

Mark looked and saw seven individuals running down the middle of the street away from them. One of them had a bad limp and was being helped by another. He looked across the street and saw that Jim had his rifle pointed in their direction, watching their every move. When they were out of sight, the four men carefully moved to behind the barricade. There was some blood and an inexpensive 9-millimeter carbine that one of them had dropped, probably the one who was hit. Once the men were sure the area was clear, they introduced themselves.

"I'm Doctor Jack Mosely." The older man stuck his hand out toward Jim. "This is my son, Robert."

"I'm Jim Davis," the tall, muscular man replied, as he shook the doctor's hand. "This is my friend, Mark Turner." They shook hands all around.

"When Mark was shaking the doctor's hand, he asked a question. "M.D.?"

"No. D.D.S. Thank you, both. We didn't know what to do. We've had a few problems with some undesirables in the last week or so, but nothing like this. If you two hadn't shown up, who knows if we would have ever gotten home? Thank you so much."

"It's no problem, Doc. In fact, if you hadn't walked into the ambush first, we would have driven right into it. It's really us who need to thank you," Mark explained.

"I guess we need to try and find the police and make a report," the dentist said, "and turn this gun in to them." He pointed at the firearm lying on the asphalt.

"You can do that if you want to, Doc, but you'll have to excuse us if we don't stick around."

"Why not?"

"I was involved in a little incident like this the other day. Only the other side wasn't as lucky. Anyway, the sheriff took my rifle for ballistic tests, and I can't afford to lose another one. So, if you wouldn't mind, don't mention our names."

"If I call them, they'll take our pistols?" The doctor seemed appalled at the idea.

"They probably will, and you could be brought up on charges, although I doubt it."

"What do you think we should do?"

"If it were me, I'd push these cars back over to the side of the road, pick up the carbine, and keep it or bury it or something, and keep my mouth shut," Mark told the man.

"Well then, that's exactly what we're going to do. We can't lose our pistols. Can you help us push the cars?"

"Sure," Mark answered.

"I'm going to run back and get the truck," Jim said.

Mark nodded, and he and the other two men started pushing one of the cars. Jim drove up in the truck and helped them push the rest over to where they'd been before they were moved for an ambush point. When they were done, the dentist asked if they lived around here. Mark told him they lived just outside the county. He didn't want to get too specific, in case the cops did get involved. The father and son thanked the men again, asking if there was anything they could do for them. Mark and Jim told them no and warned them to be careful in case the thugs came back. Then they headed home.

"You know, you were right. If we hadn't heard those shots, we would have just driven right into that ambush," Jim said soberly.

Mark didn't reply right away. "Yesterday, I was thinking it would be real easy to ambush the people walking down the road. I never stopped to think they could do what these jerks did. Ever since last Friday, I've watched my rearview mirror like a hawk. Now, I have to watch in front better, too. It's just getting more and more dangerous. I guess we've got to expect the unexpected."

"I know one thing," Alice interjected. "We felt very exposed sitting in the truck with only two little pop guns to keep us company. When we get home, Jim, you're teaching me and Abby to shoot one of those ugly guns you boys bought. Excuse my French, but I'll be dipped in shit and called a caramel apple before I come back to town without a serious rifle."

"That goes double for me!" Abby chimed in.

Mark put his hands over his ears and turned to face the women. "Please, ladies, you'll offend my sensitive, virgin ears with such language!"

They all laughed. Mark thought it strange that he could be in a shootout ten minutes ago and making jokes now. The world had changed completely in less than three weeks. What would the next three weeks bring, he wondered, or the next three months? He wished the lights would come back on. That way, everything would go back to the way it was. He had killed men. How could he do that? How could he take another human life? Oh, he'd thought about it before. When he got his CHL, he knew he might have to one day. He was sure he could if he had to, but thinking about it and doing it were two different things. He was out buying food and dickering over the price of golf cart batteries while four men were dead because of him, one of them from a shot he fired. He had actually killed a man with a squeeze of his trigger, a conscious decision he made to take a life. For what? To defend his truck? No. To defend himself and his friends. But why did he deserve to live and the men who were dead did not? Why? That was the question...why? Why had the lights gone out? Why had all of this happened? Why did he kill a man? Why could he shoot at people and then make jokes? Why did he have to wonder why?

Mark tried to think of something else, but he couldn't make his mind switch gears. It was a runaway train, and he knew where it was heading. He didn't want to go there, but the harder he fought it, the more powerful it became. He couldn't break down in front of Jim and the women. Maybe if it was Jess, but he hated even for her to see him cry. He was Billy Bob Badass Black Belt, damnit! He had to control this...to stop it. But how? He took a deep breath. There. That slowed it, if only for a second. He buried his face in his hands. Hands that had killed a man, his mind told him. That was it. He lost it. The emotional train had overtaken him. All he could do now was hope it would let him off before too long.

His whole body shuddered as he sobbed. Abby reached over the seat and patted him on the shoulder. He could hear them all telling him it would be okay. What did they know? Had they ever killed anyone? He didn't want their sympathy, and he didn't deserve it. He didn't deserve to live any more than the man he shot deserved to die. Was the man he shot a bad man? Maybe. Maybe all they had wanted to do was to scare him. Maybe not. Maybe he was a bad man. But who was he to decide the fate of another human being? Now he was a bad man...a killer...no...a murderer. He was the bad man now. He didn't deserve to live with these fine people. God, he had to stop crying. He looked like a fool, but trying to stop it only made it go faster. The runaway train had its own schedule, and Mark wasn't in control. He hated it. He hated what he had done. He hated what they had turned him into. He hated them. He hated himself.

He cried for hours, for days, for weeks, maybe, but finally, when he no longer had the strength to try to stop the emotion train, it slowed and let him off. He looked out the window. They were passing the church. Five more minutes and they would be home. No one spoke.

When they pulled up to the house, Mark just got out of the truck and went into the house. He went to his bedroom and closed the door behind him. A few minutes later, there was a soft knock on the door. He didn't answer. Jess stuck her head into the room.

"Mark, can I get you anything?"

Just leave me the fuck alone, he thought, but the words didn't come out. He had no will to say them. He just stared at her. Who was she? How could she love him? How did he even deserve to be loved?

She pulled her head out and closed the door behind her. He just sat on the edge of the bed. His mind taunted him. He had no idea how much time passed. He was completely withdrawn into himself.

He could hear people talking outside but couldn't make out what they were saying, even if he'd wanted to. Eventually, he vaguely made out Gunny's voice. "That's bullshit, George, somebody else can watch the damn gardens for a day. Someone needs to go with the women, and you're the only one can do it. I gotta teach the guards, and Jimbo and the Karate Man are s'posed to be in class, too. Abby tol' me that a lot of folks were waitin' for the water to come back on 'fore they came to the store. So, if'n you go early, you'll prob'ly be back by midmorning. Now surely it'll be alright for a couple of hours without you there."

"OK, Gunny, I'll go, but you tell them we're leaving early. I want to be back when they test out the Jeep." Mark barely recognized George's voice. After that, all he could make out were mumbles.

Later, there was a loud knock on the door.

"Karate Man, it's Gunny. I'm coming in." The door opened. "You ready to talk?"

Mark shook his head.

Gunny came in and closed the door behind him. "Good, you can listen then."

Mark just looked at the old man. He didn't want to listen; he just wanted to be by himself.

"I know how you feel. I've been there, an' I talked to lots o' guys who've been there, too. There's two things you're goin' to have to get over. One is the guilt. I can he'p ya some with that. It'll never 'pletely go away, but it'll get easier to live with. The other is feelin' sorry fer yerself."

'Damned old fart. Leave me ALONE!' he thought, as he stared at the old man.

Gunny continued. "If'n those guys you shot had been tryin' to kill Jess, Sam, or David, wouldja have any doubts 'bout whether or not you did the right thing then?"

"No."

"Well, they was tryin' to kill your family. In fact, they was tryin' to kill all of us here in Silver Hills."

"How's that?"

"If'n they killed you, who's gonna look after your family? If'n you're no longer around to provide for and protect them, wouldn't that put their lives in danger?"

"I guess so."

"I don't guess so; I know so. An', like it or not, you're a leader in this community. If'n you get killed, our chances of making it go down. Maybe not that much, but maybe your bein' here is what makes a difference for all these people. You made a difference for that dentist and his son today. You think on that for a while."

"Okay, Gunny, I will."

"The feeling sorry for yourself is somethin' you're gonna have work through for yourself. I know what you been thinking…It's not fair…Why did I

196

have to be put in that situation?…Who's gonna wanna be 'round me now? Well, life ain't fair. You were put into the situation 'cause you could handle it, and your family and your friends love you. When you decide that you've wallowed in your self-pity for long enough, kick yourself in the ass and get back to work. We got a lot to do 'round here, and while you deserve a little time to work through this, we ain't got much to give ya."

"Thanks, Gunny. I'll be out in a minute," Mark said.

Gunny left without saying another word. Mark hated it when the old codger was right. He was just mostly feeling sorry for himself now. What time was it? Mark looked at his watch. There was just enough time to run a mile or two before dinner. Mark put on his running clothes and went out on the back porch where everyone was sitting.

"Sorry about the show earlier. I'm going to run a couple of miles before dinner."

"Don't worry about it, buddy," Jim said.

"It's alright, honey. We're just glad you feel better," Jess added.

Mark ran down the hill and out of the gate. All of the barbed wire was up. He turned toward the OP that Gunny had been working on. Either they didn't get much done on it, or they had camouflaged it well. If Mark hadn't known exactly where to look, he wouldn't have seen anything. He ran down the road a ways and then turned around and ran home. When he got there, he felt better. He asked Gunny about the OP. Gunny said they needed to frame in the inside but that the outside was 90% done. The family sat and ate and then got ready for the meeting. The news had brought them no information that was useful or interesting. Perhaps the President would give them some hopeful news tomorrow. The meeting went smoothly. George told how they were coming with the gardens, and Chaparo was ready to test the Jeep first thing in the morning. Ted reported that the education committee should have something to present to the group by early next week. Gunny wanted to have a class tomorrow for the guards who hadn't had any training. Instead of training them for gate duty right now, this group would learn to pull OP duty and roving detail. Then later, he would cross-train the groups. He also told everyone they were going to put CB's in the gate guard post, the observation post and one in the CP or Command Post. He asked the group for suggestions on where to place the CP. They needed someplace centrally located. Lastly, Gunny asked for any ideas on how to call reinforcements if needed. When the meeting was dismissed, everyone got their water and headed home.

Mark and most of his group headed for the shooting range with the AK's and the Franken-FAL. The women and teenagers were able to shoot the AK's quite well, as the stocks were shorter than most American-made rifles. The controls were a little difficult for them to master, but as they shot more, they became more proficient in the operation of the rifles. Mark sat at the bench to shoot the parts gun Jerry had sold him. He fired one round and found that the rifle was very close to zeroed. He let the barrel cool and fired a second round. It was within an inch of the first round. Lucky shot, he thought. The sights on this battle rifle weren't known for their accuracy. When the barrel had cooled a second time, he fired again. This shot was touching the first. Darn, he thought, Jerry said the man told him it shot well, but this is fantastic. He loaded ten rounds into a magazine and fired them without letting the barrel cool. Now he could see why the guy had only said it shot pretty good. The first two shots were right in where the previous three had been. The third and fourth were just a little higher. From the fifth shot on, every shot was higher than the last. By the time he finished, eight, nine, and ten were three inches high. The rifle walked its groups up as the barrel heated up. He loaded five more rounds and shot them quickly. Good, once it got three inches high, it stopped going higher. The rifle wasn't the steal he thought it was after the first three shots, but it was still a good deal, and he was happy he had bought it. George shot his new Glock, and he liked it. He said he'd never owned a plastic pistol before, but he could now see why people liked them. They shot well and were easy to operate. Jim reminded him the pistol was not 'plastic.' The frame was made from a special polymer, and the rest of the pistol was steel. Mark smiled. Those Glock owners were always so sensitive to having their firearms called 'plastic.'

It was miserably hot. There was no hint of a breeze, and the humidity was stifling. This was the kind of weather that kept everyone from wanting to live in Texas. Mark tossed and turned all night. He wasn't sure how much of it was from the heat, how much from the guilt that had clobbered him today, and how much from him worrying about the future. Probably, he decided when it was time to get up, equal parts of all three.

Mark knew he'd be leading the PT for the guards this morning, so he didn't worry about working out. George had told the women that he wanted to leave by 7:30. At 7:26, he, Jess, Lisa, and Abby headed to the store in Jim's truck. It was different to see the women loading up into the truck carrying rifles. However, Mark felt better about them being in town with them. It was a different world than it had been three weeks ago, and to ignore that fact could be deadly.

Gunny began the guard training exactly at 8 o'clock. He talked to the guys about what was expected of them and how he wanted them to be in better physical condition. He told them if they had to run from one end of the subdivision to the other, they needed to be able to do it and fire a weapon with some degree of accuracy when they got there. He explained that Mark was going to do a light workout with them today and that they'd gradually increase the amount of PT. After they exercised, Gunny lectured the guards on how to man the OP first. He went over what to look for, how to call it in, and when, as a last resort, to use the OP as a firing point. He warned the guards that the OP was a lookout position first, that even if a firefight started, their primary duty was to report on enemy positions and numbers and to watch for troops that the men in the entrenched positions might not be able to see. Then he did a question and answer session with the guards. Most of the questions were the 'what if' variety, and Gunny usually had the class come up with the best answer rather than just giving it to them. Mark was even more impressed with the old vet now that he'd seen him teach. No wonder men like Breezy sang Gunny's praises so resoundingly. It was almost lunchtime, and Gunny gave the men a break and asked them to be back by 1:30.

Mark had figured that the shoppers would have been back by 11, but, even though it was now closer to 12, they weren't. He and Jim walked over to Chaparo's to see how it was going with the makeshift tractor. Chaparo had used the Jeep to pull his trailer over to the tree farm this morning in order to get the

198

plow and the disk. He was back and had mounted the plow on the Jeep's new hitch, but they still hadn't tested it. Chaparo said that George had made him promise he would wait for the old farmer to try it out. The three of them talked for a while, and then the two friends went home to make some lunch.

Not long after the men sat down to eat a sandwich, Jim's blue Chevy pulled up to the house. They had no trouble. The reason they were late was because they'd found a little mom and pop fabric store that was open and decided to buy some cloth and thread. George rolled his eyes when the women started talking about the deals they got in the store. Before they could go into detail, he excused himself to go try out the plow on the Jeep. Jess said the lady in the store was so happy to see someone with cash that she'd sold them most of the items they wanted for less than half-price. Mark asked them how long it had taken at the Kroger. Abby said that they went quicker than yesterday.

"When we got out, around 10, the line was still pretty short. I asked someone in the back if the water had come back on, and they told me 'Not yet,'" she elaborated.

Jess mentioned that when they left the fabric shop, they'd seen a couple of big columns of smoke. She said she hoped they got the water on in time to put out the fires. Mark and Jim told her the fire department probably had enough tanker trucks to put out small fires, but they would need pressure to battle any large ones. Mark was sure they could radio in and get the water turned on in a section of town if they had to.

Mark had wanted to check on how they were doing with the Jeep, but it was time to head back to class. When Gunny had been lecturing for about thirty minutes, Manny came screeching up in his Suburban with Mark's, Gunny's, and the MZB trucks in tow. He jumped out of his truck, and from the look on his face, Mark and everyone else could tell that something was very wrong.

"What happened?" Gunny asked.

"Everyone in town has gone crazy," Manny answered. "We were at the store waiting for a group to come out when a bunch of people came marching down the street destroying everything. They were setting fire to buildings, turning over cars on the side of the streets, and shooting into the air. When the police officer at Kroger went down and tried to stop them, the mob beat him senseless. We could see them coming from about three blocks away, and they were getting crazier and crazier, and the mob kept growing as they got closer to the store. They set the store on fire while they hollered about the water still being off. Some of them started running in the store and stealing everything they could carry. We had people in line and in the store. Fortunately, we got all of our people out before it got really bad. When the fire started, we packed everyone in my Sub and Gunny's truck. The other two had left before the commotion. We were leaving about the time a busload of cops showed up, and a big gun fight started. It was way worse than what happened to us last week." Manny paused and looked at Mark. "It looked like the fighting you see on the news and think 'That's terrible!' You don't realize how terrible it is until you're caught in the middle of it. Anyway, we hauled ass out of there and headed home. We saw people rioting all the way to the edge of town. A couple of people tried to stop us by standing in the road. I just put my foot on the floor, and, thank God, they all jumped out of the way. A few of them shot at us, too, but it seems

199

like they missed. We met up with the other trucks on their way back to drop off some more people and turned them around. When we topped that hill, the one just across the county line that you can see into town pretty good from, I looked in my rearview mirror, and all I could see was black smoke. I know I ain't going back there anytime soon."

Mark walked out from between the houses to where he had a good vantage point toward San Antonio. It looked like one huge column of smoke was rising from the city. It had finally happened. The shit had hit the fan.

Chapter 30

Gunny dismissed the class. He told Mark and Jim that the men were too wound now up to learn anything. They walked back to the house and told the others about what had happened. Lisa said that she could feel the tension in the air when they were in town. They decided to walk down and see how George was doing with his new toy.

They walked to Chaparo's, and he, George, and a group of folks were in the empty lot behind his house with the Jeep. Most of the people there were talking about what was happening in town and weren't paying attention to the Jeep. It had the plow mounted on it, and Chaparo was driving. Driving wasn't exactly the right word, Mark thought. The plow was down in the ground, and the Jeep was sitting in one place, digging in the dirt with only its spinning tires.

Mark walked over to see what the problem was. The vehicle didn't have enough traction to pull the plow through the hard ground. Mark asked Chaparo if he had anything they could put into the Jeep to add weight to it. He and Chaparo went into the welding shop and carried out several bags of concrete. When they'd put about five hundred pounds in the Jeep, Mark got in to try it out. He double-checked to see if the transfer case was in low range and put the transmission into first. When he eased out on the clutch, the Jeep moved about two feet and then started spinning again. He backed up and took another run at it. He moved about another foot or two and then stopped again. He gave it more fuel, and the tires just spun faster. The foul stench of burning clutch filled the air. He backed off the accelerator and turned the wannabe tractor off. One of the garden committee members came over.

"Only two tires are spinning, one on the front and one on the back. I thought Jeeps were four wheel drives?"

"Four wheel drive means that all four wheels can pull if they have equal traction, but if one wheel on an axle has less traction than the other one, that one will spin, and the other one just sits there," Mark explained.

"Wouldn't it be better if the wheel with more traction pulled?"

"Sure it would, but that's not the way a differential works. For both tires on an axle to pull, you have to have some kind of limited slip or locking differential, and I don't have that on the Jeep."

"We could weld up the spider gears," Chaparo suggested.

"I hate to do that, since it makes cornering on dry pavement difficult, but I guess we'll have to try," Mark agreed.

They jacked up the plow and pulled the Jeep into the shop. Chaparo got a bucket to drain the differential fluid into while Mark used a floor jack to lift the Jeep up. They removed the differential cover, and Chaparo got out his welding equipment. They fired up the generator and went to work on the gears. When the back was finished, they repeated the procedure on the front axle. When they took the Jeep back out to try it, they found that it worked only marginally better than it had with the open differentials. Mark and Chaparo added more weight to the Jeep by putting one of the 55-gallon water barrels in the back and filling it up with water. The Jeep didn't seem to be geared low enough to do the job. As a last ditch effort, Mark dropped the air pressure in the tires down to about 12 psi.

The Jeep started to pull the plow, and they thought they'd found the solution until the back wheels spun inside the tires and broke the bead, thereby letting all of the air out.

To say that Mark was upset would be an understatement. He cut loose with a six-dollar string of words that would have made a career sailor blush. He then regained his composure, apologized for his outburst, and asked the other men if they had any ideas. None of them did. George said they could probably use the Jeep to pull the disc, but that wouldn't really help them unless they found a tractor to use for plowing. Chaparo said he'd help George hook up the disc and try it out as soon as he aired the tires back up.

Mark decided to head back up to the house and take a shower. After he checked to see if there had been any news and filled everyone in on the lack of success with the Jeep, he went into the camper and turned on the hot water heater. The 'whoosh' of it lighting was a welcome sound. At least something was working, he thought. He remembered he had wanted to check the propane level the other night but had gotten distracted before he could. He'd filled both of the tanks just before The Burst, and since they were cooking in the house, they had only been using gas for the water heater and the refrigerator. He hoped that he still had at least one full tank. When he opened the compartment that housed the tanks, a yellow jacket flew out and stung him on the hand.

"Damnit," was the only word he said, as he shook the insect off of his hand. He went into the storage shed and got a can of wasp killer. Then, opening the compartment door slowly, he sprayed the remainder of the small wasp colony. Now that he could check the tanks, he could see that one was completely empty and that the automatic valve had changed to the second tank. Mark estimated that it was two-thirds to three quarters full. That would only last another week and half if they didn't change their usage habits. He walked over and checked the five hundred gallon tank for the house. The gauge read 40%. That was two hundred gallons, but how long would that last? He immediately thought about the gasoline and diesel. He wondered how they stood on those. He remembered that Jim had told him about a week ago that they had a hundred and fifty gallons of diesel and two hundred twenty five of gasoline. He went to the shed. Mark was shocked to find that there were only about fifty gallons of diesel and less than a hundred gallons of gas. He'd been so concerned about getting what they didn't have that he'd given no thought to conserving or replacing what they did have. He knew they could siphon gas out of the nonworking cars, but what about diesel? Was there a place that he could get some? And what about propane? How were they going to replenish that?

He went back to the camper and turned off the water heater. They'd be showering in the solar-heated ones with everyone else from here on out. He had to figure out a way to make the shower rationing fair to everyone, some way where the people who worked the hardest got rewarded with more opportunities to use them.

Mark went into the house and announced the hot water heater in the camper was not to be used anymore. He thought Sam was going to burst out in tears. She was known to sometimes take three showers in a day, and it had been a sacrifice for her to cut back to only one. The announcement that she may only get one every three or four days was more than she was ready to accept.

Mark spoke to Jim about the fuel. He was surprised at first but then reminded Mark they'd been going into town once or twice each day in every running vehicle. That would slow down now, for obvious reasons. Mark told Jim that he was going to see about getting everyone to donate the gas out of their stalled cars. He said that unless they needed the diesel truck for something that the gas trucks couldn't do, it was not to be used. They needed to save the diesel they had until they could find more. Jim agreed.

It was dinner time and time for the President to speak. They sat down to dinner and listened.

My fellow Americans, it is with a heavy heart that I speak to you. We have not made the progress with restoring the power that I was told was possible in the early days of this crisis. We are making some headway, but it has proven to be a bigger challenge than we had initially thought. However, I know that America is up to that challenge.

Another challenge facing us is the lawlessness taking place in every major city in the United States. I beg those of you living in the cities to cooperate with your local authorities. Your government is working to make sure that food and water is being supplied to everyone who needs it. We now have almost fifty cities under limited martial law, and the local authorities in five more have asked me to institute it in their cities just today. This is tying up a significant number of military personnel who could be used in relief efforts. Please do not riot or loot. Return to your homes and wait for assistance. If you have urgent medical needs, make your way to the nearest hospital for help. We are all in this boat together, and together we must work to put it back on course. I will talk to you again on Tuesday. Thank you, God bless you, and God bless America.

This is KSTX. We'll be back with the news after this...

"What do you think?" Jim asked, as a commercial came on.

"It sounds like we're going to be in the dark for quite a while. Did you notice that he didn't even hint at when the power would be back on?" Mark said.

Everyone nodded their heads.

"We need to get them towers up as soon as possible," Gunny observed. With all the riotin' in town, we're gonna see a flood of refugees just tryin' to get outta tha city."

"We can get Chaparo on the ones we have metal for tonight and get them up in the morning," Mark suggested.

"Tomorrow is Sunday, and we're going to church," Jess insisted.

"We need to talk about that," Mark responded. "I don't kno..."

"The local news is coming on," Jim interrupted.

...fires are burning uncontrolled. The death toll is already estimated in the thousands. The fire department is able to do little more than try to help evacuate the citizens in the paths of these runaway infernos. The City Water Board has stated that they are unable to provide water pressure for firefighting because of the severity of the fires around the pumping station that has the diesel- powered pump. The Red Cross is directing evacuees to the airport on the north side and Kelly Air Force Base on the south side. These two facilities have their own water supply, and the unused airfields are open enough to hopefully avoid the risk of fire. If you head to the shelters, please bring blankets or sleeping bags, as the Red Cross does not have enough bedding for the expected numbers. If you

have a tent, you are encouraged to bring it, as well. The fire department is recommending that if fire comes within two blocks of your house, you should evacuate. With the hot and dry conditions that we have experienced the past few weeks, a fire can consume a city block in less than ten minutes. Even at this station, we are unsure how much longer we will be able to broadcast. Fires are burning five blocks from here and are coming closer. If you have to leave your home, move away from the fire and make your way toward the closest shelter. Try to travel in groups with your neighbors. City busses, along with local military vehicles, are driving the major streets and transporting evacuees to the shelters.

The rioting and fires seem to be a result of the inability of the Water Board to supply pressure today. A spokesperson for CWB stated that, while they were having some difficulty, the water would have come on later. Now they are unsure of when pressure can be provided. Fire crews are fighting the fire around the pumping station with the few tanker trucks they have, but so far have been unable to control the fire.

The mayor has asked the governor to help bring the rioting under control. The mayor stated that city police were stretched to their limit before this recent outbreak of violence. No response has come from the Capitol yet, but the mayor is expecting an answer later today.

Again, our top story is the uncontrolled fires and rioting throughout the city. The mayor is plead...

Mark reached over and turned the radio off. Everyone either had tears in their eyes or looked to be on the verge of it. It was quiet at the table for a long time. Alice finally broke the silence.

"Those poor people."

After another long silence, Mark spoke. "I don't think anyone should leave the subdivision until we know what the situation is going to be like with the people leaving town. If a guy got 'testy' the other day, some people are going to be downright explosive now."

"But we promised the Preacher we'd be back this Sunday," Jess argued.

"I know we did, but that was before the world went to hell in a hand basket. I'm sure the preacher will understand."

Jess started to argue, but Mark held up one finger, which meant that he was through talking about it. Mark could see she was mad, but she'd just have to get over it. People were starting to arrive for the meeting.

Everyone was agitated by the day's events. However, for all that was happening, the meeting started out surprisingly routine. George told where they were on the gardens and about the bad luck with the Jeep. It would, he reported, pull the disc just fine, if they got to the point they could use it. The guards reported on the people who had passed by today. Even though there had been a lot of groups, there had been no incidents. Gunny asked to see all of the guards once more. Susan announced the foxholes and OP had been all framed in. She also said the gate foxhole and the OP had both been equipped with a CB by Don Wesley, the CB enthusiast. Scott Simmons volunteered his garage for a Command Post until something better could be found. Mark thanked him for the offer and asked him to get with Gunny to set it up.

Mark then told everyone of the fuel situation. He suggested they siphon the fuel from the stalled cars, so they'd know exactly how much they had to work with. Mark asked if anyone had a problem with putting Jim in charge of this project and asking him to monitor the fuel usage from now on. Mark waited for a moment, and when he was about to ask for a motion on the recommendation, a hand went up in the back. Mark pointed at the hand and said 'yes' without seeing whose hand it was. Jon Olsen stood up to speak.

"You mean, you want us to give you our gas?" He spat the words out as though they tasted bad.

Mark took a deep breath. "No, Jon, we are asking that people donate to the community stockpile. All of the fuel is going to be used for the community."

"But some of you have vehicles that you can use whenever and for whatever you want."

"That's true, and we've also provided all of the fuel to take everyone to the store for the last three weeks, the fuel for the generator that we use mostly to pump water for everyone, and the equipment we're using to till the gardens for everyone. Now we're asking people to help us replenish what's been used."

"Maybe I want to keep my gas for myself to make sure it goes for the good of the community and not for some joyride."

"If that's what you'd like, then that's fine. No one's required to give their fuel. Now, if I could get a motion to that effect, we can vote on it."

The motion was made, seconded, and passed, almost unanimously. Mark adjourned the meeting, and the kids started pumping water for everyone, even Jon, Mark saw.

A man came up to introduce himself to Mark. "Mr. Turner," he said, as he held out his hand, "I'm Craig Banks, Susan Banks's husband."

"Mark Turner. Nice to meet you. I thought Susan was divorced?"

"We were. I mean, we are, but she asked me to move back in with her."

"That's nice."

"Yeah. Well, I just wanted to let you know that I'd like to help out however I can."

"Thanks. I'm sure we can find something with all of the work we have to do. I'll get back with you, or if you see something you can help with, jump right in," Mark said with a smile.

"I'll do that. It was a pleasure to meet you," the new man said, as he walked away.

Mark and the other guards huddled around Gunny for his meeting. He wanted to go ahead and put a person in the OP and have one roving guard unit of three men working tonight even though they hadn't completed all of the training. He put Scott Simmons in charge of the team that had the 8 PM to 2 AM shift and Mark in charge of the 2 to 8 in the morning shift. He assigned the OP for four-hour shifts for the next twenty-four hours. They'd set the temporary CP up within the hour. Don was getting a CB to place there, and the OP was to call in anything suspicious. He told the rovers to concentrate on the front of the subdivision but to vary their movements enough that no one could predict where they might be. He told the guards who weren't on duty to have their weapons ready, and if they were called or if they heard any gunshots, to report to the CP as quickly as possible. Gunny announced that Chaparo was trying to get two of the guard towers ready for tomorrow and that they could use some help getting them up and securing them in the morning.

Mark decided to go over and help Chaparo with the guard towers for a while. The kids had the generator to pump water, so they cut the angle iron with hacksaws. Mark's hand was a little stiff from the wasp sting, and the sawing made it throb a little. Jon, on the other hand, made his head throb a lot. He and Chaparo talked about their disenfranchised neighbor and how best to deal with him. Chaparo thought he needed a swift kick in the seat of his pants. Mark didn't disagree but felt there had to be a better way to get him back into the fold. Mark's mind drifted off. Someone calling his name brought him back. It was George.

"Mark, I've been looking for you," George sounded exasperated.

"Well, you found me."

"Gunny said that we have to plow under some of the corn we planted. He wants nothing growing for a hundred feet from the fence, something about the guards having a clear field of view or some crap. I thought that was why you were building those towers. Hell, that's almost half of the field we spent all that time tilling and planting. I can't throw away that much work and then face the men who did it. You have to straighten him out," George said.

Mark sighed. "Let's go find him," he said.

When the two men found Gunny, it looked like they had to get in line to talk with him. Susan was bending his ear about another guard class. She stated that some of the women were interested in becoming guards, and she wanted him to start a third class. Gunny was hemming and hawing about how he didn't think it was a good idea to have the women in a position where they may get shot at or have to shoot someone. He had no problem with them manning the CP or the watch towers, but he didn't want them on the gate or as part of the rovers. Susan wasn't buying it, and she let Gunny know in no uncertain terms that she felt his arguments were without merit. Gunny looked over at Mark for help, and while Mark felt for the old Marine and even agreed with him to a degree, he knew a losing battle when he saw one. Mark just held up his hand, slightly waving it from side to side, indicating his unwillingness to jump into this fray. Gunny shot Mark a look that said 'chicken shit' and agreed to discuss the matter at the next security committee meeting. This seemed to placate Susan for the moment.

George, as soon as he saw an opening in the conversation, jumped right in with his own tirade. Mark probably would have let the crop matter wait until later. Gunny had just lost a battle, and he wouldn't be easily swayed to giving in twice in a row. Before George could finish his filibuster about why they couldn't plow under all that work, Gunny launched a volley back at him about how all the food in the world wouldn't do them a bit of good if they all got killed because the guards couldn't see someone sneaking into the subdivision because of crops planted right against the fence. Mark could see both men's points. He started asking each of them questions to find what would be acceptable to both. At first, neither one would give an inch. Mark thought both of them to be hardheaded, old farts, but deep down, he was glad that they both took their jobs so seriously. After a while, George agreed to plow under the corn within fifty feet of the fence, and Gunny agreed that they could use that space for crops as long as they weren't over knee high. The two old men shook hands and walked off, George back to the house and Gunny down to Scott's to check on the CP.

Susan had been watching this whole production in silence. "Is that what it sounded like when Gunny and I were arguing?"

"More or less," Mark answered.

"Why didn't you get involved in my argument like you did with George and Gunny?"

"Because George and Gunny were both right about what they were saying, so we had to come to some kind of compromise. In your argument, you were mostly right, and Gunny was mostly wrong."

"What do you mean…'mostly'?" Susan bristled.

"I just mean that women guards do present some problems that we're going to have to deal with."

"Like what?"

"Like the fact that some of the men won't want to be on a post with a woman because they don't think a woman can cover their back as well as a man can."

"That's bullshit!"

"I didn't say it wasn't." Mark was starting to see that she had a lot in common with Gunny. "But some will feel that way. Others won't want to because their wives might not like them spending that much time with another woman. They may feel that something inappropriate will happen."

"Guard duty is serious business. None of the people we put there would do something like that," she argued.

"You're probably right, but it only has to happen once. This community has become somewhat of a family, and everyone knows everyone else's business. If two of the guards were to have an affair, everyone would know about it, and it could ruin everything we've worked for so far. Can you guarantee it won't happen?"

Susan thought for a moment. "I don't think it would, but I couldn't guarantee it."

"Well, think about how we can work things so we can avoid those types of problems, and we'll talk about it again in a day or two."

"Okay."

"I met your husband." Mark wanted to change the subject. He'd had enough controversy for one day.

"You mean EX-husband," she said.

"He said you asked him to move back in with you."

"That lying sack of shit! God, I hate his ass. He showed up this afternoon with no place to go. He's the boys' father. What was I going to do? I offered to let him stay in the spare bedroom for now, but if he keeps telling lies, I'm going to kick his sorry ass out!"

"He seems nice enough. Offered to help out wherever we need it."

"Yeah, that's the way it starts. He's all full of hopes and dreams at first. The next thing you know, he's sitting in front of the TV all day, eating ice cream, drinking beer, and buying crap off of the Home Shopping Channel while you're at work supporting him. You keep an eye on him, Mark. He's no good."

"Okay, Susan, I will," Mark said as they reached the corner.

They each headed home. When Mark got to his house, Jim came up to him and told him that one of the new rifles had broken an extractor. Mark's initial response was one word long and cost him a dollar. He told Jim he'd take it to Jerry and Tony on Monday if he could. He wondered what else could go wrong today and decided to go to bed before it could. He asked if there was any more hot water in the showers and was told no. This time, he just thought it instead of saying it. He didn't relish the thought of going to bed without a shower. He went in the camper, took off his dirty clothes and washed up as best he could in the sink. He got dressed and went in the house to pay his black box. He couldn't remember exactly how much he owed, so he took a ten out of his wallet and put it in the box. That Murphy had sure cost him a lot of money today.

Chapter 31

When Mark showed up at the CP for guard duty, he found that the other members of his crew were already there. He looked at the men who had been assigned to him, Paul Jensen, Joe Bagwell, and Ted. Ted had asked Gunny if he could help out, and he'd been given this assignment. Gunny had told him that since they were only going to have one team of rovers, he was going to make it four men instead of three. He also told Mark what he wanted them to do in case of trouble, since they hadn't gone through the training for roving guard duty.

The men started making their rounds. Before The Burst, the lights of San Antonio had hidden all but the brightest stars. Since then, the night sky had been as beautiful as Mark could ever remember. Tonight, though, a bright, orange glow emanated from town with more intensity than the city lights had ever produced. Mark was thankful they were east of the city. The prevailing wind was from the southeast, just as usual. Not only did it keep them from smelling the burning metropolis, hopefully it would keep the fires from moving in their direction.

Mark occasionally had to remind the men to remain quiet. They walked through their community looking for any signs that something was amiss. As Gunny had instructed, Mark kept his group toward the front of the subdivision most of the time. The quiet gave him time to think.

He thought about everything: what they still needed to buy or trade for, what they needed to do, how they needed to get organized, and the million other things that, three weeks ago, he would have said weren't even worth a thought. Now he wished he'd given more thought to what could have happened. His brother had tried to get him to prepare for Y2K. Mark had ignored him. Mike had spent a lot of money putting up food and other items in preparation for TEOTWAWKI. That was what he'd called it. It stood for the 'The End of the World as We Know It.' It hadn't happened. Y2K wasn't even a hiccup. Mark had gotten a good laugh at his brother's expense, but now the shoe was on the other foot. It turned out that Mike had been right about TEOTWAWKI, just a little early. Mark hoped his brother, sister, and parents still had the food they'd put back. That would hold them for a while. Mike had told him they had enough food to last for six months easily. Even if they'd used some of it, hopefully they would be okay for another month or two. Mark wanted to go check on them, but that would be out of the question until things settled down a little.

Mark shifted his mind back onto the things he could do something about. He went over the list of things that were a priority. Water was still their number one concern. Sure, they could use the generator to pump enough for everyone to get by, but what if there was no more fuel? That wasn't likely to happen soon, but what if the generator broke? That was a real possibility. They'd been using it pretty hard, and if it broke, there was no guarantee they could get parts for it. Mark's mind drifted, as it was so prone to do lately, to what else might go wrong. They'd all been fairly lucky so far. Everyone in the subdivision was working together. Well, for the most part, anyway. No one had been hurt or gotten sick. They didn't live in town where the people were being burned out of their homes. They did have water for now, were planting gardens, and had expertise in many of the fields that were going to be so important to their survival. But Mark knew, as Murphy had reminded him so well yesterday, luck runs out. Okay, back on track, Mark thought. Back to his Boy Scout training on survival. Water, food, shelter was what he remembered. Water was number one. That was obvious. Although they were fine for now, they needed a more reliable source. They had to find a windmill or some way to pump water that didn't require the generator. Food was alright for now. They could sure use a tractor to help with the gardens, but the lack of one wasn't stopping them, only slowing them down. Shelter was no problem, other than staying cool, but fall was rapidly approaching, and it would cool off sooner or later. Mark was hoping for sooner. Security had to be their number two priority for right now. All of the planning and preparing would do them no good if a bunch of MZB's stole what they had, or worse. His mind didn't want to spend any time revisiting that possibility.

The rovers were approaching the front of the subdivision by way of the eastern fence line. They turned and walked toward the gate guards, and when they got there, Mark asked how it was going. They told him that it had been very quiet. Mark hoped that it would stay that way. They walked back up to the CP and checked in. Mark looked at his watch. It was almost 5 AM, and their shift was half over. They finished without incident.

After he dismissed his men, Mark stopped by Chaparo's to check on the towers. The first two were done, and Gunny had a crew there to move them and set them up. Mark watched them put the first one up and then headed home to get some rest. It seemed he'd just gotten to sleep when Sam came in and woke him up.

"Dad, they need you at the gate."

"What?" he replied groggily.

"They want you at the gate. Someone is there who says they know you."

"Okay." Mark's brain was starting to function. He wondered who it could be as he got dressed. He grabbed his rifle and jogged down toward the gate. Before he was halfway there, he could see Rodney's Charger. He got to the gate and told the guards to let Rodney in. They opened the gate and waved the car through. Rodney pulled up to where Mark was standing and stopped the car. Mark bent down and looked into the car. It was packed full of all kinds of stuff. Sleeping bags, blankets, and duffel bags filled the back seat to the point there was barely room for the two young boys who sat there. A woman sat next to Rodney in the front seat, clutching the old shotgun Mark had seen on his trip to Rodney's house. Only now, the barrel was much shorter. The woman had very pretty features, but her hair was a mess, and she looked like she was in shock.

"What's going on Rodney?"

"You offered to let us stay here. Does that still stand?" the parts man asked.

Mark thought about how Jon would react to him letting someone else move here. How was Jess going to react to another family in their house? Maybe he should talk it over with her first. He did make the offer, though, and he had to live up to his word. "Of course it does," he answered.

"Well, we'd like to take you up on it. We watched our house burn to the ground, and then we tried to go to the Kelly shelter. They wouldn't let us in with anything but our clothes. They said we'd have to leave everything else at the gate. The car would stay in the parking lot, and my guns would have to be checked in to the armory. Our tent and our food were to be distributed for the common good. Most people in line were going for it. Most of them only had the clothes on their backs anyway, but I wasn't going to give up our stuff. There was no way to make it to our families on the East Coast, so I thought I'd come and see if you were really willing to take us in."

"Of course we will. Drive up to the last street and turn right. My house is the last one on the right. Pull into the driveway, and I'll be up in just a minute."

"Thanks, Mark. I don't know what we would have done otherwise."

"Don't mention it," Mark said, as he patted the door of the immaculate muscle car.

Mark thanked the guards for coming to get him and asked them how their shift was going. They told him that a lot of people had been coming by, and many of them had stopped to see if they could stay here. They'd all been sent sadly on their way except for Rodney and John Greene's cousin. Mark told them to call for help at the first sign of trouble. They assured him they would, and he jogged back up to his house thinking about how he was going to explain this to the others.

When he got to the house, Jess, Lisa and Alice were all looking at the black car in the driveway through the living room window. Jess was holding one of the rifles in a non-threatening manner, but in such a way that the occupants of the car could see it. When Mark walked up, Rodney got out of the car.

"Man, you guys are really serious about your defenses around here," the newcomer said, as he nodded toward the big picture window.

"Yeah, well, we've had a few run-ins with some undesirables." Mark waved to the women to come outside.

"You told me you were putting up a gate, but that's one bad gate, and the guards were polite, but they were serious about watching me, too."

"We just want to stay safe, and we are serious about it, and, if you want, we could probably use some help with guard duty."

"Whatever I can do to help. We're just so grateful to have a place to stay," Rodney said, just as the women were coming out.

Mark made the introductions all the way around and explained the Roberts' situation to Jess, Lisa, and Lisa's mother. He expected to get one of those 'We'll talk about this later' looks from Jess, but instead they just swept Donna, Rodney's wife, and the two boys, who looked to be around eight and ten, into the house. The two men followed them in. The women were seeing what they could do to help. Donna told them about watching the house catch fire and not being able to do anything about it. Then she told them how Rodney had refused to go into the shelter at the old Air Force base. They'd spent the night in the car on the side of some old country road. The girls were trying to console her as best they could. Lisa went into the kitchen to cook them an early lunch, as they had not eaten today. Alice had her arm around the new woman, explaining that she knew exactly how traumatic it was to see your house burn down. Jess suggested they move their stuff into the guest room. At that suggestion, Rodney spoke up.

"We don't want to intrude. We have a big tent and cots in the trunk of my car. If you could just let us set up the tent in the yard somewhere, we'll be fine."

Jess tried to argue with him, but Rodney wouldn't budge. He insisted that just letting them stay here was more than they could expect. Jess kept trying to get him to change his mind. Finally, Mark spoke.

"Honey, if they want to stay in the tent for now, then let them. It'll probably be cooler than the house, anyway. When it starts cooling off, if it ever does, then we can talk about it again."

This solution seemed to satisfy both parties. They all went out onto the back porch to eat. The boys, Tommy and Timmy, were especially hungry. When they had finished eating, Mark helped Rodney unload the car and put up his tent. Jess told Mark she was going to let Donna take a shower, as she thought that might help the woman feel some sense of normalcy. Mark didn't argue.

Mark spent the rest of the day checking on how things were going. The two guard towers were up. George was supervising his crew, and they were working on garden number twenty-seven. That meant they'd be going to his place next. Jess was excited about getting the first part of their garden put in and already had everything planned out with Lisa and Alice.

Mark walked down to the gate and found Gunny there with the guards. Mark was a little surprised to see him on duty. He told Mark that with the number of refugees passing by, he wanted to be here to make sure things went as smoothly as possible. He said they were seeing at least one group passing by per hour, and some hours as many as three or four, and that quite a few of the groups were carrying firearms out in the open. The funny thing about it, he said, was that the armed groups tended to be more polite and restrained than the unarmed groups. Hopefully, that would remain the fact. The two men speculated if they were seeing this much traffic on this little farm to market road, it must be much worse on the major highways out of town. Gunny told Mark he'd like to have a security committee meeting tonight to talk about how to train all of the people who were signing up for guard duty. Gunny's other concern was communication for the rovers with the CP and how to call for backup if they needed it. He suggested if they could find some kind of bell or something to ring in case of trouble, they could use that to signal everybody. Mark agreed to have a meeting tonight. He mentioned that maybe the church had a bell the preacher would let them use. Gunny remarked that Mark looked tired and said he should get some rest because he was pulling roving duty again tonight. Mark sarcastically thanked the old Marine and headed back to the house to see if he could take a nap.

It was very hot in the camper, but Mark was able to catch about an hour and a half's worth of fitful sleep. When he woke up, it was almost dinnertime. After he washed up, he headed to the deck. When he got there, he noticed a brand new picnic table butted up next to the old one.

"Where did this come from?" Mark asked.

"Your son built it," Jess answered.

Mark looked at David. "You did a great job, son!" He looked at how the table had been built. "I didn't hear the saw running. How did you do it?"

"Mr. Roberts helped me. It's exactly eight feet long, so most of the boards didn't have to be cut. The few that did, we used a handsaw. Then we just screwed it together. I still want to paint it if we can find some paint, but I think it came out pretty good."

212

"I'll say. It's wonderful."

David beamed at the complement. Mark turned to Rodney.

"Thank you."

"David did most of the work," Rodney replied. "I just showed him how to lay it out. You have a fine young man there."

The news was mostly about the fires in town and how the fire department was doing on controlling them. They'd been able to get the City Water Board pumping station safe enough that the CWB had been able to get the pump back on. This had allowed the FD to put the fire out by the pumping station and then work to save other vital infrastructure. The Police Department headquarters and City Hall had been saved. Unfortunately, the County Courthouse had been lost. Most of the hospitals in the medical center had burned, the newsman reported, and over sixty percent of the residential and commercial areas of the city were burned or burning. The Fire Department was using the Interstate Highways as fire breaks and trying to keep the fires from crossing over them. Their spokesperson hoped they could stop the fires before too much more of the city was lost. It also was sadly reported that many people did not leave their homes in time and were trapped in their section of town by surrounding fires. The death toll was estimated at twenty to thirty thousand. The fire department was now asking anyone living inside the Interstate Loop around town to evacuate to one of the two shelters. "Once all the fires are out, and we can be sure of your safety, you will be allowed to return home," the FD spokesperson said.

'Gee,' Mark thought, 'how nice of them to allow people to go to their homes.' He also wondered about how the radio station was saved, but the announcer addressed that before he signed off. He explained that since the station was the main Emergency Broadcast System station for this area, they had been placed high on the list of necessary services and been given a high priority by the fire department. There was no mention of the mayor's request to the governor to bring in National Guard troops. Perhaps, Mark hypothesized, the governor hadn't given him an answer yet.

At least there was some good news in the weather. They reported there was a cool front that should push through the area tonight or early in the morning and bring some rain and cooler temperatures. That would hopefully help with the fires in town.

People started arriving for the meeting as soon as the news was over. They seemed to be more talkative about the happenings in town than they were yesterday. Mark figured that they were over the shock from the horrific news. He let them visit a little longer than usual before he called the meeting to order. George gave his report first, and Ted gave a report on the education committee's progress. They wanted everyone who was interested in having their children enrolled in the community school to come by his house in the morning to sign them up. He also asked anyone who had any textbooks, even old ones, to bring them by. Gunny gave the report about the people who had passed the gate today since he'd been there most of the day. After he told about the number of people they had turned away, a woman in the back raised her hand.

"Do we know who the people we turned away were?"

"Whatcha mean?" Gunny asked.

"Like were any of them doctors or other people we could use?"

213

Mark had never heard it so quiet at one of the meetings. Gunny finally answered the question.

"No, ma'am. We only asked 'em if'n they knew somebody here. If they didn't, we sent 'em on their way. I can see now that maybe that wasn't the smartest thang to do."

After another long pause, Scott Simmons spoke. "I make a motion that we form a committee to interview any people who ask to move in here. Then if the committee feels they would be an asset to the community, they present their case to the whole group to be voted on."

"I second it!" someone yelled.

"Okay. All in fav…" Mark was interrupted.

"Where are we going to put the people we let move in here?" It was Jon.

"We could ask for volunteers to let them move in with a family that's not too crowded, or we could put them in a tent in someone's yard or one of the empty lots. I'm sure if we found a doctor, we could find a place for him to stay," Scott argued with his former friend.

"Well, I can see where a doctor might be an exception, but we don't need any more people," Jon spat.

"What if some solar energy engineer came by and had a truck load of solar panels?" Susan asked with same tone Jon had used.

"Well, I think that if anyone is presented to the group for a vote, part of the presentation should be where they are going to live. AND…I think this is something only the homeowners should vote on."

"Jon, we've talked about this before." Mark was trying to keep his voice from revealing how much he wanted to put Jon in his place. He hoped he was succeeding. "Everyone here deserves a say in matters that affect us all. I believe everyone deserves a vote."

A few cheers of 'Right on' and 'Hell yeah' could be heard in the crowd.

"I do like your idea about having a place for them to live before the committee presents them to us, and I would like to amend it to the motion." Mark hoped that would satisfy Jon.

"I'm pleased you like at least one of my ideas," Jon said sarcastically, "but I still say that the homeowners should be making the important decisions. We have more guests here now than we do residents. What if they decide to vote us out of our homes?"

"Do you really think that would happen?" Mark answered with a question.

"Probably not. But it could!" Some of the homeowners, mostly those with no guests, nodded their heads in agreement with Jon.

"But what's to stop the homeowners from making us do all the work if they're the only ones with votes?" Scott's brother-in-law challenged. There were more exclamations from the crowd.

Mark could see that there was a division forming between the homeowners and newcomers. In fact, it was starting to get ugly. He didn't know what to say to calm the situation down.

"Mark, I have an idea," Ted said.

"Yes, Ted?" The history professor moved to the front.

"In the late eighteenth century, there was a debate much like the one we are having now. The solution they came up with is called 'The Great Compromise.'

That's how we ended up with a two-house legislature. We could do the same thing here. Any item that has to be voted on could have to pass both the homeowners' vote and the whole group's vote. That way, the majority couldn't throw the homeowners out of their houses, and the homeowners can't turn the newcomers into slaves."

This seemed to satisfy almost everyone. 'I get by with a little help from my friends,' Mark thought. It was strange that someone always came up with the right answer.

"As far as voting, I guess that'll work," Jon conceded, "but I think only the homeowners should be able to make and second motions."

"Jon, I don't think that's necessary. If someone makes a motion that the homeowners don't like, they'll vote it down. Right?"

"I guess so, but I don't like it," he said, as he folded his arms.

At the moment, Mark was glad that Jon had never reproduced. One of him was way more than enough to deal with. A motion was made, seconded, and passed by both groups on Ted's suggestion. Then the same thing happened with the previous motion. Mark asked for suggestions about who should be on the new committee. Lisa and Doc Vasquez were nominated since the main skills needed were medical. Manny was nominated, and Mark thought it was about time his even temperament and wisdom were recognized. Henry Patterson nominated his wife, Mary. He said she'd been in the Human Resources office at her company and was good at sizing people up. That made four. Mark knew that committees worked better with an odd number, so there could be no tie votes. When he mentioned this, Ted nominated him. Mark told him it was out of the question, as he was already on the security committee.

"That's bullshit!" Ted blurted. "You have no problem with me or Lisa being on two committees, and I suspect no one here has a problem with you being on two, either. You haven't steered us wrong yet. I value your opinion, and I suspect most everyone here does, too. So unless you can come up with a better excuse than that, consider yourself nominated!"

"Okay. I give," Mark answered. They voted on the nominations after they were seconded and accepted them by an overwhelming margin. Gunny was then able to finish his report by asking if anyone knew of a bell they could use to call reinforcements to the CP if necessary. He also mentioned that they could use some way to communicate with the roving guards at night, if anyone had any ideas. Since no one had any other business, Mark adjourned the meeting.

He called the new committee together and suggested that each one take a twenty-four hour period to respond to the gate if anyone asked to be admitted. Then, if that committee member felt they had skills or anything else that might be useful to the community, they would call the whole committee together to talk to that person or persons. This seemed to be a logical procedure to all of them, and they agreed. Mary Patterson agreed to take the first watch.

Mark then headed to his security committee meeting. On the way there, Rodney stopped him. He told Mark he was impressed with the organization they'd built in the subdivision in such a short time. He also wanted to know who the troublemaker was and what his problem was. Mark told the parts man he'd have to fill him in later because he had another meeting to go to.

"That's what I wanted to talk to you about. The older gentleman asked if anyone had a bell we could use for an alarm. Have you guys thought about using a car horn? You could tie as many together as necessary to get the volume you want."

"That's a wonderful idea, Rodney. Thanks. I'll present it to the committee right now."

"I thought you could use these, too." Rodney handed him a plastic Kroger bag.

Mark looked into the bag and saw four Motorola FRS walkie-talkies. There were also rechargeable batteries and a charger. Mark didn't know what to say.

Rodney spoke before he could say thanks. "They were in the shop, and they all work. I had them in an old metal desk, and I guess that plus the fact the building is metal, protected them from the EMP. I don't really have a use for them, and letting you guys use them is the least I can do for y'all letting us stay here. I also want to help out on guard duty, if you'll have me."

"Thanks, Rodney. We'd be honored to have your help, and thanks so much for the use of your radios." Mark smiled as he headed over to Gunny's.

The members of the security committee all slapped their heads when Mark told them of Rodney's horn idea. Then they were speechless when Mark showed them the radios and batteries. Mark also informed Gunny that Rodney had volunteered to help with security.

Gunny told the committee that he now had forty-seven more people who had volunteered for guard duty. Eighteen of them were women. Mark asked if Susan had given any thought to their discussion from last night. She told the men that, while she thought the possibility of any of the women not taking their duties seriously was remote, she felt that any mixed groups should have at least two members from each sex. That meant groups smaller than four would have to be same sex. The men agreed that would probably remove almost any possibility of accusations from spouses of the guards. Gunny conceded that women would be allowed to man any post except for one. He felt the team on the gate should be men only. Susan felt he was being chauvinistic and said so. Gunny explained that some of the refugees might feel they could push the women around more than men. Gunny agreed those men would be wrong, especially if Susan was on duty, he said with a wry smile, but the fact remained, he stressed, that women would not be able to deter a belligerent bully as well as a man could. After they discussed it for a while, a vote was taken, and Susan lost that one battle. She did get the men to agree to revisit this policy in a month or two. She also asked that the women be mixed in with the men for training and that no special allowances be made for them. If a woman couldn't cut it, just like the men, then they should be released from guard duty.

Gunny said with all the people they had now, he figured they could go to six-hour shifts and work four days on and two off. If they could get a few more people, then he could go to four on, three off, which was the schedule he preferred. He also wanted to appoint a captain for each guard shift, called Alpha through Delta. He wanted anyone wanting to switch teams to have to okay it with him. If they wanted to trade days off with one of their team members, then they would clear it with the captains. Chaparo asked if he had anyone in mind for the captains. Gunny wanted Scott for Alpha shift, Charley for Beta, Jim for

Charley shift, and Mark for Delta. Mark briefly argued that he didn't want to do it, but Gunny insisted that all of his picks were based on the person's proven ability to think on their feet and the fact that they were all respected by the men. And the women, Susan added, with a wink. The old Jarhead then told his fellow committee members that he wanted to set up the training schedule where each guard trained with his group one to two hours, four times a week. The all-day classes were just too hard to schedule everyone for. Two classes would be with Gunny, one with Jim on marksmanship, and one with Mark on unarmed self-defense and hand to hand. He told Mark that meant he'd need to teach four classes a week. Mark asked how long he'd need to teach.

Gunny just smiled as he answered. "Until they know everything you know, Karate Man."

The committee voted to accept Gunny's new schedule until he had enough men to improve it. Chaparo informed the group he still needed more angle iron for the remaining guard towers. He wanted to be added to one of the night shifts. That would let him do the welding and such that needed to be done during the day.

With the meeting over and security measures really starting to take form, Mark headed home. When he got there, he found there had been enough water saved for him to have a quick shower. Afterwards, the adults visited for a while, mostly getting to know Rodney and Donna a little better. Mark asked Rodney if he would hook up the horn at the CP like he'd suggested. The man was happy to help out. Mark also explained to Rodney about Jon and how things had gotten so bad. Before he could finish, Lisa asked if anyone else heard Jon's wife reading him the riot act after the meeting. No one had, and Lisa told them about it. It seemed Mrs. Olsen was not too happy with the way her husband was acting. She told him he needed to shape up and pitch in, or else. Lisa said she didn't say what the 'or else' meant, but it didn't sound good. Mark asked how Jon reacted. Lisa said he was mad at first, but by the time she finished, he was hanging his head and saying, 'Yes, dear.' Mark hoped that perhaps she had been able to get through to him.

Since he had to get up at 1:30 to report for Delta shift, Mark excused himself and went to bed. He hated the shift he was on. It was the coolest part of the day and the time when one could sleep the most comfortably, but he knew Gunny had given him this shift first for all the right reasons. If he got the easy shift, people could cry favoritism.

When the alarm went off, Mark was amazed at how fast he'd gone to sleep. He almost didn't remember lying down. He got dressed and reported to the CP at 1:53 AM. It was dead calm and very humid. Mark hoped the front would get here quickly. Scott was just coming off duty and told Mark that Gunny had moved him to the 8 AM to 2PM shift starting day after tomorrow. Mark had different men assigned to his crew tonight, and they were given one of the FRS radios by the CP sentry. Mark and his crew started their rounds. It started raining softly a few minutes later. Mark and his men went by their houses one at a time to pick up their rain gear. The shift again went without a hitch. It was miserable being in the rain, maybe even more uncomfortable than the heat had been. Oh well, he thought, it was a dirty job, but somebody had to do it.

As he was walking home from his shift, he noticed the water dripping out of the gutter downspouts on the houses. Shouldn't they be catching that water? He made a detour by Chaparo's. If anyone could do it, it was the plumber. He told Mark he would work on it.

Mark went home, dried off and put on some clean, dry pajamas. He crawled into his bed in the house. He was just about to doze off when he felt a warm body slip into bed beside him. The sound of the rain on the roof and the feel of his wife beside him almost made it seem as if everything was normal, if only for the moment.

Chapter 32

The next few days were almost a blur for Mark. The weather cooled off, and it was pleasant at night and not too uncomfortable during the day. The rain also helped the San Antonio Fire Department bring the fires in the city under control. Chaparo came up with a way to catch the water off of the roof for each house. It consisted of building a plywood box, lining it with plastic, then running PVC pipe from the gutters to the box. The boxes would measure four by four by eight and would hold up to nine hundred sixty gallons. Mark had never stopped to figure that one inch of rain over a two thousand square foot roof would yield twelve hundred and fifty gallons of water. Now, they only needed to find a source of plywood. Chaparo was running pipe so everyone could fill their bathtubs up, then when they got their plywood water tank, the overflow would go into it. Fortunately, Chaparo had plenty of pipe. Rodney got the warning horn, as they were now calling it, hooked up. Gunny had worked out different signals with the horn to call reinforcements to where they were needed. The FRS radios were working great for the roving teams. The gardens were coming along a little easier since the rain had softened the ground a little.

The first part of the Turner garden was tilled on Monday morning, and by that afternoon, Jess had it completely planted. Almost everyone had signed their kids up for schooling, and that meant programs had to be designed for almost a hundred and twenty kids from ages five to eighteen. That was more than the education committee had planned, but they assured everyone they'd come up with some kind of plan. Jim had finished filling the seven 55-gallon barrels with gasoline. He reported there was still about two hundred fifty to three hundred gallons in the cars that wouldn't run, but he had no place else to store it.

Mark taught his first classes for the guards on Tuesday, one in the morning and one in the afternoon, focusing on basic self-defense. He was pleased with the way they were absorbing the training. He was also enjoying the classes he was taking from Gunny and Jim. With the weather cooling off, everyone seemed to be in a better mood. Even Jon had simmered down and had signed back up to be a guard. Perhaps the little talk with his wife had worked. Gunny had wisely assigned him to Charley's crew, as Jon hadn't had any run-ins with him. Charley reported that he was doing a good job, even though he seemed a little under-motivated.

The news had little to report except the fires and the fire department putting out all of the hot spots before they released people to go check on their homes. The refugee traffic had slowed considerably since most people had already left town or checked into one of the two huge shelters. Nothing more was said about martial law or the governor bringing in the National Guard. Mark noticed a subtle change in the news. Before the fires in town, there was little, if any, local news. Now, it seemed there was no national news, as well. It was as if all of the news was being whitewashed. Even the President, in his Tuesday night speech, basically said nothing. It made Mark wonder what was going on.

After the Tuesday night meeting, Jess surprised Mark with some news of her own. It seemed that she and Lisa had volunteered for guard duty and training. Gunny had assigned them both to Beta shift, since they'd be teaching school in the morning. Mark was mad at first. He tried to talk her out of it, but she wouldn't budge. He finally agreed, hoping she would change her mind once she started pulling duty and saw what was involved.

The talent scouts, as the members of the new committee had come to be called, had interviewed a few people but none they were willing to present to the group. On Wednesday morning, that changed. Mark had just finished his two to eight shift and was taking a short nap before facing the rest of the day, as was becoming his habit. Sam came in and woke him up.

"Dad, Dad, wake up," she said as she shook his shoulder.

"What is it?" Mark said, as he looked at his watch.

"Lisa needs you at the gate. She says she has someone the talent scouts need to talk to."

When Mark got to the gate, everyone else was there except for Doc Vasquez. He looked over his shoulder and saw the good doctor just a few yards behind him. Lisa was talking to a couple Mark estimated to be in their early fifties. The man was tall, thin, and mostly bald. The woman was average height and weight, and had long, dark hair. When the whole committee was present, Lisa made the introductions. The couple's names were Steven and Jackie Hawkins. Jackie was a kindergarten teacher for one of the larger school districts in San Antonio, and Steven was a junior high school band director for the same district. Upon further questioning, they found out Steven could not only play most band instruments, he also was an accomplished guitar player and wasn't bad on the piano. He'd also been the music director for his church for the last fifteen years. The couple didn't have any children, and their only living relative was Jackie's brother who lived in Florida. They were hoping to find a place to live out of town. They only had a little food, Steven's guitar, and some blankets and clothing with them.

Mark and the others were very interested in the story of how they came to Silver Hills. They lived in a small neighborhood not too far from the airport. One of the planes that had crashed on the day of The Burst had burned most of the area around the small subdivision. Since everything was already burned, it created a firebreak around them. However, when city officials asked everyone to evacuate to the shelters, the Hawkins obeyed, like law-abiding citizens do. After a couple of days, people wanted to go home, Steven told the talent scouts. Everyone was told that the Fire Department was still making sure the fires would not re-ignite. They were told to come by the admission tent at the shelter, where the staff had a list by block where the houses weren't burned.

"Everyone I talked to said they were told that their block was a total loss," the band director said. "When I asked them about my house, I was told the same thing, but I didn't believe it. I never saw any smoke from the direction of our house, and unless someone started a fire in our neighborhood, I don't think the fire could have reached it. On Monday night, some people were starting to get pretty upset about not being allowed to leave. Some were pretty vocal about it, and the soldiers at the shelter arrested a couple of the most belligerent. That calmed the rest down, but it should have made them madder, I thought. The ones taken into custody weren't being violent. They just didn't go back to their spot when the soldiers told them to. Everyone just gave up and went back to their spot. I did, too, but I didn't plan to stay there."

220

"When Steven told me what he wanted to do, I thought he was crazy," Jackie said, taking over the story telling. "I always thought our government officials had our best interest at heart. I knew that sometimes they were a little misguided, but they meant well, right? Well, when Steven told me they had arrested people for just saying that they wanted out of the shelter, I began to think that maybe they weren't interested in what was best for us, but what was best for them."

"How so?" Mark asked.

Steven answered. "We wondered why they'd want to keep us in the shelter. We snuck out through a drainage ditch that goes under the fence. It was easier than I thought it would be. We walked to our house, and it wasn't even scratched. That's when we figured it was easier for them to have everyone in a few places. If they declared martial law, they'd need to have a lot more military personnel to keep the peace if people were out and about, especially if over half of them were now homeless. There were never more than fifty or sixty soldiers on duty at any time at the airport that I saw. They were all carrying rifles and no one came into the camp with any guns. They ran over us with those hand held metal detectors when we entered the shelter. They even took away my little Leatherman tool; you know, the one that folds out into tiny scissors. Nobody could do much of anything except for what we were told to do. There's no way they could've patrolled even a fraction of the city with that many soldiers. We think keeping us in the shelters was a simple fact of conserving military manpower."

"Anyway, we got home, ate a couple of cold cans of vegetables and went to bed," Jackie said. "About three in the morning, we heard glass breaking at our neighbor's house. A few minutes later, we heard a couple of voices cursing about how there wasn't anything good in there. Then we heard them trying our doors. Steven yelled 'Get me my gun!' and they ran off. For the first time in my life, I wished we really owned one. We didn't get any more sleep that night. We spent the rest of the night whispering about what to do. Steven has a colleague who lives outside of town on a couple of acres. We decided to ride our bikes to his place and see if we could stay there. We spent the day loading our bicycles, but we didn't really have anything but a little food and some clothes that would do us any good. We rested as much as we could, and as soon as it got dark, we took off."

Steven tagged back in. "At first, we were being really careful not to be seen by the authorities. However, except for the few times we passed close to where one of the fires was still burning, we didn't see anyone except what looked like street thugs and homeless people. One rough looking group told us to give them our bikes, but we turned around and rode away as fast as we could. Once we got to the totally burned part of town, there was nobody. A little after dawn, we got to my friend's house. His house was still there, but we couldn't find him or his family anywhere. The doors were all unlocked, and there was some blood on the kitchen floor. It looked like a tornado had blown through the house. Man, I hope they're okay. We figured it wasn't safe to stay there, so we decided to ride further out of town. That's when we saw your people at the gate."

"I was wondering what was happening at the shelters," Mark observed.

"I expect if they don't let people leave pretty soon, it's going to get violent," Steven projected.

"Mr. and Mrs. Hawkins, do you have any other skills that might be helpful to us?" Mary Patterson asked, in a voice Mark was sure prospective employees of her company had heard many times.

"The only thing I can think of is that I'm certified to teach math, as well as music. I haven't taught it in many years, but I did when I first got out of college until I got a full time music position. Lisa told me you all are starting a school and might need a math teacher and a kindergarten teacher."

Mark looked at Lisa. He'd have to talk to her about saying too much to strangers.

"Anything else?" Mary inquired.

Both of them shook their heads.

"Then would you excuse us for a moment?"

"Sure," the man answered. "Let me just say, if you all let us stay here, we will do our fair share. We don't have anywhere else to go, so we can't afford to disappoint you."

The talent scouts all nodded their heads as they moved back out of earshot from the couple.

"What do y'all think?" Manny asked.

"I say we give them some food and send them on their way," Mark answered first.

"That's pretty cold. They don't have anywhere to go, they're obviously nice people, and they could really help us teach the kids," Lisa snapped at Mark.

"Are we going to take them in because they're nice and don't have anywhere else to go? We might as well let everybody who walks by move in," Mark shot back.

"I agree with Mark," Mary said. "We don't need a music teacher, and anyone can teach kindergarten. It might be nice to have a math teacher, but he hasn't done that for a long time. The benefits just don't justify taking in two more mouths to feed."

"Mary, I expected the men to be short-sighted but not you. We can use a music teacher, and teaching young children is a lot more complicated than 1, 2, 3's and A, B, C's," Lisa said.

"I think Lisa's right. Music is important. I think this is a good opportunity to improve our teaching staff. Remember, we have a hundred and twenty kids to educate," Doctor Vasquez added.

Everyone looked at Manny. His would be the deciding vote. "I'm not sure which way to vote. I don't know that much about education, but if Lisa and the Doc think these people could help us, then I'm going to vote to present the Hawkins to the group."

"Who are they going to live with? We have to find someone who will take them in before we can take them before the whole group," Mary cautioned.

"They can move in with us," Doc Vasquez volunteered.

"I guess that settles it," Mark said. "Doc, you want to take them to your house until tonight?"

The doctor nodded.

222

"I think you need to talk to them about how this is going to work, that if the group doesn't accept them, they'll have to leave by tomorrow morning at the latest."

"Okay, Mark."

The doctor went and got the Hawkins. Everyone else headed back up to their houses. Mark and Lisa walked up the hill, and Mark mentioned to her that she should be careful about how much information she gives out to strangers. At first, she bristled at Mark's suggestion, but before they got back to the house, she understood. Jess was in the kitchen when they walked in, and Lisa filled her in on the couple they would vote on that night. Jess was very excited about both of the escapees. Mark asked her why.

"Because children need to be exposed to more than just the three R's. Art is important, and music is an important art. Music students always do better in their other subjects. There have been a lot of studies that prove it."

"Why so giddy over a kindergarten teacher though?"

"Let me ask you a question. When you get brand new, white belt students in your karate class, who teaches them?"

"I do."

"Why? Aren't they learning the most basic things? Couldn't anyone in your class teach them?"

"Yes, but I like to do it because what they learn at first is what all of their karate is going to be built on. If they don't understand what they're doing and why in the beginning…" Mark paused, realizing what she was doing. "I hate it when you do that!" he said with a smile.

"Do what?" Jess smiled back.

"You know what. Making me answer my own question. But now I see why you're excited about Mrs. Hawkins."

By meeting time, almost everyone knew about the Hawkins. Most had made up their minds, and a few impromptu polls showed that, while it was close, the couple did not have the votes they needed to be granted admittance to Silver Hills. Once all of the other business had been completed, everyone was acquainted with the prospective residents. Lisa brought them up and introduced them to the group and explained why the committee had voted to bring them before the group for a vote. Mark thought she did a good job of explaining the benefits of having them here. Obviously, everyone could see the downside to having more mouths to feed. Both of the candidates said a few words to the crowd about what they could offer and how much they'd appreciate an opportunity to help out with the education of the children. Mark felt that Lisa might have swayed enough people to her side. He asked if anyone else would like to say something before they took the vote. Jon raised his hand.

"I was afraid this would happen if we formed this committee. We said we were looking for a doctor, and you bring us a drum major and a glorified baby sitter. What's on the agenda for next week? A clown because he makes everyone laugh? Let's get real, people. We can't afford to let everyone in here just because they might be able to help out a little. I say we can't afford to take them in."

Jon had probably swayed some votes back to the 'no' side, Mark thought. He asked if anyone else wanted to say something.

Jess stood up and addressed the crowd. "I want to say that I think we need these teachers. Mr. Hawkins is not only a music teacher, he's also a certified math teacher. We can stand here and debate the merits of having some music instruction incorporated into our education program. I think music is extremely important, but not everyone agrees. However, I think everyone would agree that mathematics is very important. If the music is nothing but a fringe benefit of having him here, then he can earn his keep teaching math. Mrs. Hawkins is an experienced primary educator. The first three years of schooling are the most important in a child's education because that's what the foundation of their knowledge base is built upon. They are not just learning their alphabet and numbers; they are learning how to learn. If we can't…"

Jon rudely interrupted Jess. "You just want them here to make your job easier! You won't admit that we don't need them because you're a teacher just like them who gets paid mostly just to babysit!"

Mark saw the look on Jess's face. He'd seen it a few times in the nineteen years they'd been married, and it was never good for whomever made her look that way. He knew what was coming. Mark almost felt sorry for Jon.

"Jon Olsen," she started, with her voice barely above a whisper and speaking very slowly and emphatically even though her face was as red as a fire engine. Each word was spoken slightly louder and more quickly than the one before. "I have listened to you spew your hateful crap for long enough. You don't know what you're talking about. I have been a professional educator for over twenty years. Do you have any experience educating children?"

Jon just shook his head, having the gall to look shocked at the reaction he was getting. Mark wondered what he'd expected Jess to do. If he thought he could intimidate her into just stopping, he obviously didn't know who he was dealing with.

"Do you even have any experience raising children?" she demanded.

"No, but…"

"Then why don't you just shut the fuck up and let me finish!"

A roar erupted from the crowd. Some were cheering, others were laughing, and most were doing some form of both. It took more than a minute for the crowd to quiet down enough for Jess to finish. Mark looked, and Jon seemed to have melted to about half of his former size. The guy just didn't get it. Mark wondered if he ever would. When Mark called for the vote, the Hawkins were voted in to the community by a landslide. Mark wasn't sure if it was because Jess had convinced everyone they were needed, or if it was because she had said to Jon what most of them wanted to say. He suspected the latter. Ted asked if the education committee could meet with the Hawkins, and the meeting broke up.

Mark's alarm clock went off at 1:30. He got up and got ready to pull his shift. It was hard to get up in the middle of the night, but today was like a Friday to him, even if it was Thursday. He had to pull this shift and teach his two classes today, but then Gunny didn't have him scheduled again until Monday morning. He, David, and a couple of the other men were going down to his deer lease early tomorrow to see if they could get some meat. He was looking forward to spending some time with his son, even if Jess wasn't crazy about them going.

224

The sky was clear, and it was almost too cool. There must have been a billion stars in the sky. Mark and his men made their rounds without incident until almost dawn. Mark's radio crackled, and then a voice came over it.

"CP to Rover One and Rover Two." Both Mark and the other team leader responded.

"OP reports a large group heading for the gate from the west on foot. ETA six to eight minutes."

Mark and his crew started heading to the front. "CP, this is Rover One. Can OP estimate number of travelers?"

"Stand by, Rover One." There was a pause for the CP to relay the question to the OP and get his answer over the CB's. Mark wished they were all on the same frequency. It would make things easier. "Rover One, OP reports best estimate at twenty-five to thirty. He says they are not using any light or sound discipline. He also reports he can see a few weapons. He cannot confirm how many."

"Roger that, CP. Rover Two, this is Rover One."

"Go ahead, Rover One."

"Rover Two, proceed directly to Foxhole Two. I'm sending Ted and Joe to join you. I'm going straight to the gate foxhole."

"Roger, Rover One. Rover Two is headed to Foxhole Two."

"CP, do you read?"

"Go ahead, Rover One."

"Paul, wake Scott up and have him get some of his crew into Foxhole Three as quickly as he can. Give him the spare walkie-talkie and have him give me a call when he's in position. Have him send someone to get Gunny."

"Roger, Rover One. CP is waking Charley shift."

Mark was trotting as he spoke into the radio. Now that he didn't need to talk, he broke into a full run. It took less than four minutes from the time Paul had called him from the CP to the time he was in the foxhole with the gate guards. He could see flashlight beams from where the visitors were coming from. He hoped they would pass the subdivision by. A few minutes later, he heard Scott on the radio.

"Delta shift. This is Charley shift. I am in Foxhole Three with two of my crew. Don went to wake the old man."

"Roger that, Scott. OK, guys, this is what we've been training for. Everybody just sit tight, and hopefully they'll just waltz right by."

Mark could hear the people coming now, as well as see their lights. It was a good sign, he thought, that they didn't know what they were doing. Good for him, anyway. The group got closer and closer to the gate. Mark could see that most of the grownups were carrying bottles. He couldn't tell for sure what was in them, but from the slurred speech, he was betting it wasn't Kool-Aid. There were about twenty adults and around ten kids. When they got to the entrance of the subdivision, the leader of the pack noticed the heavy gate."

"Whoa! Look at that gate. That'll keep the riff-raff out, I bet." The man was almost hollering. "Anybody there?"

Mark and the others kept their heads down and hoped the drunks would go away. The loudmouth put one foot on the gate and started to climb.

"Hold it right there!" Mark barked authoritatively.

The drunken man jumped back off of the gate and looked around trying to figure out where the voice had come from. "Who said that? Where are you?"

"I'm on the other side of the gate. You are not welcome here. Please move on down the road."

"We want to take a little rest. You let us in," the drunken man demanded.

"I'm sorry. We don't have a place for you to rest. Please just move along, and no one will get hurt."

"You can't threaten us. We have guns."

"I see that. We have more guns, and they're all aimed at you right now."

The drunken man must have not been too drunk. He changed his tact. "We don't wanna hurt nobody. We escaped from that damned shelter, and we just want to rest up a little. Couldn't you let us take a little nap?"

"I'm sorry, but that's not possible. If you move on down the road a couple of miles, I'm sure you can find a place. Good luck."

One of the women came up and grabbed the loudmouth. "Come on, Kyle, let's go."

"OK, but these people are damn inconsiderate," he yelled. "You hear me? You're a lousy host." The group started moving down the road, still making all kinds of racket and shining their light all over the place.

Mark breathed a sigh of relief. He didn't want to get into a fight with a bunch of drunks. When the pack had ambled out of sight of the OP, Mark gave the all-clear sign. He went back up to the CP and found Gunny there. It was daylight enough to see now. Gunny told everyone to report to his house for debriefing as soon as Delta shift was over.

By 8:05, all of Delta shift and part of Charley shift was at Gunny and Abby's house. Abby had a huge dining room table, and she served the men breakfast, as Gunny spoke to them. He asked them what happened, step by step. Everyone felt the encounter had gone fairly well, but there was something that bothered Mark.

"We only had eight minutes' notice with a loud, easy-to-spot group of people walking up the road. What if they'd been quiet and hard to spot? Or if they were coming in vehicles? We may have had a minute or less. We need more time than that. We also need a way to get a backup crew of more than three men in a short time."

"Anything else?" Gunny asked.

"Yeah," Paul Jensen answered. "We could use a way to have everyone on the same radio frequency. Having to relay a message back and forth slows us down. Plus when I went to get Scott, there was no way for the Rovers to communicate with anyone."

Mark was glad Paul had mentioned that. Gunny told the men the security committee would discuss all of their concerns at their next meeting. He encouraged the men to enjoy their breakfast and told them that they'd done a good job. The teams finished eating and thanked Abby for the delicious meal. On their way out, Gunny had a request.

"Karate Man, would you stay for a minute or two?"

"Sure, Gunny, what's up?"

Gunny told Mark that he'd heard about the hunting trip that Mark and David had planned. He asked Mark not to go. When Mark asked why, Gunny said that he needed him here.

"You're right about needin' a reserve crew to call if'n things look like they's goin' to shit. I need you to be on that crew for the next few nights."

"Damnit, Gunny, no. I need a break, and I need to spend some time with David. He's looking forward to this, and I'm not going to disappoint him."

"I understand how you feel, but now is not the time to go. I'm afraid things is fixin' to go to hell in a hand basket, and we need all our best people here, not out gallavantin' around where we have to worry about them."

"Jess put you up to this, didn't she?"

"I'm not gonna lie to ya, Karate Man. She's the one who told me about the trip, but nobody's put me up to nothin' since my last commander in the Corps. I need someone here I can count on. You're still off for the next few days. You can do anything you like, just do it here. Spend the next three days with David doing whatever. I'm just puttin' ya 'on call' for the next three nights."

"NO! Find someone else. I'm going."

"You and the committee put me in charge of the guard schedules. You said I had final say. Are you gonna be the first one to refuse to comply with the schedule? What kind of example will that set for everybody?"

Mark knew Gunny had a point. He reluctantly agreed to Gunny's request.

Mark looked at his watch and saw it was time for his morning self defense class. This was to be his first class with Beta shift. Beta was almost half women. Susan, who was on Beta, had accused Gunny of stacking the women into one shift. Gunny had told her that was just the way it worked out, but Mark had also noticed that almost all of the women were either in Alpha or Beta. His shift did not have any women, and Charley shift only had two. He'd mentioned this to Gunny as well and had gotten the same answer Susan had.

When his class showed up, he first went over the benefits of a physical training program with them. He told them how to assess their physical condition and gave them a program to improve it. Next, he started going over defenses for frontal attacks. He told the guard they couldn't be squeamish or hesitant about defending themselves.

"If someone's trying to hurt you, you have to hurt them bad enough that they don't want to continue attacking you. That usually means broken bones, dislocated joints, or blood. You need to think about that. Remember, if you have to use these techniques, your life is in danger. It is you or them. If you can't pick yourself, then maybe you shouldn't be a guard." Mark wanted to make sure that everyone, especially the women, knew all of the ramifications of what they were doing.

Mark then explained how to get out of a choke and a bear hug attack. He demonstrated with a volunteer and then had the guards split into pairs and start practicing. When everyone seemed to have those moves down fairly well, he started teaching them how to defend against a punch. He showed them the steps to the defense, the same ones he'd used successfully in the Kroger attack.

Mark demonstrated the movements as he spoke. "If a right-handed punch is thrown at you, you step to the left while striking the arm of your attacker with the outside edge of both of your hands. Then you slide your right hand down to his wrist and grab it. Next, with your open left palm, smash the back of his elbow to dislocate it."

Mark asked for a volunteer to help him show what it looked like when the punch was really coming at you. Jon jumped up and offered to help. Mark was a little taken back. Jon was the last person he thought would volunteer to help. However, he had signed up for guard duty, which was an indication that he still felt some kind of obligation to the community. Or maybe his wife made him do it, Mark thought. Mark fussed at himself for thinking negatively about his neighbor. He had to give him the benefit of the doubt. Perhaps he was really trying to make amends. Yes, he had strong opinions. That was no crime. In fact, a dissenting view was good because it made you look at all sides of an issue. Jon was really an asset by disagreeing with the majority; he just needed to work on the way he presented his disagreements. Still, Mark couldn't help but wonder what was going through Jon's mind; especially after Jess had humiliated him last night.

"OK, Jon, we're going to do this about half-speed." Then he addressed the group. "When you do this with your partner, please be VERY careful when you strike the elbow. It doesn't take much force to really dislocate it." He turned back to face Jon. "Okay, go."

Jon's right hand came flying at Mark's face. If Mark hadn't been completely ready, and if Jon hadn't slightly telegraphed the punch, Mark would have been wiping blood from his nose. However, Mark's block met Jon's arm just in time to deflect it, so that the fist just barely grazed the side of his face. Mark's anger flared for just a fraction of a second. By the time he grabbed Jon's wrist, he had it under control and finished the demonstration.

Mark was pretty sure Jon had done it intentionally but took responsibility for the misunderstanding. "I'm sorry, Jon. I didn't explain myself very well. I want you to go about HALF of that speed. Let's show them again."

Mark was ready this time. He already had his weight shifted, so he could step quickly, and he was watching Jon's right shoulder for the first hint of movement, just in case he did the same thing. By the time he noticed that it was Jon's left hand coming toward his face, it was too late. There was no way for him to get his weight shifted back, so he could step to the right. He decided to go ahead and move to the left to try to dodge the punch. Unfortunately, his reflexes, now forty years old, were not as quick as they once had been. The punch slammed into his face just below his right eye. He saw a flash of color that changed from red to purple to blue to yellow and then back to red. Mark's hand was on his face, and he'd stepped back from Jon and turned sideways so he could sidekick if the jerk closed to strike him again. All of that happened without him thinking about it. What he was thinking about was how he wanted to grind Jon into dog meat. He pulled his hand down from his eye and checked his vision. Everything looked a little red. Mark wasn't sure if that was from the punch or because he was so mad. He took a deep breath. He wanted to knock Jon into next week, but he couldn't retaliate in anger. He took another deep breath.

"Jon, please have a seat and see me after class."

"What's the matter?" Jon asked sarcastically. "Seems like your Karate mumbo jumbo doesn't work too good. Maybe it'll work against one of the girls. That why you want me to sit down? So you can get one of the girls up here?"

"NO, JON!" Mark had to calm down. "I am trying to teach here, and I can't do that with you playing these childish games. Now, please sit down."

"Childish, huh? I guess nothing I do is good enough for you Turners!" Jon was starting to get a little red in the face. "You wanna teach something! Why don't you show everybody how to get your ass whooped!"

Jon lunged at Mark. He grabbed the Black Belt around the waist and tackled him. Mark fell on his back with Jon on top of him. On the ground was the last place a karateka wanted to find himself. You couldn't kick, or even punch, effectively from this position. Most people with someone on top of them would try to push them off. That used a tremendous amount of energy, and even someone in good shape would be out of breath in a short time. Fortunately, after Mark got his black belt, he took a few Jiu Jitsu lessons. He couldn't hold a candle to the guys in the class who'd been doing it for years, but it had taught him some important lessons. Ground fighting was a thinking man's game. Mark took a deep breath and made himself relax. Jon seemed to be satisfied to be in the superior position and wasn't trying to do anything except punch at Mark's face. Mark was able to block most of the blows, and the ones that got through weren't doing much damage. He dug one of his elbows into Jon's thigh. This made Jon move back over Mark's hips. Mark caught and trapped one of Jon's hands and then thrust his hips up as fast as he could. That threw Jon off balance, and he wasn't able to catch himself with his trapped hand. He rolled off and unwittingly pulled Mark on top of him. Before Jon could lock his ankles together behind Mark's back, Mark grabbed Jon's jeans at the knees and pushed down. He then jumped to the side and climbed onto Jon effectively reversing the positions they'd started in.

Jon must have had some ground fighting training, probably in the Marines. He tried to do the same thing Mark had done, but each time he tried to use his elbows to push Mark back, Mark reached down, pulled the elbow up and returned his knees under Jon's armpits. When Jon saw that this tactic wasn't working, he panicked a little and tried to push Mark off. When he placed a hand on Mark's chest to push up, Mark would swim his arm between Jon's and knock the former Marine's hand off of him. Jon was using his energy up quickly, and after a moment, he switched tactics again. He tried to punch Mark in the groin between pushes, but Mark kept his body down, and all Jon could reach was the outside of Mark's hips or his ribs. Mark asked Jon quietly if he'd had enough. Between gasps of air, Jon made an unkind comment about Mark and his mother. Then he crossed the line.

"I'm gonna kill you, mother fucker!" he screamed. "You and that bitch you're married to."

That was it. Jon had pushed the right button. Mark wasn't mad, he wasn't angry, he was outraged that someone would threaten his wife, especially with her in the group to hear it. He felt himself go cold. The next time Jon pushed up, Mark trapped his assailant's hand to his chest and jumped up. He had practiced this move so many times in Jiu Jitsu that he'd changed positions before anyone, especially Jon, who was almost out of gas, could see what happened. Mark was on his back perpendicular to Jon, with one leg across his chest and the other across his neck. He had Jon's arm with the elbow pinned between his knees creating a fulcrum. He pulled down on Jon's arm until he could see the pain in Jon's face.

Mark spoke in a low growl, where only Jon could hear him. "You will say you're sorry to everyone in this class for your behavior, and you will take back what you said about my wife."

"Fuck you!"

Mark raised his hips, moving Jon's arm to where he had even more leverage. He pulled a little harder. "Last chance, asshole!" Mark couldn't help it; sometimes there wasn't a word that didn't cost a dollar that had the correct meaning. He never minded paying his box at those times. "If I don't hear what I want in about two seconds, I'll bend your arm backwards, and you'll be left-handed for the rest of your life!"

"I'M SORRY! I'M SORRY! I DIDN'T MEAN WHAT I SAID! I'M SORRY!" Jon screamed.

Mark let his arm go. He swung his legs off of Jon and hopped up. Then he extended his hand down in an offer to help Jon up. He was starting to feel a little guilty for enjoying what he'd just done. Jon just rolled over and pushed himself up with his left arm. He started rubbing his right elbow just staring at Mark with a blank look. Mark couldn't interpret what the look meant. He held his hand out toward Jon in an offer to shake hands.

"No hard feelings?" Mark asked sincerely.

"Fuck you!" Jon yelled. He spat on the ground at Mark's feet and stomped off toward his house, still holding his elbow.

Chapter 33

The whole class was dumbfounded. No one spoke a word, and they just watched Jon walk off toward his house, most with their mouths open.

Mark decided to dismiss the class. "I guess that'll be all for today. I'll see you next week."

Some of Beta shift left, but many of them came up to Mark and told him that he had more patience than they had.

"You should have broken his arm," one man told him.

"I'm going to see Gunny right now," Charley, the leader of Beta shift, said. "I'm going to suggest that he be removed from guard duty."

Susan came up. "What a baby! I can't believe he would try something like that. You sure put him in his place, though. That ought to fix his wagon."

"I'm afraid I might have made things worse," Mark admitted.

"I don't know what else…"

"Excuse me," Jess interrupted. "I need to check on my husband's eye."

Mark noticed a little edge in his wife's voice. Could she be jealous of Susan? That might explain why she signed up for guard duty. Mark realized he had been talking quite a bit about how much he admired Susan, but if Jess thought he had any romantic feelings toward her, she was mistaken. Jess looked at his eye and then called Lisa over to check it out. Lisa said that the orbit wasn't broken and suggested he get some ice on it to keep it from swelling. They walked back to the camper and got the ice trays out of the propane-powered refrigerator. Mark looked in the mirror and noticed that his eye was already turning purple. He put the ice on it and sat back to relax.

A few minutes later, Gunny came to speak with him. He asked exactly what had happened and listened intently as Mark gave the blow by blow. When Mark was done, Gunny spoke.

"We have to kick him out."

"Yeah, Charley told me he wanted him out of the guards, and I knew you'd agree. I guess I do, too."

"I don't mean jus' outta tha guards, Karate Man. I mean we gotta kick him outta the subdivision."

"We can't do that, Gunny. He owns a home here. How are we going to kick him out of his own house?"

"I don't rightly know, but are you ever gonna be able to turn your back on him again?" the old Marine asked.

"No. But I don't know if that's grounds for kicking him out."

"Listen, Karate Man, if'n Jon can attack you, what makes you think he won't attack someone else? You know things ain't the same as they were a month ago. Our job as guards is to protect ourselves from danger from the outside. We can't be looking over our shoulders and do that job efficiently. If'n some of your MZB's get in here and kill us all because we weren't one hundred percent focused on our job, then everything else all of us have worked so hard to build here is all for naught."

"I see what you mean, Gunny. I guess we could get a group together tonight to discuss it," Mark thought out loud.

"That sounds like a good start. Who'd you have in mind?"

"The security committee, plus Manny, Charley, and Scott. Maybe Doc Vasquez, too."

Gunny agreed with Mark. He suggested they keep the group relatively small at first. If word got out of what they were talking about, it could push Jon over the edge even more, Gunny said.

Mark ate his lunch and then took some aspirin for his throbbing eye. His next class was at two o'clock. He would have checked on how things were going around the neighborhood to keep his mind off of how much his eye hurt, but he knew he'd have to tell the story about what happened a thousand times. He decided to read for a while. He had a new Stephen Hunter book that he hadn't gotten to yet, but it seemed like a waste of time to read a novel. He needed to build a chicken coop for the chickens Manny was hatching for him. He wondered if he had any books that would help him with that. As he looked through the books in his study, David came into the house calling for him.

"Dad, Dad, are you in here?" the young man called.

"Yes, Son, I'm in the study." David appeared in the doorway, out of breath. "What's up?"

"The sheriff is down at the gate. He wants to see you," David said between huffs.

"Would you mind walking back down to the gate and showing the sheriff back to the house?"

"No, sir. I don't mind at all." David took off running back down the hill.

Mark wondered what the sheriff could want. He didn't have to wait long to find out. David showed the lawman into the house, and Mark shook his hand.

"What brings you out here, Sheriff?"

"I just wanted to bring your guns back to you."

"You got done with the ballistic testing already?"

"Actually, no, but with the way things are going in the country, I don't think the lab is going to be able to get to it for a long while. Besides, the boys who ambushed you gave a full confession, and no one has shown up to claim the dead ones. I figured they were better off in your hands than just gathering dust in the evidence locker." The tall man got a quizzical look on his face. "Nice shiner. What happened?"

"Oh, I was teaching a self defense class, and we had a little accident," Mark said, praying David wouldn't say anything.

"Uh huh. Looks like your little accident has a big punch," the lawman smiled.

"Yeah. I guess so."

"What kind of self defense do you teach?"

"Just the basic stuff we use in American Karate."

"You're not a black belt, are you?"

"Yes."

"Then why haven't you been down to my office to register your hands as lethal weapons?" the sheriff said with a straight face and a gruff voice.

Mark didn't know what to say. There was no such law, but urban legend had spread this myth around so much that many people believed it. Surely the sheriff knew the truth. About the time Mark was going to speak, the sheriff got a big grin on his face.

"Had you going for minute, didn't I?"

"You sure did. I was trying to figure out how I was going to explain to you that it was an urban legend." Mark was relieved.

"Your guns are in my trunk. Come on out and get them." Mark followed the sheriff out to his cruiser. As he opened the trunk, he spoke again. "Y'all have really made some security upgrades around here. Have you had any more trouble?"

"Only a little from a bunch of drunk people the other night, but they left with only their pride wounded a little. Other than that, it's been pretty quiet."

"We've had a couple of similar incidents in Floresville and one in La Vernia. One of them went bad, though, and one person was killed and a couple more wounded before we got it under control."

"That's too bad. I guess we can't expect things to be like they were," Mark said, as he looked at his Colt Lightweight Commander like a long lost love.

"I guess not, and it's probably going to get a lot worse," the sheriff said, noticing the look on Mark's face. "But it looks like you all are pretty squared away. That's some gate you have there, and those fighting holes and lookout towers look serious, too."

Mark snapped out of his trance. "Yeah. We just don't want to get caught with our pants down." Mark thought about telling the lawman about the OP, the CP, and the other security precautions they had, but he decided he didn't quite know the man well enough to spill all of the beans. For some reason, though, he felt he could trust this man. Maybe it was the uniform. No, Mark thought, it was more than that, but he couldn't put his finger on it. He looked at the sheriff and felt as if he was being sized up in return.

"Listen, I could use some help." The sheriff hesitated as if he was unsure of what to say. "This is a route from San Antonio that I don't have the manpower to cover like I want. We're stretched pretty thin just trying to cover the two highways from the city. If I brought you a radio, would you be willing to let me know if you think we have trouble headed into the county from here? Plus, if something happens, you could contact us without having to drive into town."

"I think we can handle that," Mark said with a smile.

"Good. I'll bring the radio out in the morning." The sheriff shook Mark's hand and left in his cruiser.

Mark went back into the house and put the FAL into the safe. He also unloaded the Gold Cup Abby had given him and replaced it on his hip with the Lightweight Commander. The Gold Cup was a super pistol, but it was heavy. The Commander was a lot lighter and easier to carry. He was glad to have both of his weapons back. It was almost time for his afternoon class, so he headed out to teach.

Everyone must have heard what happened between him and Jon because no one asked about the black eye. The class went well, and when it was over, Mark went home to eat dinner. Everyone listened to the news, and then people started showing up for the meeting. Everyone was chatting, and although Mark didn't hear any specific conversations about him and Jon, he was pretty sure they were the number one item being discussed. The meeting was going as usual. Ted was telling everyone how the education committee had worked out the logistics and how they were going to start classes for the kids on Monday. He was almost done when Mark saw Jon walking up to the front. The first thought to flash through his mind was that Jon had somehow heard that they were thinking about banishing him from the subdivision, and he had come to apologize. Like that would save him. Too little, too late, Mark thought. Everyone had gotten quiet to see what Jon had to say. Mark looked at the crowd and could tell how everyone felt about Jon from the way they were looking at him. He could see disdain in almost everyone's face. Then suddenly, their looks changed to one of horror, as if he had turned into a monster. Mark looked back at Jon and saw the reason for everyone's changed expression. Jon's big Barretta was pointed directly at him.

Mark could see that the big pistol wasn't cocked, and Jon's finger wasn't inside the trigger guard. The Marines had obviously trained Jon well in proper weapon handling. From this, Mark knew that, at least at this moment, Jon had no intention of shooting him, but that could change in a heartbeat. Jon could put his finger on the trigger and complete the long, double-action trigger pull in less than a second. Mark had no doubt that he could do it with deadly accuracy. He weighed his options. Jon was too far away for him to get his hands on the gun. He practiced gun defenses regularly in his karate class, but the gun had to be within reaching distance for that to work. He could pull his pistol and hope that Jon missed, but that was unlikely. Maybe one of the other men would shoot Jon, which might make a bad situation worse. The crowd had parted in front of Mark as the Red Sea had in front of Moses. If someone shot and missed, it would definitely hit a person on the opposite side. Even if they hit him, the bullet could over-penetrate and hurt someone else, and the likelihood that Jon would still get a shot or two off after he was hit was almost a given. No, Mark decided, his only chance was to talk his way out of this, and he had to do it before someone decided to be a hero.

"Jon." Mark's voice was so calm that it even surprised him. "I know we've had our differences, but this is not the way to solve them." Mark paused for a moment. "Why don't you put the gun down and let's talk about this?"

"NO!" Jon screamed. "I'm tired of talking. You took everyone away from me. Now I'm going to show them that you're a coward. Now get down on your knees, coward, and beg for your life!"

So that's what this was about, Mark realized. Jon felt that Mark has usurped his authority, and now he wanted to get even. He probably had no intention of shooting; he just wanted to embarrass the man who'd become his nemesis. Mark knew that Jon certainly wouldn't shoot until he got what he wanted. After all, if he were dead, Jon wouldn't be able to get his way. Mark spoke again with cool confidence in his voice.

"Jon, this is not the way that grown men solve their..."

"Shut the fuck up!" Jon pulled the hammer back on the Beretta and took a step toward Mark. His hand was starting to visibly shake. "Get down on your knees and tell me you're sorry for all the shit you've done to me."

He must be getting rattled that his little scheme isn't working out the way he planned, Mark thought. He could see that Jon's eyes were glazed over like he was sleep walking. Mark was thinking about what to say next when he heard another voice.

"Jon Joseph Olsen, have you lost your mind?" It was Jon's wife. She walked right up to him, stood between him and Mark and grabbed the gun to take it away. They struggled for a fraction of a second, and a loud sound made everyone freeze. No one moved for what seemed an eternity to Mark. Then he noticed the growing red circle on Mrs. Olsen's shoulder. She half fell, half sat, on the driveway. Mark could see that she was holding her stomach. Lisa was over to the injured woman as if by magic. Jon was on his knees with the pistol on the ground in front of him, begging for his wife's forgiveness. She looked at him as a mother might look at a mischievous child, unable to allow the slight annoyance of his behavior to even slightly disguise the love she felt for him. Lisa was yelling something at someone in his direction, but they must not be listening to her. He looked around to see who she was talking to, but there was no one standing close to him. He realized that she was addressing him.

"Mark! I said get me something to use as a gurney."

Mark turned and opened the garage door. He pulled out a six-foot plastic folding table. He carried it over to Mrs. Olsen and laid it down. He realized he didn't know her first name. He then helped Lisa slide her onto the table, and several other hands appeared to pick up the makeshift gurney. Lisa led them into the kitchen, and they set the table on top of the island. Lisa pulled a pair of scissors out of the junk drawer and started cutting the blouse off of Jon's wife. Lisa sent Jim to their camper to get her medical bag. Doc Vasquez had his hands over the shoulder wound in a losing effort to slow the bleeding. Jon was holding his wife's hand, begging her to hold on. Lisa pushed him back so she could find the entrance wound. She wiped the blood off of the woman's stomach with a clean dishtowel. Mark saw the blood drain from her face when she saw where the bullet had entered. She took a deep breath and had the Doc move his hands so she could check the exit wound. It was about the size of a quarter and didn't look too bad to Mark, but he couldn't believe the amount of blood that was pouring out. He saw Lisa trace a line between the two holes with her eyes, and then put the Doc's hands back. The two medics shared a glance that told Mark more than he wanted to know.

"Jon, you need to say whatever you need to now," the tall, blonde nurse whispered to the woman's husband and killer.

"No. You have to save her. I didn't mean to," Jon yelled.

"Jon, there's nothing we can do. Even if we could call 911, we wouldn't be able to get her to the hospital in time. Her injuries are too serious, and she's losing too much blood."

Jon turned to his wife and buried his head into her good shoulder. "Oh, baby, I'm so sorry. I didn't mean it. I just wanted to scare him. Please forgive me."

The woman put her hand on the back of his head in a way that once again reminded Mark of a mother with her wayward son. Her colorless lips whispered something in a voice so low that Mark wondered if even Jon could hear it. In the middle of the second sentence, the lips stopped moving, and the loving hand slipped from the back of Jon's head.

"NO!" Jon screamed. He ran out of the house sobbing uncontrollably.

Chapter 34

Everyone left in the room just stared at the dead woman. Mark realized again that he didn't know her first name. She had most likely saved his life, and he didn't even know her name. He felt ashamed. His train of thought was interrupted by Doc Vasquez.

"What do we do now?" the veterinarian asked.

Everyone just looked at each other as if they'd been asked to find the exact value of pi to the last decimal. Lisa finally broke the silence by offering to clean the body up and wrap it in a blanket. Mark suggested they give it to the sheriff when he brought the radio tomorrow. He would be able to take her to town for a proper burial.

"What are we going to do about Jon?" Jim asked.

"I guess we'll turn him over to the sheriff, too," Mark answered, as he turned to head out the door. "Does anyone know her first name?" he asked, as he stood in the open door.

"It was Marian," Lisa answered.

Lisa's answer in the past tense hit Mark like a ton of bricks. His stomach was twisted in a knot the size of a basketball. He felt the emotional runaway train coming to take him for a ride again. He couldn't afford to let it overtake him. He focused on what he had to do, and that was to secure Jon until the sheriff arrived, hopefully early in the morning. Somehow, he felt the train would be back for him later.

Mark decided to consult Gunny on the best way to hold Jon. When he stepped around to the front of his house, he was surprised to see almost everyone still there. Many were on their knees praying. Others were just staring blankly, at what Mark didn't know. Probably neither did they, he suspected.

Charley Henderson tried to ask the question on everyone's mind. "Is she...I mean did she...uh...is she still with us?"

Mark shook his head one time. He could hear people crying, but he couldn't let himself think about it lest he join them. He looked at Charley. "Did you see where Jon went?"

"He ran off toward his house."

"Would you go keep an eye on his house and make sure he doesn't go anywhere while I talk to Gunny about how to handle this situation?"

"What do you want me to do if he tries to leave?"

"Take a couple of the guards with you and stop him with as little force as necessary," Mark advised.

"What if he still has his gun?"

"Then use whatever force you have to."

"Understood," Charley responded.

Charley called a couple of the guards to accompany him, and they disappeared around the corner. Mark walked up to Gunny, who was comforting Abby. Mark hated interrupting but felt the situation demanded it. Gunny didn't seem too displeased that Mark had called him away from his crying bride. After a brief conversation, Gunny agreed that the best course of action was to turn Jon over to the sheriff in the morning. In the meantime, he'd be placed under house arrest and guarded in his own home. Gunny and Mark walked down to Jon's house and found Charley and his men surrounding the house.

"Is he still in there?" Mark asked.

"Yes, he hasn't even looked through a window," Charley confirmed.

"I guess we better go get him," Mark said.

"Hold yer horses there, Karate Man. Since you're the one he's most upset with, I think it's best if'n you stay out here. Me and Charley will fetch him out."

"You're right, Gunny. I'll wait here."

Mark watched the house from the spot that Charley had been using, as Gunny and the guard shift leader went to the front door and knocked. No one answered, and they tried again. After a few minutes, Charley tried the door, and it was unlocked. He stuck his head inside and called for Jon. When there was no answer, the two men entered the house. Mark wondered if Jon was okay. He might have hurt himself after the accident with his wife. Mark hoped he hadn't. He already felt somewhat responsible for Mrs. Olsen's death. He had obviously mishandled the situation with Jon this morning. If he hadn't lost his temper at what Jon had said, none of this would have happened. But how was he to know? He was just a man, after all, and men made mistakes. He'd certainly made more than his fair share. He couldn't understand why all these people expected him to have the right answers. He hadn't asked to be a leader, and he really didn't want to be. Gunny and Charley coming out of the house interrupted his thought spiral.

"He ain't here," Gunny announced.

"Where could he be?" Mark realized he'd asked a question that Gunny couldn't answer. He hated when Jess asked him questions like that.

"I don't know, but we better alert the guards to keep a lookout for him." The old man didn't seem put off by the ridiculous question.

"I'll go." Mark turned and ran toward the CP at Scott's house. When he got there, Joe Bagwell was on duty. Mark asked him to let the guards know that they were looking for Jon and to report in if they saw him. When Joe relayed the message, the gate guards immediately radioed back that Jon had left the subdivision about ten or fifteen minutes ago. Mark was dumbfounded.

"Which way did he go?"

The answer came back that he had headed to the east. When Mark asked if he had taken anything with him, he was told that Jon had a large backpack and his AR-15 when he headed out of the gate. He was 'going to check on a friend down the road' was what he'd said to the guards. Mark ran back across the road and reported what had happened to Gunny.

"I can't believe they just let him walk out," Mark said, shaking his head.

"Calm down, Karate Man. All of our security is aimed at keeping people out, not in."

"Well, we better go after him."

"I wouldn't," Gunny stated flatly.

"Why not?"

"First of all, as soon as he got out of sight from the guards, he changed direction."

"How do you know that?" Mark demanded.

"Because that's what I'd do. You need to come see what we found inside. Then I think you'll see there's no point in goin' after him."

Mark followed Gunny into Jon's house. They walked to the back bedroom, and Gunny opened the door. There were boxes stacked around the walls. Three of them were open and lying in the middle of the room. One of them was empty. It said 'MRE's' on the side. One said '5.56 NATO – 1000 Rounds.' It had two long, green, plastic packages left in it that each said 'Battle Pack, 5.56 NATO, 200 Rounds.' The last half empty carton was the most interesting. Mark recognized what was in it without reading the box. It contained four baseball grenades and eight empty spots where others had been. Mark whistled.

"Yeah, that's what I said," Gunny stated. "And there's another full case in the closet. So even if you could track the sumbitch, and I don't think we could, he could give us a nasty surprise. Best just to let him go and be glad he's gone."

Mark looked at the boxes stacked around the walls, as his brain absorbed the words Gunny had spoken. Most were MRE's, but there were quite a few cases of ammo in both 5.56 and 9mm.

"How did he get all this stuff? It all says Property of U.S. Government."

"He was in supply, remember?" Gunny reminded Mark. "Those guys always have a way of getting things if'n they want. Most are honest and don't, but the ones that ain't can make out like bandits."

"You think he liberated any weapons?"

"I doubt it. You see, all of this stuff, 'cept the grenades, is considered to be consumable. If'n it gets reported as out of date and destroyed or issued to a unit, no one really questions it. It's 'spected to be used up. But a rifle is a hard asset. If'n one's missin', someone is going to want to know what happened to it."

"I see," Mark said thoughtfully. "How did he get the grenades?"

The old man shrugged his shoulders. "They always counted them going out, and we had to bring the pins back for the ones we trained with."

"Well, I agree that we better not go after him. I'll just let the sheriff know what happened and give him all this stuff."

"Like hell, you will," Gunny barked.

"Gunny we can't keep all this! It's all stolen. Plus, if we get caught with grenades, they'll put us under the jail, not in it."

"Listen up, Karate Man, you're slippin' back into the mindset that the old rules apply. We can use this stuff. Just think of it as Jon's gift to us for all the shit he put us through."

"Well...I guess we could present this to everyone and take a vote."

"You can't do that. We need to keep this as quiet as possible. If'n you're gonna tell everybody, we might as well give 'em to the sheriff because someone will flap their lips, and the whole county will know we got 'em. If you want to run it by the security committee, that's okay, but not everyone."

"Look, Gunny..."

"Look, Gunny, nothing! You put me in charge of security. This is a security matter, and I'm puttin' my foot down. If'n everyone knows about the grenades, it puts the whole neighborhood at risk...whether we turn 'em in or keep 'em. Run it by the security committee if'n you have to, but I'm tellin' ya, the fewer people know about this, the better."

"If we turn them in, how does that put us at risk?"

"Because some yahoo will think we didn't turn them all in. They'll come and try to get them with whatever force is necessary."

"I see your point. What do you want to do with this stuff?"

"We'll move it to Abby's."

"Right now?"

"No. It's gettin' dark, but there's still too many people out and about. You and Jim and Charley can load it up in my truck around 4 in the morning and then park it around back and carry it into the garage through the back door. That way, nobody will see."

"What about the rovers?"

"Oh, I reckon they'll be doing a drill 'bout that time," the old man winked.

After finalizing their plan with Charley and swearing him to secrecy, Mark headed home. He found that the women had wrapped Marian Olsen's body and placed it on a table in the garage. They'd cleaned up the blood in the kitchen and were busy sanitizing everything that it might have come in contact with. Mark offered to help, but Jess sent him out to clean the driveway. Mark restarted the generator and hooked it up to the pump. He then pulled out a hose and started to wash the blood off of the driveway. Jim showed up with an old push broom and helped to scrub as Mark sprayed.

Gunny's plan worked like a charm, and the three men were able to move all of the contraband without anyone noticing. Mark was back in bed by 5:15, and he slept in until almost 8:00. He got up, ran and did his other PT, and was just starting to fix some eggs when the sheriff arrived. He brought another man with him whom he introduced as Greg Hardy. Greg was the quiet type, but very observant, Mark noticed.

Mark invited the two men to join him for some breakfast, and they graciously declined but took him up on his offer of a cup of coffee. Mark explained to the sheriff what had happened the night before. The lawman said that he'd get a warrant for Jon's arrest for all the good it would do. Mark didn't want to tell him about what they'd found in Jon's house, but he didn't feel right not saying anything. He suggested that anyone who approached Jon should be careful. He told the sheriff that Jon had been in supply and might have hardware that law enforcement didn't come up on every day.

"I see," said the sheriff. "Do you know what he might have?"

Mark swallowed hard and hoped the lean lawman didn't notice. "No. I just suspect he might have had a bazooka or something hidden somewhere."

"Maybe we ought to look in his house and see if we find anything," he said.

"If you want to, that would be fine. We looked around yesterday, and there's nothing in there." At least that wasn't lie since they had moved it all, Mark thought.

"Naw. I guess we don't need to. We'll most likely never see him again anyway."

When Mark asked the official about Mrs. Olsen's body, he said that he could take it, but he felt that with the current state of affairs, it would be best if the community buried her here and gave her a nice service. Mark saw the logic in this. Many people had been shocked by what had happened, and a funeral service might help them deal with the situation. After Mark finished his eggs, they went out to the squad car to retrieve the radio the sheriff had brought.

As they walked down to the CP to deliver the handheld radio, Greg asked Mark a few questions, mostly about how they were getting along and how they'd come up with the ideas to do the things they were doing.

Mark was careful and selective about what he told the man but let him know that the whole community had pulled together. He was curious about why the man was asking questions and said as much. Greg explained that he and some others were trying to do the same thing on the other side of the county. Mark hoped he would elaborate but when he didn't, Mark didn't push it. On their way back to his house, Mark was questioned about the security arrangements at Silver Hills.

Mark was polite but to the point. "I'm sorry, Greg, but I don't feel comfortable discussing that."

Mark noticed that the sheriff and Greg exchanged a quick look before Greg answered. "That's fine. I understand."

When they got back to the house, they shook Mark's hand and thanked him. Then they got into the cruiser and headed out. Mark wondered what the men's real agenda had been. The look they'd given each other told Mark more was going on than they were revealing. He pushed those thoughts to a back burner in his mind and concentrated on where they would bury Marian. It only made sense to inter her in her own yard. There was a particularly large live oak tree in the back that would make a nice resting place. He would discuss it with the others.

The next afternoon, everyone gathered, and they buried Marian Olsen under the stately tree. Almost all of the men and many of the women had helped dig the grave. Rodney and David had built a casket, and Chaparo had welded a cross to place as a marker. Roberta Simmons, Marian's best friend, gave the eulogy. Brother Bob came to give a few words of comfort, and his wife sang 'Amazing Grace' like an angel. Mark thought it sad that Marian had no family at her funeral, but as he looked around at all of the somber faces around the gravesite, he realized that this community had become a big family. As sad and tragic as Marian's death was, it had served to galvanize everyone together, and Mark took comfort in that.

The next few days went quickly. On Sunday, they went to church. On Monday, the garden committee tilled the next quarter acre at Mark's house. Since Jess and Lisa were teaching school during the day now, he and Jim ended up planting most of it. On Tuesday, Mark helped Jim with his shooting classes. Each night, he pulled his guard duty shift. All of the shifts were beginning to see a few more people escaping from the city each day. The passersby were almost all small groups or families and didn't give the guards any problems. Some had places they were trying to get to, but many didn't. None of them had any skills that the community would be interested in, but the residents were able to glean some information from them. It seemed the situation in the camps was slowly worsening. There was plenty of food and water, but just not enough space or privacy. Tempers were becoming short, and some felt it was time to get out of Dodge before it really got bad. The escapees reported the camp guards were understaffed and under-motivated, so breaking out wasn't a hard thing to do. Even though none were invited to stay in Silver Hills, they were given any assistance the community could spare.

241

Enough people had signed up for guard duty after Marian's funeral that now they were working the four days on, three days off that Gunny liked. Mark liked it, too. He would have off every Thursday, Friday, and Saturday. Life was starting take on a routine that had some feeling of normalcy. Mark wondered how long it would last.

Chapter 35

Mark woke up at 1:25. It was five minutes before his alarm clock would have done the job. Mark realized he must be getting used to this schedule. He found he didn't need a nap after his shift as much, and now he was waking up without the alarm. He rose, got dressed, and reported to the CP. Some of his men were already there drinking coffee and quietly visiting. Mark went over to the Coleman stove and old percolator that someone had donated and poured himself a cup of the steaming, black nectar. He had never been a coffee drinker, but he found that he liked a cup before he started his shift. Plus, since he was out of Diet Cokes, he had to get his caffeine somehow.

Delta shift started at two o'clock, and Mark required the men to report in by 1:45. That gave him time to make sure everyone showed up and assign posts. Some of the men were having a little trouble adjusting to being on the night shift, so if one of them showed up a little late, Mark tried to be understanding. He was almost through giving out assignments when he saw Craig Banks trying to sneak in the back, as if he'd been there all along. Mark wouldn't have paid it much attention, except that this was the third night in a row that it had happened. He assigned Craig to his group of rovers. That way, he could talk to him about it without making a big deal. It wasn't long after they started patrolling the neighborhood that Mark had his chance to tell the man how important it was that he showed up on time.

"I know, Mark. I'm sorry. It won't happen again," Craig apologized.

Two things surprised Mark. The first was good. Craig had not given him a bunch of lame excuses. He had owned up to his mistake and said he would not repeat it. It was unusual for someone not to justify their behavior when they were reprimanded. The second surprise was not good. Craig was chewing gum, so Mark could not be sure, but he thought he smelled alcohol on Craig's breath. Craig seemed to be totally in control of his faculties, though, and it was only a guess on Mark's part, so he decided not to ask. These men were all volunteers, after all, and it wouldn't be right to accuse them of something without more than a suspicion.

A few minutes later, Mark got a call on his radio. Dwight Rittiman was on Command Post duty tonight.

"CP to Delta leader."

"Go ahead CP."

"OP reports eight to ten men approaching from the west. They are moving slowly and quietly. OP is unsure if they are armed or not. ETA to gate is two to three minutes."

Gunny had been drilling everyone pretty hard the last week or so, and Mark expected to hear the words 'This is a drill' any second.

"This is not a drill. Repeat, this is NOT a drill," was what he heard from the CP. It took a second for it to sink in.

"Roger, CP. Rover Two, what is your position?" Mark's mind went into overdrive. They had practiced having only a couple minutes' warning, but never had anyone actually gotten so close without being seen or heard. He had a sinking feeling in his stomach.

"Delta leader, Rover Two is at the back fence."

Damn, Mark thought. They couldn't be further away. "Rover Two, make your way as quickly and quietly to Position Three as possible. Signal me when you get there."

"Roger that."

"CP, have the reserves assemble at your location and wait. Signal me when they get there. If you hear any gunshots, sound the warning horn. Also, have the runner get Gunny. I have a bad feeling about this."

"10-4, Delta leader."

Mark was glad his group was close to the front. He turned to his men and told them to go to Position Two. He would go to the gate foxhole they were now calling Position One. After the previous encounter, they had improved the system they used for this situation. There was now a second person in the CP to get the reserves up and to wake up Gunny, if necessary. The FRS radios had call tones built into them, and they had worked out a way to use those to let everyone know when a group was in position. They had drilled on this pretty hard, and everyone was getting pretty good at it during the drills. Mark prayed they didn't have to find out how good they were for real right now.

He slipped down into the foxhole with the gate guards and looked to the west. He could just make out the shapes of men on the side of the road. They were moving slowly and cautiously. As they approached, Mark could see they were walking in single file with five or six yards between them. They all had weapons held at the ready. Whoever these men were, they knew what they were doing. Mark looked back to the east and saw Rover Two slipping into their foxhole one man at a time about the time the visitors got even with the gate. The man in front held up his hand and stopped. The men behind him, seeing this, stopped and crouched down, holding their weapons out and looking all around. The first man held an AR-15, and the second had an AK. The rest seemed to have an assortment of rifles and shotguns. Mark froze, hoping the men wouldn't be able to see if anyone was in the foxhole, as long as he and the gate guards didn't move. He turned the volume all the way down on his radio, as he knew that Rover Two would be signaling him any second. He didn't want the men on the road to hear anything. Mark watched the second man in line come up to the first. He could barely make out their whispered conversation.

"Is this it?" the second man asked.

"No," the first whispered, shaking his head. "We still have a ways to go."

"Then why did we stop?"

"I thought I saw something moving up ahead."

"What was it?"

"Are you fuckin' stupid or something, Ripper? If I knew what it was, I would have said so. God damn, I teach you boys all the shit I learned in the Rangers, and you come up and ask a fuckin' stupid question like that." Mark almost snickered at the aggravation in the first man's voice.

"Well, where was it?"

"Now that's a question I can damn well answer. It was about a hundred yards ahead and thirty or forty yards off of the road."

"I don't see anything."

"You see this gate?"

244

"Yeah. What's that got to do with what you saw?"

Mark could hear the frustration in the first man's voice. "Whoever put up this gate doesn't want any uninvited guests. I bet they're watching us right now. The movement I saw was probably some guys moving into position to cover us in case we try to get into whatever place this is."

"So what do we do?"

"They haven't made a move yet, so they probably don't want no trouble. They're most likely watching to see if we keep going, and that's exactly what we're going to do. No point openin' a big can of grief that we don't need."

"But don't you think they might have some good shit in there?"

"You are fuckin' stupid, aren't you?" The first man reached out and slapped the second on the side of his head.

"Ouch!"

"Shut up. Of course they have some good shit in there, but there are seven of us and who knows how many of them. Whatever shit they might have ain't worth dying for. Besides, we already have a place to go."

"Okay" the second man, said rubbing his head. "But can we stop soon? My feet are killing me, and I'm hungry too."

"Damn, Ripper. For a bad mo-fo, you sure do whine a lot," the leader snarled. Then his tone changed. "I got a bad feeling about this place. Let's get away from here, and then we'll look for a place to camp."

"Okay." The second man waved his hand at the others, and they slowly moved down the road.

When they were clear, Mark turned up his radio and whispered in it. "Everyone, this is Delta leader. Do not acknowledge. Just stay quiet and still. Tangos intend to pass on by. Let's not give them a reason to change their minds. Delta leader out."

After about ten minutes, Mark peeked over the sandbags that ringed the foxhole. "OP, this is Delta leader. Can you still see the tangos?" Mark whispered into the CB radio that was installed in the side of the foxhole.

"They passed out of sight a few minutes ago. It looked like they picked the pace up a little as they got past our eastern fence," the reply came back.

"Roger that." Mark switched back to the little FRS radio. With all of the security improvements they had made, they still didn't have enough radios to put everyone on the same frequency. "Rover two, resume your rounds. CP, is the old man there?"

"Affirmative, Delta leader."

"Tell him I'll be there in five minutes."

"He says you better shake your ass and be here in three." Mark could hear the amusement in Dwight's voice.

"Roger that," he groaned. At least his bad feeling had been wrong. He was grateful for that, even though he still had it for some reason.

Mark jogged over to the foxhole his men were in and had them follow him to the CP. When he got there, Gunny had two hot cups of coffee in his hand. He handed one to Mark. Mark tasted the joe as Gunny spoke.

"Two to three minutes, huh?"

"It was probably closer to four. They were moving slowly, but they got way closer to the gate before we saw them than anyone else ever has. These boys knew their stuff. I overheard the leader say he was in the Rangers. I don't think the others were, but the leader said he had taught them what he knows."

"How did our guys do?"

"Good. The drills have really made a difference."

"Rangers, huh? Those boys are pretty good. Not as good as Marines, but darn close. What else did they say?"

Mark gave Gunny the complete rundown of what he'd heard.

"Are you going to call the sheriff?" Gunny said.

"Yes, but I'll do it at the end of my shift. It's probably just a bunch of farm boys trying to get home to see their mommas. No point in waking him up for that."

Gunny agreed, finished the last swig of his coffee, and then hobbled back to his house. Mark and his men continued their rounds.

At the end of his shift, Mark radioed the sheriff. The lawman agreed that, while the men were probably harmless, a couple of things did seem a little suspicious. He especially didn't like the sound of the nickname that Mark had overheard, and if only the computers were up, he could run it through the system and see what he could find out. He said he'd send a car out to look around later. They'd had some problems in town during the night, and all of his guys were tied up right now. It sounded to Mark like he would like to say more but couldn't over the radio. Mark thanked him and signed off.

As Mark walked back to his house, his thoughts drifted to his family in Waco. He wondered how they were doing. Before The Burst, he had talked to them at least once a week. Now it had been almost a month. He knew that Mike had always thought something like this could happen and that he had prepared for it. Mark was sure they were fine, but he certainly would like to know beyond a feeling. As he approached his house, his thoughts were interrupted by the sound of Jess's voice. It had that tone that told him someone was in trouble. He walked through the door just in time to see David catch the end of a long tirade.

"I hate it!" David yelled back at his mother. "You can't make me go!"

Mark had never seen his son have this much attitude with his mother. He started to get angry and jump right into the middle of this fracas. However, he calmed himself down and waited to be invited in. He didn't have to wait long.

"Aaarrggg!" Jess turned to look at her husband. "Your son doesn't want to go to school. I can't do anything with him, and I'm already late for class. You have to talk some sense into him!"

Jess grabbed her book bag and stomped out the door. Mark loved his wife, but she sometimes had a way of alienating even him. First, why was David "his son" when there was a problem and "her son" when there wasn't? Second, why did he have to talk some sense into the boy? She was the smart one in the family. If she couldn't do it, how was he supposed to? Mark looked at the boy standing before him.

"You want to tell me what the problem is?"

"They treat me like a baby. I'm in a class with all the little kids, and I hate it. I'm not going back, and you can't make me!"

Mark took a deep breath. David was never this stubborn; that was usually Sam's department. Mark made sure his words were calm and well chosen. "If you want to be treated as an adult, then you should act like one. The last time I checked, I was still your father, and telling me what I can and can't do is not likely to help me see things from your perspective, is it?"

Mark hated this part of parenting. He guessed all parents did, but his words had the desired effect.

David hung his head. "No, sir."

"You want to try again?"

"Dad, Mom put me and Joey in the class with all the little kids. Most of them are third and fourth graders. I'm not learning anything, and I hate being treated like a baby."

"Are you doing the same work as the smaller children?"

"Not exactly, but in music class, we have to sing the kiddy songs, and the teachers talk to us like we're in kindergarten. Joey hates it, too."

"Did you try to discuss this with your mother like an adult?"

"Yes, sir, but she told me there wasn't any choice. There aren't enough kids my age to have a class just for us. She told me to get over it and get my butt to school. You know Mom." David finally cracked a small grin at his last sentence. It was a little thing that the Turner children and their father said quite often to explain the unpredictability of their mother and wife.

"Yes, sir," Mark grinned back. "I know Mom." His face took a more serious look. "I tell you what. I'll talk to your mom about this. I can't promise you anything will change, but I'll try. In the meantime, you go back to class and have a good attitude for the rest of the week, and we'll do anything you want on Saturday."

"Really?"

"Yes, really."

"I want to go to the deer lease and hunt."

Mark paused. "Well, I don't know if we…"

"You said anything I wanted!" David reminded his father.

"So I did. Okay, you got it. Now, like your mother said, get your butt to school!"

"Yes, sir!"

Mark watched the boy…young man, he corrected himself…run out the door and toward the other house where he was supposed to be. Mark swallowed hard. He didn't know if he was more apprehensive about telling Gunny that he was going to the lease or talking to Jess about David's problem. He realized he was being silly. He was way more afraid of his wife than he was of Gunny. Might as well get the easy one done, he thought. He walked over to Gunny and Abby's house and talked to the old man. Gunny argued with him a little but gave in fairly quickly when Mark said he would only be gone for the day and agreed to take two or three men with him. The two men talked for a while, and then it was time for guard class. Mark walked with Gunny down to the class. He always enjoyed Gunny's classes. He had a unique method of getting his point across, and Mark liked being the student instead of the teacher for a change. Plus, Gunny always had a drill or exercise that would test how well you paid attention, and woe to anyone who didn't.

After class, Mark went home for lunch. Jim had been working in the garden, and he was washing up in the kitchen sink. He said hello as his friend walked in.

"Hey, Jim. I promised David I'd take him to the lease on Saturday. You want to go?"

Just then Samantha opened the screen door into the kitchen. "I want to go," she said.

"We're going hunting," Mark informed her, as if she hadn't heard him right. She never wanted to go, even though her dad had invited her many times.

"Well, duh." She tipped her head to the right, doing her blonde impression. "What else would you do there?"

"But you never want to go."

"That was when I could go to the mall or the movies. Now, a hunting trip sounds like big time fun," she smiled.

"Okay, you're in."

"I'm in, too," Jim chimed in.

The three of them started setting the dining room table for lunch. The weather had finally cooled off enough that they could eat inside. Jess or Lisa had left a big pot of stew simmering on the stove, and it smelled really good. The table was almost ready when Jess, David, Lisa, and the twins came into the house. Mark turned to look at his wife, expecting that she'd be pleased with him for getting David back to school. Maybe, the thought flashed through his mind, she'll be happy enough that I'll get a little reward later. He smiled at his bride.

"David tells me that you intend to take him hunting on Saturday." The tone she had used with David this morning was now being directed at Mark. There goes my reward, he thought.

"Yeah," Mark drawled out the word, knowing that she hated it. "That's the deal I made with him to get him to go to school for the rest of the week."

"Are you going to bribe him with something every week?"

Jess usually didn't like to argue in front of other people or even the kids for that matter. Something must really be under her skin. Mark tried to bring the intensity of the discussion down to a more civilized level. "No. Just this one."

"Then what?"

"By then, I'm sure you'll have found a solution to David's concerns about his class."

Mark hoped that would at least put this discussion on hold for the moment, but he could see that his efforts to de-escalate and end the argument had backfired. Jess's face turned redder than her hair, and Mark braced himself for Hurricane Jessica. She launched into a five-minute philippic that Mark was able to make little sense of. As he stood there in the Category Five winds of anger, he saw Sam whisper something to Dave. The youngest Turner grabbed the twins and herded them outside, while Sam filled four bowls with stew and followed him. At least his children had the insight to evacuate before the terrible storm surge reached their level. Jim and Lisa just stood dumbfounded, mouths slightly ajar. It was as if they couldn't look away from the fury of the frightening power of nature displayed before them. Just when Mark thought the hurricane was blowing itself out, he found it was only the eye of the storm, and he had best keep his hatches, mostly the one under his nose, battened. The lee side of the storm was a little easier to make sense of. It seemed that the education committee as a whole had agreed on the class composition and not just her. Mark also discovered that, while there were a lot of high schoolers, there were only a few junior high school kids in the neighborhood. Not nearly enough to justify a separate class for them. The wind then switched direction suddenly as it does in a tropical storm, and blew from the 'it's too dangerous for you and David to go by yourselves' bearing.

"Jim's going with me," Mark said without thinking.

Lisa's head snapped around to look at her husband, as a tree might snap in the ferocious wind, finding its way to destroy a house or a car. Mark caught the 'Thanks buddy' look from his friend out of the corner of his eye.

"Well, Gunny probably won't let you go anyway," the howling wind taunted.

"I already talked to him, and he said it was okay, as long as I took a couple of guys with me." 'Na, na-na, na-na, na! SO THERE!' Mark thought smugly.

The wind grew silent. To the uninitiated, it might look as if the storm was over, but not to the seasoned tempest sufferer Mark had become in his twenty years of matrimony. No, the typhoon was attempting to back out over the warm sea waters, reorganize itself, intensify, and batter him again in a manner that would make the first time seem like a summer squall. Mark had seen this before, and he had to stop it right now. There was only one force that could stop a hurricane in its tracks. That was an arctic blast of cold air that Texans call a Blue Northern.

"Listen, you told me to get him to go to school, and I did. If you don't like the way I did it, then don't ask me for any more help. Now let's eat." It wasn't so much what he said, as the way he said it. His voice had that cold steely sound that he didn't use often. He knew that when he used that tone, she wouldn't say another word, maybe for several days, but he had withstood all he could take.

The four adults sat down to what was the quietest meal Mark could remember. Even the children, outside at the picnic table, were as quiet as church mice. After lunch, the girls and the kids headed back to school. Jim and Mark cleaned up the kitchen.

"That was enlightening," Jim said with just a hint of sarcasm.

"Yeah. That's what I get for marrying an Irish girl," Mark said, smiling weakly.

"No. I was talking about you. I've never seen a man get the last word in."

"My friend, I may have won the battle, but the war is far from over, and even if I win, I lose, if you know what I mean."

"I'm afraid I do," Jim said. "I know exactly what you mean."

Chapter 36

It was chilly that night in Mark's room. Not from the weather. It was still in the upper 60s and lower 70s at night this time of year. It was Jess. Mark had withstood these 'freezes' many times before. The best thing to do was to be civil and act like nothing was wrong. Then after two or three days, the 'climate' would start to warm up.

Mark was off for the next three days, so he slept in. When he got up, Jess and the kids were already gone. It was Thursday, and he had to teach his two classes, but other than that, he could do what he wanted. He fixed himself a big breakfast and sat down to enjoy a peaceful meal. Afterwards, he headed over to Manny's to see if he'd like to go hunting. Manny was excited about the prospect of getting some meat. He asked if he could bring his son-in-law, and Mark agreed. Then Manny invited his friend out back to have a look at something.

When they got to the chicken coop, Mark could see several chickens scratching in the dirt with chicks in tow.

"Your investments are growing," Manny said with a smile. "It won't be long before they're mature."

"Thanks, Manny. I can't tell you how much I appreciate this."

"*Mi amigo*, it is I who appreciates how much you have done for me and *mi familia*."

After visiting with Manny for a few more minutes and cementing the plans for the hunting trip, Mark headed over to teach his morning class. It went without incident, as did the afternoon one. The atmosphere was still cool at dinner, and even the meeting seemed subdued. Someone brought up the empty house that Jon and Marian had once lived in and asked if it should be given to someone else to live in. While a few people spoke up with ideas about what to do with the Olsen house, most seemed to be taken by surprise at the suggestion that the house be occupied. In the end, everyone agreed to think about what to do and discuss it at a later time.

On Friday, Mark spent part of the day getting ready for his trip. He checked the truck and filled it with fuel. He pulled the rifles and shotguns that they would use out of the safe and checked to make sure they were clean and ready. He got out the ammo they would need and packed it into a big duffel bag, along with skinning knives, a bone saw, and some ziplock bags. He cleaned up all of his ice chests. He'd run the generator a little longer than usual last night to freeze some of his ice bottles, and all of the ice cube trays that everyone had lent him. He would do the same tonight.

The rest of the day he spent planning out and starting on his chicken coop. He had estimated the size of Manny's coop and tried to duplicate it. He set the poles for the corners and was starting to nail the plywood up on the sides when Gunny came hobbling up.

"Hey, Karate Man, what-cha workin' on?"

"I'm building a chicken coop, Gunny. Manny has some chickens for me and they're almost big enough to move over here. I can't wait to have our own eggs."

"Man, that does sound good. Where's your trench?"

"Huh?" Mark stared at the old sergeant blankly.

"The trench to bury the sides of the coop in. You know, so's the 'coons 'n' 'possums can't dig in."

"You're supposed to do that?"

"If'n you don't, you'll have every varmint in the county stealin' your eggs and killin' your chickens. Didn't you ask George about this?"

"I didn't want to bother him. He's been so busy with the gardens and all."

"Well, you coulda looked it up in a book," Gunny chided.

"I looked for one, but I don't have any that tell how to build a chicken coop."

"Where's them books I gave ya when you fixed my truck?"

Mark looked up at the sky and slapped his forehead. When he looked back down, Gunny was smiling like the Cheshire Cat.

"I always wondered why your forehead was so flat," Gunny teased.

"I completely forgot about those books." Mark turned and walked into his shed. A moment later, he walked out with the box Gunny had given him a month ago. He pulled out the *Back to Basics* book and started flipping through the pages. When he found the section on chickens, there was a detailed plan for a coop. He studied it for a minute and then looked up to thank Gunny for reminding him about the books. The old man was nowhere in sight. Mark just shook his head and laughed to himself. The old geezer could sure move quickly and quietly when it suited him, he thought. He went back to the instructions and saw that he didn't have to change his plans much. He pulled out a spade and started digging a twelve-inch trench around the perimeter. He was almost finished when Sam called him for dinner. Normally, he would have finished what he was doing before he went in, but that would only give Jess a reason to stay mad at him longer. She hated it when he didn't come straight to dinner when it was ready. He put up his tools, grabbed the box of books, and headed into the house. He set the box down on the counter.

"Whatcha got there, Mark?" Jim asked.

"It's those books Gunny gave me when we fixed his truck. I'd forgotten about them until he reminded me. I found a plan to build the chicken coop."

"Let me look at those," Lisa requested. She pulled one of the books out and started flipping through the pages. Then she pulled another out. "Look at this, Jess. They show how to do a lot of things the old fashioned way. There's even a section on herbal medicines."

"Really?" Jess exclaimed. She moved over to look at the books with Lisa, and the two of them were oohing and ahhing over all of the information. Jess looked over at Mark. "These are wonderful! Gunny gave them to you?"

Mark nodded his head. It was the first time she had really spoken to him since the big fight.

"Remind me to thank him," she said smiling.

Everyone sat down to dinner, and the conversation quickly turned to the big hunting trip. Everyone who was going was obviously excited, and even Jess and Lisa seemed a little eager at the prospect of getting some fresh meat.

"What all are you going to hunt?" Lisa asked.

"We'll hunt for deer, hogs, and turkey first thing in the morning and late in the afternoon. During the middle of the day, we'll do a little dove hunting," Mark answered.

"Is deer season open?" Jess inquired.

"Technically only if you're hunting with archery equipment, but I don't think the game wardens are going to be very strict in these circumstances, even if they can get out into the field."

"Well, make sure you bring me a turkey or two. I just love wild turkey on the grill."

"We know, Mom," David grinned. "That's what you always tell us."

"I just have to make sure you don't forget what I like," she shot back at David but winked at Mark where no one else could see. Mark was a little confused at the signals she was sending. She should still be mad for a day or two. He couldn't think of a time since they'd been married that she hadn't been mad for at least three days after a big fight. He decided to put it out of his mind and join in with the happiest conversation he could remember since The Burst.

They listened to the news after dinner, but, as usual, there was nothing new. At the meeting, the subject of the Olsen house came up again. Someone suggested that it be saved for a doctor to live in, if they ever found one. Somehow, that suggestion didn't sit well with Mark. He didn't feel comfortable with giving the house to anyone. Evidently, he wasn't the only one with such feelings, as several people spoke up and said exactly what he was thinking. Scott Simmons suggested that perhaps the CP could be moved into the Olsen garage since it was more centrally located than his. He also said that he really needed his garage back since some of his friends had come to stay with him. This suggestion was voted on and approved. Plans were made to move everything to the Olsen place over the weekend. Scott seemed to be very pleased. Mark looked around and realized that while they weren't having the population explosion they had previously seen, their community was still steadily growing. Before the meeting was adjourned, Mary Patterson suggested that perhaps it was time for another street dance. That suggestion was met with tremendous support. Since the children now had school, next Friday night was agreed on. Mary was put in charge, since it was her idea, and the official meeting was concluded.

Most everyone stuck around for a little while, as had become customary. Mark still pumped water for those who needed it, and this was the time that the showers were taken. Most people just hung around to visit. Some of the women gathered around Mary to discuss the party plans. Manny came up and confirmed the departure time for the next morning. He told Mark he was really looking forward to tomorrow. Mark said he was anxious to go, as well. When the crowd had thinned out a little, Mark headed for his room. It would be a long day tomorrow, and he wanted to get some shuteye.

Inside his bedroom, Mark laid out the clothes he'd wear in the morning. He heard a soft knock and turned to see his wife's head poking through the doorway.

"Are you getting ready for bed?" she asked sweetly.

"Yeah, 3:30 comes early." He tried not to sound too shocked that she was talking to him.

"I wanted to tell you how sorry I am about getting mad at you the other day. I was wrong," she said, as she opened the door all the way and nervously fidgeted with the doorknob. After what seemed a long moment, she spoke again. "Aren't you going to say anything?"

"We've been married for almost twenty years, and this is only like the third time you've apologized to me. I guess I'm in too much shock to say much of anything."

"Even so, when somebody says they're sorry, you should say something." She took a step toward him.

"Okay. How sorry are you?"

"Why don't you let me show you?" she whispered, as she closed the door behind her.

*   *   *

"Mark, Mark! Wake up!"

Mark opened one eye and looked at his wife. "What?"

"Someone's at the door. She says she needs your help."

Mark had been sleeping deeply, and his brain was not in gear yet. "She who? Help with what?"

"I didn't catch her name. She said her family was being attacked!"

"Where? In the subdivision?" His brain was starting to work. He jumped out of bed and into the clothes he had laid out the night before. He glanced at his watch and saw it said 12:30.

"No. She lives somewhere else. She said her father knows you."

Mark grabbed his boots and socks and went to the living room. Standing there was one of the guards and a tall, thin, black girl he estimated to be eighteen. Mark could tell she was pretty, but she was a mess. She was dressed in black sweats and running shoes. Her hands were visibly shaking, her face was puffed up from crying, and she was perspiring to the point that her sweatshirt was soaked.

The guard spoke first. "Mark, this girl came running up to the gate asking for you."

Before Mark could respond, the girl started talking in one, long, run-on sentence. "Are you Mr. Turner? My dad sent me to get you...oh my God...he said you would help us...I hope I got here in time...he said you would know what to do...they said they would kill him and then...oh my God...what they said they would do to me and Mom...it's horrible...we have to get back and help them...you will help us won't you?"

"Calm down. Just take a few deep breaths." The girl did as Mark instructed. "Now, what's your name?"

"My name is Trini. Trini Jones. My dad is Ralph."

"Ralph Jones, the lawyer?"

The girl nodded her head.

"Okay, Trini. Tell me what happened."

The girl started to get excited again. "We woke up when they started shooting at the house. There was a cross burning in the front yard, and some men were yelling at Daddy. He started shooting back, and they all went and hid down in the ditch. He made me dress all in black and run to get you."

"How many men were there?" Mark asked.

"I don't know for sure. Maybe four or five? It could be more…I'm just not sure, Mr. Turner."

"That's OK, Trini," Mark tried to reassure the girl. "Don't worry, we're going to help you." He turned toward the guard. "Get down to the CP and have the rovers meet me there in five minutes. We'll need all of the FRS radios. Also, have the CP wake the reserves. Tell them they have five minutes, and this is not a drill. Then have him call the sheriff and tell him that Ralph Jones' house is being attacked."

"You got it, Mark." The man wheeled around, went out the door, and ran toward the Command Post.

Mark looked at Jess. "Wake Jim up and tell him what's going on. Tell him to have his truck at the Command Post in five…make that four minutes. I'm going to get Gunny. You take care of Trini."

"NO! I'm going with you," Trini insisted.

"Okay. I don't have time to argue, but you will do exactly what I tell you."

The tall girl nodded her head. Jess had already gone to get Jim. Mark ran back into his room and came back out with his FAL and a bag of loaded magazines. His Colt was already on his hip. He and Trini sprinted out to the Jeep and headed for Abby's house. One of the guards was already knocking when Mark got there. Gunny answered about the time Mark reached the door.

"Gunny, we have a situation at the lawyer's house, the one who helped us after the MZB shooting. Now he has a bunch of MZB's or KKK's or something at his house. Can you come with us and bring your truck for some of the men to ride in?"

"Sure. Didja wake the reserves?"

"Yes, sir."

"Okay, then, give me a minute, and I'll be down to the CP." Gunny disappeared behind the door.

Mark drove his Jeep down to the Command Post. Most of the men he had requested were already there. The guard who had brought Trini up to their house was filling them in. Mark spoke as some of the last men were arriving. He quickly told them what was up and said that this was strictly a voluntary mission. Jim drove up a few seconds later, and Gunny was less than a minute behind him. Gunny got out of his truck and spoke briefly with Jim and then a couple of the reserves. Jim got out of his truck, and the two neighbors climbed into Mark's Jeep. Two of the reserves climbed behind the wheels of the trucks. Every man there climbed into one of the pickup trucks. Mark climbed behind the wheel and started down the hill with the trucks in tow. The gate was already open, and the vehicles made a quick right turn onto the county road.

As they drove, Gunny asked Trini questions. "How many are there?"

"I think four or five." The girl had seemed to have regained most of her composure.

"Where are they in relationship to the house?"

"When I left, they were all in front, as far as I could tell. A couple of them had been behind the house, but when Daddy started shooting at them, they ran back to the front and got into the ditch with the others."

"Are there any houses close to yours?"

"No. We have ten acres, and it's farmland all around us."

"How much cover is there around the house?"

"What do you mean?"

"Are there lots of trees and stuff for people to hide behind?"

"Most of the property around the house is pretty clear. There are a couple of big trees close to the house, but then it's all grass for quite aways, maybe fifty or sixty yards. Then it's thick brush on the sides and in the back. There's not much between the house and the road."

"Good. How long ago did this start?"

The girl looked at her watch. "I left the house thirty-three minutes ago. It probably started ten minutes before that."

Mark raised his eyebrows. That meant Trini had run from her house to Silver Hills in about twenty-five minutes. It had to be over three miles, he thought. Mark turned onto the gravel road that the Jones house was on.

"Did they seem to be in a hurry?" Gunny inquired.

"Daddy said he knew how these guys work. They want to go nice and slow and scare their victims as much as possible. He figured I could make it to Mr. Turner's and get help before they did much beside shoot out the windows in the house."

Gunny nodded his head thoughtfully for a moment and then spoke to Mark and Jim. "Cut off the headlights and slow down. I don't want them to see or hear us."

"But Gunny, maybe we could just scare them off if they see us coming," Jim objected.

"Jimbo, you ever scare off a big rat?"

"Yeah."

"What happened?"

"He came right back."

"That's right. The only way to get rid of a rat is to catch him. Trini, tell Mark when we get about a quarter mile from your house, so he can stop."

Less than two minutes later, the convoy was stopped, and everyone was listening to Gunny's instructions. Occasionally, a shot could be heard from up the road. More often than not, it would be followed by a string of obscenities. When Gunny was finished laying out his plan, he asked for questions.

"What do I do?" Trini demanded.

"I want you to stay here and tell the sheriff where we are and what our plan is in case he shows up before we get our trap set."

"Yes, sir."

"Anything else?" the old man asked the men, as if he knew there wouldn't be any more questions. "Then let's move out."

Mark took the four men who were assigned to him and crossed the fence on the opposite side of the road from the house. Their assignment was to cross the field in front of the house far enough away that the MZB's wouldn't detect them and come back out onto the road on the far side of the house. Jim was crossing the fence on the house side and making his way behind the home with his men. Gunny had the oldest and slowest men with him. They would make their way down the road and complete the triangle. Mark and his men jogged slowly across the field. There wasn't much of a moon, and Mark didn't want any of his men falling and making noise or getting hurt. When they had reached the far side and were starting to re-cross the fence, Mark heard Jim radio that he was in position. Mark and his men, once across the fence, eased down into the deep ditch on the side of the road they had used to cross the field. They crept closer to the house until they were within a hundred yards of the MZB's. From this distance, Mark could make out almost everything that was being said between the attackers and Ralph Jones.

"You might as well come out, nigger. Sooner or later, we're gonna getcha anyway. If we have to, we'll burn you out." The voice was vaguely familiar to Mark.

A shot came from the house. "Why don't you come try, you bastards? I got plenty of ammo, and I'm not going anywhere. Just stick your head up and see what happens."

A volley of shots came from the ditch. "Suit yourself, mud duck, but if we have to smoke you out, it's gonna be hard on you. Come on out, and we'll do you quick. Then we'll let your women go. Otherwise, we'll make them scream while you watch."

The only answer Ralph gave was three quick shots from his rifle.

Mark whispered in the radio that he was ready. Gunny confirmed that he'd received the message and then asked Jim if he could see any MZB's on his side of the house.

"Negative," Jim replied. "There's not really any cover back here. We're over a hundred and fifty yards behind the house and there are only two or three places where a man could hide."

"Alright, then. It looks like they're all in the ditch in front of the house. I'm gonna tell them to surrender. If they start shooting, Mark and I will open up on them. If you still don't see anyone, move up behind the house and use it for cover. Then we'll have 'em in a three-way crossfire."

"Roger."

Mark looked toward Gunny's position. He couldn't see the old man, but he could hear him. "You men attacking the house. You are totally surrounded by a superior force. Lay down your weapons and come out in the open with your hands on your head. You will not be harmed if you..."

Mark saw the muzzle flashes and then heard the answer from the MZB's. He pulled his rifle in tight to his shoulder, concentrated on the spot where he saw the first flash, and squeezed the trigger. The .308 bucked. He let it come back to level and repeated the process. After a few seconds, the firing from the MZB's had ceased, and a moment later, so did that from his and Gunny's positions. Mark couldn't believe how quiet it was. Even the crickets had stopped chirping.

A voice shattered the silence. "Okay...we're coming out...don't shoot!"

Mark saw one man rise up out of the ditch with his hands on top of his head. A second later, two more joined him, then two more, and finally another.

Mark heard Gunny on the radio. "Jim, you and your men move up to cover these guys. Then Mark and I will move up and secure them."

"Roger, Gunny."

Mark had a bad feeling. He hoped Ralph was alright. But that wasn't really what was bothering him. It was something else. He hated when he felt this way, and it had been happening too often lately. Like the other night when…

Mark keyed his radio. "Everybody, hold your positions. Something's wrong." He moved the little Motorola from in front of his face and yelled toward the MZB's. "Ripper?"

There was a long silence, then a voice called back. "How do you know my name?"

Mark quickly spoke into the radio. "Gunny, there's another one somewhere!"

Gunny called to the six attackers. "Is that all of you?"

Mark could see six heads swiveling back and forth. Finally, someone answered Gunny. "Yeah, this is all of us."

Mark saw Gunny step out of the ditch and toward the men. He couldn't believe that Gunny bought the lie. He was going to get himself killed if he didn't stop. Mark raised the radio back to his lips to try and talk some sense into the old man. 'BOOM!' Mark was startled by the shot and saw dirt spray up just in front of one of the MZB's.

"Ya god damn liars. Ya got to the count of three ta tell me where tha other one is, or I'ma gonna shoot one of you in tha head. One…two…"

Mark recognized Ripper's voice. "He's in the ditch crawling away!"

A voice came from a spot uncomfortably close to Mark. "Ripper, you asshole!" Mark saw the hands come out of the ditch across the road only ten or fifteen yards from him. "I give up."

Mark and two of his guys handled the crawler, whom Mark realized was the leader from the other night, while everyone else patted down and disarmed the other six.

The former Ranger looked at Mark and the radio in his hand. "I heard you on the radio. How did you know there were seven of us?"

"Remember the big gate you stopped in front of the other night?"

The man nodded his head.

"I was on the other side."

"Damn. What do you figure the odds of that are? Does my luck suck, or what?"

"I guess it does," Mark agreed. Then he saw red and blue flashing lights. "But it's improving."

"How do you figure?"

"We're going to give you to the sheriff."

"How is that good luck?"

"We could just let Mr. Jones take care of you," Mark half grinned.

The look of hate in the younger man's eyes at the mention of Ralph's name was unmistakable. His jaw clenched shut, and Mark, somewhat surprised at the intensity of the hatred, had no desire to converse with him further. One of the arriving deputies handcuffed the attacker and herded him over to where the sheriff was. Mark followed. Ralph was explaining what had happened, with his wife beneath one arm and Trini under the other. Both of them were crying.

"...anyway, when they all went back around front, I had Trini run out the back and go get Mr. Turner. I knew he'd come help us." The big man looked from the sheriff to Mark. "Mr. Turner, thank you so much. Now, I owe you."

Mark smiled at the bear of a man. "How 'bout we just call it even?" The big man just nodded his head.

"Ralph, besides the obvious, any reason you can think of why these guys would want to hurt you?" the sheriff asked.

Ralph's big paw came up and rubbed his chin. "When I was a prosecutor for Bexar County, I put a lot of guys away, even some Klan guys. Other than that, I don't know."

"Well, I'll haul them to jail. Probably at least one of them will talk. I'll let you know." Then the sheriff turned to Mark. "Mr. Turner, can I have a moment with you?"

"Sure." Mark and the sheriff walked off a ways.

"You did a good thing here, Mark. I probably would have gotten here in time, but last night I was tied up on the far side of the county, and I don't think I would have made it. I feel better knowing you're here. Listen, Monday at ten in the morning, I'm having a meeting at my office. Can you come?"

"Sure I can. What's it about?"

"You'll see when you get there. Bring that old Marine sergeant with you and your friend Jim, too."

"Okay, Sheriff. We'll be there," Mark told the lawman, as he walked back toward his squad car.

The sheriff turned back toward Mark. "If you don't mind, pick up Ralph, too." With that, he climbed into his car and left.

Chapter 37

Mark walked back over to Ralph and his family. The big man was still bear hugging his wife and daughter. His huge arms reached all the way around both of the thin women. When he saw Mark, he relaxed his grip and made an introduction.

"Honey, this is Mark Turner, the man I sent Trini after. Mr. Turner, this is my wife, Valerie."

"Mr. Turner, I don't know how we can ever repay you. The sheriff told us that you called him, too. If you hadn't done that or showed up when you did, who knows what would have happened? We owe you our lives," the woman said, as she vigorously shook Mark's hand.

"I doubt that, Mrs. Jones. Besides, I was just doing what neighbors are supposed to do."

"How did you get here so quickly with all of these men? It seemed like I had no sooner sent Trini to get you than you were here," Ralph asked.

"You can thank Trini for that. The way I figure it, she ran about three miles in twenty-five minutes. I run almost every day, and I couldn't have done it nearly that fast."

It was too dark to see if Trini blushed, but she did drop her head like she was embarrassed. She kicked at some gravel in the driveway with the toe of her shoe. "I just ran as fast as I could. I guess all that time on the track team paid off."

"She is a good runner," Ralph bragged, "but you all must be fairly organized to be able to get this many men together so quickly."

"Yeah. Gunny, the older gentleman over there, has us pretty ship shape when it comes to security. In fact, we used one of our contingency plans tonight. We just modified it since it was set up for inside the subdivision."

"You must sleep better at night with that kind of security," Valerie said.

Mark nodded his head thoughtfully. Everyone just stood silently for a moment, then Mark broke the quiet. "Listen, would you all like to stay at our place for a few days? Then you can come back and clean up all the broken glass and stuff when you're ready."

"That's such a kind offer, Mr. Turner..." Valerie Jones started sounding like she was going to accept the invitation until she was cut off by her husband.

"...But we wouldn't want to impose," the bear finished.

Mark could see the woman look up toward her husband and squeeze the tree trunk of an arm she was holding. Mark had been married long enough to know that the woman didn't agree with her husband and was using her most polite form of nonverbal communication to tell him so.

"However," the big man added, "I have an old travel trailer in the pole barn out back. If you wouldn't mind pulling it over to your place, we could stay in that. I know the women folk would like to get away from here for a day or two."

Mark smiled. "I think we can handle that." He turned to Jim. "Can you pull a travel trailer back to Silver Hills for Ralph?"

"You bet," Mark's friend replied.

Ralph sent his wife and daughter into the house to get some clothes and food. He led the men around back to his pole barn with a flashlight while Jim was getting his truck. The barn was a three-sided affair made out of old telephone poles and weathered, corrugated tin. Mark could see that it was big enough to hold three vehicles. However, he couldn't see inside. Ralph shined his flashlight on the right side of the barn, and Mark saw a nice looking travel trailer. Mark could also see that the section in the middle was filled with hay.

"You have livestock?" he asked the lawyer, as he pointed at all of the hay.

"No. Trini used to have a horse, but he got some kind of nerve disease, and we had to put him down."

"That's too bad."

Jim's headlights swept across the two men, and then his backup lights came on as he backed his Chevy up to the trailer. Mark began cranking up the tongue so that it would match the height of Jim's hitch.

"This is a nice camper, Ralph. Do y'all camp much?"

"Naw. We've never used it. I had a client who owed me some money, and I took the camper instead. I had big plans for us to take a long vacation one summer, but we've never been able to get around to it. In fact, I was thinking about selling it before The Burst. Now, I'm glad I didn't."

Mark changed the subject. "You told the sheriff that you used to be a District Attorney?"

"An Assistant District Attorney," Ralph corrected. "Right after I got out of law school. I quit after Trini was born because I was scared something like this would happen, and as proud as I was of the work I was doing, I couldn't risk my family's safety."

"I understand completely."

Mark, once the tongue was high enough, directed Jim back, so he could couple up the trailer. That done, Mark hollered at Jim to pull it around front. As the camper was pulled past them, Mark noticed that one of the tires was a little low, and he asked Ralph if he had an air pump.

"Yeah, I think so," the lawyer answered, as he walked around the hay and into the left side of the barn. Mark could hear him rummaging around for a minute. "Mark, could you come hold the light for me?"

Mark pulled a small flashlight out of his pocket and walked to the other side of the building. When he shined his light into the shed, he stopped dead in his tracks.

"Come on in here and help me find the blasted air pump. I swear, the girls just use something and then throw it anywhere. It's a miracle I can ever find any of my tools," the big man grumbled. He turned and looked at Mark. "Are you okay? You look like you saw a ghost."

"You...you have a tractor?" Mark stammered, not believing he was really seeing the old, faded blue Ford.

"Yeah," Ralph answered as turned back to look for the pump. "The Burst fried it just like my truck. Are you going to help me look for the air pump or not?"

"Can we use it?"

"Sure we can use it, but we have to find the blasted thing first."

"No. The tractor."

262

"I told you, it won't start." Ralph was starting to sound a little irritated.

Mark shook his head like he was trying to bring himself back to reality. He tried to break the hypnotic trance the tractor had placed him under, but he couldn't stop looking at it. "I know…but if we could get it to run, could I borrow it to use at the subdivision?"

"Of course you can borrow it. It's just an old tractor." The irritation in the man's voice turned to humor. "You ask like it was my daughter, and you wanted to marry her." Then he got serious again. "Now, are you going to help me find the air pump, or not?" Ralph turned back to his workbench, obviously unaware of the significance of the tractor.

"How old is it?"

"The air pump?" The aggravation in Ralph's voice didn't register in Mark's head, as his mind raced ahead to telling George they might have a tractor.

"No. The tractor."

"Listen here. What friggin' difference does it make how old it is? I said you could borrow it! Now you want to get picky about how old it is?"

The tirade by the bear broke the spell the tractor had on Mark. He started laughing as if he had just heard the funniest joke in the world, while Ralph looked at him like he had gone stark raving mad. Mark caught his breath and apologized to the big man. He worked his way back into the barn and held the light while he explained how they'd been looking for a tractor and how they couldn't get any of the newer models to run. Once Ralph understood, he laughed as well. After a few minutes, they found the pump and went around front where everyone else was waiting.

Ralph hooked the pump up to the low tire and started pumping, while Mark told the men who'd come with him about the tractor. Everyone was happy as they loaded up into the vehicles to go home. Mark looked at his watch. It read 4:45. They were supposed to have left for the deer lease at 4. By the time they got back to the subdivision and settled Ralph's family, it would be close to 6. That would put them at the lease way after daylight. Plus, he needed to see about finding parts for the tractor and getting it running. He'd just have to explain to David that they would have to put the trip off for a week.

When they got home, Mark and Jim helped Ralph set up his RV. Mark was explaining to Jim about postponing the hunting trip when David came out over to where the men were working. Mark could see that he was ready to go and figured he'd been waiting impatiently for the last couple of hours.

"I guess we can't go now, huh, Dad?" the boy asked with only the slightest trace of hope in his voice. "Mr. Hernandez and Victor went home a few minutes ago, and Sam said she was going back to bed. They said to get them if we were still going."

Mark instinctively looked at his watch and didn't even see what time it was. "It's getting pretty late, son. We wouldn't get there until well after daylight. We can try for next Saturday," he said trying to cheer the teenager up.

The boy's head dropped as he mumbled, "If nothing happens then."

Mark saw the disappointment in the young man's demeanor. He hated letting his son down. After all, David had kept his end of the bargain and gone to school all week without complaining. "You know what, David? Who cares if we miss a little time in the morning? Let's go. Run and get your sister back up and

263

then run down to the Hernandez's and tell them we're leaving in fifteen minutes."

David seemed to grow six inches. "Yes, sir!" He snapped a crisp salute at his father and ran off toward the house like a lightning bolt.

"What about the tractor?" Jim asked his friend.

"Gunny should still be awake. Would you run over there and ask him if he would get with your father-in-law and Rodney in the morning about getting it fixed. They can handle it."

"Yes, sir!" Jim mimicked David's response and saluted as he headed to see Gunny.

Mark heard the back door slam, as David ran out of the house and down the road to Manny's house. Mark finished showing Ralph how to level the trailer. A minute later, Sam came out of the house and walked over toward the truck carrying a cooler full of sandwiches.

"Hi, Trini," she said as she passed.

"Hi, Samantha," the tall girl replied. It seemed to Mark as if they expected to see each other at O-dark-thirty in the morning.

A few minutes later, the hunting crew was heading down the road. Mark asked Sam how she knew Trini.

"From school. We're in the same grade."

"Are y'all friends?"

Sam laughed. "No, Dad. We have some classes together, but we don't hang out. She's nice and all, but she's a jock, and I'm a band nerd," the girl stated incredulously.

"What was I thinking?" Mark asked satirically. It seemed the sarcasm was lost on Sam. He didn't remember friendships in high school being based on extracurricular activities. It had been a long time since he was in school, though. Maybe he was just getting old. Perish the thought, he said to himself. Others may be getting old, but he was still in his prime! 'Yeah, right!' a little voice in his head told him, with the same sarcasm he'd used a moment ago.

Mark stayed on the back highways and took his time, watching for any stalled cars that might be still on the road and for any signs of danger. The way was all clear, though. They reached the lease about thirty minutes after daylight, and Mark dropped everyone off where they would be hunting as quickly and quietly as possible. Manny and Victor took separate blinds, David hunted with Jim, and Mark and Sam took the spot most likely to produce turkey. Mark was glad to spend some time with his daughter. It gave them a chance to talk about what had happened since The Burst. Sam seemed to be adjusting well to everything except the shower situation. When they had been in the blind for about an hour, a group of seven turkeys came out. One was a good-sized young jake and with Mark's whispered coaching, Sam made a perfect head shot.

At 11:30, the father and daughter made their way back to the truck. Mark had heard several shots and was anxious to see what the others had harvested. They drove around to pick up everyone. Manny had killed a big spike buck. Victor was upset with himself for missing a doe. Jim and David hadn't seen anything. The group went over to the big field where the campsite was. The skinning rack was kept there, and they cleaned the deer and the turkey, and then got the meat into the ice chests, so it wouldn't go bad. Mark made Sam help clean her turkey, but he did most of the gory parts. When they were done, they broke out the sandwiches and lemonade. David kept noticing a few doves flying into the field and was excited to get his shotgun out. He gobbled down his lunch and started hunting before anyone else. When he had downed his third bird, the men decided he'd had a big enough head start. They all pulled out their scatterguns and started hunting. Sam told her dad that she wanted to dove hunt. Mark pulled out his old Browning A-5 Sweet Sixteen he'd brought just in case of this hoped-for development. He showed her how to load it and gave her a brief lecture on the mechanics of wing shooting. The two of them found a shady spot far enough away from the others and started looking for birds. It took Sam quite a few tries to finally get her first bird, but, for Mark, the wait was worth it. To see his "mall rat" daughter enjoying the outdoors the same way he did made him very happy. A few minutes later, David came walking over.

"How many do y'all have, Dad?" the smiling teenager asked.

Mark could tell from the look on his son's face that he'd already limited out, but he played the game anyway. "Sam has three, and I have five. How 'bout you?"

"I got my twelve." His face was beaming. "I beat everybody. Jim only has ten so far, and Mr. Hernandez and Victor have fourteen between them."

"That's great son...good shooting."

"Thanks! Sam, you have three already?"

The girl nodded her head quietly. She seemed a little embarrassed that she was behind everyone else. Mark knew how competitive she was, and he hoped she wasn't too discouraged that her little brother was already limited out.

"That's fantastic," David exclaimed. "The first time I dove hunted, I only got one bird all day, and you still have the best part of the day coming. You're doing great."

Sam's face reverted back to the big smile. "Thanks, bubba!"

Mark was proud of his son for bragging on and encouraging his sister. That wasn't something he was used to seeing. It seemed that this crisis had brought some maturity out in both of his children. He was very proud of them.

Just a few moments later, Jim came and announced that he was done. He and David decided to get their rifles and hike over to the blind in the next field. Mark asked Sam what she wanted to do, and she replied that she wanted to keep dove hunting. Mark went over and talked to Manny and Victor. He told them to take the truck and go back to the blinds they were in this morning whenever they were ready. By the time he got back to Sam, she was smiling bigger than ever.

"Dad...Dad...I got two more while you were gone." About that time, she caught sight of another bird lazily making his way back from the field. Mark saw her shotgun come up with a natural ease. Sam swung the scattergun, Mark heard the shot, and then he saw the bird crumple and fall. She walked over, never taking her eyes off of the spot where the dove fell, picked up the bird and put it in her bag. When she looked back at Mark, the expression on her face was priceless.

There were more and more birds as it got later, and the father and daughter both limited just before sunset. They walked back over to the campsite and sat on the picnic table. Manny had left the cooler with the drinks in it for them. Mark opened the ice chest and removed two bottles of water. He saw that the guys had all put their birds into Ziploc bags and placed them in the ice. Mark and Sam dressed the birds while they waited for the other hunters. When they pulled back up with the truck, David and Jim had each killed a feral hog, Victor hadn't missed his doe a second time, and Manny had added a turkey to his bag. David had also taken a big gobbler. The men made short work of skinning and quartering their game, and by eight o'clock, they were headed for home. The mood was even more festive than it had been that morning.

On the way, Manny asked Mark and Jim a question. "My oldest daughter and her husband live in Austin. Do you think it would be possible for me to take a couple of trucks to get them and their stuff?"

Mark was the first to answer. "I don't see why not, Manny. I've been thinking about the same thing myself. My parents, my brother and one of my sisters live in Waco."

"How many are there, Manny?" Jim asked.

"Probably four. My grandson, my daughter, and her husband, plus his mother."

"That should be easy to do between your Suburban and Big Red here. We could even borrow Chaparo's trailer, if you think they have that much stuff," Mark suggested.

"When do you think we could go?"

"I have guard duty in the morning from two until eight, but I don't see why we couldn't go after that. Maybe leave at eleven? That'll let me get a little shuteye before we go."

"That sounds great, Mark. Again, I owe you."

"Well, maybe you can help me go to Waco later in the week."

"It's a deal."

It seemed like no time at all before the happy group of hunters was at the gate to Silver Hills. One of the guards came out and opened the gate. He held his hand up to stop Mark as he was pulling through. Mark rolled down his window.

"What's up, Greg?"

"You better get straight to your house." The man's tone was deadly serious. "Gunny and one of the other guys got shot!"

Chapter 38

Mark dropped the clutch, and the big truck seemed to leap up the hill. He'd barely stopped the red beast when everyone was piling out and running for the back door. When Mark stepped inside, the first thing he saw was Gunny sitting at the kitchen table with his arm in a sling.

"What happened? Are you okay? Who else got shot?" Mark demanded with the others standing behind him.

Gunny answered the questions in reverse order of the way they were asked. "Your friend Rodney got shot twice. He's in bad shape. Lisa an' Doc Vasquez are still workin' on him down at Doc's house." The old man paused, as he squeezed his wife's hand. Mark hadn't even noticed her sitting there. "I'm fine. I just took one to the meaty part of my arm. Not much more 'n a scratch really. We went to go get the parts for the tractor. Rodney, George, and me."

"Is George okay?" Jim interrupted.

"Yeah, he's fine. In fact, he was so cool under fire I'da sweared he was in the Corps." Gunny paused, shaking his head. "This is all my fault. I shoulda been more careful. Anyway, the three of us went to Mr. Jones' house to look at the tractor. Rodney said he had parts he thought would work, and George was so excited to see if we could get it to run that we headed straight to town to get 'em. I made you take extra guys with you on your trip, an' I shoulda followed my own advice. Drivin' through town was weird. A lot of neighborhoods were burned to the ground. Some were totally deserted, and some were trashed. A couple had people in them going about their business. In those two, other than the fact that almost ever'body was armed, it was almost like nothin' was wrong. They watched us like a hawk, but when we waved, they waved back."

"When we got to Rodney's shop, it had been vandalized. All the doors and windows were broken, and lots of his stock had been strewn everywhere. We were real careful goin' in, but no one was around. We hadn't even seen one person in the neighborhood. The cash register and some other things were missing, but Rodney said that none of 'em were really worth anything. I had George watch the front, and I watched the back, while Rodney got the parts. It took him some time to sort through the mess and find what he wanted, but he finally did. I looked out the front before we went out, but the bastards had hidden behind some cars, and I didn't see 'em. I just assumed it was all fine, and we went waltzin' out the front door like we was goin' ta Sunday School. When we cleared the door, they popped up and started shootin' from across the street. If they'd waited until we were in the car, they probably woulda mowed us down like bowling pins. Rodney got hit in the thigh and the right side of his chest. He fell back, and I pulled him back into the store. When I grabbed him up is when they got me in the arm. I found some clean shop towels and a roll of tape and bandaged him up as best I could. George was shooting back at the MZB's with his pistol and was keepin' 'em pinned down behind the cars pretty good. In fact, he did real good. I just had to remind him not to shoot from the same spot every time. The MZB's only had pistols, too, thank God, and they wouldn't penetrate the cinderblock wall unless they hit the same spot several times. If'n they'd had rifles, we'da been in deep kimchee. I had Beulah with me, and I ran up to one o' the windas and peeked out. One of 'em popped up to shoot at George, and I tagged him. The buckshot folded him in half like a dollar bill. After that, they just stuck their hands up to shoot. I got Rodney's SKS and watched for where they were all shooting from. When I knew where they all three were, I started shooting through the car bodies. Thirty seconds later, it was over. George covered me with my shotgun, while I went over to make sure they was all down for good. Then we got Rodney into the back seat of his car and headed home. I thought about takin' him to a hospital, but I figured he'd get tended to faster here. I didn't even know if'n the hospital was still there or not. We decided to take the expressway. I was afraid of runnin' inta an MZB roadblock, but we decided the risk was worth it to get Rodney here as quick as possible. We almost did, but we was too quick for 'em."

"What happened?" Jim asked.

"That car of Rodney's is a fast sumbitch, so fast it kinda scared me. We was makin' good time. Someone had bulldozed all the stalled cars off of 410, so we didn't have to worry about hitting one. They were sideways on the sides of the road. Anyway, I was doin' one-twenty, and my foot wasn't even on the floor." Gunny's eyes got big. "We were comin' up on that long bridge that crosses the river. You know the one I'm talkin' 'bout?" he asked no one in particular.

Everyone nodded their heads, but no one said anything.

"I could see a couple of cars sitting sideways just on my side of the bridge and a bunch more on the far side. I didn't give it much thought. I figured those were stalled on the bridge, and whoever cleared the road had pushed them there. As soon as we hit the bridge, I saw a bunch of MZB's come out from behind the cars on the other side and start pushing them into the road. I glanced in the mirror, and there were some more pushing the ones I'd just passed, too. I punched the accelerator, and the car rocketed up to a hundred and forty. We got past the bridge before they could block it off. If we had been just toolin' along at a normal speed, we woulda been trapped. They took a couple of pot shots at us once we passed, but they didn't hit nothin'. After that, we didn't have no more trouble, and we got here pretty quick."

"How's Rodney doing?" Mark asked.

"He was in an' out as we was coming home and havin' trouble breathin'. He lost a lot of blood. The leg wound isn't that bad, but Lisa said the chest shot went through his lung. She told me while she was patchin' up my arm that they had got the bleeding stopped and reinflated his lung, but it was touch and go. She went back down to Doc's house a little while ago to watch him while Doc got some sleep. I'm sorry 'bout this, Karate Man. I shoulda made us come back here and get a couple a more guys 'fore we went to town."

"Gunny, nobody could have done any better than you did. This could have happened to any one of us. I'm just glad you were there to handle the situation and get everyone back here quickly. We just have to make sure, all of us, that we don't forget that we can't let our guard down for even a second." This was the first time Gunny had needed a pep talk, Mark thought. "What about Rodney's family? Where are they?"

"They're all down at Doc's. Jess is with them."

Mark turned to his children and told them to unload the coolers and switch out the ice bottles, so the meat would stay cold. Manny asked Victor to help them. Mark, Jim, and Manny headed to the Vasquez house. When they got there, Jess and Rodney's wife, Donna, were sitting on the front porch on a bench. Jess had her arm around the woman who, Mark could tell, was an emotional mess. The boys were asleep on a blanket on the ground. Mark never knew what to say in difficult situations, and this one was no different. As he approached the two women on the bench, Jess looked up at him. The look on her face told Mark the news wasn't good. Mark knew he had to say something.

"I'm so sorry, Donna. We're all praying for him," he choked out.

The woman looked up at him with vacant eyes and nodded her head. Mark heard Jim and Manny offer their words of comfort and hope. Jess stood up and pulled the men to the side.

"Lisa said his chances aren't good, but that if he makes it until morning, he might have a shot," she explained. "Manny, do you know your blood type?"

"I think it's B positive."

"Rodney is O negative. We only found one other person in the neighborhood who has the right blood type. It's Sherri Henderson. Lisa took two pints of blood from her. She was looking quite pale when Lisa was done with her. Lisa said she might be able to get another pint tomorrow, but Sherri's very petite, so Lisa isn't sure."

"Maybe the sheriff could see if the hospital has any blood," Jim suggested.

"We checked with him. He checked it out but called us back and said that the hospital had run out of fuel for their generator a week ago. They got some more, but not before all of the blood went bad. He said he checked with all of the surrounding counties, and all of them were either in the same situation our hospital is in, or that they had already used up their entire supply of O negative. I didn't know it, but you can give O negative blood to anyone. Unfortunately, it's fairly rare, and those with that type can only take their type. Lisa said we were lucky to even find one person here with it."

"I've been thinking," Jess continued, "and I know what we should do with Jon and Marian's house. We should turn it into a hospital. Doc had to spend a lot of time finding the things he and Lisa needed to operate. If we turned the Olsen house into a hospital, they could have those things out all the time."

"That sounds like a good idea," Manny said.

"I agree," Mark stated. "We can vote on it tomorrow night."

Mark looked at his watch. It was almost time for him to report for duty. He excused himself to walk back to his house. He asked Manny to walk with him.

"Manny, I'm concerned about taking our little road trip tomorrow. With what happened today with Gunny and Rodney, I think we should put it off."

"I understand," Manny replied, "but I still feel like I have to go, even if it is just me and my Suburban."

"I'm not saying we won't go, Manny, but what good does it do to go if we can't be sure of the safety of those we're going to get? I'm just saying let's plan this out better, and if it means we don't go until later in the week, at least we can be confident we can get there and back without anyone getting hurt or killed."

"You're right, Mark. I see why everyone looks up to you. You always make the right decisions."

"That's a load of crap, Manny, and you know it. I make just as many, if not more mistakes as anyone else."

"But you look at the big picture and put the group ahead of yourself. That's why you're the leader."

"I never asked to be the leader, and I don't want to be the leader!"

"To the people who live here, you ARE our leader. You better get used to that fact, *mi amigo*." Manny paused, seeming to enjoy watching his friend squirm. "Tell me something, is it more likely that everyone who lives here is wrong, or that you are wrong?"

"Just because everyone thinks something doesn't make it true," Mark argued.

"That may be so, but just because you don't believe it, that doesn't make it not true. Right?"

Mark looked sideways at the Hispanic philosopher. "You told me you never finished high school. When did you take a logic course?"

"I didn't," Manny smiled. He reached up and pinched the top of his ears together. "I just used to watch a lot of Star Trek, and guess who my favorite character was?"

"Okay, Spock. I give in, for now that is," Mark smiled back. "I'll talk to you tomorrow."

"Aye aye, Captain Kirk. Live long, and prosper."

Mark winced at the corny reference and left Manny standing on the corner, trying to make the Vulcan greeting sign.

When Mark got back home, not only had the kids unloaded the coolers, but they'd also placed all of the firearms next to the safe, and David was putting up all of the ammo. Mark thanked the kids, then grabbed his rifle and headed down to the CP. He got there a few minutes early and watched as the other members of Delta team arrived. They all knew about Rodney, and the mood was quite somber. Mark gave them an update on his condition, and they said a prayer for him. Mark had planned to take gate duty tonight, but since he hadn't had much sleep, he decided to pull rover duty instead. Moving around would help to keep him awake. When it was 1:45, Mark noticed he was one person short. He looked at Gunny's schedule and noticed that Craig Banks was the missing guard. He remembered that Craig had promised not to be late again when they had talked before. Mark would be a little firmer with him when they talked this time. He gave out the assignments and told Joe Bagwell, who was on CP duty, to send Craig out to his team of rovers when he showed up.

Mark and Paul Jensen started their rounds with Mark in the lead. Mark's mind raced from thought to thought. He thought about Rodney, then what Manny had told him about being the leader, to how they could safely go to Austin and Waco. He wondered what the sheriff wanted, what unexpected event might happen, how long the lights would be out, what all this meant to the future of Silver Hills and to the country, for that matter. There were so many questions, and so few answers. Then his mind drifted back to Rodney. Who would take care of his family, if he died? Who would be the next person to get injured? How could he keep all of these people safe? How can I even...

"Hey, Mark?"

"Yeah, Paul, what is it?"

"Are we going to go around this block again?"

"I don't know. Should we?"

"Well, we've been around it four times in a row. Maybe we should move to the next one."

"I'm sorry, Paul. I've got a lot on my mind. Would you mind taking the lead?" Mark was embarrassed that he hadn't been paying attention.

"No problem," Paul responded with a smile.

Mark physically followed Paul, but his mind went back to the problems troubling him. He looked at his watch after a little while and saw it was almost time for their shift to be over. He wondered where Craig was. He called Joe on the radio and was told Craig hadn't shown up. Mark and Paul headed over to Susan's house to see if anything was up. After walking around the house and seeing that everything looked okay, Mark decided to knock. He hated to wake Susan and her boys up, but he was worried. After a minute, he heard Susan.

"Who is it?"

"Susan, it's me, Mark Turner." He heard the deadbolt turn, and then the door opened. Susan stood there in her bathrobe with the AR in her hands. Any other time it would have seemed comical. "Is Craig here?"

"No. He has guard duty tonight."

"I know, but he never showed up."

"That son of a bitch! I heard him leave about 1:30. I told you not to trust him. When he gets back, I'm going to rip him a new one." Susan was as mad as when Craig had introduced himself as her husband.

Mark thought for a second. "Don't say anything, okay? Let's give him some rope and see if he'll hang himself. I'll talk to him later and see what he says."

"Okay, Mark. I'll see you later."

Mark noticed that the usually full of spunk woman looked down. "Are you alright?"

"Yeah, I'm just tired. One of the boys is sick. He was up half the night puking. I just need some sleep."

"Maybe you should take him to Lisa."

"She and Doc have bigger things to worry about right now than a kid with a bug. How's Rodney?"

"He was still alive when our shift started. I'm going to check again as soon as we're done. If your son isn't better in a day or two, get with Lisa."

"Thanks. I will," Susan promised, as she closed the door.

Just what I need, another problem, thought Mark. He and Paul finished their shift, and Mark headed back over to Doc's. He saw a light in the kitchen, so he lightly knocked on the back door. Doc answered and invited him in.

"How's he doing?"

"He's still hanging in there," Doc whispered.

"That's a good sign, right?"

"Yes. But we're still a long way from being out of the woods. Even if he recovers from the wounds, we still have to worry about infections and the long-term effects of being shot. We don't know even how much nerve damage there may be in his leg. But, the longer he hangs on, the better his chances."

Mark nodded his head. "If anything changes, can you let me know?"

"You bet."

Mark walked home. He didn't remember ever feeling this tired.

Mark looked at his watch when he woke up. He couldn't believe it said 1:30 in the afternoon. He'd slept for seven hours. When he went into the kitchen, Jess was cutting up some of the meat they'd brought home yesterday. When she saw him, she stopped.

"That's the latest you've slept in a long time."

"Yeah, I guess I was pretty tired. Have you heard anything about Rodney?"

"Yes. Lisa came home for lunch and said his blood pressure is up a little. He's still in critical condition, but it seems he's improving."

"That's good. How are Donna and the boys?"

"The boys are okay. Donna's still a basket case. Lisa's really worried about her. If Rodney doesn't make it, there's no telling how bad she might get."

"Hopefully, we won't have to find out," Mark said thoughtfully. "Do you know where Jim is?"

"He, George, and Ralph went to see if they could get the tractor running and bring it over here."

"Good. I'm going to Gunny's. We've got a problem with Craig Banks. He didn't show up for guard duty last night."

"There's something about that man I don't like," Jess said, with a sour look on her face. "It's probably the way he acts likes he's God's gift to women. He's trouble if you ask me."

Mark laughed. "Susan told me the same thing."

"Then why did she let him move into her house?"

"She told me she did it for the boys."

"I guess I'd do the same thing. I'm just glad I was smart enough not to marry that big of a jerk."

"Thanks...I think."

"I didn't mean it like that," she winked. "But you'd better keep an eye on him. He's a snake."

"We will," Mark assured her, as he walked out the door.

Gunny agreed with Mark about Craig. If he didn't have a good explanation for skipping out, they would remove him from guard duty, but there was little else they could do. Guard duty was, after all, voluntary. Mark also talked to the old Marine about how they could safely get to Austin and Waco and back. They hashed it around for a while and finally came up with a plan. If Mark could get all the pieces in place, they would try a trip to Austin later in the week.

When he got home, Jim and Ralph were hooking the plow they had borrowed from the Christmas tree farm to Ralph's tractor. It seemed the parts Rodney had found dropped right in and, according to Ralph, the tractor had never run so smoothly. As soon as the plow was attached, George climbed on and plowed the rest of the land that Jess had staked out for their garden in only a few minutes. He pulled the medium-sized, blue tractor back over by the shed with a big smile on his face.

"We should be able to finish plowing the gardens within a week," he announced. "Then we can start on the vacant lots. They should go quickly, too."

"That sounds good, George," Mark said, as the old farmer climbed down.

At the meeting, Lisa gave an update on Rodney's condition. He was still slowly improving. Mark told everyone about Jess's suggestion to turn the Olsen house into a hospital. It was approved almost unanimously. George told everyone about the tractor, and that seemed to lift everyone's spirits a little. After the meeting, Mark found Craig.

Craig apologized and explained he had started on his way to guard duty but felt a migraine headache coming on. He went back to the house to take his medicine, but it kept getting worse. He would have come to let someone know, but it got so bad that it was even excruciating to move. He didn't want to wake Susan up to report in for him because she was really tired from little Craig being sick. Finally, his headache started getting better, and he fell asleep. Mark mentioned that Susan heard him leave but didn't hear him come back in. Craig explained that the wind caught the door and slammed it when he left but that he was extremely quiet when he came back. Mark wanted to believe the man, but something kept him from buying Craig's story. He'd check with Susan again on the possibility that things could have happened like Craig had explained.

That night on guard duty, Mark took the gate. It was quiet until 4:30, when the OP called in a small group approaching. They had already passed the westernmost border of the subdivision and were moving slowly toward the gate. Mark cursed under his breath that they hadn't seen the intruders earlier. He called the rovers and had the CP alert the backups. The men responded quickly, but by the time they were in position, the travelers had moved up even with the gate. Mark was surprised that he wasn't able to see them until they were very close. There were four of them, dressed in dark clothing, and all carrying rifles. Mark hoped they would pass on by without causing trouble.

"Hello, the gate," Mark heard someone whisper. He hunkered down into the foxhole and motioned for his men to stay quiet.

"Hello, the gate." The voice was a little louder this time. "I know you're in there."

"Yes. What do you want?" Mark responded, peeking over the edge of the foxhole.

"We don't want any trouble. We'd just like some water, if you can spare some." The man was standing in plain sight. His rifle was slung across his back, and his hands were away from his body. His companions, though, were across the road covering him. Their weapons were pointing at the ground, but they were ready if anything happened.

"What guarantee do I have that you won't start trouble?" Mark called.

"Look, we know you have at least ten or twelve guys watching us. We'd be idiots to start something."

Mark wondered who had compromised their security measures. "Who told you that?"

"No one told me. I have a night vision scope, and I saw you."

Mark was relieved and concerned all at once. Relieved that he didn't have to go on a witch hunt for a blabbermouth, and concerned that someone could just sit back and watch them without their knowledge. Mark radioed that he was coming out to talk to the stranger. The two of them cautiously approached the gate and shook hands when they got there. The two men chatted for a minute, and then the stranger waved his partners over to the gate. The three of them

273

stood up, slung their weapons, and walked over to the gate. Mark could see that it was a woman and two teenage girls. The man introduced his family. He explained they were making their way to a weekend cabin their family owned on the San Marcos River.

Mark sent a guard to get some water from the CP, and a few minutes later, he came back with a five-gallon bucket. The family all pulled out various containers they were using for canteens and filled them. Everyone drank deeply and then refilled the bottles. The man thanked Mark and said that they needed to be on their way. Mark asked if they needed anything else, and the man said that they had plenty of food to make it to where they were going. When Mark asked the man what he'd done before The Burst, he replied that he'd been a supervisor in a textile plant. Mark shook the man's hand and wished them luck. Then he watched them walk out of sight.

The next morning, when the four men that the sheriff had invited to town arrived at the meeting, they were surprised at how many people were there. The sheriff came over to the foursome when he saw them and inquired about their injured man. Jim reported that he was still improving and that Lisa now thought he had a better than even chance to make it. The sheriff said he hoped the man pulled through and then excused himself to talk with some other people. Mark hadn't expected to see this many people. He estimated there were at least sixty or seventy, and he was now even more confused about what the sheriff wanted.

A few minutes later, the meeting began. The Sheriff introduced the County Commissioners, the County Judge, the mayors of Floresville and La Vernia, and some other dignitaries. Then he took a deep breath.

"The reason we asked you all here today is to let you know some things that are going on and to get your help in deciding the best plan for our county to deal with what's happening and what may happen." The sheriff paused, as a small murmur rolled through the assembly. "Let me give you an overview of what we know. First, the shelter at Kelly suffered a massive riot Friday night, and over sixty percent of the people fled. Reports are that the airport shelter's also turning into a powder keg that'll blow at any time. We believe we'll soon see a massive amount of refugees coming through our county looking for a place to live."

A louder murmur rippled through the crowd.

"Next, the Texas Department of Criminal Justice let us know they are releasing all non-violent felons. Most of the county jails in the state have already released all of their prisoners held for misdemeanors. We're concerned that, while these criminals were non-violent, they may become violent given the current state of affairs."

A clamor of concerned voices crescendoed through the throng.

The sheriff held his hands up. "There's one more problem I need to tell you about." The audience finally quieted. "We have unconfirmed reports...not much more than a rumor right now...that there is some kind of virus on the West Coast. No one knows if it's naturally occurring, or if it is an engineered attack. However, the best information we can get indicates that it is highly contagious and that the mortality rate may be as high as fifty percent."

A pin drop could have been heard.

Chapter 39

A moment later, curious, frightened, and angry voices erupted as one and destroyed the silence. Questions were hurled at the podium from all directions like Nolan Ryan fastballs. The sheriff held his hand up in the air and asked for quiet. He had to ask several times, but finally the crowd quieted back down.

"Please, one question at a time," the lawman pleaded. He pointed to a man in the front row with his hand up. "Yes?"

Mark could hear the man ask his question, but the words didn't register on his brain. He felt as if someone had just cut a hole through his chest big enough to drive a truck through. The first two announcements the sheriff had made, while unsettling, weren't unexpected. Mark felt that they were fairly well prepared for large groups of refugees and even some groups of ne'er-do-wells, but how was he supposed to protect his people from a killer virus? He caught himself. His people? Who did he think he was? Moses? Or maybe he'd been listening to Manny and the others too much. He came back to reality in time to hear the sheriff introduce Doctor Ken Phillips to the impromptu council.

"In addition to having a practice here in Floresville for the last twenty-five years, Doctor Ken is also our county medical examiner and chairman of the Board of Health."

The doctor walked from the back of the room to the podium. "Most of you know me. I like to hope for the best, but I also like to be prepared for the worst. I don't think we need to overreact to this illness. We don't know for certain if it even exists, but if it does, and if it's truly a virus, then there's little we can do to stop it if it makes it here from California. However, we have several reasons to be optimistic. First, as I said before, it may only be a rumor. Hopefully, we'll know more in the near future. Second, if it isn't a rumor, California is a long way when transportation is as limited as it is in these circumstances. It may never make it here. Lastly, even if it does get here, it may have mutated to a less-deadly form by that time."

A few others asked some questions, but he wasn't able to tell them much more than what he'd already said. He sat down, and Curt stood back up.

"The reason we're here is to come up with responses to these threats. Any ideas?" the sheriff asked.

"Yeah," one man yelled. "Let's barricade off all the routes into the county and not let anyone in."

A large portion of the crowd seemed to agree with the man.

"That is something we've considered," the sheriff announced. "But there are several problems with that solution. First, the highways through our county belong to all of the people of Texas, not just to us. We can close down the county roads if we want, but it wouldn't be legal to shut off the state highways."

"Who cares if it's legal or not? This is a matter of survival," the same man yelled at the sheriff. He seemed to be somewhat of a hot head. However, Mark saw many of the people in the room nodding their heads in agreement with him.

"I care, and so do my deputies, but even if we tried to stop everyone from entering on the highways, what's to stop them from traveling cross country? We don't have enough men to completely surround the county. Plus some will have family and friends here who want to take them in. Others will just want to pass through. Only a small percentage will be troublemakers. We shouldn't punish everyone just because of a few."

Mark could see many of the same people nodding their heads in agreement with the sheriff now. Some of them were even saying, "That's right."

Several other suggestions were made over the next few minutes, but they all presented at least as many problems as they solved. The sheriff suggested they all think about it and have another meeting the same time next week. Everyone seemed agreeable to that, so the sheriff moved to another item.

"As most of you know, my deputies and I are stretched pretty thin. I've been hopeful the lights would come back on soon and that everything would return to normal. However, it seems the possibility of that is more and more remote with each passing day. There are two groups of people represented here today, who have formed what could best be described a citizens' militia. I want to use these groups as prototypes to organize people throughout the county into groups that can help the Sheriff's Department."

"Militias are a bunch of skin-heads and fat rednecks. We don't need any of them in our county." It was the same hothead as before. Mark didn't know who the man was, but he didn't like his attitude. He did have a point, though. Mark had seen a documentary on militias on CNN after the Oklahoma City Bombing. If fact, Timothy McVeigh, the bomber, was part of a militia.

The Sheriff took a deep breath. "That's not totally true, Barry. While 'militia' has become a dirty word in the last few years, that hasn't always been the case. Militias fought with the Colonial Army against the British in the American Revolution. Militias made up the forces that fought for Texas' independence against Santa Anna. Texas didn't have an organized Army. It was citizens who'd had enough of unfair rule from Mexico who came together to form an unorganized army that won freedom for our great state. All 'militia' really means is an unorganized group of citizens who come together to help each other. Whether they were fighting tyranny, Indian attacks, or outlaws, they were a militia. If we don't want to call it a militia, we don't have to, but that doesn't change what it will be, a group of Wilson County citizens who want to protect our county from harm."

Mark had never heard it explained that way. What the sheriff wanted to do made sense.

"The first person I want to introduce is Greg Hardy." The Sheriff pointed into the crowd, and a man stood up. Mark recognized him as the man who had come out with the lawman and asked him so many questions. "Greg lives in LaVernia and has organized his neighbors into quite a force. Four times, they have repelled groups that attacked the town. If not for him and the 'LaVernia Irregulars,' as they call themselves, some of the town's citizens might not be with us today."

The group clapped for Greg. He looked embarrassed by the gesture and sat down quickly with a wave of his hand. The sheriff continued.

"The next person I want to recognize…" Mark looked around the room, wondering if he knew the other militia leader. "…is Mark Turner from Silver Hills."

Mark was dumbfounded. He felt himself being pushed up from both sides by Jim and Gunny. His legs somehow straightened, and he was standing, as the people around him applauded. He realized he must have looked like a deer caught in the headlights of impending doom. He heard the sheriff go on about how their group had withstood a running gun battle and how he had helped the preacher and about how they'd saved Ralph Jones and his family from a bunch of hoods just a couple of nights ago. As Mark listened, his surprise slowly turned to anger. Anger that Sheriff Thompson had blindsided him. Anger that these people now though he was some kind of example for them to follow. Anger that they were clapping and cheering for him like some kind of gridiron legend. He took a deep breath to calm himself and sat down. It seemed an eternity before the applause stopped.

"What I want to do is to meet with these men and their associates to come up with a plan to train and organize our county force." The sheriff paused. "And what I'd like for all of you to do is talk to your friends and neighbors and see how many would be willing to help us out. It'll be strictly voluntary, but the benefits to us all could truly be the difference in life and death. Does that sound good to everyone?"

Everyone nodded their heads up and down like the porpoises at Sea World. The Sheriff dismissed the meeting, reminded everyone to return next week, and then asked a few people to accompany him to his office to discuss a training plan. On the way there, Mark pulled the lawman off to the side.

"You blindsided me, Curt. I didn't want to be a part of this."

"I'm sorry. I was afraid if I told you what I really wanted, you wouldn't show up. I can see now I was probably right."

Mark just glared at him.

"Look, Mark, whether you wanted to be involved in this or not, you are. You were involved before I asked you here. You were involved before those assholes in that truck tried to kill you. You were involved as soon as the lights went out. You're just beginning to realize how involved you are, and that's what you're mad about. Now you just need to accept the fact that you're in this up to your eyebrows and deal with it," Curt said, smiling. "Now, let's get to work."

Mark looked down at his boots. "I guess you're right. I'm involved up to here." He held his hand even with the top of his thinning hair. "You're not the first person to tell me this, so I guess I better learn to accept it, but that doesn't mean I have to like it."

The lawman laughed.

When they got into the sheriff's office, Mark recognized everyone but the man standing next to Greg. The sheriff introduced him as Greg's lieutenant, Rob Bowers. The lawman then turned to Ralph, whom he'd also asked to see.

"Counselor, I have some info on the guys who attacked your house. Have you ever heard the name Lee Ray Jenkins?"

The big lawyer rubbed his chin for a moment. "That sounds familiar...oh, yeah...he was the Klan boy I put away for beating up an old black man during Fiesta one year. That was back in the late 80's...I think."

"That's the one. Turns out our ringleader the other night is his baby brother looking to get even for his brother spending the rest of his life in jail."

"Jenkins only got five years. He should have been out long ago."

"That's not how it worked out, Ralph. Seems he got shanked in the shower one night and died a couple of days later."

"I see." Ralph seemed sad that the Klansman had died. Mark wondered why a black man would be sorry that some KKKer died. He didn't think he would be if he was in Ralph's shoes.

Curt addressed the group with his main topic. "I've already talked with the county commissioners and the mayor about starting our militia. At first, they wanted me to deputize an additional hundred men. I told them I didn't have the equipment to supply that many people with the minimum amount of gear required to do the job. Plus, transportation would be a major problem. We only have twelve running patrol cars. Finally, the state requirements for being a deputy sheriff necessitate a peace officer's commission, and there's no one in the county authorized to teach the class. In the end, they agreed that having a militia was the best solution. I hope to get five or six more groups like you all have. If they're spread out over the county, it should give us the ability for each group to cover a section and call the Sheriff's Department for backup. What we need to do is talk about how we're going to train the people who volunteer. Mark, your group is the biggest. Would you mind sharing what y'all are doing?"

"Gunny's actually in charge of our security detail. Why don't we let him fill you in? Gunny?"

The grizzled veteran told about the training schedule he'd set up. Members of their security detail spent about eight hours a week in training. Two with Mark on fitness and unarmed self defense, two with Jim on marksmanship, and four with him on anything and everything else. Gunny also told them how he conducted drills while the men, and women he was reminded, were on duty. Once Gunny was finished describing their training program, Curt asked Greg to fill everyone in on their program. Greg turned the floor over to Rob.

"We only train once or twice a month, but we've been at it longer than you guys in Silver Hills. We have twenty-eight people in our security detachment. Since The Burst, we've had some newcomers want to join, but so far we haven't felt we needed them. Plus, they don't have our group standard equipment."

Rob's opening statement had created several questions in Mark's mind, but before he could verbalize them, Jim jumped in.

"How long have you been at it?"

"Well, Greg started developing our subdivision four years ago. Most of our residents have been there and training with us for at least two years."

"Two years!" Mark exclaimed. "I wish we had that kind of time under our belts. You said something about group standard equipment?"

"Every homeowner has a list of standard equipment they agree to buy as soon as possible. That's part of the agreement they make when they buy a lot from Greg. It includes things like weapons and radios we use for our security force. They also agree to spend a certain amount of time per year training with the group," Rob explained.

Mark could see the raised eyebrows on the faces of his friends. Gunny asked a question.

"So, whatchur standard weapons?"

"First are an AR-15 and a Glock 17. Every adult member of the family needs at least those two, plus ammo, magazines, and web gear. After that are optional things like M1-A's and Mossberg 590's. Plus every family has to have at least two GMRS radios."

Rob went on to explain that they trained as a group on weekends, sometimes for just a few hours and sometimes for the whole weekend. Mark was beginning to see these people had done before The Burst what they had done in Silver Hills since the lights went out. He couldn't imagine how they had gotten a group to agree to all of this stuff before it became so obviously needed. He mentioned this fact to the men from LaVernia. Greg explained that he'd become concerned about the Y2K bug in 1998. He said he found a network of survival groups on the net and that some of these people helped him develop a plan. His business as a rural real estate developer allowed him to take one of his projects and turn it into a haven for like-minded individuals. He and some friends, including Rob and Curt, were the first to move into 'Promise Point.' After the Millenium bug turned out to be nothing, they felt it was prudent to stay prepared for any other kind of disaster. "Boy, are we glad now that we did," he ended.

"You sound a little like our old boss, Reginald Davis," Mark stated. He saw Greg and Curt look at each other. "Do you know him?"

"Not personally," Curt answered, "only by reputation. Some of the folks who helped us get started tried to help him, as well. I didn't know you worked for him."

"You said they tried to help him out?" Jim asked.

"According to what I heard, Mr. Davis isn't always receptive to the ideas of others. I hope this doesn't offend you, since you work for him, but he tends to be a hard-liner with his group." Greg was almost apologetic.

"I don't think we work for him anymore," Mark laughed. "We noticed 'the hard-liner thing' and told him we didn't want to stay at his ranch. He lost it. He truly could not believe that we turned him down. He never said the words, but it was clear to Jim and me that we didn't have jobs anymore."

The men talked some more about how to train the new people who would want to help. They came up with several good ideas and decided to see how many volunteers they had before determining which plan to use. When the meeting broke up, Greg asked Mark if he had a minute. The two men walked out of the Sheriff's office onto the courthouse lawn.

"I just wanted to apologize to you for not being more forthcoming when Curt brought me over to visit your place. I should have told you we had a group, but I didn't know if I could trust you or not at that point," Greg began.

"That's okay," Mark responded. "As I remember, I didn't trust you enough to answer all of your questions either. I guess that trust has to be built up slowly." He paused. "I'm still amazed you all were able to get a group together before the stuff hit the fan. It seems to me that it would be hard to keep everyone on the same page. Heck, even when solutions look obvious to me now, there is always at least a dissenter or two in our group."

"Yes. We have that problem, too, sometimes, but most of the time everybody gets along pretty well, and when they don't, majority rules." Curt, who had walked up on the conversation, concurred. "I wanted to let you know that Curt and I both were amazed at how much Silver Hills had accomplished in less than a month. It took us over a year to get to basically the same point at Promise Point. It's a real testament to your leadership."

There someone goes again, he thought, giving me credit I don't deserve. "It's really a testament to people pulling together and doing what's necessary."

"That's true, but people are funny animals. In a crisis, they almost always do one of two things. They either turn on each other, or they band together. The difference between the two is usually leadership. But I didn't ask you out here to debate human nature with you. I really wanted to ask you if there was anything we could do to help you?"

Mark thought for a moment. "Our biggest concern is water. We're pumping water out of my well for the neighborhood with a generator. It's working fine for now, but if the generator breaks or, God forbid, this thing goes on long enough that we run out of gas, we're going to be in trouble. I had tried to trade for an old windmill, but Mr. Davis wouldn't trade with us. Do you have any idea where I can get one?"

Now it was Greg's turn to think. "I just might. Let me check it out, and I'll get back to you later this week."

"Thanks. Is there anything we can do for you?"

"Actually, there is. Do you think your garden expert could come look at our gardens? They don't seem to be doing as well as they did last year, and we can't figure out why."

"I'm sure George would be glad to help you all out," Mark said. With that, they shook hands, and Mark and his crew headed home.

The trip home was filled with conversation of the day's events. Mark's mind was preoccupied with mostly two items: the killer virus and his family in Waco. He prayed the virus was only a rumor, but something in his gut told him it wasn't. How could they protect themselves from an invisible killer? He'd rather face a whole boatload of MZB's empty handed. The virus made it imperative that he go to Waco soon. If he waited, it might be too late. When they were about halfway home, Ralph asked an unexpected question.

"What would it take for us to stay at Silver Hills indefinitely?"

Mark had actually thought about that possibility, but he didn't think Ralph would want to leave his home for more than a few days. He didn't keep the former defensive end waiting for an answer. "You're welcome to stay as long as you want."

"I thought we had to be voted in by everyone or something."

"That's only if no one knows you. If you have family or friends willing to put you up, then nobody can say squat about you staying. You can stay on my property for as long as you'd like."

"So, I guess that makes us friends?" the black man asked jokingly.

"No. Family," Mark answered with his own smile.

"How do you figure that?"

"Listen, Ralph, I've heard people talking, and except for the fact you're taller than I am, they can barely tell us apart. They say we might be twins."

"Is that so? Only by our height, huh?" Ralph rolled his eyes.

"Well that and...I kind of hate to mention it, I'm so humble and all...the fact that I'm way better looking than you."

A collective groan went up from the other men. Mark's joke had lightened the mood, and the men continued to rib each other the rest of the way home.

Chapter 40

Wednesday morning, when Mark was finished with his guard duty shift, he went home to get ready to go for Manny's daughter and her family. He had a lot on his mind. His most significant concern at the moment was how the trip to Austin would go. They had practiced the convoy plan he and Gunny had come up with, and had even simulated a roadblock and the different ways that they could choose to deal with it. If this trip went well, and Mark prayed that it would, then they would go to Waco on Saturday.

The President had given his semi-weekly speech last night, and Mark noticed a subtle difference in the leader's tone. He had urged those in shelters to stay there and everyone, no matter where they were, to cooperate fully with those in charge. He warned that any civil disobedience, looting, or interfering with the government's plans to control this crisis would have to be dealt with severely, given the extraordinary circumstances. In the end, he praised the American citizens for pulling together in these difficult times, and he assured them that food and medicine would continue to be provided to all those in government shelters. Mark supposed that the man might just be tired, but it sounded as if he was almost desperate.

Rodney was holding on, but he was still unconscious. Lisa was getting a little more optimistic about his chances but said she'd feel a lot better once he woke up. Donna seemed to be doing better, and Lisa had been keeping her busy helping set up their new hospital.

Mark walked out to his Jeep with his FAL and a backpack with his spare magazines, ammo, and emergency supplies. The Jeep looked funny. Chaparo had welded a together a louvered grill guard that would hopefully protect the engine compartment from gunfire. The windshield had been lowered, and a rest for a rifle had been mounted on the dash, so the driver could theoretically shoot and drive at the same time. Mark's truck also looked different. It, too, had a new grill guard, and the stock bumper had been replaced with a huge, heavy pipe, in case they needed to ram through a blockade. Mark placed his weapon and pack into the Jeep, which would be the lead vehicle, and waited for the others to arrive. It wasn't long until Manny drove up in his Suburban with Chaparo's trailer on the back. He had Victor with him, who would drive the truck. Scott Simmons, Dwight Rittiman, and Joe Bagwell all walked up together. They would sit shotgun in the three vehicles that were already here. A moment later, Professor Petrie drove up in his Trans Am with Gunny in the passenger seat. They would bring up the rear of the convoy. The right side t-top had been removed, which would give the rider a 360-degree field of fire. They were taking the FRS radios to communicate.

The men loaded up and headed out of the subdivision. Manny, Mark, and Gunny had selected the route they would use, which was made up of mostly back roads and minor highways. Unless something compelled them to change the route, they would come back the same way. This made the round trip about fifty miles further than the most direct way, but the men felt the lesser risk was worth the extra fuel.

Mark took the lead, with Victor and Manny following about a minute behind. Ted stayed far enough back that he barely could see the trucks in front of him. His job was to keep someone from sneaking up behind them. If another vehicle tried to attack him, he would radio the trucks ahead, and they'd set up a quick ambush on the sides of the road, while Ted hauled butt up to them. Mark's job in the front was to cautiously round all curves and top all hills looking for any road blocks or attack points. The truck and the Suburban would stay back until Mark gave them the all-clear sign. If the Jeep ended up in an ambush, Mark and Joe, his co-pilot, could shoot back out of the open jeep while they backed out of the danger zone. The convoy would try to keep their speed to about forty-five miles per hour.

A little over halfway, Mark topped a small rise and saw several burned out cars at the bottom of the hill where there was a bridge over a creek. Two were completely off of the road, but one was about halfway out in his lane. He slammed on the brakes and had Joe radio for the others to stop. He was over three hundred yards from the cars and couldn't see anyone. He thought it might be the same kind of roadblock Gunny had seen the other day, but the cars didn't seem positioned right. He pulled his binoculars out of his pack and looked the area over as well as he could. He still couldn't see anyone. He radioed back to the others what was going on. Gunny had the rest of the vehicles move to the top of the hill. He instructed Victor to watch behind them and the others to cover the Jeep. Then he told Mark to slowly drive down to the choke point and see what happened. Mark eased his CJ into first gear and then placed his FAL on the dash rest. Joe had one of the AK's at the ready. The hair on the back of Mark's neck stood up as he released the clutch, and the Jeep crept down the hill. It seemed an eternity passed with each second, as Mark wished his eyes had x-ray vision. When they were fifty or sixty yards from the burned out wrecks, Mark suddenly stomped on the brakes. He still couldn't see anything dangerous, but his nose had picked up a scent that made him wretch. He looked over at Joe and saw from the hand over his nose and mouth that the smell was equally offensive to him.

"What happened? What happened?" Gunny's voice crackled over the radio.

"Something smells awful down here," Mark replied.

"Did you see anything?"

"No. Not yet."

"Move on across the bridge, then. If'n you get past the cars and still don't see anything, stop and we'll come on down, but be ready, Karate Man. If'n they's trouble after you pass them cars, haul ass on through, and we'll give 'em hell from up here."

"Roger that, Gunny."

Mark held his breath and slowly drove across the bridge and past the three cars. He drove another forty yards and stopped. Fortunately, the wind was blowing from this direction, and it kept the smell down to a tolerable level at this distance. Mark took a good look around and then gave clearance for the others to come down. He hopped out of the Jeep with his rifle and slowly walked back toward the cars. Gunny had instructed Victor and Scott to hold their position in the truck at the top of the hill and keep watch in both directions. The other two vehicles stopped at the bridge about the same time that Mark and Joe reached the first car. The two men looked into it. Joe was instantly sick. Mark, somewhat assisted by his previous experiences, but mostly because he had skipped breakfast, just gagged a couple of times. Someone had piled several bodies into the car and set it on fire. Unfortunately, the fire must have burned out before it totally consumed them, and they were starting to decompose badly. Mark called Gunny and the others over and told them what was making the terrible stench. Gunny examined the cars for a few minutes while everyone else made their way back to the Jeep for a drink of water. Mark saw the old man approach the car and look in at the bodies. He wasn't sure, but it appeared that even Gunny was struggling to keep his breakfast down. After a few minutes, the grizzled Marine hobbled up to the others and gave his report.

"It looks to me like the ones in the car were manning this road block. Looks like they bit off more 'an they could chew. The cars are all shot up from the side like they were crossways in the road and not the front, like they would be if they'd been coming down the road. There are a couple old sawed off shotguns and a .30-30 in the car with the bodies. The stocks are burned up, but you can still tell what they were. Whatever punched holes through those cars was bigger than some old scattergun or a cowboy rifle. Coulda been a group like us coming through that didn't take too kindly to being hijacked, or it could have been a meaner group of MZB's. Whoever they were, they weren't fiddle fartin' around. All of the bodies have been shot at least three or four times."

"So what should we do?" Manny asked.

"We go on, but real careful," Gunny answered.

Mark walked over to the trailer attached to Manny's Suburban and removed a jerry can of gas.

"Whatcha doin', Karate Man?" Gunny demanded.

"I think we should finish up disposing of these bodies. It seems wrong to me just to let them decompose, and we don't have time to bury them."

"Your heart's in the right place, Mark, but we don't know if we can really spare the gas, and I don't think we should send out any smoke signals that might give us away," Gunny explained.

"We can't just leave them here like this!" Mark insisted.

"I don't think we have a choice," Gunny reasoned. "Tell you what. If'n we come back this way, and it looks like we don't need the extry gas, you can finish the job up. Sound okay?"

"Yeah, that'll be okay."

The men loaded back into their vehicles, and the convoy resumed its course. The rest of the trip was uneventful. When they reached Manny's daughter's neighborhood, the entrance was blocked off with two eighteen-wheelers. Dirt had been piled up beside the road on both sides, and there were men with rifles behind the piles. Mark stopped as soon as he saw the barricade. The rest of their convoy had bunched up once they'd cleared the city limits, and the trucks behind Mark had to slam on their brakes to keep from rear-ending the Jeep. The sudden appearance of four vehicles coupled with the sound of squealing rubber seemed to make the guardians of this urban area quite nervous. Mark got on the radio.

"I don't like the looks of this," he announced to those with the other radios. Before anyone could answer him, a voice came from behind the roadblock.

"Don't move or you will be fired upon," it instructed. "Tell us what you want."

"We're here to see my friend's daughter," Mark called.

"What's her name and address?"

"I don't know…just a minute." Mark started to use his radio.

"Yeah, right, mister. We haven't heard that one before. Now you and your friends back up real slow and head on down the road before we have to show you how we deal with unwelcome guests."

"No, really. Let me ask my friend."

"No, really, yourself. You have thirty seconds to be gone, or we'll open fire."

"Manny, what's your daughter's name and address? Quick."

"Her name is Letty Washburn. I don't know her address. Her husband's name is Ed, and their son's name is Robby."

Mark repeated Manny's answer to the voice.

"Just a minute," the voice called. After what seemed an eternity, but was probably no more than fifteen seconds, the voice returned. "Okay, have the father walk up. No weapons and no funny business."

Mark turned in his seat and waved at Manny to come up to the Jeep. When he stepped out of his truck, Mark told his friend what the voice had instructed. Manny left his rifle behind and walked up to the barricade with his hands out from his sides. When he reached his destination, Mark saw a head pop up from behind the dirt pile. It spoke briefly with Manny, and then Mark saw another man run into the neighborhood. Several minutes later, the man came running back with another man, a woman, and a small boy in tow. The woman and the boy sandwiched Manny in a giant hug. The man shook his hand vigorously. A few seconds later, one of the big rigs started up and pulled forward. A man, who Mark guessed the voice belonged to, stepped out and waved the convoy through. When the Jeep pulled past the big truck, the man who had come back with the runner jumped into the back seat.

"Hi. I'm Ed. Go on up and take the second left."

He finished guiding them to his house, and then, when everyone was there, introductions were made all around. Manny explained they'd come to move the Austinites to his house if they wanted. Letty and Ed jumped at the invitation. They said that, while they were getting by, they had to rely on others more than they'd like. The grocery stores were still operating, but the selection of food had grown more and more limited over the past few weeks. Ed didn't own any firearms, and he was unable to help with the security of their neighborhood, and while those who did had been quite nice and fair, they'd also set themselves as the executive committee over the community. They made the job assignments and decided what days trips to the store would be taken. Ed and Letty were tasked with helping procure and purify water for the neighborhood. The city water had stopped working two weeks after The Burst. They were carrying water back from a creek about half a mile away and then boiling it outside over wood fires. Each person was only allowed ten gallons of water per week.

When Manny asked Ed about his mother, the younger man's head dropped.

"Mom died two days after The Burst."

"I'm so sorry," Manny empathized. "What happened?"

"I think The Burst ruined her pacemaker. We found her in her flower garden with the bucket she used to water her plants. Her heart probably slipped out of rhythm, and without the pacemaker to regulate it…" The man had tears in his eyes.

Letty slipped her arm around her husband's waist and consoled him. After a minute, she asked her father what they needed to bring, and he gave her a quick list.

The men from Silver Hills loaded the beds and the table and chairs onto the trailer. Letty and Ed packed their clothes and the little food they had into the Suburban and the back of the truck. Letty also packed most of her cookware and some of her dinnerware. Ed had a few hand tools and a chainsaw in the garage that were also loaded in the truck. Robby, when told to pack some of his most important things, came out of his room with a box of toys. Lying on top was an electronic gaming system. His grandpa got a good laugh upon seeing the video game and explained to the boy that there was no electricity at his house either. The two of them went into the nine-year-old's room to put the useless toy back. A minute later, Manny came running up to Mark with something in his hands.

"Mark! Look! Robby has a set of walkie-talkies. They're just like the ones Rodney gave us."

Mark looked at them, and they really were FRS radios. He turned their switches, but only one of them came on. Robby explained that he'd accidentally left the other one on, and the batteries had run down. Mark asked if they could borrow them, and Robby was glad to help out. Mark asked the family if they had anything else that might help. When nothing else could be thought of, everyone loaded into the vehicles, and the convoy headed out of the Washburn's neighborhood. Ed spoke briefly with the men at the entrance before they turned toward Silver Hills. The trip home was uneventful, and, except for stopping to burn the bodies at the roadblock, they made no stops.

Joe spent most of the time during the trip home talking about how he and his wife were not getting along lately. He attributed it to the big adjustment they had made in their lifestyle since The Burst. Mark listened for a while, but he soon had heard all of Joe's domestic problems he could stand. His mind kept wandering back to the attack on Ralph and his family. There was something about it that troubled him. He just couldn't put his finger on it, probably because of all the whining that prevented him from focusing. He wanted to tell Joe to shut up but knew it would hurt the man's feelings. One thing he could focus on was the fact that he would find someone else to ride shotgun with him on the trip to Waco.

When they got to the big gate, it was almost dark, and Charley shift had just come on. Jim was at the gate, and he opened it for the convoy. Mark pulled through far enough for all of the vehicles to enter. In his mirror, Mark saw Jim close the gate and then briefly speak with Gunny. Jim then made his way up to the Jeep.

"Gunny said you all didn't have any problems."

Mark nodded his head.

"That's good. Unfortunately, I have some bad news."

"What is it?"

"Rodney died this afternoon. Lisa thinks it was a blood clot."

Mark's heart fell to his stomach. He felt sad and angry all at the same time. "How's Donna?"

"Not good. Lisa gave her something to calm her down and sent her to bed."

Mark thanked his friend. He drove to Manny's house and was somewhat cheered up to see the happiness that his daughter's and grandson's homecoming had brought. After they had unloaded the trucks and trailer, Mark drove home. When he walked into the kitchen, Jess, Lisa, Abby, Alice, and George were there. The look on Jess's face told Mark that everyone was taking this badly. Mark looked at Lisa next. It was obvious she'd been crying a lot. Her face was all swollen and red. Mark had to ask the questions, but he waited for Gunny to arrive so that Lisa could relate the particulars just once. A few minutes later, the old man came in and asked what had happened. Lisa explained that she thought it was a pulmonary embolism, or in layman's terms, a blood clot that formed in his lungs, broke loose, and moved to his heart. She started crying again as she explained. George told the guys that Chaparo was building a casket and that they had tentatively scheduled the funeral for tomorrow afternoon. He had taken Abby and Alice down to talk to Brother Bob about performing the service, and he'd agreed. Mark asked about Donna, and Jess told him that she'd fallen apart. Lisa had given her some sedatives and sent her to rest. The boys were doing okay under the circumstances, although they had spent most of the day crying. They were now asleep with their mother in the tent.

Mark and Gunny then had to answer questions about their trip. They filled the others in, but expurgated the gory parts of the roadblock. Everyone was happy that Manny's family had been rescued, but it did little to relieve the sadness of Rodney's passing. Even though he had been here only a short time, he'd become a part of the family. Mark and Gunny thought tomorrow would be fine for the funeral. Everyone said goodnight and headed for bed.

Mark and Jess headed for their room. Jess lit a candle and sat down on the bed. She began to quietly sob. Mark sat beside her and held her. He didn't say anything. His thoughts bounced from the happiness of Letty's, Ed's, and Robby's homecoming to the sadness Rodney's death had brought. How would Donna, Timmy, and Tommy get along without their husband and father? How would his family get along if something happened to him? Who would take care of them? Of course Jim would step up, but it should be family who filled in if the unthinkable happened. He had to go get his brother and the rest of his family. Mike was the one he could count on if something happened. He squeezed Jess to him a little tighter.

The next thing Mark knew, the wind up alarm clock was going off. He and Jess had fallen asleep crossways on the bed in their clothes. He unwrapped his arms from around her and tried to stretch the cramps out of his back. He rolled over and looked at the glow-in-the-dark hands on the clock. They read 1:30. He got up, turned the alarm off, and threw a light blanket over his wife. He picked up what he needed from the bedroom and shuffled into the study to put on his boots and get his rifle out of the safe.

When he showed up at the CP, the radioman from Charley shift informed him that they'd seen an increased amount of traffic from town. Mark asked if there had been any trouble and was told that only one group had gotten a little mouthy with Jim. Mark was chatting with his guys when he saw Craig arrive.

286

Mark looked at his watch and noticed he had barely made it on time. The Delta shift leader made his duty assignments for the shift. He'd intended to sit in one of the towers tonight, but decided that it might be better if he was already at the gate in case of trouble. Everyone moved out to their station. Mark met Jim at the gate post.

"Heard you've been busy," Mark told his friend.

"Yeah. Eight or nine groups came through, most of them earlier. We even had a little excitement."

"What happened?"

"A group came through about eleven and gave us some trouble until they noticed we had them covered. They were demanding that we give them food, water, and camping gear. The leader kept whining it wasn't fair that we had stuff that they didn't. I told them we could help them a little on food, and they could have all the water they could carry, but that wasn't good enough for them. They had a couple of guns and said that if we didn't give them what they wanted, they would come in and take it. I convinced them that wasn't likely to happen by having the guys in the foxholes shine their flashlights at the gate. When I told the leader we had five armed guys in each hole, you should have seen his eyes get big. They were so taken back they left without the food and water we would have given them." Jim was grinning.

"Did they seem like criminals or gang members?"

"No. Just like regular people. I think the aggressiveness came from being scared. I guess if I had no place to go and no food, I'd be scared for my family, too."

Mark just nodded his head. He climbed down into the foxhole and started watching. A couple of groups came by during Delta shift, but only one stopped and asked for some water. Other than that, it was very quiet. He thought about all the things going on. When he was relieved by Alpha shift, he felt tired and looked forward to taking a nap before his morning self defense class. He trudged up the hill.

When Mark got to the house, Timmy was leading Jess out of the back door by her hand.

"What are you doing?" he asked.

"Timmy's having trouble waking his mother up and it's time for breakfast."

"I mean, why aren't you at school?"

"We cancelled it for today."

Mark didn't have to ask why. He followed Jess and the boy back to the Roberts' tent. Jess went in with Timmy. He could hear Tommy inside.

"Please wake up, Mommy. Please," the older of the two boys pleaded.

"Donna!" Mark heard his wife's voice. "I know you're sleepy from the medicine Lisa gave you, but you have to wake up. Donna. Are you lis…"

Mark heard Jess gasp, and he knew instantly that something was wrong. He rushed into the tent and saw that his wife's face was pale. He looked down at the cot Donna was lying on and noticed that she, too, was pale. He reached down and touched her forehead. It was cold. Colder, it seemed, than anything he had ever touched. He looked at the boys and knew they could see from the look on his face that something was wrong.

"Maybe Mommy needs her medicine to wake up," Timmy suggested.

"No. Her medicine is to keep her from being sad. Not for waking up," Tommy scolded his younger brother.

"What medicine?" Mark asked.

"It's in her purse," Tommy said as he reached into the bag and pulled out a vial. He held it up to Mark. "See?"

Mark took the vial. It was empty. He looked at the label. Paxil. Mark didn't know what that was. Maybe she had overdosed. He looked at Jess. "Go get Lisa."

Jess moved out of the tent, and Mark squatted down between the two boys. He pulled them to him and took a deep breath. "Boys, I know the last few days have been really hard for you, but I have some bad news for you. Your Mommy has gone to be with your Daddy in heaven. I guess she missed him too much."

"NO!" Tommy screamed, and he and his brother started crying into Mark's shoulders. Jess came back with Lisa, and they both had tears in their eyes. Lisa checked the body for a pulse and then looked at Mark and shook her head. Mark, however, already knew what she was trying to tell him.

Chapter 41

Mark had Jess take the boys inside the house. He showed the empty vial to Lisa and asked her what it was.

"Paxil is a strong anti-depressant," she answered.

"Do you think she OD'd on them?"

"No. I think she ran out. See here on the bottle. This was a 90-day script. It was filled almost two months before The Burst. If she took it everyday like she was supposed to, she would have run out around a week ago. I don't know exactly how long it stays in your system after you stop taking it, but probably like two or three days. More than likely, the benefits this gave her wore off about the same time Rodney was shot."

"No wonder she was such a basket case," Mark whispered, as if he didn't want Donna to hear him.

Lisa's eyes began to fill with tears again. "I'm so sorry I didn't know. I should have noticed the signs. If I had, maybe things would be different."

"We don't know that, Lisa. We don't even know how she died. Now, I need you to pull yourself together and figure it out," Mark said sternly.

"Okay, Mark," Lisa said, as she sniffled one last time. She asked Mark to excuse himself while she examined the body. After a few minutes, she called Mark back in.

"There are no wounds or signs of anything physical. An overdose, whether intentional or accidental, is what makes the most sense. I looked through her purse, though, and there's nothing in it that she could have OD'd on."

"Maybe it's not in her purse," Mark suggested.

"That's possible, but I doubt it. Women keep their medicine in their purses, but let's look to make sure."

The two of them looked through the tent but couldn't find anything Donna could have taken that would have killed her.

"If she didn't OD, then what else could have happened?" Mark asked.

"Maybe she had an allergic reaction to the sedative I gave her, or even an insect sting, but I don't think so. There's no trace of any kind of reaction, and she obviously died very peacefully."

Mark and Lisa stepped out of the tent. A few people had gathered around. Mark could see others coming up the street. The grapevine in Silver Hills had always been capable, but since The Burst, it had become a communication powerhouse. The speed at which this kind of news traveled was mind-boggling. Some of the residents would want to know what happened. Some would ask what they could do to help. Others were coming just because it seemed right to be with everyone else. Whatever their reasons, they came. After only a few moments, almost a third of the neighborhood was standing in Mark's yard.

"What happened, Mark?" one of them asked.

"Donna Roberts died last night."

"How?"

"We aren't sure."

"What can we do to help?" someone asked.

Mark told them there was nothing they could do right now. He promised to let them know if something was needed. They asked about the boys and the arrangements. Someone suggested Rodney's funeral be postponed and that he and Donna be buried at the same time. Everyone agreed. People hung around and talked or prayed for a while, then headed back for their houses or duties.

Don Wesley came up to Mark. "I can't believe she's dead. We saw her last night."

"When?"

"Right after our shift started. It must have been around 2:30."

"Who all saw her?"

"All of us in Rover Two. She was walking toward your house. The funny part was, she seemed happy."

Lisa heard Don and asked him a question. "Where was she coming from?"

"I don't know. I thought she was just out for a walk. She was walking up the hill."

"Could she have been coming from the hospital?" she asked.

"Yeah, I guess so. She was pretty close to there."

"Oh my God." Lisa started running toward the new hospital. Mark and Don followed her. When they got to the old Olsen house, Lisa went straight to the kitchen. Mark saw that almost all of the cabinets were open and filled with various medical supplies and medications. On the counter were three bottles with the lids off. Mark saw tears pouring out of Lisa's eyes again. Lisa started reading the bottles.

"One of these is Diazepam. It's Valium. That's what I gave her last night to calm her down. I don't know what the others are," the tall blonde told the two men.

"Don, would you mind running over and getting Doc?" Mark asked.

Don nodded his head once and was gone. Lisa started to cry almost hysterically. Mark walked over to her and patted her on the back. She spoke to him one or two words at a time between the sobs. "This...is all...my fault...She...saw...where...I got...the...tranq...qualizer...from."

"Lisa, this is not your fault. People make their own decisions, and even if the drugs did make it easy for her, she would have found another way if they hadn't been available. People always find a way to do what they want. I'm glad she did it with drugs instead of a bullet. Imagine how much more traumatic it would have been for her boys to see her with a hole in her head."

Lisa paused for a second while that image sunk in. It seemed to slow her rate of crying for a moment. "But she couldn't make good decisions in a depressed state. She needed her anti-depressants to cope. It wasn't her fault."

"That may be true, but she knew she needed her medicine and chose not to tell anyone that she was out. She still made a choice."

"But you don't understand...I...should...have...seen...that...she was...in troub...ble...I am...respons...sible...for..."

Mark had had enough. Sam used to cry like this when she was little. He had a hard time dealing with it then, and he certainly couldn't deal with it now from a grown woman. He used the voice he employed when a five or six year old was misbehaving in his karate class. It was calm but authoritative in a 'you don't want to find out what happens next' kind of way.

"Lisa, stop crying. I do understand. I understand that things are different than they were six weeks ago. Everyone has to take responsibility for themselves. We are now responsible to grow our own food, to protect ourselves, and a lot of other things we used to take for granted. YOU are the one who needs to understand these things. People are dying everywhere. We cannot help them all, especially if they don't try to help themselves. We're too busy trying to survive to nursemaid everyone." Mark realized he was started on a rant. He brought himself back on track. "This was not your fault, and I don't want to hear you say it was again. Do you understand?"

Lisa's eyes were as big as saucers. She nodded her head. It was all Mark could do not to bark "You say 'Yes, Sir' to me when I ask you a question," like he would have to that miscreant five year old. Fortunately, Don and Doc arrived just in time to break the tension.

"Hey, Doc. We've had some bad luck this morning," Mark greeted the vet somberly.

"Yes. Don told me. Let's see what she took." He walked over to the counter and picked up the first bottle. "This one is Diazepam. It's the same thing as Valium. This is Robaxin. It's a muscle relaxant…pretty strong one. And this…this is Meperidine. It's basically Demerol. The three together would make a good euthanasia cocktail. You wouldn't feel anything. Just go to sleep and never wake up. It looks to me like she knew what she was doing. Either that or she was really lucky." The doctor blushed with embarrassment. "I didn't mean…I guess I meant unlucky."

"It's alright, Doc. We knew what you meant," Mark assured him.

They walked out of the hospital and talked about getting Chaparo to work on a big metal cabinet that they could lock the dangerous stuff up in. Doc said he would go talk to the welder right now. Mark looked at his watch. It was already time for his class. He walked over to his outdoor classroom and could see that no one was in the right frame of mind to practice self-defense. He dismissed the class and sent word that the afternoon class was also cancelled.

If he had been tired when his shift was over, he was exhausted now. He didn't know why, he hadn't done anything to tire himself out, but all he wanted was to go home and go to bed. He dragged into the house, drank a glass of water, and went to his bedroom. He was pulling his boots off, they must have weighed twenty pounds each, when Jess came in.

"Mark?" she was almost whispering.

"Yeah?"

"About the boys?"

"How are they?" he asked, mad at himself for forgetting about them.

"I made them eat, and then they cried themselves to sleep in the guest room."

Mark nodded his head with his last ounce of energy.

"Have you thought about what's going to happen to them?"

"No," he said flatly, not because he was irritated, but because he was so tired. "Why?"

"Somebody has to take them," she answered softly.

That only made sense. Mark nodded his head. Maybe the music teacher and his wife would want them.

"I think I know the perfect people to take them," her voice softened even more.

Mark looked at her.

"They have a lot of experience with children, and they have room for them, too," she smiled.

She was selling him now. He knew the drill. He was supposed to ask who, but he was just too tired. Couldn't she see that? Didn't he have enough on his mind? He got angry. "Dammit, Jess! Just tell me who!" He was instantly sorry. He could tell her, but it wouldn't do any good. She would get mad and stomp out of the room. At least he could go to bed in peace. He decided to apologize anyway. It was the right thing to do. "I'm sorry, Babe. I'm just really tired."

He was surprised at her reaction. "It's okay. I know you're really stressed out right now, but I think this is important. That's why I'm talking about it right now. A lot of people may want the boys, and we need to make sure they go where they have the best chance at a normal childhood."

"Okay. That makes sense. Who do you think should take them?" he asked

"Us."

Mark didn't think he'd heard her right at first, but the look on her face told him that she had said exactly what he had heard. He started getting angry again. "What?"

"You heard me." Now her voice was forceful. "I don't want you to decide right now. In fact, I don't want to talk about it anymore right now. Just promise me you'll think about it."

He cooled off instantly and the last smidgen of strength drained from his body. He nodded his head. He finished stripping down to his underwear and somehow got under the sheets. "I'll think about it. I promise. Wake me up in a couple of hours, will you? I don't know why I'm so tired." He closed his eyes and heard the door shut. That was the last thing he remembered.

When his eyes opened, it took him a minute to come back to reality. When he did, he realized how refreshed he felt. He didn't know why, but he always slept better during the day, especially since The Burst. Maybe it had something to do with being able to relax and not having to be on alert for danger like he felt he had to be at night. He looked at the clock and saw that it was 2:45. He'd slept for over four hours. No wonder he felt so much better. He got out of bed and stretched. He owed his box a dollar, but he'd quit carrying money a few weeks ago unless he was going somewhere. He looked around on the dresser and found some loose change. He counted out a dollar in nickels and dimes and put them in the black box. Then he dressed and walked to the kitchen. Something smelled good.

He could hear Jess in the living room reading a book. He looked and saw Lisa, with Tommy, Timmy, and the twins listening intently to the adventures of Gulliver. The boys were snuggled into Jess, one on each side. Lindsey and Lacy were sitting on the love seat next to their mother. Jess looked happy to have someone to read to. He remembered how she used to read to Sam and David just like this, but they were long ago too big for such behavior. Jess really did want the boys. Her mother had told Mark before they were married about how Jess used to bring home every stray dog and cat in the neighborhood. She just had a need to nurture. But these boys were no stray puppies. They would need a lot of love and care to get past the terrible curve fate had thrown at them.

Jess looked up and saw his head sticking around the corner. "Hi, Honey. How was your nap?"

"Wonderful. I thought you were going to wake me a little after noon."

"I was, but you really needed some rest, and there was nothing important going on, so I decided to let you sleep. There's some food on the stove if you're hungry, and Alice made some cornbread. It's in the oven."

"That sounds good. Where's Jim?"

Lisa answered. "He's helping over behind the hospital."

Mark knew she meant digging Donna's grave. He also noticed that if Lisa was mad at him for scolding her this morning, she didn't show it. "Thanks," he told the women and then went into the kitchen to eat. Lisa came in a minute later.

"I asked Tommy if his Mom had ever worked at a veterinarian's office. He said no, but that she used to work for an animal doctor. Isn't that cute? I guess that's how she knew what to take."

Mark just nodded his head sadly, and Lisa went back to the living room.

He ate and then headed down to see how the digging was going. The men had finished and were just standing around looking down into the two empty holes. One had been dug yesterday and one today. Mark stared down into the graves, and the enormity of their situation came rushing back in on him. He asked Jim if they could talk. The two men excused themselves and walked down toward the gate.

"Jim, I need a favor."

"Anything. You just name it."

"I need you to stay here instead of going to Waco with me."

"I thought you needed my truck?"

"I do," Mark explained, "but I need you to stay here. If something happens to me like it did to Rodney, and I don't get my family from Waco, I need you to take care of Jess and the kids."

"Nothing's going to happen to you, Mark," Jim said with conviction.

"I hope you're right, but with how things are going, I don't think any of us knows what tomorrow holds. I can't risk something happening to both of us."

"I guess I see the wisdom in that. If something happened to me, you'd take care of Lisa and the girls, right?"

"You can count on it," Mark promised.

*   *   *

The double funeral was very emotional for everyone. The whole community, except for the members of Beta shift, who were on duty, came to the graveside service. Mark wasn't sure if people were crying more for Rodney and Donna or because this whole incident had brought the reality of what the world had become crashing home.

Mark choked out the eulogy since he knew Rodney best. Brother Bob delivered a beautiful message, and his wife sang several songs. When she sang 'Amazing Grace' as they were lowering the coffins into the graves, every eye

293

was filled with tears. Mark felt that the service was nice, under the circumstances, and did Rodney and Donna justice. In fact, except for some idiot who drove by on the county road honking his horn like a nincompoop during the eulogy, the service could not have been better. That is, unless it wasn't needed at all. Jess held Timmy through the whole funeral, and Sam was holding Tommy's hand. Timmy quietly cried the whole time, but Tommy tried to be brave. At the end, though, he ended up with his face in Sam's lap, sobbing uncontrollably. She did her best to comfort him.

When the service was over, people milled around, not sure of what to do. Mark was talking to Chaparo when one of Beta shift's gate guards came up to him. He told Mark there were two men waiting for him at the gate. They were the ones who had honked their horn. Mark and Chaparo started for the gate with the guard. Jim and Gunny spotted them heading off and fell in behind them.

"What's up Karate Man?" Gunny asked.

"I don't know. Two men at the gate asked for me. I guess we'll find out quick enough."

When the five men reached the gate, Mark could see that it was Greg Hardy and Rob Bowers. They were in an older Dodge diesel truck that was hooked to a trailer. The trailer was full of what looked like scrap metal. Mark walked up to the driver's side.

"Hey, Rob, Greg. What's up?"

"Mark, we apologize about blowing the horn. We had no idea you were having a funeral. We're really sorry," Greg explained.

"It's okay. How could you know? What's with the scrap iron?"

Greg feigned being offended. "We bring him a present, and he calls it scrap iron," he said to Rob.

Rob played along. "I guess if he doesn't want it, we could just take it to his old boss, Mr. Davis."

"I'm sorry if I hurt your feelings, if you really have any, that is," he said to get his own dig in. "So, what did you bring me?"

"Nothing much," Greg said, still playing as if his feelings were injured. "Just a windmill."

"Really? You're kidding! Thanks! Come on up to my house. Man, this is great. I don't know how to thank you. Can you stay for dinner?" Mark was talking rapid fire. "Jim, Gunny, they brought us a windmill! Can you believe it?"

The men climbed into the bed of the truck, and Greg directed Rob to Mark's house. When they got there, Mark sent David to get George. Other men started arriving at the Turner house as word of the windmill spread through the community like wildfire. The men were falling all over themselves, thanking the visitors, when David returned with George. When George saw what was in the trailer, a big grin spread across his face. He heartily thanked the men for the gift. The two gift bearers told him it was no problem, and they even offered to come back tomorrow and help put it up. Mark explained that he was going to Waco in the morning to see about his family there. Perhaps they could come later next week, he suggested. The mention of a trip piqued the interest of the men from Promise Point. They said they had some residents who wanted to go get or at least check on their extended families, but they were worried about the safety of a road trip. Mark explained how they were employing a convoy to keep the risk as low as possible. Rob and Greg were fascinated, and Rob asked if he could come along to see how it worked. Mark warned him it could be dangerous and said he couldn't guarantee his safety. Rob assured him he was well aware of the danger but that it was a risk he was willing to take to see if this was a technique they could use. Greg said he'd still be willing to help with the windmill tomorrow if there would be anyone who wanted to get it up. George and Jim immediately volunteered. Several of the other men, including Chaparo, agreed to assist. They talked about the best place to put it, and George suggested that the Hernandez well would be a natural place. It was at the top of the hill and right at the end of the road that ran through the middle of the subdivision. They could pump water into a tank, if they could find one, and gravity feed water down the hill with hoses. Manny was agreeable to the suggestion. With that decided, the gathering broke up, and everyone headed back home. Mark and his guests headed off toward the back porch for dinner when Manny asked for a minute with Mark.

"My son-in-law, Ed, wants to volunteer to ride with you in the front tomorrow. He feels he owes it to you for coming to get him."

"He doesn't owe me anything, Manny. We all went to get him, but if he wants to come, I won't stop him. Can he shoot? I need someone who can shoot pretty well with me in the lead vehicle."

"He can shoot. He was in the reserves for a while to help pay his way through college."

"Great," Mark said, thinking this was the way to get out of having to listen to Joe griping about his personal problems all the way to Waco and back. "I'll see you guys after the meeting, and we'll go over our game plan."

After dinner and the meeting, the group bound for Waco gathered at Mark's for a rundown. He reminded everyone that the primary plan was to go up tomorrow, spend the night, and come back on Sunday. Everyone needed sleeping bags and whatever else they would require to overnight. Mark went over the primary and two backup routes. He gave everyone the names of all of his family members and their addresses, just in case they needed them as they did when they went to Austin. Gunny reminded everyone what their jobs were in case of any hostile contact from either the front or the rear. They were adding another truck, but, other than that, everything would work as it had before. They had a radio for each vehicle, but the old Marine made everyone go over the hand signals, just in case one of the radios died.

"Murphy," Gunny explained, "likes to show up when you least expect him."

Gunny then made sure that Rob and Ed had weapons. Rob had a battle rifle with him, plus some kind of rig to carry his magazines in. He also had a pistol. Ed didn't have a rifle, and when he was told that he could borrow one of the AK's, he informed the group that the only weapon he was familiar with was the M-16. They lent him Jim's AR. Gunny reminded everyone to bring plenty of loaded magazines.

Mark assigned Joe to drive Jim's truck, thinking it would soften the blow of being replaced in the lead vehicle. He asked Dwight to ride with Joe and assigned Rob to shotgun duty with Manny. They would leave at first light. Rob asked if he could spend the night here and borrow a sleeping bag for the trip, so Greg wouldn't have to get up so early to bring him back. Mark agreed and had him use the camper since his family had moved back into the house with the cooler weather. With the meeting over, Mark got Rob settled in.

"Rob, what is that you have for your mags?"

"It's a chest rig made by a company called SOE Tactical Gear."

"Can I look at it?"

"Sure," Rob said as he handed it to Mark. "Almost all of the rigs and slings we use at Promise Point are from them. They're very comfortable and built like a tank."

"Man, this is exactly what we need. Carrying magazines around in a pocket or pack is a real pain. Will you show this to Gunny tomorrow?"

"You bet."

"Thanks. Sleep tight," Mark said, as he exited the camper and headed for his own bedroom.

When he got there, he noticed Jess had three candles burning in the room. At least one of them was scented. He stripped down to his shorts and sat on the foot of the bed. Getting some rest yesterday had helped his disposition some, but he still felt like the weight of the world was on his shoulders. Getting the windmill was a blessing, but now it had to be installed, and now, they needed a tank to store the water in. He had to get this trip to Waco behind him. He still needed to help train the county militia, and he had to decide what to do with the Roberts boys. No one had mentioned them at the meeting tonight, but everyone was still quite subdued from the funeral. He heard the door open. Jess came in and smiled at him.

"What's the matter?" she asked.

"Just thinking about all the things we have to get done," he answered.

She climbed onto the bed behind him and started rubbing his shoulders. She was a master at working his kinked up muscles. He felt as if she was manipulating him to get what she wanted, but he was beyond calling her on it. Besides, the massage felt so good. His suspicions were confirmed a minute later when she asked him a question.

"Have you thought about the boys any?"

"Yes," he answered. If she wanted to play him to get what she wanted, why shouldn't he play along? It wouldn't change what he would ultimately decide, but if it got him some special attention, what did it hurt? "But I need to think about it some more."

"Did you notice that no one said anything about them at the meeting?" she queried, as she dug her thumbs deep into his shoulders.

"Oooohhhh. That's good," he moaned. "Yes, I did notice." To his delight, she continued for another few minutes. She stopped and asked the next question that he was expecting.

"When do you think we might make up our minds?"

'She's good,' Mark thought. He knew her mind was already made. She had said 'we' to make sure he remembered it wasn't just his decision. He also knew if she didn't like his answer, his special attention time was over. He decided he had to tell her the truth. He really hoped that she liked it.

"Let me get back from Waco, and then we'll sit down and really talk it out." He mentally crossed his fingers.

"That sounds fair," she answered.

'What the hell did that mean?' he wondered. Was that the right answer, or had he blown it? He couldn't tell from her reaction. She smiled at him and reached into the dresser. She usually slept in flannel pajamas, but Mark noticed that the ones she pulled out were silk. 'Alright,' he thought. He leaned back in the bed and watched as she removed her clothing. When she was down to her underwear, he noticed something.

"You've lost weight," he blurted out.

She turned and faced him. "Really?" She ran into their bathroom. He knew she was going to climb on the scale. What an idiot he was. If she hadn't lost any weight, she would be disappointed and his special attention time might go down the drain. Why hadn't he just kept his big mouth shut? He heard the scale flop down on the floor with the metallic clank of inevitability. He listened as the spring wound up when she stepped on the scale, and he could see in his mind's eye the dial sweeping back and forth, not unlike a Vegas slot machine. Would he hit the jackpot, or would he crap out? He heard her squeal but didn't know if it was good or bad. She came running out of the bathroom like a teenager and leapt like Supergirl over the bed and landed astraddle him. She kissed him hard on the mouth.

"Seven pounds!" She kissed him again. "I've lost seven pounds!"

Mark's 'special attention time' had just shifted into overdrive.

Chapter 42

Mark awoke to the sound of gunfire. He looked at the clock, and it read 11:37. He pulled on his jeans and a T-shirt, grabbed his little Camp Carbine and his boots, and ran outside. The firing was coming from the front of the subdivision, but it was only sporadic. Mark ran down to the Command Post. He heard footfalls behind him and turned to see Jim with his M1A, trying to keep up. When the two men got to the CP, they asked what was going on. Peter Hogan was the radio operator, and he told them what he knew.

"Greg Gentry thinks it's a crew of six that came by the gate about thirty minutes ago. They got real mouthy with the gate crew but backed off when they saw how many guys we had covering them. They walked off to the east, but Greg thinks they came back."

"Where are they?" Jim asked.

"Tower Two says they're at the northeast corner of the subdivision in the ditch across the road."

"Can the OP see them?"

"Abe said that the angle is too steep for him to see them," Peter replied.

"Who are they shooting at?" Mark asked, as he was lacing up his boots.

"They're just taking pot shots at the gate."

"Where are the rovers?"

"Rover One slipped back into the western foxhole. Rover Two is on their way here. They should be here…"

"Right now," Don Wesley, the leader of Rover Two said. Mark noticed that Ralph was with him.

"Good! Here's what we're going to do." He pointed at the map of the subdivision that Gunny had drawn before he'd come to live here. Mark put his finger on the CP and traced the route they would take as he talked. "We'll run down Silver Mine Road to the eastern fence. Then we'll run down the fence line until we get even with the last house. We'll need to lay down some cover fire to get into the foxhole, so we'll split in half. Jim and I will go first while the rest of you cover us. We'll call in for the gate and Tower Two to give us some cover, too. We'll run down the wood fence behind the houses and jump in the foxhole. Then we'll cover the rest of you. Any questions?"

The three rover's eyes were as big as saucers, but no one said anything.

Mark turned to Peter. "Radio everyone our plan, and make sure that Tower Two knows we'll be coming up behind them. I don't want to get shot by our own guys. And call the Sheriff's Department." He turned back to his group. "Let's move."

Mark took the lead and jogged down the street. It was a cloudy night, but the almost full moon shone through the clouds sufficiently to see a few yards ahead. When they got to the fence, they turned left and headed toward the county road. Mark slowed his pace a little. The ground was a little uneven, and he didn't want his guys out of gas for the sprint down to the foxhole. A few seconds after he had turned the corner, he caught a dim flash of light about fifty yards on this side of Tower Two. He immediately stopped and raised his hand in a fist to signal his team to stop. Ralph, who had just started guard classes, had been too close behind Mark, and he bumped into the point man hard enough to knock him down. Fortunately, they were in an empty lot that George had plowed, so the dirt was soft. If it had happened any other time, it would have been funny. Mark's rifle landed in the dirt beside him. Mark picked himself and his carbine up. He rose to a kneeling position and signaled for the other rovers to get down with him. He pointed to his eyes and then toward where he had seen the light. He strained his eyes and could make out a shadow of a person. He saw the intruder bend over for a second, and when he stood back up, there were two. The second was easier to see since he had on lighter clothing. Mark caught a glimpse of another person running up to the fence on the other side, and then they disappeared. He assumed the attackers had left one or two guys on the road to create a distraction, and the others were trying to sneak in behind the watchtower. 'Clever plan,' Mark thought. 'Lucky we came this way, or it might have worked.' He figured the guards in the tower were only watching the side where the firing was coming from. Mark signaled for Don to give him the radio. He quietly radioed the CP and had Peter inform the men in Tower Two that there were some uninvited guests crossing the fence on their south side. He wanted them to wait until they were all on this side of the fence and then to shine a light on them and tell them that they were surrounded. Mark hoped they could surprise them and take them without any bloodshed. As he was talking, the cloud cover cleared from around the moon a little, and his ability to make out the strangers improved some. He watched as three more people appeared. Then, when they started to move toward the middle of the subdivision, one of the tower guards turned on a flashlight and shined it on them. At fifty yards, the light was not very bright, but Mark could see that some of the intruders were women.

The tower guard yelled, "Freeze right there! We have you surrounded! Throw down your weapons and put your hands over your head. Do it now!"

Mark thought the man had probably seen too many episodes of 'Cops,' but he hoped the authoritative voice and command would have the desired effect. The answer came in less than a second. A single shot rang out.

Mark watched the flashlight fall. It seemed to take forever for it to hit the ground. He had no idea if the guard had dropped it or if he'd been hit. He raised his weapon to fire at the raiders. The electric red dot scope was not on. He lowered the weapon back down, so he could reach the control and whispered for his men to open fire. He heard the .30 caliber booms from Jim's and Ralph's rifles. The SKS's that Don and Steve Parsons held had a distinctive sound, too. Mark reached for the rheostat on top of his scope and found that the adrenaline pumping through his system had degraded his fine motor skills to the point that turning the control was difficult. The intruders were firing back at his group now, and he could hear projectiles whistling over his head and occasionally see dirt kick up in front of his group. He finally got the scope activated and looked through it. Mark took aim at one of the attackers. He took in a deep breath, exhaled half of it, and steadied the dot on the center of the kneeling man. When the dot was where he wanted it, he squeezed the trigger. The little .45 caliber carbine went off with a pop. It almost sounded comical next to the rifles the others were shooting. Mark was shocked to see the man still kneeling in the same spot, firing his weapon back, so that the muzzle flashes winked at uneven intervals. How could he have missed? He fired again with the same result. The third, fourth, and fifth shots did no better. Mark's mind was racing. No one had hit any of the raiders. What was going on? Jim was an excellent shot. Mark looked at him. He was slowly and deliberately firing.

"Jim, why haven't you hit any of them yet?"

"I can't see my sights!" the athletically built shooter answered.

That made sense. That was probably why the raiders hadn't hit any of them either. That's why Mark liked the little red dot scope for night. But why hadn't he hit anyone? He realized all of a sudden that his carbine was sighted in at fifty yards, and his targets were over three times that far away. His fat, slow bullets were in the dirt long before they reached the target. He raised the sight so that it was centered about two feet above the head of the man he was trying to get. He pulled the trigger quickly and emptied the rest of the ten-shot magazine. It didn't appear he'd hit the man, but he must have been getting close. The attacker dropped down to a prone position and kept firing. Mark ejected the empty mag and inserted a fresh one in its place. He hit the slide release and reshouldered the little Marlin. When he had aligned the sights to where he wanted them, he pulled the trigger. Nothing happened. Mark muttered a dollar word under his breath. He checked the carbine and saw that the slide hadn't moved all the way into battery. He pulled back on the handle, ejecting a round, and let it go. The slide banged home with a satisfying clank. He looked to his left and saw Ralph struggling to get a magazine out of his pocket. Steve was attempting to reload his rifle with a stripper clip, but adrenaline had seemed to more than just slightly impair his motor skills. Mark aimed and fired twice more before the little rifle jammed again.

"Shit!"

He repeated the drill to clear the weapon, but this time the bolt didn't close all the way when he let go of it. He tried again to find that it only went about halfway this time.

"Damn it!" he said loudly enough for Jim to hear him.

"Are you hit?" his friend asked. He looked to see Jim rocking home a fresh mag. Don was looking through his sights like he was trying to thread a needle and he couldn't see the hole.

"No. My carbine is jammed. I think it's got dirt in it."

"Then get on the radio and tell the guys in the tower to put some fire on these assholes," Jim instructed.

Mark did as he was told. Then he laid the radio down beside Jim. "I'm going back to the CP to get another rifle. I'll see if I can pick up some of the reserves and come at them from the other side."

"Roger that," Jim said, as he squeezed off another round.

Mark turned and ran back the way they had come. He stayed stooped over, so he wouldn't present a good target for the MZB's. It was slow going, but he could stand up and run full out as soon as he rounded the corner. The fresh plowed dirt was like sand at the beach, and his calves were burning by the time he reached the street. As he rounded the corner, there were four strange riflemen walking toward the CP. Mark's heart jumped into his throat. The seriousness of the situation hammered him between the eyes as if it was a nine-pound hammer.

Questions flew past Mark's head like the bullets had only seconds ago. What should he do? What could he do with a jammed rifle? Could he get them all with just his pistol? How many more squads did these MZB's have? What was their goal? Did the community stand a chance? How could he warn everyone?

Mark made himself slow down and think. The quickest way to warn everyone was to get to the CP. To do that, he had to get past the four MZB's walking in front of him. He laid his carbine down on the street as quietly as he could. Fortunately, the gunfire both from the crew he'd just left and the gate guards masked the metallic click of blued steel on asphalt. He drew his Colt and ran on his toes as quickly and quietly as he could. He had nine shots in the pistol. Two rounds for each intruder with an extra, just in case. He'd done this drill at an IDPA pistol match. You started on one side and fired one round into each perp. Then you came back the other way and bestowed another hollow point to each of the targets. He had to get within five yards of the intruders to ensure solid hits in the dark. He was still over twenty-five yards away. As he ran toward them, his mind absorbed everything about them that it could. They were all different sizes. Their clothing ran the gamut from camouflage BDU's to designer jeans. They all carried their weapons differently. Twenty yards now. None of their weapons matched. One was carrying a Mini-14, one some kind of short-barreled shotgun, another what appeared to be an old Winchester lever action rifle, and the last an AR-15. He was within fifteen yards now. His toes were cramping from running on them. He noticed their shoes. Two had boots, one tennis shoes, and one, the shortest one, the one with the Winchester, had on sandals. Women's sandals. He stopped dead in his tracks. He couldn't shoot a woman in the back. But he had to. If he didn't, she or one of the others might kill one of his friends. Maybe he could shoot the men, and she would give up. Or maybe she would turn and put a hole in him with that old cowboy gun. No, he had to stick with his plan. When she crossed the fence with hostile intentions, she became an MZB, not a woman. He started running toward them again. The space had opened back up to about thirty yards. Focus on the problem, he told himself. He would start on the right and work to the left. Right between the shoulder blades. It was horrible to think about shooting someone in the back, but he had no choice. He had to warn the rest of the subdivision, and this was the only way that he could get to the…

Mark realized that all of the shooting had stopped. What had happened? The MZB's must have realized it at the same time. They froze in place for a second. Then they began to look at each other. Mark became aware that his feet had stopped moving. He was still over twenty yards away from the invaders. Could he get them from here? He raised his Colt to determine if he could see the sights. The biggest of the MZB's must have seen him move from a corner of his eye. He wheeled around to face Mark, and the other three whirled in unison as if they were playing 'Simon Says.' Mark's mind went blank. What was he to do now? He couldn't see his sights well enough to ensure a hit at this distance, and even if he could, he would get one or maybe two of the MZB's before they shredded him with their long guns. Maybe they didn't know that. Even if they did, maybe none of them would want to be the one who didn't make it. Mark had never been much of a poker player, but he prayed he could bluff his way through this

302

one. He almost didn't believe he was doing this. The voice coming out of his throat seemed as if it were coming from somewhere else.

"The first one to move dies." He hoped it was dark enough that the MZB's couldn't see his hands shaking. "Lay your weapons on the ground in front of you and step back five steps."

The intruders just stared at him. They seemed not even to be breathing. Mark saw the woman look at the man beside her, the one with the shotgun. So he was the leader. Mark barked out the order again. "Put your weapons on the ground NOW! You have five seconds, or I will have my men open up on you." Mark took a deep breath and tried to stop his hands from shaking. "ONE!" No one was moving. "TWO!" They stood like statues. "BOB! JOE! The one with the shotgun gets it first." He was running out of chips to bluff with. He wanted to look around and see if there was any cover if this didn't work, but he knew that would give him away. "THREE!"

The woman started to lay her rifle on the ground, but the leader reached out and placed a hand on her arm to stop her. He hollered back at Mark. "Mister, you've got no one else out here. Otherwise, we'd have seen or heard them. You lay down your pistol, and maybe YOU'LL live through this!"

"You can believe that if you want, but you didn't see or hear me until I wanted you to. There are five armed men surrounding you. You can't see them, but if you want to bet your life they aren't there, just move that shotgun an inch. I promise you it'll be last thing you'll ever do. FOUR!"

"You're lying," the man called back. "Tell your guys to show themselves."

Mark thought he'd heard that voice before, but his mind turned to other things. His bluff wasn't working. When he said 'Five,' they would know for sure that he was lying. Was this it for him? It had only been yesterday that he had talked to Jim about taking care of his family if something happened. Had his subconscience been aware of something? How would Jess and the kids do without him? What kind of man would his son become? How many grandkids would he have? So many questions, and he might not ever know the answers. Well, he would do everything he could to stick around for them. The odds were stacked heavily against him, but he wouldn't give up. If he could just get some kind of edge. Nothing huge, just enough to help him a little. A plan appeared in his head.

"When I count the next number, you all will be dead, but I've buried enough people in the last few weeks to last me a lifetime." That part at least was true. "I'm going to have my men step out, so you can see them. Be very careful not to make any threatening moves, or they'll shoot first and ask questions later." He couldn't believe he'd just used such a corny cliché, but it was too late to worry about it now. When the MZB's turned to look, he would open fire and move back and to his left. Maybe he'd get lucky. He called out loudly, "Okay, Joe. You and your men step out so these folks can see you."

Mark was praying with everything he had in him. He watched the leader. As soon as his head turned, Mark would try to kill him first. He strained his eyes trying to see his front sight. Movement behind the MZB's broke his concentration. Four ghosts appeared from behind some bushes in one of the yards. Had God heard his prayer and sent some deceased old veterans back to help him? They looked like they'd come from the beaches of Normandy. Four of the countless souls who had perished more than a half century ago. The apparitions moved with difficulty through the atmosphere, as a human would when walking through water. They had a mechanical gate, as if they were older than time itself. Mark blinked twice to make sure his eyes weren't deceiving him. Perhaps he just wanted to see something. Perhaps he was already dead and didn't know it, and the ghosts had come to show him to his final judgment.

"If'n I was you, I'd do like the Karate Man said an' lay my weapons on the ground!"

Mark felt tears rolling down his cheeks. Gunny's voice was the sweetest sound he had ever heard. The sound of salvation. Four MZB guns clattered to the ground with a sound that assured Mark he was still alive. Gunny, George, Abby, and Alice moved up, and each one covered an MZB.

Mark advanced and gathered the dropped weapons. The leader, who Mark now recognized as one of the refugees who had been given some water a couple of days ago, looked at him.

"You said you had five men."

"I lied," he flatly told the man. Then he turned to Gunny. "There might be other groups besides these two, Gunny."

"Don't think so." Gunny showed Mark one of the FRS radios that Manny's grandson had given them. "Jim radioed a minute ago 'n' said that the guys they captured told him there was only one other group, and you got 'em. But I got Rover One goin' 'round the perimeter, jus' in case."

"You mean WE got them," Mark smiled.

Gunny ordered the MZB's to walk to the CP with their hands on top of their heads. Mark fell in behind his four saviors and carried the captured weapons. He walked to within earshot of Gunny.

"How did you know I needed help?"

"We didn't," the old Marine replied. "When we heard the shootin', me 'n' George got up an' grabbed our rifles. The girls insisted on coming with us, and I didn't have time to argue with 'em. We was walkin' down to the CP when we saw these four comin' up the street. We hid in the bushes and was gonna ambush 'em when they got closer. We ne'er saw you 'till you started hollerin'. Why were you following them?"

"I had to get to the CP to warn everyone there might be more MZB's. They were in the way and the only thing I could think to do was to take them out."

"Where's your rifle?"

"It's jammed. All I had was my pistol."

Gunny slowly nodded his head as he absorbed what had happened. "Takes some mighty big ones to face down four bad guys by yerself," he said.

When they got to the CP, Mark got some zip ties and bound the hands of the four intruders. The guard in the tower who had dropped the flashlight hadn't been hit, but he reported that the tin roof now had a nice a hole that needed to be patched. Mark looked down the center road and saw Jim and the other guys marching their prisoners up. Peter reported that the sheriff was on his way. He told Mark that the two attackers in the front had crossed the road and entered the ditch on this side of the road. When they did, Abe Evans in the OP shot one of them, and the other had surrendered immediately. One of the gate guards was bringing him up. The one Abe had shot was dead. When Jim arrived with his charges, one of them had been wounded in the shoulder. Jim sent Ralph up to get Lisa, so she could look at the wounded man. Mark zip tied the others, two men and two women, and sat them with his four. Jim also recognized the man who appeared to be the leader of this attack. He was the man who had argued with Jim and the gate guards. It appeared that he and his small crew had set up camp just down the road and had recruited some other passers by to help them attack. They'd also scouted the neighborhood as best they could to try and find the best way in. When asked about what they intended to do if they gained control, the attackers didn't seem to have thought that out completely. When Greg Gentry marched the last living attacker up to the CP, he was promptly restrained with the makeshift handcuffs and put with his companions. After that, it seemed like only a few minutes before Curt arrived.

He and a couple of deputies were in a squad car, and they were followed by an old pickup pulling a horse trailer. The lawman pointed at the trailer and told his men to load the bad guys into his new paddy wagon. Mark noticed that bars had been welded over the windows, and once the door was shut and locked, it would be impossible to escape from. Lisa arrived, with Jess in tow, and bandaged the wounded man. The wound was fairly clean, she noted to the sheriff, but he should be checked out at the hospital. The sheriff assured her that Dr. Ken would take a look at him. Jess came to see how Mark was. He really wasn't in any hurry to share with his wife how close he'd come to dying. He asked her if she would go pick up his carbine, and she scurried off to retrieve it.

The sheriff took a few minutes with everyone who had been involved to get their stories. Mark stayed off by himself, thinking about what could have gone wrong and how lucky they had been. He had to talk to Gunny, but it seemed to him that they didn't have enough security. He realized that the man Jim had argued with had been planning this for at least two days. Now that he thought about it, that was what had bothered him about the attack on Ralph's, the fact that the attackers had watched their intended victims before attacking. What if either of the attacks had been done by a large group or, worse yet, someone who really knew what they were doing? If an experienced group of raiders watched them long enough, he was sure they could find a chink in the Silver Hills armor.

Mark looked up and saw that there were more and more people coming down to the CP to see what had happened. Jess returned about this time and handed him his carbine. She must have sensed that he wasn't in a talkative mood because she just squeezed his arm and went over to where Lisa was standing. He unloaded the little carbine and could feel that the action was gritty. It seemed as if the dirt he'd dropped it in had gotten into the inner workings. That was what had caused it to jam. He tried to clean some of the dirt out with his fingers, but he really needed to take it apart to do the job correctly.

Mark noticed that the Sheriff spent quite a few moments with Gunny. When the big officer came to talk to Mark, it seemed that everyone followed him over. Curt had a big, shit-eating grin on his face.

"Faced down four pistoleros by yourself, huh?"

"I wasn't by myself," Mark said matter-of-factly.

"You didn't know that. Gunny's right. You got some stones on you, boy."

"I was just trying to save my hide, that's all."

305

"Way I hear it, you were trying to save everyone's hide. People trying to save themselves usually just run the other way."

"Well, I was close. If Gunny and them hadn't shown up, I'd either still be running or dead."

"That might be true, but you're still JW in my book." The sheriff smiled like a Hollywood pretty-boy.

"JW?"

"Yeah, John Wayne."

The crowd behind the lawman erupted into applause, laughter, whistles, and catcalls. Mark blushed. He was no John Wayne and he knew it. Don Knotts maybe, but not John Wayne. If these people had seen his hands shaking before, they wouldn't be cheering now. This was the kind of attention he didn't want or need. It almost pissed him off, but that wouldn't solve anything. So, he did the only thing he could think of. He turned around and headed up the hill to his house.

The sheriff hollered after him. "Where you going, Duke?"

Mark wheeled around and almost told him where to go and what to do when he got there. Instead, his sense of humor kicked in, and he took a second to think about what to say. In his best impersonation of John Wayne, he said, "I'ma goin' to the hacienda to change my shorts, pilgrim."

The eruption from the crowd was twice as loud as before.

Chapter 43

When Mark woke up, there was just a hint of gray peeking through the window. He wasn't sure at first if the events of last night had been real or only a dream. As he sat up in bed, he realized that it had been real. His ribs hurt where Ralph had knocked him into the dirt. He hadn't gotten much sleep. Between Jess, the shootout, and the adrenaline, he had squeaked out maybe three hours. That would just have to do, as he had to get to Waco. He stood up and pulled on his clothes. When he walked into the kitchen, Jess had packed a small basket with food.

"Good morning, JW," she said with a smile.

"Please don't."

"Why not?"

"Because I'm not John Wayne!"

"Jeeze. It's just a joke. Don't take it so seriously," she scolded.

Mark took a deep breath in through his nose and blew it out of his mouth. "You don't understand. I can take the joke, but it only reinforces the falsehood people have about me being some kind of hero. I am not perfect. I'm just a man, a man who makes mistakes. I made a bunch last night. Some of them came this close to getting me killed." He held his thumb and forefinger a fraction of an inch apart.

"But you were so brave."

"That's just it! I wasn't brave! I was scared shitless! I was only trying to save my own ass by bluffing," he argued. "I don't want these people to see me as a hero because one day I'll disappoint them. It'll only take one little mistake to get someone killed. Then they'll lose faith in this image they have of me, and what'll happen then? Will they finally realize they can only depend on themselves, or will they lose all hope? Can you see why I don't want that responsibility?"

"I can understand your concern, but no one expects you to be perfect. You weren't just trying to save yourself last night. If that were true, then, like the sheriff said, you would have run the other way when you saw those people heading for the CP. You were putting others before yourself. *That* is why these people look up to you. *That* is why they trust what you say, because you always try to do the right thing. And *that* is one of the reasons I love you."

"But trying to do the right thing doesn't mean things will always work out right. It doesn't mean I know what's right. And, most of all, it doesn't mean I'll be able to accomplish the right thing, even if I do know what it is. I'm afraid people think that I do and I can. They think I'm some kind of fearless leader, who will never lead them astray. I'm not a leader, let alone a fearless one."

"You're right. You're not a fearless leader. A fearless leader isn't what we need around here. What we need is a fearful leader, a leader who fears for our safety and well being, and that is exactly what you are."

"I am not a leader," Mark insisted.

"Honey, a few minutes ago, you told me that you're a man who makes mistakes. Right?"

"That's right."

"Then is it possible you're mistaken now?"

"Yes…I mean no…I mean…Damn!" Mark hated it when she turned his own words against him. Plus, now he owed two more dollars to his box, in addition to what he owed from last night. "I have to go. We'll talk more about this when I get back."

"Okay, sweetheart." She kissed him goodbye. "You be careful."

"I will," he said, as he headed out the door with the basket and his gear.

"We'll have a big celebratory dinner when you get back with your family."

"That sounds great," he hollered over his shoulder.

Everyone was ready to go when Mark got to his Jeep. They all loaded into their pre-assigned vehicles and headed out of the subdivision. Mark, with Ed riding shotgun, led the way. The first third of the route was the same one they had used to go to Austin earlier in the week. Because he was familiar with the roads, Mark was a little more relaxed than he would have been.

"So, Ed, what did you do before the lights went out?"

"I worked for the State. I was an auditor in the Comptroller's office."

"I see," Mark said, "and how did you and Letty meet?"

"We met in college. She sat down beside me in Philosophy my sophomore year, and I thought she was the most beautiful girl I'd ever seen. We started dating, and six months later, we got married."

"Six months? Kind of a short time to get to know each other, isn't it?" Mark asked.

"Yeah, I guess. Letty got pregnant, and we sort of had to get married. She had to drop out of college to take care of the baby, so it was pretty rough on us for a while. Manny helped us out some, and when Robby started kindergarten, Letty went back to school. She finished her degree a couple of years ago and got a good job with the city. Things were really starting to go good for us financially, and then this happened."

"This is going to make things hard on a lot of people for a long time," Mark said, as he started to wonder if Ed's whining was any better than Joe's. He decided to try and turn the conversation to a more positive note. "On the other hand, we're really lucky to live where we have room to grow our own food and to have the good neighbors that we do."

"I guess," Ed agreed half-heartedly.

Mark wondered if this guy 'guessed' about everything. "I appreciate your volunteering to ride up front with me," he told Ed.

"You're welcome, but I didn't really volunteer. Manny made me do it. He said I owed you for coming to get us."

Mark looked over at his passenger. He didn't quite know what to make of Ed's confession. "And how does that make you feel?" 'God, I sound like a shrink,' he thought.

"I guess he's right. Letty said he was, anyway. I just don't like the thought of getting shot at, or worse yet, having to shoot at someone."

"You have a problem with defending yourself?"

"I don't know if I could kill somebody, if that's what you mean."

"But you were in the reserves. You must have known that you might have to go to war."

"I never gave it much thought. I just joined to help pay for school after Letty got pregnant," Ed explained.

Mark, all of a sudden, didn't feel so good about having someone like Ed riding shotgun. He drove a few miles without saying anything. It started misting, and Mark pulled the Jeep over to put the top up. While he was stopped, he told Ed he needed to discuss some things with Gunny, and would he mind switching places for a while. Ed seemed happy for any reason not to be in the front, so Mark radioed for Ted to bring the old war dog up to him. Once Gunny and Ed had switched places, and some of the others had used the opportunity to relieve themselves from too much morning coffee, the convoy was on its way again. Mark explained to Gunny about Ed's reluctance to defend himself. Gunny ranted about how the kid had no balls and little brains. He also had some choice words about Manny for putting them in a bad position. It seemed that the louder Gunny got, the harder the rain fell. After a while, Gunny calmed down. Unfortunately, the rain didn't lighten up with him. Mark got down to business.

"Ever since those idiots attacked Ralph's house, something has been bothering me. I couldn't figure it out until after we were attacked last night, though. The attackers watched us before they attacked. They had plans. Fortunately they didn't work, but they weren't just random attacks. None of our defenses are really geared toward a planned, well-orchestrated, multi-pronged attack. Have you thought about that?"

"Yeah. But I thought we'd have more time before we had to worry about it," Gunny said.

"You mean you knew something like this could happen?"

"Of course. If it hadn't have happened sooner or later, I'da been surprised."

"Then why haven't you trained us for it?" Mark demanded.

"Because ever'body has to learn to walk before they can run," Gunny explained, "and I didn't think it would happen this fast."

"So, what are we going to do about it now?"

"We've got to start patrolling outside the subdivision to see if anyone's watchin' us."

"I see. Any ideas about how we're going to do that?"

"I got plenty of ideas, but we have to figure out how we can cover all the posts if we pull the best guys off of guard duty, which are the ones I want on the patrols," he explained.

The two men discussed various options. However, each one had a downside. The best option they came up with was to eliminate one of the shifts, and go to three 8-hour shifts. Gunny didn't like keeping guys on normally boring guard duty for that long, but it seemed to have the least negatives. Maybe, if they got more men to sign up for guard duty, they could go back to four shifts.

Mark had another question, but he wasn't sure that he really wanted the answer. He decided that not knowing was worse than the truth. "What do you think is the worst case scenario that we might have to defend ourselves against?"

"A division of Marines with artillery and air support," Gunny said, looking Mark in the eye.

"I'm serious," Mark said, as if he was fussing at his son.

"So am I," Gunny shot back. "If the government goes any more whacko, they may try to force us into shelter camps with the military."

"What could we do?"

"Against that kind of firepower? Surrender or die."

"Well, let's hope that doesn't happen. Let me rephrase my question. What is the worst case that we could defend ourselves against?"

"I'd say three or four hundred MZB's with light automatic weapons. Any more than that, we might be able to repel, but the cost in lives wouldn't be worth it."

"How could we defend against so many? We have less than a hundred guards," Mark said.

"The defender's advantage is quoted as being three to one, but in some cases, it can be seven or eight to one."

"I see. So, how many would we lose against three hundred?"

"If'n we knew they were coming, maybe only a dozen or so. If'n they hit us by surprise, it could be fifty to a hundred or more. It depends on how many casualties they're willin' to take."

"And you think fifty to a hundred would be worth it?" Mark asked in disbelief.

"If'n it saved everyone else and our houses and gardens, yes."

Mark was quiet for several minutes thinking about what Gunny had said. He couldn't disagree with the old man. They had a place they could live for quite a while, if they had to, and it would be worth it to him to trade his life, so his kids could have a future. He wondered how they could keep the worst from happening and asked.

"We need to get everyone trained, including the women and older kids, and have at least some kind of weapon for each of them. Then we have to make Silver Hills as uninviting as possible."

"How are we going to do that?"

"I don't rightly know, Karate Man, but the way things are going to hell in a hand basket, we'd better figure it out pretty quick."

Mark was going up a hill and had an odd feeling about it. When he got to the top, he recognized why. This was the spot where they had finished burning the bodies on Wednesday, but things had changed. The rain was quite heavy now, and he'd had to look twice to make sure he wasn't seeing things. The small-car-turned-funeral-pyre had been pushed into the ditch, and the other cars were now blocking the road. Mark slammed on the brakes and skidded sideways a little as he stopped. Gunny was immediately on the radio telling the other drivers they might have a problem. Mark put the Jeep in reverse and backed up beyond the crest of the hill to where they were out of the line of fire from the potential attack. No one had fired at them, and neither of them had seen anyone manning the obstacle, but Mark wanted to check it out thoroughly before he put his men or his vehicles at risk. He and Gunny slipped out of the Jeep and crawled to where they could see the roadblock. Mark looked through his binoculars for a minute and announced that he couldn't see anyone. He handed the field glasses to Gunny. The older man fought with the focus adjustment for a second and then took several moments scanning the obstacle. When he handed the glasses back to Mark, he confirmed that no one was visible. He also informed his companion that there was smoke coming from the chimney of a farmhouse about five hundred yards past the other side of the bridge.

"Did you notice any signs that the house was inhabited on Wednesday?" Gunny asked.

"No, but that doesn't really mean anything. I suspect that most people who live out in the country are trying to keep a low profile," Mark observed.

"Maybe so. But somebody pushed those cars out into the road, and I can't think of a good reason why some farmer out in the middle of nowhere would want to do that. Especially if'n he was tryin' to keep a low profile."

"What do you want to do?" Mark asked the combat vet.

Gunny ran the options, and the two men weighed each one. The best solution seemed to be to have two men sneak down to the roadblock and make sure it was unmanned while the others covered them, then, if possible, for them to push one of the cars off of the road far enough for the convoy to pass. Gunny radioed for the other four vehicles to move up behind the Jeep. When everyone was there, the old sergeant filled them in and asked for volunteers to scout the prospective trouble spot. Manny, Victor, Mark, and Rob each had a hand in the air as soon as the request was made. Gunny looked at the men and picked Victor and Rob for the op.

"You can't send him," Mark objected, as he looked at Rob. "He's our guest."

"And he's also the most qualified," Gunny said. "After you disappeared last night, I got to talk with him for a while. He was with the San Antonio Police Department on their SWAT team. So he knows how to handle himself and this type of situation." Gunny turned to Rob. "Here's the radio. If'n the cars are empty, try to push one off the road. If you can't, radio up, and we'll send the red truck down to do it while you cover it. At the first sign of trouble, get back here while we cover you. Any questions?"

"Piece of cake," Rob said. "You ready, Victor?" He waited for his partner to nod. "Let's rock."

The two men started down the hill. Rob had Victor follow about five yards behind him. Mark noticed that he stayed in the ditch and jogged slightly bent over to keep his outline as inconspicuous as possible. The rain, though not as hard as before, was still coming down steadily. Mark was glad he had a good raincoat. He looked at what the other men were wearing. Gunny had an old GI poncho on. Some of the men had various types of jackets on, and a couple had on garbage bags they'd cut holes for their arms and neck in.

Gunny told Mark to keep his binoculars up and watch both the cars and the house for any sign of movement. Fortunately, he didn't see any. When the two men reached the blockade, they quickly looked the cars over and radioed up that all was clear. Then they easily pushed the smaller car onto the shoulder. Gunny had everyone load up and move out. The five vehicles stopped momentarily at the bridge to pick up the two men who were waiting there. Gunny told the convoy to stay together until they topped the next hill and then to start spacing out into their normal formation.

When the Jeep passed the house with the smoking chimney, Mark noticed there were six or eight motorcycles and a couple of trucks under the carport. He pointed them out to Gunny. They watched the house for any sign of life, but nothing was moving. After a few miles, the convoy had spread back out, and Mark continued his conversation with Gunny about their neighborhood's security. Mark told Gunny about what had happened with his carbine the night before. Gunny explained to Mark, that while the Camp .45 was a fine little weapon, it wasn't designed like a military weapon.

"Shoot, if'n you want somethin' that'll work when it's dirty, you oughta carry one of them AK's. I think you could bury one of them things in a mud hole for a week, and it'd still shoot every time you pulled the trigger," he said.

"I'm also worried about our ability to effectively fight in the dark," Mark said. "I could aim with my red dot, not that it did me much good after my rifle jammed, but the other guys couldn't see their sights for squat."

"That is a problem. We could try and get some of them red dots like you got and put 'em on some of the rifles, but what are we goin' to do once the batt'ries run out?"

"I don't know. I know they make tritium night sights for pistols. The Watson boys are real big on them. Maybe they make the same thing for rifles."

"That's them radioactive glow sights, right?" Gunny asked.

"Something like that. I know they're supposed to last like ten or twelve years. When we get back, maybe we should run to town and see if Jerry has any."

"Sounds like a plan to me. You want some coffee?"

Mark nodded his head, and Gunny poured two cups of the liquid gold out of his thermos. He handed one to Mark, then took a sip of his, and then made a sound that let Mark know that the warm nectar had the desired effect. Mark tasted his and found it especially satisfying. The conversation turned to the county militia the sheriff wanted to train. Gunny and Mark agreed they should dedicate one day a week to the cause, even if it hurt the training of their own men. Having a large, county-wide group to deal with problems could be very beneficial. If it stopped trouble before it got to them, well, there was no way to put a value on that. It would be a monumental task, though. Mark couldn't imagine how the sheriff could effectively train so many men. Gunny suggested that Curt already had a plan and only need some help to do it.

"Why would you say that?" Mark asked him.

"Look at how well he and those guys in that Promise Point subdivision were ready for the stuff to hit the fan. He had to have some kind of contingency plan for something like this."

"Then why wouldn't he have just told us what he wants to do?"

"Think about it, Karate Man. What does he do for a living?"

"He's the sheriff."

"And how did he get to be the sheriff?"

"The people voted for him," Mark said, failing to see where Gunny was going.

"And how did he get the people to vote for him?"

"What has that got to do with what we're talking about?" Mark asked.

"You know, Karate Man, your heart's in the right place, but you'd better learn to engage that gray matter between your ears sometimes. He's a damned politician. He got elected by getting people to think he'd do what they want him to do. He's doing the same thing now. If he insisted he was gonna do things a certain way, people might oppose him, so he gets them to think it's their idea."

"You think so?"

"I'm sure of it, and you should take a lesson from him on how to handle things like this. It mighta made things go smoother with Jon."

"Are you saying what happened with Jon was my fault?" Mark asked.

"No. Jon was totally wrong, but you coulda helped the situation. We all could have."

"How?" Mark was having a hard time believing that he could have done things much differently.

"By not making him feel and look so wrong. Once he'd alienated everyone, he could only see one way out. If we'd tried to make him part of the solution instead of the problem, maybe things would have worked out differently. That's what politics is. Making everyone feel they are part of the team and that what they say carries at least a little weight."

Mark thought about what Gunny was saying. Maybe he could have handled Jon better, but maybe he did the best he could. That was why he didn't want to be the leader. Maybe his best wasn't good enough. Maybe he could make Gunny understand.

"I know you're right, Gunny, but I don't know if I'm capable of being political. I've never been good at it. At work, I always said exactly what I thought. That's probably why I never made it out of middle management," he explained. "That's why I don't want everyone thinking I'm the leader. I'm just not the right man for the job, and I don't want it."

"That's exactly why you are the right man for the job."

"Huh?" Mark was puzzled.

"Listen, Karate Man, anybody who wants the job probably wants it for the wrong reasons. You're only doing it because you know it has to be done. I can appreciate that you don't want to do it, but you have to. A new leader would have to gain the trust of everyone, and that might take a long time, time we don't have. So whether you like it or not, you're it, and since you are, you have to try to do everything you can to make it work, even if it means learning politics."

"But, you don't understand, Gunny. I…" Mark was cut off by the old Marine.

"I understand perfectly," Gunny said, emphasizing the 'I'. "You are the one who don't understand. You don't have to like it…you jus' have to do it!"

Mark was quiet for several minutes after being chastised. When he finally spoke, his voice was subdued. "You may be right…maybe I do have to do it. But you are dead right about one thing…I don't like it!"

The two men laughed. A minute later, Mark asked another question.

"How do you know the sheriff is just being political?"

"There's politics in every job. You learn to play them, or you don't get very far."

"But it couldn't have been that way in the Marine Corps. You guys were all straight shooters, right?"

Gunny laughed so hard that the sip of coffee he had just taken shot out of his nose and onto the dash. When he caught his breath and had wiped his face off with his sleeve, he spoke. "Damn you, Karate Man. Don't you ever do that again." He winked at the younger man. "Every government job is highly political, especially if you're an NCO in the Marine Corps." Gunny's voice got bitter. "You don't know what politics is until you've have some REMF Academy puke chewing your ass, all because you didn't dot all the I's and cross all the T's on your requisition to get your men the ammo they needed to fight for a piece of shit hill that you'd taken and given back to the enemy three times in the last two weeks." Gunny smiled, and his voice returned to normal. "I almost lost all my stripes for that one."

Mark looked at his watch. It was a little after noon. He was getting hungry, and the Jeep needed to be filled. He radioed the other vehicles, and everyone agreed it was a good time to stop. Mark found a long straightaway on the little farm-to-market road and pulled the Jeep to the shoulder where they could see almost a mile in both directions. A minute later, the two pickups and the Suburban pulled in behind. Not long after that, the Trans Am pulled up. Since it was still raining, the men ate in the four door Ford or in the Jeep. There was little talking, as sandwiches were eaten with ferocity. When Mark was finished with his two, he pulled on his coat and got two jerry cans out of the back of Jim's truck. He was filling the Jeep with them when Ted came up to talk to him.

"Ed's driving me crazy. He just keeps whining about how he doesn't want to be here. He just goes on and on about how it's not fair and how Manny made him come, and he has some strange ideas about how the government should handle things. You'd think we were all subjects instead of citizens. He actually told me he thinks things would be better if only the military and police had guns."

"I understand, Ted. I'll put Gunny back with you."

"Thanks," the professor smiled.

"You need any gas?"

"No, I still have half a tank."

"Why don't you go ahead and put a jerry can's worth in anyway, as long as we're stopped."

"Good idea," Ted said, as he grabbed one of the cans that Mark had gotten.

"Hey, get your own!" Mark teased.

Ted's face got red, and he smiled sheepishly. "Sorry." He put the can back down and headed to Jim's Chevy.

Mark didn't really want Ed with him, but he couldn't pawn him off on anyone else. Or could he? Manny had made him come along. Maybe he should ride with him. Mark asked Manny if he could speak with him for a minute. Manny came over, and Mark explained that Ed was griping about being on the trip and how he said he couldn't shoot at someone in defense of himself. Mark suggested it might be best if Ed was in the middle vehicle where the chance of him having to fight was the least. Of course it was only coincidence that Manny's Suburban was the middle truck. Manny apologized to Mark and then went to find Ed. Mark almost felt bad for the young man when his father-in-law pulled him to the side and started chewing on him. Mark knew Manny's parents had moved to Texas from Mexico before he was born, but he couldn't help but wonder if there wasn't a little Italian blood in Manny from the way he was flailing his hands as he was talking. After what must have seemed an eternity to

Ed, but was really only a minute or two, Manny stomped back to the Suburban. Ed slinked over to Mark like a puppy with his tail between his legs.

"Mr. Turner, I'm sorry for being so much trouble. I really would like to ride shotgun with you. You can count on me to do whatever you say."

Mark felt awful. He wasn't sure if it was because he had gotten Ed in so much trouble, or if it was because now he had to let him ride with him in the Jeep again. Probably some of both, he figured. "Don't worry about it, Ed. Go ahead and climb in, and we'll get going in a minute."

A couple of minutes later, the convoy was back underway. Ed didn't seem like he wanted to talk much. He only responded when Mark talked to him, and then in as few words as possible. Mark was actually glad for the peace and quiet. It gave him time to think. Before he knew it, they were on the outskirts of Waco.

Mark's youngest sister, Monica, her husband and their three kids lived in an upscale neighborhood on the south side of Waco. Their house was bigger than Mark's, but it sat on a tiny lot. They called it a 'garden home,' which seemed especially silly to Mark now. You couldn't have grown a fraction of what a family would need to survive on that lot, even if it didn't have a house taking up most of it.

When Mark turned off of the Ranch Road onto the street that led to his sister's house, he immediately knew something was terribly wrong. The stench, though not as strong as he'd smelled at the roadblock a few days ago, was unmistakably the same. He mashed the accelerator down, as if he still had time to get to Monica's house before whatever had happened could reach her. Many of the houses were burned, and those that weren't had gang graffiti all over them. Mark told Ed to get his weapon ready. The young man, obviously nervous, put the AR-15 across his lap with the barrel pointed away from the driver and his hands squeezing the grip as his eyes darted from house to house. Mark was glad that Ed at least seemed ready to fight if need be. His sister's house sat at the end of the street on a cul-de-sac. When the Jeep got close enough to Monica and Jeff's house that Mark could see it, his heart jumped into his throat. All of the windows were broken out, and the doors were ajar. There were bullet holes riddled across the structure. Mark stopped in front and stared disbelieving into the house.

There were bodies lying just inside the open door.

Chapter 44

Mark turned the ignition off and jumped out of the Jeep. He didn't even think to grab his rifle or pull his pistol. He ran to the door and looked at the bodies. They had swollen up to almost twice their normal size. The stench was unbearable, and he pulled a handkerchief out of his pocket and covered his nose with it. The three faces, though badly misshapened by bullet holes and the swelling, belonged to no one he knew. The two men and a woman had tattoos all over their arms and some on their necks and legs. They all appeared to have been in their late teens or early twenties. He looked up and saw Ed, standing fifteen or twenty feet from the door, staring at the bodies like he couldn't figure out what they were.

Past the staring young man, the three trucks had stopped behind the Jeep. Mark could see the Trans Am coming up the street at a rapid pace. Ted steered the muscle car around the trucks and brought it to a halt beside the Jeep. Gunny exited the Pontiac with surprising agility and started barking orders to the four drivers. He told them to space out around the vehicles to guard them. He had the riders follow him up to the house with their longarms. When he got to the door and saw Mark without his rifle, he promptly reprimanded him. Rob looked at the bodies and told the group that they'd been gang members and, from the looks of them, had been dead for about three days. Gunny had Rob, Joe, and Dwight circle the house and make sure there were no surprises in the backyard. When they came back with nothing out of the ordinary to report, he had Joe and Dwight return to the backyard and guard the back door. With all the entrances to the house covered, he told the others to follow him into the house.

"You don't expect me to go in there?" Ed shuddered as he asked, never taking his eyes off of the dead bodies.

Gunny looked at the young man with disdain. "What's the matter? You never seen maggot chow before?"

The young man's eyes grew to the size of silver dollars. He then bent over and hurled his lunch onto the small front lawn. Mark thought he saw the faintest hint of a smile in the old man's eyes.

"Why don't you help guard the trucks when you're finished pukin'," Gunny said.

The old man assigned Rob to help Mark clear the house while he watched their backs. Rob nodded his head at Gunny then looked at Mark for an indication of where to start. Mark tilted his head toward the kitchen. The three men cleared the downstairs room by room. The rooms were full of empty liquor bottles, beer cans, and drug paraphernalia. They found another dead body in the garage. It was as lifeless as the almost brand new SUV next to it. The young man had the same type of tattoos as the other bodies and appeared to have been dead for about the same amount of time. Rob pointed out that the dead man had his throat cut. Mark was amazed how the blood covered practically the whole garage floor. They went back into the house where Mark and Rob headed upstairs, while Gunny stood at the bottom of the stairs where he could make sure that no one could sneak up behind them.

When Mark pushed open the first bedroom door, he wasn't prepared for what he saw. He'd become somewhat calloused to the sight of dead bodies since his firefight with the MZB's who had attacked the preacher. However, the sights in this room would have haunted even the most battle-hardened man. There were four more young gang members who had been bound and obviously tortured to death in the most horrible and unspeakable ways. The other two bedrooms had more bodies in them in the same condition. Mark began to visibly shake. He couldn't imagine what kind of person could do these things to another human being. He noticed that it was getting hard to see clearly and realized it was because his eyes were full of tears. Whatever these young gang members may have perpetrated during their lives could never justify the suffering they must have endured during their last hours.

When the upstairs was declared clear, Mark came back down, relieved he hadn't found any of his relatives in the house. Rob explained to Gunny what they'd found and reported that some of the bodies upstairs had been dead for only about a day.

"It looks like some of them lasted a couple of days. I've never seen anything like that," Rob explained. "I heard about stuff like this a couple of times but never seen it. I don't know if I'll ever be able to get that picture out of my mind."

"Who do ya think done it?" Gunny asked Rob.

"These kids were just wanna-be bad-asses. I'd say they ran into a group of real hardened sickos."

"MZB's," Mark interjected sadly.

"MZB's?" Rob asked.

"Yeah, Mutant Zombie Bikers."

"Fits. Anyway, I don't know if the gang was living here and the MZB's ambushed them, or if they were looting houses and pissed off the MZB's somehow. I think that's the most likely scenario. The MZB's probably chased them down the street and cornered them in here. There were a couple of bodies further up the street. They could have been the kids' lookouts, or they got capped first. Whatever happened, I'd say they made some tactically unsound decisions."

"No shit," Gunny said.

"They're probably at my Dad's house," Mark said to no one in particular. "My sister and her family, I mean. Let's get out of here. There's nothing in here worth taking, and I'm with Rob. I'm gonna have nightmares about this shit for the rest of my life." Mark headed out the front door.

Gunny and Rob came out a minute later. Gunny gave the men the PG-rated version of what had happened and instructed them to be very watchful as they drove to Mark's parents' house. The men loaded up and headed out. When they were back on the ranch road, Ed looked over at Mark and asked a question.

"Was it that bad upstairs?"

"I don't think you really want to know. Why do you ask?"

"You didn't blink twice when you looked at the dead people downstairs. In fact, you almost looked happy, but when you came back outside, you looked like you were scared."

"I wasn't happy those people were dead, if that's what you mean. I was happy it wasn't my family, that's all, and I am scared. I didn't know it was possible for people to turn into such animals. Now, if you don't mind, I don't want to talk about it anymore."

"Okay," the younger man said, as he looked nervously from one side of the road to the other. Mark noticed that he gripped the AR as though someone might snatch it away from him. Maybe what he saw will change his way of thinking, Mark thought.

It was less than fifteen miles from his sister's house on the south side of Waco to where his father's and brother's houses shared a two-acre tract on the northern outskirts of town, but it felt like it was three hundred miles to Mark. Victor had to call him three times on the radio to tell him to slow down a little. It was almost sunset, and Mark felt an overpowering desire to get there before dark. At least it had stopped raining for the moment.

Mark was a little concerned when the gate was open. As he turned down the driveway and cleared the huge, ancient oaks that obscured the house from the road, Mark felt as if his world had shattered. Both houses were burned to the ground. Faint curls of smoke rose lazily to the sky from a few lingering hot spots. They took with them the last wisps of hope Mark had of ever seeing his family again.

Mark shut off the Jeep and sat staring at the ruins. The only thing standing was his dad's metal storage building that sat toward the back of the property. It had gang graffiti across the front of it. Mark couldn't imagine that his dad and brother had succumbed to ordinary gangbangers. It would've taken some bad MZB's to take them, especially if Monica and Jeff were here. Mike had quite a collection of guns, most of them military-type rifles, and he knew how to use them. He'd attended several courses at a school in Tennessee called 'Tactical Response.' Mark wished he'd taken Mike up on his invitation to go with him a time or two. He realized now that being able to shoot a gun and knowing how to fight with one were two different things, something Mike had told him on many occasions.

Someone tapped on the plastic window of the Jeep. Mark looked and saw Gunny standing there. Mark opened the door and stepped out. "I can't believe they're all dead, Gunny."

"You don't know that. Maybe they're in a shelter in town," Gunny suggested.

"Not likely. Mike was always harping on how government had shredded The Constitution and grown into a monster. He wouldn't have gone to anything like a government shelter."

"Maybe your dad talked him into going."

"My old man was so conservative, he'd have made us look like a couple of socialists. I never once heard him say the word 'government' without a few choice adjectives before it, at least when my mother wasn't listening. He wouldn't have gone either."

"Then they could have bugged out," Gunny said.

"That's possible, I guess." Mark thought he was starting to sound like Ed with the guessing. "Mike had prepared this place for the Y2K bug that never happened. Dad bought into it some and helped out all he could. Mike tried to get me to stock up a bunch of stuff, but I just did enough to get him off of my back. I kind of got a kick out of him being so wrong. Anyway, they had everything they needed to stay here. Truth be told, I expected to get here and find them in better shape than we're in. I don't see them walking away from all of their preparations without a fight."

Most of the men were standing around listening to Mark and Gunny's conversation. Two of them were standing guard behind the vehicles.

"I'd better go see if they're in there," Mark added, nodding at the remains of one of the houses.

Gunny reached out and grabbed Mark's arm to stop him. Then he asked Rob if he had ever worked any fire scenes. When Rob nodded his head, Gunny asked him if he would have a look around. Rob moved off, pulling Victor to help him. Mark was grateful. He didn't know if he could bear to see the charred bodies. The old man turned his attention back to Mark.

"Assuming they bugged out, where would they go?"

"My house would be the logical place," Mark said, knowing the old man was just trying to distract him. "But it's too far with no transportation. There was a state park not too far from here where they liked to camp, but I don't think Mike would go there. They may have turned it into a refugee camp. Even if they didn't, there would be too many people there. There are also some woods where we used to play near here. I guess that's the best possibility."

"We'll check out the woods as soon as Rob is finished checking things out," Gunny said. He didn't have to say that it depended on whether Rob found anything or not. They all watched as Rob moved slowly around both of the destroyed houses, prodding and poking around with a shovel he'd gotten out of one of the trucks. He studied several spots intently. It make Mark hold his breath every time Rob stopped somewhere for more than a moment. Some of the places he stopped, though, seemed unlikely spots to find anyone. He looked at both driveways for a while, and he spent several minutes looking at Mike's gun safe that was in the garage. After a concise examination of the property, including a brief look at the storage shed, Rob returned to the cluster of men.

"Good news. I don't see any bodies in the rubble," he reported.

Mark was relieved. At least there was still a possibility they were alive.

Rob continued. "The houses were probably set on fire separately. There are no burn marks on the ground where the fire traveled, so unless it was from some floating embers, somebody burned them both intentionally. The houses are burned too completely for me to tell if they took any rifle fire. The shed has no bullet holes, but that doesn't really mean anything, as far back as it sits. However, there are some bullet strikes in some of the trees around your brother's house, and I found some blood on the ground. I don't think it was your family though. It's all behind the trees on the opposite side from the house, where you'd expect the MZB's, as you call them, to be if they attacked."

"You think the MZB's could have killed them and dragged them off?"

"Possibly, but not likely. If that happened, then why burn the houses? They were probably burned to get the occupants out. Do you know anyone named 'Rocky'?

"I know a stockbroker in San Antonio named Rocky. He's a friend of a friend, really."

"Anybody that your brother or dad might know named Rocky?"

"No. Not that I know of. Why?"

"Someone spray-painted 'Rocky's House' on both driveways and on the shed," Rob explained.

"It was Mike!" Mark explained excitedly. "Rocky was what we called this squirrel who lived here when we were kids…you know…Rocky and Bullwinkle. He lived in this knothole in one of the trees in the back. Dad always threatened he was going to concrete it up, and we would beg him not to. That must be what Mike means! We need to look in that knothole!"

"Which tree was it?" Manny asked.

"That one," Mark pointed, as he and the other men ran toward the tree like kids on Christmas morning.

The knothole was about ten feet from the ground. Victor, who was almost as big and tall as Jim, put his back to the trunk and clasped his hands together to give someone a leg up. "Come on, Ed. You're the lightest."

"I'm not sticking my hand in there to get bit," Ed said. Several of the men gave him a look.

"Can you lift me?" Mark asked.

"Sure. Stand on my shoulders."

Mark did as the younger man said. He was surprised at how easily Victor lifted him up. He started to reach into the hole but realized that one of Rocky's descendants might be living in there. He knocked around the opening, but nothing came out or made any sound. He carefully reached into the tree and felt a plastic bag. Upon removing it, he could see that there was a note inside a ziplock bag.

He climbed down and opened the bag. The note was short. Mark read it out loud.

September 19th

Dear Butthead,

I knew you would come. Everyone is OK. We got attacked by a bunch of nazi skinheads. We kicked their asses, but they threatened that they'd be back. Dad, J., and I figured we better go to plan B in case they did. We moved out and camped for a couple of days. They came back with a big group, and I watched them burn the place down. It was hard not to waste some of them, but it would have put us all at risk. We've decided to come see you. I've heard on the shortwave that things aren't nearly as bad in your neck of the woods. With no running vehicles and not enough bicycles, we decided to walk. We don't want to stay on the roads any more than necessary, anyway. We have a route planned out, but I hesitate to put it in this letter in case someone else finds it. I hope to be there in 10 or 12 days. Go to the tree you fell out of when you were eight. Ten yards west is some buried treasure. I hope you brought the truck. Bring it back to your house for me. Thanks.

Your Brother

"Smart cookie," Gunny said. "No names and no places for anybody to know but you."

"What's the date today?" Joe asked.

"It's the 28th. Tomorrow is ten days," Dwight said. "They may be there when we get back."

"Sorry, guys. Looks like we came up for nothing," Mark said.

"Maybe not. Where's the tree he's talking about?" Gunny asked.

"In the woods I was telling you about," Mark answered.

"It'll be dark in half an hour. Can we camp there outta sight?"

"I think so. Let's go see. Was there anything in the shed?"

"No. Looks like someone cleaned it out," Rob answered.

"Then let's load up and move out," Gunny ordered.

The men got into the trucks and cars and followed Mark's Jeep about half a mile down the road. He turned into a large, wooded lot that was probably eight or ten acres in size. That didn't seem very big now, but Mark remembered this place seemed a universe unto itself when he was young. He, Mike, and their friends spent countless days playing on this lot. Mark was able to find a path through the trees wide enough to drive to a small clearing out of sight of the road. Gunny had the drivers park the vehicles around the outside of the clearing. It reminded Mark of an old western movie where they circled the wagons. The men got out, and Gunny immediately had two of the men stand guard. He had Victor and Rob, who were fast becoming friends, scout the perimeter of the lot. The other men quickly pulled out the tents and set them up inside the circle as quietly as they could in the falling light. Rob and Victor reported that everything was clear. There was a house on the eastern side, but it appeared to be uninhabited.

When camp was set and everyone had eaten, Gunny assigned the guard shifts. Two men would take two hours each. Joe and Manny had the first shift. Mark had ten to midnight with Dwight. When that was all settled, Mark grabbed the shovel and headed for the cache his brother had left. He found the tree and paced off ten yards toward where the sky was barely pink. When he swept the leaves away, he could see where the dirt was fresh. It was easy to shovel the loose dirt, and in no time, he was down eighteen inches or so. There was a metallic clank, and he quickly shoveled enough dirt off to see the top of a 55-gallon drum. Dropping down on his knees, he swept the remaining dirt off of the top. Then, with Gunny holding a small flashlight, he read "2 of 4" in Mike's handwriting. Mark grabbed the barrel and tried to pull it out. It was way too heavy. Several of the others tried to help him, but they were only able to move it a fraction of an inch. Mark started digging around the sides of the barrel and quickly found two of the other drums. When he had cleared the dirt to a little over halfway down the side, the men were able to pull the barrel out of the hole. Victor volunteered to shovel out the next one, and Mark, now drenched in sweat, was happy to let him. Victor easily cleared out the next two. Mark saw Manny elbow Ed, so that he would take a turn. Ed reluctantly took the shovel and awkwardly climbed down into the hole where the three liberated drums had been. He hacked at the dirt ineffectively with the tool, wielding it like a six-year-old with a ten-pound sledgehammer. When he had spent almost as much time as it had taken Victor to dislodge two barrels, Manny had all he could stand.

"Give me the shovel," he ordered his son-in-law.

Ed handed the shovel up and then crawled out of the hole with the grace of a fish flopping in the bottom of a boat. Manny jumped down and finished clearing the dirt in just a few minutes. The men pulled it up. This one, marked 1 of 4, was the heaviest by far. Mark pulled out his Leatherman tool and unscrewed the bolt that tightened the clamping ring. When he had the ring off, he found that the lid had been sealed down with silicone. It was hard to pry off, but with the help of others, he freed it. The contents were encased inside a heavy plastic bag. Taped to the inside of the top, was a ziplock with a manifest in it. Mark looked at the papers for a moment and read it to the group.

"No wonder this one's so heavy; it's mostly full of ammo. It also has a Berkefeld water filter, a Coleman stove and some of the one-pound propane cylinders, plus some baby clothes for the little ones and the family photo album."

"Jeez, just this one is worth its weight in gold," Dwight said. "I wonder what's in the others."

"Mike put the contents of all four barrels in here. One contains a whole list of guns and some more ammo. That one is full of MRE's, whatever they are. Fourteen cases."

"MRE stands for Meal Ready-to-Eat. It's a self-contained military field meal," Rob explained.

"Yeah," Gunny agreed. "They taste like shit, but you can live on 'em."

Everyone laughed, including Mark. He realized how good it felt.

"The last one is full of all kinds of stuff. There's fuel stabilizer, more propane containers, extra clothes and boots for the adults and older children..." Mike's gold and silver coins were listed, but Mark didn't mention them. "...and the family Bible and some other odds and ends."

"Man, what a haul. Your brother was lucky he could hide all this stuff," Joe said.

"And luckier that you're gonna bring it to him," Gunny added.

The men loaded the barrels into Mark's truck and tied them in place. Mark considered taking the gold and silver out of its drum and putting it in his Jeep with him but decided that hidden in plain sight was probably best.

Mark washed up a little, and then it was time for him to report for his two-hour guard shift.

Chapter 45

Mark's shift had just begun when it started to rain again. It wasn't hard, just steady and cold. Mark bundled his rain parka around him a little tighter. Dwight was going to rove for the first hour, and he would watch the front of the camp. Then they would switch at eleven. Mark's thoughts were of his family. It was over a hundred and eighty miles from here to his house. He wondered if they could make it. There were eleven of them, six adults and five kids. Mike's two children were older. Jonathon was seventeen, and Jena was fifteen. They were old enough to be really able to help out, but Jeff and Monica's kids were just babies. Taylor, Luke, and Haylee were four, three, and one, respectively. They would have to be carried most or all of the way if they planned to make fifteen to eighteen miles a day. That seemed pretty optimistic to Mark. How could they carry that much food? He wondered if he could find them along the way. He went over the routes they might take. There were just too many possibilities, and if they weren't on the roads, how would he be able to locate them?

He realized that he was getting tired. He hadn't slept much the night before, and the drive plus the emotional highs and lows of today didn't help. He heard a faint rumble of thunder in the distance. It didn't register on his exhausted brain that there had been no lightning. The rumble continued to increase in volume, and Mark finally grasped the fact that it wasn't thunder. It sounded like a pack of motorcycles. The sound grew louder and louder. After another minute, it was obvious they'd come right past the woods. Mark prayed that they weren't coming into them. His radio crackled. It was Dwight saying he'd sighted the bikes. He was just off the road and could count nine headlights. Mark went to the camp to wake the others, just in case. He found them already up and getting dressed as quickly as possible.

Dwight continued to report on the bikers' progress. There were seven bikes and a truck. They were less than a quarter mile away now and moving slowly. Mark and the others moved to Jim's pickup. It was blocking the path they'd taken in here and would be the first thing the bikers saw if they came in the same way. A few seconds later, the pitch of the engines changed, as transmissions were downshifted. 'Oh, shit,' Mark thought. Most of the men laid their rifles across the hood or the bed of the truck. Mark saw Gunny drop down and worm his way underneath the Chevy. Manny followed him. Mark thought that was a good idea, but he was just too tired to crawl in the mud. He could see the headlights out on the road now, but they never turned toward him. Instead, they drifted past. Dwight came on the radio and said they were turning into the abandoned house. Mark relayed the information, and the men all breathed sighs of relief. Gunny popped back up and asked Victor and Rob to watch the house. The two men nodded, and Mark watched them move off until they disappeared.

The engines seemed to stop all at one time. Mark was thinking that if these were MZB's, his group could be in trouble when they started their engines in the morning. A second later, a car door slammed and then another. Mark listened intently to see if he could hear voices, but if there were any, the rain was drowning them out.

A woman screamed, and then parts of a sentence could be heard.

"Shu......fu...up...bi......I...kill......ri...now!"

Mark could fill in the blanks well enough to figure out what was going on. He thought maybe they shouldn't go looking for trouble and should mind their own business, but he knew that they couldn't. The last thing he wanted was to put these men, who had come to Waco to help him, in danger, but they couldn't just stand by and let lawbreakers perpetrate murder and mayhem.

Gunny spoke on the radio and then took everyone to where Victor and Rob were. Mark could see light coming from inside the house. Just outside the front door was one man standing guard. The glow of his cigarette could be seen at a regular interval. Parked in front of him were the motorcycles. They all appeared to be brand new Harleys. Mark wondered if the bikes had a simple ignition system that was easily repairable. In the driveway was an early seventies model Chevy Blazer. Rob waved the men over to talk to them.

"There are thirteen of them, nine men and four women as far as I could tell, plus a young female hostage."

"How young?" Joe asked.

"Hard to say. Mid-teens, maybe," Rob answered.

"Bastards!" Ed spat.

Rob continued. "I don't know if there were any more already in the house, but the light didn't come on until these guys went in. You can see the guy in the front, and there's one guarding the back door. What do you want to do?"

"We have to try to help the girl. What's the best way to do that?" Manny asked, as he looked at Gunny.

"This is Rob's area of expertise," the old man nodded at the guest.

"The best thing would be to take out the guards quietly and then scout for an empty room and enter the house through a window, but I don't know if we have that much time. They're probably all in the front where the light is. If we could take out the front guard, then we could probably enter through the front door with a six-man team quick enough to take them by surprise. The other four guys could surround the house and take care of anyone who comes running out."

"How do we take out the guard?" Dwight asked.

"I wish we had a suppressed .22. Since we don't, somebody's got to sneak up and knock him out or use a knife."

"What are the chances we can take these guys without having to kill any of them?" Mark asked.

"Slim to none would be my guess," Rob answered. "If things were normal, maybe we'd have a better chance. These guys look like they've been around to me, and I think that, under the circumstances, they'll fight. I won't lose any sleep if we have to kill them. If you saw the way they were treating that girl, you wouldn't either. I believe they'll kill her if we don't do something. So I'll take out the guard and lead the assault team. Who's with me?"

Everyone started to raise their hand until Mark started speaking. "Hold on a second, Rob. You're too valuable to put at risk, you and Gunny both. Your expertise cannot be replaced. This little road trip was to get my family, so I'm in charge. I'll take the guard out and lead the assault team. Tell me what to do."

Rob explained the process to everyone. Then Mark asked for volunteers. Every man raised his hand, even Ed. Mark asked him and Joe to stay with Gunny and Rob to cover the house.

"No!" Ed answered. "I'm going with you. My baby sister was kidnapped, raped, and murdered when she was sixteen, and I'm not going to stand around and let it happen again."

"Covering the house is not standing around," Manny argued. "You need to do what Mark asked you."

"I'm on the assault team, period," the young man said with steel in his voice. "The quicker you accept it, the quicker we get going."

Everyone looked shocked at Ed's declaration. He was right; they didn't have time to argue. "Alright, Ed, you're with me. Manny, you're with Rob."

Manny, after admonishing his son-in-law to do what was asked of him, couldn't very well refuse. Mark saw on his face that he didn't like it, but he agreed with a nod of his head. Mark then saw the look of surprised pride on his face when he glanced at Ed. Mark was surprised, too. His estimation of Ed had just increased exponentially.

After checking one last time to make sure everyone understood their assignments, Mark moved off to neutralize the guard. His plan was to sneak up behind him when he was looking the other way and pistol-whip him. Gunny thrust a sheathed bayonet into his hands before he left, and he stuck it down in the waist of his pants. He moved to the garage doors on the side of the house and peeked around the corner. He couldn't help but notice how well manicured the flower bed was. Too bad he'd have to run through it to get to the guard, who was a little bigger than he was and muscular. He was dressed mostly in leather and had an AR-15 slung around his neck. The man took a long drag off of his cigarette and then threw the butt out into the rain. Mark watched him look from side to side in a slow, sweeping motion. Okay, he thought, next time he turns his head the other way, I'll go. He pulled his Colt out of the holster and turned it the wrong way. It would make an effective hammer. Mark knew from his Karate training just where to hit to turn off the man's lights. When the guard should have started turning his head the other way, he didn't. Mark wondered if the man had seen him. It wasn't likely. The moonlight just barely penetrated the rain clouds, and the light coming out of the window behind the man would not help his night vision. Then the leather clad biker stepped off of the small porch and turned down the sidewalk that lead almost straight to where Mark was standing.

'Oh, shit!' Mark thought. He pulled his head back around the corner and flattened his body against the garage door as much as he could. His eyes shifted from side to side, as if he was looking to see if Murphy had somehow tagged along on his little adventure. 'Shit, shit, shit,' was all he could think. Knocking the man out was no longer an option. He put the Colt back into his holster and pulled out the bayonet. It was black and sharpened down both sides. The filed edges of the blade glimmered slightly in the pale light. Mark looked at them and shuddered. He'd never killed a man with a knife before. He wondered how it would feel to be so close to someone as the life ebbed out of them. It suddenly occurred to him it could be his life that would end. 'Fucking Murphy,' he thought, as he coiled his body to strike the guard. He could smell the man getting closer. It was a foul combination of BO, cigarettes, and beer. Mark prayed that the beer smell was fresh. Perhaps the alcohol would slow the man's reactions a little.

Suddenly, it appeared that perhaps Murphy wasn't around. The guard walked right past Mark, never turning his head to look that way. He crossed the driveway, stopping behind the Blazer. He leaned his rifle against the back bumper of the four by four and stretched. Then, with his back to the house, he stepped to the edge of the concrete, unzipped his pants, and began to relieve himself. Mark almost couldn't believe his luck. Not only could he go back to plan A, but now the man was away from the house. Mark stuck the knife back into his waistband and unholstered his pistol again. He quickly tiptoed toward the man. When he was about five feet away, he raised the pistol.

'CLANK!'

The bayonet had fallen from his waistband and hit the driveway. Mark froze. Murphy was here after all. The guard's head snapped around, and he saw Mark. Mark, wishing he hadn't stopped, charged the man. If he'd had been drinking, it hadn't slowed his reflexes much. He turned and raised his left arm to stop Mark's blow, and his right lashed out a meaty fist to collide with Mark's midsection. Mark hadn't been hit that hard since his black belt test. The man knocked the wind out of him, and all he could do was wrap up the biker and let his momentum take them to the ground. Somehow, the bigger man was able to twist around, so he ended up on top. His arm ended up across Mark's throat. That, coupled with the punch and the man's weight, which felt considerably more than Mark had previously estimated, landing on top, put him in a precarious position. All he could hear was the blood pounding in his ears. The pistol, and the hand that held it, had ended up behind his back when they fell, and he couldn't pull it out. Mark figured he had enough oxygen to try one move. He relaxed for a split second, then thrust his hips up as fast and hard as he could. He was surprised at how easily he threw the man off. He rolled over on his stomach to get up and could see why he'd had come off so easily. His assault team had come to help him. They were now standing around the man, who was on his back. His fly was still gapping open and his forehead had the crosshatch pattern of a metal butt plate from an AR-15 across it. He was out cold.

The only person with an AR was Ed. He looked at the downed biker with hatred and disgust. "Let's get the girl," he whispered.

The six of them lined up in the predetermined order at the front door. Mark crouched down and tried the knob. He could hear the girl scream as he turned it. Thankfully, it wasn't locked. Mark held the door closed until he felt the two pats on his shoulder that he knew had been passed up the line to tell him that every man was ready. He pushed the door open and entered the room, still in his crouch, moving to the right. The house was an older, ranch-style home, and the front door opened into a large living room that was connected to the kitchen by a bar. A Coleman lantern sat on it, hissing. Mark's job was to use his pistol to clear, right to left, anyone close enough to the door to impede the entry team and then to concentrate on the next closest target, as he moved into the room far enough to allow the men behind him access. He knew that Scott had the same assignment for the left side with his Glock.

Mark caught a glimpse of the young girl. Two of the men had her trapped in a corner of the room, and they were play jabbing at her with big bowie knives and making her scream. Some of the men and women were sitting on the furniture, watching the show and laughing. Fortunately, none of the MZB's were close to the door. Mark had moved into the room far enough for the two men assigned to his side to follow him, and he dropped to one knee. Ed was right behind him with the AR. His job was to start in the middle and clear to the right. Ted was his mirror for the left with his AK. Dwight was the fifth man in and was using one of the community AK's. He was charged with watching the room for any threats that the first four missed. Victor was last in, and, with a short-barreled shotgun, was to watch all the doors into the room for anyone coming through them. The entry plan had gone perfectly in the first second and a half. The MZB's, distracted by the goings on in the corner, were just starting to notice that something wasn't right. Mark yelled.

"POLICE! FREEZE!"

He prayed that the MZB's would give up, but mostly he hoped they'd left Murphy outside with the unconscious man. Mark's first prayer was to go unanswered. The MZB closest to him raised a shotgun. Before he could get it up, Mark shot him twice in the chest. The shotgun dropped, but the man just stood there. All hell broke loose from behind Mark. Mark shifted his attention to the next closest MZB. He saw a muzzle flash from the man's revolver and he covered the man's center of mass with his front sight. His finger pressed the trigger, and the gun bucked in his hand. When the sight came back down, he pressed again. The man fell to the floor, as if a cable had pulled him down. The next MZB was leveling a black rifle directly at him. He raced his Colt toward the man, knowing that he had to beat him. Mark could see down the opening of the barrel of the rifle. The hole looked to be the size of a five-gallon bucket. He was too late. His sights weren't lined up. He saw the evil grin of the MZB, as his finger tightened on the trigger. Mark feared that the look on the man's face would be the last thing he would ever see. Out of the blue, the man grew a third eye. It was small and red and right in the middle of the other two. Mark realized that Ed had just saved his life. He continued to sweep the room for threats, but the only one left was one of the MZB's with a knife. He now stood behind the girl with the blade to her neck.

Mark aimed his pistol at the man's head, but he only stuck enough of it out to be able to see. Mark didn't feel confident that he could take such a close shot to the girl. She was limp in the big biker's arms. Mark didn't know if she'd been killed, injured, or if she'd just fainted. Mark decided to try and talk the man out.

"If you kill her, there's no way you're going to get out of here alive." His voice sounded funny, like he was hearing things under water. He realized that all of the gunfire had affected his hearing. "Let her go."

"You'll kill me anyway," the man shouted.

"No, we won't. Let her go, and we'll just turn you over to the police."

"You said you were the police. You're gonna kill me no matter what. You put down your guns and let me out of here with her. I'll let her go after...."

BAM!

Mark flinched at the loud noise. He saw the knife fall, then the girl, and then the man with a third of his head gone dropped to the floor. Mark looked around and saw Ed with the AR still on his shoulder with smoke snaking out of the barrel.

"That was for my sister, asshole!" he shouted at the man who would never hear the words. Then he slung the weapon like he had carried it everyday of his life and rushed over to the girl. He picked her up in his arms and started crying. "I'm sorry, Ashley. I'm sorry for not being there." His sobbing increased, and the words became unintelligible. Mark wondered how he knew the girl's name, then realized there was no way he could. Ashley must have been his sister. Victor put a hand on Ed's shoulder and led him to the bar. The bigger man moved the lantern, which miraculously had not been hit, and helped Ed place her on the counter. Victor felt for a pulse.

"I think she's okay," Victor said.

Mark looked at the girl for the first time. She appeared to be Asian. She was extremely pretty, even with a black eye and a fat lip. He couldn't tell how old she was. Between seventeen and twenty, he would guess. She had on a khaki pair of shorts and a Baylor sweatshirt.

Mark stood up. His leg must have gone to sleep while he was kneeling. He turned around and asked his team if anyone had been hit.

"Just you," Ted answered, pointing at Mark's leg.

Mark looked down and saw that his left leg was covered in blood. He took a wobbly step backwards and leaned against the wall. Scott rushed over to help him. He eased himself down to the floor with the help. He couldn't believe that it didn't hurt. Scott pulled out his knife and started cutting the fabric away from where the blood was coming from. Mark watched in fascination, as if he were seeing it on television. Rob appeared from nowhere with Manny and Joe. He ordered the unoccupied men to check for survivors, and he sent Victor to get the first aid kit. Manny, Joe, and Dwight checked all of the MZB's. Only one of them was still alive. His breathing was rapid and shallow. Before Victor could get back with the first aid kit, it had stopped. Rob kneeled down beside Mark and looked at the wound in his hamstring. Rob had him roll onto his stomach, and he finished tearing away the jeans.

"Looks like it passed right through the meat. Exit hole is the same size as the entrance. Probably a small caliber handgun. Does it hurt?"

"No. Not really."

"Well, it will. Gonna leave a nice scar, too. Something you can brag to the ladies about," Rob said, with a hint of humor in his voice.

Rob played doctor, asking for items out of the first aid kit while Scott set them out for him. Rob wiped the excess blood away from the wound, as he told Mark that he had taken out the back guard when he heard the first shot. Three of the MZB's, weapons in hand, had tried to escape out the back door, and they were now receiving their final judgment at the feet of God. No one else came out. He, Manny, and Joe had cleared the back of the house before they came in here. They didn't find anybody. Gunny was guarding the unconscious guard. Mark noticed that it was a little tender when Rob got close to the wound, especially, on the exit side. He counted the dead MZB's in the room to take his mind off the discomfort. Eleven. Seven men and four women. Too bad they hadn't given up. Mark heard Rob ask for something. He still couldn't hear too well. He looked and saw Scott hand the acting medic a bottle of alcohol.

Rob patted him on the shoulder. "This might sting a little."

Mark nodded his head. He felt the cold liquid on the back of his leg, and then it was on fire. He jerked but found that Scott was holding his shoulders down, and someone else was holding his calf. "Sting, my ass!" he yelled. "It burns like a mother fucker." As the pain subsided, he almost had to laugh. How much money did he owe his box now? He decided he'd get the money from his brother, and a new pair of pants, too.

"Worst part's over," Rob announced.

Mark felt him apply antibiotic cream and then tape gauze over the holes. "That should get you home. It's not even bleeding much. Can you stand up?"

"Yeah." Mark felt a pair of hands under each of his arms, and they pulled him to an upright position.

"Don't put any weight on that leg. I don't want it to start bleeding again."

"You got it, as long as you don't pour any more of that liquid fire on me."

"Deal," Rob smiled.

The girl was waking up. When she saw all the men in the room, she started screaming. Ed tried to grab her to keep her from falling off of the bar, but that only made things worse. Finally, she realized that these weren't the same men who had hurt her. She quieted down and looked around the room at all of the blood and the dead bodies.

Robs voice was soft and soothing. "We're not going to hurt you. What's your name?"

"Veronica," the girl answered. "Veronica Boyd."

"Hi, Veronica. I'm Rob. This is Ed." Rob put a hand on Ed's shoulder.

"Did you all kill these son's of bitches?"

"We stopped them from hurting you," Rob explained euphemistically.

"Good."

"Can you tell us what happened?"

Veronica explained that she was at home with her parents and grandfather. "Two of these guys drove up in a truck and knocked on the door wanting to know if they could trade some food for the gas in my dad's truck. He said sure, and when he went outside to get the food, they shot him. Then the rest of the gang came around the corner. They killed Mom and Grandpa and held me at gunpoint and stole everything out of the house that was worth anything. They tied me up and left two of the women to watch me. Later, they came back. Then we came back here. They drew cards to see who got me first. Two of them drew aces, and they agreed to go at the same time. I wasn't going to give up without a fight. Then the shooting started, and one of them grabbed me. He must have hit me on the head." She touched a spot on the back of her skull and drew her hand away quickly. "Next thing I remember is waking up and seeing you guys. I hope it hurt like hell when they died." She jumped down off of the bar. Then she actually spit on one of the corpses and kicked it. It looked almost comical since she was so tiny.

"Ed, why don't you take Veronica out on the front porch?" Rob suggested.

Ed nodded his head. He reached for the girl's arm, but she swung it around as soon as he touched it. Mark didn't know if it was because she didn't want to be touched after almost being raped, or if she was just very independent. Ed shrugged his shoulders and walked out of the door. She followed him.

"How did Ed do?" Rob asked once the young man was out of earshot.

"You wouldn't believe it," Dwight said. "He must have taken out five of these guys. Every person I was fixing to shoot was dead before I could pull the trigger. It sounded like his rifle was full auto."

"I know he saved my ass," Mark added. "One of the MZB's had me dead to rights, and he put one right between his eyes just in time, and he took out the guy who was using the girl for a shield, with a shot that I would never have taken. He's either real good, or real lucky, maybe both."

The other men in the room just nodded their heads.

Ed stuck his head in the door. "Gunny says the last guy is waking up."

Everyone went outside. Victor and Rob carried Mark so that he could hop on one leg like an injured football player. They stood around the man who was just starting to move a little.

"What are we going to do with him?" Ted asked.

"Turn him over to the authorities," Mark stated.

"I would think twice about that," Rob said.

"Why?"

"Because we don't know what the situation's like up here. The police are liable to detain us all for questioning. We just killed twelve people. They're not likely to just thank us and send us on our merry way, even if these guys were wanted all over the state."

"What other choice do we have?" Manny asked.

"Realistically, we let him go. Or we shoot him," he said almost as an afterthought.

"We can't shoot him," Ted argued incredulously.

"Why not?" Ed said emotionlessly. "Twelve, thirteen. What difference does it make? If we let him go, he'll just do it again."

Everyone seemed to speak at once. They all had their opinions on what to do, and no one seemed to want to listen to anyone else. The man seemed to be coming out of his stupor and listening to what was going on. Mark tried to quiet them all down after it was obvious that the argument was going nowhere.

"Listen! Quiet! SHUT UP!" It finally worked. "We vote. All in favor of turning him over to the police?"

Mark, Ted, and Joe raised their hands.

"Who wants to let him go?"

Everyone else except Rob, Veronica, and Ed voted.

"Then I guess that's what we'll..."

'BAM, BAM, BAM.' Three small holes appeared where seconds before had beat an MZB heart. The man's eyes stared disbelieving at the dark sky for a second and then closed forever.

"There's my fucking vote," Ed said, as if he'd just ordered an ice cream cone.

A chill went down Mark's back. What had happened to Ed? And where was the switch to turn him back? Mark preferred the uptight weenie to the loose cannon. At least he knew what the weenie was going to do.

"Now the only thing you have to decide is what to do with all of the bikes and guns." Ed was ice cold. Everyone looked at Mark for the answer.

"We take them. The Blazer, too," he answered. Everyone whooped and hollered.

Mark asked Manny to go get him one of the kitchen chairs to sit in. His leg was killing him.

Chapter 46

Manny went to get the chair for Mark. Everyone was standing around so keyed up from the rescue they didn't feel like they could go to sleep. The adrenaline was still pumping, and the conversation sounded adolescent.

"Man, we hit those guys so fast, they didn't even know what hit 'em," Ted said.

"You got that right, bro," Scott said, extending his hand toward Ted to get a high five. "We kicked ass and took names."

They all started fist bumping each other. Even Rob joined in the celebrating.

"Yea, though we walk through the valley of the shadow of death, we will fear no evil. For we are the baddest mothers in the whole freakin' state," Victor proclaimed, as he smiled profusely.

Ed's voice was still icy. "All we did was take out the trash, nothing more."

"Come on, my baby brother-in-law. We kicked some serious boo-tay, and rescued the damsel in distress at the same time. How can you not be happy about that? And you, bro…you were like freakin' Batman or something. I never knew you had that in you. You were the Terminator. I never saw anybody shoot so fast."

"I just did what I had to, that's all. It was like shooting fish in a barrel, nothing special about it." Ed's voice had the faintest hint of emotion in it. Mark wasn't sure what emotion it might be, though.

"Ed's right," Gunny said sternly, trying to get everyone's head back down to size. "You boys did good, but don't go gettin' too high on yourselves. You took a bunch of untrained animals by surprise and beat 'em. Big deal. Mrs. Hawkins's kindergarten class coulda done the same thing, and they wouldn'ta got the Karate Man shot in the ass."

"Ah, Gunny, I got shot in the leg," Mark corrected.

"Sorry 'bout that," the ornery old cuss said to Mark. He turned back to the men standing around and shrugged his shoulders. "Looked like an ass shot to me…"

The men erupted into laughter, as Mark turned red. "If you guys are just going to stand around and make me the butt of your jokes, why don't you load all this shit up, so we can go home at daybreak?" The laughter increased by a factor of three.

Manny returned with the chair and looked puzzled. "What did I miss?"

"Manny, grab your rifle and come with me. We'll stand guard while these guys load up, and I'll fill you in." Gunny had a mischievous smile.

Mark sat in the chair with his leg propped up on a second one Veronica had brought him, as the men loaded the trucks. They couldn't believe the things they found in the house and garage. There was enough canned food to have fed the gang of thirteen for at least a year. It wouldn't go that far at Silver Hills with over four hundred folks, but it would help some of the less fortunate get by until the gardens came in. There was also a big stash of prescription drugs. The weapons ranged from AR-15's to cheap .25 caliber pistols. They took everything. Mark was especially happy to get the AR's. There were nine of them and lots of magazines and ammunition for them also. The garage looked like the sporting goods section of Wal-Mart. In fact, that was probably where the MZB's had stolen most of the stuff. Mark had wondered why the men hadn't put the bikes in the garage, but he now understood. There just wasn't room. There were packs and packs of batteries in all sizes, flashlights, Coleman stoves and lanterns, sleeping bags, tents, and more ammunition, including several boxes of .30-30 that they were so short on. There was some fishing equipment, several car batteries, tools, motorcycle parts, and a huge supply of liquor. There were twelve five-gallon gas cans, but only seven of them had any fuel. Mark supposed the MZB's were siphoning gas out of stalled cars as they needed it. The Blazer was still full of the items they had stolen that day.

Mark talked to Veronica, who liked to be called Ronnie, as he supervised the loading, since he was forbidden to help. He found out that she was a twenty-three year old medical student at Baylor. Her father had been a Viet Nam vet, and her mother was Vietnamese. She didn't have any other relatives who lived in the states. She was understandably emotional about losing her family, but Mark had to get her to make a hard decision. He told her that they could drop her off at a shelter, leave her with some friends, or she could go back to Silver Hills with them.

She would alternate between crying uncontrollably to acting like the situation they were in was normal. During the periods when she was rational, Mark was impressed with the intelligent questions that Ronnie asked him about her options. She was most concerned about her security. After discussing the pros and cons of each choice, she agreed to go back to Silver Hills with her rescuers.

"You can bring me back for my parents' funeral, right?" she asked.

Mark was watching as the motorcycles were loaded on the trailer. Ronnie's question took him by surprise. Maybe she didn't understand how bad things really were. "Ronnie, where do you think they're going to have a funeral?"

"Down at Duncan's Funeral Home. It's all prearranged. Daddy showed me where the papers are and told me exactly what to do. He has the funeral arrangement papers, the life insurance policies, his and mom's wills…they're all together in a lockbox in his room. Dad was real good about preparing for the future. His retirement, my college, his and mom's funerals, he had them all planned out. We just have to go down to the funeral home and tell them to come and get Mom, Dad, and Grandpa. We could just call if the phones were working."

"I doubt that anyone will be there, Ronnie," Mark said.

"Oh, there will be. They have someone there twenty-four hours a day. Daddy told me. The cards they give out with the prearrangement even have an 800 number you can call from anywhere, but since the phones don't work, we'll have to go tell them," Ronnie said matter-of-factly.

Mark was now dumbfounded. In the last few hours, this girl had seen her parents murdered, been kidnapped, almost been raped and murdered, seen thirteen MZB's sent to hell in the most violent way, and she thought they could just go down to the funeral home to arrange for her parents' funeral? Maybe she was in shock. That must be it. He had to find a way to get through to her.

"Ronnie, when the guys who brought you here attacked your house, did they make a lot of noise?"

"Yes. They were shooting so much, it sounded like the Fourth of July. Why?"

"Did it seem like they were afraid of the police?"

"No."

"In fact the police never showed up in the four or five hours that you were tied up in your home, right? Even after a bunch of gun shots." Mark hoped she would be able to see where he was going.

"Right."

"Before The Burst, how long would it have taken the police to come if that had happened then?"

"Maybe five minutes," she answered, her eyes starting to fill with tears.

"So if the police can't show up in five hours, do you really believe that people are still going to be at the funeral home?"

"But Daddy told me that they always have someone there." She was crying a little. "We have to go check!"

"Ronnie, we just can't. It's way too risky to go into town. These guys put their lives on the line to save you. They put themselves at risk to come up here for my family. We can't ask them to put themselves in harm's way to check on a funeral home, so that people who are already gone can have a funeral. It just doesn't make sense. Your parents are in a better place now, and they are watching over you. I hope you can take comfort in that."

Now she was crying uncontrollably again. Mark felt terrible. He thought about how unfair all of this was. He realized that, even though it had been over six weeks since The Burst, there were probably a lot of people still in denial. Six weeks...it seemed almost a lifetime ago. So much had happened. And what would still happen? The fabric of society was deteriorating rapidly. What had he said to Ronnie? "It just doesn't make sense." Nothing did anymore.

He watched as the men carried out armload after armload of stuff. At least it would all be put to good use now. Maybe a little good came out of this, he thought. The trucks were filled to capacity, and then the Jeep's and the Trans Am's back seats were stuffed full. By five o'clock, everything was packed. Tanks were filled and places assigned. The Jeep's top and windshield were folded down now that the rain had stopped. Mark would not be able to drive, at least not anything with a clutch. Ronnie had checked his wound and changed the bandages, as it was still bleeding slightly. She forbade him to use the leg for anything, lest he open it up again. Scott volunteered to drive the Jeep. Ed insisted on riding shotgun with him. Rob said he would drive the Blazer, and Mark decided to ride with him. He wanted to talk with the retired police officer anyway. Ronnie elected to ride with Manny.

The clouds started clearing, and the temperature fell as it got closer to dawn. Gunny and Mark decided on a new route home. It was a little longer, but they didn't want to take a chance that the roadblock was manned. At the first hint of pink in the sky, the convoy headed out. Mark actually enjoyed riding in the Chevrolet. It rode better than the Jeep, and the seats were more comfortable. There was even room to stretch out his injured leg. It was really throbbing now, and the Tylenol only took the edge off. There were plenty of pain meds in the

MZB loot. Mark recognized some of the names, but no one in the group knew the correct dosage, and he didn't want to take a chance on getting groggy. He and Rob spent lots of time talking, and that helped keep his mind off of his leg.

They talked about rescuing Ronnie and how they might have to do the same thing again. Mark asked if Rob could spare the time to work with them on dynamic entries and building clearing. Rob said he would gladly trade his knowledge for some from the 'Silver Hills gang.' Ed was another subject Mark brought up. He asked Rob if he'd ever seen anyone transform so quickly. Rob said that he had, but it was always the other way. There had been a few guys he had worked with who thought they were high speed, low drag, but turned into blithering idiots the first time they had real bullets zinging by. He'd never seen anyone go from zero to hero like Ed had. They discussed training the county militia, about some of the ideas Gunny and Mark had come up with on the way up to Waco, and how Curt could best implement them. Mark wanted to know how Rob had met Curt.

"After I left the SAPD, I started a consulting firm for small police departments and sheriff's offices that wanted training on SWAT tactics. Curt called me up one day, and we had lunch. We've been friends ever since."

"That's neat," Mark said. "How come you left the force? Did you get injured?"

"No. It wasn't an injury. You see, I wanted to be a SWAT officer ever since the show came on in the seventies. Did you ever watch it?"

"Did I?" Mark started singing the theme song. "It was one of my favorite shows. I even still have the music on a 45 somewhere in the house."

Both men laughed.

"Anyway, I was living the dream. I worked my way up from team member, to training officer, to SWAT commander. We had one of the best teams in the country. We would go to competitions, and we almost always won. I loved it. But I started to see a shift in the department's policy on how to use us. They bought us new black uniforms that didn't say 'POLICE' on them anywhere. We started going as backup on drug raids, and then they started using us to actually do the raids. We were doing a bunch of no-knock warrants, busting some big time drug dealers and getting a bunch of scum off of the street. That is, until the revolving door courts let them right out. Anyway, one night somebody made a mistake on the address on a drug warrant. We busted down the door of this house, handcuffed and dragged a half-naked man and his wife out onto the front lawn, while his children and neighbors watched, and ransacked his house looking for six kilos of cocaine. When we couldn't find anything, the narcotics lieutenant realized we had the wrong house. He was real worried that the city might be sued and that he'd get into trouble. When I was uncuffing the couple and apologizing to them, one of the narcotics officers just "happened" to find a bag of marijuana in the house that we had "somehow missed" in our thorough search. They arrested the man and took him in. He swore that it wasn't his. I believed him. I went to my superiors with it, and later the charges were dropped, but it didn't change the department's attitude about using SWAT to execute no-knocks. I was having trouble squaring some of what we were doing against the Constitution anyway. That was just kind of the straw that broke the camel's back, so I resigned and started my consulting business."

"I see. So how did you get involved in Promise Point?"

"Curt told me about it. We'd talked a few times about preparedness. He said he had this land developer friend, Greg, who was starting a new subdivision that would be totally self-reliant if things went bad. I was interested, met Greg, liked the concept, and bought in. Our group put me in charge of security, like you all did with Gunny, and you know the rest."

Around 9:30, the convoy was approaching a small town, and they tightened up their formation, as had become their custom. They saw quite a few people obviously walking to church in their dress clothes. Most were traveling in large groups. The walkers seemed apprehensive about the convoy until the drivers and passengers waved. The churchgoers would then wave vigorously in reply. Most of the men, and even some of the women, were carrying rifles, and Mark supposed that many had pistols under their coats as well.

"Looks funny to see people carrying rifles to church," Rob said.

"It does, but I'd say it's smart. I noticed there were some pretty nice weapons, too," Mark replied.

"Kind of gives a whole new meaning to the term 'Sunday best,' huh?"

"Yeah," Mark laughed. "I was wondering if it was a sin to go to church with a dirty rifle. You know, cleanliness is next to Godliness. I just never imagined that it applied to weapons."

"I'd say that a dirty rifle could get you a face to face meeting with God real quick, nowadays."

That was true. Mark had almost found out the hard way.

It appeared the men in the other vehicles were having fun with the same topic. Dwight's voice came over the radio. "Hey guys, do you think God prefers AR-15's or AK-47's?"

"That's a theological question that has divided scholars for years." Manny's answer came over the little Motorola radio. "That's why we have different denominations. Didn't you see the names on the churches? Assembly of AR's, Church of the AK, and the ever popular St. Winchester Cathedral."

Mark and Rob laughed. Mark knew that Manny was just trying to be funny, but some people did take their zeal for one type of weapon or another to a fanatical level. In fact, divisions along weapon preference lines made about as much or more sense than some of the things people let divide them religiously.

"In my experience, God loves all hard chargers and straight shooters," Gunny's Drill Instructor voice crackled over the airwaves. "Now, you boys keep the chatter down."

"Amen, Brother Gunny," Mark answered.

The two men talked more about their families and what they thought this crisis would bring to the country and their little corner of it, of how nothing would ever be the same at it was, and how that could be either good or bad. Gradually, the talk died down, and Mark was left to think about things that were troubling him.

First and foremost was his family. If only Mike had left the route in the cache, he would be able to find them, but Mark understood why he didn't do it. If anyone saw him bury the barrels or somehow found the route, they would figure they took the best stuff with them, and they might be willing to track them down and kill them for it.

337

His second biggest concern was now Ed. He was glad the guy had stopped being a weenie, but he didn't quite know how he should handle what he had become. Mark wasn't really upset that he'd killed the last MZB. The asshole had it coming for sure, but if Ed couldn't go along with group decisions, that might cause a major problem down the road. Mark certainly didn't want it to turn into a 'Jon' situation. He would have to heed Gunny's advice and find a way to work it out with him.

Mark was also a little nervous about all of the stolen property they were carrying. He knew that if he had just left it there, most probably another group of MZB's would have ended up with it, but it might be hard to explain to a law enforcement agency, especially if some of it was traceable back to an owner who was taking a premature dirt nap. But, obviously, the police were not out in abundance.

He was also concerned with Ronnie. Would she be like Donna and try to take her own life in her grief? Or would she pull through? Mark had to make sure they kept a close eye on her.

It was approaching noon, and Mark heard Rob's stomach rumble. The new route was much longer, and they weren't even halfway home with all of the detours. The smaller roads also had more curves in them that caused Scott to have to slow down a lot to check for traps. Mark called on the radio and suggested that Scott stop for lunch at the next place he thought was appropriate. Ten minutes later, the group was standing around, warming up some soup on one of the Coleman stoves. Everyone was still a little on the giddy side from the successful raid. Mark asked Manny how Ronnie was doing. He was told that she was crying a lot, but she seemed to be accepting things for the way they were. Everyone ate and took advantage of the stop. Scott was smart enough to realize that, since they now had a female with them, they needed a place were everyone could conduct their business in private. He had stopped where there was a thick grove of trees and bushes nearby.

Mark checked with Scott on how Ed was doing. He told him that Ed wasn't saying much, but when he did talk, it was about how wrong he had been about everything. Scott felt he was somewhat withdrawn, but that he would probably be okay. At least he appeared to be warming up a little as the day wore on.

After everyone was done eating, they continued on their way. Not long after lunch, Scott came up on a large tree that had been felled across the road. Upon inspection, it was not an ambush point. Manny hypothesized that it was probably just some locals trying to discourage travelers from going past their houses. They plotted a new route around and resumed their trek. Less than an hour later, they came to a bridge that was out. Again, it was scouted and found to be a benign impediment. The bridge was over a dry creek bed on a gravel road, and the sides of the creek bed weren't very steep. All of the vehicles except for the Trans Am could have made it easily through the problem area. Rob was curious about what took the bridge out, since there hadn't been any big rains since The Burst. Gunny said that it looked like someone used explosives. He figured they either had some dynamite or made some anfo. They discussed pulling the Pontiac through with a tow strap but decided that whoever didn't want anyone coming through might have more surprises up the road. Again, they re-plotted a route and continued on. Each detour was taking them farther and farther out of the way and delaying their arrival home. Mark's leg down to the knee, and now his left glute were throbbing unremittingly. There was no position that relieved the pain to any degree. It was, however, keeping him awake, even though he was dog-tired. He had to nudge Rob a few times, as the hot meal, lack of sleep, and gradually warming temperature were starting to have an effect on the driver. He and Rob cracked the windows a little to let some fresh air into the truck.

The convoy had found a way through to the minor highway that they needed to move them mostly south again. Finally, they were making good time. The road traveled through mostly rural farmland and ranches. Houses were few and far between, with long driveways leading up to them. A few of the houses had been burned, and others looked deserted. Some were obviously being lived in. They had the gates blocked off in various ways. Cattle guards were removed like they were drawbridges. Otherwise useless vehicles were blocking driveways. Gates were closed, locked, and reinforced with anything that could be pushed, piled, or stacked in front of them. Some of the properties had guards who were visible, and Mark expected that many had guards who weren't.

They were at the bottom of a hill with a long, slow grade up in front of them. Mark saw the Jeep disappear over the top without slowing down. Probably Scott was getting tired and sleepy, too. He was about to call the Jeep on the radio to caution him when he heard gunfire.

Mark looked at Rob and saw the man staring back at him with wide eyes. Rob punched the accelerator on the Blazer, and the big truck responded instantly. They were fourth in the line behind the big, red, Ford diesel and Manny's Suburban that was pulling the trailer. Mark called on the radio to Scott and Ed, but got no answer. The firing was increasing in intensity each second. The Blazer rocketed past Manny and then Victor. When they were just below the crest of the hill, Rob slammed on the brakes and stopped the truck. A second later, Jim's truck was right behind them. Rob was out and running toward the top of the hill with his rifle before Mark's injured leg would let him dismount the lifted four by four. Mark had his FAL and a canvas tool bag of magazines and half hobbled, half ran, as quickly as he could behind Rob. Dwight, with an AK, caught up to him just before they got to the top.

Rob was lying on the ground and crawling the last few feet. Mark and Dwight copied him. When Rob got to where he could see, he started pouring fire over the hill. When Mark finally pulled himself to where he could see, it put a huge knot in the pit of his stomach.

The Jeep was sideways in the road in front of a barricade built out of railroad ties. There were at least eight ambushers firing at the listing vehicle from small firing ports in the barricade. Scott was slumped over the steering wheel, not moving. Ed was behind the scout vehicle, using it for cover as best he could. From the fire being applied to the Jeep, there was no way for Ed to return any fire. There were several vehicles on each side of the road that had been caught in this trap. Mark lined up his rifle and disengaged the safety. He sighted in on one of the portholes that had a rifle sticking out and squeezed the trigger several times. The man either ducked back down or was hit, as the rifle disappeared from the port. Mark swung his weapon to search for a new target. He could hear Rob and Dwight firing rapidly. The three of them were more concerned with keeping some pressure on the attackers, so that Scott and Ed might have a chance. The MZB's started to return fire to the top of the hill. Mark and Dwight were right next to Rob, and he instructed them to space out when the bullets starting zinging off of the pavement in front of them. Mark rolled to the right, and he saw Dwight scramble to the left. When Mark was about five yards away from Rob, he looked behind him and saw Victor, Manny, and Joe running up to join them. The Trans Am was just arriving where the other vehicles were parked. He turned his attention back to the front and started firing at the ambushers again. Mark noticed the man he thought he might have hit was firing again. The MZB's had planned their ambush perfectly. The cover the railroad ties gave them seemed invincible. His twenty-round magazine was empty before he knew it. He had left the bag with his spares over next to Rob. He backed up a little, so he was out of the line of sight of the MZB's, and crawled back to the bag. Victor, Manny, and Joe were now teeming fire at the attackers. With six of them now attacking the barricade, the Jeep was taking little fire. Ed seemed to sense this and started running for the hilltop.

"Cover him!" Rob yelled.

The now eight riflemen, since Gunny and Ted had arrived, rained .22 and .30 caliber projectiles on the barricade as fast as they could. Ed was running for all he was worth and had made it almost half of the hundred and fifty yards he needed to reach safety, when the torrent of suppression fire dwindled to a trickle. Everyone needed to reload at almost the same time. Mark reached for a new mag and struggled to get it seated. A few seconds later, he started firing. He hoped the rate of fire would pick up, but it seemed that the others were having more trouble reloading than he did. Without as much enfilade, the MZB firing picked up. Mark saw Ed stumble when a bullet hit him in the leg. He managed to keep his footing and continued to run, although not nearly as fast.

"COME ON! COME ON! COME ON!" Mark yelled, not only to Ed, but also to get the others to start firing again.

Mark pulled his trigger as fast as he could while still ensuring that he was hitting the barricade. Ed was having more trouble staying up with each step. Mark tore through his third twenty-round magazine. He reached in the bag and grabbed another. As he was replacing the empty one, he saw another bullet rip through Ed. His shirt began to turn red on the right side of his stomach. He staggered and fell only twenty or thirty yards away.

"NO!" Manny screamed.

"COVER ME!" Victor yelled.

"NO VICTOR…WAIT!" Rob hollered.

It was too late. Victor was running for his wounded brother-in-law, as the men on top of the hill gave him covering fire. Victor covered the distance in a flash. He grabbed Ed under the arms and dragged him back over the hill. Mark concentrated on making every shot count. He saw two weapons pulled back through the firing ports just after he shot at them, and one of the MZB's dropped his rifle to the front. Mark figured he must have hit the SOB. Victor's strength was obvious, as he dragged his brother-in-law back out of the line of fire in just a few seconds.

The shots from the MZB's decreased dramatically with no easy targets visible. All of the Silver Hills residents rushed to Ed's side. Rob started assessing Ed's wounds and tried to get the bleeding under control. Gunny instructed Dwight and Joe to watch the MZB's.

"If'n them sum bitches come out to raid the Jeep, wait till they's almost there, then nail 'em," he said.

Rob sent Victor to get Ronnie and the first aid kit. He had Mark hold his hand over the stomach wound to try to reduce the flow of blood. Ed was turning paler and complaining of being cold. Rob had Ted hold the victim's feet up. Ed, though told to be quiet, wouldn't stop talking.

"We topped the hill, and there was the barricade. Scott hit the brakes, and the Jeep skidded to a halt, but it was too late. They started firing, and they hit Scott in the head before he could get shifted into reverse. I'm sorry I couldn't save him. I was firing as fast as I could. His foot slipped off of the brake and we started rolling closer. I pulled the emergency brake and got behind the Jeep. I don't know how they didn't hit me before I got out. Where's Manny?" The young hero looked from side to side, as his face got paler and his lips turned blue. "I have to tell him something."

"I'm here, Ed," Manny said, as he moved closer to his son-in-law.

Victor had returned with Ronnie. She knelt down beside Mark and pulled his hands away from Ed. Thick black blood poured from the hole in his stomach each time he breathed in. She replaced Mark's blood covered hands over the wound and turned to Rob. Mark saw her shake her head.

"Manny, I'm sorry I wasn't the man you wanted me to be. Tell Letty that I'm sorry. Tell her that I love her. Tell Robby that I'm proud of him and that I want him to grow up into the kind of man I wasn't."

"You'll tell them yourself when we get you home," Manny said, tears pouring down his cheeks.

Ed's eyes were getting glassy. If he heard his father-in-law, he didn't acknowledge it. He looked at Ronnie and started whispering to her. "It's okay now, Ashley. You'll be safe. I got there to save you this time." He paused and drew in a ragged breath. "I think it might have saved me, too." A small smile was on his blue lips. His eyes stared distantly at the sky. It took Mark a minute to realize he was dead.

"Son of a bitch!" Mark yelled. He looked at the other men and removed his blood-covered hands from Ed's body. Every eye had tears in it, even Gunny's.

"Gunny, these mother fuckers have to pay." Mark didn't care how much money his mouth cost him right now. "How are we gonna kill these assholes?"

Gunny looked up at Joe. "What are they doin', Joe?"

"They're holding tight. I think they know we're still here. But that's not the worst of it, Gunny. I saw one of them stand up for a second, and he had on an army helmet and some kind of bulletproof vest."

"Was the vest black or camouflage?"

"It was camo," the overweight lookout reported.

"How about the helmet?"

"It was green," Joe answered quickly.

"No, not the color, the shape. Did it have a straight lip all the way around, or did it get lower around the ears and in the back?"

"I don't remember. I think it's too far for me to tell that, anyway."

"Probably those new fangled Kevlar helmets and flak vests," the old Marine said to the group. He looked at Ted. "Would you go get me my ruck out of your back seat?"

"You got it, Gunny." Ted ran down toward his car.

"How many are there, Joe?"

"I only see six weapons sticking out of the holes. I don't know if that's all or not."

"Karate Man, you got your binoculars?"

"No, Gunny. They're in the Jeep," Mark answered.

"I have a small pair. I'll get them," Rob offered, as he ran to the Blazer.

A moment later, Ted and Rob were back.

"OK, here's what we're gonna do. Karate Man is gonna spot for me. Give him the field glasses. I'm gonna go from right to left. I need you all to cover everyone 'cept who I'm firing at. When I get one and am ready to move to the next one, Karate Man will tell you all. Then, leave that one alone, so he don't move on me. Don't just blow through your ammo, either. Just keep enough pressure on them so's they can't get a good shot off," Gunny explained. "Everyone understand?"

"Gunny, how are you going to shoot through the barricade and through body armor?" Manny asked.

"I ain't gonna shoot through the barricade. Them firing ports are 'bout 12 by 24. I'ma shootin' through them. And…" The old man rummaged around in his pack. He pulled out a Garand clip filled with ammo. The bullets looked like normal full metal jacket ammunition. The only difference Mark could see was the tips were painted black. "…this should take care of the body armor."

Mark could see a big, evil grin cross Rob's face. "AP?" the ex-SWAT commander asked.

"Yep," Gunny said, returning the grin.

"AP? What's AP?" Manny asked.

"AP stands for Armor Piercing," Rob said.

Everyone in the circle now shared the grin with each other. They all took their places to execute Gunny's plan. Mark had the binoculars and lay down beside the old warhorse. Gunny pulled out several more of the specially loaded clips and set them down beside him. He then used his rucksack for a rest and spent a minute getting into a comfortable position. When he was ready, he told Mark to tell the others. They started firing on the barricade.

"Okay, Karate Man, I'm shooting for about six inches to my right of the weapon. Tell me where they hit." Mark heard Gunny take in a deep breath and blow part of it out. His Garand barked.

"Eighteen inches low and about a foot left," Mark reported.

The dog faced Marine made an adjustment to his sights. He aimed and shot again.

"OK. Dead on the windage. Still a little low. Maybe eight or nine inches."

Mark reported that the third shot was only three inches low, and he saw Gunny raise the back sight another click. When the ancient battle rifle went off this time, a scoped hunting rifle came tumbling out of the firing port.

"You got him!" Mark yelled, as he slapped the shooter on the back. "Next target!" Mark informed the covering team.

Gunny shifted his position slightly and readied himself. It only took one shot for this unlucky MZB. Gunny swung to the next. His first shot missed, and Mark heard him curse himself under his breath. The next shot found its mark.

"Great job," Mark bragged.

Gunny moved his aim to the fourth firing hole. Mark heard the shot, then a loud 'ping.' He had become accustomed to hearing gunshots, but the metallic sound of the Garand spitting out the empty clip actually made him jump. He laughed at himself. Gunny pushed a fresh clip into the weapon and quickly removed his hand before the bolt could mash his thumb. He settled back down into his position and shot the fifth MZB.

At that point, all firing stopped from the barricade, and Mark saw two camo-clad individuals start running away. The firing from the covering team increased, as they shot at the MZB's attempting to retreat. One didn't make it fifty yards. The second got about a hundred out from the barricade before Gunny's Garand ended his escape attempt.

A collective cheer went up. Mark thought it strange that they would be so happy to see a person shot. He felt guilty about the joy in his heart and the rejoicing in his throat at another human's death, but these weren't really humans; they were predators who lived off the death of others. They had to be killed, lest they kill more decent people. These thoughts made Mark feel better about what they'd just done, but a small doubt still remained in his mind. He pushed the thoughts out of his head. He didn't want to think about it. He just wanted to be happy that these animals were dead.

Gunny made them watch and wait thirty minutes before they sent a team down to recon the barricade. Ronnie took that time to look after Mark's leaking leg. She repatched it, as she chewed his butt for reopening the wound. When the recon team got to the barricade, the MZB's were all dead. The combination of the railroad ties, the sandbags stacked behind them, and the body armor and Kevlar helmets had precluded any wounding shots. All of the MZB's had been shot in the face, the neck, or through the helmet by Gunny's AP ammo.

Scott's body was riddled with bullets. Thankfully, he had gone fast, according to Ed's account, and hadn't suffered. They wrapped his body, and Ed's, in two of the captured sleeping bags, and made room for them in Jim's truck. When they placed the bodies in the vehicle that would give them their last ride, a soberness passed through all of the travelers. Gunny saluted the bodies, and everyone else followed his lead.

When Mark was told of his Jeep's condition, he felt as though he'd lost another friend. Everything was so shot up that almost nothing was salvageable. However, the newly installed electrical parts were undamaged, and Mark asked the men to remove them. They did, unloaded the vehicle of anything else they deemed as repairable, and pushed the carcass into the ditch.

The MZB weapons and ammunition were collected. Some were on the junky side, but most were of good quality and could be put to good use. They also took all the flak jackets and helmets, even the ones with the neat little .30 caliber holes in them. A small argument precipitated about what to do with the MZB bodies. Mark decided that they weren't worth the gasoline it would take to burn them, and burying them was out of the question.

"Besides," he said, quoting one of his favorite lines from *The Outlaw, Josey Wales*, "buzzards gotta eat, same as worms."

That ended the argument. The big, red Ford was used to push the barricade down, and the convoy continued home with Rob riding point on one of the Harleys. The rest of the trip home was very quiet. Ronnie drove the Blazer, but she and Mark barely shared a word the rest of the trip. When they got to the Silver Hills gate, it occurred to Mark that he might have aged twenty years in the last two days.

Chapter 47

They drove through the gate and straight up to Mark's house. Jess and the kids were outside before Mark could exit the Blazer. As soon as they saw him and the blood on his pants, they bombarded him with questions.

"What happened? Are you okay?"

"Where are Grandma and Grandpa and everybody?"

"Where's the Jeep?"

"Where did you get the motorcycles?"

They came so rapidly that he couldn't answer. "Slow down," he said. "One at a time. I'm fine. It's just a flesh wound in my leg. Grandma, Grandpa, Uncle Mike, Aunt Monica, and their families left ten days ago to walk here. The Jeep is ruined, and the motorcycles are a long story. Help me down, and I'll fill everyone in."

David helped his father down. Mark saw people coming from all over the neighborhood to find out about the trip. He saw Letty and Robby running from Manny's house. Manny caught them before they got to the crowd and talked to them for a minute. Mark saw Letty fall into her father's arms, and Robby just stood there shaking. Mark noticed that Jess and his kids were watching, too.

"What happened, Dad?" Sam asked.

"Mr. Simmons and Mr. Washburn didn't make it," Mark said.

"Oh, my God," Jess exclaimed. "What happened?"

"They ran into a road block and were killed by the guys manning it."

"Is that where you got hurt?" David asked.

"No. That was last night. I'll fill you in later. Right now, I have to talk to Mrs. Simmons." Mark saw Scott's wife coming up the road. He moved toward her, and waved her over. "Roberta."

"Hi, Mark. What happened to you?"

"It's nothing, just a scratch really. Listen, I need to talk to you."

"Let me say hello to Scott first, alright?"

"Roberta, I need to talk to you about Scott. We ran into some bad luck. Scott and Ed Washburn were riding point in the Jeep when they ran into a roadblock. The guys who set it up started shooting at them, and they were both severely wounded."

The woman stared at Mark and blinked her eyes several times. "But Scott's going to be okay, right?"

"No, Roberta. We weren't able to save him. I'm so sorry."

Roberta shook her head. "No. I don't believe it. You're lying. He can't be dead. He promised to help me with our garden tomorrow." She spoke faster and faster until she broke down into tears. She fell onto Mark and buried her face into his chest. He had to step back on his injured leg to support the weight she had suddenly thrown onto him. It hurt him, and he quietly winced. She kept talking, even though he could barely make out what she said. "I begged him not to go. I was afraid something would happen, and now it has. He said he had to go. He would have followed you to hell and back, Mark Turner." Suddenly she stopped sobbing and pulled away from Mark. The look in her eyes was full of hate. "It's your fault, damn you. He only went because of you. And now he's dead. It's all your fault!" She turned and ran back toward her house.

The words cut through him like a knife. He had told Jess this would happen just yesterday morning. He'd gotten people killed and now everyone would hold him responsible. At least he wouldn't have to be 'the leader' anymore, he thought.

"Don't worry," Jess said, as she slid under her husband's arm. "She's just upset, and she has to blame someone. It's not your fault. It was just bad luck."

Mark looked over to where Manny, Letty, and Robby were standing. Manny now had the young boy in his arms, and Letty was hugging Ronnie, and they were crying together. Gunny was talking to a group of men with Rob, and the other travelers were gathering up their gear and heading home.

"Let's go down to the clinic," Jess encouraged. "You can unload your stuff later. I want Lisa to look at that leg."

Mark followed his wife to the Olsen house, with his kids supporting him on each side. He gave them the abbreviated version of the trip. When they got to the clinic, Lisa had him remove his pants and lay on his stomach. He was a little self-conscious about being in his shorts in front of his best friend's wife, but he continued to talk about the trip to try to cover up any embarrassment that might show. Lisa uncovered the wound and probed it from each side. She asked him a few questions, the most relevant to him being how much pain he was in. She gave him a painkiller to swallow and a big shot of antibiotics in his good hip. Then the wound was cleaned and dressed.

"You'll be fine, Mark. The bullet cut a clean hole through the muscle. Whoever patched you up did a good job. You'll be running again in two weeks." The nurse winked at him and then gave Jess a nod and a smile to let her know that she didn't need to worry.

"Thanks, Lisa," Mark said as he started to get up.

"Whoa there, cowboy. You've got to stay here for thirty minutes, so I can make sure you don't have a reaction to the antibiotics I gave you."

"Okay," Mark agreed wearily. "Can I at least get a blanket or something to cover up my half-naked butt?"

Lisa got a clean sheet and covered her patient, as he continued to talk about the trip with his family.

"Where did you get the motorcycles from, Dad?" David asked.

"The MZB's who kidnapped Veronica were driving them." Mark's eyes were halfway closed as he answered the questions. "Them and the Blazer. After we rescued Ronnie...that's what she likes to be called...Ronnie..." His eyes closed to the point where they were mere slits. "...anyway I didn't see any reason to...you know...just leave them there. Soooooo..." Both eyes were completely closed now. "...I decided...well, we all...decided...that..."

When Mark opened his eyes, he was in the room all by himself. He couldn't believe everyone had been so rude to leave in the middle of his story. Had it been that boring? The propane lantern Lisa had used when she checked his leg was still burning, but it had been turned down, so that it only produced a pale, yellow light. It allowed him to see a stack of clean clothes on a chair. He wondered where they came from, and his mind started making sense of the situation. He must have fallen asleep, and someone brought him some clothes and took all of the dirty ones. But how long had he been out? It looked like they had taken his watch and other personal items, as well. He got up, slowly, when the pain in his leg reminded him that he was injured, and pulled on the garments that had been left for him. He found a small flashlight in a pocket and turned it on, then extinguished the lantern. When he stepped outside, the sky was brilliant with stars, and a cool breeze was blowing from the north. He walked home, without seeing anyone, as quickly as his stiff leg would let him. The house was dark inside, and he used the flashlight to navigate to his bedroom. The windup alarm clock said 4:15. He crawled under the covers and snuggled up next to his wife.

"Hey, how are you doing?" she asked groggily.

"Okay, I reckon."

"Does your leg hurt?"

"Not too much, as long as I keep it still."

"Lisa left some more pain pills, if you need them, and some oral antibiotics that she wants you to take for five days," she informed him, her voice sounding a little more awake.

"I'm okay right now. Sorry about falling asleep on you all."

"That's okay." She propped herself up on her elbow. "Did you think about us keeping the boys?"

"Not really." Did she have to bring this up now?

"But you promised that you would." Her voice had that disappointed edge to it that he hated.

"I'm sorry." He really wasn't, and it was obvious by his tone. "I was a little busy."

"I know that," she snapped back. "But it's important for them to know where they're going to be staying."

"Well, excuse me for thinking that getting shot and two men dying was more important." His voice had gone up in both volume and pitch. He really didn't want to argue about this right now.

"I didn't say they weren't, did I? It's just that I think this is important, too," she said emphatically.

To the untrained ear, it might sound like she was trying to continue the argument, but Mark knew from twenty years' experience that this was her way of giving him a chance to back out gracefully. He took it. "I'm sorry, Hun. I know it's important. Okay if we talk about it in the morning?"

"That's fine," she said somewhat shortly, just so he would know that she was still a little bit ticked at him.

He wanted to smooth things out, but he fell asleep before he could think of anything to say.

When he opened his eyes this time, there was a faint light seeping through the curtains. He looked at the clock and saw that both hands were between the six and the seven. He got up, got dressed, and hobbled outside.

"Morning, buddy," Jim greeted him. He was sitting at one of the picnic tables with a big mug of coffee. "How's the leg?"

"Seems better this morning," Mark lied, as Jim ducked into the kitchen, returning a minute later with a matching mug for his friend.

347

"Gunny filled us in on everything last night. Too bad you missed your family. You think they'll be here in the next few days?" Jim asked.

"Mike said they would be here in ten or fifteen days. That was eleven days ago. It's at least a hundred and eighty miles from Waco to here. That means they'd have to hike twelve to eighteen miles a day. That's a lot when you have small children and are carrying heavy packs. I think they'd be lucky to make half that. I'm not looking for them to be here until the middle of next month, if they make it at all."

"You don't think they will?"

"I'm hopeful, but I have to be realistic. It's getting bad out there. Everywhere, really. I mean, I've been in three firefights in as many days. How much worse can it get? Anyway, if they only packed enough food for fifteen days, what are they going to do when it runs out? And that's assuming they make it that long. If they run into a big group of MZB's, I don't know how they'll survive. I would say their chances are fifty-fifty at best. If only Mike had left me the route they were going to take, we could have picked them up. Now Scott and Ed are dead for nothing, Roberta blames me, and Letty probably does, too, and they have every right. I shouldn't have risked their lives for some wild goose chase. Now everyone will see that I'm just as fallible as the next guy."

"It wasn't some wild goose chase. Remember that these guys were only doing for you what you have and would do for them. And it's not your fault they got killed. Gunny said they got careless for a minute. If they had slowed down like they were supposed to when they topped a hill, they would still be alive. We all have to remember that one little mistake can get us killed now. Plus, you saved the girl. Roberta may blame you, but no one else does."

"I should have made everybody stop and rest for a while. I could see that Rob was getting sleepy, and I should have known that the others were, too."

"Mark, you're not a mind reader. It's not your job to know everything. If Ed and Scott were getting too sleepy to do their job, then they should have gotten on the radio and told you. You said it the other day, we all have to take responsibility for our own safety."

"I suppose," Mark half-heartedly agreed.

"Anyway, that's quite a haul of loot y'all brought back. It should all come in handy, might even save someone's life. We unloaded everything and put it in your shed last night. Sorry you lost the Jeep."

"Me, too," Mark said distantly. He was thinking of all the things he had to get done today.

"Listen, Mark. I know you probably have a lot on your mind, but there's a problem that I think you should know about."

"What is it?"

"Craig Banks was seen coming out of Joe Bagwell's house while y'all were gone."

Mark didn't want to believe what that probably meant. "Well, maybe he was just helping Connie with something while Joe was gone," he said hopefully.

"At four o'clock in the morning?"

Mark's eyes got wide. "How do you know this?"

"Mary Patterson told Lisa. She said the slightest sound wakes her up, and they live right across the street from Joe and Connie. And evidently, it's not the first time she's seen it," Jim explained.

"Well, that's just great. Joe told me that he and his wife have been having trouble. I guess it's worse than he thinks it is. I suppose the whole neighborhood knows?"

"Pretty much. You know how the rumor mill around here is."

"Yeah, I do. Does Susan know?" Mark asked.

"I don't think so. What do you think we should do?"

"I don't know. I'll have to think about it." He changed the subject. "How did it go with the windmill?"

"Good. We got the electric pump pulled out and set the tower up over the well. The only problem we ran into was that Manny's well is about fifty feet deeper than the one the windmill came from. Chaparo had plenty of pipe to lower the pump, but he didn't have anything to use to lengthen the pump rod. Greg knows a guy in Floresville who deals in water systems. We drove over to see him, and he had the pump rods, plus a big twenty-seven hundred gallon tank we can pump into, but he doesn't want cash. Silver or trade only. He wanted $100 in silver, and of course we don't have that much. We talked about trading for an SKS and five hundred rounds of ammo, and he seemed agreeable, but I didn't want to make that deal without checking with you first. He went ahead and gave us the pump rod on credit, and we need the trailer to get the tank anyway. I figured we could go by after the meeting with the sheriff today."

"Crap. I forgot about that. What time are we supposed to be there?"

"At ten. Just like last week. Anyway, we got the thing pumping yesterday. With a ten mile an hour wind it puts out a little better than two gallons a minute. That's pretty slow compared to the eight gallons a minute that your pump puts out, but it should at least keep us in drinking water. Chaparo said that if we could elevate the tank about eight feet, it should give us decent pressure, and he thinks he has enough PVC to run a line down the center of the subdivision with a spigot at each street. Then people won't have to schlep water all the way from your house."

"That sounds great," Mark said.

"And if we do get the tank all the way filled, we can use the overflow to refill the three swimming pools where people have been getting water to flush their toilets."

"Good plan. Hey, did someone take Rob home?"

"No. He took the Harley he'd been riding. Said he'd give it back to us at the meeting this morning," Jim explained.

"I'm going to give it to him, along with a couple of the guns we captured. Would you pick out the nicest AR and one of the pistols for him?"

"You got it."

"What about Ronnie? The girl we brought back. Where is she?"

"She went home with Manny and his family."

"Good," Mark said.

"While we were in town, we found some old pipe to buy, and Chaparo used it to finish the guard towers."

"That's great."

The two men talked of other things for a few minutes and then decided to fix breakfast for everyone. When it was ready, they rounded up everyone for a nice sit-down meal. Mark especially enjoyed having a 'normal' morning. When David asked about when they could expect his Grandma and Grandpa and everyone else, Mark was honest about the long odds they faced. He did it as gently as he could, but he didn't leave anyone with unrealistic hopes. He encouraged them to pray for the group, for God to protect them and provide for them. Sam suggested they say a prayer right then. They did. The mood was quite somber for the duration of the breakfast.

When breakfast was over, George found Mark alone and asked him to talk privately for a minute. The two men walked outside and across the street to where one of the community gardens was. George had a notebook under his arm that Mark had often seen him carry. Mark figured that he wrote down what, when, and where everything was planted. The corn was coming up nicely in this field. George smiled as he ran his hands over the tops of the tender stalks.

"Mark, I need to share something with you, but you have to promise me that you won't tell anyone else," George said.

He probably wants to tell me about Craig and Connie's affair, Mark thought. "Sure, George. No problem."

"Mark, I have cancer. They found it about two weeks before The Burst. I was working up the nerve to tell Alice and Lisa, and then the lights went out and changed everything. Before you say anything, I decided before The Burst that I didn't want any treatment. It's in my pancreas, and even with an operation and chemo, my chances were less than five percent to make it past a year. The doctors said I would have five or six good months without treatment, and that's what I chose. I can't bear the thought of everyone treating me like I'm sick. Sooner or later, Lisa will figure it out, but until then, I want to keep it quiet. They gave me some pain medication that works pretty good and still allows me to function, but I'm almost out. I'm telling you this because I need a favor."

Mark was almost in shock. "Anything I can do, George."

"Can you see if the doctor in town can get some more pain meds? Here's my prescription."

"Of course I will, George."

"Thanks, Mark, and thanks for coming to pick us up out of that shelter, too. I know that The Burst has been a huge tragedy for so many people, but to me, it's been a godsend. I get to see my grandbabies everyday and spend time with my daughter. Gunny and Abby have become great friends to Alice and me, and I've gotten to work in the soil again. I couldn't have asked for more."

Mark fought back the tears. If the neighborhood wanted a John Wayne, here he was. Mark wished he had half the courage of this man. "George, your secret is safe with me. If you need anything else, just let me know." He put his hand on the man's shoulder and squeezed gently.

"I want you to take this. I've written down everything I can think of that you might need to know about farming. It's all in here. I hope it's useful."

Mark took the notebook and hugged it to him. "Thank you, George. It'll be really useful. This will keep us going when those who aren't as fortunate have nothing to eat. This is the greatest gift anyone could ever give." As hard as he tried not to cry, he felt a tear roll down his cheek.

350

"Enough of that," George scolded. "Don't make me sorry I told you."

"Yes, sir."

They looked over the other crops in the field. George took great pride in pointing out how well they were doing. After a while, Mark headed back to his study and put George's notebook in his fireproof gun safe.

A few minutes later, Gunny, Jim, Ralph, and Mark were on their way to the sheriff's meeting. When the meeting started, there was still some argument about the need for a militia for the county. The same loudmouth from the week before was the main opposition to the plan. However, most of the citizens felt a trained force would be beneficial. Many brought lists of people who had volunteered to help. The lists totaled over six hundred. Others estimated there were at least that many more who would also sign up. The sheriff informed everyone that they would try to have a training schedule by next Monday. Curt told of a few things he'd picked up on over the last week about how order was rapidly disintegrating in most of the medium to large cities. He asked Mark if he would share what his group had seen during their travels of the last week. Mark noticed that everyone was listening intently to his description of the two trips they'd taken. Most nodded their heads grimly at the confirmation of lawlessness and anarchy that the outside world had become. Others were shocked at some of the images he painted, even though he whitewashed them to a degree. When Mark was finished, he answered a few clarifying questions and sat down.

The doctor got up and talked a little, but he basically had no new information for the group. When he was done, the meeting was adjourned until next week. Curt asked the same small group to meet in his office.

Mark excused himself for a minute and talked to the doctor about George's meds. He was more than happy to help and told Mark to come by the hospital later. Mark asked if he could come tomorrow when he didn't have anyone with him. Doctor Ken smiled and said that would be fine.

When Mark got to the Sheriff's office, options were being discussed for training the thousand to twelve hundred volunteers. This was more than anyone had expected, and they didn't know how to train so many, let alone transport them back and forth. It was decided, after considerable discussion, to bring in two people from each group and train them to train the others. Gunny, Rob, Curt, Jim, and Mark would do the initial training. Then, perhaps later, they could bring a few of the better groups in for some special training. With that settled, the men headed outside.

"We'll help you load the Harley up," Rob offered.

"We want you to have it," Mark told him.

"I can't accept something like that."

"Yes, you can, and you will. You earned it. If you hadn't told us what to do, we never would have been able to take that house full of MZB's, and we still want you to come out and work with some of our guys."

Rob was smiling from ear to ear. "You just tell me when. Man, I always wanted a big hog, but I couldn't afford it on my salary. It was always cheapo rice burners for me. Thanks."

"You're welcome, and Jim picked out some weapons for you, too."

They walked over to Jim's truck and Jim handed Rob an AR-15 and a Kimber Custom Shop pistol in .45 caliber.

351

Rob thanked the men again as they left. The drive over to Floresville Pump and Supply was a short one. The men parked in front of the building, and Jim walked to the house directly behind the shop. A minute later, he came back with a pudgy middle-aged man, who had apparently not shaved since The Burst. Jim introduced the man to Mark.

"Mark Turner, Leo Schmitt."

"Glad to meet you, Mr. Turner"

"Please call me Mark, and I'm glad to meet you, too. Jim told me you had a fiberglass tank you'd be willing to trade for an SKS rifle and five hundred rounds of ammo. I think we can agree to that," Mark said with a smile.

Leo rubbed his chin. "I've been thinking, and I'm going to need a little more than that. After all, this is the only tank for sale in the county."

"What did you have in mind?" Mark wasn't smiling now.

"I've heard about you all from Silver Hills, and you have lots of guns. So I would think you could spare an AR-15, ten magazines, and two thousand rounds of ammo, or we could trade for $150 face in silver."

"Mr. Schmitt, that wasn't the deal you made with Jim on Saturday."

"We didn't make a deal; we just talked prices. Now the price is higher. Do you want the tank or not?" the man said emphatically.

Mark started to get mad. He would like to tell this guy where he could stick his water tank, but that wouldn't solve anything. They really did need the tank. Mark took a breath and painted on his best smile.

"We'd like to have the tank, but we don't really need it. I'm sorry, but the price you're asking is just too steep." Mark turned his head and spoke to his companions. "Maybe the windmill dealer in Kennedy will have one." He turned back to Leo and extended his hand. "Sorry to have wasted your time, Mr. Schmitt."

"Wait a minute," Leo blurted nervously. "We can talk about it, can't we? Maybe I could reduce the price a little. What if I came down a thousand rounds of ammo? How does that sound?"

"I don't have all day to dicker with you, Leo." Mark's voice was forceful but not unfriendly. "I'll give you an SKS and a thousand rounds. Take it or leave it."

"I can't take that. I need at least…"

Mark wheeled around and took a step toward the door. He motioned with his head that Jim, Ralph, and Gunny should follow him.

"Okay, okay, I'll take it," Leo said.

Mark turned back around and shook the man's hand. They gave Leo the rifle and ammo, loaded the tank on the trailer, and headed home.

Chapter 48

On the way home, Gunny told Mark and Jim that he wanted them to be the heads of the scout teams he planned to talk to the Security Committee about. He expected to get the approval today and start training tomorrow. He would promote Ted to take Scott's place on Alpha shift. Chaparo, now that he wasn't needed to weld and plumb as much, would take Charley shift and Dwight would be in charge of Delta.

Mark tried to pay attention to what Gunny was saying, but his mind kept slipping back to the Craig and Connie situation. He didn't know what to do. On one hand, he felt it was none of his business. They were two consenting adults, and they knew what they were doing. However, in the current circumstances, things weren't like they were before The Burst. Everyone in the community needed to be able to trust everyone else. That meant that if Craig was sneaking around with someone else's wife, he wasn't trustworthy. Didn't it also mean if someone knew it was going on and didn't say something, they weren't trustworthy either? Mark thought it did, but that didn't make having to tell Joe any easier. Mark knew he wouldn't take the news well. Perhaps if he told Susan first, she would kick Craig out, and that would solve the problem. No one else would be willing to put Craig up, and he would have to go. That seemed logical and easier.

When they got home with the tank, the men unloaded it at Manny's house. Chaparo had already started laying out a stand for the tank to elevate it ten feet. He just needed the actual measurements of the tank to be able to finalize his plans. David was following the big man around, double-checking his measurements for him and soaking up the knowledge given to him.

Manny was helping the men move the water tank to where it would be placed, and when they were through, Mark pulled him off to one side.

"How are Letty and Robby?"

"They're doing fine, under the circumstances."

"And Ronnie?"

"She's still having some trouble accepting things, but she and Letty are getting along well. I think they're helping each other. They almost act like sisters," Manny said.

"That's good. If there's anything we can do to help them, let me know."

"Thanks, Mark. I think having the funeral tomorrow will help Letty and Robby put this tragedy behind them and start to move on with their lives. Too bad we couldn't have done the same thing for Ronnie."

"Yeah. Too bad," Mark agreed.

"Hey, do you think we could have a memorial service for Ronnie's parents?"

"I think that's a wonderful idea. Why don't you talk to her about it, and we'll set it up if she wants."

"I will," Manny said.

Mark grabbed Jim and asked him if he wanted to go to see Jerry Watson about the night sights for the rifles. Jim was agreeable, and the two men grabbed a quick bite to eat before they left. Mark got some of the silver out of his safe to take with them.

When they got to Jerry's house, Jim honked the horn, and they waited. No one came out, so they drove down the road to the elder Mr. Watson's house. The gate was closed, which was no surprise, but Mr. Watson's new Suburban was just behind the gate. It looked like it had been used in a movie where the car gets raked over by a machine gun. Jim honked the horn, and the men waited. After a few minutes, a group of four armed guards approached the gate. They were rushing from tree to tree two at a time. When they got close enough, Mark could make out that one of the men was Tony. He didn't recognize the other three. Since Mark and Jim were in the truck, Tony had to get a little closer to recognize them. Mark saw the look on his face relax when he did. He waved to the three men he'd come down with to tell them it was okay, and they pushed the ventilated Suburban to the side. Tony then opened the gate and waved them through. Once they were on the other side, Mark could see there were several men who were stationed at the gate. The Watsons had dug foxholes not unlike those they had at Silver Hills, but theirs were camouflaged so well they couldn't be seen from the road. Mark thought that it was smart that these men hadn't revealed themselves. Tony came up to the window.

"Hey, Jim. Hi, Mark. What brings you out to our neck of the woods?"

"Never mind that. What happened here? Your dad's truck looks like Swiss cheese," Jim said.

"Yeah, we started having a little trouble after the grocery stores shut down. Let's go back to the house, and I'll tell you all about it."

The four men who had come from the house, pushed the Suburban back into place and then climbed into the back of Jim's truck. He drove the three hundred yards to Mom and Pop Watson's large house. He parked in front of the garage, which had been tuned into a large dining hall. Mark and Jim saw that it was tent city behind the house. Jerry, Mr. Watson, and a whole group of men Mark didn't recognize were waiting in the garage with weapons. Tony jumped out of the truck and spoke.

"It's okay. It's Jim Davis and Mark Turner."

Mark saw the relieved look on everyone's faces. Jerry and his dad came up and shook the men's hands. Tony began to explain the events of the past two weeks to the friends.

"Like I said, it started a couple of weeks ago. I guess quite a few people know where we live, and they started coming as individuals or in small groups, trying to buy or trade for weapons. Anyway, one guy came up, and we traded him a pistol and a rifle with ammo for an old, running Bronco. We kind of wondered why the guy would make such a one sided deal, but then we found out. Jerry and our cousin, Henry, took him home and when they got there, the guy tried to steal the Bronco back."

Jerry picked up the story. "When we got to his house, he stepped out and pointed the handgun at us. The dumbass had stuck a loaded magazine into the pistol, and he thought it was loaded, even though he never chambered a round. He told Henry and me to get out of the truck and take off. We just laughed at him and drove away. He left the rifle and all the ammo in the truck, and we brought it back home."

"Anyway, we realized it wasn't a good idea to deal with anyone we didn't know well. It's kind of ironic, really. We bought all these surplus rifles, knowing that one day things would go south, and they'd really be worth something. It finally happened, but now we can't sell them, in fear that they might be turned on us," Tony laughed.

Mark started to wonder if he had made a mistake trading the SKS to Mr. Schmitt.

"So, as more and more people came to buy guns, we sent most of them away empty handed. Some were really pissed and made threats to come back. We put a couple of guys at the gate twenty-four seven. Five guys showed up one day and shot and killed Uncle Frank and our neighbor, Mr. Barnes, while they were watching the gate. We killed three of them, and the other two ran off, wounded, we think, but we decided we had to beef up our security. More and more of the neighbors were staying here, and we put more guys on the gate, where they're hidden and protected now, and we blocked the gate with Dad's Suburban. A few more small groups tried to attack us, but we ran them off easily with the new set up. Then last week, a big group of sixteen or eighteen guys tried to get in. They shot the truck up, but they weren't able to get in. One of the neighbors got wounded slightly, but no one else on our side even got a scratch," Jerry said. "So, what are you two doing here?"

"We mostly are looking for some night sights," Mark said.

"No problem," Tony said. "Glock or 1911?"

"Actually, we need them for our rifles. We had a little close encounter the other night, and we couldn't see our sights for squat."

"Oh, we don't have any for rifles," Tony sounded disappointed.

"Tony, didn't I see a bunch of AR-15 night sights in the shop a few months ago?" Jerry asked.

"Yeah, but I sent them all back. I had ordered some Glock sights, and they sent those by mistake. I wish I'd kept them now."

"Any chance you could make some?" Jim asked Tony. "You're pretty good at that kind of stuff."

"I might be able to. I'll have to try and see what I can do. What kind of rifles do you want them for?"

"AR's, SKS's, and AK's," Mark answered. I also need to see about buying another SKS if you have any more."

"We still have a bunch, but we really don't want cash anymore. We'll take silver like we did before, or we could trade for something," Jerry said.

"What do you need?"

"Tents, cots, building materials, books, batteries, toilet paper, food, and about a million other things." Jerry rolled his eyes. "Just like everyone else I suppose. The big item we need is a tractor. We have some cattle, but we need to cut and bale some hay to get them through the winter. I don't suppose you'd have a tractor to trade, though."

"Not to trade, but maybe we could rent you one. We have an old Ford that belongs to one of our guys." Mark didn't say it was Ralph's. "Would that work?"

"How big is it?"

"Medium sized, I don't really know that much about them."

"I think my father-in-law said it was 33 horsepower," Jim added.

"That's a little on the small side, but we'll make it work," Tony said.

The men worked out the details. Mark and Jim left with the replacement SKS. They would bring the tractor over on Friday, and Tony would hopefully have something worked up on the night sights. The Watsons would rent the tractor for $10 a day in silver or trade for weapons and ammo or the night sights, if Tony could make them.

On the way home, Mark told Jim he was starting to regret trading a gun for the water tank. Jim agreed that, while it was a much better deal for them, it might not have been the smartest thing to do. With what had happened to the Watsons, they decided they wouldn't trade any more guns.

When they got home, Gunny was anxious to talk with the Security Committee, so they called a meeting. Since Jim was one of the potential scout leaders, he joined them. Gunny laid out his plans for two scout squads that would be led, at least at first, by Mark and Jim. Each squad would be comprised of five men. Gunny had selected the men he wanted. Susan asked him why no women, and she and Gunny had another argument about this subject.

"I don't see any good reason why you wouldn't want women in the scouts," she challenged. "Can you give me one?"

"Cause eventually these squads might be out overnight, or even longer, if we hafta keep an eye on a group of travelers. This is our front line of defense, and they will be in the most danger. What if they have to retreat quickly, or what if someone gets hurt and has to be carried? Do you think one of the women could carry one of the guys?"

"No, but I don't think every guy you've selected could carry Jim. Jim, how much do you weigh?"

"Two fifteen," Jim answered.

Susan looked back at the old man with her eyebrows raised, waiting for an answer. "So?"

"Any two of them could."

"Well, any two women could carry another woman. Why don't you just make one team all women?"

"Over my dead body!" Gunny shouted.

"We can arrange that, you chauvinist old goat!" Susan yelled, almost before the last syllable was out of Gunny's mouth. "Give me one good reason why one team can't be women."

"What if they got captured? Can you imagine what might happen to them? You don't know what some people are capable of."

"As I understand it, the men you found tortured to death in Waco were just as dead as the women. Are you saying that a woman's death is more tragic than a man's?"

"Yes," Gunny said flatly.

"Well, I disagree, and unless you put some women on these squads or make one all women, I'm not voting for them."

The other men had been watching the argument go back and forth. Their heads turned from side to side like at a tennis match. Finally, Mark interrupted. "Gunny, what if we train a third team of all women?"

356

"I don't know. I s'pose we could use them for a reserve team," Gunny said. It looked like he wanted to compromise at least a little.

"Would that be alright with you, Susan?"

"They would have to go on regular patrols," Susan answered.

"Impossible!" Gunny started to bristle again.

Mark jumped in, just as he saw Susan about to enter the fray again. "I make a motion that we create three scout teams, two of men and one of women. Initially, the women's team will go out one day per week, and the men's teams will split the other six days. I also suggest we reevaluate the schedule in a month. When the women's team proves themselves up to the task, we will increase the number of days they go on patrol."

"I second that," Ted said.

"All in favor?" Mark asked hopefully.

Mark, Ted, and Chaparo raised their hands. Susan and Gunny just glared at each other.

"The motion carries," Mark said.

"I get to pick the women," Susan demanded, looking straight at Gunny.

"And I get to train them," Gunny shot back. "If they can't cut the mustard, then they don't go out."

"As long as the standards are the same as for the men, I don't have a problem with that," she said.

"Good," he said.

"Good," she repeated.

"Let's not forget that we're on the same side here," Mark said. "We may have different ideas about how to accomplish them, but our goals are all the same."

"Well said," Chaparo chimed in.

"So, when do we start training, Gunny?" Mark asked.

"Tomorrow, I reckon," Gunny answered and then looked at Susan. "You think you can have your team ready by then, Missy?"

"My name is Susan, not Missy, and yes, I can have my team assembled by tomorrow."

"Okay, then, see you all in the morning," Mark said as cheerfully as he could. "Susan, do you have a minute?"

She nodded her head, as everyone else left. When they were all gone, she vented her anger to Mark.

"That old goat's got a lot to learn. I don't know why he has to be so hard headed? He thinks it's still the 1950's."

Mark looked her straight in the eye. "You're not helping any."

She crossed her arms. "What? You're taking his side? You think I'm wrong?"

"I didn't say that. I think you both have some valid points, and that's why I thought we should try your idea for an all women's squad."

"Then what do you mean?"

"You don't help yourself by opposing Gunny so strongly. All you do is make him dig his heels in. You've heard the old saying 'You draw more flies with honey than with vinegar.' Try to see things from Gunny's side, and then help him to see yours," Mark said with a smile.

"You should tell him the same thing."

"You're right, but it wouldn't do any good. You said it yourself; Gunny's from a different time. He's old, and he's not likely to change."

"But you expect me to change, right?"

"Yes, I do. Susan, you're intelligent and motivated. Those are two traits that we need around here, but we also need to work together. I'm not asking you to change what you believe, just your approach. When it comes to security around here, Gunny is the big dog. You don't piss off the big dog. Prove to him that you're right, but don't piss him off. Capisce?"

"Yeah, I got it," she said slowly. "Is that it?"

"Actually, that's not what I wanted to talk to you about, but before I change the subject, I do have one more piece of advice for you."

"What's that?"

"I don't know who you have in mind for your squad. You may be thinking of the biggest, fastest, and strongest women here. That would be logical, but there's one thing I would look for first." He stopped to emphasize his point.

"And that would be?"

"Women who won't quit no matter how hard Gunny makes it on them."

She didn't say anything for several seconds. Then she started to nod her head and smile. "You're right. He'll try to get them to quit. Thanks for the advice, Mark."

"You're welcome. Now the other thing I want to talk about." He blew out a deep breath.

"It can't be that bad. Just tell me," she said.

It is that bad, he thought, and he was embarrassed to tell her, but he had to. "There are rumors going around that Craig is sleeping with somebody."

Her eyes got big, and then her face got red. "That son of a bitch! Did he tell you that?"

"No," Mark was a little confused. "Someone else told me."

"Well, I bet the bastard is bragging it up all over the place. Listen, Mark, it was just one time. I was feeling real lonely and depressed. I knew it was a mistake, but he was there and said some nice things, and I guess I needed to believe him. I was weak for a minute, and he took advantage of it. He would do or say anything to get laid. I told you he was no good. I just wish I'd listened to my own advice. God, I hate him!"

Now Mark was really embarrassed. "Susan, you're not the one I'm talking about. He's having an affair with Connie Bagwell. Several people have seen him coming out of her house at all hours when Joe was on guard duty or on one of the trips."

Susan just stared at Mark for a long time. The muscles in her jaw clenched tighter, and her eyes got narrower. When she finally spoke, her lips only moved slightly, as her teeth never parted. "He's out of here."

"I thought you'd feel that way. I'm going to suggest, since you will no longer house him, he be kicked out of the neighborhood. I think we should give him some food and take him wherever he wants to go, within reason. Obviously, Joe doesn't know about this, and if we can keep it that way, I'd like to. We'll just say that you and he have some differences about things, okay?"

"Joe has a right to know."

"Maybe he does. Do you want to tell him?"

She shook her head. "And the other thing, can that stay between us?"

"What other thing?" He winked at her.

"Thanks, Mark." She gave him a quick hug and left in a hurry.

Mark walked back to his house thinking about exactly how he'd present his motion at the meeting tonight. When he was almost home, Jim met him.

"What did she say?"

"She wants him out."

"Good."

"Yeah, I was thinking we should give him a week's worth of food, something to cook in, a small tent and bedroll, and a weapon. What do you think?"

"The food and other stuff sounds right, but I don't know about a weapon. What did you have in mind?"

"Maybe one of the cheapo pistols we brought back from Waco. I just think it's wrong to send him out without some way to protect himself," Mark said.

"You have a point. Let's go see what we have."

The two men walked into the shed where Jim had unloaded all of the items that had been on the trucks Sunday night. The rifles and shotguns were leaning against the workbench, and the pistols were sitting on top of it. They looked at several weapons, trying to decide what would be fair to give to the future outcast. There was the potential for trouble if Craig came back with a weapon. A short range weapon would let him defend himself, but wouldn't give him the opportunity to use it offensively against the neighborhood. They narrowed the choice down to a Ruger 9 millimeter pistol or a Mossberg 20 gauge shotgun. There were pros and cons to both. Mark thought that they should get Gunny's advice, and Jim went to get their security expert.

Mark looked at the rifles they had brought back from Waco. Some of them were cheap, but most of them were quality weapons. They would be put to good use. He picked up one of the AR-15's and looked it over. Seven more AR's would definitely come in handy. But hadn't there been nine? Mark looked around. Maybe he'd missed a couple. No, there were only seven. He had probably miscounted when they were loading them up. Jim came back in with Gunny, and Mark asked his friend if he remembered how many of the 'little black rifles' he had unloaded.

"Nine," Jim said.

"I only see seven. Did you take any somewhere else?"

"We gave one to Rob, remember?"

"Right, but what about the other one?" Mark asked

"They were all leaning against the workbench. I had intended to clean and inspect all of the guns this afternoon, but I wasn't able to get to it yet. Where could it have gone?"

"You boys beat all I ever saw," Gunny said. Mark and Jim turned and looked at the old man with questioning eyes. "It's obvious…somebody stole it."

"What?" Mark asked.

"Who?" Jim was only half a second behind.

"You heard me, and if I knew who, I'd already have him hung out to dry. You should both have your butts kicked up between your shoulders for not locking this stuff up. We got a lot of people here now, and we don't really know all of them that well, do we? You can't trust everyone. I'd check to see if anything else is missing."

Mark and Jim looked at the other guns, but they couldn't remember the exact number there had been, and nothing jumped out at them as missing. Jim had counted the mags and ammo last night, and none of either were gone. When they looked at the liquor and drugs, though, it was clear that some of them had been taken. There were at least two bottles of bourbon and three bottles of painkillers missing.

"What do we do now?" Jim asked.

"What can you do? Go door to door and search every home? I don't think so," Gunny answered. "You just have to put the word out that the stuff is missing and that it belonged to everyone who lives here. Hopefully, somebody will turn the thief in, and we'll do to him what we're doing to Craig. In fact, he may be the one who stole the stuff. If'n you'll sneak around with another man's wife, I reckon you might be the type to steal, too."

"You may be right. So did Jim talk to you about what we should give him for a weapon?" Mark asked.

"Yes. But I think you're going about it all wrong. Just confront him and tell him that he's out. Don't humiliate him in front of everyone by asking them to vote if he gets the food and stuff. Ask him what he needs, and give it to him if it's within reason. No reason not to treat him like a man. Let him leave with a little dignity left. Might make it go smoother."

"You're right again, Gunny. Why don't the three of us go talk to him right now?"

Gunny nodded his head. Mark locked the shed behind them this time, and the men headed down to Susan's house. When they got there, Susan hadn't seen Craig since before the Security Committee meeting. Mark told her about the stolen items, and Susan said that she'd already packed all his stuff, and there was nothing in Craig's room. Mark told her what they planned, and she agreed it was best. She said that if it had been left up to her, she most likely would have thrown him out with only the clothes on his back. She had no idea where he might be, unless Joe wasn't home. The men figured that they would try the Bagwell house and headed that way. They spotted Craig coming down the main road.

"Hey, Craig. You got a minute?"

"Sure," he answered. Mark thought his eyes looked a little glassy, but there was no smell of alcohol. "I must be in big trouble if the three of you want to talk to me. I didn't forget a guard shift, did I?"

"Nothing like that. Where are you coming from?"

"Oh, I was just over at a friend's house." He was clearly being vague.

Mark wondered who this friend's husband was.

"Listen Craig," he began, "I'm going to be straight with you. Everyone knows about you and Connie. Susan knows too, and she's not going to put you up anymore, so you have to leave. We want to make this as easy for you as possible, but you've burned your bridges here, and there's no other choice."

The playboy stared blankly for a minute. "What if someone else volunteers to let me stay with them?"

"And who do you think is going to do that?"

Craig hung his head. "Nobody."

"Tell us what you need, and we'll try to help you," Mark offered.

"Could you give me a ride to Victoria? I have a sister who lives down there."

Mark thought for a moment. "We can't take you that far. I don't know if it's safe to drive past Gonzales. How about we take you that far, and you can walk the rest? It's only fifty or sixty miles from there. You could make it in four or five days, easy. We'll give you a tent and sleeping bag, plus enough food and water."

"I'll need a rifle, too, if I'm going to walk that far."

"No rifles," Gunny said. "We'll give you a shotgun. Take it or leave it."

"I'll take it. Can we wait until in the morning to leave?"

Mark looked a Gunny for guidance. "Alright," the old man agreed. "But you stay at the clinic tonight, and with a guard. First light, you hit the road."

Craig nodded his head. "Thanks for helping me, Mark."

Mark inwardly smiled. It was strange. He was kicking Craig out of the subdivision and getting thanked by the man he was sending away. Maybe being political was the way to get things done. "Gunny, would you take Craig over to the clinic? I'll go and pick up his stuff from Susan's. Jim, can you run and get the items Craig needs out of the shed and take them to him? You can just leave the shotgun in the shed for now." Mark handed the key to Jim.

Everyone headed off in different directions. Mark started back to Susan's, when Joe came running up to him.

"Mark, can I talk with you?"

"Sure, Joe. What's up?" Mark prayed that it wasn't about what he thought it was about.

"Remember I told you about my wife and I having problems?"

"Yes," Mark answered. 'Crap, it is about that,' he thought.

"Well, I think I have a solution."

"Really? What is it?" he asked and then thought, 'You don't know it, but I just fixed your problem.'

"Connie and I have never been able to have kids of our own. I was thinking that we could adopt the Roberts boys. What do you think?"

Mark took a deep breath. "Have you talked this over with Connie?"

"No. I wanted to surprise her."

"I think she'd have to be in on it, and we'd need to discuss what's best for the boys. This isn't like bringing home a couple of puppies for a surprise, Joe."

"I know that. Can we all discuss it later?"

"Would tomorrow be alright?"

"In the morning?" Joe asked hopefully.

"I have some errands to run first thing tomorrow, but as soon as I get back. Okay?"

"Thanks, Mark. You're a pal." Joe smiled happily and then headed back toward his house.

"Shit," Mark said to himself, not caring about the dollar.

Chapter 49

When Mark got back to his house, he told Jess what Joe had asked him. Jess's reaction was anything but calm. She ranted and raved that there was no way she or the other people in the community were going to stand by and watch while that two timing witch took the Roberts boys. Mark finally got her calmed down and told her Joe hadn't even talked to Connie about it, and he hoped when he did, she would discourage him. Jess asked if Mark had come to a decision about them keeping the boys. Mark told her that he'd thought about it, and he agreed that they were in the best position to take the boys in and care for them. He told her he wanted her to consider the first few months as a trial period to see how the boys adjusted. She happily agreed and hugged her husband.

It was almost time for dinner, but Mark wanted to check on how the water tank was coming. He headed over to Manny's house. The stand was finished, and Chaparo and David were just finishing up the plumbing. The windmill was pumping, and when Mark stood with the tank between him and the sun, he could see that there was already some water in it.

"Great job, guys," Mark praised the workmen.

Chaparo smiled. David beamed. "Thanks, Dad. By the time the meeting is over, there might be enough water that we won't have to run the generator tonight." David turned on the spigot for a second and showed his father how well the setup worked. "Chaparo said it will come out faster when the tank is full."

"That's great. I was really getting worried about what we would do for water if the generator broke or if we ran out of gas. Are you ready for dinner?" Mark asked.

"I just need to help Chaparo pick up the tools and carry them back to his place."

"I can do that. You go on home. I'll see you tomorrow after school," Chaparo told his young apprentice. "And by the way, I couldn't have finished this without your help. You're listening and learning fast. I'm proud of you."

"Thank you, sir." The wide grin almost split David's face. "And thank you for teaching me." The young man shook the journeyman's hand.

Mark couldn't tell who was prouder, him or David. It was a nice thing for Chaparo to brag on the boy in front of his father, and Mark knew he meant every word. If only someone had been studying under George like this. Of course, Mark thought, how stupid of me not to have thought of it before. His thoughts of how to implement his plan were interrupted by his son.

"Dad, when are we going back out to look for Grandma and Grandpa?"

Mark took a deep breath. He'd been going over this same question in his mind since they found the note from Mike. Unfortunately, he had only been able to come up with one logical answer. "We're not, son. There's just no way to know where they might be."

The young man was silent for a minute. "So, it would be like looking for a needle in a haystack?"

"No. It would be like looking for a needle in a field of haystacks. If I could narrow it down to just one haystack, I would have already been gone, but without knowing what route they're taking, there is no way I can ask men to risk their lives for what most likely would be a wild goose chase."

"Don't you think we could figure out the most likely route they would take?"

"Yes, but one thing this last trip taught me was that things never go as you plan, and one little detour can lead to another and another until you're so far from your original plan that it looks like you never planned at all."

"I see. So, we just have to wait for them."

"Yes. We wait and trust the Lord to watch over them," Mark said, knowing that was the only chance they had.

"When do you think they'll get here?"

Mark had spent a good deal of time thinking about that question, too. "Uncle Mike said they would be here in ten or twelve days. I think he was very optimistic with that estimate. I think it will take twenty or thirty days." Mark didn't say he was thinking that if they didn't make it in thirty days, they probably wouldn't make it at all.

At dinner, everyone told about what they had done. It was typical for a family to share the events of the day at dinner, Mark thought, but how different the stories had become since The Burst. Mark couldn't help but to see how George reacted to the various accounts of the day. He seemed to soak up every word. He listened so intently to each of the speakers that he barely touched his dinner. Or was it that the cancer had taken his appetite? If that was so, then it was imperative that Mark talk to him as soon as possible about an apprentice.

"Hey, George, I have to drop Craig off in Gonzales tomorrow morning. You want to ride shotgun? The guys at Promise Point want you to look at their gardens anyway. We could stop there on the way home."

"Sounds good," the old farmer answered.

"You need at least three or four guys for that trip," Gunny remarked.

Rats, Mark thought, he really needed George alone to be able to talk with him seriously. Plus, he would like to stop at the hospital with George and get Doctor Ken to give him a once over. Mark hoped to talk Gunny out of insisting on more than George and him for the trip. "Oh, Gunny, stop being such a mother hen. It's just a milk run over there and back. We just came home that way on Sunday, and there wasn't even a hint of a problem. George and I can handle it."

"Maybe you're right, but you need to take at least one more, just to make your mother hen feel better, okay?"

Mark knew that if he argued any more or didn't do as Gunny said, it would raise eyebrows. He'd have to find someone George would trust to be in on his secret.

When the news came on, it was the same old same old. The only interesting items were that the President's speech tomorrow was going to be very important and he'd asked that all Americans listen.

At the meeting, Mark filled the community in on the meeting at the sheriff's office and how it wouldn't mean much of a change for them. Since they were already doing what everyone else was going to do, it only meant that they might have to change their training schedule some. Mark had Gunny tell the group about the scout squads he was going to start training. Everyone saw the wisdom in being proactive. Any who would have been doubtful were on board since the attack Friday night. Gunny said that he'd start training Jim's crew in the morning and the other two would start on Wednesday and Thursday.

Chaparo got up and told everyone about the windmill and water tank and about his plan to run a line down the center of the subdivision, so that no one would have to carry water further than a block. This got an ovation from the crowd that lasted several minutes.

The last item of business was to inform everyone about the theft of the rifle, drugs, and alcohol. Mark asked that if anyone knew anything, to please let him know. Everyone just looked around like they couldn't believe that someone in their midst was a thief.

When Mark was about to dismiss the assembly, someone raised their hand in the back. "Yes," Mark asked, as he pointed at the upstretched arm.

"I heard that Craig Banks is being kicked out. Who made that decision?"

It seemed that even the crickets quieted to hear the answer. Mark cleared his throat. "Craig has decided to go stay with his sister in Victoria. I'm going to drive him to Gonzales in the morning, and he'll make the rest of the trip on his own."

"So he's not being banished?"

"Not really." Mark knew he was on slippery ground if he didn't want Joe to find out about Craig and Connie. "He and Susan, who was letting him stay with her because of their boys, don't see eye to eye on something important enough that Susan feels he can no longer remain in her home. Craig felt his best option was to go to his sister's. If he had opted to stay here, he would have had to find someone else to take him in."

The crowd nodded their heads in unison. Mark knew that they all had varying levels of understanding, but his answer seemed to satisfy them all, at least for now. Mark adjourned the meeting before anyone else could ask another question, and the whole group moved down to Manny's to get their water. They oohed and aahed over the new water system like it was magic. The tank didn't have quite enough water in it for everyone, so they went back to the Turner place and used the generator to fill the last few containers and the solar showers. When they were finished, David came up to his dad.

"Can I go with you and George in the morning?" David asked.

Mark almost instinctively said no, but his brain kicked in a split second before he did. David would probably fall asleep on the trip, and that would give Mark a chance to talk privately with George and still meet Gunny's requirements for having a third gun in the truck. David shot well enough, and Mark figured it was very unlikely they would run into trouble.

"I think we can arrange that. I'll clear it with your mother, as long as all of your homework is done."

"Thanks, Dad." David smiled. "I'll have my school work done within an hour."

"Come tell me when you're finished. I'll wait until then to talk to her, and don't you say a word about this to anyone. If your mom catches wind of this before I talk to her, we'll both be in deep doo-doo."

"No problemo," the youth said over his shoulder, as he ran off to finish his work.

Mark decided they would take the Blazer tomorrow. He filled it up and put his small toolbox and the other emergency supplies he used to carry in the Jeep into the Chevy. He checked the tires and all the fluids to make sure everything was shipshape. Whoever had owned the four by four before The Burst had taken very good care of it. Mark was still looking over the truck when David came out and told him that his homework was done. Mark walked back into the house, with just the slightest limp. His leg hadn't bothered him much today.

He found Jess helping Timmy with some of his schoolwork. She was so motherly, and Timmy seemed so comfortable with her that it would have been almost impossible for a stranger to tell that she wasn't his natural mother. She saw Mark looking at them, and she smiled at him. "Will you come find me in the study when you have a minute?" he asked.

"Sure," she replied sweetly. "I'll be there in five." She winked.

Mark was a little puzzled at her flirtatious nature. She already had his answer on the boys. What else could she want? Who could figure what women ever wanted, he thought. At least she's in a good mood. Maybe I'll only have to sleep on the couch for a night or two when I tell her I'm taking David tomorrow. He went to the study and started pulling out the guns they would take on the trip.

Jess came in the room. "What's up, Studmuffin?"

Mark didn't want to jump right into it. "How are Timmy and Tommy doing?"

"They're doing surprisingly well. I need you to spend some time with them when you get a chance, just an hour or so playing ball with them or teaching them some karate."

That was what she wanted. "Okay, as soon as I can, I promise," he told her, and she smiled back. Might as well get to it, he thought. "I'm going to take David with me and George in the morning." He braced himself for the Irish fury.

"Okay," she answered.

Mark blinked. He must be dreaming. "He has all his homework done, and he'll make up any school work he misses tomorrow, and some things are more important than going to school everyday." Mark made his first arguments, not yet realizing they were unnecessary.

"Look, I said okay. In fact, with Timmy and Tommy moving in, it's a good idea for you to spend a little extra time with David."

"Okay, thanks." Mark could not believe it.

"I have something to tell you, too. Susan came and talked to me this afternoon. She asked me to be on her scout team."

Mark blinked again. Of course, he thought, she was feeling really good about herself. That the other women looked up to her enough to ask her was a big deal for her. She had no intention of actually doing it. Mark hadn't been married to this woman for twenty years and not learned a thing or two. She just wanted his validation, too. "I can't blame her. I told her to pick fighters, and you're the best fighter around, kiddo."

"She told me you said not to pick quitters, and that's why she wanted me."

"You would have been first on my list, too," he said, smiling. "Are you going to do it?" He already knew the answer, but if he didn't ask, she would know that he was on to her. No need for her to know he was getting smart in his old age. He was becoming good at this politics game, he said to himself.

"Yes."

He heard her wrong. No, he couldn't have heard wrong. She misunderstood the question. "You're going to be on the women's scout squad?"

"Yes, that's what I said."

"But don't you have to teach school?" he asked, hoping she hadn't thought this all the way through.

"I can teach on the days I'm not on duty," she informed him matter-of-factly.

He finally blurted it out. "But I don't want you to do it."

"I knew you wouldn't." She wasn't angry. "But this is important, and unless you can think of a valid reason why I shouldn't do it, I'm going to give it a shot."

He put his brain into overdrive. Teaching the children was more important than this, right? He could use that argument. But hadn't he just said that some things were more important than school? He couldn't come up with one reason that she wouldn't chop to ribbons. He would just have to hope Gunny could wring the desire out of her. "I see you've given this a lot of thought. If you want to try it, I won't stand in your way."

She hugged him. "Thanks, sweetheart."

"I just hope you know what you're getting yourself into. Gunny is going to run the dog crap out of you guys."

"I know. Susan told me that, too. I can do it." She squeezed him a little tighter. "I need to finish helping Timmy."

He kissed her on the head, and she left him with his thoughts. He kicked himself for being stupid enough to think that he'd been in control a few minutes ago. The people in the neighborhood might look to him for guidance, but in the Turner household, there was no doubt about who was in charge.

He went out to the shed to get some ammo. It was almost dark, and he had to use a flashlight inside the metal building. He was still mumbling to himself about how Jess had played him. When he stepped through the door, he thought he saw movement out of the corner of his eye. He swung the light toward the corner, thinking it was some varmint. Two shocked faces blinked into the blinding light. 'The thieves!' flashed through his mind. His hand shot down to his pistol. The faces were familiar, too. He looked at them. One of them was his Samantha. The other one was Ted Petrie's son, Alex. What was wrong with his face? It had red marks on it. And what were they doing in here? Had Jess sent them to get something? If so, then why didn't they have a flashlight? Was it possible that they were the thieves? Mark refused to believe that.

Suddenly it was clear. It was Sam's lipstick on his face. He heard his own voice. "What are you two doing in here?" What a dumb question, he thought.

"We weren't doing anything, Dad," Sam stammered.

Mark didn't know how to deal with this. MZB's were easy. They were the enemy. You killed them before they killed you. Simple. But this threat came from the inside. It was something Mark had known for a long time he would have to face. Yet here it was, and he didn't know what to do or say. An idea flashed through his mind. He could just shoot the kid and say he thought he was a burglar. No, he couldn't do that, but he wondered how many fathers had

367

thought the same thing. He had to say or do something. "That's not what it looks like to me. Young lady, you get into the house."

"Yes, Dad," Sam said. Then she did the strangest thing. She kissed the young man on the cheek, whispered something in his ear, and then ran out of the shed and toward the house.

Mark just stared at this gawky kid for a minute. He was so skinny. And he was such a nerd. What was Mark going to say to him? Before he decided, Alex spoke.

"Mr. Turner, I can explain."

"I'm sure you can," Mark replied sardonically.

"Sam and I have been seeing a lot of each other lately."

Mark wasn't sure how true that was. How much of a person could you see in the dark with your face stuck to theirs?

"We have become quite fond of each other."

'No shit, Sherlock,' Mark thought. He didn't like where this talk was going. He had to side track it. This was his little girl that this…this…this whatever he was and he were talking about. "What did she tell you?"

"Sir?" Alex asked.

"Sam. What did she whisper to you before she left?"

"She told me not to be afraid." He stood straight and tall when he said it.

"Well, you should be afraid. Now you run on home."

"But Mr. Turner, I really need to talk to you, man to man."

"Fine. When you're a man, come and find me. I'm not talking man to man with some kid who has my teenaged daughter's lipstick all over his face and has to hide out in my shed to do God knows what."

Alex tried to wipe the red marks off of his face. "But I really need to talk to you now."

"Maybe you didn't hear me the first time. I said 'NO.' You get on home." Mark's voice was cold and flat. The boy just stared at him. "NOW!" Mark yelled.

The young man jumped at Mark's last command. He ran out of the shed, appearing to be all knees and elbows. Mark grabbed the boxes of ammunition that he'd come to the shed for. When he went out, he locked the door. He and Jim had moved all of the weapons, drugs, and alcohol out earlier in the day. There was no need to lock it for that reason. There was something the shed held that was still valuable, and becoming scarcer every day. Privacy was becoming harder and harder to find with all of the people moving in. It was a futile gesture, Mark knew. The pit in his stomach confirmed it. The young would always find a place to be alone if they wanted, but it made him feel like he had some control.

He walked back into the house and told Jess what he had walked into. She laughed. Mark was flabbergasted. How could she laugh? He asked her.

"You weren't kissing girls when you were seventeen?" she answered him with a question of her own.

"That's beside the point. What if they're doing something else?"

"Like what?" She laughed again. "Plotting to overthrow the world? Maybe they are the ones who caused The Burst. Oh my God." Her eyes opened wide, and she clutched her hands to her heart dramatically.

"You know what I'm talking about." He was on the verge of getting angry.

"Mark, you don't have to worry about that."

"How can you be so sure?"

"Because, number one, we've raised her right, and we have to trust her and what we've taught her. Is she going to make mistakes? Yes. But she's smart, and she's not going to make a big mistake that could affect her future. And, number two, if she was going to do that, she wouldn't go to a place where she's sure to be caught."

Mark was confused again. That seemed to be happening a lot lately. "You mean she wanted me to catch her?"

"What do you think?" Jess smiled.

"I don't know. I'm finding that how I think has nothing in common with how you females think. Why don't you clue me in?"

"If I was sixteen and liked a guy who was too scared of my father to ask me out on an honest to goodness date, I might set up an 'accidental' meeting to force his hand."

"Is that what that was about?"

"That would be my guess," Jess answered.

"God, I thought the boy was going to ask me if he could marry her," Mark said, in a relieved tone.

"You are naïve." She laughed again. "But that's why I love you." She blew him a kiss.

"Thanks, but I think you love me because you know how to push all of my buttons," he said sarcastically.

"That doesn't hurt either," she winked.

The next morning, Mark got up before dawn. He got dressed, woke David, and they carried their weapons out to the Blazer just as the sky was starting to lighten. George was waiting for them, and he had his AK and the Glock Jim had bought for him. They drove down to the clinic to pick up Craig. When they pulled in, Mark saw Connie sitting on the front porch with a big duffle bag. He figured that she'd come to say goodbye and to give him some food and stuff for his trip. He admired her generosity, misplaced as it might be. He got out of the truck and walked up to her.

"Connie, we're giving Craig enough food and equipment for the trip. I don't think he'll be able to carry that, too."

"This is for me. I'm going with him."

Mark stared blankly at her for a minute while the full weight of what she had said fell upon him. "Does Joe know?"

"I told him last night. We fought about it, but I finally won."

At least this would put any talk of Joe and Connie taking the boys to rest, Mark thought. "Okay, then. Let me help you with that bag."

"I can get it. You just get Craig, and let's get out of here."

Mark went inside and relieved the guard who was watching Craig. They walked out to the truck, Craig with the pack that Jim had given him. Connie hugged him when he came out and whispered in his ear for a moment.

Craig took her by the shoulders and held her at arms length. "Are you sure?" he asked.

She nodded her head, and the two of them climbed into the Blazer's back seat. David sat behind them in the cargo area, and George rode shotgun. Mark suggested that perhaps he should check on Joe before they left.

"He's sleeping," Connie said. "We were fighting pretty late. I think I really broke his heart. Let him sleep."

Mark nodded his head in agreement and drove out the gate. The trip was quiet and uneventful. Mark knew where all of the stalled cars on this route were, and there weren't many. They were in Gonzales in less than two hours. Mark stopped to let the couple out. They took their bags. Mark remembered what had happened to Jerry Watson when he tried to drop off the man he'd sold a gun to. Mark told Craig that he would leave the shotgun and ammo up the road about fifty yards. That would give him time to be gone before anything could happen. Better to be safe than sorry, Mark thought. He dropped off the weapon, turned the truck around, and they waved at Craig and Connie as they passed them on their way back home. Craig waved back, but Connie gave them the one finger salute.

Chapter 50

Mark wondered why Connie would have a reason to be mad at him. It was her choice to go with Craig, and he had chosen to go to his sister's, mostly of his own accord. Well, he thought, since when did women need a good reason to be angry?

Mark put it out of his mind. Craig and Connie weren't his problem anymore. It was going to be a beautiful day. It had been chilly early in the morning, but it was warming up nicely now that the sun was overhead. The windows were down on the Blazer, and Mark had on his sunglasses. The sky held a few wisps of white clouds that were hurriedly making their way north. If only the radio would play, it would be perfect. He looked in the rearview mirror and saw that David's eyes were closed. George was looking out his window. Mark decided that now was a good time.

"George."

The older man turned his head toward the driver. Mark could see that he was smiling, but his eyes held a sadness. "Thanks for bringing me, Mark. Nowadays, a trip anywhere is a treat. I'm really going to miss seeing the fields of crops when I drive by. You can just catch a glimpse down each row as you pass, and then it's gone, and you see the next for an instant. That's how the days are. Each one passes so quickly."

Mark smiled at the analogy. Everything must take on a deeper meaning when you know your time is short.

"Did you want to ask me something?" George asked.

"Yes. I wanted to know if you thought it might be a good idea for you to take an apprentice. I know the book will help us a lot, but some things are better passed on in person."

"I've been thinking the same thing." George seemed a little surprised.

"Good. Do you have anyone in mind?" Mark asked.

"I was thinking about Alex Petrie. He's in FFA, and he really has an interest. He's always asking me questions and pestering me to let him drive the tractor. I think he would be the natural choice."

"Alex Petrie?" Mark asked. "A little young, isn't he?" That wasn't Mark's real objection.

"He's almost eighteen, and he's sharp. No one else in the neighborhood really has the fire to learn like he does. Don't get me wrong, everyone wants to help, but they just want to do what I tell them. Alex is the only one to ever ask why."

"Hmm," was all that Mark said. Mark wished that the fire to learn was the only fire the boy had. 'Alex the farmer.' Mark thought about it. Maybe that would work. Sam would never have any interest in a farmer, would she? She wanted to be a doctor. What would a doctor and a farmer have in common? This might work out. "If you think he's the right one, then let's go for it."

"Okay. I just have one concern," George said.

"What's that?"

George looked over his shoulder at David. "People are going to wonder why I'm teaching him. Someone might put two and two together and guess that I'm sick."

"I see what you mean." Mark nodded his head thoughtfully. "What if we assigned apprentices to everyone with crucial knowledge? We really ought to do that anyway. I don't know why I haven't thought of it before. We need backups for Lisa, Doc, Gunny, Chaparo already has one, you, and probably some others. If we did it that way, no one would suspect anything, and we should have them write down things like you did, too." Mark was excited about this proposal.

"That sounds like a good idea," George agreed. He smiled a happy smile this time.

They had just crossed back into Wilson County when Mark heard an all too familiar sound. It sounded like firecrackers, but he knew instantly that it was gunfire. He slammed on the brakes and brought the Chevrolet to a stop. David woke up and looked around confused. George had a worried look on his face, as well. The firing was coming from in front of them. Mark couldn't imagine that someone had set up a roadblock in the little time since they had come this way. He eased the truck almost to the top of the hill and stopped. He grabbed his FAL and hopped out of the truck. George and David were grabbing their gear and getting out of the truck behind him.

"You two stay here and let me check it out," Mark told them.

David's shoulders slumped, and George looked at Mark with disapproval.

"Would you tell Gunny and Jim to stay in the truck?" George asked.

"No, but they have experience with this stuff," Mark answered.

"And how did they get experience?" George followed up.

Mark realized that George had a point. If the lights didn't come back on soon, everyone was going to be faced with this kind of situation sooner or later. Might as well see how he does, Mark thought, looking at his son. "Look I don't have time to argue. You can both come, but stay behind me, and don't do anything unless I tell you, okay?"

"Okay," George answered.

"Yes, sir," David replied.

Mark waited for his two teammates to get out of the truck with their gear. He then headed for the crest of the hill at a trot. When he was close, he bent over, so that his head couldn't be seen on the other side. About ten yards from the top, he dropped and crawled the rest of the way. He checked over his shoulder and was pleased to see George and David copying him. He crept the last few feet and peered over the top. He was surprised to see there was no roadblock. The firing was coming from a house about three hundred yards off of the road at the bottom of the hill. The residents were firing at a group hiding behind a couple of huge bales of hay about a hundred yards in front of the house and next to the driveway. Right next to the hay was a large garden plot. A sign next to the main gate said 'Calvert's Horse Farm.' Mark pulled his binoculars out of his pack and glassed the area.

There were four people behind the bales, but only two of them were firing. One had a handgun, and the other had a small rifle, probably a .22 from the looks and sound of it. There were at least four rifles being fired from the house. It almost appeared the people behind the bales of hay were on the defensive.

They only fired occasionally and only took quick, poorly aimed shots. Mark would have been surprised if they managed to hit the house at all. The people in the house, however, were shooting regularly at the bales of hay. Mark didn't know what to make of the situation.

"Are we going to help them, Dad?" David asked.

"I don't know who to help, Dave."

"The ones in the house have to be the good guys," David said.

"Not necessarily, son. It looks to me like the ones behind the hay would like to leave but they can't. Plus, if you were going to attack that house you would need a lot more than two guns," Mark explained.

"So you think the ones inside are the bad guys?"

"I didn't say that. I really don't know what to think." Mark looked at George and only got a shrug of the farmer's shoulders for an answer. A second later, Mark thought he heard a siren.

"Did you hear that?" David asked excitedly. "The cops are coming."

Mark definitely heard it now, and the siren grew stronger each second. He looked down the road with his binoculars. From this vantage point, he could see two or three miles. As he focused, a squad car came over the hill and into his view. A moment later, the van that the Sheriff's Department was using for a paddy wagon followed it. The squad car quickly covered the distance, and when it reached the gate, it stopped. Mark heard Curt's voice over the loud speaker.

"This is the sheriff. You people behind the hay. Put down your weapons and put your hands up. Jack Calvert, you and your people, hold your fire."

Everyone complied with the sheriff, and he drove up to where the four outsiders were standing with their hands over their heads. The paddy wagon was right behind him, and a total of six officers got out of the two vehicles. Four of the deputies were using AR-15's to cover the men and women, while the sheriff questioned them. Mark decided to drive down and see what was going on.

George, David, and Mark walked back to the truck and drove down to where the sheriff was questioning the four who had been behind the hay bales. When Curt saw Mark he walked over to the Blazer.

"What are you doing here?" the sheriff asked.

"It's good to see you too, Curt," Mark smiled.

"I'm sorry. How are you?"

"Fine, thanks. We were driving by when we heard the shooting. We stopped and were watching from the top of the hill." Mark pointed behind him. "I was trying to figure out what was going on when we heard you coming. So what's going on?"

"That's what I'm trying to figure out. The four here say that they were walking by and saw the garden. They claim they called to the house, but no one answered, so they helped themselves to some of the produce. Then someone started shooting at them. They said they tried to leave, but the people in the house kept them pinned down, and they couldn't make it back to the road. This is Jack Calvert's place, and he's kind of a hot head, so I don't doubt the kids are telling the truth."

Mark looked over at the quartet and noticed that they were very young. "Where did they come from?"

373

"I haven't asked them yet. Come with me while I finish questioning them," Curt said.

The four young people told Curt they were from San Antonio and had escaped from the airport shelter about a week ago. None of them had ever met before their internment in the camp. All of them were single and had their own apartments on the north side of town. They didn't know the status of their families and could get no help in determining the condition of their loved ones from the shelter staff. They decided to band together, escape, and see if they could find out about their parents and siblings. Two of them had families in San Antonio. One of the houses was burned, and there was no sign of the girl's mother and father. It was possible that they hadn't escaped the burned out neighborhood. The other house had obviously been attacked, and the young man's family had been murdered. The house had been ransacked, but the murdering thieves hadn't found his .22 rifle or the .38 Special revolver that were hidden in his old room. One of the families lived in Minnesota, and it was way too far to try to reach their house. The last family lived southwest of Houston in the suburbs. They had decided to try to make it there.

The sheriff went to the house to talk to the residents and get their side of the story. Mark couldn't hear what Curt was asking, but he could hear Mr. Calvert's answers. He was hollering about how he was sick and tired of people just helping themselves to his garden produce and about how someone had even stolen a couple of horses last week. He even yelled at the sheriff for not doing enough.

"Only when I take matters into my own hands do you show up!" Calvert barked.

Mark had stayed with the refugees, and he was glad he did. He didn't know if he could be as patient as Curt was with the irate homeowner. The 'vegetable thieves' were all young and strong. It was a good thing they were, Mark thought. Only the strongest would be able to make a journey as far as they planned. It would be hard on them still, but it would be almost impossible for a typical, middle-aged person to hike that far. Mark looked at the gear the young people had. It was inadequate for even a backyard campout, let alone a trip of the magnitude they were attempting. They had no tent, just blankets to sleep on, a few pots, fewer clean clothes, almost no food, and cheap backpacks to carry it all in. Mark felt sorry for them, but there wasn't much he could do. He asked them what they did before The Burst, but none of them had any skills that were needed in Silver Hills. Three of them were college students, and one was a telemarketer. They looked scared and hungry. Mark made up his mind that he had to help them somehow if he could.

The sheriff spoke a few more minutes with Mr. Calvert and then came back over to Mark. "Dern fool," he exclaimed. "If he would have just fired a couple of warning shots, the kids would have run off, but, 'NO!' He was going to get even with these kids for all the wrong that's been done to him since The Burst. I told him that if he had answered them when they called to the house they probably would have gone away. He's as much to blame in my book as these kids are."

"What are you going to do with them?" Mark asked tipping his head toward the four scared youths.

"Let them go." The sheriff shrugged his wide shoulders. "I don't have room in the jail for them even if I wanted to take them in. They're almost out of the county anyway, and then they won't be our problem. Why?"

"I was thinking of taking them to Silver Hills."

"What for?" the sheriff asked.

"Just to let them clean up and maybe give them some food and gear to help them make it."

"Going to be a Good Samaritan, huh?"

"Not really. I just feel bad for them. Tomorrow, I'll take them to Gonzales. That'll get them a little closer to their destination," Mark explained. "I need a favor from you, though."

"Name it. But first you have to tell me what you're doing out here."

Mark explained about how they had dropped Craig and Connie off in Gonzales and the circumstances that brought that to pass. Mark asked the sheriff how he knew about the little shootout and the lawman told him one of the residents up the road a little had one of his radios, just like Silver Hills did. Mark then asked Curt if he would drop George off to look at the Promise Point gardens with Greg and Rob. Curt agreed, and then he told the four travelers that he was going to let them go. They thanked him profusely. He told them they could thank him by not trespassing anymore. They assured him they wouldn't. Curt then explained that Mark had volunteered to take them back to his house to clean up and rest, and then he would take them to Gonzales in the morning. If they wanted to take him up on it, he added. The four of them jumped at the offer. Mark explained to George that Curt would take him over to Greg's house and he would come and pick him up after he got the kids squared away. George left in the squad car, and Mark loaded the kids into the Blazer with David.

The trip home was fairly quiet, as the kids seemed to be reflecting on the big bullet they had dodged. Both literally and figuratively, Mark thought. When they got to the subdivision, Mark found Manny and informed him of what he had in mind and then put the young people under the grandfather's watch and care. Mark chased David off to school after he made the youth promise to let him tell Jess about the so-called gunfight. No need to get her worked up for nothing, he thought. Then he headed out to pick up George.

He thought about the long trip the four kids had in front of them, and that naturally made him think about his mother, father, brother, sister, and their families. Mark said a little prayer for them. He also said a prayer for Joe. He had meant to check on him when he got home, but he'd been in such a hurry to go get George that he'd forgotten. He would make sure that was the first thing he did when he got home.

He pulled up to the entrance to Promise Point and noticed they had added some of the big radiator punching spikes to their gate. Greg really had liked that idea. A guard asked him what he wanted, and when he said he was here to pick up George, the guard said they'd been expecting him and opened the gate.

Mark drove to Greg's house, and the Promise Point leader and George were outside talking. Mark parked the Blazer and got out. George had already looked at the gardens and determined the trouble. He had instructed Greg and the others to get some nitrogen and put it on the soil. Greg thanked the farmer for helping and then turned his attention to Mark.

"Nice bike you gave to Rob," he smiled. "He told me you have several. Any chance we could buy or trade you for another one?"

"I'm sure we could work something out." Mark rubbed his chin and smiled comically. "What did you have in mind?"

"What do you need?" Greg smiled back mischievously.

"Lots of stuff," Mark said, as the reality of their situation pressed the joviality out of him. "Let me check with my people and get back to you. What do you want it for?"

"We plan to use it for our convoy point vehicle."

"That's a good idea," Mark said. He then looked at George. "Ready to go?" The older man nodded his head.

Mark shook Greg's hand. "Sorry to run, but we have a lot to do."

"I understand," Greg said, as he finished shaking Mark's hand and then shook George's. "Thanks again for your help, George. Maybe you can come back in a couple of months and see how our crops are doing?"

George nodded his head stoically. He and Mark climbed into the Blazer and headed to the hospital in Floresville. Mark noticed that George was staring out of his window without saying anything for a long time. It seemed Greg's invitation to come back in two months had struck a nerve. Finally, the farmer turned to Mark and spoke.

"Do you think I'm doing the right thing not telling anyone that I am sick?"

Mark looked over at the man and could see the pain in his eyes. He thought about the question for a moment before he answered. "I don't know if I'm the right person to ask, George. What's right for one person may not be right for another, and I'm no expert on how to best handle things." He paused for a second. "I can tell you one thing, though. If it were me, I'd do the same thing you are."

"Thanks, Mark." George looked like a burden had been lifted from his shoulders. He smiled faintly.

They arrived at the hospital, and Dr. Ken was expecting them. He had instructed one of the staff to escort them to his office. He greeted them and invited them to sit down.

"So, George, Mark gave me your prescription. I have it here, but I'd like to ask you a few questions before I give it to you. I promise no poking, prodding, or probing. I'm sure you've had enough of that already. Just a couple questions, okay?"

"Alright, Doctor."

"Mark, would you excuse us?" the doctor asked.

Mark nodded his head and put his hands onto the arms of the leather chair to push himself up. Before he could rise, George's hand was on his arm, stopping him.

"It's okay, Doc. He can stay. In fact, I want him to."

"Whatever you want, George," the doctor smiled. "Mark told me you decided against chemo. Are you sure about that? We could possibly provide you with several more months to spend with your family."

"I'm sure, Doc. I discussed it with my oncologist in Uvalde at length. I prefer quality time to the quantity."

The doctor nodded. "I just had to make sure. Now, how much pain are you having?"

"Not too much. It comes and goes."

"I see. And your appetite, how is it?"

"Just so-so," George answered.

"Any other problems? Headaches? Nausea? Bleeding?"

"Yeah, I get a little sick to my stomach at times."

"Nothing else?" the doctor asked, as if he were a detective questioning a witness.

"That's it," George assured him.

The doctor opened a desk drawer and pulled out two vials. He pushed the first one across the desk. "This is your pain medicine. If one doesn't work, you can take two, but no more than that."

George nodded his understanding.

The doctor continued, "and this is for the nausea. Take one when you need it. You need to make sure you're eating." The doctor's eyes cut to Mark when George looked down at the vial. "You must keep your strength up. Understand?"

"Yes, Doc."

"I want to see you again when you run out of medicine or in a month, whichever comes first."

"Thanks, Doc. How much do I owe you for the medicine?"

Doctor Ken waved his hand. "Nothing. Besides, I have plenty of kindling, and dollar bills don't make good TP."

George actually laughed at the joke. It seemed to help him. Mark was impressed with the way that Doctor Ken treated George. He didn't talk down to him or treat him like a number.

"Thank you, Doctor Ken," Mark said, shaking his hand heartily.

Five minutes later, the two men were on their way back to Silver Hills. George was talking and laughing like a teen-aged girl.

When they got home, Mark went straight down to see Joe. He knocked on the door, but no one answered. He checked the door. It was locked. The back door was also locked. Mark figured he must be over at someone's house or working at one of the community gardens. 'Good for him to keep busy,' Mark thought. 'I'll check on him later.'

Mark spent the rest of the day checking on projects and people. He dropped in on Gunny's class with Jim's scout team and watched them endure the old man's charm for a while. He was riding them pretty hard if they made a mistake. His turn would come tomorrow. Then Susan's team would be the next day. He didn't think Jess would like this side of Gunny. He hoped she wouldn't.

The day passed quickly, and the next thing Mark knew, it was dinner time and time for the President's big speech. They tuned the radio and listened.

...is KSTX. Please stay tuned for the President's address.

There was a moment of dead air, then the sound of the President clearing his throat could be heard.

My fellow Americans, it was six weeks ago today that we were hit by the most devastating attack we have ever seen on our soil. While this was not a conventional attack, the results have been devastating. Many of us have lost friends and loved ones to the panic and lawlessness that have resulted from the loss of electricity. I, and the rest of your government, hoped this would be a short-term problem and that we could pull together and overcome like we have in times past. However, it has become obvious to me that The Burst has caused problems beyond what we are capable of dealing with using normal means and solutions.

The President paused. Mark wasn't sure if it was for effect or if he needed a deep breath.

I have been reluctant to enact many of the actions that my advisors assured me were necessary to ensure the continuation of our way of life. It is now painfully clear to me that these things must be done. The epidemic of lawlessness throughout the country must be brought to a halt. Our ability to feed, shelter, and protect our citizens has been taxed beyond what we ever thought possible, and we now face a new threat that must be stopped.

The Center for Disease Control has identified a new strain of flu. We do not yet know where it came from, and we are not sure if it is naturally occurring or if it was bioengineered. The CDC has been hampered by the lack of electricity, as have most of our government assets. What they are telling me is that, while any strain of flu can be deadly, this one is very dangerous. It weakens the immune system to the point that the possibility of a secondary bacterial infection is very strong. The risk to the elderly and very young is especially alarming. With our current situation making it difficult for people to travel or call for help, many may develop pneumonia, which if left untreated, could prove deadly. This virus, being called the 'Burst Flu' has infected over ten percent of Californians. It is spreading to California's neighboring states at alarming speed. For these reasons, I must implement the following acts.

First, all active and reserve military units, along with local, state, and federal law enforcement are temporarily placed under the command and control of the Federal Emergency Management Agency. I am recalling all of our overseas military personnel, except for the bare minimum to keep our bases open and protect our interests and allies, to aid in serving and protecting our own citizens. FEMA will coordinate all of these military and law enforcement assets to ensure that no omission or duplication of services is occurring. They will make sure that help gets to where it is needed.

Second, any citizen living in a county or parish with a population over fifty thousand will be required to temporarily report to a FEMA shelter. We can no longer ensure the delivery of food to numerous locations. This measure, that we expect to be very short lived, will allow us to provide for many people with minimum resources. As soon as we get a larger percentage of our trucking industry back on its feet, you will be allowed to return to your homes if you wish. Counties and parishes with smaller populations will have different requirements to meet their residents' needs. FEMA will work with the assets available in these areas to develop the best plan on a case-by-case basis.

Third, all travel without the proper authorization is prohibited. This is necessary to prevent the spread of the Burst Flu. No one is allowed to cross out of his or her county or parish without written permission from FEMA. Again, this measure is only temporary and is done with the country's best interest at heart.

In order to make certain these orders have the chance to accomplish the desired goal, FEMA will be empowered to detain lawbreakers and deal with insurgents until our justice system is operational again.

I know these may seem like extreme steps to many, but these are extreme times, and they call for extreme measures. I assure you that I do not invoke these powers lightly. I believe they are necessary to assure the survival of our country and government. I ask that you assist FEMA officials in any way that you can and that you pray for a speedy recovery for our country. Thank you. I will speak with you again on Saturday. God bless you, and God bless America. Good night.

Mark reached over and turned off the radio. No one said a word for a long time. Jim finally shattered the silence with the question that all of the adults were asking themselves.

"Can he do that?"

"I guess he can," Mark answered.

"But is it legal?" Jess asked.

"Legal…yes," Ralph answered. "But not Constitutional. All of the authority for what he's doing came from Executive Orders that Presidents have signed over the past few decades. There is no power granted to the President by the Constitution to create law, but that's what an Executive Order does. No one has ever challenged the legitimacy of this practice, and before today, none of the orders have been enacted where there was a need to ascertain their constitutionality."

"So what you're sayin' is that he ain't supposed to do it, but until the lights come back on, there's no way to stop him?" Gunny stated more than asked.

"That's right," the lawyer answered.

"But if it helps our country, isn't it a good thing?" Sam asked.

"Not necessarily, sweetheart. We have a Constitution to keep our government under our control, and while it might look like they are trying to help us, the President just put us under total government control, and not even under our elected officials, but under a bunch of bureaucrats who were appointed and are not beholden or accountable to us," Mark explained.

Everyone around the table nodded their head. David had a different question.

"Do you think Aunt Mary, Uncle Allen, Myra, or Max could have the flu?"

Mark had asked himself the same question about his sister, who lived in California. "Probably not, son. Most of California's population is along the coast. They live up in the mountains. I'm sure they're all right, but if they did get sick, the town they live in is so small that the doctor still makes house calls. Aunt Mary told me he's even done it on horseback if the roads are closed with snow."

David was happy with the answer. "Maybe we should get some horses from that horse farm, Dad."

"Could we?" Sam asked excitedly.

"That's not a bad idea. We'll look into it," Mark answered.

The group headed for the meeting where opinions on what the President had done were mixed. With everyone wound up about the speech, and the spirited debates over the pros and cons, no business was accomplished. Just before Mark was going to adjourn the meeting, he noticed that Joe wasn't there. He asked if anyone had seen him over the course of the day. No one had, so Mark dismissed everyone and hurried back down to the Bagwell house with a large, self-appointed delegation in tow. He knocked on the door vigorously, but received no reply. With the doors locked, he pushed in a screen on one of the windows and entered the house.

"Joe, are you in here? It's Mark. I know you're upset, but keeping to yourself is not going to make things any better."

Mark didn't get an answer from Joe. However, when he went into the kitchen, he did get an answer to one mystery. Lying on the counter were two of the missing pill vials that they had brought from Waco. There was also an empty scotch bottle that he thought he recognized from the same place.

He walked into the master bedroom and found Joe in the bed, just as Connie had said she had left him. He had a broken heart all right. It had been broken by a jumbo-sized butcher knife that was still sticking out of his chest. And he was asleep. Permanently.

Chapter 51

When Mark called the sheriff's office on the radio, the dispatcher told him it might take the sheriff three or four hours to get there. Mark didn't think it would matter. Joe wasn't going anywhere, and they probably wouldn't go look for Connie, if they even had the manpower, until the morning anyway. Mark went back home to wait for Curt, and when he got there, Manny was waiting for him with the four young people from the shootout at the Calvert farm.

"Mark, the kids are wondering what the President's order means for them. Can they still go, or do they have to stay here?" Manny asked.

That was the question for all of them, wasn't it? What did it mean for these kids, for his family trying to get here, for those like Brother Bob and his wife, who lived in a county where they would have to report to a shelter? "Tell them not to worry. We'll get it figured out, and they can stay here until we do."

"Okay, Mark. That sounds like a plan. What about your family?"

"I was just thinking about them, Manny. Hopefully, they can still make it here. We'll just have to wait and see." Mark prayed that they would make it. What would happen to them if they got caught traveling? Would they be put in a shelter or worse? Mark didn't like the sound of what the President had said about FEMA. How did he say it? "FEMA will be empowered to detain lawbreakers and deal with insurgents until our justice system is operational again." It might be a long time before the justice system was up and running. Could FEMA imprison people without a trial until then? And "deal with insurgents" could be translated many ways. Most of them were ways Mark didn't like. He'd ask Curt what his opinion of the speech was.

With Manny taking care of the youths, and Mark realizing that there was nothing he could do at this point for his family, he turned his thoughts to the preacher. Mark found Jim and asked him what he thought they should do.

"It's probably not my place to say," Jim began. "After all, I'm a guest here, too, but I think we should offer to let them move here. We can put them up in a tent, if nothing else."

"I agree. We can't let them go to a shelter. Would you get whoever you think should go with you and talk to him?"

"You want me to go in the morning?"

"I think you should go right now," Mark suggested.

"Okay, I will."

"Good. By the way, how did it go with Gunny today?"

Jim whistled. "Man, he was rough today. I've never seen him so ornery. I think he's just being that way, so he can treat the women the same and not get called out for discriminating. I don't think the girls can cut it. I had to keep talking to my guys today to keep them from quitting, but he still managed to make two of them walk. I'd get a good night's sleep. You're going to need it."

"Thanks for the warning. Let me know what the preacher says."

"You got it," Jim said, as he headed off to gather his delegation.

When Curt arrived, Mark took him down to Joe's house. He looked over the crime scene and asked his technician to bag the murder weapon, dust for prints, and take some pictures. He told Mark he'd put out an APB for Connie. Mark asked if they were going to go look for her. Curt told him she was out of his jurisdiction and had more urgent things to deal with right now. He assured Mark someone would pick her up and deliver her back to him. Mark informed the sheriff that he was sure she'd stolen the AR-15 in addition to the liquor and drugs. He also said she wasn't knowledgeable enough to steal any magazines or ammo for it. The lawman wrote the information down in his notebook.

"You got time for a cup of coffee?" Mark asked..

"Sure. José is going to need some time to finish his work," Curt said, referring to the crime scene tech. "Lead the way."

When they got back to Mark's house, Curt sat down at the kitchen table, and Mark put a percolator on the stove. "So, how did you like the President's speech?" he asked.

"I didn't," Curt replied sharply. "I work for the people of this county. They elected me, and they are my bosses. I have no intention of kowtowing to FEMA. In fact, any Feds who try to come into our county and tell us what we can and can't do can kiss my ass." Curt had fire in his eyes and steel in his voice.

Mark was surprised by Curt's candor. He'd never seen him so passionate. "Why don't you tell me how you really feel?" Mark said to break the tension.

Both men laughed. Then Curt continued, "I'm sorry. I shouldn't have vented at you like that."

"Don't worry about it," Mark replied. "I may need to do the same thing sometime."

"Any time," Curt smiled. "It's just that I'm afraid what FEMA might do isn't the best thing for the country. With the declaration of Martial Law...I know he didn't call it that, but that's what it is...the Constitution can be suspended. That means they can confiscate just about anything they want. Firearms, gas, vehicles, and even any food they consider being over a family's immediate needs. There are Executive Orders to cover all those things and more. A lot of people...Greg's one of them...think the government's been wanting to do this for a long time and has just been biding their time until the situation was right."

"And what do you think?"

"I don't think the federal government is that devious. It's just too big and unorganized. There may be small parts of it that have plans, but the government as a whole can't even work together in the best conditions. I don't see how they could pull something this big off in the current situation."

"What does Greg say?" Mark asked.

"I haven't talked to him yet, but I think he's going to see this as part of the UN's New World Order conspiracy he blathers about from time to time."

"But you don't think so?"

"No. Maybe. Hell, I don't know what to think anymore." The lawman rolled his eyes. "It sure goes along with what the conspiracy theorists have been saying was going to happen, but then, even a broken clock is right twice a day. I'm just concerned with what FEMA has planned for our county at this point."

"What do you think they'll do?"

"Well, we're under the fifty thousand threshold the President talked about for mandatory relocation. I'm hoping FEMA will see we don't really need any help and leave us alone. That's what I'm going to try to diplomatically convince them to do, but I have no idea what they have in mind. I can tell you one thing. I will not stand idly by and see them stomp on our God-given rights."

"That's good to know." Mark stood up and poured two cups of coffee.

"Something that really bothered me was what the President said about FEMA having the power to detain and deal with lawbreakers and insurgents. I can kind of understand the lawbreaker part, but what do you think the insurgent part means?" Mark asked, as he placed a steaming cup in front of the sheriff.

"Thanks. Yeah, that bothers me, too. As long as the lawbreakers retain all of their rights to a speedy trial, a lawyer, and a jury of their peers, I don't have a problem with them being detained, but it sounds like the President's giving FEMA the authority to hold them indefinitely. That's not right. And what laws are we talking about? If he means that murderers and rapists can be held for a couple of months until we can try them, then that's okay in my book, but if we're talking about misdemeanors, or if we can't give even the most hardened criminal a trial in less than six or eight months, then I have a big problem with it. And I'm not sure what 'insurgent' means to FEMA. To me, it means looters and raiders. To FEMA, it may mean anyone who refuses to jump through hoops for them. I just don't know, and that's why I'm so uneasy."

"I guess we'll just have to wait and see, huh?"

"I guess we will," Curt agreed.

The two men talked about the virus. Curt didn't know how the government could effectively keep people from sneaking county to county. He said that hopefully the great expanses in the western states, coupled with the lack of fast transportation, would at least slow it down. Mark asked him what he intended to do with anyone coming in to their county. He explained that it was kind of a catch-22 situation. He would instruct his people to turn anyone approaching the county line away, but if they snuck in on a back road or trail, he wasn't sure of the best course of action. If he arrested them, then he had to put them up in the jail. It may be better to just let them pass on through. Mark didn't envy the sheriff's job. The two men chatted about other subjects for a while and then walked back down to Joe's house. The tech was done, and he and Curt left.

A few minutes later, Jim drove back up to the house. The preacher had agreed to move to Silver Hills. Jim had a truckload of the minister's possessions and asked Mark if he'd help him unload them. As the two men walked outside, Mark realized he hadn't even thought about where to put the minister.

"I guess we can let him stay in my camper, at least for a while," Mark suggested.

"Abby insisted they move into her house," Jim informed him.

When they got to the truck, Mark noticed that a large part of the cargo was fishing equipment. It seemed that Brother Bob, like several of Jesus' disciples, was a fisherman. Mark commented as much, and Jim informed him that he still needed to pull the pastor's boat over. They unloaded the contents of the truck into Abby's garage, and then Jim left to pick up the next load. Mark needed to get some sleep in preparation for his upcoming day with Gunny, so he went home and quickly made his way to bed.

When the training began the next morning, Mark felt that Jim might have understated how tough Gunny was being. Mark had what he thought was a first-rate team. Victor was on it, as were three other promising young men who had previously been on guard duty. Gunny had them run, roll, crawl, climb, and jump with their weapons and packs. By the end of the first hour, they were all sucking wind. Then he started telling them how to move as a unit and how to cover each other. Anytime it looked as if anyone's attention strayed, Gunny questioned that person and berated him if he couldn't give the correct answer. Mark could see the younger men get upset, but he had already warned them, and none of them lost their cool. When the trainees were finally given a short break, they flocked around Mark.

"This is a crock of shit," one of the young guns said. "I understand we need to know this stuff, but he doesn't have to treat us like crap if we don't get it right away."

The other young men nodded their heads in agreement. Mark smiled back at them.

"Allen, he probably just wants to see if we have any quitters in the group." Mark paused and looked at each man for an instant. "Do we?"

The men looked at one another and then slowly shook their heads.

"Good," Mark continued. "Now go get some water before the break's over."

Gunny continued to quiz the men hard. The old Marine did his best to extract a negative reaction from each man more than once, and Mark couldn't tell if he was happy or disappointed when his best efforts failed. A little before four in the afternoon, Gunny had the men do more physical training. It was very difficult, since he'd worked them out hard in the morning and then let them sit in comfortable chairs for the classroom portion, causing their muscles to cool down and tighten up. Mark, even with his disciplined training regimen, felt the pain in his legs as they ran up and down the hill in short rushes with all of their gear on. Mark didn't have to guess how the others were feeling; he could see it on their faces. After they'd run up and down the main subdivision road for what seemed like the hundredth time, Gunny took them to one of the empty lots where there was a large puddle. He made the men get down into pushup position, still wearing their packs, in the middle of the puddle. He had them do pushups, and they were required to put their face into the water when they were in the down position, but they weren't allowed to put their body on the ground. The old goat called out 'Up...Down' in his best Drill Instructor voice. If one of the men dropped his weight down onto the ground, Gunny was on him like a cat on a mouse, calling him names that would have made the most hardened seaman blush. Then he'd switch tactics and sympathize with the struggling trainee, telling him he didn't have to take the abuse. The old man was cruel and relentless. He rode them until he got what he wanted. After fifteen minutes of pushups and humiliation, Allen stood up, cursed at Gunny and walked off. Gunny spent a few more minutes on the remaining four before he dismissed them. He instructed them to report back Friday morning for further training.

It was Mark's day to get a shower, and he enjoyed it after the hard training. He was used to running, but wearing a heavy pack and carrying a rifle while doing it elevated the aerobic exercise to almost torture status. He wondered how the women would hold up tomorrow. He didn't see how they would be able to make it. He knew that Jess wouldn't make it. It was just too bad she'd have to find out the hard way it wasn't for her. Mark decided he'd try to stop by several times and see how they were doing.

After dinner, the family listened to the news and then attended the nightly meeting. Mark noticed that Brother Bob and his wife were there. The only major point of business was about letting the four young adults who were heading to Houston stay in Silver Hills until the travel restrictions were lifted. The group voted to let them camp in one of the vacant lots. They could help and become part of the community, but at the first sign of trouble, they would be asked to leave. They were grateful and assured everyone that there would be no trouble.

After the meeting, Mark was tired and headed for bed. He encouraged Jess to get a good night's sleep. He thought about warning her more, but decided against it. She told him she was right behind him. He fell asleep almost as soon as his head hit the pillow and never felt her come to bed five minutes later.

The next day, Mark had little to do except teach his classes for the regular guards. They were also going to bury Joe late that afternoon, so he checked on the arrangements for the funeral a couple of times. With nothing else pressing, he had plenty of free time to observe Gunny's class. In the morning, the trainer had the five women running with packs and rifles just like his group had done. Mark noticed that all of the women were having at least a little trouble, but none of them said a word. He figured that Susan had given them all a pep talk before the class started. Jess was the oldest in the group, and she was struggling more than the others. When she cast a look in Mark's direction, he just shrugged his shoulders at her to let her know there was nothing he could do. The look on her face hardened with determination. Mark had really been hoping she would quit, but he couldn't help but feel sorry for her. Gunny was just getting warmed up, and it would be a long day for the woman he loved.

The group Susan had assembled impressed Mark. In addition to herself and Jess, she had Olga Jensen, Paul's wife. Olga was a big-boned, tall, blonde woman in her early thirties. She reminded Mark of a Viking. She was almost six feet tall, and while you wouldn't call her fat, she was no lightweight.

The youngest member of the group, Christina Greene, or Chris as she liked to be called, was the daughter of John and Laura. She was nineteen or twenty and had been about to start her sophomore year at UTSA when The Burst hit. She had gone to high school in La Vernia and had lettered in almost every sport. She wasn't drop dead gorgeous, but she was cute. With her tomboy attitude and athletic physique, she was one of the most pursued young females in the area.

The last and most surprising member on Susan's team was Manny's daughter, Letty. Although she was the smallest female, she was by far the fastest. Mark figured she must be a runner, because she was having the least trouble. If it weren't for the pack and rifle, Mark deduced that she'd be flying up and down Gunny's obstacle course.

Mark watched what Gunny was doing. The man was a master. Mark hadn't been able to see what he was trying to do when he'd been in the middle of it yesterday, but Gunny had a method to his madness. It was all so clear to Mark, now that he was sitting on the sidelines. Gunny ran the women until they were tired enough that it began to interfere with their cognitive ability. Then he started instructing them to do this or that, knowing they'd have a difficult time following directions. Then, when someone messed up, he scolded them in a manner not to correct them, but in a way that would make them angry. Mark realized that this would let Gunny evaluate how they most likely would perform in the field when exhaustion and fear took over. Fear was a hard emotion to invoke without danger present, but anger could be a close substitute.

Although the women were making mistakes, Mark noticed they were doing better than his group had yesterday. They seemed to have more focus. This observation dovetailed into what he'd seen in his karate classes over the years. Females were much better students than men.

After lunch, Gunny had the women sitting in chairs as he lectured about small unit tactics, escape and evasion, and reconnoitering. When he was through with his lecture, he quickly began the next phase.

"Okay. I want y'all to grab your packs 'n' rifles and run down to the gate 'n' back as fast as you can."

The women groaned as they stood up and tried to stretch out their stiff muscles. They slowly started reaching for their gear. Gunny watched for a second. When none of the women were looking, he had a smirk on his face that, had any of the day's victims seen it, would have ruined his plan. Mark saw it from his distant spectator's seat and couldn't help but laugh inside.

"MOVE!" Gunny screamed, his face now deadly serious.

The women jumped at his command and quickly began to run toward the gate, hoisting their packs into place as they ran. Mark watched as the individuals made it to the gate and back as quickly as they could, which wasn't that fast. Letty came back first, and Jess again brought up the rear, huffing and puffing. When she reached the rest of the group, Gunny opened up on them with a barrage. He censored what he said to them a little compared to the language he had used with the men, but only slightly.

"Do you all have shit in your ears, or are you just stupid?" he yelled. "We just spent several hours working on moving as a unit and covering each other, and you all act like you're in the sack race at the company picnic. Just run off and leave the others behind. I've seen kindergarteners who rode the short bus do better than you five wannabees. Now do it again!"

Three women took off down the hill with two covering them. When the three had gone twenty-five or thirty yards, they knelt down and covered the two, as they ran past the first group a ways. Then the process repeated itself until they'd made it to the gate and all the way back.

"That was slightly better, but you're slower than a three-legged turtle. Do it again."

"But, Gunny…" Susan gasped, with her hands on her knees trying to catch her breath.

Instantly Gunny was screaming in her face, his nose just inches from hers. "But, Gunny, WHAT? When I tell you do something, MISSY, you don't 'But, Gunny' me. You just damned well do it. YOU GOT THAT?"

Susan's eyes were the size of manhole covers when Gunny jumped in her face, but upon the expulsion of the word 'Missy,' they narrowed to angry slits that Mark didn't know how she could see out of. She grabbed Jess by the shirtsleeve, and they started down the hill.

Mark watched as Gunny ran them up and down the hill three more times. Then he took them to the puddle. He explained the drill and had them get into push up position. Mark noticed that he'd let them take their packs off.

"UP! DOWN! UP! DOWN! UP!" he barked.

Letty was the first to fall to the ground. Although she was the fastest runner, it seemed she had the least upper body strength. Gunny pounced on her like a spider on a fly.

"I told you I only wanted to see your hands and your toes touching the ground. Did I not make myself clear? Or maybe you can't cut it. I guess I could let you do girl pushups. Is that what you want, to do girl pushups?" Gunny's tone was venomous.

"No, Gunny. I can do them," Letty said, as she struggled back into the up position.

"DOWN!"

All of the faces went into the water.

"You don't need this shit, Letty." Gunny's tone changed, as he seemingly reasoned with the woman. "You've got a little boy who needs you. Have you thought about that? A little boy who doesn't have a father anymore. What's he going to do if something happens to you? UP! Just get your stuff and go home. You don't want to do this."

"Yes, I do." Letty yelled back at the old man. "I have to do it for my boy, so he can see that men and women can do anything if they stick to it." Mark couldn't tell if the water dripping off her face was from the puddle or tears.

"DOWN! UP! DOWN! UP!"

Susan was the next to drop. Gunny seemed to really enjoy going after her.

"You're supposed to be the leader of these Girl Scouts!" He screamed at her. "Why don't you get a real Girl Scout troop and take them out to sell some cookies, Missy? DOWN! Come on, Susan. You need to go home and take care of your boys. They need you. Letty's son has his grandparents if something happens to her, but what about your boys? They don't have anyone but you. Quit this silly charade and go home to them," he pleaded. "UP!"

Susan stared hatefully at the Marine when her face came out of the water.

"Stick it," was all she said through clenched teeth.

Olga and Chris eventually fell and then withstood Gunny's debasing discourse and feigned sympathy. Both passed the test.

Jess was the last one to fall. Mark was surprised she'd made it the longest. In fact, he was beginning to believe she'd be successful. Gunny moved to her side. Mark cringed at what was coming. He knew Gunny would push every button until he could find the one that would get her to quit. He'd failed to get a quitter yet, and he wouldn't be happy until he had one. He would be relentless. Until a few minutes ago, Mark had been hoping that Gunny would get his wife to resign, but somehow he now wanted Jess to be successful. He held his breath as Gunny verbally attacked.

"Get back up! Right now!" he yelled, as she pushed herself back up. Then his tone softened. "What's your story, Teach? You've been lagging behind all day. You can't stay with these young girls. I hear you're one hell of a teacher. Why don't you go back and do what you're good at? DOWN!"

Mark saw Gunny get close to Jess and whisper in her ear, as her face was in the water. He couldn't make out what the old devil dog was saying. Mark found himself whispering a prayer for Jess.

"UP!"

Jess and the other women pushed themselves out of the puddle. Mark saw the look on his wife's face. It was as if she was in pain, more than would be caused by the physical stress of the push-ups. Mark could see her bottom lip quivering. His shoulders slumped, as he realized what was happening. Gunny had won. She was going to quit, just like she had quit karate, aerobics, jogging, and countless other things.

"DOWN!"

Four of the women stuck their faces back into the water, but Jess was frozen in the up position. Tears were streaming down her face. Gunny had broken her. 'I should have helped her last night,' Mark thought guiltily. Now he'd have to build her back up, and it wouldn't be easy. He cursed himself for agreeing with Susan about a women's team. His life would be hell until Jess got her self-confidence back.

Gunny continued his pleading. "Come on, Teach. You don't need some old fart like me to tell you what you can't do. You know you're in over your head. Save yourself the embarrassment. Just get up and go home. UP!"

Mark knew her. She would silently stand up and walk home as Gunny had suggested. His emotions and thoughts were as jumbled as he knew hers were at this moment. He found himself holding his breath.

"DOWN!"

Mark was a little surprised when Jess's arms bent, and her face went into the water.

"Jess, you don't need this crap." Gunny really did sound sincere. "The neighborhood needs you to teach their kids. That's your calling. What are you trying to prove? Just go home and take a hot bath. Trust me, you'll thank me tomorrow. UP!"

Jess pushed back up. Her face was screwed up like someone was twisting it from the inside. 'Here's where she stands up and leaves,' Mark thought.

"FUCK YOU, GUNNY!" she screamed.

Mark was shocked. The four other women whooped and laughed at her outburst. It seemed somehow to unite them. It became their mantra. They repeated it over and over, quietly at first but slightly louder each time.

"I am good enough! I may have to work twice as hard, but I will!" Jess snarled at the old man. After staring him down for a minute, she joined in a chorus of 'Fuck you, Gunny!'

Mark was dumbfounded. Jess wasn't quitting. She had made it. Somehow Gunny had pulled something out of her he'd been unable to find in over twenty years. The five women had fused into a cohesive unit before his eyes. Mark now wondered how Gunny would react to the unified response he was receiving from this team. He didn't have to wait long for an answer.

"Okay. Get your gear. Class is dismissed for the day. Be back here at 8:30 in the morning."

The women sprang up and all high fived and hugged each other. They grabbed their gear, and as a team, started walking out of the field.

"Ladies!" Gunny called. The women turned around to face the old man. "I'm only gonna say this once, so listen good."

Gunny cleared his throat. "I was wrong."

Chapter 52

The next morning, all three of the scout teams met with Gunny. Mark was tired. The evening before had been busy with Joe's funeral, which went about as well as could be expected, and the meeting, where there was more and more speculation about the President's address. In addition, Mark had nightmares about his family. It seemed each time he managed to go to sleep, some new terror manifested itself in his dreams. First, it was the MZB's after them, then it was the Burst Flu, and the FEMA goons, or they just ran out of food and starved to death. Each nightmare woke him up in a cold sweat, and it seemed an eternity until he could calm down enough to go back to sleep, just to have the process repeat itself.

Mark was somewhat surprised by how Gunny started the meeting.

"I wanna congratulate the twelve of you for making it through the first day of training," the old man smiled, "but don't get a big head just yet. The toughest part may be over, but ya still have several more tests to pass. The part that'll prob'ly be the hardest for some of you is the physical test. It's divided into two parts. First, you have ta run a mile in eight minutes or less. Then you'll all wear a pack that weighs twenty-five percent of your body weight, plus your rifle, and complete a three-mile obstacle course in less than fifty minutes. The course will include push-ups, sit-ups, pull-ups, belly crawls, shootin' from different positions, shootin' and reloadin' while on the move, and anything else I can think of. You have to be able to do this three weeks from today. So, if'n runnin' ain't your strong suit, you better start training." He looked right at Jess, as he said the last sentence and paused. "And if your marksmanship ain't up to par, you better work with Jim." Another short pause. "I know all of you can pass this test if you put your mind to it. You may ask why I'm making this a requirement. Scouts are just that. They find the enemy, not fight him. If'n you get into a tough situation, I want you to run back here, lickety-split if possible, and if you're forced into a firefight with a larger force, you better be able to shoot if'n you want to survive. Any questions?"

Gunny looked at each person, and no one asked anything for a few seconds. Finally, Jim raised his hand, and Gunny pointed at him.

"Are we going to replace the men who quit?"

"I was coming to that. We're not going to replace them right now. Later, we'll train some others, but for right now we're goin' to go with two six-man...I mean six-person teams. This'll let us get you all out in the field the fastest, and if a couple of you don't make it, we'll still have two five-man teams. Mark, all of your team except for you will be assigned to Jim. Victor will be second-in-command. Mark will move to Susan's team, and he'll now be in charge of it. Susan will back him up."

Susan crossed her arms, and her eyes narrowed. "So you don't think we women can handle ourselves without a man to tell us what to do?" she said venomously.

"No, Susan." Gunny emphasized her name to show that he wasn't calling her 'Missy.' "It's not that at all. Mark is the logical choice to put with your team. We need to split the teams equally, and since his wife is with you all, no one can be accused of any hanky-panky. Mark has the most experience, so it only makes sense to put him in charge. Plus, this is only temporary. When we get more people trained, I'll probably put him in charge of a new team."

"So, we're going to have the same assignments as Jim's team?" Her voice still had a razor's edge.

Mark leaned in to her. "Susan, you need to cool it."

She now glared at Mark the same way she'd looked at Gunny.

"If you have enough team members after the test, you'll be treated the same as the men's team," the old Marine answered.

Susan didn't say anything else. Mark didn't know if Gunny's answer had satisfied her or if she was being quiet because he had said to.

Gunny spent the next couple of hours lecturing about what the teams should look for if they encountered a group of possible bad guys. He went over numbers, weapons, supplies, organization, and other things that would be helpful for them to know if they had to defend against an attack. When Gunny was satisfied with the answers everyone was giving, he moved them to the rifle range and had Jim go over some advanced techniques. Everyone seemed to do pretty well, except for Letty. She really had a problem shooting the AR-15, even though she did well with a pistol. After a couple of hours of rifle and pistol training, the two teams were dismissed until the next morning.

On the way back home, Mark realized he was supposed to have gone over to the Watsons' to check on how Tony was coming with the night sights. He mentally kicked himself for not remembering. He wondered what else he was forgetting.

Dinner was good, even if beans and rice was becoming an every other day occurrence. The news mostly went over the new FEMA rules the President had explained on Tuesday night. Everybody in Bexar County was advised to make their way to one of the two established shelters in San Antonio, or the new one in the far northwest corner of the county, as soon as possible. Anyone who had a running vehicle was instructed to bring it and any gasoline they might have to the shelter closest to them. FEMA would then use them to help those who were too infirm or too distant to make the trip without assistance. Those who were unable to relocate without help should remain at home until a FEMA representative came by to make arrangements for transportation. Mark was glad they weren't faced with having to leave their homes. It made him hope Curt could convince FEMA to leave their county alone. He certainly didn't want to turn over any of their vehicles or other supplies to some bureaucrat.

The talk at the meeting was mostly about FEMA. The populace of the subdivision was split almost exactly down the middle by two opinions. Some felt it was about time the government did this, and that it was their duty to do whatever they could to help, even if it meant lending their cars, trucks, fuel, or whatever FEMA needed within reason. The other half argued the government had no right to commandeer any private property. Besides, one man argued, who got to decide what was 'within reason?'

"What if they ask for your food?" he demanded. "What if they tell you that you have to work for them for free because it's a national emergency? Do you think that is within reason?"

"They wouldn't do that," someone answered.

"Probably not," Ralph said, joining the fray, "but there are laws and executive orders on the books authorizing them to do those things and many others. I did a paper on executive orders in law school. If you read them, it's scary what they can do if they think they need to. Look at what they're doing to the people in the next county. Most of you probably think that if the people who live in Bexar County don't report to a shelter, they won't be able to eat, but I know some people there who live outside of the city and are probably better off than we are right now. They already had water wells, gardens, and farm animals before The Burst. I know a guy who has all those things plus a big tank full of catfish and bass. His wife cans what they get out of the garden every year, and he shoots two or three deer a year from his back porch. He told me once that he could live for a long time without ever stepping foot off of his property. Put yourself in his shoes. Do you think he should have to leave it all behind, just because the government said so? Doesn't he have the right to decide what's best for him?"

No one said a word, and after a minute, Ralph continued. "We have all worked very hard to make sure we can take care of ourselves. We've even helped some people less fortunate than we are. What if FEMA comes to our county and wants to move us to a place where they say what we get to eat and what we get to do and where we can and can't go? What'll we do then?"

"No government toady is going to make me to move off of my property!" Don Wesley yelled to a chorus of applause with some chants of 'You tell 'em' and 'Hell, yeah' thrown in.

"That's the way I feel, too," Ralph said, after the clapping had subsided. "But what if they use the National Guard to try and force us to move at gun point? I don't think that will happen, but each of us needs to decide how we'll react if it comes down to that."

Again it was quiet. Ted asked a question after a moment. "How do you think we should deal with that, Ralph?"

"I'd start with passive resistance. If all of us refuse to go, they'll probably decide that we're not worth the effort."

"And if they decide to force the issue?"

"Then we actively resist." Ralph's tone carried more meaning than his words.

The residents started talking quietly in small groups. It was obvious to Mark that most of them hadn't considered this possibility. If he hadn't spoken with Curt on Tuesday, he probably wouldn't have either. He thought it might be good to let what Ralph had said sink in for a while.

"Thanks, Ralph, for telling us about this. I think it might be good for all of us to think about what we should do and talk about it again tomorrow evening."

The crowd nodded their heads as one. No one had other business, so the meeting was adjourned.

After the meeting, Susan came up and talked to Mark.

"I guess you know I didn't like you telling me to be quiet this morning?"

Mark nodded his head, as Susan continued.

"In fact, it pissed me off pretty bad, but I was quiet because you're in charge of our group, and it wouldn't look right if I argued with you in front of everyone."

"That was the right thing to do," Mark said. He wondered why she couldn't extend the same courtesy to Gunny.

"I do want to talk to you about it, but I didn't want to do it until I calmed down."

"And are you calmed down now?"

"Yes," she said. "I've been thinking about it all day. I was right to say something. Even Gunny saw that I was right and said he'd treat us the same as the men, but if I hadn't have spoken up, I don't think he would have been fair with us. I expect that from him, but I don't expect it from you. You made me feel like I was wrong." Her face got redder by the minute. "I thought you were on my side!"

Mark didn't think she was as calm as she said she was. He felt more like he was dealing with a teenager than a grown woman. She seemed to take this equality thing too literally. Her 'me against the male dominated world' attitude was becoming a problem. He had to make her see the reality of the situation. "I think you were wrong, and I'm not on anybody's side. You were right when you said the women should get a chance to prove they could do the job as well as the men can. I stood up for that, and you're getting your chance, aren't you? But when Gunny assigns us a job, you can't question our orders. You need to separate being on the Security Committee from being on the scout team. On the committee, we're all equal, but on the team, Gunny's our boss, and when he says 'jump,' the only question out of your mouth should be 'how high?'"

"But, I think it…"

Mark interrupted her. He had to bite his tongue not to call her 'Missy,' as immature as she was acting. "Susan, I'm not going to argue with you about this." His voice was firm and authoritative. "I'm going to tell you that you'd better wake up and smell the coffee. You and the other women passed Gunny's first test. In fact, you did better than the men did, but you better take a hard look at our team. We have a big test coming up in a couple of weeks and the only person I'm sure can run the three miles within the time limit is Letty, and I don't know if she can pass the marksmanship part."

The color drained out of Susan's face. "You don't think we'll pass?" She seemed shocked at this revelation.

"Not if the test were today. I think you all can pass if you work at it, but all this 'he's not being fair' whiney shit of yours is a distraction not only to you but to the rest of the team."

"I'm not whining! I'm just trying to make sure everyone gets treated the same!"

Mark was getting mad. "Then I hope you get just what you want." He turned and walked off before he said something that would cost him. He walked into the house and took a few deep breaths to calm himself down. It didn't help much.

Jess walked into the kitchen. "What's the matter?"

"Nothing, really, just something Susan said." Mark tried to decide if he should tell her. She decided for him by changing the subject.

"Honey, I need three favors," she said sweetly.

"Just name them," he said, hoping he wasn't in too much trouble.

"First, I need you to spend some time with Timmy and Tommy like you promised. I know you've been busy, but it's really important that they get to know you."

"I'll do it tomorrow," he agreed. "What else?"

"I need you to run with me in the morning. I have to get a lot faster if I'm going to pass Gunny's test." She smiled seductively. "And as for the last favor...I'll let you guess what that is."

The next morning, Mark and Jess ran three miles. She did better than he'd expected, but her assessment of needing to be faster was dead on. Mark's leg was feeling much better. He noticed that he wasn't favoring it at all today. Even Lisa was pleased with how it was healing. When they finished the run, Jess made Mark promise to keep working with her.

Brother Bob held Sunday morning services in one of the empty fields. Most of the neighborhood attended, regardless of their denomination. Mark, Jess, and their now four children were there, too. The preacher kept it fairly short, since everyone was standing. Mark prayed that his family was safe wherever they were, and that God would keep the neighborhood safe from MZB's, FEMA, and anyone else who would destroy what they'd worked so hard for.

After lunch, Mark and David played catch with Timmy and Tommy. Mark was surprised at how good the boys were for their ages. Tommy told them Rodney had been their baseball coach since they were old enough to play T-ball. Later, Mark pulled out David's old Stevens single shot .22 and started teaching the boys how to shoot. They'd never shot more than a BB gun before, but they caught on quickly. Afterwards, the three of them returned the rifle to the safe, after they'd cleaned it together. When they were done, Mark sent the boys to clean up for supper. Before Timmy left, he hugged Mark's leg quickly and then ran off after his big brothers.

Chapter 53

On Monday, Jim, Gunny, and Mark went to town to train those who were training their own small groups. Mark found a few minutes to talk with Curt. The sheriff said he hadn't heard anything from FEMA yet. He was a little surprised they hadn't been to see him, and he told Mark he'd be sure to keep everyone up to date when they did show up.

On Tuesday, Gunny spent the morning with Mark's scout team. In the afternoon, he sent them on a short recon mission. Gunny divided them in two fire teams. Mark and Susan would be the leaders of each team. Susan was assigned Jess and Olga, while Mark was given Letty and Chris. Everyone was carrying AR-15's except for Mark, who had his FAL, and Olga, who had the Franken-FAL Jerry had sold to Mark. This gave each fire team a heavy battle rifle to go with the 'poodle shooters.' That's what Gunny called the AR's. Gunny also gave everyone a chest rig for their magazines.

"Where'd you get these?" Mark asked, noticing they were made from heavy canvas.

"Rob lent me his, and Abby used it for a pattern to make some for us. They don't have the velcro or nice buckles like the original, but I think she did a great job on them."

"I'll say," Mark smiled as he put his on.

The rig had pockets for magazines in the front, and the straps spread the weight across his shoulders, so that it was quite comfortable. Mark had thought several times that they needed a better way to carry their extra mags. He gave Gunny a grin and a thumbs-up. The only other gear anyone carried was a canteen and handgun. Mark and Susan also had FRS radios.

They circled the subdivision, trying to stay about a half mile away from their home base. There were no residences within that distance. Everyone did well, except for a few times when they had to be reminded not to bunch up. As far as his team went, there were no surprises. They didn't see anyone during their trek, but two things did intrigue Mark about the ground they covered. The first was a cut fence to the northeast of the subdivision. It was fresh, and there were still footprints where a small group had gone through. The second was the utility easement running south of their homes, just on the edge of the half-mile circle. It was over the hill and hidden by the trees behind Silver Hills. Mark had no idea that a natural gas pipeline ran that close to his house. The real surprise was how a path had been worn down through the easement. He and his team followed it a ways, and they found evidence of two recent camps and several other signs humans were using the pipeline to escape from the city.

It made sense to Mark, once he thought about it. The easement was mowed, and it had gates in each fence it crossed. It was a lot easier to climb a gate than it was a barbed wire fence. Plus, people didn't like to build their houses too close to the pipeline, so the chances of running into the property owners were slim. Mark imagined that the people using the easement were ones who didn't want any trouble, and it was probably a lot safer than walking down the road. They'd have to keep an eye on this. If MZB's started using it, there could be big trouble. Fortunately, MZB's were usually lazy and not that smart.

When they got back to the subdivision, the team was debriefed by Gunny. He told Mark his ideas about how to watch the easement and that they would talk with the security committee after they found out a little more.

That night after the meeting, Roberta Simmons came up to Mark and apologized to him for what she'd said when Scott died. Mark told her it was understandable, and he accepted her apology. She told him she wanted to help out any way she could. Mark made a suggestion that she check with Jess and Lisa to see how she could best contribute. Mark also expressed his sincere grief about Scott's death.

The next night at dinner, Mark got two surprises. The first was Alex Petrie joining them for the meal. The second was a small bowl of radishes on the table.

"Are these out of our garden?" he asked.

"Yes, they are," Jess beamed.

Mark wasn't crazy about radishes, but these were delicious, probably because he hadn't had any fresh produce in over a month. He noticed that Alex was quite reserved. In fact, he never looked directly at Mark during the entire meal. Mark thought he probably had his bluff in on the youngster. He hoped so.

After dinner, there was an impromptu domino tournament. Everyone partnered up with his or her significant other. When Mark and Jess played Sam and Alex, Mark was impressed by the boy's adroitness for the game. Mark had to pull his A-game out to beat the young team. If he and Jess hadn't been playing together for so long that each knew what the other partner was thinking, the outcome might well have been different.

When Mark went to bed, his thoughts were mostly about his family. It had been twenty days since they'd left Waco. His hopes that they would make it here were diminishing. Now, he prayed that they were safe wherever they were.

Thursday morning, Mark's team reported to Gunny for training. He ran them through some quick drills and informed them what he wanted them to do for the remainder of the day. They were to make their way east along the easement cautiously and see if they could determine where the people using it were coming from. The refugee traffic had started picking up again since the order to report to shelters. They were seeing eight or ten groups a day making their way past the gate. Some of these groups had a place to go, but others didn't. Gunny wanted to know how many people were using the pipeline and where they were entering it. Once Mark's team reported back on the entrance or entrances to the pipeline, he planned to send Jim's team out on a two or three day patrol to determine how much it was being used. Then they could decide on the proper precautions.

When Susan heard that the other team was going on the first overnight patrol, she started to protest.

"We're the first team up," she argued. "We should get the overnight patrol."

Mark saw the irritation on Gunny's face. He started to say something to his second-in-command, but before he could, Jess spoke up.

"Would you gentlemen please excuse us for a minute?"

The other four women pulled Susan with them just out of earshot of the two men. They watched the animated conversation, wondering what was being said. Jess and Olga did most of the talking at first. It wasn't hard to see that Susan didn't like what they were telling her. Her responses were punctuated by her arms moving as much as her mouth was. After a few minutes, the five women came back over. Nothing was said, and Susan just stood there with her arms folded and a sour look on her face.

Before Gunny sent them off, he gave them a pack frame that had a CB radio, a motorcycle battery, and an antenna mounted to it. Gunny also gave Susan a codebook with frequencies that would be monitored in the CP 24/7. They varied by time of day and day of the week. Don Wesley had built the single-side citizens band radio at Gunny's request, and he estimated it should work easily up to a range of ten miles. Gunny quickly showed them how to operate the radio, how to read the codebook, and told them to call only if they needed help. Susan shouldered the radio pack, and the team made their way to the pipeline easement.

They spotted two groups. One was a family of three, and the other was a group of eleven. The second group was moderately armed, but they didn't appear to be looking for trouble. Mark's team had no trouble avoiding contact with these groups, as they were making way more noise than they should have. They also found a few more campsites along the way. Mark was most concerned about stumbling into the camp of a group traveling by night and resting during the day. That's how Mark would have traveled, if he had to. He made sure everyone kept an eye out for such a camp. Traveling stealthily, it took them until late afternoon to make it to where evidence pointed that most people were entering the pipeline. It was where the easement went under Anderson Loop, the outer loop around the city of San Antonio. Mark estimated they were eight or nine miles from Silver Hills and at least fifteen miles from San Antonio proper. They crossed under the loop and followed the pipeline a few hundred yards, but it was obvious that this section was very lightly traveled.

Mark huddled his group together. "What do you all think?"

"Looks like this is it," Susan said. She seemed to have cooled off considerably since this morning. "I don't see any reason to go any further, do you?"

"No," Mark answered. "Anybody else?"

The others just shook their heads.

"It's getting pretty late," Mark continued. "Why don't we get back across the loop and then double time it home? Not too fast, just a steady jog. It should be safe since we'll be going the same way as everyone else. Susan, how about your team taking the point, and we'll bring up the rear?"

"Sounds good," she smiled.

"I can take the radio if you'd like."

"That's okay. It's not very heavy. I hardly notice it's there."

"Well, the offer stands if you change your mind," Mark said.

They were making good time. Susan set a good pace for everyone, and even Jess was keeping up. The running and other exercises she'd been doing with Mark were making a big difference. It had even helped her lose a little more weight, and she was getting stronger, too. The other day, she had playfully hit Mark on the arm, and it had left a bruise, but Mark didn't mind. He'd made her feel guilty about it, and she'd felt the need to make it up to him.

They were two-thirds of the way home when Mark heard a woman scream from where Susan, Jess, and Olga were. They were next to the trees on one side of the easement about twenty-five yards in front of him. He knew it wasn't Jess, the voice was too high for Olga, and he didn't think that Susan would scream so girl-like. He dropped down to one knee and saw Letty and Chris do the same. Susan's team looked like they didn't know what was going on or what to do about it.

"It's okay! It's okay! We're not going to hurt you!" Susan shouted. She had one hand up in front of her like a traffic cop trying to stop the cars at a busy intersection.

Suddenly, a man burst from the opposite side of the easement with a rifle on his shoulder. He was walking forward in a crouched position, and he and the rifle were sweeping back and forth looking for targets. Mark was instantly alarmed.

"FREEZE, MISTER!" he called out in his best command voice.

The man instantly swung the rifle toward Mark's voice.

"Just relax," Mark continued. He now had his hand up like Susan. "We don't want to hurt anyone. Just lower your rifle, and everything will be okay."

The man looked confused. He lowered his rifle, so it was no longer pointing at Mark and his team, but he still had it on his shoulder where it could be used in an instant. He was looking from Susan's team, who now had their rifles trained on him, to Mark's team and back, when a woman came running out from behind a large bush pulling on the top of her trousers.

"I'm okay, Honey. They just startled me," she said, as she approached him.

He seemed to relax a little, and Mark motioned for his team to drop the muzzles of their weapons. "Sorry about that, mister. We didn't expect to run up on anyone." Mark stood with his rifle held non-threateningly and took a few steps toward the couple. He noticed that the man's rifle was a lever action with an octagon barrel, and it looked fairly new. Mark switched his FAL into his left hand and reached out to shake the man's hand when he was close enough. The man copied his movements.

"Pat," the man said. "Pat Rigsby. This is my wife, Gladys."

"Mark. This is Susan, Olga, and Jess." They had moved behind Mark. "Over there are Letty and Chris." Mark didn't want to give their last names. He noticed that the rifle was the type used in Cowboy Action Shooting. The man also had a pair of single action revolvers in a two-gun rig. "What are y'all doing out here?" he asked the couple.

"I was trying to pee when you ran up on me and nearly scared me to death," Gladys answered, as she blushed.

"That was pretty obvious, ma'am. I mean, why are you out on the pipeline easement in the middle of nowhere?" Mark smiled like he was making small talk.

"We're trying to get to my uncle's place south of Stockdale. We didn't want to leave our home, but I'm not going to some camp where some pointed-head, pencil pusher is going to tell me what to do, so we decided to hump it over to Uncle Fred's. I figured we'd be safer on the pipeline than on the road."

Mark had figured as much. He spoke with the man and woman for a few more minutes, and then he and his crew continued on home. Mark wondered if Mike and the others could be using a utility easement to make their way south.

Mike had said they weren't going to use the roads any more than they had to. Mark pondered if he could find a map with the easements marked on it.

When they got back to the subdivision, dinner and the meeting were over. Gunny, Jim, Chaparo, and Ted debriefed them. When Susan told about scaring the crap out of the lady squatting down behind the bush, everyone got a good laugh. When they caught their breath, Gunny warned the scouts that it could have gone badly for them and said they should be more careful in the future.

"Not really, Gunny," Susan commented. "The man only had an old rifle. If he would have shot at us, we'd have chewed him up with our AR's."

"Maybe. Maybe not," Mark corrected her. He explained about the rifle and revolvers and told her that the man seemed very skilled, based on the way he moved with the rifle.

"Plus," Jim added, "those Cowboy Action Shooters can fire really quick when they get good, and they're not shooting a little .22 caliber bullet. Those cowboy rifles can make some big holes."

Susan seemed to dismiss what the men told her. Mark wasn't happy about it, but he let it slide. Gunny was right. It was stupid for them to move that fast, even if they had been through the area a couple of hours before. If someone had set up a trap, they would have fallen right into it.

After discussing what Jim's team would do for the next two days, Mark made his way home, ate some dinner, and headed to bed. His body was so tired that he felt like he could sleep for a week, but his mind kept racing from thought to thought, and it wouldn't stop. Besides thinking about where his family might be, he wondered what FEMA would say when they talked to Curt. He worried about all of the training they still needed to do for the county militia. How was George doing? He hadn't really had a chance to talk to him in over a week. And what about Susan? She'd started off as a real asset, but now she was turning into a royal pain in the butt. Maybe Jess and Olga would straighten her out. He still needed to go see the Watson brothers about the rifle night sights, too, but that was across the county line. What if he got caught crossing it?

Mark desperately wanted to get off this mental carousel that refused to let him go to sleep. It seemed as if it was controlled by some Machiavellian operator, who rebuffed every request to let him off. Mark forced himself to think of all of the good things they had going. The gardens were coming along nicely. Their security teams were shaping up well. The windmill was a Godsend. Things were going fairly well, he thought. Maybe too well. They hadn't had a major setback. In fact, they were probably overdue for one. How would everyone react if the windmill broke? What if something happened to the gardens? They wouldn't have enough food without them. What if they got attacked, and several of them died? Most of the people living here still hadn't come to grips with the total reality of how bad the situation was and how much worse it could get.

Mark's fears and worries continued to spin in his brain, and they became more farfetched and unreasonable as they exhausted his mind, matching his weary body. Finally, sleep overtook him. It gave him little peace, though. His subconscious, now unfettered by his conscious mind, ran amok though his dreams.

First, he dreamt he was on a big hill overlooking Silver Hills. It was like looking down on a colony of ants performing their duties. Each person in the neighborhood did his or her job to near perfection. It was as if he was watching a perfectly choreographed ballet of efficiency. He felt pride at what they'd worked so hard to accomplish. He heard something behind him and turned to see a boulder rolling down the hill toward the workers. He stopped it before it could disrupt the harmony below, but then another boulder came rolling down. He forced himself to stop that one, as well. Another came, and another. Now, it was all he could do to stop the new boulders and hang on to the ones he'd already stopped. A feeling of dread spread throughout his being as he realized he couldn't stop them all. It was only a matter of time before one escaped his best efforts. Finally, a big one avoided his grasp. He watched as it rolled through the subdivision, leaving destruction and chaos in its wake.

Suddenly, he found himself looking down the pipeline his team had reconnoitered. He could see Mike and the rest of his family coming toward him. He felt joy at seeing them. Then he saw a bunch of men in some kind of uniform coming up behind them. The men were dressed in white shirts with black trousers and blood red ties. Each had on a hardhat with some official-looking, red, diamond-shaped emblem on it. If Mark hadn't known better, he would have guessed they were Orkin exterminators. As they closed in on his family, who were unaware of their presence, they stretched out a net to snare his kin. He tried to yell at his family to warn them, but no sound would come out of his mouth.

He woke up in a cold sweat, with his heart trying to pound its way out of his chest. After realizing it was only a dream and getting a drink of water to calm himself down, he went back to sleep, only to find himself looking down the same pipeline. However, this time, it was the virus chasing his loved ones down. At least this time, they were aware of its presence and were running to him as fast as they could. It was a big, pink blob rolling up on them like a tidal wave. Mark watched, powerless to help, as his feet weighed so much he was unable to move them more than an inch or two at a time. He felt horror as the virus engulfed them and then looked for its next victims. It saw and zeroed in on him with a menacing look that he wasn't sure a faceless blob could have. The terror again jolted him from his sleep like it had the first time.

He wiped the sweat from his brow and lay down again. Sleep didn't come as quickly as it had last time, but when it did, he was again on the pipeline easement. The evil this time was the band of MZB's who'd kidnapped Ronnie in Waco. Only now, they really were zombies. Mike, Jeff, Becky, Monica, and Jonathon shot at the MZB's, while Jena ran with Mark's mom and dad, all three carrying the babies and running as fast as they could. The AR-15 had little to no effect on the undead marauders. It was like shooting a charging elephant with a Daisy Red Rider BB gun. Mark knew his FAL could stop the MZB's, and he took careful aim on the lead monster. Mark recognized him as the biker who'd held the knife to Ronnie's throat. Half of his head was still missing from where Ed had so skillfully used his weapon to end the man's natural life. Mark wished Ed was with him now. He squeezed the trigger and felt the hammer fall when the sights were perfectly aligned with the center of his target. Mark's pleasure at making a perfect shot was quickly shattered when he saw his bullet exit the barrel of his rifle at a snail's pace. The normally deadly projectile went about ten feet and then fell to the ground with the force of a spit wad. Mark pulled the trigger again, with the same results. He quickly emptied the entire twenty-round magazine to find a nice, neat pile of bullets stacked up on the ground in front of him. He tried to change magazines but found that the mag release lever wasn't where it was supposed to be. He dropped the twelve hundred dollar club and reached for his Colt. It wasn't there. Mark thankfully awoke again. There was the faintest hint of gray coming through the window, so he got out of bed.

He pulled on his clothes and boots, then strapped his .45 on his hip and patted it twice to make sure it was where it belonged. He picked his watch up off of the dresser, and the luminous hands said it was 7:03. Mark thought it should be much lighter by this time, and he looked out the window to see that is was drizzling. Since The Burst, there had been no real weather forecasts. Not that it really mattered. Before the lights went out, weathermen usually only batted about .500 anyway, but now, it was a crapshoot at best.

Mark walked quietly to the kitchen and started preparing breakfast. A few minutes later, Jess walked in and kissed him good morning.

"You tossed and turned all night," she said quietly.

"I've got a lot on my mind."

"You want to talk about it?"

"Maybe later," he replied, putting on his best smile. He knew it didn't fool her.

"I'm here when you're ready."

The silence said more than words, as the two of them worked in harmony to prepare breakfast. Finally Mark could stand it no more and had to find some way to break the silence. But he really didn't want to talk about what was bothering him. Speaking it out loud might make it true. Finally, he thought of something to say.

"What did you girls tell Susan when you pulled her off yesterday?"

"We told her if she didn't stop objecting to every little thing we're told to do, we wouldn't follow her orders anymore."

Mark's eyebrows went up. "And what did she say to that?"

"She said she was just trying to make sure you G.I. Joes didn't treat us like a bunch of Barbies, and that if we didn't listen to her, Gunny would kick us off the squad. We told her the results would be the same; she wouldn't have a team to lead. That seemed to get her attention."

"I guess it did," he agreed.

The silence returned, and Mark wondered why Jim hadn't come in for a cup of coffee yet. Then he remembered Jim's team was going to observe the pipeline for a couple of days. Mark realized it must be miserable out there in the drizzle.

"What do you have planned today?" Jess asked, breaking his train of thought.

"I need to go see Jerry and Tony about some rifle sights. I was supposed to go last Friday, but you know how that goes."

"Are you taking someone with you?"

"I don't know. I don't know how hard crossing the county line might be. I wouldn't want to get someone else between a rock and a hard place," he explained.

"I understand. I wish I could talk you out of going, but I'm not going to waste my breath. I'd feel better, though, if you took someone to watch your six."

"What did you say?" He was almost laughing. "Watch my six?"

"You know, watch your back."

"I know what it means. I just never heard you say anything like that before."

"Well, maybe I've been hanging out with you G.I. Joes too much. You, Gunny, and Jim are turning me into a G.I. Jess."

"I guess we are."

After breakfast, Mark asked Ralph if he'd like to go to the Watson place and explained the possible risk. Ralph agreed, and after thinking they might have to ditch whatever vehicle they took, Ralph suggested they take a couple of the motorcycles. Mark wasn't real keen on riding in the rain, but the bikes were the only expendable vehicles they had. If they had no problems, they could go back in one of the trucks. Ralph, it turned out, rented and rode hogs with some of his buddies on a regular basis, and he had a nice rain suit. Mark had to make do with some of his duck hunting wardrobe. They set out with their rifles slung across their backs. Mark figured they must have looked like something out of *The Road Warrior*. They didn't see any signs of anyone watching the county line, and it didn't take long to get to their destination. When they pulled up to the gate, Tony was on guard duty, and he let them in.

"Nice hogs," he said, as Mark and Ralph pushed the Harleys through the gate and around the shot up Suburban. Tony had them push the bikes out of sight of the road, and then the three men walked to the house.

"I figured you guys wouldn't go to the FEMA camp," Mark stated.

"You got that right!" Pop Watson replied. "We've got everything we need right here, and we're not leaving. Some of the neighbors left the day after the President made his decree. Others are waiting for FEMA to come pick them up, but we're staying here come Hell or high water."

"You know you're all welcome to come to our place if you need to," Mark offered.

"Thanks," Jerry said, "but we're pretty set on staying here."

"Well, the offer stands if you change your mind."

A few minutes later, Mark asked about the night sights. Tony reported that he wasn't successful in fashioning them. The tritium lamps, as small as they were, weren't small enough to fit in a factory front sight post. He tried to make a larger front sight, but none of his equipment was intended to mill, shape, or thread such a small piece of metal. Mark was disappointed. Jerry quickly spoke up and told them he might have another solution. He had some high quality electronic sights and some mounts that went on the carry handle of an AR-15. Plus, he had a bunch of mounts for the AK-type rifles.

"How many AR mounts do you have?" Mark asked.

"Eight."

"And how many scopes?"

"About fifteen, and I have extra batteries for them, too. I counted the mounts because I knew I didn't have a bunch of them, but if any of your AR's have the removable carry handle, we can mount a scope right to the receiver," Jerry informed him. "The bad part is that it's quite a bit more expensive than if

Tony had been able to make the night sights. I don't think we'd ever be able to use the tractor enough just to trade for them."

"How much are we looking at if we took all of the handle mounts, five AK mounts, fifteen scopes, and as many extra batteries as you can spare?"

Jerry looked up at the ceiling for a minute. "That would come to, let's see, call it $220 in pre-65 silver."

Mark had always been impressed with Jerry's ability to calculate numbers. Mark knew he didn't have that much silver. He did some quick figuring on his own. "How many days do you think you'll need the tractor?"

"Dad?"

"Maybe ten days, at the most," the elder Watson answered.

"And what all did you say you'd be willing to trade for?" Mark asked.

Jerry quickly went down the list, but there was nothing of any significance the Watsons needed that Silver Hills could spare. Mark was rubbing his chin, trying to think of a solution when Tony spoke up.

"Jerry, Mark told me they have some Harleys donated to them by their late owners. We could really use another vehicle. What if we traded that stuff and some more ammo for one of the bikes?"

"That would be great!" Mark exclaimed.

"That could work," Jerry agreed, "I'd rather have a truck, but beggars can't be choosers, can they? How much do you figure the bike's worth?"

"They're the nice ones," Ralph jumped into the conversation. "I was looking at one before The Burst, and they run about $18,000 new. The used ones are a little cheaper, but not much. Harleys hold their value pretty well."

"Any way you figure it, the bike is worth a lot more than the scopes and mounts. That wouldn't really be fair to you, Mark."

"I don't care. We need the scopes a lot more than we need the motorcycle."

"Give us a minute," Jerry said, and he walked out back with Tony and his dad. A few minutes later, they came back carrying several boxes. "How about this? I have seventeen scopes and forty-four extra batteries. I give you all of them, the mounts you asked for, and throw in six cases of ammo for your AK's. We still want to rent the tractor and will pay you in silver, ammo, or whatever you want."

"You don't have to pay to use the tractor, Jerry."

"I know I don't, Mark, but I think it's a good deal for both of us. I know it is for me. If you don't think it's fair to you, then say so, and we'll talk about it. Otherwise, shut up and shake my hand."

"No, it's more than fair," Mark said, as he shook Jerry's hand.

Later in the day, Mark and Ralph delivered the tractor and the Harley and picked up the scopes and ammo in return. It was now raining steadily, and Mark was glad they were in the truck. The trip home was, again, uneventful. He and Ralph both seemed lost in their own thoughts, and it was quiet except for the rhythmic swish of the windshield wipers. Mark was still thinking about the nightmares he'd had. He prayed tat they didn't turn into reality.

Chapter 54

Mark got some sleep that night. He wasn't sure if it was because he was tired from getting so little rest the night before, or if it was because of the rain. He always slept well when it rained. In fact, he had a hard time getting up in the morning. When he did, he counted the days since his family had left Waco. Twenty-three. He was losing a little more hope every day.

He made himself think of something else. Jim and his crew had spent the night out in the rain to watch the pipeline. Mark wondered how much good it had done. How many people would move in the rain? After breakfast, he'd check with the front gate and see how many people had gone by in the last twenty-four hours. Finally, the coffee was ready, and he sat down at the kitchen table with a hot cup and listened to the pouring rain hit the roof.

There was a knock on the back door. It surprised Mark a little. The kitchen had become an open area to everyone who was close to the Turners. They respected the rest of the house, but no one knocked to get into the kitchen. Mark said come in, and Curt walked through the door.

"Hey, Curt. This is a surprise. I didn't hear you drive up. How about a cup of coffee?"

"Coffee sounds great," the lawman said. "The way it's coming down out there, you couldn't hear a tank driving up."

"What brings you over to this neck of the woods?"

"I met with the FEMA man yesterday, and I wanted to fill you in."

"Really? How did it go?" Mark asked eagerly.

"Better than I expected. Thanks," Curt said, as Mark put a cup in front of him. "I didn't really like him. He was a little too self-absorbed for me, but I was able to get some good information because he likes to hear himself talk. He's been charged with evaluating the needs of twelve rural counties and reporting back to FEMA's Central and South Texas headquarters in Austin. Then, they're going assign what resources they can to each county, based on need."

"So, what does that mean for us?"

"I told him we're in pretty good shape, that if they could just get us some food for those who need it, we could take care of distributing it. He seemed to like the idea that he wouldn't have to do much around here. I got the impression he's allergic to work."

Mark laughed. "Aren't all politicians and bureaucrats?"

"Hey! I'm a politician, remember?" Curt said, acting like his feelings were hurt.

"Sorry," Mark snickered. "I didn't mean you."

"Well, alright then," the lawman finally laughed. "Anyway, since Mr. FEMA Big-Shot has eleven other counties, I think he's going to leave us pretty much alone."

"That's great. What about our vehicles? Do you think they're going to try and confiscate them?"

"I don't think so. He told me if I needed any vehicles to distribute the food, I could 'request' them from the citizens of our county, and if I didn't get what I needed to let him know. I don't know if that means he'd get us some trucks or make the citizens 'volunteer' them. Whatever he meant doesn't really matter to us because we'll take care of it ourselves."

"Good," Mark said. "Did he say if they knew anything more about what caused The Burst?"

"He said they think it's some form of terrorism, but they haven't ruled out some kind of solar event. I'm not sure if he really knows anything, or if he just likes using a bunch of big words."

Mark laughed. "I know the type," he said.

"Yeah," Curt agreed, laughing with Mark. After a minute, his face got serious. "He did tell me something that really concerns me, though. They're having trouble getting a lot of the citizens of Bexar County to leave their homes and report to the shelters. They don't really have the manpower to go around and make everyone do it, so they're going to turn the water off in about a week."

"Are they going to announce it on the radio?"

"No. They don't want to give people a chance to store a bunch. Then, when they don't have any, they'll have to leave. They figure most of them will report to the shelters then, but they're going to post National Guard troops at the county lines to catch anybody trying to leave."

"That's kind of dirty pool, isn't it?" Mark asked.

"I think so."

"What'll they do with those people?"

"He told me they were just going to take them to the shelter and make them report," Curt answered. "I hope that's all they do. Making people leave their homes against their will is bad enough in my opinion. Thank God we're not faced with that here."

The two men sat quietly, thinking about what would happen if FEMA tried relocating all of the citizens in this county. A thought occurred to Mark that concerned him.

"What about the people who have their own water wells? What are they going to do about them?"

"I don't know," the sheriff answered. "It's been illegal since the late eighties for anyone in the city limits to have a working well without a special, and hard to get, permit. Even most of the people outside the city are on some kind of water system. There can't be too many folks who have wells *and* the ability to get water from them without electricity. I think those who do would fly under the radar, as long as they kept a low profile."

"I hope so," Mark said quietly.

"Let me tell you what I'm concerned about," Curt said. "This is the real reason I came over. There are a lot of gangs still roaming the streets of San Antonio. FEMA's aware of the problem, but I don't think they know how bad it might be. Most of the gangs are looting abandoned houses for food and keeping their heads down, from what I hear, but when the water goes off, it's going to force things to a head. They'll kill if they have to for water, and some of them might come our way. The FEMA man said they'd have troops at every road leading out of the county, but what if some of them are smart enough not to stay on the roads? No doubt some of the released felons have returned to or mixed in with the gangs. I want us to be ready in case some of them make it past the

National Guard. I wanted to get you, Jim, and Gunny to come back to town with me for a meeting with some of the other guys."

Mark explained that he and Gunny could come but that Jim was out watching a pipeline being used just as Curt was concerned about. Curt asked if they could go see it, and Mark was happy to oblige him. He pulled down two large thermoses out of the cabinet and emptied the rest of the coffee into one of them. He started a fresh pot and went to get his rifle, vest, and rain gear. When he returned to the kitchen, Curt was standing ready with a camouflage poncho on over his uniform. Underneath, it was obvious that he had on a chest rig like Rob had. In his hand, he held a M1A with a stainless barrel and synthetic stock. Mark filled the second thermos with coffee and put both of them in his daypack.

Mark knew where Jim's team was going to observe from, and it didn't take him and the lawman long to cover the distance. Jim and his guys were thankful for the coffee, and they finished it in no time. Jim reported that they'd seen three groups go by yesterday morning before it started raining hard, but that no one had moved by since. Mark took Curt down to the trail and showed him how worn it was. Curt agreed that they'd have to watch this route once the water was turned off in the city. They went back up to Jim's observation post, and Mark talked him into coming back home. The rain was getting harder, and the sky showed no sign of it letting up anytime soon. It seemed foolish to leave the guys out in this mess if there was no one moving.

When they got back home, Jim changed into dry clothes, and then he, Mark, and Gunny rode back to Floresville with the sheriff. They talked of the problems they might face and what they needed to cover in the meeting. At a break in the conversation, Curt changed the subject and gave them some news.

"I went to the tax assessor's office and looked up who owns the property around you. A corporation in California owns the tracts on either side of the subdivision. There's a copy of a lease attached to the agricultural tax exemption that shows they've been leasing both tracts to a farmer named Roy Wilkins in Floresville. The large tract behind you is part of Rancho Borrego. Guillermo Borrego started the ranch after Texas won its independence from Mexico. Supposedly, it had been a Spanish land grant to a Don Federico before Mexico broke away from Spain. When Federico sided with the Mexicans in the war, he was sent back to Mexico with Santa Anna. Borrego had fought with Seguin and his boys on our side, and supposedly Sam Houston himself gave the land to Borrego. The ranch was originally over ten thousand acres. Parts of it have been sold off over the years, and I don't know how big it really is now. It straddles the county line, and there's still over two thousand acres in Wilson County. I'd guess there's at least that much in Bexar County where the ranch headquarters are. Guillermo the Fourth runs the ranch now. They call him Billy the Kid, even though he's over sixty years old."

"Fascinating story," Jim commented, "how much of it do you think is true?"

"Most of it, I reckon," Curt replied.

"How do you know all of this?" Mark asked.

"You don't get to be sheriff without knowing the influential people in and around your county," Curt smiled. "Anyway, where we were on the pipeline is part of Borrego's ranch. I'm sure where you all live used to be part of it, too."

"Interesting. Who did you say had the lease on the tracts next to us?"

407

"Roy Wilkins."

"Can we talk to him? Maybe he would sub-lease it to us."

"No chance of that," Curt said dryly.

"Why not? Do you know him?" Jim asked.

"I did. He and his family were killed by a small group of gang members about two weeks ago. Roy's place was isolated down a county road off of Highway 181. The gang members attacked them in the middle of the night, sort of like those guys who attacked Ralph's house, but unlike the Joneses, they didn't have anyone to help them. The next day, one of my deputies got a report from a guy down the road from Roy that they'd heard some shooting. Cole, the deputy, checked out the house with his binoculars and saw some guys he didn't think belonged there. They all had bandanas tied around their heads, and their jeans were hanging down off of their butts. He called me on the radio, and we hit them just after dark. They gave up quickly. I have never been so close to becoming judge, jury, and executioner in all my life. It was like what you told me you saw up in Waco inside your sister's house. Anyway, they're in my jail now, and I think if you want to farm that land, ol' Roy wouldn't mind." The look on the sheriff's face was as somber as Mark could ever remember seeing.

When they got to the sheriff's office, there were ten or twelve men waiting. Mark knew all of them, as he'd been training most of them on Mondays for the last few weeks. Curt brought out a big map of the county and briefed everyone about his fears and where he felt the greatest threats could come from. He informed everyone of the pipeline Mark had shown him and told them that there were also several electrical easements that might bear watching. He asked for recommendations and received several. The discussions were spirited and even bordered on heated a few times, but everyone realized they were in this together, and no one got hostile. In the end, they all agreed to a plan tendered by Rob Bowers. They'd post a small group at each point of egress from Bexar County to watch for groups who looked like trouble. Each observation group would have a radio and could call for one or both groups of responders who would be assembled. These responder groups would be a combination of citizens' militia and law enforcement. They'd use school buses for transportation, and each would be at least thirty men strong.

They identified eleven points along the county line that needed to be watched. Curt mentioned that Silver Hills had already placed an observation group on the pipeline, and he asked for Gunny's advice.

"I noticed you had six men in the group I saw this morning. Is that how many you think we need at each place?"

"Naw," the old veteran drawled. "If'n we're gonna have a static OP at each point, you could get by with three man teams. We have five or six 'cause they're designed to move around. With three men, one is on duty, one can sleep, and one is on support, like cooking and such. Each man spends eight hours on each assignment."

Everyone liked Gunny's suggestion. Curt asked if Silver Hills could provide and train the observation groups, since they already had a head start on it. Rob and Curt could then assemble and train the responders. Everybody agreed, and they resolved to meet on Thursday to evaluate their progress.

On the way home, Gunny asked Curt what he thought the biggest group they might face would be. Curt answered that he expected most would be fifteen or twenty people, but that it could go as high as fifty. Gunny knit his brows at the answer.

"Why do you ask, Gunny?" Curt inquired when he saw the Marine's concern.

"If'n this was a military operation, then thirty guys could take out fifty easy with the right ambush, but since this is a law enforcement scenario, you hafta give up the element of surprise and wait to see what the other fellas do. I don't think thirty's enough for that situation."

"I was thinking we'd use both groups of responders if we had that big of a gang," Curt said.

"I guess that'd work," Gunny responded. "Some of us should go scout each site and find where we want to put the observers and where we'd intercept a gang on that route," he added.

"Good idea," Curt answered. "What if I bring Rob over early next week and we go look them over?"

"Sounds like a plan."

Mark could see that something was still bothering the old man. There was no sense in asking him, though. If he wanted to say something, he would.

Curt dropped them off at Mark's house, and they assembled the rest of the security committee. They were quickly filled in, and then Gunny told them what he wanted to do. He planned to create fifteen teams to cover the eleven sites. That way, each team could work three on and one off. They had twelve members on the scout teams, and each of them would be put in charge of a team since they were pretty well trained already. Gunny would take one team, so they just needed two more leaders. Chaparo and Ted both volunteered, but Gunny told them he'd rather they stick around the neighborhood, just in case. Jim suggested Manny and Dwight, since they both had experience in tough situations. Everyone agreed that they were good choices. Mark asked how they would select the other thirty people they needed. Gunny didn't want to take anyone else who had regular guard duty. Susan suggested they ask for volunteers at the meeting tonight. It might give some people a chance to see if they liked helping out with the security details. Gunny took the opportunity to compliment Susan for a great idea. Mark was tickled that she didn't seem to know how to accept the praise and finally stammered out an embarrassed 'thank you.'

Gunny asked if she'd mind taking down the names at the meeting and then for them to get back together tonight and make their selections. Everyone agreed, and the meeting broke up.

The President's address, or Candlelight Chat, as one of the media's talking heads had dubbed the twice-weekly speeches, was mostly more of the same. One thing did strike Mark as a little odd. The President implored the members of the National Guard to trust the authorities to protect their loved ones while they were doing their duty.

"I understand the need to make sure your families are secure," he said. *"But it is imperative for you to stand your post in this, America's greatest hour of need."*

Mark wondered if they were having trouble with Guardsmen deserting their units to go home and take care of their own families.

At the meeting, Mark explained the plan the sheriff wanted to implement. He told them that, while the assignment they'd drawn wasn't dangerous, it was very important and should not be taken lightly. He told them to see Susan after the meeting if they wanted to volunteer.

When the security committee got back together that evening at Gunny's, Susan informed them that thirty-seven people had signed up. She started reading the names, but Mark had a hard time paying attention. His mind kept drifting back to what the President had said. 'What does it mean?' he wondered. He was mentally in his own world trying to figure it out when one of the names Susan read smacked him back into the here and now. He shook his head to clear it. He must have heard her wrong. She couldn't have said David. A moment later, she read the last name, and he knew that he hadn't heard wrong.

"And the last one is Samantha Turner," Susan said.

"Well, we can't let teenagers do this," Mark stated.

"Mark, I don't know if you were paying attention or not, but eighty percent of the names she read are teenagers," Ted informed him.

"Then I guess we'll just have to go ask people to volunteer."

"Wait jus' a second, Karate Man. Why couldn't we use the young folks? You said yourself that it wasn't dangerous," Gunny said.

"Yeah, but they have to go to school," Mark insisted.

"Mark," Ted said, "I know how you feel. Alex signed up, too, but this could be an excellent learning experience for the kids, and it's only going to be for a week or so."

"Sides that," Gunny said, "them kiddos got better eyes than us old farts."

Mark didn't like this. Everyone was talking and looking at him like he was wrong. He wasn't wrong. He was right! They were all wrong!

Those last two thoughts rattled around in Mark's head for a minute. All of them were wrong, and he was right? How likely was that? He realized he was the one being hardheaded. He admitted it and apologized. They went through the list and eliminated four of the volunteers right away for eyesight or mobility problems. They divided the list by gender and found they had one too many males and two extra females if they were going to keep the teams one gender. Everyone agreed that they should. They went through the boys' names first to see if there was someone who shouldn't go. When they got to Alex's name, Mark spoke up.

"Alex is George's backup. He should be learning from George instead of being on a team."

"But, Mark, isn't David Chaparo's backup?" Ted asked. "Shouldn't the same go for him?"

Ted had a valid point. However, he didn't know everything Mark did. Mark wondered how he could keep Alex off without tipping his hand about George's illness. "That's true, but we only have one extra guy. I think it's more important for Alex to stay on his regular job because the planting and harvesting of crops is more time sensitive than what David's learning. Unless Chaparo has some project where he really needs David or something that David can't learn another time, I say Alex should come off the list."

Everyone looked at Chaparo. "We're not doing anything we haven't done before, and I don't know of anything coming up that can't wait. Let him do it if he wants."

That seemed to satisfy all of the committee members, and they looked at the female list. No one could see any reason to disqualify any of the girls, so they drew names out of a hat. Doc Vasquez's daughter, Amanda, and Brittany Jordan, Dwight Rittiman's niece, were the two names drawn. Susan volunteered to let everyone know who was selected, and to divide them into teams. Gunny told her to tell them they'd all meet after church the next day. He asked Jim to make sure all of them could shoot well enough not to kill each other.

The meeting broke up, and Mark walked home. His two children, wanting to know if they'd been selected, greeted him at the door. He told them they had, reminded them of the importance, and told them he expected them to set an excellent example for the other kids.

The next morning, Brother Bob kept the church service short since it was still raining. Gunny mustered his new recruits and their leaders right afterward. They were standing in one of the empty lots, right in the middle of the downpour. Between the claps of thunder, Gunny thundered about how this wasn't going to be some kind of picnic and that if they didn't like standing in the rain, then maybe this wasn't for them. He told them it might be a cold, wet, and miserable job, but it was important, and no matter how unpleasant the weather, it had to be done. He said if anyone had a problem with any of their team members, they better work them out. No disagreements could get in the way of performing the tasks at hand to the best of their ability. He told everyone they were responsible for providing their own equipment, including a rifle and at least a hundred rounds of ammo. They'd have to prove to Jim that they could handle the weapon safely and shoot it accurately. He told anyone who wanted out or who couldn't meet these requirements to come see him. Otherwise, they were to go get their rifles and report to the shooting range. No one went to see Gunny.

When they got to the shooting range, Mark saw the most eclectic array of weapons he had ever imagined. There were shotguns in pumps, autoloaders, and double barrels. Rifles ran the gamut from old lever actions to the latest pistol caliber carbines. A few of the youths even brought .22 rifles. Mark asked Gunny if he thought they should make them get something a little more potent.

"Naw," he answered. "If'n that's what they're comfortable with, let 'em carry 'em. Chances of 'em gettin' into a situation where they have to use 'em is pretty slim. 'Sides, that might be all they have, and we don't have enough community rifles to lend one to everybody."

Jim had the shooters come to the line one at a time, load their weapon and fire five rounds at a target. From observing them, he dismissed the ones who were adequately skilled and had the others remain for some further instruction. Samantha was in the latter group.

On Monday, Curt came with Rob and picked up Gunny, Mark, and Jim. They surveyed each place that needed to be watched and picked out a place where their group could observe. They set the OP's close to the county line on the utility easements, but the ones on the roads were set far enough away from the line so if any group went around the National Guard roadblock, they had

411

plenty of room to go back to the road. They found great cover for the OP's in almost all of the locations. There was only one spot where they couldn't find a place as far from the road as they would have liked. Gunny said he'd make sure the team he placed there could be very quiet.

Jim snickered, and the old man asked him what was so funny. Jim did his best Elmer Fudd impersonation and said, "Be vewy, vewy quiet. I'm hunting wabbits."

All five men had a good laugh.

The rest of the week, Gunny lectured, drilled, and tested the observation groups, or OG's as they had started calling them for short. He made sure each member could give an accurate report about a traveling group regarding size, arms, and apparent skill. The rain gradually subsided over the first three days of the week, and by Thursday, it had cleared off and cooled down. By Friday, every OG was performing at or above the standard Gunny had set. He announced that, starting tomorrow, they'd be watching the routes and reporting on any movement they saw. Mark hoped this whole exercise proved to be unnecessary, but something in his gut told him it wouldn't.

Chapter 55

Eight o'clock on Saturday morning found Mark at his OP. Along with two of the younger volunteers, he was watching a small road that crossed the county line in the southern part of Wilson County. Albert Michaels was 'almost fourteen' as he put it. He was in the eighth grade with David, and the two of them were good friends. He lived with his mother and younger brother on one of the one-acre lots. The third member of their Observation Group was a young man named Roman Santana. He was seventeen and had moved in to his grandparents' house with his mom, dad, and two sisters shortly after The Burst. He was a very quiet boy. Albert was carrying his .22, which was the only rifle he owned. Roman had his grandfather's beautiful old Winchester bolt action.

OP-Ten was on the south side of the road about a thousand yards from the county line. It sat almost at the top of a small hill, seventy or eighty yards from the road. The hill provided a good view in both directions, and Mark figured they'd be able to see the National Guard roadblock when it was set up. They had piled up brush in front of a medium-sized oak tree to hide the observer. It was pretty comfortable to sit against the tree on a folded blanket, and, as long as the person stayed still, there was little chance anyone from the road would spot him or her. They had a small campsite on the opposite side of the hill. Mark took a piece of olive drab cord and ran it from the OP to the campsite where it was tied to one of the pup tent poles. The observer could then pull the tent down if he needed to let the other two know he saw something.

Gunny had scheduled each person to take two four-hour shifts a day. The boys both wanted to go first, so Mark had from 4 to 8 PM and then 4 to 8 AM. This suited him fine, as sunrise and sunset were his favorite parts of the day. Mark had instructed the boys to signal him if they saw anyone. He wanted to make sure they were evaluating the situations correctly. On the noon to 4 PM shift, Roman pulled the ripcord, and Mark and Albert belly crawled around the hill. Before they could get to the OP, they saw a young couple walking down the road. They were carrying large gym bags and no obvious firearms. Mark waited until they were well past and then finished crawling to the OP. He asked the young men what they thought, and both of their assessments coincided with Mark's. The couple was no threat and did not need to be reported.

When four o'clock rolled around, Mark took over in the OP. With nothing to do but watch the road, his thoughts had plenty of time to torment him. He recounted the days since his family had left Waco. He prayed that he'd made a mistake and miscounted, but to his disappointment, he was right. It had now been thirty days. Even if they only walked six miles a day, they should have been here by now. Mark didn't see how they wouldn't have made at least eight or ten miles a day. Mike, in his note, had estimated fifteen to eighteen miles a day. That might have been optimistic. It would be hard to keep that pace up day after day, but even Mark's most pessimistic estimate of seven and half miles a day would have seen them here almost a week ago.

Mark's mind raced over every possible scenario that could have caused them to take this long. Unfortunately, none of them were apt to produce a happy ending. He almost hoped the FEMA goons he'd dreamed of the other night had captured them. The other nightmares were too scary to even consider.

Mark noticed the sun getting close to the horizon. He leaned back and watched the sky change colors, as the fireball sank lower and lower. Just at dusk, he was surprised to see a group of twelve or thirteen feral hogs cross the road. Soon it was dark, but the white gravel of the road gave off an eerie glow in the starlight. He saw nothing else move during his shift except for rabbits and fireflies. Time crept by slowly, as his thoughts hammered his mind into a mush of chaotic goo. Finally, Albert came to relieve him.

Mark made his way back to camp, warmed up a can of soup, and then tried to get some sleep. It wasn't hot out, but it was humid. Sleep came in fitful bouts. Finally, it was 4 AM and time for his turn in the OP.

Mark leaned up against the oak tree and waited for his eyes to adjust to the dark. Now that he needed to stay awake, he found it hard to do so. He fought the urge to nod off for a long time, and then, finally, the eastern sky started to lighten. He watched as the stars became invisible and he was able to see more and more of his surroundings. Just before the sun peaked over the horizon, the group of hogs Mark had seen the night before came back across and disappeared into the brush on the south side of the road. Mark wondered if this was a daily occurrence. At 8 o'clock, Albert showed up to relieve him.

Mark, when he was back in camp, started cooking breakfast for himself and Roman. When they were almost finished eating, the pup tent fell. Both of them grabbed their rifles and started toward the OP. Mark fell to his belly once he saw the road and started crawling. Roman mimicked his movements. Mark watched for signs of people on the road, but saw no one. He wondered if Albert had seen someone who wasn't on the road. He slowed his advance and looked around thoroughly. He couldn't see anyone or anything that seemed out of place. Eventually, he spotted Albert who was frantically waving his arm for Mark to hurry up. Mark quickly crawled the remaining distance.

"What's up, Albert?"

"Gunny called for you," the young man answered.

"What does he want?" Mark wondered out loud.

"He didn't say, but there was a lot of chatter on the radio about a dog attack at OP-Three," Albert said with a frightened look.

Mark took the radio and called the CP. Gunny answered.

"Mark, David was attacked by a pack of dogs. Lisa and Doc are on their way over right now. I'm sending another squad in my truck to relieve you. As soon as they get there, come back here. Lisa and the Doc should be back with David by then."

"How bad is it, Gunny?"

"I don't know, Karate Man, but we've all got our fingers crossed."

"Where's Jess?"

"I'm sending someone to get her right now. Sam's here. She's already at the clinic, waiting on Dave," the old man said.

"Okay, I'll see you in a minute. Out," Mark said calmly.

All of a sudden, all the problems he'd been worrying about seemed trivial. Mark breathed a prayer for his son. He knew wild dogs could be very dangerous. As Mark thought about it, he realized there must be thousands of dogs whose owners could no longer feed them. 'Just what we need,' he thought, 'another threat to worry about.'

When the truck arrived, Olga Jensen's team got out, and Mark, with his OG, loaded into the truck. He turned the old Dodge around and tore down the gravel road. It didn't take long to get back to Silver Hills. Mark pulled through the gate and raced up to the clinic. When he went in, the only people there were Sam and Ronnie. Sam was holding a piece of gauze in the crook of her elbow and crying. Ronnie had her arms wrapped around the crying girl, trying to console her. When Sam saw Mark, she rushed to embrace him.

"Oh, Daddy, it's horrible," she cried. "I don't believe it."

Mark couldn't remember the last time that Sam had called him 'Daddy.' He shushed her, as he wrapped his arms around her. She seemed so small. "It's okay, baby. He'll be all right. He's a tough cookie." He squeezed her tight. "What happened to your arm?"

"Lisa had me donate some blood for David. She started it before she left and told Ronnie to unhook it when the bag got full. She said, that way, she'd have some for him when she got back, just in case he needs it."

"Good thinking. Ronnie, I'm the same type as David, too. Do you think you could get me started?"

"I really don't know how to stick a vein, Mr. Turner. I can get all of the stuff out, so you'll be ready to go when Lisa gets back, though."

"I thought you were a medical student."

"I am, but I was just starting my second year. You don't learn how to do procedures until the third year," she explained.

Mark nodded his head. "Then, yes, please get all of the stuff ready."

He made his way out to the garage where the CP was. It was packed with people. They all moved out of Mark's way, and he walked up to Gunny who had the radio in his hand. Before Mark could say anything, Gunny spoke.

"Lisa and the Doc are still at OP-Three. Jess is already on her way back."

"How is he?"

"I don't know," Gunny stated. "Victor just radioed in a minute ago and said they're still working on him. He did say that David is conscious."

"I guess that's good," Mark said flatly.

A minute later, Jess came roaring up in Jim's truck.

"Where is he?" she demanded, almost in tears.

"He's still at the OP," Mark explained. "Lisa and Doc Vasquez are working on him there."

"Then why are we standing here?" she shouted. "Let's go."

Mark looked over at Gunny, and the old man spoke into the radio. "Victor, what's the situation?"

A hiss came over the handheld, followed by Victor's voice. "They're loading him up in the truck right now. I'm sending Tony with them. He got a few bites, too. Nothing serious, but they need to be dressed."

"Roger that, Vic. Do you want me to send someone to relieve you?"

"No. I'm fine. I can watch it for a while."

"I'll check back with you in a while." Gunny signed off, then he looked at Jess, "They'll be here in a couple of minutes."

Jess paced back and forth in the main room of the clinic. Mark wanted to try and calm her down by pulling her to him and hugging her, but he realized she needed to work off the nervous energy.

After what seemed two eternities, the truck pulled up to the clinic. When the tailgate was lowered and David was pulled out of the back of the truck by a couple of the men, Jess screamed and buried her face into Mark's chest. The boy was covered in blood and lifeless. Lisa sat on the tailgate and then let her long legs reach down to the ground.

"It looks a lot worse than it is," she told her friend. "He only has one bad injury on his arm. The rest are shallow wounds."

"Why isn't he moving?" Jess cried. "He looks…"

Before Jess could finish, Lisa reassured her. "I gave him something for the pain. It's working, and he fell asleep a few minutes ago. He's going to be fine. Why don't you come help us clean him up?"

Mark and Jess followed Lisa into the clinic. Jess was quickly put to work cleaning the bites on her son's legs. Lisa assigned Ronnie to clean and dress the bites on Tony's arm and hand. Doc and Lisa hovered over David's left triceps that had taken a brutal attack. Lisa shielded Jess from seeing how bad it was, but Mark was shocked at how mutilated the area was. Lisa was draping the arm and getting out the tools they'd use to mend the injury, while Doc Vasquez was washing up for the surgery. Mark walked over and spoke to the vet.

"How bad is it, Doc?"

"Mark, I'm not going to lie to you. Dave is in no mortal danger. Most of the bites aren't too severe, but the injury to his arm is pretty bad. Some of the muscle is missing. I've seen a lot of dog attacks on cows and horses in my business, and they often cripple animals beyond repair, but David's young and strong, and that's in his favor."

"Thanks, Doc."

"You're welcome. Now, why don't you get everyone out of here, so we can get to work?"

Mark herded everyone but Doc and Lisa out of the room. They made their way into the garage where the CP was located. Chairs appeared, and the worried family and friends sat down to wait. Ronnie was wrapping Tony's arm in gauze, and it looked like a mummy's when she finished. Gunny asked the young man to tell them exactly what had happened.

"Victor was on watch, and David and I decided to cook up some breakfast. He was frying up some Spam, and I was cracking eggs into a bowl when the dogs just came out of nowhere. There were eight or ten of them. The biggest one jumped on David. His head looked like a bear's. Some of the others attacked Dave, too, and three or four charged me. I managed to get my shotgun up, and I killed one before the others got my arm and knocked the gun out of my hands. I started punching them and trying to knock them off of me. I could see David, and he was just rolled up into a ball trying to protect himself. The dogs were biting him like crazy. I wanted to get over to help him, but the dogs kept knocking me down. Suddenly, I saw Victor come running up, and he kicked the big dog off of David like he was kicking a football. Even though that dog was skinny…all of them had ribs showing…he still must have weighed a hundred pounds. He went flying like twenty feet, and I heard his ribs break when Victor made contact. The other dogs on David must have figured they were next because they went running. Victor ran over to me and cracked the skull of biggest dog attacking me with the butt of his rifle. He killed it with one hit. Man, I'm glad he's on our side. He kicked the other two, and they ran off behind the others. Victor started shooting at them with the AR, and he must have hit one or two of them. They yelped, but they kept on running."

"Why do you think they attacked y'all?" Tony's father, Henry, asked.

"I think they were hungry, Dad. I didn't see them do it, but all of the food we were cooking was gone. I guess some of them ate it while the others were attacking."

"Were they wild dogs?" Ronnie asked.

"They acted like it, but at least three of them had collars on, including the two we killed."

"What kind of dogs were they? Could you tell?" Gunny inquired.

"The one I shot was some kind of mutt. The big one that attacked Dave was mostly Rottweiler, I think. The one Vic cracked over the head was a German Shepherd, and the only other one I recognized was one of the smaller dogs. He was a Beagle about this big," Tony held his good hand about fifteen inches off of the floor. "The others, I couldn't tell. It all happened so fast."

Mark didn't like this. It had now been almost nine weeks since The Burst. Many people probably couldn't care for their pets and had turned them loose. Others may have left them behind when they reported to the shelters or left the city. There was no telling how many hungry dogs there might be roaming the countryside. They'd have to be very careful when they were out. They also needed to stop everyone at the OP's from cooking. Before Mark could say anything to Gunny about that, the old man was on the radio telling all of the posts that cooking was now a big no-no.

A few minutes later, the sheriff showed up to check on David. His office had monitored the transmissions and informed him of what had happened. Mark filled him in on David's condition and gave him the play by play of what had transpired. Curt informed them that, while there had been a few reports of dogs harassing livestock, nothing like this had happened. He felt bad that this had happened on an operation for him, and he apologized to Mark and Jess. Mark told him it wasn't his fault and that the operation was for all of them. Jess reached out and squeezed the lawman's arm with a weak smile.

Curt sat down in an empty chair, and it was quiet in the CP until Doc Vasquez came out. He told Mark, Jess, Sam and the others that it had gone as well as could be expected. Lisa was bandaging the youth up, and he could go home and sleep in his own bed in just a short while. They were giving him some strong antibiotics to fight possible infection, and they wanted to make sure he didn't have a reaction to them. He also told them David might need some skin grafts on his arm, but they'd have to take him to someone who had experience with that. Curt told them he would bring Doctor Ken out to look at the boy and then left. Doc Vasquez also mentioned that there were a few bites on David's face that would probably leave some scars but nothing disfiguring. He said they would be 'tough guy scars' that the girls would probably like.

Thirty minutes later, David was resting comfortably in his own room with Jess sitting at the foot of his bed watching every breath. After a few minutes of staying with him, everyone except Jess left. Mark led Sam, Timmy, and Tommy into the kitchen to fix a late lunch. They warmed up some leftover soup and sat down at the table. No one spoke much for a while. Finally, Timmy started crying.

"Uncle Mark, is David going to heaven with my mommy and daddy?" he sobbed.

Mark was shocked by the question. Not because Timmy had asked it, but because he'd been too oblivious to see it coming. He kicked himself for not expecting the young boys to be overwhelmed with anxiety. They'd lost their parents just a short time ago, and now part of their new family was ailing. How would they not expect the worst?

"No, Timmy. David's not going to heaven, not for a long time," Mark reassured both of the boys. He reached out and put his arm around the young boy's shoulders. "But the dogs hurt his arm pretty bad, and he's going to need you two to help him. Can you both do that?"

Timmy sniffed and nodded his head. Tommy's head also went up and down.

"Good. Now let's eat some soup, and then we'll go outside and play catch for a while."

That seemed to cheer the two boys up considerably, and they dug into their soup bowls with vigor. Sam agreed to clean up, and Mark took the boys out in the front yard to toss the baseball. Before long, Curt drove back up with Doctor Ken. Mark took him in to see David, while Curt volunteered to take over coaching the boys. Mark introduced the doctor to his wife, and then the M.D. unwrapped the arm to look at it. Word had spread quickly that Doctor Ken had come, and Lisa and Doc Vasquez, as soon as they heard, were at the Turner house. After a brief inspection of the injuries, Doctor Ken rewrapped them and told Jess her boy was going to be fine.

"What about skin grafts? Will he need them?" she asked.

"Maybe," he replied, "We'll see how it heals, and if we need to get a plastic surgeon to work on it, I know a good one. Don't you worry, he'll be up and around in no time."

When the doctor left the room, he asked who had patched up the arm. Doc Vasquez and Lisa introduced themselves to the county's top medical official and told him they'd done the work. He told them they had done a masterful job.

"In fact," he added, "most trauma surgeons I know couldn't have done any better. Would the two of you be willing to come help us out at the hospital from time to time?"

Both members of the Silver Hills medical team blushed at the compliment and agreed to help out however they could. Doctor Ken asked Mark to bring David to see him in five days, and he invited Doc and Lisa to tag along. They agreed, the doctor apologized that he had to run, and Curt drove him back to the hospital.

That night, Mark's nightmares came back to haunt him. Only this time, in addition to his other fears, there was a new threat confronting all he cared for.

Chapter 56

The next morning, Mark woke up early. He softly padded to David's room and saw that his son was still asleep. Jess was sleeping on the floor next to his bed. He closed the door and walked to the kitchen. He put on a pot of coffee and pulled on his boots. Just as the coffee was starting to emit its delicious aroma, there was a soft knock, and the back door opened. George came in and took a deep whiff of the brewing black beverage.

"Boy, that smells good," he said.

"You want a cup?"

"You bet."

Mark pulled two cups from the cabinet and set them next to the stove.

"Still needs to percolate for another couple of minutes," he said with a smile. "How are you feeling?"

"Pretty good. Some days are better than others, but I'm doing okay," George smiled back. "How is David doing?"

"Sleeping like a baby right now, and his mama's likely to spoil him rotten as long as he's laid up."

"Isn't that the way it's supposed to work?"

"I reckon so," Mark agreed.

The men sat quietly with their thoughts for a minute. The only sound was the rhythmic belching of the percolator. Finally, George broke the silence.

"I came over to talk to you about the tractor. You said the Watsons would need it for ten days, and today's the tenth day. Can we go pick it up this afternoon?"

"Gosh, George, I'd forgotten all about it. The National Guard is due to post guards at the county line any time now, if they haven't already. We might get over there and not be able to get back. Can it wait a week or so?"

"Not really. I've already put off planting some things because we lent it out. I really need it back for us to stay on the plan we have for our crops."

"George, I'm really sorry, but I don't think there's any way for us to get over to pick it up until the Guard leaves. Could you borrow the tractor from Promise Point? I'm sure they'd lend it to us since we helped them out," Mark said.

"That's a good idea. I'll go over and ask after you pour me that cup of coffee you promised. It'll give me a chance to see how their gardens are coming along."

Mark poured the two cups full, and the two men chatted casually, as if neither had a care in the world. Mark finally got around to asking how Alex was doing as George's apprentice. George reported that the young man was doing quite well and he seemed to have a good head on his shoulders. Mark took the last comment with a grain of salt, but he had to agree that the boy at least had good enough sense to be interested in Sam.

A few minutes later, Jess stumbled into the kitchen and poured herself a cup of wake-up juice. She looked as if she hadn't slept a wink.

"What's up, Sunshine?" Mark teased.

"Ugh! Not me. Sleeping on the floor sucks," she complained.

"How's David?" Mark asked.

"He's awake. He wanted to get up, but I told him to stay in bed. He's hungry, so that's a good sign. You guys want some breakfast?"

"That sounds great," Mark rubbed his stomach.

"Thanks for the offer, but I have to go borrow a tractor," George explained. "I'll come back later and check on Dave."

George put his mug in the sink and headed out the back door. Mark walked down the hall and knocked on the door to his son's room.

"Who is it?"

"It's me, Dave."

"Good. Come in and help me," the young man requested.

Mark pushed the door open. His son was sitting on the edge of his bed, his left arm in a sling, trying to pull on a pair of athletic shorts with just one arm. The look on his face was a cross between determination, frustration, and mild pain. Mark walked in, grabbed the left side of the shorts and pulled up, while David pulled the right side. The shorts slid into place, and David let out a sigh of relief.

"Thanks, Dad."

"You're welcome. How do you feel?"

"Pretty good. My arm hurts some, and some of these bites on my legs do, too, but I'll be alright," David assured his father.

"Can you tell me what happened?"

"I'd just gotten off watch, and Tony and I were fixing some breakfast. The next thing I remember is getting knocked down and this big dog biting me. His head looked like it was as big as a basketball. I tried to push him off and hit him, but he was too big, and then some other dogs were pulling and biting my arms. I remembered seeing on TV about how people who were attacked by bears rolled up in a ball to protect themselves, and that's what I did. I really thought I was going to die. I was thinking about how sad you and Mom and Sam would be at my funeral. I could see the three of you crying and hugging each other over my grave. The funny thing was, I wasn't scared or upset. I just knew that I'd miss y'all as much as you missed me. Then the dogs weren't on me anymore. I heard one of them cry, and when I looked, Victor was standing over me. Tony told me that Victor kicked the big dog off of me, but I didn't see it."

"Yes, Tony told us the same thing," Mark said.

"After the dogs ran off, Tony called in on the radio while Victor worked on my arm to stop the bleeding. I was kind of in and out, and the next thing I knew, Mrs. Davis was working on me. Then they put me in the truck, and you know the rest."

"And you weren't scared at all?"

"Not when the attack was happening," David explained. "But I got scared when it was over. The looks on Victor's and Mrs. Davis's faces told me it was pretty bad, and I heard what she and Doc V. said about my arm, even though they were whispering. Doc said he didn't know if they could save it or not. Lisa told me she was going to give me something for the pain. I tried to stay awake, but I couldn't. I remember thinking as I dozed off that I'd probably wake up without my arm. Dying didn't scare me, but cutting off my arm terrified me.

420

Anyway, I was glad when I woke up, and it was still there. Does that mean that it's going to be okay?"

"It looks like it, Son, but the dogs did a lot of damage, and we're going to have to see how well it heals. It'll probably not be as good as it was before, but it'll be close if you're willing to work hard at it, and I mean harder than you've ever worked at anything. Do you understand?"

"Yes, Sir. I'll do whatever it takes," David nodded his head.

"Good. You hungry?" Mark asked, even though he already knew the answer.

David affirmed his ravenous state, and the father and son walked into the kitchen to see what smelled so good. Jess started scolding both of them for David being out of bed, but she quickly relented. Mark wasn't sure if it was because of the look he flashed her or because she was relieved that David was doing well enough to get up, but the reason didn't really matter. The aroma of cooking breakfast brought Timmy and Tommy into the kitchen where they were both overjoyed to see David. A few minutes later, Sam entered the room. She called her brother 'squirt,' which was her usual nickname for him, and she acted as if nothing out of the ordinary had happened. This seemed to put David more at ease.

The family ate breakfast and enjoyed each other's company. Mark realized that his concerns about all the other things he'd been worrying about had impaired his ability to be thankful for what they had. He spent the rest of the day with his family, except for a short time he spent talking with Gunny. Mark told the old veteran that he and his team would work three days to make up for the extra day they got off. Gunny said that would be fine. He also told Mark he was pulling a couple of the guards to fill the holes left by David and Jess in the Observation Groups.

The next morning, Mark, Roman, and Albert were at OP-Two. This was the post that watched State Highway 87, one of the two main highways that crossed Wilson County. A little more than a mile from the county line, the National Guard roadblock couldn't be seen, since it was around a bend and on the opposite side of a small hill. The Guardsmen had shown up around noon on Sunday, not long after David had been attacked. Since then, the flow of refugees had been reduced to a trickle. Every OP in sight of the county line had reported that a lot of people were intercepted as they tried to leave the now waterless Bexar County. Mark, since he had the third shift, climbed to the top of the hill with his binoculars to watch the goings-on at the roadblock.

When Mark peeked over the hill with the field glasses, he saw two Humvees and a two and a half ton truck. Each Humvee was straddling a lane and most of the shoulder on the highway, so that a vehicle couldn't pass without going into the ditch. One of the highway blockers was covered in antennas, and the other had a belt-fed machine gun mounted on the top. The deuce and a half was off to one side of the road, thirty or so yards behind the big 4x4's. There were fifteen or twenty Guardsmen milling around the trucks. Most of them looked to be chitchatting or playing cards. A few were watching the road from behind the Humvees or in the machine gun turret. There were also two soldiers guarding the back of the deuce and a half like there was something in it worth stealing.

Before long, a group of six refugees came walking down the highway toward the county line. The Guardsmen, who'd been doing other things, picked up their weapons and seemed ready for trouble. As the travelers got closer, they seemed unsure as to what to do. One of the Guardsmen waved them in and seemed to be telling them something. Mark was too far away to hear what was said. The man in front dropped the duffle bag he was carrying and put his hands above his head. Then he turned his back to the trucks, knelt down, crossed his legs, and put his hands on his head. The people behind him mimicked his movements, and then eight of the soldiers scurried from behind the trucks up to the travelers. Six of the soldiers carried rifles, and each one stood six or eight feet behind a person kneeling on the road. The other two pushed the surrendered refugees to the ground and pulled their hands behind their back where they were zip tied. Then each prisoner was searched. The troops didn't really mistreat any of the former citizens, but they weren't exactly gentle with them, either. When all six had been handcuffed and patted down, the two searchers went through the bags the travelers had been carrying. Once the bags were searched, each of the rifled guards pulled his charge to their feet and led them to the back of the deuce and a half. The cover was pulled back, and Mark could see that there were several people in the back. The six new prisoners were herded into the truck, and their bags were tossed in behind them.

Mark was thankful he wasn't in those people's shoes. He realized they were breaking the directives of the President and FEMA, but they were just trying to get by. He didn't like the idea that his family might have already been treated this way, and he had mixed emotions about what he would do, if he saw them being herded into a truck like common criminals.

A few minutes later, another deuce and a half showed up and parked behind the one with the detainees in it. Mark watched for a while and saw two more small groups stopped, searched, and seized. One of them tried to turn around and leave when they saw the roadblock, but the soldiers chased them down. When the first truck was full, it pulled out to take the prisoners to, Mark hoped, the FEMA shelters. He didn't want to consider any other option.

Mark went back to the OP camp and tried to get some rest. When it was time for his next watch, he reported to the post and relieved Roman. He hated just sitting here. It gave him time to think. Before The Burst, he would have welcomed it, but now it only allowed his mind to worry about things he was powerless to do anything about. He laughed to himself. Before The Burst, he worried about things that now seemed so insignificant. Was he saving enough money for retirement and the kids' educations? Would he be considered for the next promotion at work? Could he afford to buy a new truck? Now he worried that they might not have enough food to make it through the winter. He worried that some group of MZB's could kill them in a surprise attack. And now, since the dog attack, he worried about what he wasn't worrying about. That was his biggest fear. The things he could see as threats, he could do at least something about, but what about all the things he hadn't thought about? He should have known dogs would become a problem. What else had he missed?

Finally his shift was over. Albert showed up to relieve him. He hadn't seen anyone pass during his shift. In fact, the three of them hadn't seen anyone get past the National Guard roadblock in the last twelve hours. Thinking about it, there hadn't been one report over the radio from any of the OP's during his shift. He asked Albert if anyone had called in a sighting on his first shift. The boy told him 'no.'

Mark made his way back to camp. He asked Roman if he'd heard anything over the radio today. The answer was negative. It seemed strange to him that no one had reported anything in twelve hours. What could that mean? He went down the list. The National Guard could be doing a really good job. The guys at this one were watching the road pretty well, but Mark thought that he could detour around them without much problem. The refugees could all be walking straight into the roadblocks, but that didn't seem likely. Surely some of them were smart enough not to get caught. Maybe all the ones who were getting through looked harmless, and the observers didn't feel the need to call them in to the CP. He hoped so. But, even if that was true, how long until it changed? Or perhaps the OP's weren't in the right places. Maybe people were taking wider detours than they'd predicted. Maybe some, but surely not all. As Mark crawled into his sleeping bag, he felt that he'd never be able to go to sleep with all of the random thoughts rattling around in his head. Fortunately, he was wrong.

"Mark. Mark! Wake up!" Albert whispered, as he shook the snoring man.

"What? What's the matter?" Mark, still half asleep, mumbled.

"Roman pulled the cord. Didn't you feel the tent fall?"

"No," he answered, as he slowly came back to reality. "Let's go."

Mark unzipped his bag and pulled on his boots. He grabbed his rifle and chest rig and started toward the OP. The hands on his watch glowed, and they told him it was almost one o'clock. He realized he'd been sleeping very soundly and not even dreaming. It was too bad he hadn't gotten six or seven hours. He could have used them. They crawled up to Roman. The youth put his finger up to his lips and pointed down the road.

"What you got, Roman?" Mark asked in a whisper.

"Eleven people crossed the road, most with rifles. I could see them good when they crossed the road. Right now, they're under that big oak tree on our side of the road. Here, look through the binoculars, and you can make them out."

Mark took the field glasses and looked at the spot Roman had indicated. He couldn't see anything at first, but then he made out a group in a circle. He couldn't tell how many. They were being very still and quiet. He handed the binoculars to Albert.

"Did you call it in?"

"Yes. The sheriff said he'd be here in twenty minutes. That was three or four minutes ago. He said to call him back if they moved out," Roman answered.

"Alright, let's keep an eye on them."

About ten minutes later, the group stood up and started walking away from the OP on the side of the road. Roman called it in to the sheriff, and he said they were still about five minutes away. Mark and his crew had a good view of the direction that the group was heading. Whoever they were, they were very careful. They were walking slowly on the side of the road in the highest grass that grew next to the fence. They had gone about a quarter of a mile when, all of a sudden, they hit the dirt. A second or two later, Mark heard the hum of tires on the asphalt. A minute later, he could just make out the lights on the bus. He called Curt on the radio, and told him that the group had hidden in the grass next to the fence.

"Okay, Mark, I read you. I want you to stop me at least a hundred yards away from them."

"Roger that," Mark answered.

He could make the bus out quite well now. It was obviously slowing down, as the whining of the big tires got lower and lower.

"Stop, now!" he ordered into the radio. The highway behind the bus became red from the brake lights, and the brakes squeaked like fingernails on a chalkboard. "You're about a hundred and fifty yards from them. They're right up against the fence on your left side."

"Got it. Thanks," Curt's voice crackled over the radio. A second later, the same voice came over nothing but the cool, crisp air.

"This is Sheriff Curt Thompson of Wilson County. I know there are eleven of you up against the fence. I want you all to stand up with your hands over your heads. Leave your rifles on the ground. I've got thirty men here. Don't give us any trouble."

Mark could barely make out the reply. "We don't want no trouble, and we ain't done nothing wrong. We're just on our way to Luling to see my cousin. You just leave us be, John Law, and we'll be out of your jurisdiction in no time."

"I'm sure that's true, but I can't have a large, armed group of pilgrims wandering through my county. Not only is it not safe for my constituents, it's not safe for you all. Some of the people around here are getting real jumpy about strangers. They figure it's better to shoot first and ask questions later. Now, you all come on out. We'll gather up your guns, and if everything is as you say it is, we'll give you a ride across the county. Save you two, three days of walking maybe."

"Mister, that sounds like a good offer, but we ain't giving up our guns for nobody. Not no sheriff, not no FEMA people, not even for the President. The second amendment says I got a right to keep and bear arms, and that's one right I ain't giving up, no matter what."

Mark found himself in a moral dilemma. The man was right, but Curt was just trying to do his job and protect the people in his county, even these eleven people. Mark put himself in each of the two men's shoes. He would do the same thing each of them was doing if he was in their places. He hoped Curt had a solution.

"Listen, mister," Curt said. "I'm not going to stand here and debate Constitutional law with you all night. I agree that you have rights. I'm not disputing that, but I took an oath to uphold the law in this county, and I can't do that if I let every Tom, Dick, and Harry who sneaks into my county with a bunch of rifles run loose. Y'all come on out without your rifles and show me your ID's. If none of you have any warrants out on you, I'll ask you to get on the bus. We'll pick up your rifles, and when we get to the other side of the county, you'll get them back. Until then, I'll guarantee your safety. I give you my word."

"And what if I say no?"

"Then you leave me with only two choices. My men and I can try to disarm you, but that could get real bloody, real quick, and we all have families to go

424

home to, or I can get on the radio to the National Guard. I'm sure they'd be happy to have the men on the roadblock you went around come over here and take you back to one of the Bexar County shelters. Those boys are getting paid to do the dangerous jobs, so I guess I'd let them come over here and earn their money. Yeah, that's what I'd do."

"You can't do that. We heard they got a special camp for the ones who don't go in voluntarily. Sumbitches! We weren't bothering nobody. We had food for at least another six weeks, but they had to go and turn the water off, so's no one could stay in town. They came through the neighborhoods shouting over the bullhorns that we had to turn ourselves in. Well, we decided we weren't going into no Nazi concentration camps. We made a plan to get the hell out of Dodge, and that's what we did. In fact, we just got finished having a little prayer meeting to thank the Lord for delivering us out of Bexar County. Had it back there under that big oak tree. Now, you're gonna hand us over to those goons?"

"Mister, that's not what I want to do. You all come peacefully, and I'll see you across my county safely."

"You drive a hard bargain, Sheriff. I reckon we got no choice. You give me your word that you won't send us back?"

"Sir, you have my solemn word that, as long as none of you are wanted felons, I will not send you back," Curt promised.

"Alright then, here we come."

Mark saw the group stand with their hands above their heads. They walked out to the road where Curt had two people cover each of the travelers. He got an ID from each of the adults and got back on his radio to what Mark assumed was his office. Wherever it was, it was a different channel than the OP's were on. Mark decided to walk down and see what was going on. When he got to the bus, he could see that the group being detained seemed to be three families. The leader was still half-heartedly grumbling about his rights. Mark thought that if he saw how the people on the other side of the county line were being treated, he wouldn't be griping so much. Mark found Curt.

"Hey, Mark," the Sheriff said. "How's David doing?"

"He's doing okay. He's hungry, so that's a good sign."

"Yeah, I guess it is."

"Hey, Curt, I heard you say you were going to check to see if these people had any warrants on them. How can you do that? Your computer isn't working, is it?"

"No, but I have a hardcopy of all the warrants issued in Texas from the day before The Burst. See, our old computer system was pretty crappy. It seemed like it was only working half the time, so I had a list printed out every Monday morning, just in case our computer went down. It's not as easy as checking on the computer, and not as up-to-date, but it's way better than nothing when the system is down. Of course, the list is about nine weeks old now, but I still feel better checking it."

Just then, Curt's radio came to life. "They're all clean, Sheriff."

"Thank you. Out," Curt said into the two-way. He then asked the group to get on the bus. While they loaded up, Mark asked Curt one more question.

"Is this how you're going to deal with all of the groups we call you to check out?"

425

"I hope so," Curt said, stepping up on the school bus. It belched black smoke, as the engine came to life, and then the yellow beast lurched into reverse to turn around. "As long as they let me, that is," the sheriff added, as the bus backed up. The gears grinded, as the driver looked for a forward gear, and then the bus pulled away.

The next two days at OP-Two were rather boring. Only two other groups of travelers came past the OP, and neither one looked troubling enough to call in. The traffic did seem to be picking up at some of the other OP's, mostly on the utility easements where there wasn't anyone blocking the county line and on some of the minor roads where it was easier to go around the smaller National Guard blockades. On Thursday, the response teams were called three times. Each time, the results were the same as they had been on Wednesday morning; the travelers were seen safely to the opposite side of the county.

Friday morning, Mark's group was relieved for their day off. Mark, when he got home, took a shower, ate a huge, hot breakfast, and then accompanied David to the doctor along with Jess, Lisa, and Doc Vasquez. Doctor Ken was happy with the way David was recovering. He sent David and Jess down the hall to see a Physical Therapist, so that they could get started on strengthening his injured arm. While they were gone, Doctor Ken talked to the others.

"Doctor Vasquez, I know that veterinary medicine is often looked down upon by the rest of the medical community, but I want you to know how much I admire you vets. You have to be able to treat so many different species, without the benefit of your patient being able to tell you where it hurts. I'm impressed with the repair you made on young Mr. Turner's arm. You're really the only trauma surgeon we have in the county. I've talked it over with the rest of my staff, and we'd like to be able to call you in when we need some help. Would that be alright?"

"Doctor Phillips," Doc Vasquez began.

The older doctor's hand shot up. "Please, call me Doctor Ken, or just Ken. That's what everyone calls me," he smiled.

"Okay, Doctor Ken, I'm happy to help out however I can, but I have to tell you that David's arm wouldn't be in as good of shape if Lisa hadn't been there to help me."

"I realize that, and I want her to come with you as your surgical nurse if we call you in, but I'm also in desperate need of nurses here in the hospital. Lisa, would you be willing to come and work here two or three days a week?"

"I don't know. I have the twins to take care of, and I teach school every day. I guess my mother could watch the girls, and we could maybe see about rearranging the teaching schedule," Lisa half-asked, looking at Mark.

Mark gave her a quick nod. Before she could say anything else, Doctor Ken started talking.

"Why don't you see what you can work out and get back to me next week? I can't really pay, except in medical supplies, which we would give you anyway, if you needed them. Other than that, all I can offer you is the satisfaction you get from helping people."

"That's fine, Doctor. You know no one goes into nursing for the money, anyway," Lisa said, with a big smile on her face. The doctor smiled back.

"Doctor Ken," Mark interrupted, "have you heard any more about the virus?"

The color drained out of Doctor Ken's face. That was more answer than Mark wanted, and he barely heard the words the doctor spoke.

"I'm afraid that it is real, after all. From what I've heard, they still aren't sure if it was engineered or not. Either way, it's taking its toll, especially on the very young and the very old. There are now reports of it in Phoenix, Las Vegas, and Salt Lake City, and the numbers being quoted are still around a fifty percent mortality rate. I'm hopeful that it won't spread east of the Rockies, but we'll just have to see what happens."

Mark looked at the other faces in the room. They seemed paler than they had a minute ago. It also seemed the air in the room had thickened. Mark felt it harder to pump the oxygen into and out of his lungs, and it didn't appear that he was the only one that felt this way. Everyone was quiet for a moment.

"I have another question," Mark stated, "hopefully, one that has a more cheerful answer. What happened to David got me thinking that we need some trained medics who can go out with our militia. Doc Vasquez and Lisa are too important to us to put them in harm's way. I was wondering if you had anyone who could train three or four people to be medics for us?"

"I have a great paramedic who could train some people."

"That's great! You want me to bring the trainees here, or do you want to send him out to us?"

"Her," Doctor Ken corrected, "and I think we should bring your people here. Some of the other groups might want to send a couple of people, too. Let me get back to you on when."

"Sounds good," Mark said.

"Bring that boy of yours back next Friday, and, Lisa, maybe you could have an answer for me by then?"

"I'm sure I can, Doctor," Lisa answered. "We'll see you next Friday."

The trio went down the hall to where David and Jess were. They were almost done, and soon they were on their way back to Silver Hills.

The next morning, Mark was back at an observation post with his team. OP-Seven was on a small, paved road that didn't continue to the east very far after it crossed the county line. Mark snuck over to see what kind of manpower the National Guard had assigned to this location. There was only one Humvee with about six men. He watched them for a while, but no one was using this route to escape the city. The first twelve hours of his group's duty hadn't yielded any activity. Some of the other OP's were seeing some action, and OP-Two, where Mark's group had been before, reported a brief firefight between a group of twenty or so gang members and the troops at the roadblock. Evidently, the liberal application of .50 caliber bullets from the machine gun had kept the conflict quite short. Mark almost felt sorry for the gang members.

Just before dark, OP-Six reported a large armed group coming across the county line. That observation post was the one on the natural gas pipeline, and the National Guard wasn't blockading that route. Mark couldn't put a face with the voice, but it was one of the female teams, and the voice sounded on the young side. She estimated thirty to forty travelers, moving at a moderate pace and requested that both response teams come to confront this large band. Curt's team was on the other side of the county dropping off a small group who'd been spotted by OP-Twelve. Rob's group wasn't too far away and said they'd set up at the north-south road that crossed the pipeline about three miles east of OP-Six. Curt radioed that he'd be there as soon as he could. No more than fifteen minutes later, Rob radioed Six and asked them for an update. There was no answer. Mark heard him call them again, but still no answer. Mark knew he was only about a mile and a half south of Six's position. He thought that perhaps their radio wasn't receiving Rob, so he called them. They didn't respond to him either.

"Mark, is that you?" Rob called.

"Yes, Rob, it is."

"What do you think is going on?"

"I have no idea. It could be anything," Mark answered.

"I'm worried. We're going to take the bus and knock down the gates and go down the pipeline as far as we can. Hopefully, we'll be there in eight or ten minutes."

"Roger that. I'm only a little over a mile away. I'm going to leave one guy here, and two of us will take off on foot. You'll beat us unless you can't make it all the way in the bus."

"That sounds like a good plan. I'll meet you there. Out," Rob said.

Mark pulled the cord and then hollered for the boys to come quickly. He explained the situation to them, left Albert with the radio, and then he and Roman took off for the silent post.

Chapter 57

Mark and Roman were running across a large field toward OP-Six. Run might have been a strong word; it was more of a jog, but in the dark and carrying their rifles, it was as fast as they dared go. Mark strained his eyes looking for holes or irregularities in the ground that could trip them. The field, thank goodness, was fairly smooth. As near as Mark could figure, it had been used for hay. There were no cattle on it, and the grass was cut ankle high and very even. He could barely make out a thick grove of trees on the other side, but it was impossible to judge the distance in the poor light. He hoped that the OP was just on the other side.

His mind was racing faster than his feet. What could have happened? Who was assigned to OP-Six? He wished he'd asked the Command Post before he left. Would Rob be able to get there before it was too late? And, too late for what? Just like everything else since The Burst, it seemed there were many questions and few answers.

He noticed that his breathing was starting to get a little labored. He looked over at Roman and saw that he wasn't breathing hard at all. The young man held his grandfather's prized Winchester in both hands with the barrel pointed at two o'clock and ran with an easy, smooth gait that Mark envied. Youth truly is wasted on the young, Mark thought. His mind switched back to OP-Six. He played out various scenarios in his mind and worked out the best response to each one. Whatever was happening, he needed to approach quietly and find out what the problem was. If he burst out into the open, he could find himself in deep doo-doo.

They were approaching the tree line, and Mark could see there was a fence separating it from the field they were in. Mark wondered if there was a gate, but he couldn't see one. He took Roman's rifle and the young man climbed the fence and was on the other side so quickly Mark almost thought he must have jumped over. He handed the two rifles over the fence to the agile young man and started to negotiate the fence himself. His weight, which was around forty pounds more than Roman's, made the wires give enough that he was nervous the old rusty fencing might break. He slowly increased his weight on each wire as he went up to make sure it would hold. Finally, he was high enough to swing his leg over. This was the part all men hate. If one of the wires broke at this point, a man was guaranteed a seat in the soprano section of the church choir. He slowly swung his right leg over, holding his breath and whispering a prayer. His foot found the wire on the other side and he carefully transferred his weight to that side. Not wanting to stay in the precarious position any longer than necessary, he quickly swung his left leg up, but it caught on one of the barbs, that somehow, after years in the elements, was still razor sharp. The barb dug into the back of his leg, just above his knee. Mark bit his tongue to keep himself from saying the word that the pain had automatically triggered in his mind. He moved his leg away from the wire, and the small, knife-like protrusion excoriated a piece of flesh, as it freed itself. Mark had to bite harder this time to save his dollar. He stepped down onto the ground and gave thanks to be on terra-firma almost as much as he had the time he'd gotten sea-sick on an offshore fishing trip. He didn't kiss the ground this time, though. Roman handed him his rifle, and they looked for the best way through the woods. The underbrush was thick, and every plant seemed to have descended from the rusty barbed wire they'd just climbed. This, coupled with the almost moonless night, made the going very slow and painful.

Mark estimated they'd gone fifty yards when he heard the first shot. It seemed to have come from right in front of them. They froze and listened, both subconsciously holding their breath. An eternity passed while the entire planet held its breath with them. Even the wind stopped. Then, hell's gates opened. The gunfire was so fast and furious that it sounded like one long artillery barrage. A bullet whistled over Mark's head, and a second later, one thwacked into a tree he was standing next to. He and Roman instantly went horizontal, not even feeling the heretofore irritating and hurtful spines, needles, and stickers abundant in this spot. Mark gestured in a direction perpendicular to their previous line of travel, one he thought would take them out of the line of fire but still keep them parallel to the opening of the pipeline. Roman nodded, and both pulled their feet under them and ran in the direction Mark had indicated. Under normal circumstances, the noise they made would have been sufficient to alert everyone within a mile of their proximity, but the constant enfilade would have masked the sound of a herd of charging elephants. They dashed a hundred yards in Olympic class time, with the briars and brambles clawing unmercifully to slow them down. The angry buzzing of supersonic projectiles lessened as they moved to the west, partly because the rate of fire was slowing with each passing moment, but mostly because they had moved out of the path of the bullets. Now, only an occasional shot whizzed high over their heads. Mark stopped behind a huge tree he and Roman could use for cover as they tried to catch their breath. Mark smelled the cordite in the air, and it left a putrid, acidic taste in his throat with each gulp he took in. The rate of fire continued to slow until it sounded like the last few kernels of Jiffy-Pop finally deciding to give in.

Mark's breathing slowed to where he was only gasping for air, and he heard a familiar voice from what sounded to be several hundred feet away.

"This is the Wilson County Sheriff's Department! Put down your weapons and come out into the open! You will not be harmed!" Rob's voice called out.

The answer was another round of rifle fire. This one didn't last as long. A minute later, Rob yelled again.

"You boys can sit over there and shoot up all your ammo if you want, but we're not going anywhere. Why don't you make it easy on yourselves and surrender?"

A short two-word sentence punctuated by few shots was the only answer proffered by the group, who sounded like they were positioned right in front of where Mark and Roman were when the shooting started. Mark's breathing was now close to normal. He tapped Roman on the shoulder.

"The OP is right across the pipeline from these guys," he whispered. "That's probably why they couldn't answer. These guys were probably taking a break right on top of them or something. Let's quietly move on down another couple hundred yards, and then we can sneak across and work our way back up the other side."

Roman nodded his head and gestured for Mark to lead the way. It was excruciatingly slow to move without making any noise. As they picked their way through the thicket, shots occasionally rang out from each side. Mark was pretty sure that only a couple of the guys on Rob's response team had any kind of night compatible sighting devices on their rifles. He doubted if these MZB's, or whatever they were, had any. The two sides could shoot thousands of rounds at each other, and they would, at most, score an occasional lucky hit. They needed to find a way to inflict enough damage on these troublemakers to make them want to give up without putting themselves in too much danger. Mark's mind was in jackrabbit mode, while his body moved at turtle speed. He wondered how many men and rifles the MZB's had. He knew Rob had almost thirty, and the report said there were thirty or forty in this group. Even if he used the high side numbers, he didn't know how seventy rifles could make that much noise. It sounded more like seven hundred to him, but that was impossible. The observer could have underestimated, but not by that much. Perhaps there was double what she said. No more than that, surely. He felt a tap on his back.

"Mark, that's three hundred and fifty steps," Roman said softly. "We should have gone at least two hundred yards."

Mark was embarrassed that he hadn't been paying more attention to the task at hand. Fortunately, Roman couldn't see him blush. "Thanks," he said quietly.

He turned toward the clearing, and a minute later, they were standing on the edge. They looked both directions, but it was impossible to make out much beyond a hundred and fifty yards or so. Mark saw some flashes from the direction they had come, and a split second later he heard the shots.

"Do we dash across together or separately?" Roman asked.

"Neither," Mark answered. "I don't want to take any chances. We'll belly crawl. I'll go first. When I'm across, then you come."

"Okay."

Mark hit the dirt and started crawling. It was about fifty yards to the other side, but from the ground it looked like a mile. The chest rig Abby had made worked wonderfully, as long as he was upright. When he tried to crawl on his stomach, the corners of the magazines dug into his chest and stomach. He raised himself on to his elbows and knees to take the weight off of his torso and crawled halfway across. His unprotected elbows couldn't take any more, and he rose up a little more and put his weight on his hands. He scampered the rest of the way and then turned to watch Roman. The young man seemed to make it in half the time Mark had, and he stayed down on his stomach the whole way. 'Bet you couldn't do that with all these mags stabbing you,' Mark thought.

The two men slowly tracked their way back east. The brush was, thankfully, not quite as thick on this side, but they didn't want the girls from OP-Six to shoot them by mistake. They moved very quietly, and as they got closer, they were more and more careful. Mark stopped every few yards to listen and whisper.

"OP-Six, this is OP-Seven. Can you hear me?"

There was no answer. Mark's mind started imagining all of the horrible things that could have happened to the girls. After the sixth or seventh time he called, he heard an answer.

"Mark, is that you?"

It was Susan.

"Yes. Me and Roman," he whispered. "Where are you?"

"Right here…in the OP. I can see you. Come forward about five more yards," she answered in a hushed tone.

Mark and Roman took a few more cautious steps, and then Mark saw the OP. It was just inside the tree line. Since there wasn't a good natural hide here that afforded a good view of the pipeline, a nicely covered spider hole had been dug. It was well camouflaged, and the men might have walked right past it if Susan hadn't heard and seen them. Mark slowly approached the back of the OP. They were almost exactly across from where the MZB's had obviously been setting up camp before Rob's guys had shown up. There were a couple of small fires burning and some half set up tents reflecting the flickering flames in a strange dance-like fashion. The wind was blowing gently toward the hide, and the smell of burning mesquite made Mark's mouth water. All three girls were crowded, sardine like, into the OP. Mark knelt down at the back and could see that the two younger girls were crying. Susan looked as if she had seen a ghost.

"Are y'all alright?" Mark asked. Before any of them could answer, a short burst of gunfire came from across the clearing. The younger girls flinched at the sound. Mark now understood why it had sounded like so many guns when the firing began. The quick burst of three or four shot had come from the same spot. Mark saw the almost continuous muzzle flash and heard the distinctive sound of an AK-47. The MZB's had fully automatic rifles.

"Oh God, Mark. It was horrible," Susan's voice started to increase in volume, as her eyes opened wider with each word. "They started setting up…"

Mark put his finger up to his lips. "Shhhhh." Susan hadn't really answered his question, but the three of them looked okay, physically, and the fact that she started telling what happened told him that none of them were hurt. He knew the men on the other side couldn't hear her. The wind was blowing the sound away from them, and their ears were probably ringing from all of the gunfire, but he didn't want to take any chances. There was no sense in staying at the OP either. It would be best to get the girls back to their camp and calm them down. Then they could move over to join Rob.

"Sorry," Susan more mouthed the word than said it.

"Come on, let's get out of here," Mark told them. "I want you to, as quickly and quietly as you can, crawl back to your campsite. Roman and I will bring up the rear.

The girls wiggled backwards out of the OP and quickly snaked their way back into the trees. Roman followed them, and Mark took one last look across the pipeline. The MZB's were all back in the woods on the other side, using trees for cover from Rob's team. Mark could shoot some of them from this angle. The red dot scope he'd bought from the Watsons would allow him to make the shots, but he'd bet that before he could get the third one off, they'd turn those full tilt boogie rifles in his direction and cut him to ribbons. He followed the direction Roman had gone. The sharp corners of the FAL magazines were now no more than a minor annoyance as he crawled on his stomach.

When he got to the campsite, Mark could see the two younger girls, whom he now recognized, crying. Debbie Friesenhahn had her head buried in Roman's shoulder, crying uncontrollably. Susan was comforting Maria Gutierrez robotically. Mark crawled up next to the normally boisterous Susan.

"Why didn't you answer us on the radio?"

"It broke."

"What happened?"

"When Debbie saw the large group coming, she called it in and then signaled us. We crawled down to the OP, and when Maria climbed in, she broke the radio with her elbow. We were trying to see what was wrong with it when those bastards started setting up camp on top of us. We couldn't get out of the OP without them seeing us. We watched them for a while and tried to figure out what to do. Debbie told us the Response Team was going to set up at the county road. We decided to wait for the campers to go to sleep, and then we were going to sneak out and go find the team. Debbie had underestimated the number of intruders, and we needed to let them know that the number was closer to sixty. Almost half of them are women, but they have guns and look like they know how to use them. All of a sudden, here come some guys from the other direction. We figured out they were the response team when they ordered the MZB's to put their hands up. One of the MZB's shot and killed one of our guys. Everyone just stared at him for a minute, and then all hell broke loose. Eight or nine guys got hit, as the two groups backed up into the trees. I never imagined it would be like this. The first guy just crumpled when he got shot, but most of the others lived for a while after they were hit. Some of them were screaming and crying. It sounded like it was out of a horror film. I don't know if I'll ever get the sound out of my head. One of the MZB's kept trying to get up, but his legs wouldn't work right. Each time he took a step, he fell. It was worse than I ever imagined. One of our guys ran out to help a wounded guy who was trying to crawl back with his group. All of the guys yelled for him not to go, but he took off running. He almost made it to the guy, and those sons-of-bitches shot them both. All we could do was watch. We didn't know what to do. If we fired on them, they would have known where we were and killed us. The girls were really too scared to do anything. Thank God you came along."

"Okay, Susan, you all did the best you could. Now we need to go over to where Rob is and help him. Debbie, Maria, I know you're scared, but you've got to suck it up for now. Do you hear me?" Mark's voice was stern. He wasn't mad at the girls. On the contrary, he felt bad for them. Seeing real violence for the first time was sobering to anyone, let alone teenage girls, but he had to get their attention and make them pull themselves together. The trick worked; both of the girls nodded to Mark while they sniffed to stop the flow of tears. Roman shot Mark a look that said he really didn't appreciate Mark causing Debbie to separate herself from him. "Alright, let's move out. I've got the lead. Roman, you bring up the back."

"You got it, Boss," Roman replied, matter-of-factly.

The group traveled quietly, parallel to the clearing, and slowly made their way toward Rob's group. Mark called to the response team, as he had to the girls. He didn't want any of the guys shooting them. Finally, one of the team members heard him and told him to hold his position. The man called for Rob, who came back and recognized Mark's voice. Rob ordered his men to hold their fire, and then he invited Mark in. The five of them stood and walked to Rob. Mark shook the man's hand.

"Thank God the team's okay. Why didn't they answer us?" Rob asked.

"Their radio broke. How many men did you lose?" Mark inquired.

"We only lost two in the initial exchange," Rob explained. "I was stupid. I was in such a hurry to get here, and I just assumed we were the superior, better-armed group, so I wasn't careful enough. I never expected to run up on fully automatic weapons. Anyway, three guys got wounded, and two of them made it back into the trees with us. They'll be okay, I think. One of the guys was hurt bad and couldn't move. He was lying out in the open, and Jimmy Ramsey tried to go get him. Now, they're both dead."

"Susan told me about that," Mark said sadly, as he nodded his head. "Don't beat yourself up. It could have happened to any of us. The rules are changing faster than we can accept. I guess we just have to start approaching everything from the worst-case point of view. I'm kicking myself for not thinking about how dangerous wild dogs could be, and that oversight almost got my son killed."

"I appreciate your encouragement, but I still have to go tell three wives and a mother that their husbands and son aren't coming home." Rob was almost in tears.

Mark patted the man on the back. "Right now we have to figure out how we are going to deal with this. Do you have any ideas?"

"I'm not sure. This is more of a military operation than a law enforcement one. Curt should be here in a few minutes. Gunny's sending us some help, along with your doctor and nurse. I figure when everyone gets here, we can make a plan." Rob took a deep breath.

A few shots came from the MZB's, and Rob's men answered back in kind.

"You told Curt to be careful coming in?" Mark asked.

"Yeah. I sent two guys back to the bus; it's about a quarter mile away, one to bring Curt and the other to bring your Silver Hills crew in through the woods."

"Good, Gunny's probably sending some of our guys with rifles that have some of the red dot sights we bought. Susan said there are closer to sixty in the group than forty. Debbie underestimated, and when the radio broke, they couldn't let you know. They're behind some pretty big trees. You could shoot all night and not hit any of them without a lucky shot. Anyway, when the guys with the red dots get here, I think I should take three or four of them and try to flank these SOB's. Then, you can distract them with covering fire, and we can try to pick them off a few at a time. If there's enough noise from everybody shooting, maybe they won't figure out what's going on until it's too late."

"That sounds like a good plan," Rob said.

Mark tried to think of what else they could do. He wondered what the MZB's were planning. If they rushed Rob's guys before Curt got here, would they be able to hold the aggressors off? He hoped so.

Fortunately, Curt showed up just a few minutes later. Rob went over everything that had happened, and then Mark presented his plan to the sheriff.

"How many of them are there?" Curt asked.

"Fifty or fifty-five now," Rob answered.

"I don't know, Mark. That's a lot of guys for you to take out four of five at a time. I think, at most, you might be able to use that tactic two or three times before they figure out someone's behind them. Do you think Gunny might send ten guys with rifles?"

"He might," Mark speculated.

"I think if you had ten guys, and we could take out twenty of them before they figured out what was happening, we might get the rest to surrender. Let's see how many he sends and then talk about it again," Curt suggested.

The men waited. Every few minutes, the MZB's would fire across the easement. Curt told all the men on his side not to shoot back unless they had a definite target. No one could see anything except for an occasional muzzle flash. After a few minutes, fire was only coming from the invaders. Finally, the MZB's quit firing. A minute later, a voice came from the opposite camp.

"You Pigs, we know we got you outnumbered. Leave your guns where they are and come out, and we'll let you leave. You have one minute," the voice said emphatically.

It sounded confident, but Mark wondered if it was just bravado. And a minute to what? If they rushed now, Curt and Rob should have enough men to easily stop a charge. Of course, the MZB's didn't know that, did they? Curt must have thought the same thing because he quickly passed the word that no one was to answer or shoot back unless the bastards charged.

It was deathly quiet. Mark felt like he was a kid in a graveyard at midnight. The hair on the back of his neck was standing up. He knew the rush was coming. There were about the same number on each side. Under normal circumstances, the defenders would have the advantage. The attackers would have to cross the open ground, and fifty yards was a long way when you were being shot at, but how would the full auto weapons play into the scenario? Would they even the odds back up, or even tip them in the MZB's favor? He wished the guys Gunny was sending would get here. Having more rifles with sights that worked at night would help them a bunch.

He could hear mumbling from the MZB's. Fortunately, the wind was still coming from their direction. Unfortunately, he couldn't make out what they were saying. He readied himself for the blitzkrieg. Would they come in one big group, or would they split up and attack from different directions? Either way, he'd try to take out the guys with the machine guns first. He could hear his heart pounding in his ears.

Suddenly, another voice yelled out from the other side. Here they come, Mark said to himself. He thumbed the safety off of his big rifle and hugged it in tight to his shoulder, as he looked through the scope, but the voice didn't say what he thought it would. It took his mind a second to register what his ears had heard.

"Fuck you, Smitty! I ain't going over there to see if the mother fuckers left. You do it!"

"Me, neither!" another voice chimed.

Mark almost laughed out loud. He had worked himself up for nothing. It looked as if there was a little dissension in the MZB camp, and as Mark thought about it, he wasn't surprised. Why would they want to face an armed group when there were so many others who were easy pickings? Mark was almost surprised they hadn't retreated. The only reason they were probably still here was because all of their equipment and supplies were in the clearing.

A few seconds later, the MZB leader called out with a different plan. "You Pigs can just leave. We don't want no trouble from you. You just take your guns and go, and we'll call it even. Okay?"

No one answered.

"Are you Pigs fuckin' deaf? Leave! If you're still there in fifteen minutes, we'll kill every one of you. Then we'll go find your old ladies and have some fun before we kill them and the rest of your families. Just go on home and nobody else has to get hurt. You know you don't stand a chance against our assault rifles, so make it easy on yourselves. You now got fourteen minutes and forty-five seconds."

It was so quiet that Mark would have sworn he could hear the tree he was behind growing. A second later, there was a tap on his shoulder. One of the men pointed back in the trees and whispered that Curt wanted to see him. He wiggled backwards until he could get turned around without exposing himself. He crawled up to where Rob and Curt were.

"What do you think?" Curt asked him.

"I guess we could leave, but I don't like letting these guys go. No telling what kind of trouble they'll cause. Even if they leave us alone, somebody's going to have to deal with them," Mark answered.

"I agree," Rob said. "So how do we handle this?"

"Curt, why don't you call FEMA and have them send some of their National Guard troops to mop up this mess. Didn't the FEMA guy tell you to call if you needed anything?" Mark asked.

"I could do that, but I don't think it's a good choice. First no telling how long it would take them to get here, if they could even find the place. Second, they killed our guys. No way do I want to let someone else clean this up, and last, and probably most important, I'm afraid asking for help might set a bad precedent. I don't want to give Mr. FEMA any reason to think we can't handle things on our own. Next thing you know, he thinks we need help blowing our noses and wiping our butts. I'd rather take care of this in-house."

"We could just wait for them to come out after us," Rob suggested. "We should be able to take them out before they cross the opening, or we could go with the plan Mark came up with, when his guys get here."

"Well, let's see how many guys Gunny sends," Mark said. "Normally, I think we could wait them out, but those full auto rifles kind of worry me."

"They worry me too, Mark," Curt said, "but probably not for the same reason they bother you. Full auto isn't really as effective as aimed fire is. It's really hard to shoot accurately on automatic, but if these guys are smart, and thankfully they haven't shown any sign of that yet, they could use them for covering fire. If they could keep our heads down with them long enough to get their guys across the pipeline, it could get ugly for us. Close quarters is where full auto is an advantage."

"Hey, Rob, the Silver Hills guys are here," someone whispered loudly.

"Bring them here," he instructed.

Mark strained his eyes to see how many Gunny had sent. He hoped it was at least fifteen. With that many, his plan should work. He hoped they were the best ones, too. He didn't want to say anything, but most of the guys with Rob and Curt had never seen the elephant, as Gunny put it. Mark didn't know how well they would do under fire. He saw a shape coming out of the darkness. It was a big guy. Mark recognized Chaparo's silhouette. The big man knelt down with the threesome.

"How many guys did you bring with you?" Mark asked.

"Just Doc and Lisa," Chaparo responded.

"Damn it!" Mark exclaimed. He was pissed. "Gunny said he was sending us some help!"

"He did," Chaparo smiled.

"I know. I'm sorry I got mad. I know you're great help, Chaparo, but I was hoping for a few more men."

"You've got enough men," Chaparo answered. "What you need is an equalizer. That's what I brought."

The plumber took off his backpack and opened the top. In the dark, it was hard to make out what was in the pack. It looked like green baseballs. 'How in the world were painted baseballs going to help?' Mark wondered.

"HELL, YEAH!" Curt said, a little louder than he intended. "I don't even want to know where they came from, but I'm glad you've got them."

The two former soldiers grinned at each other evilly. Then it hit Mark. It was the stuff Jon had left behind. Mark's smile nearly split his face. They had hand grenades.

"Okay, here's what I'm thinking," Curt said. "We take five guys directly across from where the perps are. We have Rob and the rest of the guys draw their fire. When we spot their muzzle flashes, we send them some presents. That should take the starch out of them pretty darn quick."

"Sounds good," Rob agreed.

"Okay, Chaparo, you and I know how to use these. Who do we take with us?"

"I'm in!" Mark insisted.

"I figured that," Curt smiled. "Who else? We need someone who can throw."

"I have a kid with me who told me he was the closer on his high school baseball team," Mark said, referring to Roman.

"That'll work. Hey, Rob, didn't Jack play quarterback in high school?"

"I think he did."

Thirty seconds later, Chaparo was giving an impromptu class on hand grenades. A minute after that, the five grenadiers were moving toward the OP. Mark had a strange feeling of mixed emotions. The closest he could come to describing it was the feeling he got before riding on a roller coaster, kind of a scared-excited mix of anticipation.

Before Mark knew it, they were to the OP. Curt spaced them out about five yards apart. He put Roman in the middle, with him and Chaparo on either side. Mark and Jack, whom Mark had only met once before, were on the ends. Each man was assigned an area and was given a grenade.

"Okay, Roman," Curt instructed quietly, "when we see where they are, I want you to throw at the middle. Mark, Jack, when Roman's grenade goes off, you two throw yours. Jack, you aim for the right edge, and Mark, you've got the left. When yours explode, they should be totally confused. Chaparo and I will throw at any big bunches of them we see. Remember, we'll just barely move out into the open. Lob them in; don't try to fast ball them, and don't forget to pull the pins. If this works right, it should completely break their will to fight. Everybody ready?"

Heads nodded all around. Curt pulled his radio up close to his mouth.

"Rob, we're ready," he whispered.

A second later, Rob's voice could be heard yelling to the aggressors telling them to give up or else. Shots rang out, and Mark could see the muzzle flashes from the MZB weapons. The five grenadiers moved out of the trees with a quick stealthy crawl. The full auto AK's across the clearing belched fire like dragons. Mark saw Roman hurl his fragmentation grenade toward the thickest concentration of automatic fire. It shrank in size as it journeyed toward its victims, then it was gone into the darkness. It seemed almost comical that a little, green ball could have so much power, and it gave Mark a feeling of sick giddiness. As he wondered why he felt this way, the explosive detonated, and the firing from the invaders immediately ceased. Mark pulled the pin on his, and tossed it at the shocked MZB's. A few seconds later, the frag chewed through them as Mark imagined a lion chewed a gazelle. As the pale moonlight reflected off of Curt's grenade, Mark realized his elation had turned to dread. When the last two grenades exploded, the fight was over, and Mark felt like he needed a shower with a full-pressure fire hose to wash off the feeling of dirtiness he now had.

Chapter 58

The cleanup on the pipeline was not a fun job. Mark was still sickened by the loss of life, even if the MZB's had it coming. There were nineteen dead and thirty-seven injured invaders. The injured were treated at the scene by Doc and Lisa and then were taken to the hospital. Only two of them died on the way. The dead were taken to the county morgue. What bothered Mark the most were the dead women. The hand grenades had shown no prejudice and had ripped through flesh and bone, no matter its gender. Almost all of the casualties looked to be in their thirties or forties, too old for a run of the mill gang. Rob said they were members of a biker gang known as 'Los Muertos.' It was a particularly dangerous group with ties to organized crime. He recognized them from a small tattoo of a skull most of them had on their necks. There were ten or so MZB's unaccounted for, and it looked like they'd retreated the way they'd come. Some of them must have been injured, as there were blood drops along the route they had trampled.

The grenades had destroyed some of the weapons left behind by the MZB's, but many of them were still serviceable. There were quite a few AK-47 types, including eleven full-auto weapons. In addition, a hodgepodge of handguns and a few shotguns were recovered. Some of the destroyed weapons looked like parts might be scavenged or repaired to make them useable again. Mark could take them all over to Tony Watson and see what he could do with them.

A fresh team of observers had been sent to OP-Six, and Curt had left them another radio. He was pretty sure his radio tech could fix the damaged one. The men packed all of the weapons, ammunition, and camping equipment into the buses. Then everyone loaded onto the old, yellow, school buses and headed home. When they stopped at Silver Hills, Curt asked Mark if he needed any of the confiscated property.

"Not really, we're a lot better off on weapons and stuff than a lot of the newer groups are. I wouldn't mind having a couple of the full-auto rifles and some of those big 40-round mags, though. We could use them at the gate, in case it got swarmed, but if you think someone else needs them more, then that's okay."

Curt walked to the back of the bus and returned with three rifles and fifteen magazines. "Here you go."

"Thanks, Curt, but I only need two."

"Take them. I know Gunny will make sure your guys know when and when not to use them. Some of the others might just waste a whole bunch of ammo with them."

"Alright. I really appreciate it. Hey, any word on how much longer the Guard's going to watch the county line?" Mark asked.

"Shouldn't be too much longer, according to what the FEMA man told me. The latest over the short-wave is that China's getting ready to push into Taiwan. Supposedly, the President has said he won't stand for it. Rumor is that he's sending two carrier groups back over there, and the National Guard's going to assume some of the duties the regular military was doing. Wouldn't surprise me if they were gone tomorrow, but I think we ought to man the OP's for at least another week."

"Great," Mark said. "Just what our country needs right now, another crisis." He took a deep breath. "I agree on the OP's. No telling how many bad guys might be left in San Antonio."

"Let's hope not too many," Curt responded.

"Amen to that. Anyway, I need to go pick up our tractor when the National Guard leaves the county line. It's over at my gun dealers' house. If you want, I can take all of the broken rifles to them and see if they can be fixed."

"Sounds good." Curt and some of the others took all of the nonworking firearms out of the bus and carried them into Mark's shed. After that, Curt shook Mark's hand, and the buses left.

Mark went into the house and found everyone asleep. He woke Jess and filled her in on what had happened. He asked her to check on Susan and the other two girls in the morning and make sure they were doing okay. She agreed, and then Mark gave her a kiss and headed down to the CP to talk with Gunny over the radio. He informed the security chief that he was going to have someone drive him and Roman back to OP-Seven. The old man agreed and said he'd see Mark the next morning to debrief him about the fight.

Twenty minutes later found Roman and Mark at the OP. It was almost 3:30 in the morning, and Mark went ahead and relieved Albert who'd been on duty for over eight hours. The young man reported that he hadn't seen anyone pass by. He told Mark he'd never heard so many gunshots at one time in his life, and he wanted a play by play on what had happened. Mark gave him the high points and then sent him and Roman to get some sleep. Mark, alone with his thoughts, found it difficult to think of anything but the badly broken bodies the grenades had left behind. It wasn't as grotesque as what he'd seen in his sister's house in Waco, but it was the worst thing he'd ever had a hand in. It was much worse than the shootout in the trucks or the one at the roadblock. Bullet holes were neat compared to the mess the shrapnel made. He tried to put it out of his mind. Finally, the sun rose, and the family of feral hogs crossed the road. They were the only ones to use it that day.

The next morning, Gunny spoke with Mark and Chaparo about the fight with the MZB's. He thought they'd done a good job, but he said wouldn't have used so many grenades, at least not at first.

"You don't gotta kill all of the enemy," he lectured. "All you gotta do is take the will to fight away from them. One grenade mighta done that. We hafta to be careful with these, 'cause the chance that we can get more is slim to none. Chaparo, I know you and Curt are Army pukes, and you guys usually get plenty of supplies, but you need to start thinking like a Marine on the front lines where re-supply is iffy at best."

"I get the point, Gunny," Chaparo said, obviously trying to not take the scolding personally.

Gunny had a good point. They needed to treat every bean, bullet, and Band-Aid as if it was their last, Mark thought.

In the afternoon, word came back from the OP's that the National Guard troops had pulled out from all of their posts along the county line. George, as soon as he heard the news, was knocking on Mark's door to go get the tractor.

Mark didn't argue with the man, who was now much thinner than when he'd arrived. Mark wondered how much longer he could hide his illness, perhaps a while longer, since almost everyone had dropped at least a little weight.

"Okay, George, let's hook up the trailer, and find a couple of guys to go with us."

"Alex is already hooking it up, and he can go with us."

'Just what I need,' Mark thought. "Okay, that's one," he said, trying not to let his displeasure show. "Let's see if Gunny's up for a little road trip."

"I'll go get him," George said quickly.

Before Mark could answer, George was out the door and scurrying down the street. Mark saw that Alex had the trailer hooked to the Ford, and he got the young man to help him put the broken rifles in the back of the truck.

"Where's your rifle? If you're going with us you have to have a rifle," Mark admonished the young farming apprentice.

"I don't have one. George has been teaching me how to shoot some, but my Dad never believed in guns before The Burst."

Mark saw this as his opportunity to leave Alex behind. "Sorry, but you can't go without a weapon. It's just too dangerous, and we never know what we might run into."

The young man hung his head dejectedly, but he didn't say a word. Mark knew that a trip anywhere had become a real treat. He felt a little bad for not letting Alex go, but it was a rule that everyone had to be armed outside of the subdivision. A second later, George returned with Gunny. The master farmer was carrying an old Marlin .30-30 in addition to his own rifle. Mark thought he recognized it from the roadblock on the way back from Waco. Much to Mark's chagrin, George gave the old cowboy gun to Alex, who immediately beamed. The four of them climbed into Mark's truck and headed west.

The trip to the Watsons wasn't far, but it seemed to take a long time. Once they crossed the county line, it was obvious that things had changed. Some of the houses along the route had been burned. Others had windows broken and doors kicked in. There wasn't a sign of anyone living in any of the houses. Before, when they drove through, they'd see a few people, and Mark could feel the eyes of many more. Now, it felt like a ghost town. Mark expected any minute to see a tumbleweed roll across the road.

As he turned onto the road the Watsons lived on, he realized no one in the truck had said a word since they crossed into Bexar County. The houses he could see appeared to be undamaged, but there was still no sign of anyone. When he saw the Watsons' gate, his heart sank. The gate was ripped off of its hinges and bent. The big Suburban they'd been using to reinforce the entrance was on its side. Mark felt it would have taken a bulldozer to damage the gate and push over the truck like that.

"Stop the truck," Gunny ordered. Mark obeyed immediately and pulled the truck off to the side of the road, thirty or forty yards from the gravel driveway. "I don't like the looks of this," the veteran continued. "George, I want you and Alex to stay in the truck. Keep it running, and if there's any sign of trouble, I want you to get the hell out of here. Go back home and get Chaparo and Jim. Tell them we'll meet them at the little church we passed about a mile back.

Mark and I are going to check out the house. If it's safe, we'll come back and get you. Clear?"

"Crystal," George answered, tight lipped.

Mark looked over at Alex and noticed his face was whiter than normal. Gunny got out of the truck, and Mark followed him. The pair crept toward the gate with their rifles ready and their heads down. When they got to the driveway, Mark could see no signs of bulldozer tracks, but it was obvious that there had been several vehicles making their way in and out of the place. Mark looked down toward the house. It was obscured by trees, trees that had many round, white spots on the trunks, where the bark had been blasted away. The knot in the pit of his stomach twisted into a tighter ball. The two men made their way down the driveway in three to five second rushes, one covering the other as they leap-frogged each other to the house. When they could see it, it was apparent that a major fight had taken place. Every window was broken, and the brick exterior was pock marked with various size fissures that could have only been caused by bullets. The two men worked their way over to the side of the house where the garage was. The big doors were open, and the door from the garage into the kitchen was swinging in the breeze. Mark made his way to the open door and quickly peeked into the house. He didn't see anything, and a moment later, he and Gunny were searching the house. There was shattered glass everywhere and several places where dark, misshapen circles stained the beige carpet. The house had clearly been ransacked, with anything of value taken. Mark wondered what could have happened. Could FEMA have come for them, and they resisted? The Watsons would have at least taken a few of their attackers out, but there were no bodies. MZB's weren't likely to cart off their casualties, or those of their victims. Whatever it was, it hadn't gone well for the Watsons. The two men took a quick look around the back and found nothing threatening. All of the tents and RV's were gone, as was the Watsons' Jeep. The tractor was next to the big storage shed, but the gas cap was laying on the ground next to it. The storage shed was open, and it was practically empty, but the cargo containers were still locked. Nothing made sense.

"Who do you think did this?" Mark asked.

"I don't know, Karate Man. It don't add up."

"I was thinking the same thing."

"Why don't you go get George and the kid? I'll look around here for clues, and we'll see if we can figure this out."

"You got it, Gunny." Mark trotted back out to the truck. George and Alex visibly relaxed when Mark waved them in. When George had pulled the truck through the gate, he stopped to let Mark get in. He climbed onto the bumper, and they drove up to the house where Gunny was looking in the grass around the biggest trees.

"What are you looking for Gunny?" Alex asked.

"Someone threw a bunch of shots at the house, but there's almost no empty cartridge cases out here. I've only found two so far. None in the house, either. What does that tell you?" The old man answered the question with one of his own.

"That whoever did this is picking up their brass to cover their tracks, or to reload, or maybe both?"

"That's what I was thinking. Help me scout around and see if we can find some more."

The four of them spent the next thirty minutes looking for empty cases. When they got together, the results of their search had only produced twenty-one empties.

"Lookin' at all the impact marks in the brick, how many shots would you all say was fired at the house?" Gunny asked, sounding like a trial lawyer.

"Hundreds," George answered.

"Thousands," Mark said, with Alex nodding his head.

"I would say at least a thousand," Gunny said, "and that's just what was goin' in. Yet we can only find twenty-one empty cases? Somebody was real thorough cleaning up. I found some pretty good signs that they took at least a few casualties, but the bodies are gone. If it was the military, they would have taken the bodies, but not the brass. MZB's might be smart enough to pick up their brass, but why would they haul the bodies off? And where are the Watsons? If they got taken to a camp or to jail, that would explain it, but what else would?"

"Maybe they got overwhelmed and ran away," Alex suggested.

"Maybe, but, from the size of some of the bloodstains inside, it looks like some of them were probably killed. What happened to them? They didn't run away."

"Perhaps the others came back and buried them after the MZB's left," George said. "Maybe they knew they were going to be attacked, and the women and children left before the battle and took the tents and stuff with them, and if the MZB's picked up their brass so as not to leave any evidence, wouldn't they take their dead for the same reason?"

"That makes the most sense so far, but I just don't see your run of the mill MZB covering their tracks like that," Gunny argued. "Let's look at the evidence we have." Gunny set the cartridge cases on the hood of the truck. "What do you all notice about these?"

"They're mostly rifle cases?" Alex asked, trying a little too hard for Mark's taste.

"Yes, but what else?"

"They're all military. Most are NATO rounds, but a couple of them are 7.62 by 39 that are used in AK's and SKS's like we bought from Jerry and Tony," Mark stated.

"What about this one?" Gunny asked, handing Mark what the younger man thought was a 9mm.

Mark took it and looked at the head stamp. It read R-P .40 S&W. "This is a police round," he said. "At least most of the police departments I know of around here use it. I don't think the military has ever used it."

"And look at this one."

Mark took a piece of rifle brass from the old Marine.

"Why is it striped?" Alex asked.

The case had several black stripes running along its length.

"That was my question," Gunny responded. "Look at the head stamp. It says LC 63. That stands for Lake City Armory. It's where a lot of our ammo for the military comes from, or at least used to. The 63 stands for 1963, when it was made, but I've never seen one striped like that."

"Me neither," Mark added. "Maybe some kind of reloading marks? Jim will know what it is. We'll ask him when we get back." He took a breath as he looked at all twenty-one empty cases. "What jumps out at me about this is, while it's almost all military brass, it's not all our military's, which would point to MZB's, but with the exception of the group the other night, who all had AK's, we haven't seen a group that didn't have strictly civilian caliber rifles like .30-30's and .243's."

Gunny nodded his head. "I would tend to agree with you, Karate Man, but maybe we just didn't find any brass for them. Bolt and lever action rifles would put the brass in an easier to pick up pile than a semi or full auto would. Maybe they had some civvie rifles, and they picked up all the brass for them. Either way, it looks like an organized group, but not military. That leads me to my next question. Why would a well-armed group attack here? What did the Watsons have that would make someone spend thousands of rounds of ammo to get?" he asked, like he already knew the answer.

"That's easy," Alex answered. "They wanted the guns."

"Maybe," Gunny said, trying to let the kid down easy. "But they already have guns, lots of them, and it's not that hard to get more."

"They wanted the food and the RV's," George said. "That's why the house is cleaned out, and the trailers are gone."

"Could be," Gunny answered, "but I think it was something else, and those were just a bonus, or maybe you were right before, and the Watsons knew they were gonna be attacked, and they moved that stuff before the MZB's got here."

"Ammo!" Mark blurted. "They wanted the ammo. What good are guns without ammo?"

"Bingo! That's the answer I was looking for."

"Last time I was here, some of the ammo was on the shelves in the shed. That's all gone, but the unbroken cases were in one of the shipping containers that are still locked. Maybe they couldn't get them open."

"Maybe not. Let's go look."

All four of them walked into the shed. Mark pushed the door open all the way, but it was still too dark to see well except in one corner of the shed where some old, rusting shovels and rakes were stored.

"Alex, would you run and look under the front seat of my truck. There's a big flashlight there."

The young man nodded his head once and dashed off. Seconds later, he was back with the light. Mark clicked it on and shined it on the lock. His mind cycled through the possibilities. Maybe they hadn't gotten in, but there were no marks on the lock or the door that looked like someone had tried to break in. Maybe they got the key, but then why would they relock it? Mark verbalized his thoughts to the others.

"Only one way to find out," Gunny stated. "Now, how do we get the lock open?"

"We can just shoot it off!" Alex said, like the answer was so obvious he couldn't believe he was the only one who thought of it.

"That only works in the movies, kid!" Mark answered. "I've got a big tire iron. I'll get it."

A few moments later, Mark had the tire iron through the hasp of the lock, and he, Alex, and Gunny were pulling on it for all they were worth. George held the flashlight, since there was only room for six hands on the curved tool. It was hot in the shed, and after just a few minutes of pulling, all three of them were drenched in sweat. The lock was apparently high quality, and it hadn't yielded one iota to their attack. Mark felt that if whoever had been here before had gotten in, they must have used the key. The three of them tried and tried again, pushing, pulling, and jerking. After a few more minutes, Mark was worried about how red Gunny's face was turning, and he called for a break. They went outside where a breeze, even though it was warm, felt like heaven.

The three of them breathed in the fresh air, trying to catch their breath. George walked over to the truck and returned with a canteen of water that they all passed around. Mark was bending over with his hands on his knees, wondering when was the last time he'd worked so hard for nothing.

"What do we do now?" Alex asked, getting on Mark's last nerve.

Before Mark could launch into the ten dollar tirade that he figured was worth it, George, who must have sensed what was coming, patted Mark's arm and spoke. "Let me see if I can find something to help." He disappeared into the shed, and a moment later they heard the sound of metal singing across the concrete floor. George appeared out of the darkness, dragging a long pry bar. He handed it to Mark, who felt the weight of the long, round, piece of steel. It felt as if it weighed fifty pounds. One end was pointed, and the other end of the six-foot long cylinder had a chisel tip.

"Goodness, George, that's a big ass pry bar. I think it might work. Where'd you find it?" Mark asked.

"It's called a breaker bar. It's for breaking and prying rocks out of the ground. I found it with the hand tools in the corner."

"Let's give it a try," Mark said with a smile, his first of the day.

They went back in the shed and threaded the tapered point into the lock. All four of them pulled against bar, but the lock still held.

"Let's give it a quick jerk," Mark suggested. "One, two, THREE!"

The lock yielded with a metallic crack, and three of the four men landed on their butts. Only Alex had kept his footing, barely. No one was hurt, and they laughed at the outcome that would have been obvious to anyone who wasn't so focused on the task. Mark jumped up after a minute and opened the door to the container. George picked up the light and shone it into the twenty-foot abyss. It was as empty as a cookie jar with a bunch of unsupervised three year olds around. Mark wondered why anyone would lock an empty container. A second later, Alex, voiced the same question.

"I don't know," Mark answered, slightly annoyed, "but last time I was here, this thing was at least half full."

"Should we look in the other one?" George asked.

"Can't hurt nothing," Gunny replied.

It took three tries to open the container the Watsons had kept the guns in. The lock was the same, but the men were a little more cautious about how hard they pulled. Finally, the hasp popped free. Mark set the breaker bar down and removed the lock from the handle. He lifted the handle and turned it. George had the light, and the other two were positioning themselves to see what, if anything, this big, metal box held.

As soon as the door cracked, Alex and George doubled over and retched. Mark recognized the rancid smell of death immediately, and he barely kept his breakfast down. Gunny's hand was over his nose and mouth in a flash, and with the other hand, he pulled George outside. Mark copied his example and half dragged Alex by the back of his belt, as he spewed a month's worth of food across the concrete floor. Once outside, George and Alex stopped throwing up. Mark didn't know if it was because of the fresh air or if they had emptied the entire contents of their stomachs and had nothing left to heave. He had to swallow hard several times not to puke himself. Gunny looked at him with knowing eyes. Mark knew what he was saying without words, but he didn't want to admit it to himself.

"Somebody's gotta see who they is."

"I'll do it," Mark said stoically, praying it wasn't who he thought it was. He walked toward the door and pulled his t-shirt up over his mouth and nose before he entered. It had been two days since he'd taken a shower. That, combined with the sweating he'd done working on the lock in the stagnant shed made his body odor as strong and pungent as he could ever remember. However, compared with the smell of rotting flesh and vomit, it smelled like the hundred dollar an ounce perfume he'd once given Jess. He walked to the container and pulled the door all the way open. He wished he smelled worse, as the putrid stench from inside seemed to permeate every cell of his being. He tried to hold his breath, but when he did have to breathe, he inhaled through his mouth. He shined the flashlight on the first face. It was swollen to almost twice its size, but he didn't think he recognized it. The same with the second, but the third man was Jerry Watson. Mark, upon seeing his misshapen face, could no longer hold his breakfast down. He ran out of the container and heaved the contents of his stomach onto the floor with those of the others. Mark wiped his mouth off and returned to look at Jerry. He'd been shot through the chest where it looked like he would have died quickly. As Mark made his way toward the back of the container, he discovered that, except for the six men in the front, the others had been shot in the back of the head. Because of this, they were unidentifiable, but he thought he knew which ones were Tony and Mr. Watson, and Mark was pretty sure all the others were part of the Watson clan. He was able to determine one thing for certain; they were all men. Perhaps the women and children had left before the fight. He prayed that was what had happened.

He returned to report his findings to the others. As he looked at them, he noticed that not even Gunny's eyes were dry. He reached up and touched his own cheeks to find them wet, as well. Perhaps it was from the smell, he thought. It wasn't because he was sad. He was way beyond sad. He was pissed.

Chapter 59

"So what do we do now?" George asked.

"We load up the tractor and go home," Mark said coolly. "I closed the container back up."

"We aren't going to report this to the authorities?"

"How would we get a hold of them?" Mark asked. "And even if we could, I don't think it's a good idea to involve ourselves in this mess. There's nothing we can do to help them anymore. It'll be dark soon. We might be able to come back and bury them tomorrow or the next day. Right now, we'll get home and call Curt, and then he can call whoever he thinks should know. Then maybe we can come back."

"That sounds like a good plan to me," Gunny seconded.

"How are we going to load the tractor?" Alex asked. "They siphoned all the gas and stole the battery."

"We could borrow one of the batteries out of Mark's truck, since it has two, and there may be enough gas in the fuel lines to get it started and drive it up on the trailer," George said.

George's plan worked, and thirty minutes later, they were on their way back to Silver Hills with the tractor in tow. When they got home, George and Alex busied themselves with the tractor, while Mark and Gunny went to find Jim to tell him the news and have him look at the striped brass cartridge case. A check at the CP revealed that Jim was manning OP-Five, and Mark and Gunny had the radio operator tell him they were coming to see him. Then, Mark called Curt and asked if he would come out.

"Can you tell me what you need, Mark?" the lawman's voice crackled.

"I'd rather not say over the air, Curt."

"I can be there in a couple of hours. Is that okay?"

"That'll be fine."

Mark signed off about the time Gunny drove up in his old Dodge truck, and they drove to the observation post.

"What's wrong?" Jim said, as soon as they got out of the truck.

"It's the Watsons," Mark answered.

"Are they okay?"

"I'm afraid not, Jim. They're dead," Mark said, the anger still in his face. "At least all the men are; we don't know about the women and kids."

"How did it happen?" Jim said, as his eyes started misting up a little.

"It looks like they was in a hell of a firefight," Gunny explained. "Anyway, it appears some of 'em were killed, and the others surrendered for some unknown reason. Then they was executed."

"Oh, my God! Who did it?"

"We don't know," Gunny continued. "If they took any casualties, they removed the bodies, and they picked up almost all of their empties, but we found a few and wanted to know what you can make of this."

Gunny handed the case to Jim. The tall man looked at it for a minute and then spoke. "It's a Lake City .308 case that's been reloaded and fired out of an Heckler & Koch model 91."

"I knew it was Lake City, and we figured the stripes had to do something with it being reloaded, but how can you tell what kind of rifle it was shot out of?" Gunny asked.

"The stripes don't have anything to do with the reloading process. They're what tell me the kind of rifle. Well, them and the sizable dent here," Jim explained, as Mark and Gunny's looks became more confused. "See, the HK91 has a fluted chamber. It's supposed to make the case extract easier or something. They are the only ones I know of that do that. Anyway, the fluting lets the burning gas discolor the brass like this, and the 91 is notorious for denting cases."

"How can you tell it's a reload, then?" Mark asked.

"That's easy. See the primer? It's silver. Military primers are all brass colored, and they get crimped into the case. This case has had the crimp swaged out, so a new primer could be put into it."

"I see," Mark said, as Gunny nodded his head.

"H&K's aren't cheap rifles, and 91's usually bring twenty-five hundred or so, even used. Whoever did this has expensive taste in weapons. You know, some of the European militaries use H&K's, I think. You don't think the President has let the UN bring troops into the country, do you?"

"I doubt that, Jim. Besides, Europe has her own problems, and we found some commie ammo and even some .40 S&W ammo, too. I don't think it was any kind of military unit that killed them in cold blood," Mark said. "More than likely, it was group of organized MZB's who stole some good hardware somewhere along the way."

"Unless that's what the government wants us to think," Gunny said.

"I think you've got your tinfoil hat on a little too tight there, Gunny," Mark said. "I think the government is slow, lazy, and sometimes stupid, but I refuse to believe that, as a whole, they are evil. Besides, what would be the point in hiding the bodies if you wanted it to look like a bunch of MZB's?"

"He's right, Gunny," Jim told his friend. He paused thoughtfully for a moment. "Hey, didn't they have a bunch of H&K's at Mr. Davis's ranch?"

"Now who's the conspiracy nut? Mr. Davis might be a control freak and a bigot, but I got no indication that he, or anyone else we knew down there, is a murderer and looter," Mark said.

"I know that!" Jim argued. "I was thinking maybe someone stole one from them."

"Maybe," Mark weighed the possibility.

"Now you boys need to give your 'maginations a rest. That would be a little too coincidental, dontcha think? Someone steals a rifle from your boss and then uses it to attack your friends, three counties away? You couldn't sell that story, even in Hollywood. For all we know, that case might have come from one of the Watsons' rifles," Gunny admonished the younger men.

"Yeah, you're right Gunny," Jim said.

The three men talked a few minutes more, and then Gunny and Mark drove back to Silver Hills. It was fully dark when they got there. Mark, half asleep, took a shower and then sat down to eat some dinner. Jess kept smiling at him across the table. As he was eating, Curt knocked on the door.

Jess opened the door, and the lanky lawman came in and removed his cowboy hat.

"Hi, Curt. Sit down. Would you like something to eat?" she asked.

"No thanks, but I'll take a cup of that coffee I smell," he said, as he pulled out a chair at the table.

"You got it." She poured a cup and set it in front of the sheriff. "I'm going to put the boys to bed and read them a story." She kissed her husband on the head and winked at him.

"Thanks for the coffee, Jess."

"You're welcome, Sheriff. You boys don't stay up all night talking. You both look like you need some sleep. Besides that, I need to talk with Mark before he's totally brain dead."

Mark wondered what she wanted to talk to him about this time. "Okay, Jess," he answered. "I only need five or ten minutes with Curt, then I'll come find you."

She smiled sweetly again and then walked out of the kitchen, calling for Tommy and Timmy. Mark filled the sheriff in on what they had found. Curt asked him some questions and promised to let the authorities in Bexar County know about it. He made Mark promise not to go back.

"If they catch you there, you'll be in deep shit, my friend. Plus, whoever did it could come back. I know you want to make sure your friends get buried, but let the cops over there take care of it."

"Okay, Curt, I promise."

The lawman left, and Mark went to find Jess. She was reading the boys Treasure Island, and they were sitting up on their cots, listening intently to the practiced storyteller.

"I'm headed to bed, sweetheart," he said when she paused.

"I'll be there in a few minutes," she promised. "Don't go to sleep until we talk, okay?"

"Okay. Night, boys."

"Good night, Uncle Mark," they chimed in unison.

Mark trudged into the room and lay down to wait for her. He was so tired. All of the problems and worrying had worn him out. He closed his eyes. 'I'll just rest them for a second,' he thought.

When he opened his eyes, sunlight was filtering in through the curtains. He looked at his watch, which read 6:30. Jess was snuggled up next to him. He got up as quietly as he could and dressed. He didn't feel like he'd gotten any sleep at all. In fact, he felt more tired now than he had last night. He leaned out, placed a hand on the wall, and tried to collect his strength. 'The stress must be taking more out of me than I realized,' he thought.

He looked up at the calendar. He had placed it on the wall over his dresser a few weeks ago and had started marking off the days. He'd found it difficult to remember what day it was since he wasn't on any kind of normal schedule anymore. In some ways, it was liberating, but at times, it was frustrating not knowing what day it was, so he'd started using the calendar. He picked up the pen and marked the day, Tuesday, October 28th. He counted back. It had been ten weeks since The Burst. It seemed like a lifetime. He wished the lights would come back on and everything would go back to the way it was. He started to the kitchen, and when he got to the bedroom door, he stopped and flipped the light switch, wishing. He heard a giggle behind him.

"What did you do that for?" Jess asked.

"Just hoping maybe they'd come on," he answered, a little embarrassed that he'd gotten caught.

"Yeah, I was hoping to talk to my man last night, too, but trying to wake you up did about as much good as flipping that switch."

"Sorry."

"That's okay, I know you were tired. You want some breakfast?"

"That would be great," he said.

"Come help me?"

He nodded his head, and they went into the kitchen and started the wordless ballet of preparing breakfast that had been perfected over many years. He finally broke the silence. "What did you want to talk to me about?"

"It's not that important. You have to go pretty soon. It can wait until we have more time to talk about it."

"It seemed like it was pretty important last night. I don't have to leave for an hour. What is it?"

"I was thinking that we need a couple more bedrooms. The boys really need something better than the dining room, the way it is, anyway. It's just too open, and they don't have any privacy. I was thinking we could convert your study into one room and close the opening between the entryway and the dining room off to give whoever's in there some privacy."

"I see what you mean about the dining room, but the boys don't need separate rooms. Mike and I shared a room until he left for college."

"I know that." She paused like she was fishing for the right words. "It's just that we need…"

The back door burst open, and George appeared suddenly and out of breath. "Mark!" he exclaimed, trying to catch his breath. "Mark, something knocked down the corn across the road. Come quick."

"Be right back," Mark called over his shoulder, as he followed the flustered George out of the door, across the road, and through the field.

Mark could normally run circles around the old farmer, but in his excited state, George was setting quite a pace. Mark also noticed his left hamstring was a little stiff, and that was slowing him down a smidgen. That gunshot hasn't bothered me for a couple of weeks,' he thought, 'must be the weather changing.' When they'd gone not quite halfway across the five-acre field, George stopped suddenly.

"Look!" he said as he pointed.

A large area of the corn had been flattened, and some of the small, young, tender ears had been eaten. Mark knew immediately what had done it.

"Hogs," he said calmly.

"That's what I think, too," George said excitedly, as he launched into a tirade. "We have to do something! This is over a quarter acre of ruined corn! We can't afford to take this kind of loss! If they come back, they could wreck everything! We have to stop them! What are you going to do about this, Mark?"

Mark felt his face go hot. "I don't know, George. Let me see, the fucking lights went off, I don't have a job anymore, my family is probably dead, someone killed some of my best friends, the sheriff won't let me go back to bury them, my wife wants me to build two new bedrooms in our house, I'm trying to keep your secret from my best friend and his wife, my damn leg hurts, and you interrupt my breakfast to know what I'm going to do to stop a bunch of fucking pigs that ate your corn? You know what, George? That's what fucking pigs do; they eat corn. I don't know how to change a million years' worth of instinct. I'm sorry, but I'm just not that smart, and I don't have all the answers to everybody's fucking problems!"

The red in his eyes faded enough to where he could see the hurt look on George's face. He was immediately filled with regret. "I'm sorry, George. I just have a lot on my mind. I'm not mad at you. Please forgive me."

"I'm sorry, too. I know you're upset about the Watsons. I shouldn't have dumped this on you, and I never realized how hard it's been for you to keep my secret."

"It's not that hard. I was just blowing off steam. That's the least of my problems. I had no right to throw it up in your face. I'll tell you what; Jim will be back in an hour or so, and he's the best hog hunter I know. Why don't you get with him and see what he thinks is the best way to handle this."

"I will, Mark," George said dejectedly.

"I'm really sorry, George. I didn't mean it," Mark pleaded.

"I know you didn't. Go eat your breakfast. I'll take care of this. Don't you worry about it," the older man said, as he turned and started out of the field at a fraction of the speed he'd entered it.

Mark walked back to the house, slightly limping on his aching leg. He went back inside to find the four kids sitting around the kitchen table as Jess scraped scrambled eggs onto their plates. She saw the look on his face.

"What's wrong?"

"Oh, some feral hogs got into the corn last night and trampled it."

"Well, that's nothing some of you hunters can't take care of," she said cheerfully. "Come sit down and eat some breakfast before you have to go."

"Dad, I could watch for them tonight. My arm's getting better, and I know I can shoot my deer rifle," David volunteered eagerly.

"You can check with Jim when he gets back," Mark told his son. "George is going to talk to him about how to keep them out of the crops. As long as Lisa and your mother are okay with it, and Jim needs the help, it's okay with me, but no whining if any of them say no. Alright?"

"Sure thing, Dad."

"Uncle Mark, can I help David?" Tommy asked.

"Me, too," Timmy interjected.

Mark took a deep breath and searched for the right words.

"We'll have to see about that," Jess said, saving Mark from having to be the bad guy. "Besides, I'm not sure David's as well as he thinks he is."

Mark shot his wife a thankful glance and then picked up his fork and stabbed at the eggs. He put the bite in his mouth. They didn't taste like anything. He realized he wasn't hungry, put the fork down and pushed the plate away.

"I'm sorry." He wondered how many times he'd said that this morning. "I'm not very hungry, and I've got to go. You kids mind your mom, and I'll see you in a couple of days."

He stood up and headed for the study to get his rifle and gear. Jess followed him into the room.

"What's really the matter?" she demanded.

He turned to tell her 'Nothing,' but her look stopped him. She always saw through him. He hated it.

"I lost my temper with George when he asked me what *I* was going to do about the hogs, and now I feel like shit about it." He wondered how much he owed his box now. He'd lost track.

She came up and hugged him to her and started to say something. She pulled back, and her hand went to his forehead.

"Holy crap! You're hot. Really hot. Do you feel okay?"

"Just tired. I'll be okay. I've got to go."

"Not before Lisa looks at you," she insisted.

"No. Really, I'm fine."

"Then you won't have a problem letting Lisa have five minutes to look at you. Sam?" she called.

"Yes, Mom?" Samantha answered from the other room.

"Run down to Abby's and tell Lisa I think your dad's coming down with something and I'm sitting on him until she can get here."

"Okay, Mom."

A second later, they heard the screen door slam. Mark wanted just to go, but he knew if he did, he'd pay for it later. He stacked all of his gear on the table, so he would be ready when Lisa cleared him. Each second seemed like an hour as he waited with Jess standing in the door with her arms folded. Finally, Lisa and Sam came into the room.

"So what's the problem?" the nurse asked.

"Mark's running a fever. He says he's fine, but I don't think so," Jess said before Mark could say anything.

Lisa put her hand on Mark's forehead. "You're right, Jess." She pulled a thermometer out of her bag and stuck it in his mouth. A few minutes later, she pulled it out. "A hundred and one and a half," she said.

"I feel fine," Mark protested.

"Uh huh," she said disinterestedly. "Open up and say *AH.*"

He obeyed her commands as she poked, prodded, and probed, asking if this or that hurt. His response was always negative.

"Nothing hurts at all?" she finally asked.

"Nothing," he answered. "My leg's just aching a little where it got shot."

"Here?" She reached down and grabbed his thigh.

It made him a little uncomfortable to have someone besides Jess touching his upper leg. He looked at her, and she seemed oblivious to the fact that her hands were so close to his crotch. "No lower, just above my knee."

Her hand slid down. "Here?" She squeezed the area he had indicated.

The pain wasn't severe, but it did surprise him. He jumped a little. "Yes."

"That's not where you were shot. Drop your pants," she ordered.

He was embarrassed, and for so many reasons. He felt the blood rush to his face. Then he was more embarrassed that he was embarrassed. He hoped the girls hadn't seen him blush.

"Sam, will you check on the boys?" Jess asked, but it wasn't a request.

452

Sam silently left the room, and Mark slid his trousers down to his knees, as he looked at his wife and mouthed the words 'Thank you', hoping she would think that was all he was embarrassed about.

"Oh my God, Mark. What did you do to your leg?" Lisa asked excitedly.

"Nothing," he answered, as he looked down and saw the reddish, purple streaks running up his thigh.

"Turn around."

He turned as best he could with his pants around his knees.

"You cut yourself or something right here above your knee in the back, and it's infected. Bad."

"Oh, yeah. I got stuck by some barbed wire crossing a fence the other night."

"Come on over to the clinic," she said. "I want to give you a shot of antibiotics and a tetanus shot right now."

"Then can I go?" he asked expectantly.

"Yes," the tall, blonde nurse replied. "You can go to bed and rest for a couple of days. No work of any kind until we get this infection knocked down."

"But..."

"But, nothing!" This was the firmest Mark had ever seen her. "This is serious. You want to lose this leg?"

He shook his head, finally realizing why she was so concerned.

"I didn't think so. Now, pull up those pants, and let's go." She looked over at Jess and spoke to her, as if he wasn't in the room. "I think we caught this in time. Good thing you called me. I'm going to give him the shots and some oral antibiotics, too. When he gets home, you're to make sure that he rests. I'll tell them at the CP that he's on medical restriction for at least the next few days," Lisa said, as she marched out.

Mark buckled his belt and sheepishly followed her out of the room. When they got to the clinic, she gave him a big shot in his hip. He felt a little humiliated. First, Jess and Lisa had acted like he was a kid by not including him in their conversation, then he had to get a shot in the butt. He had asked for it in the arm, but Lisa had refused, saying it was too much medicine to inject there. She did give him the tetanus shot in the arm. When she was done, she instructed him to sit in one of the chairs for twenty minutes.

"I have to make sure you don't have a reaction to the antibiotics. I have some work to do in the other room. I'll come get you in a little bit, and then you can go home and rest. Understand?"

"Yes, Lisa, I understand," he said in an exasperated voice.

She pretended not to notice his attitude, wrote something on a clipboard hanging on the wall, and walked out of the room.

Mark sat in the chair for a few minutes looking around. He wished he'd brought something to read. He stood up and walked over to the clipboard to see what she'd written. Her handwriting looked like a doctor's. "Sheese, Lisa," he whispered to himself, "your writing is worse than mine." He looked at the top line on the chart. Someone with good handwriting had written the labels. Date, Time, Patient, Reason Seen, and Attending were written across the first line. His entry was about two thirds down. He tried to make out Lisa's hen scratches. He could make out the date, time, and his first initial and last name, but what she wrote in the other two columns was indistinguishable from children's scribbling to him. He looked up the chart. Doc Vasquez's writing wasn't that good, either, but at least Mark could make it out. He looked at some of the other entries Lisa had made to see if he could find some similarities to what was written on his line. He saw nothing similar as he ran down the 'Reason Seen' column. Some he could make out, but most were Greek to him.

Halfway down the page, one of the entries he could read said 'Preg. Test.' He wondered who in the neighborhood might be pregnant. He knew he shouldn't look, but he couldn't help himself. When he saw the name, his anger exploded. In fact, if the anger he'd felt in the cornfield this morning was a firecracker, the fury he felt now was an atomic bomb. The name read S. Turner.

He stomped out of the clinic with the clipboard under his arm. With a burning, single focus, he made his way home, each step increasing his anger exponentially. When he burst through the front door, he bellowed like a mad elephant.

"Samantha!" he screamed.

Jess came running into the entryway, wiping her hands on a towel. "She's on the back porch with the boys. What's the matter?" she asked worriedly.

Mark was so angry he couldn't find the words to express himself. Finally, he took the clipboard out from under his arm and pointed to the line that had upset him so. "Did you know about this?" he demanded.

She looked quickly at the chart. "Of course."

His anger doubled. "And when were you going to tell me?"

She now was starting to get upset. "Well, I've been trying to find time to tell you about it, but you're always too busy."

"Was the test positive?"

"Yes."

His fury rocketed off of the charts. However, he was no longer yelling. "I'll kill that boy," he spewed through clenched teeth.

"Who?" she asked.

He couldn't believe she'd play dumb with him about this. His mind whirled so fast that he couldn't focus, and the room seemed to spin. "That, that boy! Alex!"

"Why?"

He couldn't believe she was so stupid. How could she not know? "For getting my baby pregnant!" he roared so loud that it made him lightheaded.

"Have you lost your mind?" She was laughing now. "He didn't get me pregnant, you idiot!" she rebuked him. "YOU did!"

Mark had a strange feeling. His legs felt like rubber. The walls were closing in on him. He wondered briefly why he was looking up at the now useless chandelier. Then everything went black.

Chapter 60

He heard her voice from a distance. "Mark, Mark, wake up," she called. He didn't know why. It made no sense. He was wide-awake, yelling about something. What was it? He couldn't remember; it was so aggravating. Now he could see her, but she was blurry, like he was looking through an out-of-focus camera. He could hear someone else, too. "He's waking up," the second voice said. He thought he recognized it. Now he remembered. He was mad because Sam was pregnant. Or was she? Maybe it was someone else. He heard her voice again. "Mark, are you okay?" He could see her more clearly now.

It all came to him suddenly, almost as if someone had twisted the focus on the camera lens so that the image became sharp and clear. He had been talking, if you could call it talking, to her about Sam being pregnant, when she told him it was she who was expecting. But then what? He couldn't remember. Why was he lying on the floor with Jess and Lisa bending over him?

"What happened?" he finally formed the words.

"I think you had a mild reaction to the antibiotics I gave you," Lisa answered. Then her voice became stern. "I told you to wait for me. Also, who said you could look at, and take, the medical log?"

"Sorry," he said automatically.

"Well, sorry isn't good enough, mister. People have a right to their privacy. Guess I'm going to have to lock up the log from now on. If it wasn't for the fact that Jess wanted you to know she's pregnant, I'd kick your ass myself, black belt or no black belt!" Lisa said, as she drove home her point by poking Mark in the shoulder emphatically and in time with her last six words.

"I believe you would," he replied sheepishly, as he propped himself up on his elbows. He turned and looked at his wife. "So, you really are pregnant?"

"Yes, I am."

"How did that happen?"

"What?" Lisa interjected, before Jess could say anything. "Did you hit your head when you passed out, and now you have amnesia, too? How do you THINK it happened, you big stud, you?" she said with a wink and humor in her voice.

Mark failed to see the humor. "I didn't mean that. I know how it… I mean, I thought you were on birth control? And the chart says 'S. Turner…'"

"That's not an 'S,' Mark," Lisa said. "It's a 'J' in my lousy handwriting, but if you had minded your own bees-wax, you wouldn't have seen it, gotten the wrong idea, and then gone ballistic," she switched back to the stern voice.

"You're right, but maybe you ought to put a magazine or two in that room, so people have something to do while they're waiting on you," Mark snapped back. He didn't like her chewing him out twice for the same thing. "And aren't you on the pill?" he turned and asked Jess.

"I was until I ran out of them eight weeks ago," she explained. "I thought I was being careful, but I guess I goofed up. Are you mad?"

He didn't answer right away. "No, I'm not," he said, surprised that he wasn't. "Three months ago, I would have been, but now, I don't know. I guess I'm kind of happy, as long as you're okay. Everything is okay, isn't it?"

Jess smiled and nodded her head at her husband.

"She's as healthy as a horse, Mark," Lisa said. "It's you who worries me. Can you stand up?"

He nodded his head, and the two women helped him to his feet. He almost lost his balance and put his hands on the wall to steady himself.

"I guess I'm still a little dizzy."

"Then let's get you to bed, so you can rest like Lisa said," Jess suggested.

He walked through the house toward his bedroom, a woman on each side to steady him. He felt a little like a condemned man taking the long walk to the electric chair, with a guard on each side to make sure he arrived safely for his appointment with fate. Once he was in bed, Lisa admonished him once again to take his meds, and then they left him to rest. He tried to get some sleep, and probably did for a few short spurts, but his mind wouldn't stop long enough for him to get any real rest. Thoughts of a new baby both excited him and scared him to death.

He got up and snuck out to the shed. He tried to hurry, but his leg was bothering him quite a bit. When he opened the door, he could see that a lot of the ammo they'd bought from the Watsons was still stacked on the floor. Most of the weapons that had been leaning on or sitting on the workbench had been moved to the CP or loaned out. The liquor was still in the shelves over the workbench, but the medication had been moved to and secured in the clinic. Mark walked up and looked at the bottles. He recognized a lot of the names. Not that he was much for drinking, but he'd seen almost all of these brands on the big billboards along the highways. The MZB's had obviously only stolen the very best stuff.

He spun around and looked across the metal building. The opposite wall was lined with the 55-gallon drums that had fuel in them. He limped over to the row of barrels lined up like a bunch of fresh recruits in front of their drill sergeant for the first time. He envisioned them standing as straight as they could and listening to some old, grizzled veteran, who, in his mind, looked surprisingly like Gunny. The DI was explaining that he was now their daddy and their mama and that life as they'd known it was now over. Mark looked them up and down as if he were the DI. He walked up to one in the middle and thumped it to see how much gas was in it. It was full. So were the next two. The fourth one he checked was only about two-thirds full. The three to the left of those were bone dry. Mark looked at them with the distain that a hard-assed, gung-ho NCO would reserve for a long-haired, mama's boy. He snorted his displeasure and wheeled around to see if the right side of the formation was more to his liking. From this angle, he could see that the last four barrels weren't quite in line with the others.

"Are you boys stupid, or are you just trying to piss me off?" he barked at the misaligned containers. He half marched, half limped up to the transgressing drums. He looked down his nose at them and saw his brother's handwriting on the lids. It took him a minute to realize that these were the four drums they'd dug up in Waco. Since he'd been hurt when they got back, someone else had put them in here.

'I should go through these,' he thought. He walked to the workbench to get some tools to remove the lids. He grabbed a crescent wrench and turned back

456

toward the drums. He stared at them for a long moment. Somehow, opening them meant there was no hope for Mike. Mark knew that after this many days, the chances of his family making it here were slim at best, but going through Mike's stuff might squash even that slim chance. All of a sudden, he felt tired. He threw the wrench down on the bench, went back into the house, and slept.

Two days later, Lisa cleared Mark for normal activities. It was just in time for Curt to declare that the OP's were no longer needed. Mark went back to his scout team, and Gunny wasted no time in sending them out. He briefed them in the CP.

"I want you all to make a circle 'round the place, just out of sight of the guard towers. Move slow and look for any signs of travelers that we didn't see. When you finish that loop, move out about half a mile and make another pass, then move another half mile and make another one. You'll leave at first light, and I want you back here day after tomorrow by sundown. Then, we'll send Jim's group out the next morning to pick up where you all left off. Any questions?"

All six members shook their heads.

The next morning, they started their first loop and finished it before noon. They didn't find any signs that surprised them. The second loop proved just as uneventful. They moved out another half mile and had just started the third circle when it started getting dark. They set up camp and prepared some dinner. Mark wondered why Gunny had them stay out when they weren't that far from the subdivision. 'Probably,' he thought, 'he doesn't want to hear Susan griping about the all-man team being treated differently.' After dinner, he assigned guard duties. He and Jess would take the middle shift, and they climbed into their tent. She snuggled up next to him. He'd tried to talk her out of staying on the team now that she was expecting, but she'd insisted that pregnancy was only a normal, biological function and that she would stay on the squad until she got to the point where she couldn't keep up.

The following morning, they resumed their patrol. This loop, even though they were only half a mile further out, was over twice as big as the previous one. They found a couple of sets of fresh human tracks, and they followed each set for a short way. However, they all appeared to be from no more than two or three people, and none of them headed toward Silver Hills. Later, they found a set of horse tracks, but Mark didn't know how to tell if they had riders or not.

Mid-afternoon, they found another set of fresh tracks. Mark could make out at least five distinct sets of footprints in the soft dirt, and unlike the sets from in the morning, these were pointed almost directly at the subdivision. The six scouts started following them, with Mark praying they would turn away from the direction they headed. They didn't, and the closer they got to Silver Hills, the more nervous Mark became. He put himself on point and moved slower and slower, not just because he wanted to be careful, but also because the signs this group left behind were becoming more difficult to find and follow, as they moved closer to home. When Mark could no longer find any tracks to follow, he stopped and looked around. Several hundred yards ahead of him was a hill that he'd been on top of during a previous scouting trip. One could see quite a bit of Silver Hills from the crest. It was probably about a thousand yards from the hill to the closest fence line, but with a good set of binoculars or a decent spotting

457

scope, it would be an ideal location to watch the subdivision. Mark pulled out his own set of binoculars and glassed the hill. He didn't see anything out of the ordinary, just bushes and small-to-medium size trees. He went back and slowly scanned every spot on the hill looking for anything that seemed out of place. He could find nothing suspicious. He waved the five women up to his position and told them what he was thinking. Then he handed the binoculars to Chris.

"You have the youngest eyes," he whispered. "Give the hill a good once over and see if you see anything that looks like it might be a person, or even just part of a person."

Chris put the field glasses up to her eyes and slowly moved them back and forth. After three or four minutes, she handed them back to him and shook her head. He had Letty look next, and she also saw nothing out of the ordinary. Mark thought that whoever's tracks they'd been following had probably turned off somewhere, and he missed it. He decided to go back to the last sign he'd found and see if his new theory was right.

"Let me look," Susan said.

"Okay," Mark answered, figuring that he might as well use this opportunity as a teaching experience. He handed the field glasses to Susan and briefly explained what she should look for. She spent over five minutes looking the hill over, only to hand the binoculars back to Mark.

"Everything looks okay to me," she said.

Next was Olga's turn. She looked for only a minute or two, when she quickly pulled the binoculars down from her eyes.

"A bush moved!" she whispered excitedly.

"Where?" Mark asked.

"On top of the hill, a little on one side."

"Maybe it was just the breeze."

"No, it, like, twisted and moved over about a foot," she insisted.

"Look back through the binoculars and find it again," he ordered.

She pressed the lenses back to her eyes and moved them around only slightly. A moment later, she froze in one place.

"Got it?" Mark asked.

"I think so," she answered. "But it's not moving any more. Maybe my eyes were just playing a trick on me."

"Maybe. Maybe not. Look at the landmarks around it so you can tell me exactly where it is."

Olga described the terrain around the mysterious bush and then handed the binoculars to Mark. It only took him a moment to find it. It really did look like a bush. Mark checked the rest of the hill but couldn't find anything else exactly that color. That meant either it was the only bush of that type on the hill, or it was someone in a camouflage suit. He watched it for a few minutes and started to think that it really was a bush. Then, he saw it move, not much, but enough that he knew it wasn't natural. He memorized the spot where the man was and then searched for more strange bushes. He couldn't find anything else by size or color that could hide a man. He knew there were at least five of them, so where were the others?

He figured they probably had a camp set up at the base of the hill or somewhere that he couldn't see with all of the scrubby trees and cactus in the way. He looked for any sign of smoke and listened as hard as he could. There was nothing. 'These guys are good,' he thought. Yesterday, Mark and his team had walked past the foot of the hill on the other side. He wondered if the observers had watched them walk by. On the second loop yesterday, they were well within where the intruders had left little to no tracks. It was just luck that they'd found any tracks today.

Mark had his team follow him back the way they had come. He wanted to call Gunny and see what the security chief wanted him to do, but he wanted to make sure he was well out of earshot of the intruders. Since they weren't looking for tracks, it only took a few minutes to make their way back to the first footprints they'd found. He set up the radio and made his call. It took the CP a few minutes to go get Gunny. Finally, his crusty voice came over the radio.

"What's your problem, Scout One?" he sounded slightly out of breath.

"We found five sets of tracks heading toward your position, CP. We followed and tracked them a ways. We lost the tracks but spotted one of them on the hill about a thousand yards east-south-east of the eastern fence line. He's camouflaged real good, and it looks like he's observing the subdivision. I think the others have a camp out of sight like we did at our OP's. Do you want us to see if we can find it?"

"No. It's too dangerous."

"He just doesn't think we can handle it," Susan spat angrily.

Mark shot her his best shut-up look. "Roger that, CP," he answered.

"What's your position right now?" Gunny asked.

"We're about half a mile south of the hill, back where we found the tracks."

"Okay, Scout One, you've got a little over an hour before sunset. Why don't you track backwards a ways and see if you can find where they came from. I'm going to stay here in case you find something."

"Ten-Four, CP. Scout One out." Mark turned off the radio. "You heard the man, let's see where these tracks came from."

The five women fell into Ranger file behind Mark. He had little problem following the trail the intruders had left. Mark wondered who they could be. They'd become careful as they got close to Silver Hills, but they must not have expected anyone to find their trail this far from their observation post. They came to a fence and crossed it into a very large grass field that had been cleared of all but the largest trees. The grass looked like it had been recently cut and probably baled for hay. There were enough bare spots to see footprints every few yards. Mark found a small rock that had been kicked over. He knelt down and touched it. The bottom, which had been in the ground before someone kicked it over, was still slightly damp. Mark figured it had probably been turned over today, or last night at the earliest. He was still kneeling and examining it when something whacked the ground about six feet away from him. It sounded like a big nut or something had fallen out of the tree he was under. Mark looked and saw that whatever it was had made the ground erupt like a small explosion. He was confused. A split second later, he heard the crack of a gunshot and knew what had hit the ground.

He jumped behind the massive trunk of the tree and saw his team scrambling for cover. Mark heard a couple of the shots thwack into the big oak tree and two or three others go whistling by. Again, the sound of each shot came a split second later. Whoever was shooting at them was a good distance away. Mark dropped down on his hands and knees and peeked around the tree trunk. There was a slight rise up to a ridge line about four hundred yards in front of him. He felt like an idiot. It had never occurred to him that the intruders might leave someone behind them. He wondered why they would do that. Another bullet ripped into the tree spraying bark across Mark's face. He pulled himself back behind the safety afforded by the ancient hardwood. Maybe, he thought, I should worry about why later. He rolled to the other side of the tree and sent four of his own bullets back toward whoever was up there. He had no idea where to aim, but maybe he could get the attacker to give away his position. He watched for a second, and several bullets came a little too close for comfort. He pulled his head back and cursed under his breath. He hadn't seen a thing; only now, from the different sounds, he knew there were two or more people shooting at them, and at least one of them had some skill. One rifle made a cracking sound, and the other had more of a boom. The shooters weren't wasting any shots either. They only fired when they had a target, and they weren't missing by much. Mark looked at where each member of his team was. Everyone was behind good cover except for Chris. She was down in a patch of weeds that looked like they'd grown up since the grass was cut. It probably kept her out of the sight of the shooters, but it certainly wouldn't stop a bullet.

"Chris," he called only loud enough for her to hear.

"Yes, Mark?"

"I want you to move behind this tree across from me," he pointed to a tree about ten yards from him as he spoke. "Wait until I tell you to go."

"Okay."

"Everyone else, when I say go, I want you to shoot three or four shots at the top of the ridge. It's a long way, so turn up the elevation on your sights a little."

Everyone gave him an affirmative response.

"Okay, ready, GO!"

He stuck his rifle out and fired three shots. He saw Chris out of his peripheral vision, and when she was behind the tree, he pulled his head back around. Now that everyone was safe, he needed to come up with a plan to retreat, or, as Gunny so appropriately called it, to de-ass the area. If he could figure out where the shooters were, they could use covering fire and pull back three at a time. He pulled the binoculars out of his pack.

"Chris, catch," he said, as he tossed them to her. "When I shoot, I want you to see if you can see where those guys are."

"You got it, boss."

Mark stuck his head back out and let two shots fly, he hoped, in the right direction. He pulled his noggin back just in time for a bullet to hit the tree and another buzzed by angrily. He looked over to Chris.

"I saw one of them. He's at about one thirty, just below the top, behind a pile of rocks," she said.

Mark stuck half of his head out the left side of the tree just far enough to see with one eye. He saw the spot Chris had reported. He still needed to find the other guy.

"Okay, one more time. Look for the other one," he told her.

He switched his rifle to his left shoulder and squatted down. He shot from the low left side of the tree. He didn't want to give them the same target they'd come so close to hitting a minute ago. He shot four quick shots at the rock pile and must have come close enough, even left-handed. He saw dust fly, and the man behind the rocks ducked down. He came back behind the natural barricade long before a returned bullet hit the ground four feet away.

"Anything?"

Chris nodded her head. "There are two of them behind a log about fifty yards left of and a little below the first guy. One has a scoped rifle, and the other one looked like he was talking into a radio."

Mark could only think of two reasons why one of them would be talking into a radio. The first one was that they wanted to get out of here, and they were calling their buddies to meet them at an alternate rendezvous site. The other was to call for reinforcements. Mark figured it was the second one, because if it were the first, they'd most likely be calling their friends while they were on the move.

"Ladies, we have to get the hell out of Dodge!" Mark said. "We're going to fall back by squads. Susan, you, Jess, and Olga are going first. Go to the next trees behind us and get behind them. Then, you can cover Chris, Letty, and me while we run to the next set. Did everyone hear where Chris said the MZB's are?"

Mark heard four 'Yes' answers.

"Good. And keep an eye out behind you. The guys we tracked may be on their way back. Ready…GO!"

Mark swung his big rifle out and opened up on the guy in the rocks. He wondered which target Chris and Letty had chosen. He stopped firing for a moment and looked up the hill. Thoughtfully or luckily, each one had picked a different sniper to engage. Unfortunately, both of the young women were shooting quite low. He pulled the trigger on his rifle again and watched the man in the rocks try to make himself invisible. Then he swung over to the log and gave that position something to think about. A moment later, his bolt locked back. He couldn't believe he'd already gone through twenty rounds. He retreated behind the tree and changed magazines. By the time he was done, Susan's squad had reached their cover. Letty and Chris continued to fire, but only for a few seconds more. Mark could see them both grabbing for a reload.

"Chris, Letty, you both need to turn your elevation dial on your rifles. Turn it up to between the 4 and the 5. When you're reloaded, let me know. It's our turn to haul ass," he told them. "Susan?" he called a little louder.

"Yeah, Mark?"

"Make sure your squad has their sights turned up to about 500 yards. Also, make sure that you don't all shoot at just one guy, and please make sure you don't shoot us. Are you ready?"

Mark could hear her talking to Jess and Olga but couldn't quite make out what she was saying. A moment later, she called back, "Yeah, Mark, we're ready."

"Okay, when I say go, we're going to go twenty or thirty yards on the other side of you. Don't blow through all of your ammo. Just a shot every two or three seconds should make them keep their heads down." He looked at Chris and Letty. "You two ready?"

They nodded their heads grimly.

"Ready...GO!"

Mark let the girls go first, and then he took off after them. He pumped his legs as fast as they would go. He wasn't falling behind the girls, but it was all he could do to keep up with them. Darn, they're fast, he thought. He heard a bullet buzz by him like a hornet. He ran past Susan's squad and dug in harder to cover the distance to the next tree behind them. It was the longest thirty yards he'd ever run. He saw the girls disappear behind the huge tree. A second later, he joined them. His breath was coming in huge gasps. He wasn't sure if it was more from the running or the adrenaline. He leaned back against the mammoth trunk to try and get his wind back. He bent over and rested one hand on a knee, as he wondered how far they had to go to get back to the fence. Before he could look up to find the answer, a couple of bullets smacked into the tree above his head and sprayed stinging pieces of bark onto the back of his head and neck. He snapped his head up, and what he saw took away the little breath he had left. A group of men were shooting at them from the fence line.

Chapter 61

Mark had been concerned about the snipers on the hill, but he knew his team could use covering fire to make a clean escape with little chance of a casualty. Now, caught between two groups, he was frightened. He pushed the girls down. "Other side. Quick!" he shouted, as he thought how the second group of MZB's made it here a lot faster than he figured. Letty and Chris scrambled to the other side of the big tree. Mark fired two quick shots back at the men on the fence line and then joined the girls. "Fire at those guys! Don't let them get across the fence." Letty fired from a squatting position on the right side of the tree, only exposing a fraction of her body. Chris threw her AR-15 up to her right shoulder and stepped out on the left side of the trunk, uncovering almost her whole body. Mark grabbed her and pulled her back before she could get a shot off.

"Damn it, Chris! Are you trying to get yourself killed? Don't show yourself like that. Shoot left-handed, so you can stay behind the tree."

Chris struggled to put her rifle on her left shoulder and lean out to shoot. Mark called out to the other squad.

"Susan, we're in deep shit! The guys we tracked are by the fence. You and Jess keep those guys on the hill from shooting at us. Olga, get on the horn and tell Gunny we're caught in a crossfire and need some help RFN!"

"RFN?" Olga asked.

"Right now! Tell him we need help right now."

Mark assessed the situation. It would take Gunny a while to get some guys here. He'd have to get them together and brief them. There were no close roads where they could drive any closer than they already were. It must be at least two miles, and even if they ran all the way, it would take fifteen or twenty minutes. Mark glanced at his watch. It might be dark before his reinforcements could get here. If he and his team could hold out that long, they could probably get away. They might be able to keep the MZB's at bay, if they had enough ammo. Each of them had about a hundred and fifty rounds. He figured quickly and deduced that, even if they were really careful, they'd need about three times what they had to make it that long. 'Okay, what's plan C?' he thought. He realized Chris hadn't fired a shot.

"Chris, shoot!" he barked.

"I can't see through the sights like this, Mark," she cried, as she tried to get her right eye in line with the rifle on her left shoulder.

"Get out of the way," he pulled her into the middle so he could shoot. He leaned out and fired a couple of shots where the men had been standing a minute ago. He couldn't see them anymore, but they continued to fire. Fortunately, they weren't coming any closer to hitting their targets than Mark's group was, at least not at the moment. Mark realized how hopeless the situation was. It was only a matter of time before the MZB's got lucky. All of the members of his team were exposed to one group of them or the other. The fence line was only two hundred and fifty or three hundred yards away, not an extremely difficult shot for anyone with a little skill. The guys on the hill were over five hundred yards from the scouts. It took a better marksman to make a shot at that distance, but with scoped rifles and enough ammunition, it was only a matter of time. He fired three more shots when he saw a head pop up by the fence. The head ducked back down just as quickly as it popped up. It reminded Mark of one of those amusement park games where you had to hit the quick, little gophers with a club as they popped out of their holes. You had to be really fast to get them before they ducked back down to safety. Mark looked over at Chris. She was shaking like a leaf. He turned and looked at everyone else. They seemed to be doing okay. More than likely it was because they were concentrating on their shooting and not thinking about how much trouble they were in. He needed to get Chris back into the fight.

"Chris, take a step back from the tree and then lean out the right side and shoot over the top of Letty. Be careful. Letty, make sure you stay down," he instructed.

Letty nodded her head, and Chris did what Mark had told her.

"Neither of you shoot unless you see someone," he added.

Maybe one of us will get lucky, he thought. It would take luck. The MZB's were holding all the aces. All they had to do was wait for Mark's group to run out of ammo or do something dumb. Any one of a thousand other things could go wrong. Mark was really scared. Not for himself, but for the rest of his team, especially Jess and the baby. This could be it for all of them. He was sad that his new son or daughter would never have a chance to have a life. The unjustness of it made him angry.

"Mark, Gunny says he has some guys on the way RFN!" Olga called, breaking him out of the trance into which he'd momentarily slipped. He looked at her, and she was giving him a 'thumbs up' and grinning at figuring out what 'RFN' meant. Mark was almost shocked that she could be lighthearted in this situation. She obviously didn't comprehend the severity. It must be television's portrayal that the good guys never get shot, he thought, that or they think our guys can get here in time. Maybe it was good that she didn't get it. Hopefully none of them realized how much trouble they were in. He was afraid, though, that when the first one of them got shot, the rest of the team would fall apart. He had to do something. He stuck his rifle back out and waited for a gopher head to pop up. When one did, he sent two quick rounds toward it.

"Mark," Chris said excitedly, "two of the guys are moving to the right!"

"Where?"

She pointed, and he watched a pair of the MZB's bent over, so as not to expose themselves, making their way down the fence. They were about forty yards from their original position and moving fast. He stepped back clear of Chris and sent several shots their way. The men disappeared completely, but a second later they returned fire. Things were going from bad to worse in a hurry. If the guys on the fence line spread out enough, the team wouldn't be able to make all of them stay down. Mark knew if they were going to have a chance, if his baby was going to have a chance, he had to do something quickly. A plan formed in his mind. He looked at the trees between here and the fence. They were further apart than he would have liked them to be, but it could work.

"Chris, watch those guys. If they stick a little toe up, blow it off."

"Okay, Mark."

"Susan!" he called. "I need you over here. Everybody cover Susan when she says go."

A second later Susan yelled. "Ready, GO!"

Mark leaned out and fired his rifle until the bolt locked back on the empty magazine. He pulled back in to change it, and Susan was standing beside him. He was thankful the tree was large enough to cover all four of them. He dropped the empty magazine on the ground and rocked a fresh one into place. He didn't bend over to pick up the expended mag. Susan looked at him as if he had just committed heresy. Gunny had drilled into them to never leave a magazine behind if they could help it.

"Here, hold this," he told her, as he thrust his rifle her way. She took it, her eyes still wide. He unbuckled his pack and dropped it. Her face screwed up into a look of confusion. He reached out and took his FAL back. "I'm going to try and get close enough to the fence to take those guys out. Then we can get the hell out of here. I want you all to cover me as I move tree to tree."

"Mark, no! Wait for the reinforcements to get here. We can hold them off until then."

"We're going to be out of ammo long before Gunny's guys get here. This is our only chance."

"But it's suicide."

"So is waiting here for help that ain't coming quick enough to save us. I'd rather go down trying than wait until we have no ammo left. Now listen. I'm going to sprint to the next tree. When I get there, I'll catch my breath real quick and then go for the next one. You watch me, and when you see me move, try to keep those bastards from shooting at me. Don't blow through your ammo, though. Only shoot if there's a target. Got it?"

"Mark, you can't do this."

"It's not up for discussion. Do you understand what I want you to do?"

"Yes," she said solemnly.

"One more thing…if something happens to me, I want you and the others to make a break for it that way." He pointed west. "Drop your packs, so you can move faster, and make sure you cover each other. And tell Jess I love her."

Susan just nodded her head. Mark tore out from behind the tree and put all his energy into making it the thirty yards to the next tree. He heard the women firing behind him and was pleased they were only firing sporadically. If this didn't work, they'd need all the ammo they could spare. Mark heard one shot come close to him. He remembered hearing somewhere that, during the Viet Nam war, our soldiers fired a hundred thousand rounds for every hit in battle. Mark hoped that number applied to this situation, and that the bullet that had just whizzed by wasn't round number 99,999. He stopped behind the tree. This one wasn't nearly as large as the last one, and he checked to make sure he wasn't exposed at all. He was okay as long as one of the snipers didn't get lucky. Jess and Olga seemed to be keeping them under control. Mark breathed in and blew out several deep breaths and then took off for the next tree. This one, unlike the last, was at an angle. That was good and bad. The good part was that he wasn't running straight at the MZB's. The bad part was that he couldn't use the tree to shield himself at all like he'd done last time.

He ran for all he was worth, praying his feet would grow Mercury-like wings. He heard several bullets rip past him this time. He wondered what number they were and if there were any more coming that might have his name on them. He knew as long as he heard them, he was all right. If one got him, he'd never hear it. He made it unscathed to his interim destination and looked at the next tree. It was close to seventy yards, he figured. He took a few extra breaths.

"Dear Lord," he whispered, "please help me."

He came out from behind the tree and launched himself toward his next waypoint. The MZB's must have figured out what he was doing because he heard several screaming projectiles rush past him at Mach Three. It motivated him to run faster, but that was physically impossible. His steps and his heartbeat were coming almost in time with each other. He glanced up, but the tree looked no closer than it had from behind the last one. He wished he could run faster. He wished Gunny was here to tell him if he was doing the right thing. Hell, he wished Jim was here with his M1A. His buddy could have taken out the snipers from a long range, and Mark wouldn't have to do this damned kamikaze run. A couple of more shots flew by. Shit, as long as he was wishing, he might as well wish for the cavalry to come save his ass. A bullet ripped into the ground between his feet. How much further, he wondered. He looked up and was almost there. A few more steps, and he skidded to a stop behind the most beautiful tree he'd ever seen. It was old, knurled, and insect infected, but it stopped several bullets that otherwise might have exterminated him. He gasped for breath, patting the old elm to thank it, since words to express his gratitude would have been insignificant, even if he'd had enough wind to speak them. He looked to his next haven. Good, this one was only twenty or twenty-five yards. He glanced toward the fence and saw that he was only a little more than a hundred yards from it. The closer he got, the easier it would be for the MZB's to get him. They came close enough last time.

He decided to try a little head fake on them. He darted out like he'd done before but then quickly pulled himself back behind cover, as several shots zipped by. He side-stepped to the other side of the tree and shot three times at the surprised MZB's. He didn't think he hit any of them, but that would give them something to think about. He started the short distance to his next spot. When he'd gone no more than a couple of steps, he heard the girls open up rapid fire. He wanted to see what the problem was but knew if he slowed down to look, he was dead. It couldn't be good, no matter what had caused them to start shooting like they had all the ammo in the world. Mark wondered if one of them had gotten hit, and the others had panicked, or if the MZB's had somehow closed in on their position. The only good part was it was keeping the MZB's from shooting at him. He pulled up behind the tree and wheeled around to see why the women were firing like there was no tomorrow.

What he saw terrified him, not because it was bad, but because it was impossible. It wasn't the girls shooting; it was the cavalry he'd wished for a minute ago. Wishes like that didn't come true, did they? Not in this life. Then he realized…he must be dead. He stared at the horses racing toward him to see if one had a chariot behind it. He didn't see one. All he could see was seven horsemen shooting at the fence line from a full gallop like they were Roy

Rogers. Maybe the chariot was following the horsemen, or maybe he rode double with one of them. He looked down and checked for the bullet hole. He couldn't find it in any part he could see. They must have hit him in the head. At least it didn't hurt, but if he was dead, why was he still breathing so hard?

He turned back toward the MZB's. They were running the other way. Who could blame them? If he had seven angels riding toward him and unleashing the wrath of God, he'd haul ass, too. He turned back and looked up the hill. He was too far away in the failing light to see if the snipers were running away, but no more shooting was coming from that direction. Mark watched the riders gracefully slow their mounts, while their rifles continued to encourage the MZB's to remain at their current course and speed.

The lead angel stopped his horse just feet from Mark. The heavenly steed was all white. He was huge, and Mark could see the rippling muscles beneath his perfect coat. His eyes were wild, but they held a knowing look of a creature not of this world. They looked at Mark and blinked, as if to say 'poor little mortal.' Mark hoped that if he had to ride to heaven on one of the horses, it would be this one.

The earthly being looked up at the rider. God had sent not just angels, but Spanish angels. Seven Spanish Angels. Mark seemed to remember a poem or song about that. The angel was the most beautiful creature Mark had ever seen, not feminine beauty, but with the look of rugged, masculine perfection. His face was weathered, but his arms had a young man's muscles, rivaling those of the beast he rode. His skin was dark, and his eyes were the color of the sky. His hair was short and dark, with just a trace of silver at the temples. His teeth beamed a flashing white smile that would have made a movie star jealous. He opened his mouth to speak, and Mark prepared himself to hear the most eloquent and perfect words ever spoken on earth. He was sure the voice would resonate like a choir in a cathedral. He was surprised when the first sentence came out.

"Mister, that's the bravest fucking thing I ever saw in my life," he said in a raspy voice. "You must have one humongous set of cajones on you."

He stepped down off of the horse, as Mark stood there dumbfounded.

"I...I...I..." Mark stuttered.

"Well, shit, there's no need to thank me," the horseman said, with a toothy smile.

He must be a man, Mark thought. Surely an angel wouldn't talk this way.

"Thank you," Mark stammered. "Where'd you come from?"

"We were over on the western edge of this pasture, following tire tracks from some assholes who cut my fence. We heard the shooting and came over to see what the deal was. I would have helped you sooner, but we couldn't really tell who were the good guys and who were the bad guys. As far as we were concerned, you were both trespassing, so we just thought we'd let you thin each other out. Once we saw you rushing the position of the other guys, we all said we had to help you, even if you was old Beelzebub himself. Bravery like you showed shouldn't be wasted."

The men heard some engines start up on the other side of the sniper's hill. One of the other riders nudged his horse over to the head horseman. This squat man had a big, ugly scar on his face from his mouth to his ear on one side.

Except for the color of his skin, he was a complete opposite of the man with whom Mark was talking.

"You want us to go check that out, Billy?" he asked.

"I reckon not. They'll be gone before we could get there. Besides, I have a feeling they won't be back. Leastways not without a lot more men."

"Your name's Billy?" Mark asked curiously.

The man offered a hand that Mark gladly shook. "Yes," he replied. "Billy Borrego. Guillermo Borrego the Fourth to be exact."

"You're Billy the Kid!" Mark exclaimed, as he shook the man's hand like he was star struck.

The man laughed. "Nobody's called me that to my face in a long time, mister, but yeah, that's who I am."

The women had made their way over, and Mark, still pumping Billy's arm up and down, introduced them to the rancher. "Guys, this is Billy the Kid who saved us!" He said it as if he was introducing Babe Ruth. "Billy, this is Letty, and Chris. That's Susan, and the tall one is Olga, and this, Billy, is my wife Jess. Girls, this is Billy the Kid. He's famous!"

"I don't know if I'd go that far. My great-grandpa was the famous one," the man grinned. "Do you think I could have my hand back now?"

"Oh, sorry, Billy."

"That's okay. Let me introduce you to my boys," he said, as he waved the other men over. "This is Pete, Marty, Juan, and JD," Billy said, as he pointed at each one. "The fellow in the back is Mick." Billy put his arm around the man who was his opposite. "This ugly, mean sum bitch is José Vella, my ranch foreman, and my best friend in the whole world."

"It's really nice to meet you all," Mark said, "and I'm not just saying that. If y'all hadn't helped us, we'd probably be buzzard chow."

A voice called out from the fence line. "Mark, is that you?" It was Jim.

Everyone turned their heads and looked toward the spot where the MZB's had been a few minutes ago. No one appeared where the voice had come from, but it was getting fairly dark.

"Yeah, Jim, it's us. Come on over here. There are some people I want you to meet," Mark called back. "That's my best friend, Jim," he said to Billy and his men. "We called them for help, but I think they would have been too late."

Jim and the eight guys he brought with him came over, and introductions were made all around. Mark made sure everyone knew that Billy's great-grandfather fought in the war for Texas' independence. Billy put on an 'Aw, Shucks' show, but he seemed to enjoy the notoriety.

"So now I know who everyone is but you," Billy said to Mark.

"Oh, crap, I'm sorry!" Mark said. "My name's Mark Turner."

"Mark Turner?" Now it was Billy's turn to act surprised. "Well, Sheeee-it! Hey, boys, this here's Mark Turner. You know, the Karate Man! Hell, Karate Man, you're the one who's famous, and now I can see why. Your buddy was rushing five or six men by himself," Billy told Jim. "I don't know how he can even walk around with a big set of huevos like that," Billy winked.

Mark hung his head and kicked his toe into the ground, hoping it was dark enough that his reddening face couldn't be seen.

The new acquaintances made small talk for a few minutes. Mark noticed Chris flirting with one of Billy's young guys, but he seemed more interested in Letty, who was oblivious to the fact. Mark half listened to Jim's and Billy's conversation while he ran through the events of the last hour in his mind.

"So, Karate Man, what were y'all doing on my ranch?" Billy asked, snapping Mark out of his thoughts.

Mark explained how they'd started scouting for groups that might cause them trouble before they just showed up on the doorstep. He told Billy they'd found a group that seemed to be watching the subdivision and the scout team was backtracking to see where they had come from when his group started taking fire from the hill. Then the others showed up and caught them in the crossfire. "And, you know the rest," Mark said.

"Yes, I do," the older man said, with a grin that embarrassed Mark again.

"I better go call the CP," Jim said. "Gunny's probably having a cow about now."

"Thanks, Jim," Mark said. "I forgot all about that. I'm going to get my ass chewed real good when we get home, I bet."

Jim walked over and got the radio from Olga. Mark watched him carry on an animated conversation over the radio. He couldn't tell what was being said, but he figured Gunny was pretty mad. Billy asked the obvious question.

"Who's Gunny?"

"He's our security chief," Mark explained. "He's an old retired Gunnery Sergeant from the Marine Corps. He's older than the devil and twice as mean."

"Sounds like a good man to have on your side."

"Yes, he is, unless you piss him off." Mark was the one grinning now. The two men talked for a minute more. Jim came over and interrupted.

"Gunny said he wants us to come home. In fact, he told me to tell you he wants us there 'RFN,' whatever that means." Jim shrugged his shoulders.

"It means 'Right Fucking Now,'" Mark whispered to Jim and Billy. They both laughed.

"Listen, Billy, we're having church services at Silver Hills at 10:30 in the morning and dinner at my house after that. I insist you all come, so I can thank you and your men properly. I don't know what we'll be having for dinner, but I'll make sure it's good."

"Sounds good," Billy said. "But tell me, can I wear my spurs in this church?"

"You can wear your spurs and your hog leg."

"Then we'll see you tomorrow, Karate Man."

"Don't be late, Billy the Kid," Mark called out, as everyone lined up to move out.

Jim was on point, and one of his guys was bringing up the rear. Mark's team was in the middle, since they'd seen enough adventure for one day. This gave Mark some time to think about the guys who were checking them out. He really needed to talk to Gunny about what he thought it might mean. Before he knew it, they were home. Gunny was at Mark's house. Mark noticed his truck and the Blazer were gone. He asked about them, and Gunny said he had to send some guys out on an errand. Mark wondered what it could be, but he didn't want to tick Gunny off any more by asking.

469

The old fart surprised him by not immediately ripping him a new one, but he did want to debrief the team while the events were still fresh in their minds. They all sat down on the back porch around the picnic tables. Mark told most of the story, trying to down play the parts that made him look good. Jess and Susan made sure to fill in any part they thought he didn't elaborate on enough. Jim even told Gunny and all the others, who somehow miraculously showed up to hear the story, about what Billy the Kid had said about Mark.

Gunny finally commented. "It sounds like you all did okay. You should have called me at first contact, but other than that, not too bad. Lucky that Billy came along, though."

Mark couldn't believe Gunny was being so...so...well, so un-Gunny like.

"However," the old Marine started again and then paused.

'Uh-oh,' Mark thought, 'he's fixing to drop the other combat boot.'

"I would like to hear what our guest expert has to say about you, Karate Man," Gunny finished.

Mark wondered what 'guest expert' Gunny could be talking about. Maybe it was Rob or Curt. Mark didn't know who else would have much constructive input on what had happened.

"I think he's a butthead," said a voice coming through the screen door between the kitchen and the back porch. The voice was familiar, but Mark couldn't figure out who it could be. It didn't sound like Curt or Rob. "He's always been a butthead," the voice continued, "and he'll always be a butthead."

Mark jumped up and spun toward the door. It opened and a tall, very thin, bearded man stood there in ragged clothes. Mark ran up and almost tackled the haggard looking man with a bear hug. It was his brother, Mike.

Chapter 62

Mark released the vice grip on his brother's neck, only to have Jess immediately squeeze him with her own hug.

"Where's everyone else?" she demanded, with her arms still wrapped around her brother-in-law.

"They're camped about fifteen or twenty miles from here. Your friend sent some people back with Jeff to pick them up in your trucks," Mike explained.

"Is everyone okay?" Mark asked.

"Pretty much. The trip was real hard on Mom and the babies, but they'll be okay. As soon as they get a little nutrition and rest, they should be as good as new. The trip was a lot harder than I thought it would be."

"How?" Mark asked.

"Well, it obviously took us a lot longer than I thought it would, and we didn't have the right stuff for bugging out on foot. I never imagined a scenario where we wouldn't be able to drive our vehicles to your place. I knew we might have to drive some back roads, but I never expected to have to walk. I mean coming here was just a backup plan anyway. I really expected to be able to ride out almost anything at home, and I just didn't understand the reality of bugging out on foot for what ended up being around two hundred and thirty miles. In fact, even though I thought I was prepared, I found out I was about as close to a real survivalist as an armchair quarterback is to Joe Montana. We started out with things we didn't need and left behind simple things that really would have made a difference."

Mark was intrigued by his brother's comments and was about to ask him to expound on them, when his truck and the Blazer pulled up. He bounded to the truck and found himself in an embrace with his mother. She looked very tired, and her normally flawless appearance was absent.

"Mom, it's so good to see you. I was starting to think you'd never get here."

"I was afraid we wouldn't either, Son. I can't tell you how happy I am now that we are," Patricia Turner said. When her son let her out of the bear hug, he saw tears in her eyes. He hugged her to him again.

"It's alright, Mom."

When he released her from the second hug, she was immediately clasped by David, who told his grandmother how worried he'd been about her. Mark hugged and greeted each member of the arriving party. All of them were much thinner than they had been the last time he'd seen them. When he got to his father, he was shocked at how gaunt the eldest Turner was. His clothes hung on him like a weathered scarecrow. Mark was almost afraid to squeeze him too tightly, for fear of breaking him in two. His fear was quickly relieved, however, when his father clinched him in a vise-like grip that defied his seventy years.

"I've prayed every day that you'd get here, Dad."

"Then both of our prayers were answered, Son. I've prayed every day that you'd be here. I don't think your Mom or the young ones could have made it much further," Andrew Turner said, as he looked at his son. The older man, though much thinner and older looking, had a look in his eyes that Mark couldn't remember ever seeing before. He wondered about it for a second.

"I hate to be rude," Andrew told his son, "but do you think we could get something to eat? We haven't had a decent meal in weeks."

"Of course, Dad!" Mark slung his arm around his father's shoulders. "Jess, can we get the kitchen going?"

"That's just what I was thinking," she replied. "Okay, everybody, you can have whatever you want, but I can have eggs and biscuits ready in a flash."

Everyone agreed that eggs would be wonderful. The newcomers all sat down around the picnic tables, and several people followed Jess into the kitchen to help her cook. Manny sent David, whose arm was healing miraculously fast, to his house to get more eggs.

"Tell us all about your trip," Gunny prodded.

Mike took in a deep breath through his nose and then blew it out of his mouth. "Well, we started out on September nineteenth, but you all already knew that from the note I left you. Gunny told me you found it. I should really start out by telling you that I never expected a situation where we'd have to leave home for more than a few days, and I never dreamed we wouldn't be able to drive. We were totally unprepared to bug out on foot. Thank goodness Jeff and Monica had done some backpacking before they had the kids. They had a couple of good packs and some other stuff that really saved our bacon. I only had an old army pack and frame that I'd bought on a whim once. Other than that, all we had were the kids' school backpacks and a camo daypack I used for hunting. Oh, and a duffle bag with shoulder straps. Monica's kids had a big, red wagon, the kind with the wood sides that go up about fifteen inches. It would hold all three of the kids, even if they were asleep. They were packed in tight, but it was a lot better than carrying them. Also, Dad had that big flatbed wagon he uses in the garden. Without the wagons, we'd have never made it. Anyway, we loaded up sleeping bags and tents, a couple of tarps, a bunch of MRE's and canned food, plus some dry goods, along with canteens, some pots and pans and a few clothes. Then we passed out a long gun and a handgun with ammo to everyone except the little kids. A couple of us took some extra guns in our packs. Mostly pistols, but some .22 rifles, as well. The packs were all pretty heavy, but I figured we'd eat up the canned goods first, and that would lighten the load up quickly."

"Well, we started out early the first day. I knew the roads would be dangerous from what I'd heard over the short-wave. So, we discussed all the options and decided to try traveling on the train tracks. That would keep us off the roads, and we wouldn't have to cross any fences, as we would if we tried to travel cross-country. The obvious course would have been to use the tracks that come straight down Interstate 35 to San Antonio, but those go through a bunch of medium and large towns. Plus they're in sight of the highway for most of the way. We knew we had to take a more secluded route, even if it meant we had to walk further. I have an atlas of Texas that breaks the state up into about a hundred pages, and it shows all the major tracks."

"After studying the maps, we picked the route we thought would be the safest. It increased the distance here by about thirty miles, but I figured we'd just go a few miles further each day or, at worst, take a couple of extra days to get here." Mike rolled his eyes again. "The good news was the tracks we needed to start on were only about a mile from the house, so we left before sunup to be on them by the time it got light. The tracks ran to the little town of McGregor about twenty miles west, and then they intersected with a set that ran north and south. We didn't make it nearly as far as I thought we would the first day. We only went about seven or eight miles, but I figured we'd get better as time went on. We found a nice, wooded area about a hundred yards from the tracks that was secluded enough to camp in. We set up the two tents, and everyone ate an MRE. All of us were griping about how bad they were. It was kind of funny, after we ran out of MRE's, we were all wishing we had more of them. We took twelve cases of them on Dad's big wagon. I figured that would give everyone at least one good, high-calorie, nutritious meal a day until we got here. That with the canned food and dry goods we had, I assumed we could make it, no problem." Mike stopped and took another big breath. "A big miscalculation on my part." He shook his head from side to side.

"Don't be too hard on yourself, Mike," his dad said. "You got us here."

Mike smiled at his father gratefully, as some of the cooks brought out plates of scrambled eggs and set them in front of the beleaguered travelers.

"The biscuits will be ready in a little bit, but we didn't want you to wait," Abby explained, as she and Samantha made sure everyone had a plate.

Mike winked at his niece and then took a bite of eggs. "Man, I never knew scrambled eggs could taste this good. I'll tell you, if I never eat another tough, old squirrel or rabbit as long as I live, it'll be too soon."

Almost everyone laughed at that comment. Mark noticed the newcomers were all too busy stuffing eggs into their mouths to laugh. When the laughter died down and Mike had eaten a few more bites, he continued his story.

"Where was I? Oh, yeah, we set up the tents. We only had room enough for seven in the tents. Jeff and Monica had a good two-man tent and a cheaper, family-sized, dome tent big enough for the five of them. The old canvas tent I had was too heavy to bring. We put the women and kids in the tents, and the rest of us slept out under the stars. Two of us were on sentry duty at all times."

"The next day, we started out a little after daybreak. We were pretty sore."

"Yeah, it helps to be in good shape if the world suddenly ends," Mike's wife, Cathy, interjected, with her mouth full of eggs.

Everyone laughed again, even though Cathy hadn't meant it to be funny. She smiled at the humor the others had seen in her comment.

"We walked for about an hour and then stopped to rest," Mike continued. "After about thirty minutes, we took off again, but we were moving pretty slow. We had the kids in their wagon, and Dad's cart was pretty heavy with all the food on it. We took turns pulling them, and I noticed the interval to change off was getting shorter and shorter as the day wore on. After lunch, we were resting more than we were moving. The babies were getting fussy, and it was all we could do to try and keep them entertained and quiet. We must have stopped around four. As best as I could figure, we'd only gone four miles, but everybody was beat. It was still pretty hot, and I was worried about us getting dehydrated. Everybody had canteens or water bottles, and we had two five-gallon buckets of water on the wagon with the food, but those were empty, and the canteens were getting low, too. Jeff, thank goodness, had a good backpacking water filter, and we found a creek nearby with running water in it. Jeff and I filtered enough water to fill every container we had. We took them back to the camp, and I made

473

sure everyone drank all the water they could hold. Then we went back and refilled all the canteens and bottles for the next day."

"The next morning, we all ate a good breakfast of Spaghetti-O's and canned peaches. Everyone seemed a little less sore, and we actually made about eleven miles that day. We reached the southbound tracks at McGregor and got about two miles south of the little town. We got some strange reactions from the citizens as our little convoy walked down the tracks. Some of the people just stared disbelievingly, but a few talked to us. Most people ran into their houses, and I saw several rifles covering us from inside as we passed. Dad and I were on point with Jeff and Jonathon in the back. I told everyone not to make any threatening moves, and we all kept our rifles slung. It seemed like we'd never get out of the town. We felt very vulnerable. Thank goodness it was before things really got bad."

"We camped that night next to a stream where we got more water. Everyone took a bath, and we washed our clothes. We were all feeling better, and I felt like we were going to start making good time. I was right for a day or two. Temple was about twenty-five miles away, and we made it to the northern outskirts of town in two days. After the reception we'd gotten in McGregor, we didn't want to chance going through Temple. We looked at the maps and picked a route around the western side of the city." Mike paused to take a bite.

Andrew picked up where he'd left off. "When we looked at the map, we figured the area was mostly ranch land. Some of it was, but a lot of it was farm land. The fields were soft plowed dirt, and it made walking difficult and pulling the wagons almost impossible. We ended up carrying the kids since the hard rubber tires on their wagon just sank right down. The big wagon was sinking, too, until Jeff let some air out of the tires, and then it did a little better. Crossing the fences was a real bear, too." Mark unconsciously rubbed the spot on his leg where the barbed wire had stuck him, as he listened intently to his father speak. "Some of them we could crawl under or through, but others we had to climb. Either way, we had to unload the cart and hand all of our food and packs over and then load everything back up. It made us really appreciate the gravel and wood walkway of the railroad tracks."

Mike took back over. "During lunch, we decided this route was too hard and that we'd chance going out on the road. After we ate, we made our way out toward a gravel road, and when we were almost there, we heard a bunch of whooping and hollering. Jeff and I snuck up for a peek and saw several guys ransacking a house. It looked deserted; at least we didn't see anyone but the hoodlums, so we just watched. They carried out anything of value and loaded up three old pickups. They even siphoned the gas out of the car and lawnmower in the garage. Then they set the place on fire, got in their trucks and took off down the road screaming like they'd just hit the jackpot. Jeff and I looked at each other, and we could tell what the other was thinking. Traveling the fields looked pretty good, even if the going was slow."

"The guys were scary looking, and no telling what they would have done to anyone they found on the road," Jeff elaborated. "We were carrying a fortune compared to what they stole from the house. I'm still hoping there wasn't anyone there when they arrived. If there was…well…" his sentence trailed off.

"We went back to where everyone else was and told them what we'd seen," Mike said. "We stayed in the fields and started walking around the edges of them. It was further, but at least the ground was harder. By mid-afternoon, everyone was exhausted. We set up camp and ate."

"That night, I came to several realizations. We'd made maybe five miles that day, and it was day six of our journey. I pulled out the map and saw we'd come fifty-two of the two hundred and ten miles I was estimating. That was right at a quarter of the way. The best day of traveling had seen us do thirteen miles. That was nowhere near the twenty miles a day we needed to average to have enough food to get here without resupply. We had to supplement our food somehow, and we needed to find a way to make better time. I decided to talk with everyone in the morning. I also decided to start keeping a little journal about out trip." Mike reached into his shirt pocket and pulled out a small notebook encased in a plastic bag. "On the inside cover, I wrote your name and address and a note to whoever found it to please make sure you got this, just in case," he said, as he looked Mark right in the eyes. Mark could see the faintest hint of a tear in his older brother's eye. "Boy, am I glad I got to bring it myself."

The arrival of the biscuits interrupted what was becoming an emotional moment. They were followed closely behind by a big bowl filled with more scrambled eggs. All of the food quickly made its way onto plates. Mark looked around the table. The smaller children were each eating a biscuit, and even the baby had one clutched in each of her tiny fists. This gave Monica a chance to concentrate on her own plate. Mark's sister had always been thin, except for when she was pregnant, but she almost looked anorexic now. She dug into the heap of eggs on her plate, and Mark hoped she'd look better in a few days. He wondered how much of her food she'd given to her children on the trip.

"Anyway," Mike continued, "we talked about it in the morning and decided that, except for the little ones, we'd only eat half of an MRE each day. That gave us another twelve days' worth. We had our rifles, and we decided we'd take whatever game we could find along the way to help stretch our food. We continued on around Temple and pushed hard that day. Even so, we only made about seven miles."

Mike flipped open his small journal and flipped through the pages. "I almost have the whole thing memorized; I've read through it so many times. The next day, we hit our first big problem. In fact, what I'd thought before this point was bad luck, turned out to be nothing. We hadn't crossed a creek or stream in a couple of days, and we were almost out of water. My map showed all the bigger creeks that weren't seasonal, but there were none close to us. The next running water on our current course was still at least a day away. We found a farm pond and took water from it. Jeff said it was always best to get water from a running source in the sun, but we didn't see any choice. We filtered enough water for everyone and filled up all the containers. I figured the filter would take out anything harmful, but there was some bug in the water the filter didn't get.

Jeff had the package for the filter, and it said it would remove 99.9% of harmful bacteria. That's why I figured we'd be okay, but I guess that .1% can really get you. By lunch time, we were all sick. Everyone had diarrhea and stomach cramps. We knew it was the water. In hindsight, we shouldn't have let the little ones drink it until we knew it was good; in fact, we shouldn't have let anyone drink it until one of us had tested it. At least then, only one of us would have been sick. We had a real dilemma then. We needed to drink a lot of water to keep from getting dehydrated from the diarrhea, but the only water we had was contaminated. We only had two choices. We could go find some good water, or we could try to clean up the water we had. We decided to do both."

"If we'd just brought some chlorine bleach to treat the water with, it would have made the water taste bad, but it would have killed the bugs. Unfortunately, all the bleach I'd stored burned up with the house. I just didn't think about it, and some other stuff, until it was too late. I'm sorry; I'm digressing. We found an old dilapidated barn that was about half fallen in, but at least it gave us some shelter from the sun. We set up camp inside, and Dad and I started looking for wood to start a fire with. There were woods fairly close, and we found plenty of fallen limbs, but most them were damp. There was enough old, dried wood from the fallen parts of the barn to burn without putting out any smoke. The only problem with it was it burned too fast. We only had a few pots, and the biggest one was only a gallon and a half in size, so we needed some wood that would burn for a while. We ended up using the barn wood to dry the damp logs, and then we started a second fire with them to boil the water."

"In the meantime, Jeff and Jonathon, who were the least sick, took the two five-gallon buckets and strapped them to a couple of the pack frames. They took the filter and headed out for the next stream. It was five or six miles on the map, and we hoped they could make it there and back by nightfall." Mike nodded at Jeff, indicating he wanted him to take over the storytelling for this part.

"Jonathon and I headed out about one in the afternoon," Jeff started. "Between the diarrhea, the heat, and not having any water, we were getting dehydrated quickly. We didn't make anywhere near the time we'd hoped. At first we had to keep stopping for the diarrhea. Later, we had to stop and rest frequently because our legs were cramping up from dehydration. Plus, it was hard to stay focused, and we kept drifting off course. By five o'clock, we were getting close to the creek when Jonathon tripped and twisted his ankle. It swelled up right in front of my eyes, and I knew it was at least a bad sprain. He tried to get up and walk on it, but we only got a few yards before it was obvious to both of us that he couldn't go any further."

"It was this big around," Jonathon said, as he held up his hands in a circle about the size of a cantaloupe. "And it was all green and purple."

"We hadn't brought anything with us except for the buckets, water filter, and our rifles. Oh, and a roll of toilet paper," Jeff added. "Really, it was pretty stupid, looking back on it, but at the time, we thought it would let us move faster. We should've at least taken some food and a small first aid kit. I didn't even have an aspirin to give him. I stashed him in some bushes, strapped both buckets to my pack, and took off. The creek was only about a half mile away."

"I had two extra filter cartridges, and since the one we used at the pond was contaminated, I'd put a new one in before we left. I pumped a little water through it to try and flush it out, and then I pumped about a gallon into each bucket and washed them out as well as I could. Then I pumped some drinking water into them and drank. It tasted so good. I must have drunk half a gallon, and I started feeling better almost instantly. I refilled the bucket and started back to where Jonathon was. It was starting to get dark, and I didn't know what to do.

When I got back to him I gave him some water and checked his ankle. It wasn't any worse, but it wasn't any better, either. There was no way he could walk back. I didn't know if I should head on back, wait until the morning, or wait for Mike to come looking for us. I really didn't like the idea of leaving Jonathon alone. Plus, I wasn't sure I could find my way back in the dark, so I decided to stay put until morning. We were hungry and cold that night, but at least we had plenty of water. I was praying that Mike and Andrew had been able to boil enough water to keep them going and that Jonathon's ankle would be good enough to walk on in the morning."

"In the interim, we were going nuts wondering where they could be," Mike said. "We'd gotten the water boiled, and everyone had plenty to drink. The biggest problem we had with the water was waiting for it to cool off enough to be able to drink it. By nightfall, everyone was quite a bit better. Only Mom and the babies were still having diarrhea. I was really worried about the little ones, but they were all improving by morning. Anyway, we didn't know what could have happened to Jeff and Jonathon. Cathy was going ballistic about her son. I kept trying to tell her it was nothing to worry about, but she wouldn't hear it."

"I don't care if he's almost eighteen," Mike's wife said. "He's still my baby."

"Mom!" Jonathon whined in protest.

"Well, you are!" she retorted.

Mike launched into his tale again before they could argue any more. "It was too dark to go looking for them. We decided we'd give them until lunchtime the next day, and then a couple of us would go follow their tracks. Cathy wanted us to start out at first light, but I was afraid they might not take the same path back that they took there, and we'd miss them. I figured if they didn't make it back by mid-day, something was really wrong."

Jeff leapt back in at this point. "When it started getting light, I woke Jonathon up. We'd covered ourselves with leaves and branches to stay warm. It helped some, but I was still pretty stiff from the cool night and the hard ground. Jonathan's ankle looked a little less swollen, but he still couldn't put any weight on it. We were both starving. If I'd just brought a .22 and some matches, there were tons of squirrels and rabbits around the creek we could have eaten. I decided I had to take the water back and get some help to come back and get him. I drank as much as I could out of the bucket we'd been using and left the rest with him. With only forty pounds of water and my Mini-14, I made it back in about two hours."

"Cathy was watching for us, and when she saw me coming by myself, I thought she was going to lose it. I told her that Jonathon just sprained his ankle and couldn't walk on it. She cussed me up one side and down the other for leaving him by himself," Jeff grinned at his sister-in-law.

"I told you I was sorry," she said.

"Once she calmed down, we decided everyone was well enough to travel," Jeff continued. "I drew Mike a map, gobbled down an MRE, put my pack back on the frame, took the first aid kit and the now empty bucket, and headed back to Jonathon ahead of the group. I took him an MRE, too."

"Even though the day before we'd decided we'd ration ourselves to half an MRE a day, we figured everyone should eat a full one since we'd been sick," Mike added.

"When I got back to Jonathon, he wolfed down the MRE like he hadn't eaten in a week. I gave him some ibuprofen and headed back to the creek to refill the buckets. I knew it would take the rest of the family almost until dark to get to where we were, so I scouted around a little. There was only one house within about a half a mile radius. It was deserted and had been ransacked like the one we'd seen two days before. At least whoever looted it hadn't burned it like the other one. I went through the house, but couldn't find anything we really needed. There was some bleach, but it was the kind that has other stuff besides chlorine in it."

"You wouldn't have stolen anything, even if you could have used it, would you?" Mark asked, as if the very thought repulsed him.

"Mark, I struggled with that as I was looking. I know it's immoral to take stuff that doesn't belong to you, but how moral is it to watch your kids go hungry? You guys don't know how lucky you have it here," Jeff almost sounded a little angry. "It's bad out there, and the answer to your question is yes. I would have taken food or anything else that would have helped us from a deserted house. If I hadn't, someone else would have."

"That doesn't make it right," Mark argued.

"No, it doesn't, but right and wrong are a lot easier to discern when you're warm, sheltered, and fed. I would've taken the food if there had been any, and later we did take some things we found. I'd never hurt anyone, or take anything from someone's possession, but if something's abandoned, I consider it finders-keepers. I guess it all comes down to where you draw the line."

"I guess so," Mark said, not wanting to argue the point in front of everyone.

"Anyway, after I saw there was no one around, I went back to check on Jonathon, and then I snuck back down to the creek and shot some squirrels with my .22 pistol. By the time everyone else arrived, they were skinned, cleaned, and cooking on spits over a fire. We opened a few cans of vegetables and had ourselves a big feast of tree rats," Jeff said.

"We HATE tree rats!" all the newcomers said in unison. Everyone laughed.

"That night it started raining. Gently at first, but then it got harder and harder," Mike explained. "The small tent kept the water out, but the larger one leaked. We strung the tarps up over it, and that helped some. Monica and the babies stayed in the good tent since we didn't want them to get sick. We kept the fire going, even though the wet wood smoked. Someone would have had to trip over us to see the fire or the smoke anyway. It was miserable, and we even talked about going over and staying in the abandoned house, but we decided it was too risky. It rained hard for two days straight, and we didn't go anywhere. In a way, it was good. It gave Jonathon's ankle a chance to heal, and everyone got plenty of rest. Jeff was able to get everyone all the tree rats they could eat."

"We HATE tree rats!" they said again, to another chorus of laughs.

"That kept us from having to eat any of our food except for a few canned fruits and vegetables. One other thing I should have mentioned was that Monica had a big bottle of kids' vitamins. We all started taking one a day since she had plenty. I don't know for sure how much it helped, but I think it made a big difference. The next morning, let me see," Mike looked at his little journal, "yeah, it was the eleventh day, the sky was clear, and it had cooled off a little. We made real good time since everyone was rested. Jonathon was still limping a little, so we put his pack in the cart, and he was able to keep up just fine. We followed the creek south for a couple of miles and then came to another set of tracks. I hadn't intended for us to use them since they ran east west, but it was so much easier to walk on the tracks, and with no fences to cross we decided to follow them. They ran through Belton to the west of us and back to Temple if you took them east. We didn't want to go through either city, but we saw that we could go toward Belton and then cut cross country for just a mile or so and get on another set that would take us back east and intersect the north-south tracks we needed. We got that far and even made it about a mile south of the intersection that day. I figured we walked over fourteen miles that day. Of course, we only made six or seven as the crow flies, but we were all happy to be back on course."

"The next couple of days went well. We made good time, and there was plenty of good water with all of the rain. By the end of the second day, we were just north of Granger. I should also mention that we saw a couple of things we hadn't seen before during this period. The first is that we saw our first dead train. It was kind of ironic. It was a car carrier, and it must have had hundreds of new cars on it. Too bad it wasn't loaded with '57 Chevys. Maybe we could have used one." Mike paused.

"The second thing we saw was another group using the railroad tracks. It was a group of young people, who said they were from the University of Texas, and they were trying to get home to the Dallas-Ft. Worth area. We talked to them for a few minutes. They had good backpacks and plenty of freeze-dried food. In that way, they were better off than us, but they only had one gun. It was an old pump shotgun and a couple of boxes of shells. They seemed like good kids…I hope they made it home and found their folks. I'm afraid even to think about what Dallas is like."

It was deathly quiet at that comment.

Mike consulted his notebook again. "The next day, it started raining again mid-morning. We'd only gone a couple of miles, and we talked about going on, but the women were afraid the kids might get sick if they got too wet and cold. We stopped and set up camp. It stopped raining late in the afternoon, but we decided to stay put until morning."

"It was very cool the next morning and we all felt great with brisk air and extra rest. We'd gone seven miles by lunch, and I felt like we were going to make some good time. Right after lunch, the kids' wagon broke. One of the front wheels just fell off, and the wagon tipped over. The kids tumbled out and started crying from the surprise. Luckily, none of them were really hurt. We tried to fix it for almost an hour, but with no tools to speak of, it was hopeless."

"We'd been lightening our packs by putting stuff on Dad's cart as we ate the food and there was room. We could have taken the extra stuff off and let the kids ride on it, but since it was a flat bed, there was no way to keep them from falling off if they fell asleep or lost their balance. We tried to adapt the stake sides to the big cart, but again without any tools, we couldn't make it work. We took them with us, though, just in case we could figure something out. The two bigger kids would have to walk or be carried, and there was no other choice but to carry Haylee. Since everyone else had a pack, Mom insisted on carrying her."

"Between spending time to fix the wagon and slowing down for the kids, we only made three miles that afternoon. The next day wasn't any better. It started getting hot and humid again, like we were going to get another storm. We only made five miles the whole day. The kids were miserable, and so were the adults. Taylor and Luke didn't have any good hiking shoes, and they complained that their feet hurt. We ended up carrying them half of the time. It wasn't horrible if they were awake, but it seemed like they fell asleep as soon as you picked them up, and then they were just dead weight. Mom didn't have any heavy shoes either, and carrying the baby started to take its toll on her. Her feet started hurting so badly she could barely walk even when we took the baby. It was obvious we had to figure something out, or we'd never get here."

"That night we emptied out Jeff and Monica's packs and my hunting day pack Cathy had been carrying. We cut leg holes in the bottom of them and made baby carriers. We had to load the cart down pretty good with the stuff that had been in the packs. The next day, it was harder to pull than it had been when we started out. It wasn't just the weight, either. The gravel between the tracks had become more uneven as we made our way south. That's probably what broke the other wagon."

"That wasn't our biggest problem, though. Mom's left foot was killing her. It was swollen, and she could barely put any weight on it. She must have injured it or strained it somehow when she was carrying Haylee. She did the best she could, but we only made three miles that day. We saw more people on the tracks, too. One of the groups was pretty creepy looking. They gave us a wide berth, and we gave them the same."

"I was getting pretty depressed with how slowly we were going and how bad our luck was running. It was our sixteenth day, and we weren't even halfway here. I felt like we really needed to start pushing hard, but we decided we had to let Mom's foot heal first. I was afraid we might run into a group looking for trouble. The last thing we needed was to get into a shootout with a bunch like the ones who had burned our houses. We talked about it and thought we might try moving at night and resting during the day. We figured most groups were doing the opposite, like we had been, and this would be safer."

"In the morning, Mom's foot was still swollen. We moved camp to a more secluded location, under some big oak trees. Everyone spent most of the day trying to sleep to get ready for traveling at night. The exception was the kids. We tried to keep them up and entertained during the day so they'd sleep all night. By dark, Mom's foot was a little better. She said she could go, but we decided to give it one more day of rest."

"The next night, we took off, and I couldn't believe how well we did. I thought moving in the dark would slow us down. However, I didn't realize how much time we were spending tending to the kids. They slept almost the whole time we were moving, and since it was a lot cooler, we didn't need as many rest stops either. We passed through Taylor, which was the biggest town we'd gone through. It seems like a strange thing to say, but I felt a lot better about going through it after dark. I don't think anyone saw us. We went almost fourteen miles that night. Just as the sun was coming up, we found a nice spot next to a big creek to camp. Jeff killed us some more squirrels, and the teenagers tried to spear some fish. I wish I'd brought some hooks and line. We could've caught all the fish we wanted. As it was, they got a couple of good-sized perch, and we cooked them. Everyone got a bite or two of fresh fish for dessert. It tasted real good compared to the monotonous diet we'd existed on for the last two weeks."

"Mom's foot was hurting a little and slightly swollen again, but by nightfall it was better. The next couple of days' traveling went well. We went through Elgin one night and made it almost to Bastrop the next. Jeff was having better luck with the hunting, and one day we ate rabbit, which is just a little better than tree rat in my opinion. The next day, we got a real delicacy. Jeff shot a wild turkey, and we all agreed it was the best thing we'd ever eaten. Mom's foot was still bothering her some but not enough to slow us down. We just kept her on aspirin and Tylenol, and she did okay."

"I was worried about going through Bastrop. It was big enough that I felt like we might have trouble even in the dark. The tracks went right through the middle of town, and on the map, it looked like we'd have to go far out of our way to skirt town. I wasn't thrilled with either option. The big problem was getting across the Colorado River. It's big, and there are no little roads that cross it. The tracks didn't cross until well south of town, and then they started heading more to the east. We really needed to start moving in a more westerly direction, so we were at a loss for what to do. We discussed all the options, but there just wasn't a good solution. Sometimes it's funny how things work out though." Mike laughed, and the other newcomers nodded their heads and laughed along with him.

"What do you mean?" Jim asked curiously.

"Well, I was trying to get some sleep, but the problems of getting through Bastrop and across the river kept me up. It must have been late morning when we heard the gunshots. They sounded close, and we weren't sure of what to do. We were hidden pretty well, so we decided Jeff and I would go see what was going on. The gunfire was further away than it sounded, but when we got close, we could see some ratty looking dudes attacking an old farmhouse. Jeff and I knew we had to help whoever was in the house. We were between three and four hundred yards away, and there was no way to get closer because it was all plowed field between where we were and the house. We spread out about fifty yards and each got behind a big tree. The goblins were using the trees around the house for cover. They seemed to think they were safe as long as they had a tree between them and the house. When Jeff and I started shooting at them, we clipped one of them in the leg before they could figure out what was going on. When they scrambled around to get out of our line of fire, they took a hit from the house. That must have been enough for them because they ran off; well, two of them limped off. A minute later, we heard a car or a truck crank up and tear off down the road."

"Jeff and I walked up to the house to see if anyone was injured or if they needed help. When we were within fifty yards, we heard her voice. 'You boys hold it right there,' she said. I can still hear it. It sounded like a cross between a creaking board and a squeaky hinge. I told her we'd just come to see if anyone needed help. She stepped out onto the porch and told us that while she was appreciative of that and that she was grateful for what we'd done, no one needed any help. She looked like she was at least eighty years old. In fact, she reminded me of Granny Hawkins from *The Outlaw Josey Wales*. You know, the old lady in the store by the ferry?"

The movie Mike had mentioned was one of Mark's favorites, and he knew exactly who Mike meant.

"Was she smoking a corn cob pipe?" he asked his brother.

"No. I'd say she was more of the chewing tobacco type," Mike smiled. "She was holding an old Savage lever action rifle. She never pointed it at us, but the way she held it, you knew she could use it. I told her I was glad everyone was okay and that we'd go on back to our families. She looked a little taken back by that comment. She asked if we had kids. Then she asked where we were from and where we were going. She seemed to relax a little after we answered those questions. She asked if we had plenty to eat. I told her while we didn't have plenty, we were doing okay."

"She insisted we go get everyone and come back to her place for dinner. We didn't argue, and were back in no time. We introduced ourselves, and she told us her name was Roberta Pruett but that we should call her Bert. Bert fed us so much food that we couldn't even move. She just kept opening mason jar after mason jar of vegetables and was frying up venison like it was going out of style. I almost got sick, I ate so much. She told us she and her husband had never had any kids, and after he died twenty-odd years ago she still worked the two hundred-acre farm. She said all the canned vegetables had come out of her garden over the summer, and the fresh ones had come out of the fall one, along with the deer, who'd been eating her lettuce until the day before."

"She talked our ears off. I think she was glad to have company. When she asked us to spend the night, I told her we were traveling at night and needed to get going. She said if we would stay the night, she'd take us as far as the county line, since travel was now restricted to within the county, and she didn't want any trouble with the law. Dad asked if she had a running car and she said 'No.'"

Mike paused to yawn. Mark looked at his watch and saw that it was after eleven. He should have sent everyone to bed, but he wanted to hear the rest of the story. His dad took over for a few minutes.

"I asked her how she was going to take us anywhere without a vehicle. She said her tractor still ran and she could hook up her hay wagon and take us in that. Mikey told her he'd have to think about it, and then as soon as he could, he went and sneaked a look at the map. When he came back, he told her that we'd be happy to take her up on her kind offer. After hiking and living in a tent for three weeks, it was sure nice to sleep in a bed. We all took baths and even washed our clothes."

"How did you do that? Did she have a generator to run the water pump and the washer?" Sam asked.

Andrew laughed. "No, sweetheart. She had a well with a hand pump, and we pumped water into buckets and carried it inside for baths, and we washed the clothes in the tub, too. We scrubbed them on washboards, and she had an old ringer we put the clothes through before we hung them out to dry. In fact, Bert said she barely missed the electricity. She had kerosene lamps, and a big propane tank for cooking and heating. She said if she used her wood stove for heating, the propane would last her several years. She didn't own a TV and said she only used to listen to the radio for the news."

Jenna, Mike's fifteen year old, jumped in with a comment of her own. "I used to hate it when Mom made me wash the clothes. After washing them by hand, I swear I'll never complain about doing them in a washing machine again!"

Everybody laughed, and Mark noticed Sam's head nodding vigorously in agreement. Mark thought about how soft their lives had really been before The Burst.

Mike took back over the story telling. "We really slept well that night. I can't tell you how good it felt to be clean. Since there was no hurry to leave the next day, us men cut and split a bunch of oak firewood for Bert's wood burning stove, and the women helped her with canning some of the vegetables out of her garden. Late in the afternoon, she hooked an old wagon up to her tractor, and we took off toward the county line."

"Now a tractor doesn't go all that fast, but after walking for the better part of a month, twenty miles an hour seems like flying. She dropped us off at the Caldwell County line at Highway 20 in less than an hour. It would've taken us two or three days to walk that far, probably more if we'd stayed on the tracks. She gave us a week's worth of fresh vegetables, some the girls had helped her can, and some deer jerky she'd made herself. That was the last good food we had until tonight." Mike picked up the mug of hot coffee that had been placed in front of him and took a sip. "You don't appreciate the little things until you have to go without them," he said. It was quiet for a moment as he drank.

"Where was I? Oh, yeah. We got on the tracks that ran right beside the road at the county line and started walking toward Lockhart. As lucky as we'd been finding Bert and her helping us, it seemed we were doomed to pay for it with a run of bad luck. First, the tracks were in bad shape. I mean, the actual tracks were fine, but the gravel and ties between them were uneven, and it made for some very slow going. Even if we tried to pick up the pace, the bumpiness would make things fall off of the big cart. We even broke some of the mason jars of food Bert had given us."

"We only made six miles that night. Plus, my boots started falling apart. I taped them up with duct tape as best I could, but the *coup de gras* was that one of the tents fell off the wagon at some point, and none of us saw it. It was the big one that leaked, but we still needed it. We didn't notice until we started setting up camp that morning. Jeff and I backtracked and found it almost back to where Bert had dropped us off. By the time we found it, I'd worn through the duct tape on my boots. I hadn't taken the roll with me, and since the boots were so sloppy on my feet, I had blisters you wouldn't believe when we finally got back to camp. We had to rest for two days until my feet healed enough for me to walk."

"The next day we traveled, we only made five miles, but that got us to Lockhart. We needed to head south, but there were no tracks that ran north and south, plus everyone was sick of the tracks. We decided to try the roads, as long as we could stay out of the cities. I was a little nervous about all of us traveling on the roads, so we started scouting ahead. Each morning, two of us would take as much food as we could carry and go seven or eight miles down the road. We'd find a good campsite, hide the food, then go back to the group, and all of us would walk to the new camp as soon as it got dark. Only one time did scouting keep us out of trouble, but it was worth it. Plus, having a hundred pounds less to carry at night really made a difference. We weren't making a lot of distance each day, but seven or eight miles every day beat what we'd been averaging."

"So, what day did you get to Lockhart?" Mark asked.

Mike checked his little notebook. "October fourteenth."

"I don't understand. Lockhart's only fifty miles from here. You should have been here by the twenty-first at the rate you were going."

"That's true, but remember I said that scouting kept us out of trouble once?"

"Yes," Mark answered.

"Well, we'd crossed into Bexar County on the eighteenth, and guess what we saw on our scouting trip for the nineteenth when we got to the Wilson County line?"

"The National Guard roadblock," the younger brother replied.

"You got it. Dad and I were the scouts that day, and we saw them take a group into custody. We watched until almost dark, and they took every person and group who tried to cross the line and hauled them off somewhere. We went back to the camp and decided we couldn't chance getting caught when we were so close. We decided to lay low until we could cross the county line."

"Why didn't you try going cross country?" Manny asked.

"We talked about it, and we would've had to try in a day or two because we were almost out of food for the little ones, but we didn't want to take any chances that the Guard would catch us and take us who knows where."

"I see your point," Manny conceded.

"We found an old, abandoned, pole barn that looked like it had been used to store hay. It was closed in on three sides and offered a little protection from the elements and kept us out of sight, so we set up camp there. It was close to a windmill that worked, so we had plenty of water. We laid low and didn't do anything to call attention to ourselves. There wasn't much game to hunt, but Jeff found a few tree rats and rabbits for us. We saved all the vegetables for the little ones. For the last thirteen days, two of us made the walk to check and see if the Guard had left. It was frustrating to only be a few miles from you and not be able to get here."

"Yesterday, Dad and Monica saw that they were gone, and Jeff and I decided we'd walk here and see if it was really safe or not. I hoped that once we got here, you all would have some sort of transportation you could use to get the others. Thank goodness I was at least right about that." Mike yawned.

Mark looked at his watch. It was now after midnight. "Why don't we all hit the sack, and we can finish catching up tomorrow," he suggested.

"That sounds good to me," Mike answered, as everyone else nodded in agreement.

Sleeping arrangements were made, and everyone went to bed. Mark thought that with the worry of his family finally gone, coupled with the fact of how tired he was, sleep would come quickly. However, something wouldn't let him doze off until just before dawn.

Chapter 63

Church services the next morning were joyous and crowded. Not only were many people happy Mark's family had made it, the local legend, Billy the Kid. Billy and his boys showed up in full regalia, wearing their best cowboy duds down to the spurs and six-shooters Mark had assured the rancher would be welcomed. Most of the residents of Silver Hill were there. Even a few others, who had to travel further than was becoming customary, came to the service. Curt, Rob, and Greg from Promise Point brought their families to the service and then stayed for the barbeque afterwards. Even Dr. Ken made an appearance.

The luncheon became even more joyous when the news that Jess was expecting was revealed to everyone. The only person who expressed any reservations was Mike's wife, Cathy.

"How in the world are you going to bring a baby into this world when there's no electricity?" she asked Mark in admonishing tones after she pulled him to the side.

"Gee, Cathy, I hope the lights are back on by the time the baby comes, but if they're not, can you tell me how many thousands of years people had babies before electricity was invented?" Mark asked.

"Smart ass!" she shot back with half a grin.

"I love you too, Cathy."

Her only reply was a quick right jab to his shoulder.

When the celebration started to die down, Mark told Gunny and the other security committee members that he wanted to have a meeting. He also invited Jim and Mike to attend, and since the visitors from Promise Point were still there, he invited the three men to join them, as well. On his way to the meeting, he ran into Billy the Kid and dragged him along, too.

After making sure everyone knew each other and giving a short brief on his team's mêlée, Mark started. "I know we would have met tonight, but I didn't think this should wait. I am, and I'm sure you all are, too, very concerned about the group we had the run-in with yesterday. The fact that they were watching the subdivision makes the hairs on the back of my neck stand up. They were also probably the best-trained group we've come up against. If it wasn't for Billy and his men, I probably wouldn't be here right now. I want to hear what y'all think it means. Are they a threat to us, and if so, what should we do about it?"

Gunny spoke up first. "I'm sending Jim's group out this afternoon to check out the hill they was using to watch us from. In fact, I plan on goin' with 'em. I can only think of one reason why they'd be watchin' us like that."

"And what would that be, Gunny?" Susan asked.

"To see if they can whip us. I expect some are gettin' mighty desperate by now, and we're a big, fat target. Too many people know we got food, water, and guns."

Mark looked at the sheriff. "Is that true, Curt? Are we well known?"

"Mark, I don't think 'well known' even comes close to describing it. You and Silver Hills are downright famous. I doubt there's anyone in the surrounding counties who hasn't heard of you. Heck, even the FEMA man asked me about you. I downplayed it and told him y'all were just looking out for each other and that all the stories were gross exaggerations. It doesn't change the fact that people talk, and they talk about you all a bunch."

Mark would have been embarrassed if what Curt said hadn't scared him so much. Before he could stop himself, he verbalized his fear. "That's pretty scary!" He hoped his face didn't give away the extent of his alarm.

"No!" Greg interjected. The Promise Point leader's eyes were wide. "Let me tell you what's scary. Anyone who even contemplates taking on Silver Hills is a threat to us all. Even if they decide that you're too big and well organized, they'll come looking for easier targets. Other than perhaps the city of Floresville itself, and God knows they're not organized, no community in the county can match the manpower or firepower you all possess."

It was quiet for a long moment as Greg's words sunk in. Finally, Chaparo broke the silence.

"I think we have to go on the assumption that they are a threat and figure out how they might try to attack us, so we can come up with a defense plan."

"Gunny, how would you do it, and how many men would you need?" Ted asked.

The grizzled veteran rubbed his chin. "I'd try to sneak a few men under the back fence and set up a diversion. Then I'd hit from all four sides at once, while the men on the inside took out the CP and any other targets of opportunity. With a well trained crew of Marines and the element of surprise, I could do it with fifty or sixty men."

Mark whistled. "Only fifty or sixty? If we have over a hundred armed men, shouldn't they need at least three hundred?"

"That's what the books say, Karate Man, but in real life, things seldom go as the books say. Remember, most of the guys here have never had to fire a shot when the chips are down. When the shit gets deep, only 'bout half them will keep their heads. The good part for us is that they no longer have the element of total surprise. They may have some training, but they aren't the kind of heartbreakers and life takers I was talkin' 'bout. We can pro'ly handle a hundred or more, but I can't make no promises."

"Besides, there's no way for them to sneak in a diversion team with the lookout towers," Susan added.

"I wouldn't say that," Jim countered. "We have hogs coming under the fence almost every night, and most of the time, the men on guard duty don't even see them."

"Then maybe the MEN should get their eyes checked. They should at least stay awake and do their job," she shot back.

"Maybe you ought to sit up there on a cloudy night and see if you can spot them before you throw any stones," Jim said through clenched teeth.

Mark was a little surprised to see his best friend let a comment like Susan's bother him. Jim was usually the cool one. "Guys, this isn't the time," he said. "Gunny, what do we need to do?"

"We really ain't done nothin' to our security preps since the first few weeks after The Burst. I know other things have been more pressin', but we need to get back on it. The biggest problem we still have is the backside. The woods come right up to the fence. If'n we could thin 'em out some, so we could see people before they got up to the fence, I'd feel a lot better. The second prior'ty is to stop vehicles from coming through the fields on the sides and driving right through the barbed wire. We need to dig ditches down the sides like the one we got in the front. Then, we need foxholes to fight from on the sides and in the back at least every couple of hundred yards."

"That's a lot of work," Ted said. "How long do you think we have?"

"Not very long. The fact that we scared 'em off is good. Maybe they didn't finish their recon, or maybe the fact that we surprised 'em will make 'em think twice, but my guess is that we have a couple of days to a week at most if'n they plan to hit us."

"There's no way we can get all of that done in a week."

"The hell of it is, I'm doubling the guards because of this, and we need to keep sending out the scout teams, too," Gunny added.

"Me and my boys could take over the scouting for a while," Billy the Kid said. "But don't you think you could be overreacting just a little? You're talking about a group one hundred or more strong. I haven't seen or heard of any group that big. The biggest group I've seen has been about twenty, and they were harmless. Ten or twelve troublemakers at a time is what we've dealt with a few times. I don't think you have to worry about so many."

"I agree," Susan said, smiling sweetly at Billy. "I think you men are overreacting to this. We certainly don't need to double the guards. If you do that, where are we going to get help for all these projects you want to do?"

Mark noticed she received several irritated stares in response to her statements. While Billy's was a sincere question, Susan appeared to be playing gender politics again or was just kissing up to the rancher. Probably both, Mark thought.

"Curt, have you heard of any groups over a hundred men?" Gunny asked, making a point of ignoring Susan.

"Not officially, but there are rumors there could be some 'Super Gangs' out there. That's what they're calling them. We saw that group of sixty come down the pipeline, so a hundred or more isn't that far of a stretch. It makes sense, too. A lot of criminals were released after The Burst. They were supposedly just the ones who were in for non-violent crimes, I know, but that just means they were in jail for non-violent crimes. Just because Little Johnny Bad-ass is in the slammer for burglary doesn't mean he hasn't done worse, just that we didn't catch him or couldn't prove it beyond a reasonable doubt. Now, all the Little Johnnies who are gang members, which is most of them, go back to the gangs they belong to. That might be anywhere from ten to fifty members. As the deserted places dry up, they start hitting the easy places, like Roy Wilkins' house I told you about a few weeks back. Once those become few and far between, and only the well-armed places are left, some of the gangs will put the past behind them and join forces in an attempt to survive. Even if there are no groups that big right now, there will be."

"How big do you think they could get?" Billy asked.

"Five hundred is the number FEMA estimates."

"Holy shit!" Billy's panache for saying exactly what he was thinking showed through again.

"You can say that again," Susan said quietly, as the number took everyone by surprise. Mark thought it might change her mind about whether they were overreacting or not.

"I don't think we'd have a group that big yet," Curt quickly added. "In fact, Rob and I have discussed this at length, and we don't think a group bigger than about three hundred would be probable. Any more than that, and we think there would be a power struggle, and the group would split."

"Well, that makes me feel a hell of a whole lot better!" Billy said sarcastically.

"Why haven't you two discussed this with me?" Greg asked accusingly.

"Because there was no way for us to defend against those kinds of numbers at Promise Point, so we decided not to worry you with it," Rob explained.

"So you two are now like the Federal boys and decide what we peons need to know and what we don't?" Greg seemed more hurt than mad.

"You're right, Greg. I'm sorry." It was the first time Mark had seen the lawman remorseful.

"Anything else we ought to know?"

"No, not that has any bearing on this problem."

Mark caught the look Greg shot at Curt. The contractor didn't say anything in response, but Mark was sure there would be a spirited conversation between the two in the near future.

Rob jumped in and broke up what was becoming an uncomfortable moment. "Look, this isn't just a Silver Hills problem. This is a problem for all of us. We need a countywide solution. If there are any 'Super Gangs' out there, they'll sweep through the countryside like a swarm of locusts. We need to be able to stop them in their tracks. It was hard enough to stop those sixty 'Los Muertos' gang members with the automatic weapons. We lost four good men in that fight and had two others wounded. How in the hell can we stop three to five hundred?"

Everyone began talking at once. The meeting had spiraled out of control, and they were accomplishing nothing. Mark had to get everyone back on the same page.

"Listen, everyone."

The chatter continued.

He raised his voice a little. "Can I have your attention, please?"

No one paid any attention.

"Everyone! This isn't accomplishing anything!" He was almost shouting now.

It didn't do any good. Susan was arguing with Jim. Billy and Gunny were having their own animated conversation. Rob, Greg, and Curt were talking back and forth, while Ted and Chaparo whispered back and forth. Mike was the only one not actively involved in a conversation. He just sat wide-eyed and looked like he was trying to absorb everything. Mark realized that if the situation wasn't so serious, this would almost be comical. Well, he thought, time to go to plan B. It would cost him a dollar, but if it worked, it would be worth it.

"HEY! EVERYBODY! SHUT THE HELL UP!" he shouted at the top of his lungs.

Ten heads snapped around to face him. Twenty eyes looked at him with surprise, shock, anger, or some combination thereof. Most importantly, it was quiet.

"Sorry about that," Mark said with a slight smile. "Back to business. I think we all agree we need to treat this as a threat of some kind. Right?"

The ten heads nodded.

"We also agree that Super Gangs, if or when they exist, are not just a threat against Silver Hills, but one that the whole county will have to deal with, if not now, in the future, for sure."

Again the heads nodded.

"And that we're all in this together."

More nods.

"So, how do we protect all of Wilson County?"

"That's what we were talking about," Rob said. "We have the response teams already. What if we just try to expand on that strategy? We put a radio and a school bus or two in every neighborhood or area where there's enough firepower to call on. If an attack occurs, the attackees call for help and hold the attackers off or fall back until the cavalry arrives."

Mark glanced at Billy and thought about how "the cavalry" had saved him last night. It seemed like a good plan. Everyone else seemed to think so, too.

"I can get that set up and organized in the morning at the Monday training classes," Curt volunteered.

"I hope you'll excuse us if we don't show up," Mark said. "I think we need to start on the things Gunny suggested."

"I think we should cancel the classes and come help y'all," Greg said. "Please forgive me for being so blunt, but our best hope for stopping a Super Gang is if they do attack Silver Hills. We should help you get your stuff done. Then you can help us."

"That's very kind, Greg. We'd be happy to have the help and then to help whoever helps us." Mark smiled. This was coming together.

"One other thing," Greg said. "I have about eight hundred feet of chain link fence that we put around a building site when we're constructing a house. It's eight feet tall and has razor wire on the top. We use it to keep tools and materials from walking off after hours. I don't think it'll go all the way across the back of your subdivision, but you could put it across part of the back, and it would discourage people from crossing there."

"That would be a great help," Gunny said. "That'll cover about half of the back fence. We'll put it in the middle and force them to cross closer to the corners. Thanks, Greg."

"You're welcome. I'll bring it tomorrow and help you set it up. We'll probably need six or eight guys."

"Chaparo, can you put together a crew to set the fence up?" Mark asked.

"No problem."

"Susan, can you be responsible for the foxholes?"

She nodded.

"I'll help you, and once they're done, we'll get started on the ditches. Ted, can you start on clearing behind the old fence? When Chaparo gets the new fence set up, then he can help you. We can start first thing in the morning."

"Sounds like a plan," Ted agreed, and Chaparo gave him a nod.

"Gunny, if you'd get with Billy on the scouting, I don't see any reason not to take him up on his offer. Also, I agree that we need the additional guards, at least for a while. I know that's going to make manpower around here hard to come by, but with some outside help, maybe we can get all of this done in a week. Does anybody disagree or see a problem?

Everyone in the meeting shook his or her head.

"Good. Anything else we need to talk about?" Mark asked.

"Yeah, Mark," Curt said. "I was wondering if I could borrow six of the Harleys you brought back from Waco. I have six deputies who can ride, but no bikes. That would let me put more men out on patrol. The bigger these Super Gangs are, the harder it'll be for them to stay out of sight. With more men out, maybe we'll see them before they can attack anyone."

"No problem, Curt. Just come get them, or you can borrow my truck and Chaparo's trailer and take them today if you want. Is that okay with you, Chaparo?"

"Fine by me."

"Anything else?" Mark asked as a formality.

"Just one more thing, Mark," Rob said. "Gunny, you said you were going to look at the hill your scouts saw the observer from."

"Yeah?"

"Two things. First, can I come with you?"

"Sure. Be glad to have you along."

"Second, are you assuming he was part of the group that shot at Mark and the others last night?" Rob asked, as Gunny nodded his head. "Chances are they were all together, but you have to consider that it may have been two different groups. I know your background is in the military, where you only battle one enemy at a time, but this is a different ball game."

"You're right," Gunny agreed. "I was just assuming that. Jim, why don't you and the boys go recon that hill and call me when you're sure it's clean. Then Rob and I will come look at it with you. Don't let your guys trample everything."

"You got it, Gunny. Are we done? I have a job to do," Jim said.

"We're done," Mark said.

Everyone got up and walked out. Mark and Mike headed back toward the Turner house.

"What's the deal with the Harleys from Waco?" Mike asked.

"It's kind of a long story, but when we went to get you, we camped where you'd cached your barrels. A bunch of bikers had moved into the house on the west side of the woods."

"You mean the gray colored, ranch style house?"

"Yes. We were in the woods when they came home with a young woman they'd kidnapped. We went into save her and ended up killing all of the MZB's. Since there was no way..."

"Did you say 'MZB's'?" Mike asked.

"Yeah. It stands for Mutant Zombie Biker."

"I see."

Mark thought his brother would be amused at the acronym, but he didn't even crack a smile. Mark continued his story. "Anyway, since there was no way to involve the local police without it probably complicating our lives considerably, we took the bikes, the Blazer, and a bunch of stuff they'd obviously stolen."

"That's a little hypocritical, don't you think?" Mike asked.

"What do you mean?"

"Well," Mike explained, "last night you were quite 'holier than thou' when Jeff said something about going through an abandoned house and looking for food for his kids. Now I find out you took a bunch of stuff you really didn't even need from a house where you killed all the occupants. I'd say that's being hypocritical."

"This was different. Everything we took had obviously been stolen, and there was no chance for the rightful owners to get it back." Mark was a little defensive.

"Do you know that for a fact? Maybe one of the bikers lived there. Maybe some of that stuff was really his? You really don't know for sure, do you?" Mike shot the questions out rapid-fire.

"No, but..."

"But nothing!" the older brother snapped back. Then his tone softened. "Listen, Mark, that house belonged to Patrick and Maggie Fielding, an old retired couple. The closest thing to a motorcycle I ever saw Patrick on was a riding lawnmower. We tried to get them to come with us, but they wouldn't budge. Said they'd lived there for thirty years, and they weren't moving away for a little blackout. God only knows what happened to them. Hopefully one of their kids came and got them. I have no doubt all the stuff you took was stolen and that the MZB's, as you call them, got what was coming to them. In fact, they were probably some of the same bikers who burned down our houses. The point I'm trying to make is that you did what you thought best at the time. That's what Jeff did. It's easy to judge right and wrong when you're not standing in the shoes of the person who's in the situation. Just remember that, Bro."

"You're right, Mike. I'll apologize to Jeff." He was quiet for a moment. "You really think they could have been the same guys who attacked you?"

"Possible. When we ran them off the first time, they had at least a few bikes that I could hear. When they came back, they must have parked a ways off because I didn't hear any cars or bikes. I just happened to be going back to the house for some stuff when I saw them. Luckily, they never saw me. There were way too many of them for us to fight. They shot at the houses, and when no one shot back, I guess they figured out we'd left. One of them had a jug of gas that he split between dad's house and mine. Then they put a road flare into each house. The houses went up quick. When they were fully engulfed, they left."

"It must have been hard not to shoot them."

"It was, but there was no way to get all of them, and what good would that have done us? I'd have been dead, and the houses still would have been destroyed."

491

"You're right again, big brother." Mark threw his arm around Mike's shoulders like he was going to hug him. "Have I told you how happy I am to finally have you here?"

"About a hundred times."

"Yeah, but not officially." Mark swiftly turned the sideways hug into a headlock and rubbed his knuckles on his brother's scalp. The two scuffled briefly, as they had a thousand times before. Mike quickly accepted the inevitable and let his brother perform the ritual that had been shared by brothers for generations. Once he quit struggling, the fun was quickly gone, and Mark stopped.

"Why don't you show me around?" Mike more insisted than asked.

"You got it."

Mark spent the next few hours showing Mike around and introducing him to many of the Silver Hills residents. Before dark, they saw Gunny and Rob walking toward the CP.

"So, did you get to look at the hill?" Mark asked.

"Yep," the old Marine answered. "We found the campsite the others was staying at, too. It was right at the bottom of the hill in some heavy brush. It don't look like they was there too long."

"How could you tell?"

"They had some wood stacked up for a fire, but never lit it. They was pro'ly waitin' for dark. Also, the grass on the top of the hill was matted down where the observer was watchin' from and where they had walked up the hill from the camp, but the grass wasn't dead like it woulda been if they'd been watchin' for several days."

"Any clue where they could have come from?"

"Not a one, Karate Man. They didn't leave nothin' behind. Hopefully that's 'cause they weren't there long and not 'cause they were well trained."

"I hope so too, Gunny," Mark said, then he shifted his attention to Rob. "You need a ride home?"

"No, Dr. Ken is still here, and he said he'd give me a ride. I'm going to the clinic to find him. I'll see you in the morning, though."

"Good," Mark said, as he shook Rob's hand. "Thanks for all your help."

Rob nodded and then headed to the clinic, while the other three men walked home. Mark wanted to get a good night's rest. It was going to be a long, hard week.

Chapter 64

Early Monday morning, they started on the security measures Gunny had outlined. The men in Mark's family insisted on helping with the work, but Mark felt they hadn't recuperated enough from their long trip to work as hard as the jobs would require. Gunny agreed with Mark. Guard duty, though, wasn't so physically strenuous, and the security chief put the four newcomers there. They didn't really know the ropes, but with the doubled numbers on watch, there were plenty of 'old timers' to help them learn.

Greg and Rob had shown up with the fence materials early, and with the help of Chaparo's crew, it was tied to the barbed wire fence in just a few hours. Then they started helping Ted and his crew with the brush in the back of the subdivision. With only a couple of working chainsaws, it was slow work. All types of handsaws were put to use. Anything that was usable as firewood was dragged into the subdivision and stacked, while all of the brush was stacked in a row that would be hard for an attacker to crawl through about fifty yards behind the fence.

The biggest team was Susan's digging crew. It included Mark and Jim. They started on the foxholes. Gunny had marked where he wanted them with Susan the day before. He told her to skip every other one for now. Then, they'd come back after the first half was done and do the second half. That way, he explained, if they only got halfway done before the MZB's attacked, they wouldn't just have fighting positions on one side of the neighborhood. Susan went further and broke the men into eight man squads and dispersed them around the subdivision. Mark found her organizational skills to be excellent, even if she didn't get along with everyone all the time.

Unlike suitable saws, shovels weren't in short supply, and the work progressed nicely. As the day wore on, people from outside the neighborhood showed up to help with the digging. With the help they were getting, Mark estimated they'd have all the foxholes dug by the next afternoon. Then they'd start on the ditches. That would be a monumental job, since the subdivision was right at three quarters of a mile deep. The only equipment they had to help them was the tractor with the plow attached, and all it would do was break the ground and make the first eighteen inches or so easier to dig. Mark had asked Greg and Rob, who had stayed to help after the fence was erected, if they knew of any available heavy equipment. Unfortunately, they didn't, but they promised to keep an eye out.

Mark was thankful it was November. It was still warm but nowhere near as hot as the Texas summer. If it had been August, when The Burst happened, the heat would have allowed them to do only half the work, even with the longer days. When it got too dark to see, they called it a day.

As Mark was walking home, Jim caught up with him.

"Mark, got a minute?"

"Sure, what's up?"

"Mark, you have got to do something about that witch!"

Mark knew he was talking about Susan. Tension between the two of them had been building for the past few weeks. "What happened now?"

"She went off on us because we moved one of the foxholes over a little. We hit a big rock about a foot down. I mean this thing was more like a boulder, so instead of taking the time to dig it out, we moved the hole over about six feet. When she saw what we did, she went ballistic. I tried to explain to her why we moved it, but she just kept on screaming. Gunny heard the commotion and came over and told her it was alright. For a moment I thought she was going to yell at him, too. She turned around and stomped off like a three year old. The guys I was digging with were so mad, they wanted to quit. The only reason they didn't was because I told them if they quit, she won."

"Maybe she's just having a bad day," Mark suggested.

"I don't think so. She's always on everyone's case. Like yesterday in the meeting when she suggested the guys weren't doing their job. You know how hard it is to see a black feral hog after dark, but she thinks that just because the guys don't see them, they're sleeping on the job or something. It's like she expects everyone to be perfect. She needs to take a good, hard look in the mirror. Everyone's getting tired of her crap. If you don't fix this, it's going to blow up...big time."

"I know she was out of line yesterday, and I'm sure she was today, too, but I don't know if I'm the one to talk to her about it. After all, I haven't really seen the kind of behavior you're talking about that much."

"Of course you haven't," Jim countered. "She doesn't do it around you. She always goes with whatever you say. That's why you have to talk to her. You're the only one she really listens to. I'm telling you, Mark, this needs to be nipped in the bud, or it's going to turn ugly!"

"Okay, Jim, let me sleep on it, and I'll figure out how to handle it."

"Thanks, Buddy."

In bed that night, Mark talked with Jess about the problem. He told her about what happened in the meeting and about the run-in she'd had with Jim and the other guys.

"Jim says I have to talk to her since I'm the only one she'll listen to, but he's the one having a problem with her, not me. I think he should talk to her."

"No, he's right. You're the only one she'll pay attention to," Jess said.

"Why's that?"

Jess laughed. "You really don't know, do you?"

"No!" he said seriously. He didn't like being laughed at, especially when he didn't know why.

"Mark," she said, still snickering, "you're as blind as she thinks the guys who can't see the hogs are." She paused. "The reason she only listens to you, heck it may be the reason she acts the way she does, is that she has a crush on you."

"What?"

"You heard me. I can't believe you haven't noticed the way she looks at you, although, you may be losing some of your charm. Yesterday, I noticed her making puppy eyes at Billy the Kid."

"So, what should I do?" he asked. "Now that I know that she likes me, I don't know if I'm comfortable talking with her one on one."

"Just reason with her like you would one of the guys, and play dumb about the other thing. That shouldn't be too hard for you," she said with a big smile. "Playing dumb that is."

"Duh," he teased back.

"Well, at least we know she doesn't want you for your brains," she laughed.

The only answer he could come up with that wouldn't cost him a dollar was to stick his tongue out at her. She laughed again. He pulled his wife to him and kissed her. He couldn't imagine how he would make it without her.

"Well," she teased when the long kiss ended, "I guess I really can't blame her, you being such a stud and all."

"Stop it, or you're going to get it," he threatened.

"Why, whatever do you mean, Mr. Turner?" she said in her best Scarlet O'Hara voice. She smiled at him and then turned and blew out the candle on the nightstand.

The next morning, Mark rose, dreading the task before him. He knew he needed to do it, so he might as well get it done. He asked Susan if she had a minute when she came by the hole he was digging with some of the men from outside the neighborhood. The two of them walked out of earshot of the other men, but not so far that they weren't in plain sight. Mark was surprised that the talk went so well. Susan agreed with everything he told her. He couldn't help noticing the doe-eyed look she gave him as he spoke. He hoped she couldn't tell he'd noticed. He hoped even more that she was really listening to him.

Later that day, he saw Jim. Mark asked his friend if he'd seen any difference in Susan.

"Yeah," Jim answered. "I sure have. Did you tell her I talked to you?"

"No, of course not."

"I guess she figured it out then. She's so mad at me she won't even look at me, but at least she's not yelling at everybody, so I guess that's an improvement. We'll just have to see how long it lasts."

Mark thought she'd get over it in a few days. He'd watch and see. If it looked like things were getting out of hand again, he'd step in quicker this time. He was finding it was better to face problems head on than to let them seethe. Plus, he couldn't afford to let her rile the men up so much that they didn't work.

Meanwhile, the preparations were going fairly well. The digging crew finished all the foxholes by lunchtime on Wednesday. The brush crews were making good progress and estimated they'd be done by Friday. The foxhole crew moved on to the vehicle ditches. They split into two teams, one for each side, and started at the front of the subdivision. George and Alex had mowed down the grass and then plowed as deep as they could with the tractor to make the work easier. When all of the plowed dirt had been scooped out of the section they were working on, they brought out the big tiller to help break up the deeper dirt. Although using the tiller made the digging a little easier, it didn't really speed the process up any. In addition to digging out the ditches, something had to be done with the dirt. Someone suggested they pile it up against the side of any houses that might be susceptible to gunfire if there was a big attack. They only had two effective ways to move it. The easy way was to pile it up on Chaparo's trailer, pull the trailer where they wanted, and shovel the dirt off. Unfortunately, the trailer reached its weight limit long before it was full volume-wise. The other was by wheelbarrow, which was slow and tedious. They tried using the pickups to haul the dirt, but the beds were too high to shovel the dirt into easily. George voiced his wish for a front-end loader for the tractor to Mark. However, no one they talked to knew of one.

The first half-day of work on the ditch provided less than a hundred yards of progress on each side. With over twelve hundred yards to go, it would take another six days or more to finish the digging at the current rate. The big problem was that, as they moved back, the dirt would have to be carried further and further to get it where it was needed. Mark hoped if an attack came before they were done, the attackers wouldn't have vehicles.

That evening, they held a security committee meeting. Everyone who'd been at the meeting on Sunday was invited, and they all came, except Curt. They reviewed the progress of the projects. Mark noticed that Susan was still treating Jim coolly, but she spoke with him if it had to do with the work. Mark didn't expect her to be friends with Jim. As long as they could work together, he was happy. Billy gave a report about the scouting. They were basically following the same route Mark and his team had followed a week ago. The big difference was that on horseback they could do in one day what had taken Mark's team two days on foot. Each day, they were making the widening circles around Silver Hills and so far hadn't seen anyone or anything suspicious. Before the meeting was adjourned, Gunny asked if anyone had anything else.

"I do," Rob said. "I noticed that the vehicle ditches are only about ten yards from the fences. Aren't you worried attackers may be able to use them for cover and concealment?"

"That's a good question, Rob. I was thinkin' 'bout that, too. To answer your question, yes, they might be able to use them, but the guards in the towers should be able to see 'em. We pro'ly ought to add some more towers, just to be sure, but I think the protection the ditches give us from a vehicle attack far outweighs the small advantage they may provide to any MZB's," Gunny said almost eloquently.

By midday Friday, the brush cutting was done, and Ted's crew started helping with the ditches. They started in the back on one side and worked toward the front. Their crew wasn't as large as the other two, and they had to move the dirt further, so they didn't make a lot of progress. However, every little bit helped. Mark made a point to tell each person how much everyone appreciated his or her work.

The weather was unseasonably hot by the end of the week, and it had also become more humid each day. Between the hard work, the hot weather, and the stress of an impending attack, everyone was tired, sore, and cranky. Mark thought they should take Sunday off, even though they wouldn't be finished. He talked to everyone about it at the meeting on Friday night, and they all agreed that a day off would be a good thing. One thing he hadn't said was that maybe there would be no attack since the week was almost over. With each moment that passed, he felt more and more like they had dodged a bullet. Not that they shouldn't finish what they had started. At some point, he was sure the defenses would be needed, but thankfully, perhaps not for a while. He suspected some of the others were feeling the same, but it seemed as if no one wanted to verbalize their hopes, just in case doing so might jinx their good fortune.

The next morning, Mark received a pleasant surprise. Curt showed up to help with the defenses. Mark made sure the lawman was assigned to his team. The two men worked side by side, talking on their breaks about families, hobbies, and anything else they could think of that didn't remind them of the chaotic mess the world around them had become. By two o'clock, it had become a scorcher, and no one could work more than fifteen or twenty minutes without a break.

Mark and Curt walked over to get a cup of water and stand in the shade for a few minutes.

"Man, I can't believe how hot it is," Curt said, as he took a big drink.

"I know," Mark replied. "It's almost like The Burst stopped the calendar and it's August twentieth instead of November the eighth. I bet we're setting a record today. I just hope somebody somewhere is keeping up with such things for posterity's sake."

"I know what you mean, but I wouldn't bet on it. From what I can gather, the Federal Government is just barely keeping their heads above water, and I suspect tracking the weather is pretty low on the priority list right now."

Mark decided to broach a subject the two men had been trying to steer clear of all day. "How bad of shape is the government in?"

"I don't really know many facts, just what I can pick up here and there. From what I hear and what I can see, I'd say it's pretty desperate. That scares me a little, because if the Feds think they're losing control, they may try anything to…"

"What are you two doing?" Susan interrupted, as she walked under the canopy. She stopped right beside Mark, almost pushing him over, so that she was directly facing the Sheriff.

"We're taking a water break, Susan," Mark answered, annoyed that she interrupted Curt just when he was getting to the interesting part.

"I see," she cooed. "Sheriff, I really want to thank you for coming out to help us. It's so kind of you. I can see now why people speak so highly of you."

Mark almost couldn't believe it. He watched Susan, expecting her to start batting her eyelashes at Curt any second. Was she interested in him, too? Rumor was she was dating the president of the bank before The Burst. Mark deduced that she'd go after any man in a position of authority. He was almost disgusted, as he saw her make goo-goo eyes at the tall, thin lawman.

He was glad he'd never noticed her doing that to him. It was sickening the way she was throwing herself at him. He looked at Curt. If Curt noticed, he sure wasn't letting on. Mark was sure Curt was no stranger to women throwing themselves at him. As he understood, it happened all the time to peace officers. Something about the uniform, he guessed. He noticed that Curt spoke with the flirt as if he were giving her directions or a speeding ticket. He was all business, or maybe Curt was just as clueless as he was. Perhaps most men needed a woman to translate for them like Jess had done for him.

Mark listened to them make small talk, as he wondered which group Curt fell into. He barely heard the words, but he could hear Susan's sweet southern drawl and the sheriff's courteous but cool demeanor.

In the middle of one of Susan's advances, Mark felt a cool breeze come from behind him. It hit his sweaty shirt and instantly cooled him off. It felt as if it was the first breeze of the day. It really wasn't, he knew, but it was the coolest and strongest one he could remember. Mark noticed that Susan had stopped talking and that Curt had picked his arms up parallel to the ground to take full advantage of the wind. He thought to do the same, but with Susan beside him, he could only pick up one arm.

He started to take a step to the side when he heard a sickening, wet smack. It instantly took him back to his junior high school days, when he was an undersized seventh grader and the titan-like eighth graders would pop him with damp towels as he tried to shower after gym class. The memory engulfed Mark in a feeling of total helplessness he didn't enjoy.

When Mark saw Curt recoil, he came back to the here and now. 'Who popped Curt with a towel?' he wondered. No one could have. The lawman crumpled to the ground, and Mark's brain calculated what had happened just at the instant that his ears received confirmation that he was right. The gunshot echoed back off of the nearest house and spurred him to drop down.

Mark hit the ground just as another bullet screamed past him. The sound of the shot's muzzle blast came at least a full second later. He tried to figure where the thunderous boom had come from but could only guess at more than a general direction.

"Everybody, get down!" he yelled. He looked around to see men diving for cover. He looked back at Curt. It was obviously hopeless. The lawman looked like a busted balloon, transformed from a full, happy being into an empty shell that had the life exploded out of it. He looked to his left and saw Susan's legs and feet. He looked up at her face and saw her standing there frozen. She was staring at Curt like a magician had just made him disappear and she couldn't quite figure out the secret of the trick. Mark realized that, although Susan was veteran of several battles, she'd never looked directly into the face of death.

"Susan, get down!" He reached up for her hand to pull her down. He heard another smack, and his face was covered in something that felt like warm oil. He wiped his eyes and spit the thick, salty liquid from his lips. When he could see, Susan was no longer standing next to him. She was in a heap, like a broken, forgotten toy. Mark heard the last gasp of air leak out of her, and he knew that she, like Curt, was gone.

Mark turned his attention back to the direction he thought the shots had come from. Some of the guards were returning fire. He hoped they had a better bead on the attackers than he did. He heard a few more shots from the gun that sounded like a cannon, as they echoed across the field and then back off of the houses behind him. The constant popping of the guards' AK-47s rebuffed his attempt to zero in on the perpetrators. As quickly as it had started, it was over. The firing stopped, and the high pitched exhaust notes of small, two-cycle engines, the kind used on dirt bikes, could be heard in the distance.

Mark looked back at the two casualties. Just seconds ago, the three of them had been standing here talking. How was it possible they were dead? Who could do this? Who would do this? Fear chilled him down to his very core. The only thing that stopped it was a tiny spark of anger that started in the center of his being. That spark spread outward at lightning speed until the anger overwhelmed him.

He jumped to his feet and shook his fist in the direction the shots had come from. He heard his voice shouting endless obscenities at the faceless killers, daring them to come back and face him like a man. He felt hands pulling on him and voices trying to calm him, but it only enraged him more. He screamed at the top of his lungs, like a wounded animal, and thrashed his body to rid it of the restraining hands. His hatred, although he didn't know for whom, was pure and perfect. He knew it would burn in him until he made this right or he died, whichever came first. After what seemed an eternity, but in fact was only a few moments, he was quiet. He quit fighting the calming hands and stood still, looking across the field the silent death had crossed to do its evil bidding. He started to shake, just a little at first but then uncontrollably. He collapsed to the ground, much as his two comrades had, and cried.

Chapter 65

After a couple of minutes, Mark pulled himself together and stood. He looked around and saw several people standing around. Mark didn't see anyone with dry eyes. Others were running toward them, and he saw Gunny doing a stiff-legged run, as he barked into one of the walkie-talkies. Guards were scurrying to and fro. Mark was sure it was in response to Gunny's instructions. They kept scanning the horizon, as they jumped into the freshly dug foxholes. Mark could hear Gunny's raspy voice as he got closer.

"Get down!" he yelled. "Have you all lost your marbles? They may not be gone. Get down now!"

Mark was sure the old man was wrong. The snipers had left. Somehow, he knew it. He felt someone gently push him down, and, too tired to fight, he complied. Mark looked and saw Gunny roll under the fence and then crawl, with surprising agility, the twenty-five feet to where he was.

"What happened?" Gunny asked when he got next to Mark.

"We were standing here talking when they hit Curt. They must have been a long ways off because the sound of the shot came way after the bullet. Susan froze, and I tried to pull her down. They hit her just as I was reaching for her hand."

"Where were they?"

"I'm not sure. Somewhere over there." Mark used his hand to point out a wide area across the field.

Gunny keyed the radio again. "Did any of you in the towers see anything?"

The radio crackled. "Gunny, this is Steve Parsons in Tower Five. I saw two guys get up from all the way across the field and run into the brush. They were just a little ways down from the back corner. Holy crap, that has to be over a half of a mile, Gunny. Who could shoot that far?"

"That's what we gotta find out, Tower Five. Thank you," Gunny said, meaning he didn't want to discuss it over the radio.

Gunny spoke into the radio again and had the CP relay a message to Billy. A few minutes later, the CP called to say that the old cowboy and his men were in position and the area looked clear. Gunny radioed back, and Mark could see Billy and his boys ride out of the brush on the south side of the big field. They spread out, side by side, and walked their horses down the far edge of the plot looking for signs of the perpetrators. Finally, one man threw up his hand. Everyone stopped and backed their horses up and then rode to where that man was. The cowboys dismounted and walked to look at the spot. A moment later, Gunny's radio cracked.

"They found it, Gunny," the man at the CP relayed. "They said it looks like there were two of them and there are some tracks leading southwest."

"Tell them to stay put and not to disturb anything."

"Roger that."

"Any word back from the sheriff's office?" the security chief asked, as he stood up. Everyone followed his lead.

"Yes, they have a car coming with a couple of deputies. They're going to pick up Dr. Ken on the way."

"Okay, call me when they get here." Gunny clipped the little radio to his belt.

Greg and Rob arrived at the site, and their faces drained of all color when they saw Curt. Mark looked at the others who were gathered around and noticed that most of the men were fixated on Susan and doing their best not to cry. Mark had heard of this happening in combat. If a female got killed, the men would stop and stare at the body, not able to accept the fact that she was dead like they could with a man. Mark had to agree that, as disturbing as it was to see anyone killed, looking at the dead woman, who he'd fought with side by side, bothered him more. Mark had to make himself look away from her crumpled body. He saw Rob shake his head, as if to wake himself up, and then the ex-policeman took on a cold, clinical look Mark was sure was the result of years of training.

"Tell me exactly what happened," he requested.

Mark gave him the same sequence of events he'd given to Gunny.

"Where were you standing?" Rob asked.

"Right here beside Susan." Mark pointed at the spot.

"Lucky shooting," one of the helpers from outside the neighborhood said.

"I don't think it was luck," Rob said. "They shot from almost a half mile away. It took someone with considerable skill to make a shot from that distance. I think he hit Curt on purpose."

"Why would someone want to kill Curt?" Greg asked.

"And Susan?" someone added.

"That's the question, isn't it?" Rob said matter-of-factly, as he looked at the bodies without touching them. "Since Curt was shot first, I'd say he was their target. You don't stay in law enforcement as long as Curt did and not make a few enemies. The other shots were probably just to create confusion, so the snipers could get away. Since Susan froze, she was just a target of opportunity." He said it as if he were giving a boring lecture to a bunch of disinterested college freshmen. He squatted down next to Curt. "This is strange," he said more to himself than anyone else.

"What's that?" Gunny asked.

"The bullets hit them both through the chest cavity at about the same place, in through one side and out the other. Susan has damage to both arms, but Curt's arms weren't hit at all."

"That's because his arms were up, like this," Mark demonstrated.

"Why?"

"There was a nice breeze just before he was shot, and he picked up his arms to let it cool him off."

"Which way did the wind come from?" Rob asked, as if he were disturbed by Mark's revelation. His all-business disposition melted into one of confusion.

"That way." Mark pointed behind him. He saw Rob and Gunny exchange a glance that he didn't understand.

More and more people were coming.

"Gunny, can you get some of your guys to keep everyone back?" Rob asked.

The old devil dog barked at several men, and they formed a line and pushed the onlookers back. Gunny was looking at them when Jim came running up behind the human barricade.

502

"Rob," Gunny said softly, "Jim's one of the best long range shooters I've ever seen. You want to see what he thinks?"

"Yeah."

Gunny told one of the guys to let Jim through. He walked up to the now small group standing by the bodies. Mark noticed that the sight of Susan's body had the same effect on him as it had most of the men. "What happened?" he finally asked, swallowing hard.

Rob told him Mark's story, almost word for word.

"Where were the shooters?" Jim asked.

"Over by Billy and his boys," Gunny answered, as he pointed west.

Jim put his hand to his forehead to shield his eyes from the relentless sun. "Holy crap, Gunny, that's over a thousand yards!"

The old Marine nodded his head.

"Mark said there was gust of wind from the south just before Curt was shot."

Jim's head snapped around to look at Mark. "How strong was it?"

"I don't know," Mark answered in an aggravated manor.

"Ten, fifteen miles an hour?" the sharpshooter prodded.

"Somewhere in there, yeah."

"How long did it last?"

The anger was coming back, but now it was directed at Jim. What was it with these guys and the wind? Couldn't they see two people were dead? Two people he was friends with? He didn't mean to, but he found himself yelling at his friend.

"What difference does it make? Curt and Susan are dead. The wind isn't going to bring them back. Just forget the fucking wind, okay?"

Jim took a deep breath and slowly blew it out. He looked at Gunny and then Rob. They both gave him a single nod. "Mark," he said, turning his head back to his friend, "the reason we're interested in the wind is that we don't think the snipers were trying to kill Curt. We think they wanted to kill you."

A hot knife couldn't have pierced Mark's heart like those words did. His knees buckled a little, and Gunny had to steady him. Curt and Susan were dead because of him? Who would have wanted to kill him? And why? A thousand thoughts ran through his mind in a millisecond. Jim explained how the wind had pushed the bullet off of its intended course. Mark knew what had happened the second Jim had said the bullet was aimed at him, but he let his friend explain. Hearing anything was better than listening to the doubts, fears, and questions running through his mind.

Jess showed up at the fence and called Mark. He walked over to her, trying not to show the fear on his face that he felt in his heart.

"Is it true? Are Susan and Curt dead?" she asked.

He nodded his head. He was afraid to speak. If he started, he might not be able to stop, and he certainly didn't want to tell her he was the one who was supposed to be dead.

Jess burst into tears. He hugged her as best he could across the barbed wire fence. After a couple of minutes, she pulled herself together.

"What about Susan's boys? They don't know yet, do they? You want Lisa and me to go talk to them? Should I bring them to our house?"

Mark hadn't even thought about the boys. This was going to be as hard on them as it had been on Timmy and Tommy when they lost their parents.

"Yeah, I think so. Thanks. Why don't you get Brother Bob to go with you and Lisa? And wherever you and Lisa think they should stay until we find someone to take them permanently is okay with me."

She turned to leave and then turned back around. "Are you okay?"

"I will be," he promised.

When the deputies arrived with Dr. Ken, they pushed everyone back and let the doctor look at the bodies. When they saw the sheriff, the younger deputy became emotional, and Mark noticed he had to swallow hard several times. The older one didn't seem affected at all. Mark figured he was and just wasn't showing it because of his experience. Mark also found out that the good doctor was also the Wilson County Medical Examiner. The older deputy pulled a small notebook out of his pocket and started asking questions. Mark recognized him as the one who had resentfully babysat the trucks after his rolling shootout with the MZB's. He hadn't been very happy, having to sit there until the crime scene photographer could come take pictures that hot day. Mark was the first one he questioned. Ralph had come over and was standing with Mark as he answered. Any time Mark began to volunteer anything, he felt the beefy paw of the big lawyer on his shoulder telling him not to say anything more. Mark was slightly annoyed that Ralph wouldn't let him tell the deputy what he thought, but he shut up when told. He noticed the sourpuss deputy only asked for the bare facts and didn't follow up on anything Mark tried to say before Ralph stopped him. It seemed a little strange to Mark, but he figured the investigator had his reasons. When the deputy, whose nameplate said 'Barnes,' was finished with his questions, he tersely thanked Mark while completely ignoring Ralph and moved on to see who else had witnessed the attack.

Mark turned to Ralph. "What was that about? Why wouldn't you let me say anything?"

"Because I don't trust that son-of-a-bitch," Ralph whispered.

"Why not?"

"I'll tell you later."

The Deputy asked several times if anyone had seen anything. Many people had heard the shots, but it appeared Mark was the only one to see Curt and Susan actually shot. Rob started to tell the investigator about the wind and the probability that Mark was the primary target, but the deputy cut him off.

"Rob, I know Curt was your friend and that you helped him from time to time, but unless you directly witnessed something, just be quiet. I'm not interested in your theories. You need to let the Sheriff's Department run this investigation. Clear?"

"Crystal," Rob replied shortly.

Mark didn't know why Ralph didn't like Barnes, but it looked like there was no love lost between him and Rob, either. In fact, Mark was beginning to dislike him, too. The deputy trudged across the field to see the spot Billy had found. When he got there, he ran the horsemen off with some wild waves of his arms and started looking the area over. In the meantime, the photographer had arrived, and Dr. Ken was telling him what pictures he wanted of the bodies. As the cameraman started to shoot the grisly shots, Dr. Ken walked over to the group who'd had been watching him.

"Mark, I understand you saw what happened?" the doctor asked.

Mark nodded his head.

"Did Curt have his hands up over his head?"

"No. He had them out like this." Mark demonstrated again. "There was breeze, and he was trying to cool off a little."

"That explains it," Doctor Ken said.

"Yeah, Rob noticed it, too." Mark nodded in the ex-policeman's direction.

The doctor looked at Rob like he couldn't quite place him, then his face indicated he'd figured it out.

"Of course, you're Curt's cop friend from his neighborhood."

Rob nodded.

"I've never seen damage from a single gunshot like that," the doctor said. "Have you?"

"No, Doc, I haven't, but then, I was with SWAT, and we didn't do much in the way of investigation."

"Well, hopefully, I'll be able to tell more as I do the autopsies."

The younger deputy walked up with two body bags. He and the doctor went back to the remains. They waited for the photographer to finish, and then, as respectfully as possible, donned gloves and put the bodies into the bags. The photographer spoke briefly into his radio and then trudged over to the other side of the field.

After Barnes ran them off, Billy and his boys had crossed the field, leading their horses. Billy and his foreman, José, came over to where Mark was standing with the other men.

"Sorry to hear about the Sheriff and Susan," Billy said. Even his eyes were on the moist side. "I didn't know either one of them well, but Curt was as good as they come, from what everyone said, and that Susan, she had a lot of spunk."

Mark thought that was a nice way to put it. "Yes," he agreed, "she sure did. We didn't always agree on everything, but we sure are going to miss her. She was a valuable asset to us." He saw everyone nodding their heads. "And I don't know what we're going to do without Curt," he continued. "He was the one the whole county looked to and depended on to get us through this mess. I hadn't known him that long, but I can truly say that he was my friend."

There was a long silence.

"What did you see over there?" Rob finally asked, as he pointed to where the shots had come from.

"We were told by the guy on the radio not to get too close to where they were, so we didn't. We could see two sets of footprints coming in and going out and the place where they lay down to shoot. Other than that, we really couldn't tell." Billy's voice changed. "What's the deal with that asshole deputy? I know he just lost his boss, but there's no reason for him to act like that. We were at least seven or eight yards from the tracks, and he goes off on us for messing up his crime scene. It didn't even seem like he was sad."

"He's probably not," Greg said, halfway under his breath.

"What do you mean?" Mark asked.

"I mean he probably figures someone just did him a big favor."

505

"How's that?"

Greg took a deep breath. "His name is Fred Barnes. He's the lieutenant, which is the highest ranking deputy. He's also the nephew of the sheriff Curt worked for when he first moved to Wilson County. When Hank Barnes, Fred's uncle, was getting ready to retire, it was a foregone conclusion that Curt, who'd worked his way up to lieutenant by then, was going to get his job. Hank made Curt promise to look after his nephew, who was just a rookie at the time. You know how Curt was about a promise? Barnes has been a pain in the neck for Curt ever since. He never did anything, or maybe I should say never got caught doing anything, bad enough to disqualify him from being a deputy or to keep him from receiving promotions based on his time served. However, to say his ethics are a little questionable is being generous."

"I'll say," Ralph interjected. "He beat the crap out of one of my cousins and a friend of his once. Claimed they attacked him. They said otherwise, but they were legally drunk at the time, so the county prosecutor, who just happened to be friends with Big Hank, didn't think they made good witnesses, and he refused to prosecute the son-of-a-bitch."

"That's a pretty typical story in the career of Fred Barnes," Greg said. "Curt would have fired him if anyone could have gotten charges to stick, but Fred's a lot smarter than he looks. Plus, with his uncle's influence, a lot of people looked the other way. Anyway, even though Curt wouldn't fire him, he still made him do his share of the dirty work. That's a fact Fred didn't like. So, I don't think he's that sad. The jerk probably thinks he's going to be sheriff now. I doubt he'll even break a sweat trying to figure out who did it, but even if he does stumble over the killer, he'll probably just give him a medal for getting Curt out of his way."

Dr. Ken and the young deputy had recruited two men to help them, and they were carrying one of the body bags to the ambulance. The group of talking men grew silent as they passed. They watched as the body was placed gingerly aboard and as the helpers made a second trip for the other bag. When both bodies were loaded, Dr. Ken came back over to the tightly knit group.

"I'll let you know if I find out anything," the doctor said as if he was reading their minds.

"Thanks, Ken," Greg said.

Doctor Ken climbed into the passenger side of the ambulance, and it drove off.

A few minutes later, Barnes and the photographer came back. As they passed the men, Barnes looked over and nodded his head at them.

"Rob," he acknowledged the former policeman. His actions were right, but his demeanor said he didn't mean it. His voice was semi-cheery, and the big smile on his face was out of place.

"Barney," Rob said back flatly.

Barnes face twisted up immediately, almost as if he were in pain. His steps became stomps, as he headed straight to his car and left.

"What was that about?" Jim asked.

"A couple of years ago, Curt asked me to help him set up a team of his deputies who could function as a SWAT team. They'd have their normal duties and drive their own squad cars, but if they were needed, they could work just like a big city team. Fred thought since he was the lieutenant, he should be the team leader. Curt agreed to let him try out for it but told him the final decision was mine. Well, Fred didn't have the skills it took to even be on the team, let alone be team leader. I cut him, and he hasn't exactly been friendly towards me since."

"I meant why'd he get so mad when you called him 'Barney'?"

Rob smiled. "I found out from the guy I picked to be team leader that when Fred was a rookie, he responded to a domestic violence call way out in the country. When he got there and got out of his car, this big, mean-ass dog comes charging at him. Fred got scared and went to pull his service revolver. Before he even cleared leather, he fired his weapon and shot himself through the calf. The old timers started calling him 'Barney' after Barney Fife. No one calls him that to his face anymore since he's the lieutenant, but he pissed me off, and I don't have to work with him."

As sad as things were, all of the men had a good laugh.

"Let's go see what we can tell from where the shooters were," Gunny said.

The men walked across the large field, each one deep in thought and mourning. When they reached the snipers' site, it was evident that Fred Barnes had been smiling like the cat that ate the canary for a reason. The place where the snipers had shot from had been wiped clean of tracks and impressions. Rob was so mad Mark thought he might pop a gasket.

The footprints, coming in and going out of the field, though, were still mostly intact. The men followed them until they found the spot where the getaway vehicles had been parked. The tracks weren't those that would have been made by a two-wheeled dirt bike with skinny tires. They were fat and had been made by something with four tires.

Mark and Jim looked at each other.

"Look at this!" José exclaimed. He'd forged ahead of everyone else, following the four-wheeler tracks, as they headed toward the road. He bent over and picked up something. "This thing's a monster! I've never seen one this big."

As he turned and showed it to the other men, it was obviously an empty cartridge case. It was a very large case, in fact, a .50 caliber Browning machine gun case. The same cartridge used in a Barrett M82A1 rifle. That was the kind of long-range rifle that sat in the armory of the New Age Ranch.

Chapter 66

"I don't give a rat's ass what Barney might do! I'm going!" Mark was yelling at his friends again. He wasn't mad at them, but it had been an emotional day, and he was passionate about what he wanted to do. It was almost dark now, and they were at his house.

"Mark, I'm not trying to talk you out of it," Rob explained. "I just want to make sure you understand everything that could happen. Barney told me he didn't want to hear any theories, and that's all we've got right now. Even if he would listen to us, I wouldn't expect him to do anything about it. I don't feel the slightest inclination to tell the son-of-a-bitch anything, but, if push comes to shove, we could possibly be charged with obstruction of justice."

Mark took a deep breath. "Sorry for raising my voice. I understand what you're telling me. I also agree that the Sheriff's Department isn't going to do anything. Does anyone think we shouldn't go see what's going on at the Ranch?"

All of the heads shook negative responses. The fact was, it was too big of a coincidence that Mr. Davis's ranch had .50 BMG rifles and running four-wheelers.

"Then who's going with me?" Mark asked.

"Hold your horses, there, Karate Man. Who decided you were going?" Gunny challenged.

Mark took a deep breath, preparing to yell again but caught himself at the last second. "I'm going because I'm the one Mr. Davis wants dead," he said flatly.

"That don't mean you're the best one for the job. In fact…"

"Gunny, I'm going. End of story," Mark said flatly. "Now, am I going alone, or is someone going with me?"

Every man on the porch volunteered to go. After several minutes of spirited discussion, it was decided that Chaparo and Rob would accompany Mark. They'd take the MZB truck and leave at two in the morning. The plan was to drive within five miles of the backside of the ranch and then to hike in and be at the ranch by sunup. They'd do their recon and then be back home before dark. The MZB truck was chosen in case they were discovered and had to leave it behind. They would take the scout radio and a little food in case their exit strategy went to hell. Three alternate rendezvous points were set up that would be checked if they weren't home by midnight. The radio was just in case that plan backfired, too.

With the details worked out, the three man recon team wanted to get some sleep, so the meeting was adjourned. Rob was invited to spend the night at Chaparo's house, which he graciously accepted. Mark went inside his house, followed by Mike.

"Hey, Bro, tell me again why this Davis character has such a sore spot toward you?"

"He invited me and Jim to come live at his ranch. It's a real survivalist's dream. It has everything for a hundred people or so to make it for years. The

509

catch was we couldn't bring any of our extended families. We respectfully declined his offer, and he went ballistic."

"Why would he want to kill you for that? It doesn't make sense," Mike said.

"Since when did crazy people have to make sense?"

"Is he really nuts?"

"That was the rumor at work, before The Burst," Mark explained. "I never met him until we went to the ranch, but by the way he reacted when we said no, I'd say he's certifiable."

"Well, you be careful, little brother. You seem to have acquired quite a knack for finding trouble. You should know I didn't walk all the way here just to see you killed."

"I'll be careful. I promise."

*   *   *

Oh-two-thirty found the recon team heading southwest. They stayed off of the major highways as much as possible. A few times, there was no choice but to use one of the main roads. These short legs of the trip were quite eye opening. Mark hadn't realized how insulated from the violence they'd been. Almost every home and business close enough to the road for them to see in the moonlight had been burned. Forsaken roadblocks had been pushed aside, and vehicles that must have been running after The Burst were shot up and abandoned every few miles. The three men were sitting on pins and needles whenever they were on one of these roads. Whether it was because of the time of the day, or because all of the ne'er-do-wells were dead, Mark, Rob, and Chaparo didn't see anyone.

By four o'clock, they had parked and covered the truck with brush to hide it. This was a task made easier by Jim, who had stayed up and spray painted some camouflaging stripes on the body and taped over all of the shiny surfaces of the truck with flat black duct tape.

Each man grabbed his pack and weapon and headed in the direction indicated by Chaparo's compass. It took almost two hours to traverse the four miles in the pale moonlight. The trek wasn't difficult, but the team moved cautiously and quietly. Just as the sky was turning pink in the east, they reached the still shiny new fence. Mark could see the trail where the four wheelers had killed the grass next to the fence, but it looked like the grass was starting to grow again. Perhaps they weren't patrolling the outside fence any longer. Gunny had said it was a waste of time trying to watch eight or ten miles of fence line. Maybe Mr. Davis had figured that out.

The eight foot tall fence, with its three strands of barbed wire along the top, was intimidating looking, patrols or no patrols. The tightly-woven mesh that made up the bottom six feet gave no place for a toehold. The heavy, sharp four-point barbed wire at the top would make it almost impossible to pull oneself over the fence with just arm power. Chaparo took off his pack and pulled out three small, aluminum items.

"What's that?" Mark asked.

"They're called Lobo Hi-Steppers. Watch this."

The big man attached the lightweight steps to the metal T-shaped fence post. They stuck out three or four inches on each side of the fence and provided

510

an adequate foothold. Chaparo placed one about every two feet, then climbed over the fence with ease.

"Throw me your packs."

The two men on the outside threw the packs over the fence, and Chaparo caught them. Next, Mark climbed to the top of the fence and steadied himself there, as Rob checked to make sure the safety on each rifle was engaged and then handed them to him. He handed them back down to Chaparo. He climbed down, Rob scurried over the fence, and Chaparo removed the Hi-Steppers and put them back into his pack.

They moved toward the compound in the middle of the ranch, moving slower and more cautiously as they got closer. When they topped a small rise and could see the living complex, it looked deserted. When Mark had visited, many of the residents were up and doing their chores by this time. He took out his binoculars and pulled them to his eyes, careful not to lift them where they might reflect the rising sun. Mark wondered if they should have come in with the sun to their backs, but that would have put them close to the road leading into the compound.

He slowly scanned the compound and saw that foxholes had been dug inside the fence every hundred yards or so. That was another recommendation Gunny had made. Mark wondered if Old Man Davis had somehow bugged him and incorporated all of Gunny's recommendations into his security measures. Mark looked for guards in the holes, but either there were none, or they were well hidden. He continued looking, trying to figure out what was out of place. When he looked at the garden, it was apparent that it had been neglected. Weeds were choking out some of the plants, and others were already dead and brown. Mark looked back at the cabins and noticed the grass around them wasn't manicured like it had been for their visit. Perhaps things other than landscaping had taken a priority, but for Mr. Davis to let the garden go seemed strange.

Mark continued to glass the compound. He looked at where the vehicles were parked. They were in the parking area, but not perfectly aligned as he remembered them. Some of the three-quarter and one-ton pickups were missing, but all four of the newer Jeeps were still here. One of them had some damage to the front fender, but the others still looked like new. There were four vehicles Mark was pretty sure hadn't been here before. That only made sense. They probably belonged to some of the new people Mr. Davis had recruited. Maybe one of them belonged to the shooter. Mark quickly studied each one to see if he could tell anything about the owners. The first was an old Dodge Ram Charger. Mark stared at it, but he didn't even know what he was looking for. The next car was an early seventies model Ford Torino. The third one really caught his eye. It was a Jeep CJ-5, a slightly smaller version of his Jeep. In the early morning shadows, he could just make out that it was painted camouflage like it had been used on a deer lease.

Mark squinted his eyes trying to make the distant image clearer. With each passing moment, the rising sun made the colors of the vehicles change from gray shades to the color they really were, and with each of those passing moments his blood boiled hotter and hotter until he was positive.

"That son-of-a-bitch," he whispered hatefully through clenched teeth.

"What?" Rob asked.

"That older Jeep down there belongs to my gun dealer friends who were killed a few weeks back. I don't know how Davis found out about them, but he's the one who killed them and stole their inventory."

"Are you sure?" Chaparo asked, as he held out his big hand in a request for the binoculars.

Mark handed them over. "Yes, I'm sure. It's their Jeep. I drove them down to Cotulla to get it. Somehow I knew it was him. When we found that striped .308 brass that came out of an HK-91 at the Watson's place, I knew it was him," he said, as he shook his head from side to side.

Chaparo handed the binoculars to Rob, and he looked over the compound for a couple of minutes. It looked like the place was empty. The sun was fully over the horizon now, and they had yet to see a person.

"What do you think, Mark?" Chaparo asked.

"I don't know. Maybe we should go in for a closer look."

"Couldn't hurt to get a little closer, I guess."

Mark started to push himself up off of the ground when Rob's hand grabbed his arm. "Mark, wait. Somebody's coming out of one of the cabins."

Mark dropped back down. "Where?" he asked.

"Second cabin from the right. Here, use these." Rob gave the field glasses back to Mark.

He put them up to his eyes. With their aid, he could see that the figure was dressed in camouflage clothing. It was the "Multicam" camo Mr. Davis had bought for his guards. It seemed big on the person they were watching. The figure also looked nervous. It looked from side to side several times before it came completely out of the cabin. Then she, Mark assumed it was a she from the size and the way the figure moved, walked gingerly across the front porch and looked around again. After making sure no one was around, she briskly walked across the compound to the garden. Once there, she hid in the overgrown plants for a moment and rechecked behind her for several minutes. Mark saw her drop down to the ground. The undergrowth around the fence kept him from seeing her for several minutes. When she popped into view again, she was on his side of the fence. One quick glance over her shoulder, and she was headed away from the compound at a brisk pace.

"What was that about?" Chaparo asked.

"Looks like a prison break to me," Rob said. "Did you recognize him, Mark?"

"I think it's a her, but I couldn't tell who it is. I'm thinking it could be one of the Watson women. They were missing when we found the men. Mr. Davis may have had them brought back here."

"Well, let's go get her. She can probably tell us more about this place in five minutes than we could learn watching for a week."

"Let's go. I'm in front," Mark said, as he picked up his rifle and backed down the hill. The men moved at a quick jog on an interception angle to the escapee. They had to stop a couple of times to reacquire their hard-to-see target and adjust their bearing. While the woman wasn't moving fast, she was keeping a steady pace. That, combined with the head start, made catching up with her harder than Mark had thought it would be.

The three men didn't want to shout at the woman, in case someone else might be in the area. Finally, after what seemed like more than a mile, they were within normal talking distance. The woman had given no sign that she knew they were there. She had stayed on her deliberate course, and the soft ground had allowed the men to approach with little sound. When Mark was about fifty feet away, he spoke to the woman.

"Hey! Wait up. We want to talk to you."

The woman spun around with shock in her eyes. Mark couldn't see the rest of her face. It was covered with a dark colored bandana. The wide eyes narrowed, and she turned back and sprinted away. Mark handed his rifle to Rob behind him without breaking stride. When he felt Rob grab it, he accelerated to catch the fleeing female. Her top speed was no match for his. In less than a minute, he'd closed the gap and grabbed her by the arm. He'd expected her to struggle, but to his surprise, she stopped.

She started turning to face him. He released his grip, so she wouldn't think he was trying to hurt her and started to tell her that they meant her no harm. As she turned counterclockwise, he saw that her right arm was coming around as if she was going to hit him with a windmill punch. He almost laughed. The woman weighed no more than a hundred and ten pounds. Even if she connected with the swinging punch, it would do no more than cause him mild discomfort, and the chance of her connecting was slim, since he was already starting to lean back out of the range of her arm. Then the laugh caught in his throat.

In her hand was the biggest butcher knife he had ever seen. It really wasn't the biggest, he realized, but the fact that it was being swung at his face made it look twice its actual size. The extra twelve inches of reach the blade gave to this small woman made leaning back out of the way a fifty-fifty proposition at best. He jerked his feet off of the ground as his arms came up in front of his face. It seemed to him that gravity had ceased to work, as he hung suspended in the air while the large piece of kitchen cutlery rapidly circled to make his acquaintance. Just when it looked as if the knife would cut at least one of his arms, someone turned the pull of the earth back on, and the knife sliced harmlessly over his head. The ground that had seemed so soft that it made running difficult didn't seem at all soft as he landed on his lower back. The wind rushed out of his lungs on impact, and the breathless state he found himself in forbade him to move. As the woman whirled around three hundred and sixty degrees from the momentum, he heard her shriek.

"You can't make me go back!"

Mark, able to take his eyes off of the huge knife for a moment, saw the look in her eyes. They held the look of a cornered animal. She was frightened and enraged at the same time. Those eyes told him she had nothing to lose and would fight to the death to keep from going back to what she was escaping.

"I won't go back!" She raised the knife high over her head and stepped in to drive it through him. He was powerless. Having the breath knocked out him had temporarily paralyzed him. Just as he knew his number was up, the look in her eyes changed to one of disbelief.

"Mark?" she whispered.

He couldn't answer her in his breathless state, not that it mattered. A split second later, a freight train named Chaparo slammed into her. The knife went flying one way and the woman another.

Mark got some of his wind back and scrambled to his feet to see the woman gasping like a fish out of water. Chaparo was standing over her like a fisherman trying to decide whether to throw her back or put her on the stringer. Mark walked over and looked down at the woman.

"It's okay, Chaparo," he said, breathing hard, as he studied her. She was the right size to be Debbie Watson, Tony's wife. "She knows me. Don't you?"

She nodded her head, still unable to talk.

"Are you Debbie Watson?" he asked hopefully.

She shook her head from side to side and pulled the bandana off of her face. Mark thought he recognized her, but he wasn't sure until she removed the camouflaged hat, and her long, blonde hair fell down onto her shoulders. It was the office worrywart, Suzy Sullivan. Only she didn't look like herself. She was fifteen or twenty pounds leaner, and her always-immaculate hair was unkempt and had about four inches of brunette showing at the roots. Mark wondered what kind of ordeal would have changed Suzy from the type of woman who would climb up on a chair at the sight of a mouse to the type who would fight a man almost twice her size.

"Suzy, what happened? Why are you running away?" He helped her up.

She held up one finger while she tried to take in enough air to speak. When she did, she didn't answer his questions. She had questions of her own. "How can you be here? He told us you were dead. They all got drunk last night celebrating. He said he saw the bullet hit you. He described it over and over again as he got drunker and drunker. He said Bullseye's first bullet missed and hit someone else, but that the second shot hit, and you dropped like a rock. I didn't think he was lying. He seemed way too happy about it to be lying."

Mark was shocked at this revelation. Why would Mr. Davis say he'd been hit? Mark looked questioningly at Rob.

"It makes sense, Mark," Rob answered, without hearing the question. "You said you dropped down to the ground just as the second bullet whistled by. He must have thought you were hit."

Mark nodded his head. Of course it made sense. He looked back at Suzy. "He missed me, Suzy. Now, why are you running away?"

"It's horrible, Mark. We're just property to them. Assigned to this one or that one every night, and if we don't do what they say, we get a beating, or worse. I'm not doing it anymore. I decided they could kill me if they caught me, but I wasn't going to do it anymore."

"Where's your husband?"

"They killed him. One of the cretins wanted me, and Paul stood up and said 'Over my dead body.' The asshole pulled a knife and stabbed him. I remember him laughing in Paul's face and saying 'If that's the way you want it, Doc,' as he died." Suzy buried her hands in her face and started weeping uncontrollably. She was still speaking, but it was impossible to make out her words. Mark could only pat her on the back, a gesture he knew did no good. Mark figured Mr. Davis must have gone off the deep end and was recruiting lowlifes to do his dirty work for him. He must have realized he didn't have enough men to defend the ranch and had to take whatever help he could find. Probably some of them had military training. That's where the foxholes had come from. This 'Bullseye' Suzy had mentioned was probably ex-military, too. Davis was probably letting his new recruits have their way with the women to try and keep them in line. It didn't make sense that he'd allow them to kill the doctor, though. Mark supposed it was possible that he was really off his rocker or that he didn't have very good control of his MZB troops. After a few minutes, Suzy pulled herself together.

So many questions were running through Mark's head, he didn't know which one to ask first. He decided he needed to find out about the Watson women.

"Suzy, the woman I thought you were, Debbie Watson, do you know her? She and a bunch of other women and kids would have come with that old camouflaged Jeep they brought back two or three weeks ago."

Mark wouldn't have thought it possible, but the look on Suzy's face saddened even more. "I know who you're talking about," she said despondently. "They killed her. She and two of the others tried to escape. They caught them and shot all three of them in front of everyone to make an example. The other two died from beatings for not giving in to the animals."

"What about all the other women and children who came with them?"

Suzy shook her head. "They only brought five women back from that raid. They only bring back the young ones. I've heard them say they tell the men they'll let the women and children go if they give up. They say they are just going to take them long enough to insure that whoever they're raiding doesn't get any ideas about following them. They take all the women and children and haul them off while the men load up all the supplies. There's less fuss that way, they say. They all co-operate because everyone thinks they're going to be back together. Then, when the men finish doing all the work that the cretins want done, they're killed. They also kill all of the older women and kids they don't want. Most of the women that they bring back are so traumatized after seeing their kids and relatives executed, they're little more than zombies. Those Watson women were fighters, though. They wouldn't give up."

Mark felt the same intense rage he'd felt after seeing Curt and Susan murdered. He choked it down. He couldn't afford to lose control out here.

"Suzy, how many of these cretins does Mr. Davis have?"

Suzy looked at him with a shocked expression. "Mr. Davis is dead. Big 'O' killed him right after he surrendered. That rat bastard used the same kind of tactic on us. Telling us they just wanted some of our supplies and then they'd leave. Yeah, right. Mr. Davis should have never given in. Big 'O' only had twelve or thirteen men then. Now he has over seventy-five. He had more, but he killed eleven of them when they wanted to break away."

Mark was a little shocked. He realized he shouldn't have been. Gunny had said the ranch was vulnerable. Mark had wanted a face to put with his hatred, and that's probably why he'd made himself believe Mr. Davis was at fault. This Big 'O' sounded like a truly evil MZB of the worst sort. Mark started to ask more about him when he heard a horn honking.

"Oh, no," Suzy said. "It's the raiding party coming back from one of their trips. They'll wake up the others, and when they find out I'm missing, they'll come looking for me."

"Then let's get you out of here. We've got a truck, and we'll take you back to Silver Hills with us."

The foursome followed Chaparo's compass back to the truck at a brisk pace. It only took about an hour to traverse the remaining distance. They checked to see if anyone had approached the hidden vehicle, and when they were sure it was secure, they loaded up and drove home. Chaparo drove, and Suzy sat in front. Mark and Rob sat in the bed of the truck. Mark didn't want to crowd her, and being in the back would let them defend themselves better if they were chased. Mark wished they'd brought a few sand bags to stack against the tailgate, just in case. He would have like to be up front with Suzy to ask her questions, but they'd decided that since he and Rob had the more powerful rifles, it made sense for them to be in a position to defend against a vehicle attack. Fortunately, they didn't see anyone on the way home. Unfortunately, Mark had about a million unanswered questions that ran through his mind over and over again.

When they got home with Suzy, the women took over. Lisa examined her, while Jess fixed them all something to eat. Suzy was fed in the clinic, and Mark found out she'd eaten and fallen asleep before he could ask her the questions he wanted. Lisa forbade him to wake her up. She said Suzy had been through enough and needed to get some rest. Lisa felt that she was suffering from post-traumatic stress disorder; probably the result of seeing her husband killed and then being assaulted herself.

Mark, Chaparo, and Rob met with the other official and unofficial members of the security committee and filled them in on what they knew. In order to come up with a plan, they really needed Suzy to fill in some blanks for them. Gunny felt it would be too costly to try and take the compound if they had seventy-five skilled defenders and the security upgrades Mark had seen. Everyone thought it was imperative that the women who were still at the compound be rescued. After discussing it for a while, they came to the conclusion that they had to turn it over to the authorities. Unfortunately, that meant Barney. They had proof now that the shooters had come from the New Age Ranch, and Barnes would have to follow up on the leads.

Mark trudged down to the CP and called the Sheriff's Department. The dispatcher had him stand by for several minutes before she came back onto the radio. Senior Deputy Barnes would try to come by tomorrow afternoon, if his schedule wasn't too busy, she informed Mark. Mark's blood began to boil, but there was no reason to kill the messenger, he thought. He thanked the dispatcher and signed off.

Much to Mark's dismay, Suzy slept for eighteen hours straight. Lisa brought her to the Turner house to eat when she awoke. While Jess and Lisa fed her breakfast, Mark and Gunny sat down behind their plates and prepared to ply her with questions. Mark really wanted to know who this MZB leader was and why he wanted Mark dead, but he decided to let Gunny go first.

"Suzy, you said there are seventy-five guys in the gang at the ranch?"

"Yes, but there could be more now. Sometimes they bring guys back with them from the raids."

"How does that work?"

"I don't know exactly. Guys they meet up with when they're out on raids, I guess. I've heard them talk about making the new guys earn their membership by having to kill somebody. No telling what else they make them do," Suzy said and then shook her head like she didn't want to think about it.

"Tell me about these raids. How often do they go out, and how many men go?"

"It depends, sometimes they go two or three times a week, but usually just once every week or so. They always send out a ten-man group to watch any place they want to hit. Then, when they come back, if it looks like they can take the place with no problem, anywhere from twenty to fifty of them go raid the place. They leave one day and usually come back by the next night."

"I see," Gunny said. "Did they send a team to watch us?"

"Yes. Big 'O' was really mad when they came back earlier than planned. Snuffer, that's the guy who always leads the watchers, said it was too dangerous to hit you all with less than two or three hundred men. Big 'O' was fuming, and he kept telling Snuffer that there had to be a way to do it. Snuffer's the one who always comes up with the attack plans, too. Anyway, Snuffer told him there was no way. Big 'O' asked if he thought they could take out one guy. Snuffer said if he was patient that it would be simple. I didn't know it was supposed to be you, Mark, until Big 'O' and Bullseye came back, and they all got drunk."

Mark could stand it no longer. "Why does this Big 'O' want me dead?"

"He hates you," Suzy said matter-of-factly.

'Well, duh!' Mark thought. "Why?"

"I don't know. I guess you did something to him."

Mark was confused. What could he have done to some gang member? Could it be the leader of the gang that attacked Brother Bob and then attacked him in the truck? That didn't make sense. Who could it be?

All of a sudden it came to Mark. It was so evident; he didn't know how he hadn't seen it before. Who knew about the Watsons, the New Age Ranch, and him? Big 'O' was Jon Olsen.

Chapter 67

Mark was sick. If it truly was Jon, and who else could it be, then it meant it was at least partially his fault that Susan, Curt, the Watsons, and the people at the ranch had died. If he hadn't pushed Jon out, all of them would still be alive. He had to make sure. He asked Suzy if she knew Big 'O's real name, but she said the band of criminals never used anything but their nicknames. He asked if she knew anything else about the gang leader.

"The only other thing I know is that he was married. They say he killed his own wife for defying him."

The knot in the pit of Mark's stomach twisted even tighter. He excused himself to go get a picture from Jon's old house to show to Suzy. Once outside, his remorse turned to anger. He may have had a hand in Jon's predicament, but Jon had made his own choices. He'd chosen his own path and turned into what he said he feared at the beginning, a monster.

When Mark showed the picture to Suzy, the look of hate on her face confirmed his fear. He felt guilty for the part he'd played in creating this nightmare. He hoped Barnes would allow him to help in ending it. There was no way Barnes could arrest all seventy-five gang members without help. He'd probably ask the National Guard to assist him. Perhaps, Mark thought, he'll take me along as an advisor since I've been there. He knew it was a long shot, but he was hopeful.

The work on the ditches continued. Gunny pulled all the workers to one side so he could protect them. A team of guards patrolled the side of the field from where the snipers had fired. Gunny also made sure Billy's patrol changed their schedule each day. They'd been using the same pattern each day, and that may have let the snipers plan their actions around the predictable cowboy patrol. The shooting had scared many of the volunteers off, so most of the workers were from inside Silver Hills. Mark helped with the digging. It was hard for him not to relive the events of two days ago. He tried to lose himself in the work, but the images of Curt's and Susan's bodies haunted him with almost every shovel of dirt.

Barnes finally showed up in the late afternoon. Mark, Gunny, and Ralph met with him. Ralph had insisted that he accompany them, in case Barnes tried any 'funny business,' as the lawyer put it. Mark had expected Barnes to be in a foul mood, but he was surprisingly pleasant as he said 'hello' to the trio. Mark's hopes rose that Barnes would let him help with Jon's capture. He started to explain why they had called him.

"Deputy Barnes, we asked y...."

"Sheriff Barnes," the man interrupted.

"I beg your pardon?"

"You can call me Sheriff Barnes. The County Commissioners appointed me Interim Sheriff until we can have a proper election. Seems they want to make it official as soon as possible, too. They're calling for a special election in a month. I expect I'll have no trouble earning enough votes to be the new sheriff. So, you can call me Sheriff Barnes, or just Sheriff, if you prefer." The man was gloating.

Mark was flabbergasted. He looked at Gunny and Ralph, and they both looked as shocked as he was. "Sheriff Barnes," he said, not believing he was saying it, "we asked you out because we've discovered some evidence about Curt's shooting."

"You have, have you?" he said belittlingly. "And, what, may I ask, did you discover?"

"Members of a gang from McMullen County shot Curt. They've taken over a ranch down there and are holding fifty or sixty women hostage. The leader of the gang lived here until a couple of months ago. His name is Jon Olsen, and he escaped after he shot and killed his wife. He came back to shoot me, but he hit Curt instead."

"I remember that. You all let him get away, right? You see, that's why you should leave law enforcement to the professionals. Now, because of your bumbling, Curt's dead."

The words stung, and Mark winced. Even though he knew Barnes was just being cruel, the statement had some truth to it. He swallowed hard and continued.

"We know where he is, and I'd be glad to take you down there."

"To do what?" Barnes asked, as if the thought was ridiculous.

"To arrest him." Mark wondered if the Interim Sheriff was really that dumb or if he was just playing the part.

"I'm sorry," Barnes said in a voice that revealed he wasn't, "but that's out of my jurisdiction. I can try to get a hold of the McMullen County Sheriff and pass your information on to him, but unless this Olsen character comes back to my county, there's nothing I can do."

"I see," Mark said, realizing that Barnes probably wouldn't even make an effort to reach the McMullen County Sheriff.

"We also found this close to the four-wheeler tracks." He held up the spent cartridge case. "They have two .50 caliber rifles down at the ranch."

Barnes took the case as if it held no interest to him. "Anything else?"

"No. That's it."

"Then how do you know it's this Olsen and that he intended to kill you?"

Mark started to tell Barnes about Suzy, but then thought better of it. "When we found the case, I suspected it was someone from the ranch, so we went down and had a look. We saw Jon there, and since he didn't even know Curt, as best we can tell, it only made sense that his intent was to shoot me."

"Uh-huh." Barnes pulled a notebook and pen out of his shirt pocket. "And who is the 'we' who traveled out of the county?"

"I'm sorry, did I say 'we?' I meant 'me.' I went by myself. I hope that isn't a problem?"

"Not for me," Barnes said, with a wicked smile as he scribbled on the paper. "But I don't know what the FEMA rep is going to say about it next time he comes around." The acting sheriff paused for effect. "By the way, I understand that Curt gave you three full auto rifles from the 'Los Muertos' shootout. I'll be needing those. I can't have civilians running around with full auto rifles, now can I?"

Gunny, who had remained silent to this point, turned red in the face. "Now listen here, you sumbitch, Curt gave..." he started.

Mark grabbed his arm and cut him off. "What Gunny's trying to say is that we don't know what you're talking about." Mark mimicked the evil smile he'd seen Barnes give a minute before. "But if you can find a judge who will give you a search warrant for every house in Silver Hills, you can come and look for them yourself. Isn't that right, Ralph?"

"Sure is," the lawyer replied with his own smile, as he folded his arms.

"We want to thank you for coming out, Interim Sheriff Barnes," Mark said in a sickeningly sweet voice. "Now, if you don't have any more questions for us, we have work to do. I think you know the way out." It was all Mark could do not to put 'Barney' at the end of the last sentence. However, there was no sense in further taunting the fill-in.

Barney made half a face and then went back to the cruiser that had been Curt's. He started the engine, put the car in gear, and stomped on the accelerator. Smoke and dust hung in the air as he made his way out of the gate.

"You were smart not to tell him about Suzy," Gunny said to Mark. "What do you think we should do about the AK's Curt gave us?"

"I don't know. Do you think he could get a search warrant, Ralph?"

"Not likely and certainly not for every house here. I'd just keep them out of sight and out of the obvious places he might search, like your two houses and the CP."

"Good idea," Mark said, as he pulled his keys out of his pocket and turned to head toward his house. "You two coming?"

"Where?" Gunny asked.

"To help me talk Rob into running for sheriff. I'll do anything to make sure Barney doesn't get elected."

"We're right behind you, Mark."

*　*　*

"Yes, we heard," Greg said. He and Rob were standing out in front of the builder's house talking to the three man delegation from Silver Hills. "I'm good friends with several of the county commissioners, and one of them told me about their decision. A few of them aren't too excited about Barnes even being the interim sheriff. That's why they want a special election so quickly, in hopes he won't be elected."

"Do they have someone in mind to run against him?" Ralph asked.

"Not yet, but they hope someone will step up to the plate. Barnes and his uncle still have a lot of influence around here. On the other hand, there are just as many people who don't like their heavy-handed tactics. If the right person was to run, I think they could beat old Barney. Why are you asking? Are you thinking about running, Ralph?"

The volume of Ralph's laughter was some where between a grizzly's roar and a clap of thunder. "Me? No. I'm just a humble law-YER, not a law-MAN!"

Everyone laughed. When they stopped laughing, the big lawyer's face tuned from jovial to dead serious. He looked right at Rob. "Actually, Mark dragged us over here to talk you into doing it, Rob. Since you were a cop before, we think you'd make a great sheriff."

"You're crazy!" Rob exclaimed. "I got out of the cop business because of politics. Now you want me to become a politician? That's what a sheriff is, you know? Politician first and peace officer second. Thanks, but no thanks."

"Rob, if you don't do it, who will?" Mark said rhetorically. "I understand how you feel, but we need you. Barney's not interested in doing what's best for the citizens of this county. He's only in it for his own benefit. Curt seemed to find a way to be a peace officer first. I'm sure you could, too."

"Mark, Curt was a long-time resident of this county. Everyone knew him and respected him. Some didn't like him, but they still respected him. He was one of a kind. I only moved here a couple of years ago. No one really knows me. Even if I could beat Barney, and trust me, nothing would please me more, I still couldn't do the things Curt could do. People just naturally followed his lead. There's going to be a big power struggle in county government no matter who ends up being the new sheriff. That's tough enough under normal conditions, but with the situation as it is since The Burst, it could be tragic. Curt's primary goal the last several weeks was making sure FEMA stayed out of our business, something he was able to do not only because he knew how to let the federal bureaucrats think they were choosing to leave us alone, but also because everyone here in county government showed solidarity with his plans. If you let the feds smell any hint of discord, they'll take that as an open invitation to come in and ride roughshod over us. I hate to say it, but we might be better off if no one challenges Barney. He probably stands the best chance of holding this thing together until the lights come back on."

Everyone considered Rob's point of view for a long moment.

"I'm sorry, I disagree," Mark said. "First, I think you could do as well as Curt did. True, it might not be as easy for you as it was for him, but we'd all help you however we could." Mark paused a moment for effect. "Second, we haven't told you about the meeting we had with Barney this afternoon." Mark went on to tell the Promise Point leaders what the interim sheriff had said earlier. Their faces got redder and redder as they listened. When Mark got to the part about the rifles Barnes wanted back, Rob could hold back his anger no more.

"That rat bastard!" he spat. "I'll do it. I'll run against him just to piss him off."

"Good. We've only got three weeks until the election, so what do we need to do?"

"Let me get together with some influential people I know who don't like Barnes and don't want him as our next sheriff," Greg said. "Then we'll set up a meeting, probably day after tomorrow, and come up with a campaign strategy."

"Sounds good," Mark agreed.

"Sounds real good," Gunny said, speaking for the first time since saying hello. "We need to talk about somethin' else, too. What are WE gonna do about Jon since it's clear Barney don't intend to do nothin' about him?"

"What did you have in mind, Gunny?" Rob asked.

"We talked about a few options on the way over here, but I'd like to have a meetin' in the mornin' with our extended security committee and see what everyone thinks. Can you two make it?" he asked Greg and Rob.

"I can't," Greg said. "I need to get on this election thing, but Rob can speak for me."

"I'll be there," Rob promised.

The three men said their goodbyes and headed home for dinner. The next morning at ten, Gunny called the meeting to order. In addition to the regular members and the guests who had attended the last meeting, Olga Jensen was there. She had been selected, mostly by the women, to take Susan's place.

"We're here to determine what, if anything, we should do about Jon and his gang of MZB's." Gunny was using his formal 'report to the Commander' English, Mark noticed. "It's apparent that the interim sheriff intends to do nothing about the situation. Jon believes Mark is dead, and if he finds out that the Karate Man is still alive, there's no telling what he might do. Does anyone have any suggestions?"

"What do you think, Gunny?" Ted asked.

"Ted, I have an opinion, but I'd prefer to hear what you all think first."

"What did you mean, 'if anything'?" Olga asked her first official question.

"Just that. One option is to do nothing." Gunny explained.

"That may be an option," Olga contested, "but it's one I can't see us doing. Curt and Susan were our friends. They can't stand up for themselves anymore, so we have to do it for them."

"I agree," Chaparo chimed in. "If we let Jon get away with this, we're no better than that 'do nothing' deputy. I think we have to hit them before they hit us again. If Jon thinks Mark's dead, maybe we can use that to our advantage."

Most everyone's heads nodded in agreement with Olga and Chaparo.

"It almost sounds like we're looking for revenge," Ted said. "Is that what we want? I mean, Lord knows I'd like to see Jon pay for all of the wrong he's done, but I want justice, not vengeance."

"That's not what I meant, Ted," Chaparo said quickly, "but we can't do nothing. Can we?"

"To me, this situation is no different than the one we had in Waco," Rob said. "We have a bad group that's hurting other people. If we have it in our power to stop them, then we have a moral obligation to do just that. It's not about getting even, it's about doing the right thing."

Mark spoke for the first time since the meeting was called to order. "Ted, I don't think anyone here wants to do this for revenge. If anyone's in a position to want that, it's me. Not only did Jon kill Curt, Susan, and the Watsons, he tried to kill me. I don't want revenge. I want justice, just like you said, and, like Rob said, we have an obligation to stop Jon from hurting others if we can. Hopefully, we can get him and his group to surrender, and we can turn them over to the proper authorities. If all goes well, we'll turn Jon over to Rob, who will hopefully be next sheriff, but we need to go into this with our eyes open. The chances of getting Jon to surrender are slim to none. More than likely, people will get killed if we do this. Possibly a lot of us could be killed. We've been very lucky so far. Compared to most, we've only lost a few of our friends and family to violence since The Burst. One day our luck will run out. So, think about that before we commit to this."

Everyone was quiet for a long moment.

"Gunny, will you tell us what you think now?"

523

"I think we have to do it. None of us are safe as long as Jon is running around free. Mark may have been his target, but remember, Suzy said he wanted to take out the whole subdivision. The only reason he didn't was because he didn't have enough men. If he keeps growing his group, soon he will have enough. We have to stop him before he gets that strong, not just for us, but for everyone who's trying to hold things together until the lights come back on."

They took a vote, and everyone voted to strike Jon and his band of MZB's. Several plans were discussed, but no final decision was made about how to do it. A little after noon, everyone agreed to go away and think about it, and they'd get back together the following morning. Rob was invited to eat lunch at the Turner house, and he graciously accepted.

When they were about halfway through their meal, Greg showed up with news from his political contacts.

"I talked to the people I told you about, and they were thrilled that Rob's willing to run. They want to get together tomorrow afternoon and form a campaign committee. With no power, it's going to be hard to get the word out to the voters, but we think we may have a few ideas that'll work. I also talked to one of the county commissioners, and they've come up with a plan for the election. The polls are going to be open on December ninth, tenth, and eleventh. Since not too many people have transportation, they're going to use the running school buses to bring the voters to the polls. There aren't enough buses to do it all in one day, so they're going to do it over three days."

"What are they going to do for ballots?" Jess asked.

"They're still working on that. The biggest concern they have is making sure that everyone who's eligible to vote knows about the election."

"Then why don't they just put the election off until they can be sure all of the voters know?" Abby asked.

"The County Commissioner I talked to said they considered that," Greg explained. "They feel we need to have a properly elected sheriff as soon as possible, since the office of sheriff is the most recognized and depended-on office in county government. "

"That doesn't give us much time," Rob said.

"Don't worry, I'm sure the best man will win," Jess said with a smile.

After lunch, Jim and Lisa cornered Mark and Jess.

"We want to talk to you about something important," Jim started.

Mark was concerned they'd figured out George's secret. The old farmer was hardly eating anything, and he'd lost a considerable amount of weight in the last month. His clothes just hung on him like an old scarecrow.

"What is it?" Jess asked.

"We've been talking about it, and we want to adopt Susan's boys," Lisa said. "I know it may not be permanent if their father shows back up, but who knows what's going to happen with the way things are right now? At least they'll be in a family for the time being."

"I know Susan and I were often at odds," Jim explained, "but that doesn't mean I didn't respect the job she did raising the boys mostly by herself. We've always wanted to have sons to go along with our daughters, and we want to help out if we can. Lisa and I talked to them earlier and asked them if it would be okay if we looked after them for a while. They agreed, but we wanted to get your blessing, too."

"I think Susan would be honored and grateful if you would look after her boys," Jess said with a smile.

"I agree," Mark said. "Where will you put them? There's not really room in your camper, is there?"

"We can fit. It'll be a little tight, but we'll get by. Compared to the people still living in tents, we're lucky," Lisa said.

"Why wouldn't you just move into Susan's house?" Jess asked. "There's no reason to make the boys move. It'll be easier for them to adjust if they're in familiar surroundings."

"Don't you think that might cause problems with some of the people in the neighborhood?" Lisa asked.

"I don't know why. The house technically belongs to the boys. If you're taking care of them, I don't see how anyone could say anything about it," Mark answered.

"We don't want anyone to think we're doing this just so we can move into Susan's house," Jim said.

"Don't worry about that. People are going to think what people are going to think. You know you're doing it for the right reasons, and that is all that counts," Jess said in a voice that ended the conversation.

Susan's funeral was the next morning. Everyone from Silver Hills was there, as well as Greg and Rob and their families from Promise Point. She was buried in her own backyard. It was very hard on her boys, but having Jim and Lisa to lean on seemed to help them.

The expanded security committee met over lunch and voted to accept an attack plan Gunny and Rob had collaborated on. They'd send a three-man scout team to watch the compound. If a large raiding party was sent out, one of the team members would drive back to tell Gunny and Rob. They would have a seventy-five or eighty man attack force ready to go on an hour or two's notice. The attack force would take the compound, hopefully with little or no bloodshed, and then use the defenses that Jon had emplaced to defeat the returning raiders. It seemed like a good plan to Mark.

Curt's funeral was late that afternoon. It seemed as if half the county showed up. The service was quite emotional. Mark shuddered several times, realizing this should have been his funeral. He went back and forth between feeling guilty to being thankful he was still alive.

At the cemetery, when the short service was over, Mark and Jess got into the long line to give their condolences to Curt's widow. When they finally approached the front of the line, Mark saw that Greg Hardy was sitting next to her. Greg, when he saw Mark, leaned over and whispered into Mrs. Thompson's ear. She looked up at Mark as if she recognized him. When it was his turn to speak to the widow, Mark took her hand and squeezed it gently. He always felt so awkward in these situations. He never knew what to say.

"I'm so sorry for your loss, Mrs. Thompson. Curt was a great sheriff, and although I didn't know him long, he was a great friend, too."

"Thank you, Mr. Turner. Curt always spoke so highly of you. I want to let you know that he valued your friendship."

"Thank you, ma'am. I appreciate that."

"We're having a few people over to our house after this. I hope you and your wife will come," she smiled weakly.

"We'd be honored," Mark said, as he took a step to the side to let Jess shake the woman's hand and say a few words. When she was finished, they walked over to a group standing around making small talk. A minute later, Rob and his wife joined the growing circle of friends. Rob squeezed Mark's shoulder and gave him a nod.

While everyone was chit chatting, Mark saw Barney walking toward the group. When he reached the now good-sized circle, he spoke in a loud voice that seemed irreverent in the small cemetery.

"Rob, I heard you've thrown your name in the hat to run against me for sheriff."

Mark was amazed the lack of electricity and phone service hadn't seemed to slow down the small town grapevine.

"I have," Rob said quietly and humbly.

"Well," Barney said, making a conspicuous display of extending his hand to Rob, "I just want to wish you good luck."

"Thank you," Rob said, shaking the offered hand. "Good luck to you, too."

Barney pulled himself in close to Rob and whispered in his ear. Mark was close enough to make out what the insincere man said.

"I don't know what you're thinking, Bowers, but if you run against me, I'll crush you."

Chapter 68

When the interim sheriff pulled back from Rob's ear, the vile grin on his face made Mark so mad he could have spit.

"Thank you very much," Rob said coolly. He smiled. "I feel the same way about you, Fred."

Mark thought that Rob might be a better politician than he thought himself to be. He smiled as he watched Barney's grin turn into a sour look at his failing to get a rise out of his opponent. The acting sheriff stomped off like a child with hurt feelings. Mark gave Rob a pat on the back and a wink.

A short time later, Mark and Jess arrived at Curt's house. It didn't take long for the men to move out onto the deck behind the house, while the women stayed mostly inside. Most of the men were residents of Promise Point, Mark noticed. The topic of conversation had turned from stories about Curt, to how horrible a sheriff Barney would make, and to how they could make sure Rob got elected. Mark tried to be sociable, but his mind kept thinking about Jon and the New Age Ranch. Should they really try to take it back? Maybe they should wait and see if Rob was elected? If he was, he could officially be involved.

"What do you think, Mark?" Greg asked.

Mark had no idea what they were talking about. "Think about what?" he said in a startled voice.

"Earth to Mark," Greg laughed. "We were talking about having Rob debate Barnes. We could do it in front of the courthouse several days before the election, maybe on a Sunday afternoon."

"That sounds okay, but how many people would show up? It's a long walk to Floresville for most people. How much good would it do if only a few people show up?"

"Even if just a few actually come, I think the results will spread by word of mouth. I believe it'll give at least some of the people a chance to see Rob and how he responds to their concerns."

"But what if I blow it?" Rob asked.

"You won't," Greg responded confidently. "Besides, you're already the underdog. What have you got to lose?"

"Nothing, I guess."

"Then I'll talk to the county commissioners about it," Greg said. "We can set it up for about ten days before the election, which should give the grapevine enough time to work."

All of the other men thought it was an excellent idea. Only Rob and Mark seemed to be on the tentative side. Mark looked at his watch and excused himself, saying he wanted to get home before it got too late. He went inside, found Jess, and told her he was ready. The couple offered their condolences to Mrs. Thompson once more and headed out to the Blazer.

As they were climbing in, Greg came running out of the house.

"Mark! I'm glad I caught you," the real estate developer was slightly out of breath. He stood next to the door of the big Chevy and spoke through the window. "Rob was just telling me about the plan y'all came up with to take care of the guy who shot Curt."

"Yeah," Mark said, prompting the man to make his point.

"Look, Rob can help you plan and train, but he can't go. He can't do anything that's the slightest bit unlawful, or it may ruin his chance to get elected. If Barney found out about it, he'd throw the book at him just to eliminate him from the race."

Mark was quiet for a moment. They really needed Rob's expertise and leadership on the incursion, but they needed a sheriff they could depend on more. "You're right, Greg. Thanks." He patted the man on the arm and backed out of the driveway.

On the drive home, Mark filled Jess in on the planned debate. She thought it was a good idea and agreed that word would get around, no matter how many people saw the actual deliberations.

As Mark pulled through the heavy gate into Silver Hills, he glanced at his watch. He needed to tell Gunny that Rob wouldn't be able to go to the ranch with the attack force, but it was getting fairly late, and he figured the old Marine would be in the sack by now. It could wait until morning. When he pulled the Blazer behind the house, he was surprised to see a group of men sitting at the picnic tables. Gunny was one of them. Jim, Mike, Chaparo, Ted, and Ralph were with him.

"Looks like another meeting, sweetheart," Jess said. "I'll see you later."

"What's up guys?" Mark asked.

"I picked the two teams who are gonna do the recon. Jim, Mike, and Ted are leaving in the morning. You, Chaparo, and Ralph will relieve them in two days. I know these are new groups for you all, but this job ain't the place for women and kids. If there's a screw up out there, our plan is ruined at best and if'n worst comes to worst, somebody might get dead."

The men all nodded their heads to signify they understood the seriousness of the situation.

"Now, I wanna go over how I want you all to operate out there. Jim and Mark will be in charge of their respective groups. I want you..."

"Excuse me, Gunny," Mark interrupted, "but shouldn't Chaparo be in charge of our group? He has military experience, after all."

"I already talked to Chaparo and explained to him that you have more recent experience. He doesn't have problem with it, and neither should you."

"Besides," Chaparo said, as he laughed, "I was just a grease monkey."

"Anyways," Gunny began again, "I want y'all to use the four hour shift rotation like we did when we watched the roads. The camps are to be cold...no exceptions. That means no cooking of any kind. If'n someone catches a whiff of cooking food, the whole jig might be up. And you'll sleep under the stars. No tents for someone to see. If'n it starts raining, you can string up a tarp, but it is to come down as soon as the rain stops."

"Be careful with your field glasses, and don't let the sun reflect off of 'em. Chaparo told me you watched the compound from a small hill a little over three hundred yards from the fence," the old man said, looking at Mark. He pulled a small hand drawn map from a folder. Mark was amazed at the accuracy of the diagram. Gunny could have been a professional mapmaker in a bygone era. "Chaparo said you parked the truck here and walked into here and set up your OP."

"That's right."

"Jim, I want you to take this map. Park and set up in the same place they did last time. You'll take the MZB truck and cover it up real good far enough off the road that no one can find it. If more than two thirds of the men leave the compound on a raid, then whoever is due for OP duty next is to come back. That way, whoever it is will have had at least four hours of rest."

"Okay, Gunny," Jim affirmed.

"If'n two days go by and nothing happens, I'll send Mark's group out to relieve you. At first light, send one of your men back to the truck. He'll meet Mark's group so'n they know everything's alright. When Mark gets to the OP, you can head back. Bring back the truck Mark and his guys drove over and leave the MZB truck hidden. I don't want to drive in an' out so much we start makin' a trail that someone can see. You should scruff up any tire tracks near the road, too. Everybody understand?"

Heads bobbed up and down around the table.

"Alright. Your main job is to watch for a large group to leave on a raiding party. I'd like to wait for fifty or sixty men to leave. That way we'll outnumber them three or four to one. Until that happens, I want you to watch and take notes about everything you see. Try to figure out how many people are there, how many of 'em are in Jon's group, and how many are captives. Make notes about how they work their guard duty and schedules, the weapons you see, what the daily routine is, and anything else, no matter how unimportant it might seem."

"If'n a group of forty-five or more leave out for a raid, normally early in the morning, according to Suzy, I want you to send two men back to me as soon as they leave. The one left will continue to watch the compound. You'll have the portable CB with you, and I'll call you on it before we come in. I had Dwight fix it up, so you can listen in on an earplug. I won't call before oh-two-hundred, so you don't have to worry about it until then. We'll wait and hit them at first light. Hopefully they'll all be asleep. Rob and I will look at the intelligence you all bring back at each shift change and see if we need to modify our plan."

"Gunny, about Rob…Greg said he shouldn't come on the raid with us."

"Why the hell not?"

"Greg thinks it might ruin his chance to get elected."

"I reckon it could," Gunny said. "I could still use his help on the planning end."

"Greg said that wouldn't be a problem."

"Good. Once we take the compound, we'll use their own defenses against the raiders when they return. Now, does anyone have any questions?"

No one said anything.

"Alright then," Gunny said, "Jim, you and your boys better hit the hay. You leave at oh four hundred. Just one more thing." He took a deep breath. "This is some serious shit, a lot more serious than anything we've done up to this point. These boys are trained and motivated. If you screw up, you're probably gonna take a long dirt nap, but if you do live, I'll make you wish you hadn't. Got it?"

"Aye, aye, Gunny," Jim said seriously. Mark half expected him to salute.

Mark couldn't tell if the old sergeant was impressed or put off by Jim's response. He wheeled around and marched off toward his house without saying another word.

The next two days went fast for Mark. He spent most of them working on the defensive ditches. A few more days, and they should be finished. The afternoon of the second day, he went to a meeting with Rob's campaign team. The debate they'd discussed at Curt's house was on. It seemed Barnes was reluctant at first, but when someone hinted that he might be chicken, he agreed. The debate would be Sunday after next. Questions would come from the onlookers, and each candidate would have a chance to respond and then comment on his opponent's response. Mark hoped Rob would do well.

The next morning at four, Mark found himself sandwiched between Chaparo and Ralph in Gunny's truck. He felt almost like a child with the two huge men on either side. The ride to the rendezvous point was uneventful. They talked some on the way down, but whether it was the earliness of the hour or the seriousness of the task before them, it was quiet for most of the way. Mark knew what they were doing was important, but he also wished he didn't have to do it. He wasn't sure why he was so apprehensive, but he had a real feeling of dread.

When they got to where they were supposed to meet one of Jim's crew, they stopped and got out of the truck to stretch. Before long, Mike came out of the brush. He quickly conversed with the new group.

"We set up where you did last time. No one left or came in while we were watching. There was a big fight between two men late yesterday afternoon. We couldn't tell what it was over, but it didn't last long. One of the men pulled a knife, and it looked like he really knew how to use it. The other guy must have bled out in under a minute."

"Is that all that happened?" Ralph asked.

"No, but it was the most violent thing we saw. The women aren't treated very well. The men hit them all the time. Ted saw one get beaten pretty badly. He said they had to pick her up and carry her into one of the cabins. It happened two days ago, and he's still upset about it."

"Anything else we need to know?" Mark asked his brother.

"Not really." Mike reached out and gave Mark a quick hug. "Y'all just be careful, and I'll see you in two days," he said, as he shook Ralph's and Chaparo's hands.

"We will," Chaparo promised.

The three men shouldered their packs and moved into the brush. The trip was much easier than it had been before. They knew where they were going, and it was daylight this time. They arrived at the OP in just under forty-five minutes.

"Hey," Jim whispered. "Glad to see you."

"You, too," Mark replied. "How'd it go?"

"Okay, I guess. We've got some activity going. It looks like they're sending out a couple of trucks. It might just be their recon team, but I can't tell for sure. Other than that, there's nothing significant. Mike saw a knife fight yesterday, and Ted saw a woman get beaten half to death the day before."

"Yeah, Mike told us. Have you seen Jon?"

"A couple of times. He was watching the fight last night," Jim answered.

"That doesn't surprise me. Any counts on their numbers?"

"Not anything I would count on. We've seen twenty-five to thirty men in the courtyard a couple of times, but I'm sure that's not everyone. There are a bunch of women and a few kids, but just like with the men, we haven't seen them all at one time."

"Okay, I'll take the first watch," Mark said, mostly to Ralph and Chaparo. Then he turned back to Jim. "See you in two days, buddy." He belly crawled up to the top of the small rise and patted Ted on the shoulder. He gave the professor a thumbs-up. Ted didn't return the gesture, and the look of anger in his eyes shocked Mark a bit. He figured seeing the woman beaten had a stronger effect on him than Mike had told him. Mark wondered how he would react at seeing what the professor had seen. Ted slid backwards down the hill, and Mark saw him and Jim head out the way his team had come in.

Mark turned his attention back to the compound, and he could see the activity Jim had described. There were two pickups in the center of the courtyard. Men were scurrying about, filling them with fuel and supplies. After a few minutes, ten men lined up in front of the trucks. Mark saw a man run up to the cabin that used to belong to Mr. Davis and knock on the door. A minute later, Jon came out.

Mark was instantly angry. It was irrational, he knew, but he couldn't help himself. He watched Jon walk over to the men lined up in front of the trucks and talk with the man on the end. Mark looked through the field glasses and made a mental note of the man Jon was addressing. He was short, but powerfully built. The two men talked for two or three minutes, then Jon stepped back and spoke to all ten of the men. Mark wished he could hear. When Jon finished his short speech, the ten thugs whooped and hollered and climbed into the trucks. A minute later, they were gone. Mark looked again at Jon. The murderer seemed to have lost some weight. His mannerisms told Mark that he was even more cocky and brazen than he had been at Silver Hills. Mark watched his nemesis walk back into Mr. Davis's cabin. If looks could kill at three hundred yards, Jon would have been dead.

Mark snapped himself out of his hate-filled trance and made some written notes. He listed the trucks that had been used, the time they left, and the number of men they held. He also wrote down a short description of the man who seemed to be the leader of the probable scout party. He then counted how many people were still out in the courtyard. Eight men, who appeared to be visiting with each other and watching the women, were visible. He could also see thirteen women doing various tasks. He wrote those numbers down as well.

The three men spent the next two days watching the compound and noticing nothing extraordinary. Mark saw a couple of women slapped or kicked at, but nothing that would have seriously hurt them. Still, it was hard seeing someone being abused. Ralph saw a woman hit hard enough to knock her down. He thought she wasn't moving fast enough for the man who hit her. He reported that she got right back up and quickened her pace. Ralph said she acted as if the treatment was nothing new.

The greatest number of men they saw at one time was thirteen, and once they saw twenty-eight women and four children in the open. Guard shift changes were noted. There were always seven men on guard duty, although only the two rovers could be seen, except when shift changes were made three times a day. The other five were assigned to the foxholes. They were rarely checked on, though. Mark hoped they were spending most of their shifts sleeping.

Sunday morning at the first hint of light, Mark sent Chaparo to meet Jim's team at the rendezvous spot. About two hours later, Jim showed up at the OP. After a brief exchange to let the fresh team know how little they'd seen, Mark and Ralph made their way back to the truck. Then the two of them and Chaparo drove back to Silver Hills.

They arrived just in time for the men to eat, take a quick shower, and go to the church service. After lunch, Gunny met with the small squad to debrief them. Each member reported what he'd observed over the two-day period. Mark asked Gunny about Ted's reaction to what he'd seen on his first rotation.

"He was pretty upset," Gunny confirmed. "He tried to convince me to let Jim pick Jon off at the first opportunity. I told him that if we thought it would stop what was going on, we would, but we all know that one of the other ruffians would take over, and things would go on like before. You also know our plans to capture or take out all of the MZB's at the ranch would go out the window. He had a hard time with it. I even had to get the preacher to talk to him, and he finally agreed that we had to stick with our plan."

"I'm glad you got him calmed down," Mark said. "The last thing we need is someone going off half cocked."

The meeting adjourned, and Mark tried to enjoy the next day and a half. The defensive trenches were done. Olga, after her appointment to the security committee, had taken over responsibility for them and was able to maintain worker morale so well that the work got done very quickly. Mark helped in the garden and spent some time with the kids. Timmy and Tommy were adjusting well, and they wanted to do everything David did. David told his dad that now he knew how Samantha had felt when they were younger. Mark made sure to spend some time just with David, and he tried to make himself available to Sam, but she seemed to want to spend all of her free time with Alex. As much as he tried to make himself relax, the thoughts of having to go back to the OP, and the eventual conflict that would bring, hung over his head like a dark cloud. The minutes and hours seemed to drag by, but the two days were gone in a flash. It was such a paradox. Mark woke on Tuesday morning, the feeling of dread heavy on his heart. The trip back to the OP was uneventful, again. Mike met them at the truck, and the news he had was interesting. The MZB scouting party had come back Sunday afternoon, and twenty-two men had left yesterday morning in three trucks. Other than that, nothing extraordinary was happening. Mark visited with his brother briefly, and then he and his team made the hike to the OP. When they arrived, Mark noticed that Ted seemed anxious to go home. Mark didn't blame him; he, too, was starting to hate this job.

About four o'clock that afternoon, horns could be heard honking in the distance. Ralph was on watch, and he waved the other two men up to see what was happening. The three trucks Mike had told them had gone on the raid were pulling through the gate, and they parked in the center of the compound with the drivers still sounding the horns. Men rushed out of every cabin like ants from a disturbed anthill. All three onlookers immediately started counting. Mark, looking through his binoculars, had to start over several times, as the men were moving around too much for him to tell who he'd already counted. A few minutes later, Jon appeared in the doorway of the big cabin. He walked over and shook hands with the short, muscular man Mark had seen leave with the scouting party. He assumed this man was also the leader of the raiding party. Suzy had identified him from Mark's description as the one called Snuffer. The two men spoke for several minutes. Mark wished he could hear what they were saying, but he was just too far away. The men in the compound had stopped scurrying around when Jon had appeared, and Mark was able to get an accurate count. There were forty-eight men standing around the trucks in the courtyard including Jon and the short man. No one except for Snuffer had gotten out of the trucks yet. Since the fronts of the vehicles were facing Mark, he couldn't tell how many men they held. If all the men had come out of the buildings, and if Mike's count of twenty-two was correct, and if all five of the hidden guards were still at their posts, that made seventy-four. Mark was excited by this revelation. If it was correct, then Jon hadn't increased his group size, and the plan they had should work. All they needed now was for him to send out a big group.

"I count forty-eight standing out where I can see them," he whispered to Chaparo to confirm his number.

"I only got forty-seven."

"I got forty-eight," Ralph volunteered.

"If that's all of them, then including the guards and the men who should still be in the trucks, they have seventy-four men. That's good news for us," he whispered.

Chaparo nodded his head, and Ralph gave him a thumbs-up. Mark turned his attention back to the compound. Looking through his Steiners, he saw Jon wave his arm. Mark figured that Jon wanted the men in the trucks to get out. His assumption was confirmed a minute later, as men appeared out of the three vehicles. Most of them jumped out of the beds of the trucks and ran toward the back of the truck they had ridden in. A minute later, they could be seen walking toward Jon, each carrying a box or bucket that appeared to be heavy. They made a line and set their bundles on the ground in front of them.

Mark counted eighteen men in the line. Mike had said that twenty-two had left in the trucks. Including Snuffer, that meant that only nineteen had come back. The Karate Man wondered where the other three were. Maybe they'd been killed. He hoped so. He found it strange that he was wishing for people to be killed, but the world had changed in the last three months, and he'd changed with it, he realized. If anyone had told him before The Burst that the world could fall apart in ninety days, he would have laughed at them. He never realized what a fragile society they lived in. His mind drifted over the events since The Burst. He had attended more funerals since August than in the previous ten years. Jon moved toward the first man in line, and Mark snapped out of his daze.

Jon walked down the line, looking in each container. On most of them, he looked back up at the bearer and shook the man's hand or slapped him heartily on the back. Toward the end, he looked in one box and seemed upset when he looked back up. Mark could see that the man Jon was in front of was talking and making gestures like he didn't understand. Jon reached down into the box, pulled out a portable radio, and shook it at the man. He then turned and threw it as far as he could. Mark could see the anger on his ex-neighbor's face. When Jon turned back toward the man with his hands on his hips like he was waiting for an explanation, the man said a few words and then crossed his arms like he

533

was through defending himself. Jon's right hand exploded off of his hip and crashed into the man's face. With his arms folded, there was no way the attacked man could block the punch. Mark doubted he could have blocked it even if he'd been expecting it; it came so fast. Mark had seen some quick hands back when he was going to tournaments, but only a special few had been as fast as Jon just was. The thin man fell to the ground with blood squirting from his nose. Jon moved down the line, as if the event that had just transpired had never happened. He looked in the last two boxes, their contents evidently more to his liking.

Jon stepped back from the line and stood next to Snuffer, rubbing his hands together quickly as if he was trying to warm them up. Mark had seen people at the dinner table rub their hands like that before they dug into an especially delicious dessert or favorite food. Jon made a wave at the trucks, and the three men Mark had hoped were dead appeared out of one of the trucks. Each pulled a woman out of the bed, and they roughly pushed the charges toward 'Big O.'

Mark looked closely at the women. They all seemed to be young and strong, although they were dirty and haggard looking. Their hands were tied behind their backs. Mark could hear the catcalls and some of the obscenities being directed at the women. They were wide-eyed with fear, as they were herded toward Jon. When the men had them arrayed, shoulder-to-shoulder, in front of their leader, they stepped back a few feet. Jon looked at the captives as if he were at a cattle auction trying to decide what heifer to bid on. He circled the trio. Mark could now see they were really nothing more than girls, about the same age as Samantha. Jon's mouth was moving, and Mark strained to read the lips of the Marine-turned-MZB, but he couldn't. Jon moved back around to the front and grabbed one of the girls, as if he was testing a piece of fruit at the market. The girl cowered in fear. He did the same thing to the next one and received the same response. He turned back to the men in the courtyard and said something. Judging from the laughter he received in reply, it was probably disgusting and demeaning. Jon moved to the girl on the end. She seemed to have suddenly grown a backbone, as she now stood straight and proud. When Jon put his hand on her, she spit in his face. Mark, although he didn't know her, was proud of the young woman.

Mark saw Jon's right hand shift into high gear again. Only this time, instead of moving toward her, it moved away. An instant later, the big Beretta pistol Jon had murdered his wife with was in that hand. It came up to a point between the eyes of the girl who, three months ago, was probably a very pretty young lady. The pistol barked once. Mark flinched at the sound. The woman stood there for what seemed an eternity, and Mark wondered if Jon had missed or used blanks in the pistol.

Finally, the girl crumpled to the ground like a discarded rag doll. The cheers that rose from the pack of MZB's reminded Mark of the cheers he imagined the Romans gave when a lion ate a Christian. Mark's anger went from zero to sixty in a heartbeat. The thought of pulling his rifle up and shooting Jon flashed through his mind. Just as quickly, he heard the words Gunny had said to Ted, and he knew that even if he could kill that son-of-a-bitch, it wouldn't stop what was going on at the ranch. No, they had to wait for the right time.

Mark promised himself that when it was the right time, no matter what it took, he would kill Jon himself. 'I have changed, haven't I?' he thought coldly.

Chapter 69

Mark could see the two living girls being led into Mr. Davis's cabin by Jon and Snuffer. The dead girl was being carried into the barn by several very unsavory looking characters. He didn't want to imagine what they would do to her lifeless body. Somehow, he was there in the barn, being forced to watch. He could actually feel the dirty MZB hands on her cold skin. It was horrible. He couldn't bear to watch, but something wouldn't let him look away. As the cretins began to ravage her, he felt he could take no more.

Mark woke, sitting upright in his bed with cold sweat dripping from every pore. He felt a hand on him and recoiled in fear. A split-second later, he realized he was at home, and the hand that had touched his back belonged to Jess.

"Another nightmare?" she asked softly.

"Yeah," was all he had the breath to choke out.

"Which one this time?"

"The dead one." He'd been having nightmares about the three girls at least two or three times a night since he'd seen their ordeal at the ranch over a week ago. He had to go back there in the morning, and he dreaded it more than death. He looked at the wind-up alarm clock. It was only a little after midnight. He was so tired, not just from the lack of sleep that the almost constant nightmares caused, but also from the dread and hate he held for watching the compound. Ted had been pulled off of Jim's team, as he wasn't able to stand, night after night, hearing the screams of the women and the evil laughter of the MZB's that invariably followed. Paul Jenson, Olga's husband, had taken over for him, although he looked like it was quickly wearing on him, as well. Gunny had taken to having Brother Bob debrief the men with him, to try to bolster their spirits. It helped some, but they all hated the job. Mark knew the only thing that kept them going was the knowledge that someone had to do it.

"Try to go back to sleep, Honey."

Sure, he thought. That was easy to say. It wasn't so easy to do, though. "Okay," he said.

He lay back down and felt her arm wrap around him. Maybe it would protect him from the bad dreams. A few minutes later, he was sleeping again. The next thing he knew, the wind-up alarm was singing its annoying song, and the hands were pointed at three-thirty.

When they arrived at the OP, Jim reported that nothing had happened. Mark had hoped Jon would have at least sent a scout party out. He needed this to be over, although he knew if a large raiding party did go out, it meant that lots of people were going to die. He felt conflicted like never before in his life. The only good news they'd gotten in the past week was that Jon sent twenty-five men out on the last raid, and Snuffer only came back with eighteen and no loot or prisoners. Jon had appeared very upset at the team when they returned. Mark first feared, and then hoped, that Jon would take it out on one or more of his MZB buddies, but he didn't.

Mark climbed up the small hill and took the first watch, like he always did. At least it was usually quiet this early in the morning. Today was no exception. In fact, it was unusually quiet the whole day. In the early afternoon of the second day of Mark's team's watch, activity around the compound increased to a pace the observers hadn't witnessed before in the sixteen days they'd been observing. Mark, who was looking forward to the debate between Rob and Barney day after tomorrow, wondered if something big was brewing. If it was, he might miss the debate. Again, he was conflicted. He didn't want to miss the debate, but he needed this to be over, too. His question was at least partially answered when seven trucks pulled into the middle of the courtyard. They were checked over by a couple of guys and filled with fuel. Mark wondered how many men Jon would send out in seven trucks. He'd sent twenty-two men in three trucks before. That ratio would indicate that as many as fifty might go in seven. That was way too many for a scout team. If Jon was planning a raid without sending a scout team first, it went against his normal MO. Mark wondered what could be up. He was hopeful this was the one they'd been waiting for, but he refused to let his spirits get too high. He didn't think he could take another big disappointment.

The next morning, they traded out with Jim's team and made the trip back home. It was only an hour and a half later that Mike and Paul arrived with the news that forty-four men had left the compound in the seven trucks. Even better news was that Jon had gone with them. That meant only twenty-three were left to guard the ranch. Preparations for the assault on the ranch kicked into high gear.

Mark and his group were ordered by Gunny to get some rest and be ready to go by eleven PM. Mark went home and tried to sleep, but the excitement or fear or some strange mix of the two wouldn't let him doze off. As he lay there, a terrifying thought leapt into his mind. He jumped out of bed and ran to find Gunny.

The old sergeant was barking orders at several men who were going over the vehicles they'd be using this afternoon. When he saw Mark, he gave him a how-dare-you-not-follow-my-orders look. "What are you doing out here?" he demanded.

"Gunny, what if they're coming here?"

Gunny snorted. "Karate Man, you need to calm down a little. Jon may not be no George Patton, but he ain't no dummy either. He knows there's no way he could take Silver Hills with forty-four men."

"But why did he go with the men this time? We know he doesn't usually do that. Maybe he's coming back to do some more sniper work."

"Relax, Mark." Gunny put his hand on Mark's shoulder. "You only use two or three men for that kind of job. Besides, I have Billy's boys and a group from here out making sure nobody gets close without us knowing 'bout it. Now, I want you to go back home and get some shut-eye. Got it?"

"Okay, Gunny, I got it."

Mark trudged back home, but he didn't feel like sleeping. He went into his study and pulled out everything he would take with him tonight. He pulled ten extra magazines for his rifle out of the closet and loaded them. He got out his cleaning kit and meticulously cleaned and oiled his rifle and his pistol. When he was sure everything was exactly like he wanted it, he went into the kitchen and made himself something to eat. As the minutes dragged by, Mark could find little to do. He went back into his study and pulled a book off of the shelf, went

536

into the living room and sat in a big chair to read. The L'Amour novel pulled him in, even though he'd read it several times before.

Jess and the three boys arrived home from school a few minutes after three. She admonished him to get some sleep and had David take the younger boys outside to play, so it would be quiet in the house. He went back into the bedroom, closed the curtains, and tried to doze off. Fear of the nightmares kept him awake for a while, but soon the fatigue overtook the fear, and he drifted into a deep slumber.

Jess woke him at ten. He groggily got up and realized he'd slept for almost seven hours with no nightmares. The dreams he remembered were about cowboys and ranchers trying to build a new life in the frontier, while evil tried to destroy their dreams. He dressed and went to the kitchen and sat down for the meal his wife had prepared. He finished and then got his gear. Jess had allowed the boys to stay up so they could see their father off. Mark hugged each of them, as they wished him good luck. It was hard for him to say goodbye. He knew it could be permanent. Even though he'd been in several shooting situations before, they had taken him by surprise. This was the first time he was going out the door on a job where he knew someone was going to die. The boys seemed to be okay, but Mark could tell that Jess was nervous. He gave her an extra hug and kiss.

"Where's Sam?"

"I'm right here."

He turned around to see her throwing a daypack over her shoulder. She also had a pistol on her hip. "Where are you going?"

"With you," she said.

"For what?" he demanded.

"I'm on the medical team. I'm going to help Lisa and Doc Vasquez in case anyone gets hurt."

"Like hell you are! It's way too dangerous." He didn't raise his voice, but it was obvious that he was upset.

Sam's face screwed up into a look of hurt and confusion. "But, Dad..." she started.

"But, nothing!" Mark said, his voice just slightly elevated now.

Sam looked at her mother who came to her rescue. "Mark, you know she's been taking the EMT training. Lisa said she's doing great, and she asked Sam to go with them. Gunny told me they wouldn't be close to the fighting, so I gave her permission," Jess said.

"But, what if something goes wrong?"

"Like what? Like the lights going out? Like society as we know it falling apart?" she asked sarcastically. "Everything is already wrong. The world has turned into a dangerous place, and her staying here doesn't guarantee her safety. You, better than anyone, should know that. You said in one of the neighborhood meetings that we all need to do what we can to help. This is what Sam wants to do. Now, unless that speech only applied to everyone else's families, I suggest the two of you get going."

Mark didn't want to admit it, but what Jess said was right. How would it look if he didn't let his daughter help just because she might get hurt? "Okay, let's go, but if anything happens where you are, you keep your head down. You got me?"

"Yes, Dad."

Sam walked past Mark and out of the door. Mark gave Jess a quick smile and followed his daughter out.

"You'd better keep your head down, too, Mark Allen Turner!" Jess called out.

He didn't turn around, but waved his hand at her as he walked away to let her know he'd heard her. He caught up with Sam so he could talk to her.

"Sorry, honey," he said. "I just don't want you to get hurt."

"It's okay, Dad, but you have to stop treating me like a baby."

"I know," he said, as he squeezed her into his side.

As they approached the CP, Rob saw them.

"Hi, Mark, Sam. You ready to go?"

"Yes," he replied, as Sam walked over to her team. Mark noticed that Ronnie, the girl from Waco, was going with them, too.

"Sorry I'm not going with you all."

"No need to apologize, Rob. Getting elected sheriff is the most important thing you can do. Barney's only going to look out for himself, not the community as a whole. I appreciate your helping Gunny with the planning."

"It's the least I could do. Y'all be careful and try to get back by noon on Sunday for the debate. I'm going to need all the moral support I can get."

"You'll do fine," Mark assured his friend.

Gunny called everyone who was going on the mission together and went over the plan with them one more time. Then, everyone loaded up into the vehicles, and the convoy pulled out of Silver Hills. Mark had climbed into the bed of his red truck. He wasn't in a talkative mood, and the wind noise would allow him to be alone with his thoughts.

Before he knew it, they were pulling off of the paved road. It was only a few miles to the rendezvous point, and the knot in his stomach twisted a little tighter. He glanced at his watch. It read three fifteen. They were a little ahead of schedule. He went over the plan in his mind once more and rechecked his equipment, as they went down the bumpy gravel road.

When they stopped, everyone got out of the vehicles. Gunny drew them together and reminded everyone that this was the real thing. Any mistake, he said, could cost lives. He wished everyone luck and passed out an FRS radio and one grenade to each squad leader. Then he had them group up into their twelve-man squads. Each one of the five squads was led by one of the scouts who'd been watching the ranch for the last two weeks. Jim, the sixth scout, was still at the OP, and would help Gunny coordinate the fight from there. He'd also provide long-range cover with his M1A, if needed. Since Mark's squad was assigned the position closest to the gate that entered the compound, his group left first, as they had the furthest to travel. Gunny went with them.

When Mark came to the high fence that circled the ranch, he pulled out a small set of wire cutters. He cut the fencing next to one of the tall t-posts to a height of about four feet. Chaparo, whose group would come through last, would put the fence back into place and make it look undisturbed, just in case.

A few minutes later, Mark pointed Gunny toward the OP and led his group in a wide arc to their designated spot. When they reached it, Mark checked his watch, and saw they were well ahead of schedule. He had his men settle down and told them they could grab a little sleep if they wanted. There was over two hours before it would be light enough to start the attack. He reminded them that they must be absolutely quiet. He knew he wouldn't be able to sleep.

The trip from Silver Hills to the rendezvous point had gone quickly. Now, that they were waiting for sunrise, time slowed down to a crawl. The feeling of dread came back over Mark even stronger as he waited. He prayed the attack would be successful and that no one would be hurt, but the gnawing feeling in his stomach told him otherwise. Finally, he detected a lightening of the horizon to the east. A shot of fear rushed through him, as he thought it might be headlights from the trucks Jon took on his raid. A few seconds of watching told him it was only the sun giving its very first hint of the dawn.

Mark checked all his men to make sure they were awake. It seemed that they, like he, had been too nervous to sleep. As the light gradually revealed the outlines of the buildings in the compound, Mark turned on his radio and held it to his ear. Ten minutes later, he heard Gunny's whispered voice asking for all the squads to check in.

"Squad one, ready to go," Mark said quietly into the little radio.

He heard the other four squad leaders affirm their level of preparedness. Gunny gave Mark the command to commence the attack. Mark threw his grenade in a perfect arc, and the explosive fell into the foxhole closest to the gate with a dull thud. The gate guards never heard or saw anything. Mark briefly wondered how well trained they were, or if they had been asleep. The grenade went off with a deafening roar. Almost before the sound had quit reverberating, Mark heard Gunny's voice over the homemade PA that Don had rigged up using one of the CB radios.

"You in the foxholes, put your hands up an' come out, or the next grenades will be in the holes you're in. Everyone in the cabins come out and show us your hands. I've got armed men surrounding the compound, and they'll shoot first and ask questions later if'n they see any sudden moves. Now, get out in the open."

Mark almost couldn't believe his eyes. He didn't know if it was the grenade going off in the foxhole or the no-BS sound of Gunny's voice, but the men in the foxholes immediately put their hands up and stepped out. It took the men in the cabins a little longer to come out, but they did. Many of them were only half dressed. They stumbled out in a stupor, with the women and children timidly coming out behind them. Mark tried to count the men and see if the number matched up with how many they thought were left.

"Is that everyone?" Gunny screeched through the battery-powered amplifier.

"No," one of the women said, "one of them is still in there." She pointed at a cabin.

"You better come out," Gunny yelled. "If'n we have to come getcha, you'll be comin' out feet first."

A pair of hands appeared out of the front door, followed by the MZB they belonged to. He walked cautiously into the courtyard.

539

"Now, is that everyone?"

"Yeah," one of the MZB's answered, "this is all of us."

"Good. Now I want you to listen real good. I want all the women and children to go into the mess hall and lock the door behind you. Don't come out until we come and get you. Understand?"

The women didn't even answer. They quickly grabbed the children and did as they were told.

"Now, I want you men to walk to the middle of the courtyard. When you get there, lay down with your arms and legs spread eagle. Once you lay down, don't even twitch. I got an ol' boy here with me who can shoot the hairs off a gnat's ass, and I'm tellin' him to make sure anyone who moves only does it once."

The men did as Gunny said and lay like toppled statues in the dirt. Gunny called Mark on the radio and had his group open the gate and then cover the MZB's. When Mark and his men were in position, two of the other groups moved past them and circled the prostrate dirtbags. In a matter of just minutes, all of the MZB's were handcuffed with big tie-wraps. A few of the Silver Hills men went through each building and cleared it. It looked to Mark as if Rob had been working with them; they moved like a veteran SWAT team. As each cabin was cleared, another team went in and retrieved any weapons. Gunny hobbled up and asked who was in charge with Big O gone. The men seemed a little surprised at an outsider knowing the name of their leader. No one said anything. Gunny prodded one of the captives with the toe of his boot.

"I said, who's in charge?"

"He is," the man tilted his head toward one of the others.

Gunny made his way over to the indicated man and motioned for Ralph to pick him up. The Silver Hills resident pulled the MZB up onto his knees.

"You in charge?"

"Yeah, what of it?"

"Tell me when the raiding party will be back and what the procedure is when they get here," Gunny demanded.

"I ain't tellin' you shit, you old fart."

Several things surprised Mark. First was the speed of Gunny's fist. Second was the power he generated with the punch. It contacted the MZB just below his cheek and drove him back down into the dirt. The Karate Man was also a little surprised that Gunny would resort to violence so quickly, not that he had a problem with it. These cretins had terrorized the women relentlessly, and they deserved whatever they got.

"Pick him back up."

Ralph did as he was told. Although the MZB was not a little man, he was no match for Ralph's size, and the big man lifted him as if he was a child.

"Now, I want to know when the raiding party is due and what the procedure is when they come back!"

The hate in the MZB's eyes was evident. So was the swelling on the side of his face that got bigger with each passing second. He spit blood onto to the ground and told Gunny where he could go and what he could do when he got there. There was no trace of anger on the old Marine's face as his fist plowed into the same spot.

'That's gonna leave a mark,' Mark thought.

This time, Gunny let the man writhe on the ground for a moment before he nodded at Ralph to once more pick him up. When he was back on his knees, Gunny pulled out his .45 and stuck it in the man's eye.

"I ain't got time to fuck around with you. Tell me what I want to know, or I got no use for you."

Mark hoped Gunny was bluffing, but he really couldn't tell. The man looked at Gunny out of the other eye, trying to discern the same thing for himself. A second later, the grisly interrogator clicked off the safety on his pistol and put his finger on the trigger. Mark thought the old man was really going to do it, and so did the MZB. He spilled his guts faster than if someone had sliced him stem to stern.

"I don't know! I don't know! Please don't kill me! Big 'O' never left me in charge before. I've only been here a couple of weeks. He just told me to keep up the guard schedule. He didn't say nothin' about doing something special when he gets back or any kind of signal. That's all I know, honest. I just wanted to do a good job while he was away, so I could be in his inner group. Now, he'll kill me if he gets the chance."

"I don't think you'll have to worry about that," Gunny told the man, as he returned his pistol to safe and placed it back in its holster.

Gunny had the prisoners taken into the barn and secured. Then, he sent Jim to retrieve the women. Once they realized the group was here to free them and not just a rival gang wanting to take over the ranch and continue their ordeal, they were overjoyed. A few ran from rescuer to rescuer, hugging and thanking each one. Most just cried. Some weren't even capable of that. Gunny radioed for the medical team to come in and look after the liberated captives. Mark walked around the compound for a while and took note of how things had changed since he'd been here before. He wandered into the mess hall where Doc and Lisa were treating the women and children. Lisa told him that, despite some mild malnutrition and lots of bumps and bruises, most of them were in decent physical shape. However, she said, the psychological damage might take years to heal in the best cases. Many would never recover. Mark couldn't understand how one human being could treat another the way these women had been treated.

Sam came over to her father with tears in her eyes and posed the same question to him. Mark hugged her, not knowing exactly what to say. He'd been concerned with his daughter getting physically hurt, and hadn't considered that she might be hurt emotionally. "Baby, I don't know how anyone could do this. There's just evil in this world. We just have to find our comfort in the fact that good will eventually prevail. I promise these men will pay for what they've done." His hatred for Jon, although he didn't think it possible, intensified. He almost felt guilty for wanting his former neighbor dead…almost.

Half an hour later, Gunny called the squad leaders together to brief them on his new plan for when Jon returned. They quickly set up the ambush. The first part of their plan had been executed without a shot having been fired. Mark wondered if they could be that lucky when Jon came back. For now, they just had to wait to see.

Chapter 70

Mark went over the group's attack plans in his head. It was different than what they'd come up with originally. They hadn't expected for things to go as easily as they had. That, coupled with the info they'd gotten from the MZB's, had convinced Gunny to come up with this plan. Instead of using the defenses Jon had put in place and attacking the raiders from the inside out, they would let them come inside and ambush them from the outside in. The man Gunny 'interviewed' had said Jon's raiding party was due back at noon, but that could vary by several hours. He told Gunny that between the time the scout team had first evaluated a small ranch about thirty miles south of here and the time the raiding party had gotten there, another group had evidently taken over. They were more than the raiding party was prepared to deal with and killed three of Jon's men. Four others were badly wounded, so Snuffer had put them out of their misery. That was why Jon had gone on this raid and taken all of his most experienced men with him. They weren't looking to bring anything or anyone back on this mission. It was purely for revenge.

Further questioning of the captured MZB's and the women revealed that the man Jon had left in charge was telling the truth. The returning raiders would drive right into the compound as long as they didn't see anything out of the ordinary. Gunny had six of the men find some clothing out of the cabins and put it on. All but two were to be in the courtyard, as if they were MZB's watching the women do their chores. A half dozen of the women had volunteered to help make things look normal to the arriving cretins. The other two men were to open the gates when the convoy arrived and close them once the last truck came through. That was the signal for the rest of the Silver Hills gang to pop up in the foxholes around the perimeter and cover the trucks. Gunny wanted to show them what they were up against, before they could get out of the trucks. He felt that, with as easy as the MZB's Jon had left behind had given up, perhaps they could also take this group without a shot being fired, and even if they did have to shoot, with no hostages to worry about, the men could open up with no fear of innocent casualties. The crossfire would be a deathtrap to anyone caught in it. The foxholes had been dug to defend the compound from attack from the outside, but they would work for this ambush just as well. Jon had apparently never seen this possibility, or he would've had an all clear sign before the raiders just drove through the gates.

"Hopefully," Gunny said, "we'll take 'em without a fight and be home in time fer supper."

It seemed a solid plan. Simple, but solid. 'That was supposed to be the best kind, wasn't it?' Mark thought. Somehow, he just had a bad feeling about it, but he didn't know why. He voiced his concerns to Gunny in private.

"I think you're just bein' paranoid, Karate Man, but if it makes you feel better, I'll ask again to make sure we're not steppin' into a trap."

Gunny re-questioned several of the men and women specifically about an all clear signal, but all of them told him the same thing. There was no such system in place. He asked about the honking Mark had witnessed when the raiders had come back one time. They explained that it only happened when 'fresh meat,' as Jon called it, was brought back. Since the women at the small ranch had probably been killed by the other group, and Jon's plan was to destroy them and the house they were in totally, no one was expecting them to bring any new captives back. From everything Gunny could discern, it looked like all they had to do was to wait for the rats to come back to their hole and then spring the trap. Mark was still nervous, but maybe Gunny was right. Maybe he was just being paranoid.

The medical team had taken all of the women who weren't helping and the children back to the trucks. Almost everyone else was making themselves as comfortable as possible in one of the foxholes. Jim, Mark, and Gunny were each positioned in the second story of three of the cabins: Gunny so he could coordinate the attack, and Jim and Mark to serve as sharpshooters. They all had a commanding view of the courtyard. Jim and Gunny were in two of the smaller cabins, but Mark had drawn Mr. Davis's cabin. He could see not only the courtyard, but also the gate and the way into the compound. It was his job to watch for Jon's return and give as much warning as possible to the others. As he sat and waited, he fought back his paranoia by going over his own plan.

He hoped Jon and his gang would fight. He didn't want to see any of his friends get hurt, but that way he could put a 150-grain bullet in his former neighbor. He would look for Jon if fighting broke out and permanently part his hair. If they surrendered, he'd have to hand 'Big O' over to Barney, who'd probably end up bumbling the case and letting him go, intentionally or not. Mark didn't want that to happen. He wanted to make sure Jon got his just desserts.

The wait seemed endless. Mark looked out the window in the direction the convoy would come from almost every minute. Between looks, he'd try to take his mind off what might happen by thinking of other things. His family was foremost in his mind, how the neighborhood had all pulled together was not far behind, and how much they still had to do and how hard the future would be close behind that. What was the future? Would the lights ever come back on? How would Rob do in the debate, and would he be elected sheriff? Mark's mind raced from thought to thought like a chronic channel surfer held the remote control to his brain. It was maddening, but he couldn't focus on one thought for more than a few seconds at a time. He always ended up on the same thought, though: how he would finish Jon if he had the chance. He wondered how guilty he'd feel, and he told himself it didn't matter because it had to be done. Then he would look out the window for his nemeses, and the process would start all over again.

The six liberated women who'd stayed behind fixed soup and sandwiches for their rescuers. The food took Mark's mind off of his troubles for a while. These women had been raped, beaten, and terrorized for weeks, and they still went to the effort to feed the men who'd come to stop the terror. Some of the women the medical team had taken back to the trucks couldn't function at all. Others, like the ones who had volunteered to help with the charade in the courtyard and had cooked without being asked, still could. Mark was amazed at their resilience. He didn't know how they could go through what they had and still seem normal. He figured some of them wanted to do whatever they could to help punish their captors. It may have been the thought of getting revenge that kept them going. If that was the case, they would soon have it, especially if there was a fight. He wondered what they'd do if he really did kill Jon, or if he didn't. Although he'd taken a psychology course in college, it certainly never addressed this type of situation.

In the middle of his second sandwich, Mark spotted a cloud of dust on the horizon. He radioed it in to Gunny, and the old man had everyone get ready. Two of the MZB costumed men jumped into the foxholes on each side of the gate. The other four took positions as if they were watching the women. Mark looked over the courtyard. It looked just like he remembered from his two weeks of watching it. He didn't see anything that he thought would give away the ambush. He hoped the MZB's didn't see anything either.

It took several minutes for the lead vehicle to come into view. The other vehicles followed closely behind. The last one was the Watson's Jeep and the sight of it threw a log on Mark's burning hatred for Jon, as if the fire could burn any hotter. As the Jeep approached behind the other vehicles, Mark could see through his binoculars that Jon was in its front passenger seat. Mark was pleased that he knew where Jon was and that the open top on the Jeep would give him a shot before Jon could even get out of the vehicle. Mark looked over the courtyard again. Everything seemed to be in place. There was even a woman getting firewood from a pile close to the gate and one of the fake MZB's watching her. As the convoy stopped in front of the gate, the two men who were assigned to it jumped out of the foxholes on each side and pulled it open. The convoy stopped well back of the gate. This struck Mark as a little unusual, but it was probably just a different driver, he told himself. Mark turned his focus back to his enemy. He could visualize where the Jeep would pull to, and how he'd put his sights squarely on Jon's head. At the first sign of trouble, he would squeeze the trigger and end Jon's reign of terror over the ranch.

The convoy didn't pull through the opened gate. It sat there for a long moment. Mark wondered if something was wrong. He looked to see what the matter was. At first, it looked like nothing was out of place. Then he noticed that the woman who was getting wood was staring at the convoy, her face filled with hatred, as she slowly walked toward one of the cabins. Mark knew all of the women he'd observed at the ranch walked with their heads hung as they did their chores. None of them would ever 'eyeball' one of the MZB's. Mark couldn't see through the glare coming off of the windshield of the lead truck, but he imagined they were noticing the same thing. Mark realized the driver was probably waiting for the man watching her to punish her somehow. If Mark had been in his place, he would have knocked her down with the butt of his rifle, as he'd seen done to the women many times. He would have done it easily enough not to hurt her, but hard enough to make it convincing to the men in the truck. He, however, could not be that man since Jon might recognize him. In picking men Jon didn't know, Gunny had been forced to pick some of the newer ones. This one was obviously unaware of what was happening right in front of him. It would be his last mistake.

Mark looked back at Jon and saw him listening to a small radio. The MZB's in the lead truck must have been reporting the problem to him. Mark realized the plan was going to hell in a hand basket. Jon's mouth was in overdrive, and Mark figured he was telling the driver to get the hell out of Dodge. Mark pushed the

545

muzzle of his battle rifle out of the window so he could shoot the MZB leader before he made his getaway. As he was pulling the rifle into shooting position, two men stood up in the back of the lead truck and aimed their AR-15 rifles at the counterfeit gate guards. An instant later, Mark realized that the rifles weren't AR-15's. They were the fully automatic version that the military called the M-16. The two automatic rifles fired so fast it was hard for Mark to differentiate between the shots. When the two men by the gates were down, the rifles found their way to the defiant woman and the man watching her. They were cut down in less than a second. Mark could see that the others in the courtyard were running so they wouldn't be next. The Karate Man wanted badly to use his first shot on Jon, but he knew he had to silence the two M-16's. He aimed at the first one and jerked the trigger twice. He missed, but the shooters were too intent on the shooting gallery of running targets in the courtyard to notice they were being targeted. By this time, all of the trucks were in reverse. Mark took a deep breath and blew half of it out. His next shot hit home and the man crumpled. His lifeless body hit the ground beside the truck. The other shooter looked up at where the shots had come from. He pulled his rifle around and up and let off a burst in Mark's direction. Mark pulled himself back from the window just in time to hear the bullets impact the outside wall. He was thankful Mr. Davis had built the cabins out of heavy logs. While that was happening, the vehicles in the convoy were picking up speed in their rearward retreat. Some of the Silver Hills men in the foxholes began to fire at them. The men in the back of the pickups retuned fire. A second later, the air was consumed by the sound of gunfire with smoke and dust hanging thick. Mark peeked back out the window and tried to get a steady bead on the second shooter in the lead truck. He was still spraying pellets of death across the compound, as his vehicle backed up. Mark fired at him several times. He didn't think he hit the man, but at least he was able to make him duck for cover. He got a few more shots off at the fleeing trucks, but they were just potshots. He hoped that somehow someone had hit Jon before he got away, but he knew the odds were against it. He changed magazines in his weapon, just in case they came back. He noted there were still four rounds in the old one. He had only expended sixteen rounds in the encounter that had lasted probably less than fifteen seconds.

After a few moments, it became evident that Jon wasn't coming right back. The dust that the retreating convoy was raising disappeared over the horizon in a reversal of how Mark had seen it approach. He heard Gunny's scratchy voice on the radio.

"Mark, are they gone?"

"Yeah, Gunny, I think so."

"What went wrong?"

Mark gave a brief synopsis of what had happened with the woman from the ranch and how it had tipped the MZB's off.

"Damn," the old Marine growled. "I never thought about that."

"None of us did."

"Well, you know what they say about hindsight. Alright, I'm gonna send someone up to relieve you. Come find me when they get there," Gunny instructed.

"Okay."

Mark heard the old man radio for the medical team to come look after the wounded. A few minutes later, Charley Henderson came up the stairs to take Mark's place. The Karate Man made his way out into the courtyard. The initial report on casualties was five dead and seven wounded, three of them seriously. Gunny was having the wounded put into the mess hall when the medical team arrived. Two of the seriously injured were beyond the help of the team, but it looked like one had a fighting chance. Lisa continued to watch over her, Doc Vasquez was doing what he could to make the other two as comfortable as possible, while the rest of the team turned their attention to the less critical patients.

Mark was depressed they hadn't gotten Jon. He was equally saddened by the losses they'd taken. Most of the casualties were the men and women who'd been in the courtyard. The only person Mark knew well was José Santana. He lived on a lot behind Mark's, and his grandson, Roman, had been on Mark's three-man observation team. Mark dreaded the thought of having to go back to Silver Hills and tell José's family.

Mark found Gunny, and the old man called his squad leaders together. He filled them in on what had happened.

"We've got several things to figure out," the old man said. "First, what are we gonna do with the pris'ners we got? Next, Lisa tells me none of the women wanna stay here. What are we going to do with them, and what do we do with the ranch?"

Jim started to say something, but Gunny held up his hand.

"The biggest thing we gotta figure out is what we think Jon's gonna do, and what do we do about him?"

"What do you think he'll do, Gunny?" Mark asked.

"I think he'll go somewhere to regroup, maybe to the place he just hit, then I think he'll do one of two things. He'll set up a new base, forget about this place, and continue to do what he was doing, or he'll come back here and try to retake the ranch."

"Gunny," Mark asked, "what if he knew it was us and heads to Silver Hills?"

"There you go being paranoid again, Karate Man. Look, even if he did head for Silver Hills, there are still too many men there for him to be able to take it. Even with all of us here, our defenses are just too good for about forty men to do much more than annoy us."

"I know you're right, but I just have a bad feeling."

"Of course you do. We're all worried about our families and friends, but the simple truth is that they're way safer at home than we are here. You ever hear of Occam's Razor?"

Mark nodded, surprised that Gunny knew what it was. The old ground-pounder was a lot smarter than he let on. "It says that the simplest solution is the most likely."

"That's right, and the simplest solution is definitely not that he knows it's us and is headed for Silver Hills, is it?"

"I guess not," Mark said, glad Gunny felt so sure of the situation and yet still feeling something wasn't right.

547

"I think he'll come back here," Chaparo said. "There's too much stuff here for him to just leave it behind. Plus, we all heard he went out on the last raid for revenge. You think he won't want to get even for us taking his base?"

Everyone agreed with the big plumber.

"So what do we do?" Paul Jenson asked.

"That depends on what we wanna do with the ranch," Gunny replied.

"I was thinking that some of the families from Silver Hills might want to live here," Ralph said. "Especially the ones who are doubled up in someone else's house or living in a camper or tent."

"I wouldn't advise that," Gunny said. "Unless you put three or four families in each cabin, I don't think you'd have enough people here to provide the security the place requires, let alone all the other work that needs to be done. It's a nice place, but anyone living here could find themselves in the same position as the previous residents. If it was closer to Silver Hills where we could help protect it, it might be a different matter, but it's just too far from home.

"Well, we at least want to take everything we can use back to Silver Hills," Mark said. "I think we owe it to the women to take them back with us or to take them wherever they want to go, within reason, of course."

All of the men nodded their heads.

"It'll take weeks to haul all this stuff," Jim noted. "I was looking around earlier, and, although it's really disorganized, there's tons of food, ammo, fuel, and other stuff that Mr. Davis bought or Jon stole. We have to protect the ranch until we can get everything we want, and we have to protect the trucks hauling the stuff, too. That's going to take a lot of manpower."

"I'll tell you something else," Chaparo added. "I was looking at the cabins and they were built from kits on a concrete foundation. There's no way to move the slabs, but the cabins could be taken apart and put back together again on another slab or even a pier and beam foundation. It's a huge job, but we could add twenty-six houses and a barn to Silver Hills."

This suggestion got everyone's attention.

"How long would it take?" Jim asked.

"And how many men would you need to do it?" Mark added.

"The more men, the faster we could do it," Chaparo answered. "Putting them back together would be easier since we have so much help at home. It's tearing them down and getting them back that's the problem. If we had fifteen men working on it, we could probably disassemble and ship two cabins a week."

Mark whistled. "That's three months' work."

"Who would get them?" Paul asked.

"We can figure that out later," Mark said. "The main thing is do we agree that we want to take everything we can, including the cabins, back to Silver Hills?"

Everyone said yes.

"As far as the women and kids from here, do you think the majority will vote to let them stay with us if they want?"

"They will if you think we should, Mark," Jim said, as if it was an afterthought.

The comment struck Mark, but he didn't let it distract him. "Then we'll have to work it out so we can guard this place and the trucks until we're finished or Jon is no longer a threat. Gunny, when do you think he'll attack?"

"That's hard to say Karate Man. Could be tomorrow, could be a month from now. Whenever it is, we'll be ready for him. Next time, I'm gonna slam the back door shut so's there ain't nowhere for him to run."

"Good. That takes care of the ranch and the women. Now what are we going to do with the MZB's in the barn?"

"Let's go find the sheriff of this county and have him come haul them off," Chaparo said.

"What if we can't find him, or worse, what if he comes out here and wants all this stuff for himself?" Jim asked.

"Let's take them to him, then," Paul suggested.

"That could be problematic, too," Ralph said. "If you tell the sheriff why you're bringing them in, he'll want to see this place. If he's another Barney or some FEMA lackey, we could all be in hot water. "

"So what do we do?"

"Kill them," Mike said flatly. "They've all murdered, raped, and looted. They have it coming, and it doesn't get us in hot water with the locals if we shoot, shovel, and shut up."

"No way," Mark said angrily. He couldn't believe his brother would suggest such a thing. On the other hand, that's exactly what he planned to do to Jon if he got a chance. Were these men any different than 'Big O'? Maybe not, but he wasn't going to be a party to it. He'd witnessed Jon killing his wife, and they knew he was responsible for Curt's and Susan's deaths as well. He had no first hand knowledge that the captives in the barn had done anything as vile. He wouldn't just shoot them like Ed had the MZB in Waco. There had to be another solution. "We are not going to be judge, jury, and executioner for those men," he said emphatically.

The room, even with only seven voices in it, erupted into argument.

After a few minutes of arguing, a vote was taken, and Mike's plan was dismissed with a four to three vote.

"So, what are you going to do?" Mike asked, looking at Mark.

"If things go our way, Rob will be our new sheriff in a week. Maybe he can help us with the local sheriff then."

"And what do we do with them until then?" Paul, who had voted with Mike, asked. "We got plenty to do without having to guard a bunch of MZB's for a week and a half, and what if Rob doesn't win, or he can't help us? We're right back in the same boat then."

"What if we made them work for us?" Ralph asked. "They could help tear down the cabins and load them. It probably wouldn't take more than three or four guys to guard them if we had them work in one area."

Everyone seemed to like Ralph's plan, and it was agreed the prisoners would be housed in the barn and fed as long as they worked. With that decided, the plan was to take the women and children back to Silver Hills, where they could be looked after. Then, if any of them wanted to go somewhere else, arrangements would be made if at all possible. Since they now had several more vehicles from the ranch, there was also room for some other items on the first run. Although not deemed the most important, the remaining weapons and as much of the ammo and reloading supplies as could be carried were taken first. Since the firearms were in the barn where the prisoners would be housed, they had to be moved, and it only made sense to move them once. Almost all of the left behind weapons were of the hunting variety. However, Jon had only taken one of the Barrett .50 caliber rifles with him, and the other was still in the armory with some ammo and the reloading equipment. It was the first thing loaded into one of the trucks. Jim was almost salivating on the big rifle, and he made sure it was packed securely.

Gunny assigned Mark, Mike, Ralph, and a handful of other men to go back with the convoy. As soon as they arrived home, Mark and Olga would pick twenty-five men to come back to the ranch to reinforce the guard, in case Jon attacked and to bring back the trucks for the next load. The next evening, Mark would return with twenty-five to relieve some of the original attack force. They would try to rotate a third of the ranch crew home each day. Even though they'd still have to pull a guard shift at home, at least they would be able to see their families. All of the men would be on seven-day weeks until everything from the ranch was moved. Mark planned to ask any of the men who weren't serving as guards to go down to the Ranch and help with the work. The sooner they could get finished, the better for everyone.

Gunny and the others stayed behind and started preparing for Jon's return. Mark hoped it was soon. He knew what a toll waiting could take on the men, but he prayed Jon would wait at least two days, so he'd be there to ensure that the evil leader was dead. As he drove and thought about all that had happened in the last twenty-four hours, he felt like a hypocrite. He wouldn't consider killing the captives but couldn't wait to put a bullet in Jon. It was wrong, he knew, but he couldn't take a chance on the bastard getting away. The only way out Mark saw was if Jon didn't attack until Rob was the sheriff. If that happened, and Jon surrendered, then he could turn the murderer over to the law and know that justice would be served. It was a long shot, but it was the only way he could see out of this moral dilemma. As his thoughts turned to the liberation of Jon's captives and all of the useful things they were getting from the ranch, his spirits lifted. The closer they got to home, the happier he was.

Before he knew it, they were crossing the Wilson county line. Mark looked at his watch and couldn't believe they were going to be home in time for dinner. It had been a long day, and he envisioned a peaceful evening at home. Then, tomorrow, he'd go to church and attend the debate between Rob and Barney. As they topped the last hill before they got to the subdivision, Mark's vision of dinner and time with his family was shattered, and his heart jumped into his throat. There was gunfire coming from the other side of his community. Lots of gunfire. Silver Hills was under attack!

Chapter 71

Mark slammed the brakes on the big Ford and skidded to a stop. 'Stupid, stupid, stupid,' he thought to himself. He knew he should have listened to that little voice. It seemed both Gunny and Occam were wrong this time. It was possible it wasn't Jon, but it seemed too big a coincidence. Mark grabbed the FRS radio and turned it on.

"CP, this is Mark. How long have you been under attack?"

"Only for five or six minutes," the voice answered.

"What's happening?"

"They started out shooting at the towers with some big gun that punched right through the sandbags. They killed one and injured another before we could get all of the tower guards down. They're across the field to the east, shooting at the guards in the foxholes, but they aren't hitting anything now. We're not sure how many there are. We were shooting back, but Olga just came on the radio a minute ago and told the men to shoot only if they see something."

"Good," Mark answered. "Have you called the sheriff?"

"Yeah," the man said. Mark finally recognized the voice belonged to Henry Paterson. "They said he's tied up with a situation in town. They checked with him, and he said he might be here in an hour or two."

"Wonderful," Mark said, rolling his eyes for no one to see. He wasn't surprised, though. "What about the County Rapid Response Team? Are they coming?"

"Evidently, Sheriff Barnes has all the keys to the buses for the RRTs with him," Henry answered. "Someone went to find him to get the keys."

Mark's stomach started churning, mostly because Barney had neutered the RRTs, but hearing Henry call him 'Sheriff Barnes' hadn't helped. "How about Billy and his boys? Have you talked to them, Henry?"

"Yes, but Olga wasn't sure what to tell them to do."

"Where is she?"

"I'm here in the CP, Mark." Olga's voice came over the radio.

"Call Billy back and have him try to flank the shooters. Tell him to be careful; there's forty of them, give or take. Tell him it's probably the same group we were fighting with when we met him. They came…"

"You mean it's Jon's group?" Olga interrupted.

"I think so," Mark said, realizing he was doing no good out here on the road. "Listen, can someone get the gate open so we can get in?"

"I'm sure one of the gate guards can crawl up and open it," she answered. "I'll call them on the CB and get it open for you."

"Thanks, Olga. Make sure they get everyone off the road. We'll be coming in fast."

"Roger that."

A minute later, Mark saw the big gate swing open. He stuck his hand out the window and waved to the trucks behind him to follow. He accelerated as he made for the gate and only slowed down enough to make the turn without wrecking. He continued up to the CP with his convoy in tow. When he entered the garage of Jon's old house, Henry was talking on the radio to Billy, and Olga was looking over his shoulder.

Mark looked at Gunny's big map of Silver Hills and the land around it. Why would Jon attack the front corner of the subdivision? Surely he knew they were weakest in the back. What was he doing? Mark's mind raced from possibility to possibility. 'Of course,' Mark thought. It was a diversion. He wanted the grenades he'd left behind. He probably thought they were still here in his old house. That would make sense to him. That's why he shot at the towers, to get the guards out of them, so he could try to get a small group through the perimeter. Then, while most of his men engaged Silver Hills, he could bring a few of his best here to take the CP. He probably hadn't figured on anyone from the ranch making it back so soon. Mark wondered if he'd seen them come in. If not, maybe they could ambush him. 'No,' Mark thought, 'Better to figure that he knows we're here.'

"Mike! Ralph!" Mark called.

"Yeah, Mark?"

"Get your rifles; Jon could be coming this way. Have Doc Vasquez and Lisa come in here and take a look at the wounded man. Get these women out of sight. Take them to Roberta's house next door and get them inside ASAP."

"You got it, Mark," Mike replied.

"Olga, you got any men who can help us guard the CP?"

"We're pretty thin with all the men who went to the ranch. I have almost everyone down where the fighting is," she answered.

"I think we need at least ten more men to guard the CP. We can't afford to lose our communications center and clinic. What are the tower guards doing?"

"The ones on the east side are helping fight the invaders, the others are in the closest foxhole to where they were and are still watching for anyone trying to get into the neighborhood. You want to get them to come guard the CP?"

"Yes," Mark answered, thinking Jon had already come across when the tower guards were climbing down. 'Was that right?' he thought. He wished Gunny were here. The old man would know exactly what to do. Mark shook the thought from his mind. Gunny wasn't here, and they'd just have to make do without him. "Wait," he stopped Olga before she spoke over the radio. "No, pull ten men from the corner instead and have them come back here. Tell them to double time. Then call the tower guards and have them look for intruders inside the subdivision, as well as anyone trying to get in."

"You got it, Boss."

"Tell Billy they had seven trucks. We may have shot some of them up too bad for them to bring them all, but there's probably five or six. Tell him to find the trucks and do whatever he has to, so they can't get away in those vehicles," Mark instructed.

Henry relayed the message over the proper radio.

Mark turned his attention back to the map. He had to figure out what Jon was doing. The grenades were the obvious target, but is that what he really wanted? Mark tried to put himself in his adversary's shoes, as he stared at the map. If Jon's plan was to hit the CP, then he really should have been here already. It made no sense to give Silver Hills time to mount a better defense. Mark put his finger on the map where the fighting was taking place. If it was a diversion, what from? Usually, you'd head fake one way and then go the opposite. He looked at the opposite corner. The southwest corner held nothing of tactical importance. In fact, the closest house to that corner was his.

Mark's stomach felt like someone had just carved a gaping hole through it. If Jon wanted revenge, the Turner house was the best place to get it. Mark choked back his fear and tried to convince himself that he was just being paranoid. The fear came roaring back as his logic failed to overcome his paranoia. He had to find out. He turned and saw Mike and Ralph coming back from Roberta's house.

"Ralph, you and the other men stay here with Olga. Mike, you're with me."

As Olga and Ralph stared vacantly, Mike followed Mark out of the converted garage. Mark turned and started cautiously running up the hill to the back of the subdivision.

"Where are we going?" Mike asked.

"I have a bad feeling about this," he explained to his brother. "I've had a bad feeling all day, and now I think I know why. I think the attack at the front is just a diversion. Jon hates me, and he might try to take it out on Jess and the kids."

"Then why are we going by ourselves?"

"Because it's just a hunch, and we can't take men off of the CP where it becomes an easy target."

The two men quietly jogged up the moonlit road toward the back of the subdivision. Mark was lost in the fear that he might be right. He wondered what Jon would do to his family. When the two brothers were half a block from Mark's street, Mike grabbed him by the arm and pulled him down into some small bushes on the side of the road. Mark looked at his brother and saw that he had his finger to his lips. He then took that finger and pointed at three shapes walking across the intersection. Mark instantly recognized the shape in the lead. It was David. The muzzle of a rifle held by one of the larger shapes was pushing him along. Mark wasn't sure, but he thought it was Jon's right hand man, Snuffer.

The sight both terrified Mark and calmed him. The unknown is sometimes worse than the known, he thought. Mark now knew what the score was and what he had to do.

Mark pulled his rifle up to eliminate the threat to his son. The moon was bright enough that he could make out the shapes, but not bright enough to see his sights well enough to insure clean hits on the MZB's. If Mark wounded one or both of them, they might shoot David. There was even the possibility that he could hit David. He pulled the rifle down.

They'd have to follow them until they could get a good shot at Snuffer, or whoever it was, and the other guy. Mark could do that by himself. He would send Mike to check the house. Was that right? Jon could be at his house right now, but David was definitely in danger. Maybe he should send Mike after David. He wasn't sure. One thing he was sure of was that he had to do something.

As the two figures disappeared behind the house on the corner, Mark whispered to Mike. "Follow David and the MZB's. They're probably forcing him to take them to the hand grenades at Gunny's. Take them out if you get a chance at clean shots or if it looks like they are going to hurt Dave. I'm going to our house to see what's going on there."

Mike gave Mark a quick nod and then took off after David. Mark moved as fast as he could toward his house. From the front, it appeared dark inside. Jess usually had some candles burning that could be seen through the front windows. Mark listened and could hear nothing. He went around to the back. Again, it was dark. There was always an oil lamp burning in the kitchen if anyone was home. Maybe they'd gone somewhere when the fighting broke out. But where? They could have gone to Gunny and Abby's house, but then why did David come from this way? Mark decided he had to find out. He pulled back the screen door as quietly as he could and stepped into the kitchen. It was pitch black inside the house. He strained his eyes, willing them to see through the darkness. He wished he had a flashlight. As he stood there, he thought he heard some whimpering coming from the living room. He set his rifle on the kitchen table and pulled his pistol from its holster. It would be easier to navigate the hallways without the long arm.

He carefully and quietly inched his way toward the front of the house. He hoed the moon would shine in through the living room windows enough that he could make out what was going on. It seemed the hall was miles long as he crept forward. As he reached the doorway, his prayers were answered. There was some light in the room. He could see several people sitting on one side of the room in a huddle while a man on the other side was holding a pistol on them. There was no light behind Mark, so the man, it had to be Jon, couldn't see him. He silently prayed Jon hadn't heard him. The MZB leader had probably figured he would use a light or make more noise coming in. Well, Mark would make him pay for his mistake.

He slowly raised the pistol to eye level. Mark used his left thumb and forefinger to ever so slowly disengage the safety without the normal metallic click. He didn't know if he barely heard it, or if he more felt it, but Jon didn't turn his head. Mark spread his feet a tad and took a good two-handed grip on the firearm. He was moving his finger into the trigger guard when he felt a severe pain at the base of his neck. The force of gravity seemed to increase a hundred fold.

The floor raced up to meet him before he could get his hands down to slow its approach. His beloved Colt slipped from his grasp, as he heard the thud of his body impacting the hardwood floor. He felt his breath expel in reaction to the collision with the floor. What had happened?

A second later, a flashlight clicked on, and a voice came from behind him. "Turn on that electric lantern, Bullseye."

Mark turned his head, despite the pain, to verify the source of the voice. All he could see was the beam of the light originating from just behind where he'd been standing. A moment later, the flickering florescent bulb of a Coleman battery powered lantern illuminated Jon's hateful face.

He was holding his Berretta in one hand, with the business end pointed right at Mark. A long, metal flashlight, that had probably been used to knock Mark down, was in the other hand. A pair of night vision goggles was pushed up on his head. Two of Jon's goons were behind him holding rifles.

"So kind of you to join us, Karate Man," Jon spat venomously. "I've been waiting for this for a long, long time."

Mark's mind went into overdrive wondering what Jon meant. 'How could Jon have been waiting for this if he thought I was dead?' he asked himself. He wondered what Jon would do to his family. He knew he was dead, but maybe he could disrupt Big O's plan enough that his family could get away. Mark looked to see where his .45 had gone.

"I'll be taking that," Jon sneered, as he stepped around Mark, not letting his nine-millimeter pistol stray off of him. He carefully set the flashlight down and picked up the Colt. Sticking it in the waistband of his BDU's, he placed the muzzle of his pistol in the small of Mark's back. "I think I'll take this one, too." He reached down and removed the little Kel-Tec from Mark's back pocket.

Mark wondered what was going on. He looked over at his family, crammed into the corner of the room, and saw the same bewilderment in their eyes that must have been in his. Jon must have seen it, too.

"I know what you're thinking," the head MZB said. "You thought that I thought you were dead." Jon laughed wickedly. "Well, my plan worked perfectly. You fell for it hook, line, and sinker."

"You mean, you didn't try to kill me with the .50 caliber?"

"No. We tried to kill you alright. We would have, too, if it hadn't been for that sudden gust. Then you ducked down just as Bullseye squeezed off the second shot. I saw the whole thing in the spotting scope like I was standing right there. I was so mad we missed you, but then, on the way back to the Ranch, it came to me. I knew you'd suspect someone from the ranch had done it when you found the empty shell casings and four-wheeler tracks. I knew you'd come take a look, so we arranged for you to see that bitch, the doctor's wife, escape."

"You mean Suzy was in on this?" Mark asked.

"Not knowingly. We knew she'd planned to escape. We were going to catch her in the act and make an example of her, but then decided to let her go, so she could tell you I thought you were dead. All we had to do was wait for you to show up and then give her the opportunity to get through the fence. You did all the rest. God, you're so predictable. You really made it too easy."

Mark's stomach began to churn. Had he been led right into this trap? 'But why would Jon give up the Ranch? Just to be able to have a chance to kill me?' he thought.

Jon continued to talk, obviously enamored of his own genius. "See, we knew you were watching us and waiting for a chance to take us out. I figured you'd wait for most of us to leave and then take over the compound. I could have left almost right away, but I figured Gunny might get suspicious, so we waited two weeks. I left behind my newest and weakest men and took the hard chargers with me. I knew those pussies I left behind would fold. The only thing I didn't know was when you'd come back here and how many people you'd bring. I thought I might have to wait a few days, but you came right back. I couldn't believe it when they called me from my own OP at the ranch and said…"

Mark felt the blood drain from his face.

"That's right," Jon said, obviously enjoying Mark's surprise. "You aren't the only ones who know how to set up an OP. We have one on the other side of the compound from yours. We changed men each night when you couldn't see. Anyway, when they called me and said you were coming back with just a couple of men and all the women, I almost didn't have time to set up my little ambush." Jon was grinning so big now that it looked like his face might crack.

"If you had an OP, then why did you come back to the ranch?"

"To keep up the illusion. That's what you expected us to do, so we did it. If we hadn't, you would have suspected something was up, and all of you would have come back here. I couldn't have that if I wanted my plan to work, which it obviously has." Jon was really stroking his own ego now.

"There's no way you can take Silver Hills with only forty men," Mark said. "Even with some of our guys gone, our defenses are too good for that size group."

"You're right," Jon agreed, smiling bigger than before. "You see, the last couple of times we went out, we weren't going on raids. We were coordinating with a gang that really needs some supplies. I made a deal with them that if they helped me, I'd give them everything in Silver Hills except for you and your family. They're waiting for my signal down at the church where you rescued the preacher." Jon pulled a handheld radio off of his belt and showed it to Mark. "There's only a little over a hundred of them," he said, as if one hundred was the same as ten. "I have a couple of guys with me who are quietly taking out your west side sentries as we speak. Once they're dead, we'll cut the fence and put the wooden bridge we built over your trench. My new friends will have no trouble coming in and crushing your remaining defenses."

The churning in Mark's stomach stopped. It was now knotted so tightly that nothing could churn. Mark's mind raced to figure out how the guards, most of whom were occupied with Jon's diversionary force, could stop a hundred men once they got inside. He went through scenario after scenario as fast as he could, but the answer came up the same every time. They couldn't.

Jon must have seen the look on Mark's face. "Yes," he said slowly, as if he were relishing the taste of a perfectly aged and cooked steak. "You are fucked!"

Mark had to do something. Maybe he could lie his way out. "Not really, Jon," he said with all the confidence he could muster. "We have a County Rapid Response Team of over a hundred and fifty men. We already called them, and they should be here any minute."

Jon tipped his head back, and the laughter roared out of him. "I'll give you one thing, Mark, you are funny."

"I'm serious!"

"Oh, I know all about your little RRT. I just don't think they're going to be getting here anytime soon without their buses."

The knot in Mark's stomach was now the size of a boulder. How did Jon know Barney had the bus keys? Were Barney and Jon in bed with each other? What would the wanna-be Sheriff get out of the deal? Mark didn't know. What he did know was that everything they'd worked so hard for in the last three months was going to be destroyed in one night. Mark's mind raced to find a way out of this predicament. It occurred to him that maybe Jon was lying. Mark tried to find out.

"I think you're lying. If you really had an extra hundred men, you'd have had them here already."

"I told them I wanted to make sure I could find you and get the revenge I wanted. I really just needed them to stay out of the way long enough so I could get my frags back. I never really thought things would turn out so well for me with you coming back so quickly, but if you don't want to believe me, that's alright. You'll never live long enough to know for sure that I'm telling the truth, anyway."

If Jon was lying, he was doing a masterful job. Mark realized how really stupid he'd been, how stupid they'd all been. He'd tried to play by the old rules. The problem was there was no one to enforce the old rules, but he'd continued to observe them, and now he'd lost. Jon would kill him, of that there was no doubt. Mark wondered what would happen to his family. Jon might take them back to the ranch with him, a fate that might be worse than death. Despair was the only emotion he felt. There was no way out. He looked at the faces of his family and saw their fear. How he wished there was something he could do to change things.

"Big 'O', you got a copy?" Jon's radio squawked.

"Yeah, Snuffer, what is it?"

"We found them, Boss."

"Good. Bring them back here. Out," Jon said. He switched to another channel and pushed the Talk button. "This is Big 'O'. Snake bite. I say again, snake bite."

"Roger, Big 'O'. We copy snake bite," a voice said over the handheld.

Jon grinned big at Mark. "Ten minutes from now will be the beginning of the end of Silver Hills." He watched for a reaction, but Mark was too numb at this point to have one.

"Scorpion, Digger, take the women and kids out and lock them up inside the shed in back," Jon said. The order confused Mark a little, but he was glad his kids wouldn't have to see him shot. "We'll need some new workers and playthings when we re-take the ranch," Jon continued, as he smiled wickedly at Mark, confirming his worst fear. "One of you guard the shed and the other guard the back of the house. Keep an eye out for Snuffer and Porkchop with the grenades. Put the kid in with the others and get ready to haul ass as soon as I'm done. Listen, I don't want anyone coming in here, understand? I just have a little business to conclude with Mr. Turner here, and then I'll be right out."

The two goons did as they were ordered. Mark reached out and squeezed Jess's hand as she walked by. He tried to tell her with his eyes that he was sorry, but hers only showed the fear of what she knew awaited her and the kids at the ranch. They exited the house through the front door. When it was open, Mark could hear sporadic gunfire coming from the opposite corner of the subdivision. Finally, the door closed. Mark looked to see that only he, Jon, and Bullseye were left in the house. Maybe he could take out the two of them. Without any of his loved ones in the line of fire, he was sure as hell going to try. His mind struggled to form a plan. He tried to figure out where the two thugs would be standing when they finally finished him off. There was no way to tell, but he would do something. If the two of them got close enough for him to grab them at the same time, maybe he'd have a chance. It was a long shot, but it beat nothing.

"Bullseye, move that coffee table out of here," Jon instructed.

Now Mark was confused. Why would Jon care if the coffee table got blood on it? Jon's sniper did as he was told and then returned to his spot, never getting close enough for Mark to grab him.

"Okay, you son-of-a bitch," Jon said, smiling as if he were joking, "Last time we fought, you beat me with that Kung-fu shit." Jon walked carefully over to his accomplice and handed him not only his pistol, but Mark's two, as well. "This time, it's going to be a little different. I've been training hard for this, and I'm going to kill you with my bare hands. Bullseye here is not just a hell of a shot; he was a Golden Gloves champion back in the day, and he's been working with me. Said he never seen hands as fast as mine, isn't that right, Bullseye?"

"That's right," Bullseye agreed.

Mark had seen Jon's speed, and while fast, he'd seen faster, and he suspected Bullseye had, too, but he knew his forty-something year old hand speed was no match for Jon's. He wondered why Jon didn't want all of his men to see this. He almost taunted Big 'O' with that question, but he thought better of it. If Jon brought more men in, he'd have no chance to escape. He did think of another question to ask.

"Jon, I saw you punch one of your guys, and you're right, you do have the fastest hands I've ever seen. I remember when you punched me before you started training; I knew it was coming, and I couldn't block it. You're way faster now, so what do we need Bullseye for? Send him outside, and we'll finish this like men."

Jon laughed hysterically again. "You think you've got a chance to beat me, don't you? Blowing all that sunshine up my ass. Good, I'm glad you think so. You'll fight harder that way. No, I think we'll keep old Bullseye right where he is, just in case something goes wrong."

Maybe Jon wasn't as confident as he appeared. Maybe that's why he sent everyone else outside. Maybe Mark could goad him into having Bullseye leave, too. "What's the matter, Jon? You afraid I might kick your ass again? I ain't fighting you until he leaves."

Jon, who in the past would have lost his cool at the taunt, must have learned a little self-control since he'd been away. "Oh, you'll fight. You'll fight, or I'll drag your ass outside and kill everyone I have locked up in your shed one by one until you agree to fight. Understand?" he asked with ice in his voice. He waved his hand at Bullseye, and the man moved across the hall into the dining room. That position would make it extremely hard for Mark to get to the man with the guns. "Okay," Mark answered, changing tactics, "but if I fight, you have to promise to let my family go."

Jon laughed again, this time louder and longer than the last. "Sure, I will," he replied sarcastically. "You're in no position to be demanding anything. The only thing I'll promise is that they'll live, at least for a while. Now let's go!"

Jon stepped back into a traditional boxer's stance. By contrast, Mark moved his left foot back behind him. This placed his best kicking leg in front, and he hoped the different stance might confuse Jon a little.

"If he steps onto the hardwood in the hall, kill him," Jon said to Bullseye.

Mark slowly circled, staying just out of Jon's reach. Perhaps he could stun Jon and use him for a shield. He stepped in and threw a single jab at Jon. Jon blocked it and countered with a jab of his own that caught Mark just above his right eye. Mark, although he thought he was prepared for it, was shocked at the speed of the punch. Fortunately, it hadn't landed with enough force to daze him.

Mark slowly circled back the other way, looking for any weakness his opponent might show. He threw another jab and watched as Jon's hand flew to intercept the punch. This time, Mark backed out before Jon could retaliate. Mark wondered how Jon would react to a three shot combination. He sidestepped in and struck at his target with a backfist strike, followed by a punch, and ending with a ridgehand strike to the side of the head. The first two techniques were blocked, but the third found its intended target. Mark paid dearly for the brief victory, as a left jab hit him in the chest, and a right cross found the same spot above his eye that the first exchange had. Mark felt a trickle of blood coming from that spot.

"Good," Jon taunted. "You're a bleeder. I like bleeders."

Mark tried to take advantage of Jon flapping his lips instead of fighting. He stepped in quickly, locking his leg out into a sidekick at Jon's midsection. Jon's quick reflexes caught the foot and used it as a lever to tip Mark back onto his behind. Mark jumped up quickly.

"That karate shit ain't going to cut it, today," Jon said, as he closed the gap. His hands became blurs as he pummeled the Karate Man with a flurry of head and body shots. Mark was able to deflect most of the headshots by sacrificing his body. To stop the brutal attack, he snapped his knee up hoping it would collide with Jon's groin. He missed but was able to use his foot to push the aggressor off of him. Mark now knew there was no way he could win using his traditional sparring tactics. He had to find another way. He knew he could take out Jon's knees, but that would end the fight too quickly, and then Bullseye would shoot him. There had to be a way to stop Jon that would keep him more or less on his feet.

He stepped forward and jabbed at Jon's face, not to hit him, but so his hand would block Jon's vision. Mark saw the counter punch coming and leaned back some to try and lessen the blow. At the same time, he cocked his right leg and sent a round kick to the outside of Jon's left thigh. As soon as he felt the satisfying thud, he mirrored the action on the other side. Jon had been throwing punches like a machine gun. Most of them were landing, but Mark was doing his best to ignore the pain. The two leg kicks seemed to take a toll. Now the punches weren't coming as fast or as hard as they were before. Mark chambered for another kick and whipped it out. Jon tried to step out of the way, but in doing so, he put most of his weight on his left leg just as the kick landed six inches above his knee. He staggered a little, and Mark could see the anger starting to smolder in his eyes. Mark cocked his left leg again, but this time only faked the kick, as Jon diverted all of his energy toward blocking it. Mark stepped down and in and landed his own barrage of body and head punches. When Jon's hands came back up to block the hand techniques, Mark sent another devastating roundhouse kick to Jon's left leg.

The leg buckled, and Jon dropped down on one knee. Mark backed off. If the situation weren't so serious, he would have enjoyed the look on Jon's face. The invader returned to his feet, the anger in his eyes beginning to blaze, and attacked in a straight line. His punches weren't straight and hard like they had been at first. He was attacking with the windmill motion that an untrained fifth grader might use. Mark was ready and kicked his opponent's right leg again. Jon didn't fall this time, but it staggered him again. The rage was building in him, and Mark was beginning to believe his plan might work.

Jon was initiating the attacks instead of countering them, as he'd done at first. With each rush, he'd make some contact, but Mark made sure he received at least one good leg kick in return. Mark could see the fight draining out of the man and figured that, with two or three more good kicks, he could try his plan. He'd try to turn Jon around and put him in a headlock. Then he could worry about Bullseye.

The next kick sent Jon down to his knees again. Mark took a half a step back to allow his old neighbor to regain his footing. Jon stayed on one knee, resting his arms across the other leg and took several deep breaths.

"You've improved, too," Jon admitted to Mark. "But how are you going to stop THIS?" he said, as he leapt up and forward with his hands reaching for Mark's neck. The move surprised Mark, and he felt himself falling backwards. His martial arts training kicked in, and he pulled his chin down to his chest so his head wouldn't hit the floor. Jon's head smashed into Mark's face and made his head snap back, and he hit the back of his head anyway. Even though the living room was carpeted, the impact was still severe. Mark could feel Jon's weight on top of him, and the cretin's hands around his throat. He had tunnel vision and knew he was close to unconsciousness. Mark fought it, as he knew if he passed out, he was dead. The blow to his head seemed to keep his arms from working properly. He was trying to push Jon off him, but he didn't have the strength to do it. As he felt the life being choked from his body, he began to panic. The faces of those he loved flashed before his eyes, not just the faces of his family, though those were the first he saw, but the faces of his friends and neighbors.

This was it for him. He'd tried his best to build this community just so the faces he saw would be safe from the fate that was now inevitable, but he had failed. Jon would take his family. The MZB's would terrorize and destroy Silver Hills. The remorse Mark felt overwhelmed him, and he was sorry, not only for failing, but that this would be last emotion he felt before he departed this life.

Chapter 72

'NO!' Mark told himself. 'I won't go out like this!' He made himself calm down, and he quit expending all his energy and oxygen trying to push Jon off. He pulled in as much air as he could. His vision widened back out, and he began to think. Jon was lying across his body, using the blade of his forearm to choke him. Mark's arms and legs were free, but they felt weak from the impact with the floor. He took his legs and wrapped them around Jon's hips. Pulling down with his legs, he was able to lessen the pressure that Jon was putting on his throat. This allowed him to draw in more air. He crossed his arms over his chest and inserted the four fingers on each hand into Jon's shirt close to the collar. He slid the hands up until one was on each side of his attackers neck, then he clamped down on the heavy material of the BDU blouse by making a fist and twisting his hands so that the backs were toward him. Then by simply moving his elbows out, he placed Jon in a chokehold twice as devastating as the one the murderer was using.

Mark could see the instant panic in Jon's eyes. The MZB leader removed his arm from Mark's throat, and the Karate Man took in a deep, sweet breath. Jon started scratching and clawing at Mark's head and face. Mark pulled him down close to his own body, increasing the pressure on the cretin's neck. From this position, Jon could no longer reach Mark's face to continue his sissified attack. Jon switched tactics and pushed on the floor, trying to space himself from the vise-grip on his throat. Feeling the strength creep back into his extremities, Mark simply held on and made Jon try to pick up his weight in addition to his own. It proved to be too much for Big 'O'.

"Shoot him! Shoot him!" Jon croaked out to his associate.

Mark could hear Bullseye's footsteps cross the hardwood floor of the hall. He knew time was up for him. He only wished he could send Jon to hell before he was dead. He imagined that if he focused all his energy into it, he could keep choking Jon even after he was shot. In the past, he had focused so deeply during board breaking that he couldn't remember hitting the stacks of boards, but this would require a focus far beyond that. He didn't know if he could do it, but he would give it his all. He slowed his breathing so that he was taking long, deep breaths. He willed his heart to slow and focused all of his energy into his hands and arms. He was as ready as he could be. He prayed a silent prayer that he could hang on long enough to choke all of the life out of Big 'O'.

Mark saw the shadow of Bullseye positioning himself for the shot. He expected it would be hard for the man to get a clean shot with the way he was holding Jon. He hoped that might give him just enough time to finish this last task. He barely heard the shot; he was so intent on the job. It was working. He didn't feel any pain, and he still had Jon in the death grip. A second later, he heard another shot, but he didn't feel that one, either. Jon quit struggling and went limp. Mark thanked God that he'd sent Jon to his final judgment before he went to face his.

"Mark, Mark, are you alright?"

It was Mike. Mark looked up and saw his brother, not quite believing his eyes. He pushed Jon's body off him and stood up. He was still a little dazed, and he staggered some. Mike grabbed him by the arm to steady him. Mark saw Bullseye lying on the floor with two bullet holes in his chest, and a red circle slowly spreading in the carpet underneath him.

"Mark, are you okay?" his brother asked again.

"Yeah, I'm okay. What happened? Is everyone okay? Did you get everyone out of the shed?"

"Yes, everyone's out of the shed, and the two guys outside are dead," Mike answered. Mark could tell he was holding something back.

"Mike," Jess called from the back of the house as if on cue. "Is everything okay? Can we come in?"

"Yes."

Everyone rushed in. Jess wrapped her arms around her husband like she hadn't seen him in years. She pulled back to look in his eyes. "Did you tell him?" she asked, looking over at her brother-in-law.

"Tell me what?" he asked.

"David got shot," Mike confessed. "He's gonna be okay. They just got him in the arm. I took him straight down to the clinic, and Lisa said the only problem is that they re-damaged the arm the dogs tore up. That's why it took me so long to get back here." Mike took a deep breath.

"Why aren't you down there?" Mark asked his wife.

"I sent your mom. You're going to need my help with the hundred attackers from the church."

Mark had almost forgotten about the MZB's Jon had called on the radio. "That's right. We've got to go."

"There's more bad news," Mike added. "George is dead."

"What happened?"

"I followed Dave and the two MZB's to Gunny's house. The MZB's made David knock on the door, and George answered it with a pistol in his hand. He dropped it when he saw they had David covered, and he took them to the garage. He lit a propane lantern that lit up the whole garage and backlit the two gangsters. I think he must have known I was there from the way he set it up. I had great shots at them. I was just starting to squeeze on the first one when George tried to jump him. I couldn't shoot with George so close. I heard George yell for David to run, and Dave was making a beeline for the door when the other one shot at him. David went down, and I moved my sights over to the other MZB and shot him. In the meantime, the first one wrestled his gun free of George's grip and killed him before I could get back on him. I'm so sorry."

This was the first time Mark had seen Mike upset since he'd arrived. Mark patted his brother on the back. "Don't be too hard on yourself. George was real sick. No one knew, but he only had a few weeks to live. That's probably why he tried the hero stuff. Listen, we've a got a big problem. There's a hundred MZB's on their way here right now. We've got ten minutes if we're lucky. Let's go."

"What about him?" Mike asked, pointing at Jon.

"What about him? Forget him!" Mark wanted to use another word that started with 'F,' but the children were in the room.

"No, I mean he's still breathing!"

Mark was shocked. He put his finger on the cretin's neck and found a strong pulse. He thought he'd killed Jon, but evidently he'd only knocked him out.

Mark was disappointed he hadn't finished Jon off, but he'd have to figure out what to do with him later, as right now he had to deal with the hoard coming from the church. "Dad, there's a roll of duct tape in the kitchen. Can you tape him up before he comes to? Jess, you cover him with my .45 until he's secured. Mike, run back to Gunny's and get the grenades and bring them to the CP. The rest of you, get your rifles out of the safe and meet me at the CP. Jess, you stay with the kids."

"I will not!" Jess said. "You're going to need every gun you can get to fight Jon's buddies."

Mark knew she was right, but he didn't want to put their baby at risk. "Look, we can't afford to take a chance on Jon getting away again."

"Then your dad and I will lock him up in the shed."

"Alright! Just do it fast," Mark said over his shoulder, as he ran toward the kitchen to retrieve his rifle.

Mark raced out of the house and down to the CP. When he got there, he saw that Ralph had set up a good defense around the CP. He called all the men and told them to go inside the converted garage, so he could explain to them what was happening. Then he took a quick peek into the clinic to check on his son. Lisa was standing over the young teenager.

"Hey, Bubba, you hanging in there?" he asked David.

"Yes, sir," the young man responded. "It only hurts a little."

Mark could tell he was lying. He looked at Lisa. "Take good care of him for me."

"He's going to be fine," Lisa said reassuringly. Mark didn't know if the reassuring tone was for him or for David. He wanted to tell Lisa he was sorry about her father, but he didn't know if she knew yet. He certainly didn't have time to tell her what had happened and deal with her emotions right now.

Mark walked out of the house and into the garage, where Olga had some bad news for him. "Mark, Billy and his boys are pinned down. He said they were ready for him, and they've got him in a crossfire. One of his guys is dead, and one's wounded. What are we going to do?"

'Crap,' Mark thought. 'What else could go wrong?' "Where is he?" he asked out loud, trying to sound like it was no big deal.

Olga pointed to a spot on the map. "Best I can tell, he's around here."

Mark tried to think faster. He couldn't leave Billy hanging out to dry, but they had to stop the mob coming to destroy the subdivision. He couldn't personally do both, and his first priority had to be to the subdivision. He'd have to send someone else to help Billy. He looked around the room. The men around him were mostly older and less trained. Billy was almost a mile away, and there was no way any of these guys could run that far with rifles. He could send a few of the younger guys off of the corner where the diversion was, but who would lead them? Could Mike do it? With a trained crew, he might be able to, but most of the young guys only had training for guard duty, and they didn't know Mike well enough to trust him. It would take a tight knit group who knew how to move quickly and quietly, one that could run the whole way with rifles and ammo, a group whose members trusted each other implicitly. If only Jim were here with his scout team, they could do it.

563

The answer hit Mark like a ton of bricks, but he didn't like it. He made himself run through the options again, hoping for a different solution. There wasn't another one that stood half a chance. He swallowed hard and spoke, hardly believing the words coming out of his mouth.

"Olga, where are Letty and Chris?"

"They're down at the corner, helping the guards."

"Well, get them back here. I'm sending you three and Mike to help Billy."

"What about me?"

Mark turned to see Jess walking into the CP with her rifle. "I need you in the CP to coordinate our defenses over the radios."

"That's bullshit!"

"Look, Jess, I don't have time to argue."

"Good! If Billy's in trouble, and you're sending Olga, then I'm going! I'm on her team, and Gunny taught us to stick together."

Mark wanted to protect his wife and their unborn child, but Jess was right. The mission stood a better chance with her.

"Okay. Olga, you five are gonna have to haul ass. Cross the road and stay out of sight. When you get to where Billy is, get in position and put one of the groups that has him pinned down between you and him. You'll turn the tables on them by putting them in a crossfire. Once the first group is eliminated, start working on the second, assuming they haven't bugged out. If it's safe, you and Billy move up behind this group that's trying to distract us. When you're there, radio Henry, and he'll tell the guards. Then y'all can play hammer and anvil on those boys."

As Mark was talking, Mike came in with a box of Jon's hand grenades.

"Take some of these with you," Mark continued, "but use them sparingly."

"Roger that, Mark," Olga said, as she stuck three of the frags into her gear. Letty and Chris showed up a moment later.

Mark grabbed Mike and gave him his rifle and homemade web gear that held the FAL's magazines. "Take this. You might need another heavy rifle if they're dug in."

Mark squeezed his brother's arm hard and looked him straight in the eyes. "You've got three of my babies," he whispered, nodding at the rifle and then toward Jess. "You better bring them all back to me."

Mike just nodded once and followed the four women out of the garage.

Mark turned and looked at the rag-tag group he had left. There were ten or twelve of them. Could they turn away a hoard of MZB's? They'd had to. Mark went over to the rifle rack and pulled down one of the full-auto AK's Curt had given them. He tossed it to his Dad and gave the second one to Manny. He took the third one for himself.

"Ralph, can you carry that box for me?"

"You got it," the bear of a man answered, as he slung his H&K across his back.

"Alright, let's go."

Mark jogged toward the western fence line. Fortunately, the moon was illuminating the ground enough that it wasn't too hard to see. When he got even with the last houses on the street, he slowly crept forward and peeked around the corners. Looking toward the road, he saw nothing, but not far in the other direction, he could see four men dragging something toward the defensive trench. It looked like they were even with the next street over. Mark backed up and motioned for his impromptu squad to follow him. He cut through the two yards of the houses along the fence line, keeping the structures between him and the MZB's as much as possible. When he got to the next street, he could hear a faint rumbling in the distance. Each second it got louder, and he knew it was the marauders Jon had sold them out to. He could see the men with the makeshift bridge dropping it into place, and a section of the barbed wire fence had been cut between the bridge and the street. Mark didn't know how strong the bridge was. He figured anything four men could drag wouldn't be strong enough to support a car or truck. Perhaps the MZB's would just drive their vehicles to the bridge and then bring their men over on foot. Whatever they had planned, he had to figure out a way to stop them, and he had to do it fast. There was no house on the opposite side of this street to use for cover, so they'd have to work from this side only. That was a disadvantage, but on the plus side, it was only fifty or sixty yards to the bridge from here. Surely even this ragtag crew could hit a man size target at that range. Mark prayed they could, or this would be a short battle. Now he just had to figure out a strategy.

His first thought was to shoot the four men who'd placed the bridge and move it before the attackers arrived. It seemed like the simplest plan, but he realized it was too late when he saw them drop down into the trench. A small flashing red light appeared on each side of the bridge. If Jon's men were already signaling, then the attack force must be closer than he thought. He looked into the field, and the moonlight let him see about a dozen motorcycles and five or six trucks turning toward the lights. They had no lights on, were much quieter than Mark had thought possible, and were already halfway across the field. That many vehicles could easily hold over a hundred men, and they'd be at the bridge in less than a minute. Mark wondered if they were too late. Whatever he was going to do, he had to do it now.

He turned and looked at his team. He didn't see how such a group would be able to stop a determined group of a hundred men. The only advantage he had was the hand grenades. He grabbed a couple out of the box Ralph was holding.

"I need someone to help me take out the bridge with these," Mark said, as if it was some menial task.

"I'll do it," Alex said.

"Alright," Mark continued, "Grab a couple. Manny, take half of these guys and go to the opposite side of the house and cover us. Ralph, you stay here with the other half and do the same. We'll try to take out the bridge and turn these bastards around before they can cross."

Manny and Ralph only nodded their affirmations of the order.

Mark looked at Alex. "Let's go."

Mark, though his estimation of the young man had just gone up a couple of notches, wasn't thrilled with Alex being his backup. The boy had almost no training for this kind of thing, but he was the only one in the group who could keep up with Mark. In fact, as they raced into position to hurl the grenades at the wooden MZB crossing, Mark was surprised that he was the one struggling to keep up. When they reached halfway between the house and the trench, Mark

565

figured they were in range, and he stopped. Alex, who was a step ahead, continued to run.

"Alex," Mark hissed, as he found the pin ring on his first grenade.

The youngster didn't hear him.

"Alex!" he called a little louder.

His daughter's boyfriend raced on, now fully four or five yards in front of his team leader.

"ALEX!" Mark barked at the youth.

The young man stopped on a dime and turned toward Mark with an inquisitive look on his face.

"Now!" Mark told him.

Mark had already pulled his pin and was just waiting for Alex to stop before he threw his first grenade. He tossed it in a high arc, hoping it would land dead center of the bridge. Mark reached into his pocket for his second grenade. He saw that Alex was groping for the pin on his grenade when he saw the muzzle flashes from next to the bridge. The men in the ditch had probably heard him yelling at Alex, and now they were shooting at the two of them. He heard the shots whistle by, and a few seconds later heard return fire from behind him. He hoped the covering fire would give him and Alex enough time to finish their mission and get back to the safety of cover. Mark saw the young man in front of him start his throwing motion. At that instant, a red spot appeared on Alex's back, and the grenade dribbled from his hand as he fell forward onto the pavement. Mark knew he had a couple of seconds before the grenade went off, and he pulled the pin and sailed his second frag toward the bridge. As it made its way, the first grenade Mark had thrown exploded. He had evidently missed the bridge by a few feet to the right. Mark could see the bridge was still standing. He hit the pavement and waited for Alex's M67 to go off.

It seemed to take forever. At least the firing from the trench had stopped, he noticed. The frag finally exploded, and Mark felt a searing pain in his left hip. His hand instinctively went down to the injury, and he felt that it was warm and sticky. He wondered how bad it was, and tested his legs. They seemed okay, so he got to his feet to run to where Alex lay. His left leg didn't want to work quite right, but he limped as quickly as he could to the fallen defender. Mark could see the young man was dead. He knelt down and checked for a pulse. There was none. If the bullet hadn't killed Alex instantly, the grenade certainly had. Mark was saddened by the loss. He wondered how Samantha would take the news. At least the young man had gone out a hero. Mark's second grenade detonated, snapping him back to reality. He looked to see what had happened and was terrified at the results.

The explosive had landed on the bridge and gone off, but somehow it was still standing. Either it was constructed much more sturdily than he'd thought, or the frags weren't very effective on wooden targets. He heard another bullet zip by his head, and he looked to see if the guys in the trench were firing again. It wasn't them. It was the guys on the motorcycles. They'd be crossing the bridge in a matter of seconds.

Mark's first thought was to run back to the cover of the house, but with his wound, the MZB's would likely overtake him before he got there. He quickly glanced from side to side to see if there was anything close that might at least provide some concealment. There wasn't even a small bush. He looked back at the rapidly approaching MZB's. They were bouncing across the last few yards of dirt before traversing the drawbridge into his kingdom. The uneven soil had kept them from getting a good shot off at him, but once they reached the smoothness of the bridge and then the street, they'd cut him to ribbons. Mark could hear his friends behind him firing at the marauders. They weren't having any effect on the bobbing targets. He could hear them calling him to run back to them, but it was strange. He only barely heard them.

"Oh, no you don't!" he said to the invaders, but only he heard it.

He stood up and unslung the rifle off of his back in a smooth motion, as if he'd rehearsed it a hundred times for a movie scene. The short rifle came up easily to his shoulder, as he moved the safety to the fire position. Mark took aim at the lead biker and squeezed the trigger. The rifle bucked, and the muzzle climbed as eight or nine rounds erupted from the weapon. Mark mentally kicked himself for forgetting the rifle was full auto. He aimed again at the biker, who was now just on Mark's side of the bridge, and squeezed off a short burst. By starting a little low, the rifle climbed so Mark's last shot was right in the upper torso. The motorcycle fell over. Mark took aim at the next target and fired another three or four shot burst. The bike and driver went over the side of the bridge, and Mark repeated for the next rider, who went over the opposite side.

Mark was oblivious to the bullets screaming by him and continued to shoot the MZB's as they attempted to cross the bridge. It didn't feel real. It was almost as if he was playing some sort of video game, and he was racking up the points by the boatload. On the seventh biker, his magazine went dry, and he reached for a new one. He dumped the empty one on the ground and seated the fresh one just as the next biker was rolling across the wooden bridge. Mark thought it strange they'd continue to come, as he leveled one after the other. He pulled the little commie rifle back into position and let off another burst. This time, the biker fell off, and the bike turned onto its side, right in the middle of the bridge. That blockage made the other bikes stop on the far side.

Mark could see the trucks were coming to a halt, and the men in them were pouring out. Several of them dashed toward the big motorcycle blocking the bridge. Mark took aim and sprayed them with 7.62-millimeter bullets, as they rushed forward. Only one of the men made it to the bike, and his quest to remove the blockade was cut short. He landed on top of the motorcycle, and it began to burn. Mark figured he must have punched a hole in the gas tank, and some gas must have ignited on a hot part of the engine. That would keep them from using the bridge, he thought.

He could see the rest of the men who'd been in the trucks making for the trench. He ripped off several bursts, and his rifle's magazine ran out of ammo for the second time. Mark reached for another and again became aware of his team calling his name. He could see the first of the MZB's jumping down into the ditch, and he knew it was only a matter of time before they'd get a good shot at him. In fact, he thought, I've been real lucky not to be hit. He decided it was time to get out of Dodge. As he half ran, half hobbled, back to his friends, he could see the muzzle flashes and hear the reports of their weapons laying down covering fire for him. He also heard several shots zinging by his ears, but he made it back to the corner of the house without any additional injuries.

"Alex?" Manny asked.

Mark shook his head, and Manny's look told the Karate Man that he already knew the answer. "Anybody here hurt?" Mark asked.

"No."

"Good. I'm going to the other side to check on Ralph. Don't shoot unless you have a target, and don't get carried away with that AK. Just short bursts."

"Roger that," Manny replied.

Mark went around the corner and checked on his fighters. Mark's father was kneeling down and firing the AK over the top of another man who was prone, firing a bolt-action rifle at the unwelcome visitors. Ralph was standing and firing his H&K over both of the other men. Just as Mark got to the trio, Ralph pulled back to change magazines.

"Y'all okay?" Mark asked.

Ralph nodded his head. "Too damn many of them," he hissed, as he stuck the muzzle of the big rifle out toward the attackers. Mark leaned out from behind the ex-football player and let off a burst or two of his own. He noticed that almost each time Ralph's .308 barked, the sickening smack of a hit returned. He looked at the rifle and could see the glow of the tritium insert in the front sight. Mark wished they had night sights for all of their rifles. He leaned back out and ripped off the last few shots in his magazine.

"Look," the elder Turner said excitedly, "they're running!"

Mark looked, and sure enough, four or five of the attackers were running back to the trucks.

"Let's get 'em!" the prone man exclaimed.

"No!" Mark yelled. "Let them run. Keep the pressure on the ones in the trench. If they see the others making a clean getaway, maybe they'll run, too."

"You got it," Ralph answered.

Mark semi-ran back to Manny's side and repeated his command. "Don't shoot the trucks, either. Let's make it easy for them to leave," he added, as he saw three more of the attackers retreat. Mark sent them a few more reasons to leave. However, no one else pulled out of the ditch. Mark wondered if perhaps the men had gone back for more ammo. Perhaps the "get-out-of-jail-free-card" he'd given to the runners was a mistake.

Just as he began to regret his decision, he saw another person jump out of the trench and run toward the truck. That one was followed by two more, and those two by four. The number of men running away seemed to increase exponentially. Seconds later, there was no shooting coming toward the subdivision other than an occasional hurried shot fired over the shoulder of one of the retreating force. Mark quit firing, and a second later, the first truck lurched forward and turned away from Silver Hills. It was quickly followed by the rest of the four wheeled vehicles, and their tail lights jumped and bounced, as they rapidly retreated.

"Woo Hoo!" Manny yelled. "We turned them!"

"We sure did," another man agreed, as he held his hand up for a high five. Manny slapped the hand with a satisfying smack.

"We're not out of the woods yet," Mark cautioned. "We still have people fighting on the other side, and we lost Alex."

"You're right, Mark," Manny said, becoming instantly reverent.

"Ralph!" the Karate Man yelled, noticing that his ears were ringing. A second later, Ralph, Andrew, and the other man rounded the corner. They jogged over to where Mark and the others were standing. Mark noticed they all had looks on their faces that appeared to be halfway between relief and elation. Mark returned their nervous smiles. "Ralph, Manny, I want you to go check on our guards on this fence line. Everyone else, you're with me."

Mark headed back toward the CP at what looked like a gallop. He would see how the battle was going on the southeast corner and figure out how he could help. When he was almost back to Jon's old house, the firing from the corner became as rapid and loud as what he'd just experienced in turning the MZB hoard away. He quickened his pace as much as he could with the weapons he was carrying and the injury to his hip. He dashed into the garage to see Henry smiling.

"What?" Mark asked, confused by the look on the radioman's face.

"It's Greg and the RRT. They're here!"

"Yes!" Mark yelled, pumping his fist in the air.

A few seconds later, the firing stopped. Mark heard the report over the radio that all the invaders who'd been at the diversion point were dead or wounded and that the area was secure.

"Has Olga radioed in?" Mark asked.

"Yes," Henry answered, "they're on their way back with Billy and the injured men."

People began to show up at the CP. Some were the guards and fighters from the southeast corner, others were residents who just wanted to know what had happened. The mood was jubilant as the participants told their stories. Manny and Ralph emerged from the crowd.

"Anyone?" Mark asked, inquiring about the guards on the western fence.

Manny just shook his head sadly. Ralph took his index finger and traced it across his throat.

"How many?"

"Four," Manny answered.

Mark was saddened by the news, but he wasn't surprised. If eight men, including George, Alex, Billy's man, and the first guard shot with the .50 caliber rifle, were all they lost, they'd been lucky. Not that it would be any comfort to the loved ones of those who had died, but Mark knew it could have been much worse.

Greg walked into the CP.

"Hey, Greg," Mark called, as he rushed over to shake the man's hand. "Thank you so much for coming."

"Sorry it took so long. That damned Barney had the keys to all the buses. We had to hotwire them. Plus, he locked up all the full auto AK's and took the keys to them, too. Hopefully, Rob will be in charge soon, and we won't have any more problems like this."

"Where is Rob?"

"Since we sort of stole the buses, we decided he'd better not come. Barney would probably love to lock him up, even if it was on some bullshit trumped up charges. How many of your people are hurt?"

"We have eight confirmed dead and I don't know how many wounded. Doc and Lisa are checking on everybody now."

"Do you know who the attackers were?" Greg said.

"Yes. It was Jon Olsen and a group he sold us out to just so he could get even with me."

"I thought you went down to ambush him yesterday."

"Things didn't go like we expected. It seems Jon's a lot smarter than I gave him credit for." Mark went on to explain what had happened. Greg could hardly believe the intricate trap Big 'O' had set and almost pulled off. As Mark continued to talk to Greg, he became aware of people looking in his direction. He'd seen them look at him this way before, and it made him uncomfortable. He could see the ever-growing crowd whispering to each other, as they took reverent glances in his direction. When he stopped talking and listened, he could hear bits of their conversations. They were talking about him and the AK he used to hose down the MZB's Jon had hired. He knew what they were thinking, and they were wrong.

He'd only done what he did because he was trying to save his own skin. If there had been a spot to hide behind, he would have never stood out in the open. He only kept shooting at the attackers so they wouldn't be able to get a clean shot off at him. No one was telling how he'd run back to safety at his first opportunity. The way the crowd was looking at him, you would have thought he single handedly stopped the six hundred thousand Persians at Thermopylae. He hated it when people got the wrong idea about him.

Mark snapped out of his compunction when he saw Lisa and a litter being carried by four men. Lisa looked at him but not like the others were looking at him. Her's was a look of sympathy. Mark's stomach dropped to his knees. Jess and the baby were his first thoughts. He was quickly relieved to see her running up behind the litter and said a quick prayer of thanks. As his wife approached, he could see that she was holding his prized rifle. His stomach sank a second time.

He ran up to the litter and saw his brother. Mike's face was ashen, and Lisa was holding a pressure bandage on his chest. He fell in beside Jess and followed the litter into the clinic. Lisa had the men set the litter down on a table and instructed one of them to hold the dressing for her. She quickly began to scrub up.

Mark looked down at his sibling and wondered how long he would last. It was obvious he was close to death, if he hadn't already passed through that door. Mark prayed, and his prayer was answered at least in part.

Mike's eyes flickered open and looked around. They locked on Mark, and he weakly waved his little brother over to him. Mark went and grabbed the hand.

"I'm here, bro."

Mike's mouth began to move, but the words were too weak to hear. Mark put his ear down close to Mike's face.

"I brought your babies back. Now, you better take care of mine," Mike whispered, as his eyes closed.

Chapter 73

Mark asked Manny to drive to the ranch and bring back Gunny and Jim. He told his neighbor to pick two or three men to go with him. Two trucks pulled out in less than five minutes. Greg and the RRT had taken off in the buses to see if they could find the MZB's with whom Jon had struck the deal. They headed back toward the church, hoping to catch up with the remaining attackers before they escaped or hurt anyone else.

Then Mark found his wife and asked her for details about what had happened to Mike.

"By the time we got to Billy, the RRT was already there and had taken out the small groups that had him pinned down," she explained. "We all moved up to engage the group that was shooting at the subdivision. We spread out behind them, and everyone found some cover, then we engulfed them in fire. It was over quickly. The MZB's quit shooting, and Mike, for whatever reason, jumped out from behind cover and started moving up. Olga yelled at him to stay down, but it was too late. One of them shot him. We opened up again, and when we were finished, none of the SOB's were left."

"It's my fault for sending him out with you all. I was so worried about you that I didn't even think about him not having the training to go on that kind of job," Mark moaned, putting his head in his hands. "I should have gone."

"And who would have stayed here to defend the subdivision?"

Mark sighed. He knew she was right. "I don't know." He pulled his hands away from his face and looked at his wife with a blank stare.

"No one else would have or even could have done what you did, Mark. You should hear what everyone's saying. They think you're the bravest man alive. Some of them are comparing you to Superman. They think you must be bullet-proof or something."

Mark started to get mad but instantly realized it wouldn't change anything. People would talk. It didn't make what they said true. "They're wrong," he sighed. "I did the only thing I could do. As soon as I had half a chance, I ran like a rabbit."

"Well, you're pretty okay in my book, mister," she said, obviously trying to cheer him up.

It didn't work. "We have another problem," he confessed. "Alex is dead."

"Oh, no," Jess cried. "What happened?"

Mark relayed the details to his wife. They talked for a while and decided to tell Sam together. She was still at the ranch but would probably come back with Gunny.

Doctor Ken arrived from Floresville twenty minutes later to work on Mike. He relieved Doc Vasquez who was then able to take a look at Mark's hip in one of the other rooms.

"How's he doing, Doc?" Mark asked, almost afraid of the answer.

"It's not good, Mark. He lost a lot of blood, and there's a lot of damage. The good news is that he's strong and a fighter. Plus, after seeing them work together, there's no one I'd want working on me more than Doctor Ken and

Lisa. If he can be saved, they're the ones to do it. It may be a long shot, but I believe he'll make it."

Mark didn't answer. He hoped Doc Vasquez was right. To think of the alternative was too painful. At least Mike had a chance. That was more than he could say for Alex.

The vet pulled a small piece of shrapnel from Mark's glute after he'd deadened the area with a local anesthetic. He put a couple of stitches in the wound, bandaged it, and gave Mark a big shot of antibiotics. Then he herded the Karate Man into David's room and admonished him to wait there for thirty minutes to make sure he didn't have a reaction to the shot as he'd had the last time. David was sleeping, and his light, rhythmical snoring had Mark sawing logs of his own in just a few minutes.

Mark woke with a start. Lisa was in the room, checking on David. Mark looked at his watch and saw that it was a little after ten. He briefly wondered if there wasn't something else in the syringe than what he'd been told. Lisa looked at him with sad eyes.

"Mike?" he asked.

"He's holding his own. We were able to repair most of the damage. Now it's just a waiting game. Every minute he hangs in there, the odds move more in his favor. If he makes it to twenty-four hours, he has a good shot."

"I'm sure you heard about your dad."

Lisa nodded her head, and tears rolled down her cheeks.

"I'm really sorry, Lisa. There's something you didn't know," Mark continued. "He was really sick. He didn't want anyone to know."

"We all knew, Mark," Lisa stopped him.

"How?"

Lisa gave him a sad smile, and he knew the answer. It was obvious, especially to someone with medical training. How could she not have known?

"He went out a hero, Lisa. He saved David. You can take comfort in that."

"I do, Mark. In a way, it was probably for the best. He couldn't have believed he was hiding it from us for much longer, and the pain would have been horrible at that point. We would have had to keep him so medicated that he wouldn't have had any quality of life. At least this way, it was quick and painless. I'm just going to miss him like crazy," she said. The tears turned from a trickle to a stream.

Mark stood up and hugged her. "I'm going to miss him, too. We all are."

"Thank you, Mark," she said, as she patted his back and then pulled away, turning her attention back to David. Mark was impressed with how well she was taking the loss of her father. He remembered just a few short months ago when the same woman nearly fell apart when they couldn't find her parents. The events of the last hundred days had changed them all.

"How's David?"

"He's going to need a lot more physical therapy on his arm. I don't know if he'll ever get it back to a hundred percent, but we'll do whatever's necessary to make sure he gets the best chance for a full recovery."

"Thanks," he said, as he headed for the door.

"You should really get some more rest."

"Sorry. I have to go visit an old neighbor."

Mark unlocked the shed and used a flashlight to find his lantern. He lit it and hung it up in the center of the storage building. It swung back and forth on the nail, making the shadows dance wickedly. The hissing of the burning gas sounded evil.

Jon was lying on his stomach with his wrists and ankles taped. There was also a strip of duct tape over his mouth. He kept moving his head from side to side in order to get a look at who was in the shed with him. However, the position he was in prevented it. Mark walked up behind him and roughly flipped him over. Jon's eyes were wide with fear or curiosity; Mark couldn't tell which. When the criminal saw who it was, the look changed to one of hate. Mark reached down and took pleasure in ripping the tape off of Jon's face.

"Hi ya, Jon. It's so good to see you again," Mark said contemptuously. "I think we need to catch up a little."

Jon's only response was a hate-filled stare.

"I want to know how you knew the RRT wasn't coming. Did you make a deal with Barnes?" Mark demanded.

Jon didn't say a word. Mark reached down and pulled the murderer to his knees.

"I'm only going to ask you one more time. Do you have a deal with Barney?" Mark was yelling now.

Jon didn't answer. Mark's fist impacted just above Jon's left eye and drove him back to the concrete floor. It was the hardest Mark had ever hit someone. His knuckles hurt, but it wasn't enough to diminish the immense pleasure he took from striking the captive. Mark let him lay on the floor for a moment and then pulled him back to his knees.

"You'd better talk to me, Jon. I'm really pissed right now, and I'm going to take it all out on you unless you tell me what I want to know. My brother's on his deathbed because one of your guys shot him, and one of them wounded my son, too."

"I hope they both die," Jon said through clenched teeth.

Mark reacted without even thinking. His right hand smashed into Jon's face only a split second before a left hook spun the MZB leader around and back down to the floor. With his hands taped behind him, there was nothing Jon could do to stop his face from hitting the concrete. Mark, still enraged from Jon's comment, jumped down onto his adversary's back and began to pummel the back of his head with rapid-fire blows. This unconscious reaction only served to hurt his fists more than it did the hard skull he was assaulting. After about thirty seconds, he began to tire. He realized he was holding his breath. 'What am I doing?' he asked himself.

He began to shake. He was so filled with hate and rage that he could have killed Jon. To kill him in a gun fight or when they'd fought earlier was one thing, but to beat a man to death when his hands were tied behind his back was quite another. If he did that, was he really any different than Jon? He drew in a deep breath and slowly blew it out, trying to calm himself. It took a couple of minutes, but he composed himself to the point that he at least didn't hear his heart pounding in his ears.

He needed information from Jon. That's what he came in to get, and that's what he had to accomplish. He walked back over to his prisoner and rolled him onto his back. Mark inwardly winced at what he saw. The impact between the floor and Jon's face had definitely come out in the floor's favor. Jon's nose was pushed to one side, and the skin was split right down the center of it. Blood was gushing out of both nostrils. If Jon could see the horrified look on Mark's face at all, it was most likely out of one eye, as the other was rapidly swelling shut. Mark could see that Jon was bleeding from his mouth, too.

Mark lost his will to interrogate the man further. However, he still needed to know if Barney had been in on Jon's attack. He pulled his Colt from his hip and pointed it right into Jon's good eye. He wanted to make sure the cretin could see it, and he hoped it might also keep that eye from seeing that the interrogator was bluffing.

"Jon, I have to know if you made a deal with Barnes or not. Tell me, or I'll shoot," Mark said, keeping his teeth clenched. He hoped that would make him sound like he meant what he said.

"Do it!" Jon said, spitting blood everywhere. "I'm not telling you shit!"

Mark knew it was hopeless. He didn't have the stomach for it. He put his gun back into its holster.

"Come on, DO IT, you pussy!" Jon yelled with contempt.

Mark shut off the lantern and walked out of the shed, with Jon launching a stream of expletives at his back. The dejected man locked the door and headed back to the clinic. He wasn't sure if he was more disappointed in himself for not being able to get Jon to talk, or for what he had almost allowed himself to turn into. When he got to the clinic, he found Doc Vasquez.

"How's the hip feeling, Mark? Are you in pain? You look a little pale."

"I'm fine. The hip's okay. It hardly hurts at all. Any word on Mike?"

"No change," the vet said. "He's still hanging in there."

Mark nodded. "Listen, Doc, I need you to go have a look at Jon Olsen. He's tied up in the shed behind my house. Here's the key. He's pretty messed up, and he'll probably need some stitches. Whatever you do, don't untie him. He's dangerous, and he'd kill you in a heartbeat to get away. In fact, take Ralph with you to cover him, and make sure you lock the shed when you're finished."

"Okay, Mark."

Mark looked into the room where Lisa was tending to his brother. She buzzed over him like a bumblebee over a patch of flowers. When she saw Mark at the door, she waved him in. Mark stepped in and saw Mike's wife asleep in a recliner in the corner of the room.

"I gave her something to calm her down," Lisa said.

"What about his kids?"

"Jess took them back to your house."

Mark just nodded his head.

"Sit and talk to him while I go check on David and the others," she said, pointing at a chair close to the bed.

"Can he hear me?"

"I think so. Even if he can't, it won't hurt, will it?" She scurried out of the room before he could answer.

Mark pulled a chair over to the side of the bed. He sat and hung his head, looking down at his hands. They were both starting to swell from hitting Jon in the back of the head.

"I sure screwed up this time, Bro. I got you and a bunch of others shot or killed. You'd better make it, Mike," he said, as a tear rolled down his cheek. "I need you. We all do, but I really need your help. I've got no clue what I'm doing here. I don't know why people expect me to have the answers. Well, at least they did until this fiasco. We've been really lucky up to this point. Some of us knew that, but a lot of the residents here thought that with all of our defenses, we were impregnable. Now that everyone knows we're not, no telling what they'll do. They'll probably want another leader, and that's okay by me. I never wanted the job in the first place, and when they find out what I did to Jon, they'll realize I'm no better than him. They have this illusion that I'm perfect or something. Well, I'm not, and now everyone will know it."

"Nobody 'spects you to be perfect, Karate Man." The unmistakable voice came from behind him. Mark twisted to see Gunny standing in the doorway.

"How long have you been there?"

"Long enough," Gunny said. "No, you're not perfect. Hell, none of us 'round here are. If I hadda listened to that gut feeling of yours, 'steada thinkin' I knew more than everyone else, we wouldn't have been in this position."

"But I should have tried harder to convince you," Mark argued.

"Maybe so. Fact is, there's plenty o' blame to go around, but that's not what's important. The important thing is that most everyone is safe. It coulda been a lot worse, you know. Everyone mighta been dead if it weren't fer you. Manny told me most of what happened. You did the best anyone could have. Nobody can see the future, Mark. We all do the best we can. We learn from our mistakes and move on. People look to you 'cause you always try to do what's right, and you put others before yourself."

"Yeah, well, if that's true, then why's my brother lying here, and why are George and Alex dead, and why did I beat the shit out of Jon when he was tied up? I came two inches from killing him!" Mark held up his thumb and forefinger to demonstrate the distance.

"You prob'bly beat Jon 'cause you were angry at him. I reckon a lot of us woulda done the same, but most of us wouldn't have stopped until he was dead, and as far as who lives and who dies, we don't get to make that decision."

"Yeah, I guess you're right." Mark felt a little less guilty but not much.

"Now, tell me everything that happened," Gunny commanded.

Mark told the whole story from the point where he first heard the gunshots. He glossed over the part about him standing in the middle of the street, mowing down biker after biker with the AK. He finished by telling the old man of his suspicions that Barney might have known about the attack and his failed attempt to get Jon to talk.

"It seemed like he really wanted me to kill him," Mark concluded. "Why would he want to die like that?"

"Cause as bad as he hates you, he hates himself ten times worse. He's been dead inside since he killed his wife, and he wants the outside dead, too. Beatin' him and killin' him is just what he wants," Gunny explained.

Mark could have slapped himself on the forehead. It made sense. "How did you get to be a psychologist, Gunny?"

"Karate Man, you don't live as long as I have without learnin' a thing or two 'bout human behavior."

"I guess there's no way to get him to talk. If he wants to die, he'll never talk in hopes that we'll grant his wish."

"I wouldn't say that," the old man retorted. "The threat of death might not work, but everybody has things that scare them more than dying. I'll get him to tell us what we need to know."

"How?"

"Don't you worry 'bout it. Just come help me a little."

The two men walked up to where Jon was being held. Doc Vasquez was just finishing up with him. Jon had a line of stitches running down the bridge of his nose and a bandage over his left eye. Gunny looked over at Mark with a what-the-hell-did-you-beat-him-with look.

"How is he, Doc?" the old man asked.

"He'll be alright, only a busted nose and a black eye. I'd say he's pretty lucky."

"I'll say!" Ralph agreed. "If you'd let some of those women from the ranch have at him, he'd be singing soprano about now."

Mark was surprised they didn't seem upset about Jon's condition. Doc and Ralph started heading to the door. Gunny stopped Ralph by asking him for some help for a couple of minutes. Doc continued out the door, but Mark noticed the curious look on his face as he disappeared. Gunny began to rummage through the large shed. Even though he'd only been in it a few times, he seemed to know where everything he wanted was. He found some nylon rope, a two foot square piece of plywood, and a set of jumper cables.

"Mark, go in the house and bring me a big bowl of water, a container of salt, and a pair of those yellow rubber gloves Jess uses to wash the dishes. Oh, yeah, and bring me a couple of those sponges on the sink, too."

Mark didn't question the old man; he did as he was told, noticing that Jon was silently watching what was going on out of his one good eye. When Mark came back out, Ralph and Gunny had Jon up against the big, wooden, support pole in the middle of the shed. He was standing on the plywood, and Gunny was taping his ankles to the pole. Next, the old man put a few wraps around the prisoner and the support at waist level. Mark set the items Gunny had requested down on the workbench, wondering what in the world the old man was up to. He watched as the retired Marine pulled out his pocketknife and cut two sections of rope, each about eight feet long. He tied one to each of Jon's wrists, just above where they were taped. He took the free ends and threw them over the horizontal roof support that the beam Jon was tied to held up.

"When I cut his hands loose, you two pull his arms up with the rope. Then tie them off, not too tight, just snug," Gunny instructed Mark and Ralph.

The two assistants did as they were told, and when they were finished, Jon looked like the letter 'Y'.

Jon could hold his tongue no longer. "You gonna beat me again? Go ahead. I ain't telling you shit. You can't make me talk. You might as well go ahead and put a cap in me."

Gunny paid no attention to what Jon was saying. "Now bring me four of those golf cart batt'ries."

Mark and Ralph looked at each other for a second, and then did what Gunny had requested. When Mark set two of the heavy batteries down in front of Jon,

576

he could see that the outlaw was still trying to figure out what Gunny was going to do. Ralph set the other two batteries next to Mark's.

"Now get me them batt'ry cables you bought from Rodney," Gunny told Mark.

Mark went over to the wall and pulled the short cables he'd bought to hook the batteries together off a hook on the wall. The old man took the cables from Mark and started hooking the batteries up, not in parallel, as Mark had intended to do with them, but in series. Wired positive on one battery to negative on the next, they would produce twenty-four volts. Mark saw the look on Jon's face when he figured out what the old man was doing. It was one of complete horror, but it went away as fast as it had come and was replaced by the burning, hate-filled stare.

"Jon," Gunny began, "we're going to get some honest answers from you. You might as well tell us what we want to know now and save yourself a whole lot of misery. You will talk. Everyone always does. It's only a matter of how much time it's going to take. You understand?"

Jon said nothing. He just continued to stare.

"How'd you know about the Rapid Response Team and that they wasn't coming?"

Jon pressed his lips together.

"I really don't want to have to resort to the batt'ries, Jon, but if'n you don't talk, I will."

Jon looked Gunny square in the eyes. "Screw you, old man. You're just trying to scare me. You can't shock someone with just a few old car batteries. You need at least 110 volts to even give a little shock."

"You've been watching too many movies, Jon," the interrogator said, as he hooked a heavy pair of jumper cables to opposite sides of the string of batteries. "This will work, and you're gonna find out just how well it does, if'n you don't tell me what I want to know."

"I got nothing to say!"

Mark watched as Gunny poured some salt into the bowl of water and then stirred it with his finger. He then donned the rubber gloves and dipped the two sponges into the salt water and wrung them out just so they weren't dripping. Next, he carefully placed them into the alligator-like clips on the free ends of the jumper cables.

Mark wondered if this would work, or if it was just a big bluff like Jon believed. The only time Mark had seen this done was in the movies, and they always used some kind of contraption where they could dial up the power as the interrogation wore on. Usually, in the movies, the lights would flicker as juice was sent through the twitching victim. He figured that was just Hollywood hype, but he really didn't know for sure.

Gunny took the cables in his yellow-gloved hands and held them in front of Jon about three feet apart. "Last chance, Jon," the old man said, as if he was about to perform some daily routine.

Mark decided it was a bluff. The old man was playing it too cool. The batteries would probably give Jon a little shock, but not enough to cause any real pain.

Jon's answer came not in words, but in the form of a large gob of spit that landed on Gunny's face. Mark expected Gunny to wipe it off, but what happened surprised him. The look on Gunny's face turned to what Mark imagined the Grim Reaper's face would look like as he did his never-ending morbid duty. It was devoid of any emotion or any resemblance of humanity. In that instant, Mark knew it wasn't a bluff, and he smiled.

A split-second later, Jon found out what Mark knew, as Gunny pressed the two wet sponges to his forearms. The MZB stiffened as if rigor mortis had instantly occurred. The visible eye rolled back into Jon's head, and the muscles in his face and neck constricted so tightly that he looked like some kind of monster. It did surprise Mark that there were no sparking or crackling noises, but the horrid sight of his former neighbor made all the special effects he'd seen in films pale in comparison.

After what must have seemed an eternity to Jon, but was probably no more than a few seconds, Gunny removed the sponges. Jon's body relaxed and was held up only by the tape and rope as he tried to catch his breath. It only took a few seconds for Jon to regain his composure. He stood back up straight with a look of indignation and shock.

"You can't do this to me, you old fucker!" he screamed in disbelief. "I've got rights. You'll never get away with this!" He blinked his eye as if he had just wakened from a nightmare and was trying to shake off the effects. "When I get a lawyer and tell him what you did to me, you'll all go to jail."

Gunny got right in Jon's face and spoke through clenched teeth. "Who says you're ever gonna get a lawyer, Jon? We might just take your advice and Triple-S your ass. You know what that is, right? Shoot, shovel, and shut-up!" Gunny paused. He pulled back, and his face and voice relaxed. "Even if we don't kill you and turn you into the Sheriff, when you getchurself an attorney, who do you think the authorities are going to believe? You," Gunny raised his thick, gray eyebrows, "or us?" The old man looked at Ralph and then at Mark. Jon squinted his eye.

"Back to business, then," Gunny said flatly, when Jon didn't say anything. "Now, that wuz just a little taste, Jon," the old Marine said. "Are you going to tell me what I want to know, or am I going to give you a good zap this time?"

Jon pressed his lips together tightly and glared at Gunny like an infant who refused to eat his carrots, daring his parent to make him.

Gunny, his face again blank, pressed the sponges to Jon's arms again. This time, he put them just inside the elbows. Mark didn't know if them being closer to the torso increased the pain or intensity of the shock. Jon's face contorted again, as Gunny held the crippling electrodes for almost twice as long as the first time.

When he removed the cables, Jon crumpled again, the rope and tape again supporting his weight. It took him longer to regain his breath and his composure this time. When he stood up, his jaw was clenched, and his eyes burned with hate. Sweat dripped from his head and face.

"Fuck you!" was all he said.

Gunny laughed like he'd just heard the funniest joke of his life. The old leatherneck's reaction surprised not only Jon, from the look on his face, but Mark, as well.

Could Gunny really be enjoying this? Mark had thought he would, but now, it was almost more than he could stomach. It would take a truly evil person to get pleasure from something like this. 'Maybe Gunny has a dark side I don't know about,' Mark thought. He could see from the look on Jon's face that the same question was running through the interviewee's mind.

Suddenly, the laughing stopped, and the old man's face turned back to stone. "Let's try it in the armpits this time," he said, as he moved the snake-like cables back toward their victim.

Jon's eyes widened, and he began to shake. "Don't! Don't!" he screamed. "Please don't! I'll tell you whatever you want to know." He began to cry, his words now coming in short gasps.

"How did you know about the RRT's?" Gunny asked.

It took Jon a few seconds to stop sobbing enough to answer. "We had a police scanner from the ranch, and we heard the conversation between your radio operator and the sheriff's office."

"And you never met with or planned anything with Fred Barnes?"

"No. I didn't even know who he was until I heard him on the radio."

"Where would the gang you recruited to help you go?" Gunny demanded.

"Probably back to the ranch where we found them," Jon spoke in a whisper now, all the starch removed from his body. "I can show you on a map."

Gunny nodded and then looked at Ralph. "You believe him?"

Ralph nodded his head. His experience as a prosecutor probably gave him a good idea as to whether a scumbag was lying or not, Mark thought. Gunny turned and looked at Mark. Mark nodded his head in agreement.

"Please kill me," Jon begged Gunny, crying again.

"You're not gonna be that lucky, Jon. Least ways, not today."

Gunny and Ralph cut Jon down and rebound him to the post in a sitting position. He seemed less like a monster and more like an errant child as he sat on the floor, still sobbing quietly. Mark could barely believe the change in him. The three men turned the lantern down to a dull glow and left Jon locked in the shed alone.

"Where did you learn to do that?" Ralph asked Gunny.

"I saw a lot of shit during my stays in Southeast Asia. This particular trick was used by the South Vietnamese to get VC prisoners to talk. It always worked. I ne'er 'spected to use it myself, but as you could see, it does work and don't leave no marks."

"It was damn quick, too" Ralph said frankly.

"Usually is. Only seen a few men take more 'en one or two jolts. I'm just glad Jon wasn't one of 'em."

"Me, too," Mark added sincerely. Although he'd wanted Jon to suffer greatly at one point, he discovered it was only hate and anger, the same kind of hate and anger that had turned Jon into a killer. Mark vowed never to let them take him over again. He wondered how Gunny had been able to do what he'd done and have it not affect him.

A second later, Mark realized he was wrong again when Gunny doubled over and retched up his dinner. Mark and Ralph each grabbed an arm and held their sick friend up. Gunny puked uncontrollably until there was nothing left and he was only heaving. Finally, the nausea subsided, and the old man stood back up and wiped his mouth with the back of his hand.

"Must be getting a touch of the flu," he mumbled.

Mark and Ralph's eyes met. "Yeah, I heard there was some of that going around," Mark said, as Ralph nodded.

"What are we going to do with him?" Ralph asked, obviously referring to Jon.

"I think I'll turn him into Barney during the debate tomorrow. Even though he had no prior knowledge or hand in the attack, he facilitated it by taking the keys to the buses and playing politics with us. I'll make him squirm in front of everyone," Mark vowed.

"What about the other gang? Do you think they'll be back?" the big lawyer inquired.

"Prolly not," Gunny answered. "Least ways, not for some time. You boys gave 'em some wounds they'll want to lick for a while, but just to make sure, I'll get a map and have Jon show me where their base is. I'll leave the batt'ries where Jon can see 'em, just to be sure. Wednesday morning, we'll send a scout squad to check it out and decide what to do."

"That sounds like a good plan, Gunny," Mark agreed. "Now, if you two will excuse me, I have to go tell Sam about Alex," he said sadly.

/

Chapter 74

Mark was running late. He'd gone to bed just before dawn, and Jess had let him sleep until the last moment. His hip hurt, and it was slowing him down. He got dressed, choked down some Advil and a couple of bites of eggs, and hurried to check on David and Mike. David was up and complaining he was hungry, which was a good sign. Mike was still unconscious, but alive. Lisa, who'd stayed with him all night, told Mark it was still touch and go. Mark chatted with his son for a few minutes before he had to leave for the debate. As he limped home, he thought about the events of the day before.

Telling Sam about Alex had not been easy. Not surprisingly, she hadn't taken it well, and neither had his parents. It seemed everyone had lost a family member or close friend in the battles yesterday. Greg and the RRT had swung back by at three-thirty in the morning to say they could find neither hide nor hair of the gang Jon had made the deal with. Mark had a feeling that somehow they hadn't seen the last of that group.

Jim, Gunny, Ralph, Manny, and Mark's dad were waiting for Mark when he got home. They pulled Jon, who'd been fed and cleaned up some, out of the shed and loaded him in the back of the truck. All of the duct tape had been removed, and only a large zip-tie held his hands behind his back. Ralph and Jim sat in the back with the almost catatonic prisoner. He was extremely quiet and reserved and seemed resolved to face whatever punishment awaited him. The other men climbed into the front of the truck. Then, Manny drove down to the gate and waited for the guards to open it. Mark noticed that almost every other running vehicle in the subdivision had already left for the courthouse. Even the vehicles that had been captured from Jon's men the night before were gone.

"Go get 'em, Mark!" one of the guards called, as the red truck pulled through the open gate.

"Yeah, give 'em hell!" the other chimed in, giving a hearty thumb's up sign.

Mark lifted his hand and waved at the two, trying not to notice the way the young men stared at him. The trip to Floresville seemed to go quickly since Mark was concentrating on what he'd say when he turned Jon over to Barney in front of the crowd. He hoped to put the "Interim Sheriff" on the spot enough to swing the vote to Rob's favor. He wanted to do it as if he didn't have an axe to grind with Barney. Better, he figured, to be politically correct.

They had to drive several blocks past the courthouse, as all of the closer parking places were taken up by an eclectic array of conveyances. Trucks, cars, tractors, motorcycles, ATV's, bicycles, and horses, either saddled or hooked to buggies and wagons, lined the streets. It looked as if some mad scientist's time travel experiment had mixed the past, present, and bizarre into one era. Manny found a spot three or four blocks away and parked the truck.

The men unloaded and walked as quickly as possible toward the debate that had already started. Mark estimated they were about twenty minutes late. His hip seemed to loosen up as they walked, and he was still deep in thought about how he could make Barney look bad. When they got to the crowd, it was much bigger than anyone had imagined. They stood in the back. Microphones had been rigged so the public address system on several of the squad cars could be used to amplify the voices of the debaters. Mark snapped out of his fog and focused on what Barney was saying.

"...should take complete advantage of whatever help FEMA or any other agency can give us. FEMA will provide food and safe drinking water to anyone who needs it in the county. I don't know how any rational person could turn down this offer. By bringing FEMA in, we can free up Sheriff's Office personnel to work on other problems. Let's face it, until this crisis is over, we can use whatever help we can get."

There was some light applause for Barney's statement.

"Thirty second rebuttal, Mr. Bowers?" the moderator asked.

"Thank you, Judge Hickman," Rob answered. "As you can see from my previous answer, my view on this is quite different from Deputy Barnes'. I believe, as did Sheriff Thompson, that we're better off making do on our own. The system set up by the leaders of our county and local neighborhoods is working. It requires very little time of any of the Sheriff's Office employees. By allowing the churches and other community groups to organize and oversee this program, it puts control in local hands, where we have the best knowledge of who needs help. Yes, there are things FEMA can do for us that might make things a little easier, but it comes at the cost of kowtowing to their dictates and desires. I believe we're wiser to continue to 'fly under the radar' and keep the feds out of our business."

The applause for Rob's view was about equal to Barney's.

"Thank you gentlemen," the County Judge said. "Next question. How do you plan to deal with the increased lawlessness we are experiencing? Deputy Barnes, it is your turn to go first."

"I have a two-pronged plan for dealing with any criminal activity during this crisis. First, I plan to integrate the five police officers who work for the city of Floresville, who have no transportation, and the constables from the four county districts into the Sheriff's Office. In addition to this, I plan to hire several more deputies. The local FEMA director has assured me they can get us all the fuel and running vehicles we need. Second, by asking FEMA for help, we have access to National Guard troops to help us bring in line any group that does not follow the rules. I know these actions might seem a little extreme to some, but these are extreme times, and we may all have to do some things we don't like. The local FEMA director is telling me that the roving gangs are getting bigger and bigger. Just last night, one of the small communities on the edge of the county was attacked by a group of twenty men. Fortunately, the Rapid Response Team I sent to help them arrived just in time and was able to save the neighborhood. The RRT's were a good idea when this crisis first began, but the situation is getting where we need professionally trained responders. What if the attacking groups had a hundred men or more? A forty-man RRT made up of poorly trained individuals wouldn't have a chance against an army like that. They are too small and too slow to be effective against more than a handful of bad guys. Most importantly, the last thing we need is to have forty of our own citizens killed because they were overwhelmed by a superior force or because they weren't trained or equipped to deal with the threat. We need the National Guard to deal with threats like that, and any small sacrifices and inconveniences we have to make to the National Guard and FEMA are worth our safety!"

Over half of the crowd was applauding. Mark was hot, not because many of the listeners were agreeing with Barney, but that he was flat lying through his teeth. Hopefully, Rob would set the record straight.

"Your turn, Mr. Bowers," the judge said.

"Thank you, Judge. I believe we already have a system set up to deal with this issue. Unfortunately, Deputy Barnes has seen fit to hamstring and belittle the efforts of so many of our citizens and especially the hard work of our late sheriff. Sheriff Thompson, along with help from others, myself included, trained the two Rapid Response Teams to be able to meet this kind of trouble head on. The RRT's have been professionally trained by law enforcement professionals and by men who spent their entire careers defending this nation in our armed forces. These are men who have volunteered to put their lives on the line for their neighbors and friends. To imply that they're just a bunch of half-cocked farmers with pitchforks is reprehensible. Deputy Barnes took it upon himself to take the keys to the buses that serve as transportation for the RRT's and lock up some of the most effective weapons they use. If the team was slow to react last night, it's because Greg Hardy, the team leader, had to chase him down to get the keys. Then when they got to where Deputy Barnes was supposed to be, he wasn't there, and they ended up having to hotwire the bus and go without the automatic rifles. Saying the RRT's can't handle a large group is not true. In the attack on Silver Hills that Deputy Barnes spoke of, the twenty man gang that the RRT mopped up was just a diversion. On the other side of the subdivision, a group of at least a hundred men attacked and were turned back by a small group of twelve highly-motivated residents. I'm sure some of you have heard the same stories I have about how bravely they fought. I say if twelve can beat a hundred, then a well-trained, forty-man RRT can defend anything a National Guard company can."

There was some applause and cheering from a few of the people. What they lacked in numbers, they made up for in enthusiasm.

"One last thing I want to say. Silver Hills lost several men last night who might not have been killed had the RRT been able to get there earlier. Do we really want a sheriff who puts politics ahead of human life?"

"NO!" the same few cried. It seemed to Mark that perhaps a few more were yelling this time. Rob's question had at least caused most of the crowd to look around as if they were searching for an answer. 'Good job, Rob. You're turning them,' Mark thought.

"Thirty second rebuttal."

Barney seemed a little taken back by the reaction from the crowd, but he quickly regained his composer and fired a volley back at Rob. "I never said the men on the RRT's were a bunch of farmers with pitchforks. I just think the job they're doing can be better done by the National Guard. Why should we send our own people into harm's way when we pay, with our own tax dollars, someone else to do that for us? And if I kept the keys to the buses, it was only to ensure that the RRT was really needed in an area before they took off and left the rest of the county unprotected. I'm sorry that I got another call I had to respond to before Mr. Hardy could get there. Once we have the National Guard taking care of our security, there will be no need for assault buses and assault rifles."

This answer really ticked Mark off. He hoped the rest of the folks could see how Barney was talking out of both sides of his mouth. The RRT's were no good, but he didn't want to send them out and leave the rest of the county unprotected? Too bad Rob didn't get to rebut his rebuttal, or he could point this out. Besides, that was why there were two RRT's.

"Those are all the questions the candidates were told beforehand would be asked. For this next part of the debate, we'll take questions from the audience. The same rules will apply. Both candidates will have two minutes for an answer, and then the first will have thirty seconds, if needed, for rebuttal," the judge said. "Mr. Bowers is up first."

It was as quiet as church on Monday morning. It seemed no one wanted to break the ice. It was too bad Barney wasn't up first. Mark had a question or two for him. Finally, someone spoke up.

"Mr. Bowers, earlier you said you worked for the San Antonio Police Department and then were a law enforcement consultant. How does your experience relate to running a rural sheriff's department?"

"Good question," Rob started. He seemed less sure of himself now that they weren't answering the questions they'd been told would be asked. "My area of expertise is SWAT teams. That's what I did for the SAPD, and that's the area I've consulted in since I retired. I've helped numerous small departments and sheriff's offices set up and train teams to respond to the type of problems common in rural areas. That includes this county. Sheriff Thompson hired me to set up and train a team of his deputies in case a SWAT-type situation happened here in Wilson County. They're one of the finest teams I've ever seen. Because of this, I'm familiar with the personnel of this Sheriff's Department, and, coupled with living here in the county for the past three years, I'm familiar with the politics as well."

The response to Rob's answer was lackluster. Mark wasn't impressed with how Rob came across, either.

"Deputy Barnes," the judge said, "can you answer the same question about yourself?"

"Yes, Judge, I can. Everyone here knows I've spent my career dedicated to this department and this county. I think that speaks for itself. Mr. Bowers is well qualified to run a SWAT team; I'm not disputing that, but in a county where barroom brawls and domestic disturbances are the bulk of our calls, do we want a sheriff whose training is basically to shoot first and ask questions later? I've lived here all my life, and I know almost everyone else who lives here. I know how to handle the day-to-day problems and the out of the ordinary ones."

Many people cheered at Barney's answer.

"Mr. Bowers, thirty seconds."

Rob got defensive. "SWAT training is not 'shoot first and ask questions later.' It's simply a tool to address problems that one or two deputies are not likely to be able to handle on their own. Most SWAT deployments end up without a shot even being fired. My training includes negotiation and conflict de-escalation. The day-to-day problems of today are not the day-to-day problems of yesterday, and you need a sheriff who knows that!"

A few people cheered and said 'That's right!' but not many. Rob had gotten a little too hot under the collar at Barney's accusations. Mark didn't fault him for that; he knew he wouldn't have done any better, but his answer did make him look a little hotheaded.

"Question for Deputy Barnes?"

"Yeah, I got one!" Mark yelled out, almost before the judge finished speaking.

All heads turned back to where Mark was standing. He could see eyes in the crowd recognize him, and he heard mouths whispering 'Karate Man.' The crowd parted to let him through, as if he was Moses and they were the Red Sea. He ignored the stares, as he strode toward the front where everyone could hear him better.

"Deputy Barnes," he started. Mark couldn't help but say the name like it left a bad taste in his mouth. "What would you do if you were told the whereabouts of a murderer this county had an arrest warrant out for?" Mark smiled inside. He had Barney now. No matter what the wanna-be sheriff said, Mark would show it was a lie.

"I would follow the protocol set forth by Texas law to arrest him and bring him back here for trial. I assume you're talking about Mr. Olsen? Is that right, Mr. Turner? After you spoke with me about him and his whereabouts, I tried to contact the McMullan County Sheriff's Office, as, according to your information, he was in their jurisdiction. I know you would have liked me to go get him, but I have no authority to affect an arrest down there. I don't think anyone here would want another sheriff just coming up here and hauling off one of our residents without the proper paperwork being done. Unfortunately, with the communication difficulties, I haven't been able to get a hold of them. I assure you that when I do, Mr. Olsen, if he is there, will be brought to justice."

Damn, he's smoother than I figured, Mark thought. That didn't go exactly like I had planned, but I'll get him with this one.

"I have another question for you then. What if someone told you…"

"I'm sorry, Mr. Turner, but I believe that it's Mr. Bowers' turn to answer your question," Barney said with a sickeningly sweet smile. "Isn't that right, Judge Hickman?"

"Yes," the Judge stammered. "Only one question at a time. Mr. Bowers?"

"Thank you, Judge. I know what Mr. Turner is talking about here." Rob looked down at Mark and smiled. "Interim Sheriff Barnes was given good information and evidence that Jon Olsen, the suspected murderer of Sheriff Curt Thompson, was holed up at a remote ranch about sixty miles south of here. He could have acted on that information. Texas law says that a law officer can cross out of his jurisdiction to effect an arrest, within the state, without the permission of the other jurisdiction, if he feels that a suspect, for whom he has an arrest warrant, would otherwise escape capture if he were to wait for permission. Every sworn peace officer is taught this law and tested on it before they can wear a badge and a gun. Mr. Barnes chose, for whatever reason, to ignore this law, and because he did, people have died."

"Because Deputy Barnes wouldn't do anything, Mr. Turner and some of his associates went down to the ranch to place Mr. Olsen under citizen's arrest and bring him back here. Unfortunately, Mr. Olsen and some of his accomplices had planned to attack Silver Hills at the same time. The story is too long for me to tell in my allotted time, but because of the courage of Mr. Turner and his team,

585

the women who were held captive and tortured at the ranch were freed. Mr. Turner also was able to place Mr. Olsen under citizen's arrest. Mr. Olsen, who, in addition to being the number one suspect in Sheriff Thompson's murder, also has a warrant out for murdering his own wife. In fact, I believe Mr. Turner wishes to turn the suspect over to the authorities here today. Isn't that right, Mark?"

"That's right!" Mark was happy that Rob had been able to do to Barney what he'd failed to do. Mark waved for Jon to be brought forward. Chaparo and Ralph dragged the prisoner to the stage. Barney, wide-eyed with surprise, motioned to a couple of his men to take Jon.

"Way to go, Karate Man!" someone in the back of the crowd yelled. The rest of the crowd began to cheer and chant Mark's nickname.

After a moment, Judge Hickman began to pound his gavel, and the crowd slowly quieted.

"Deputy Barnes," the judge said, "you have thirty seconds."

While the crowd had been cheering, Mark had watched Barney's expression turn from surprise to anger and back to smugness. Mark wished the crowd hadn't given the deputy time to collect his composure.

"First, I want to thank Mr. Turner for bringing in this dangerous fugitive. However, I want to remind all of our civilians that confronting known felons is very dangerous and should only be done by trained law enforcement personnel. I think Mr. Turner's attempt to bring this man to justice is a perfect example of this. Although the ultimate goal was achieved, at what cost?"

Mark fumed at what Barney was saying. It wasn't so much what he said, but how he said it, as if Mark was some errant schoolboy.

"Also, Mr. Turner broke the President's Executive Order about crossing county lines, and while I'm certainly not going to arrest him for it, if he'd been caught by the National Guard or some other official branch of the government, he would be in almost as much trouble as the man he went to get."

A few boo's drifted up from the crowd.

"We must follow the letter of the law during these difficult times. That is what is best for all of us. We need a sheriff who will observe all the laws, and I assure you that I will enforce the letter of the law when I am elected sheriff," Barney said emphatically.

There were a few cheers, but they came from a small group of hardcore Barnes supporters who were in a tight knot in front of the stage. They quickly died in the vast sea of silence from the majority of the observers. From the middle of a crowd, a lone voice rang out. "You're wrong, Barnes. Laws be damned. Just because some politician who never had a real job in his life got a majority of his cronies to agree with him and passed a law, don't make it right. We need a sheriff who'll do what's right!"

The crowd erupted. The sounds of "That's right!" and "Hell, yeah!" were sweet music to Mark. Everyone does see through Barney, he thought. He looked up on the stage and saw Barney shrink from the jeers, while Rob stood straight and proud. He reminded Mark of the painting of Washington crossing the Delaware. Rob would be the new sheriff, it was obvious now, and he would be a great leader for the county. Mark, despite the trials and tribulations he'd recently experienced, was jumping for joy on the inside. In fact, it was all he could do to keep his enthusiasm from overflowing and publicly displaying his elation.

Judge Hickman's gavel struggled to quiet the commotion. It slowly overcame its opposition, and finally the judge was able to ask for the next question.

A young man stepped forward. "Mr. Bowers, you've mentioned the group that went with Mr. Turner down to McMullen County to bring back a fugitive from justice. Did you go with them?"

"Well, I, I ..." Rob's voice trailed off. He cleared his throat. Mark's elation plummeted. Rob continued, "I wasn't able to go with Mr. Turner's group, but I did help them plan their attack on the ranch."

"Why didn't you go help?" the young man asked sincerely.

Rob looked like deer caught in the headlights of a speeding truck. "Well, I, I, I think we have to give Deputy Barnes a chance to answer your first question," he said weakly. It was obvious he was trying to avoid the question.

Hisses and catcalls came from the crowd with shouts of "Answer the question!" and "What are you hiding?" thrown in. Judge Hickman didn't come to Rob's rescue, as he, too, appeared interested in the answer. The shoe was on the other foot now, and Barney seemed to be enjoying it immensely, gauging by the vile smirk on his face.

"I didn't go because of the election. I had to help with my campaign and get ready for this debate," Rob explained defensively.

"So you put politics ahead of your friends and neighbors?" someone yelled.

Rob stood frozen on the podium. The blank stare on his face told that he didn't know what to say. The jeers from the crowd continued for several minutes, but finally died down. Mark didn't think that anything could be worse than the booing and hissing the crowd had thrown at Rob, but the sound of Barney's voice, saying what Mark imagined everyone was thinking, was worse.

"I think this all comes down to integrity. You can see now why I'm the logical choice for sheriff. While everyone might not always agree with my position, you know where I stand and know I'll do what I say, unlike Mr. Bowers, who advocates one thing, but does another."

The words stung. Mark, so sure just a minute ago that Rob would be the new sheriff, was now sure his friend would lose the election. His stomach twisted into a knot that almost made him physically ill.

A voice from the back of the assembly rang out. "You got no room to talk, Barney! You're as two faced as they come."

Barnes visibly bristled. Mark didn't know if it was the accusation or being called by his nickname that riled him.

"Now you look here," Barnes shouted back, "I say what I mean and mean what I say!"

"Sell it to the fertilizer plant, Barnes!" someone else yelled.

"Yeah, everyone knows you're full of shit!" another agreed.

Barney's mouth was moving, but his words of rebuttal were lost in a wave of heckling that made him turn redder by the second. He finally shut his mouth and stood on the stage shaking in anger. The vocal insurgence of the crowd finally died enough that the pounding of the Judge's gavel could be heard. When it got almost quiet enough that Mark could hear himself think, one of Barney's supporters yelled something derogatory about one of Rob's supporter's mother. This caused the din of both camps to crescendo beyond the decibel level of a heavy metal rock concert. The yelling quickly turned to pushing and rapidly degraded to slapping and then punching.

Mark couldn't believe what he was seeing, as the fighting spread to almost half the crowd. The other half pulled back into a big circle and watched, as if it was the Super Bowl. Mark looked up onto the stage, hoping Rob would say something to quiet the crowd. His friend had more the look of soon to be road kill in his eyes than understanding that someone needed to take charge of the situation. Mark looked at Barney and saw him grinning at the melee. Well, somebody has to do something, he thought.

He jumped up on the stage and got behind the microphone.

"Hey, quit it! Everybody, stop!" His words had no effect on the pugilists. "I SAID STOP!" he yelled as loud as he could.

The last command had the desired effect. Not everyone stopped at once, but within a few seconds, the punches had stopped flying.

"What are you doing?" Mark asked in disbelief. "We're neighbors. We have to stick together if we want to make it through this crisis, not fight against each other. You should all be ashamed of yourselves."

Almost everyone hung his or her head. Mark could hear nothing but the breeze wafting through the treetops.

"The debate is obviously over. Now we have a decision to make." Mark wanted to come right out and endorse Rob, but he knew he had to be neutral as long as he was on the stage. He almost couldn't believe the words coming out of his mouth. "Both of these men have laid out their plans for the Sheriff's Office and our county. They both have strong convictions and feel that their way is the best. Our job now is to decide whose plan is better for us. Now go home and think about it. Not just what is best for you personally, but what's best for all of Wilson County, and no matter what the results are, remember we're all in this together. We have to stand behind whichever man is elected. Petty fighting amongst ourselves will only give the evildoers a foothold on our families, friends, homes and community. To paraphrase an old saying, we have to stand together, or we will surely fall apart. Now go home peacefully and remember that we have to live together, no matter what happens."

The crowd stood frozen. Finally, men and women began to nod their heads and look at the neighbors they had only a minute ago been fighting with. Hands were shaken in apology, and the crowd slowly dispersed.

Mark, with bile churning in his stomach, hopped down and made his way to his friends. He wasn't sure if the feeling in his stomach was from his distaste for how everyone had acted, or because he'd said something nice about Barney. He decided it was probably some of both. He felt that, overall, Barney had done better in the debate, and that bothered him, too. He imagined the outcome would be determined not by how many voted for the candidate they liked, but by voting against who they didn't like.

Chapter 75

Monday was a very sad day. A single funeral was held for all the residents who'd been killed. Brother Bob did his best to console those who had lost family and friends. Mark couldn't imagine a more heartrending day. It was depressing that each person wasn't able to have a separate funeral, but Mark wondered if the living would have been able to endure eight separate funerals in such a short time frame. He didn't think he could. After the funeral, the community had a large potluck dinner. While a somber affair, it seemed to promote the long journey of healing that needed to begin. Mark watched as the younger children, unconscious of the seriousness of the day, ran and played.

After lunch, a large crew gathered the bodies of the attackers and buried them in a large grave in the field on the west side of the subdivision. Brother Bob said a few words over the site after it was covered. No marker was placed, and Mark found it ironic that this small area would probably be the most productive in the field for years to come and that, one day, people wouldn't have a clue as to why. Civilization would return, maybe many years from now, but it would, and all of this would be forgotten. It was the way of the world.

Tuesday was the first day of the elections. Mark woke up early and dressed. He went to the kitchen and started preparing breakfast for everyone. Family and friends drifted in and began to help cook and set the table. The mood was better than the day before, as everyone was excited about the election. Even though many of the new residents of Silver Hills weren't registered to vote in Wilson County, they still intended to help. Some had volunteered to drive those voters in the neighborhood without a car to the polls. Others had plans to pass out handmade flyers in front of the courthouse. Breakfast was abuzz with chatter and speculation.

Even among all the enthusiasm, Mark was a little depressed. Losing George and Alex really had him in a funk. Not only because George was his best friend's father-in-law and Alex was his daughter's boyfriend, but they were the neighborhood's farming experts. Mark wondered who would take their place and what it would mean for Silver Hills' food production.

He was still concerned about Mike, too. His brother was getting better, but he wasn't yet out of the woods. Mark would feel a lot better if Mike woke up. David was home. At least that was good, even if they didn't know how much use he'd get back in his arm.

He also feared Rob would lose the election and they'd be stuck with Barney. He was glad he was going with Ralph and Manny to recon the small ranch where Jon had met his MZB allies. They planned to leave late this afternoon. As soon as he and Manny got back from the courthouse, they'd pack up and then have one last briefing with Gunny.

After breakfast, Mark, Jess, Manny, and his wife, Olivia, climbed into the Blazer and set off for Floresville. Mark was deep in thought when Jess spoke.

"A penny for your thoughts," she smiled.

"You won't get your money's worth," he answered.

"Try me."

"Yeah, Mark, what's wrong?" Manny added.

"Oh, I'm just worried about the election. If Rob doesn't win, I don't know what'll happen to us. What if Barney screws up, and FEMA decides to put us in camps like they did to the people in San Antonio? Or what if he goes through with his plan to disband our RRT's and County Defense Force, and the National Guard can't protect us? I mean, we already know there are gangs that have over a hundred members. What if they get up to three or four hundred or even more? What if…" Mark's voice trailed off. There was no need to depress everyone else. "I think you see what I mean."

"Look, Mark," Jess said beseechingly, "you just need to trust that the right man will win. The citizens of this county aren't a bunch of idiots. They see Barney for what he is."

"I hope you're right."

"Besides," Manny jumped in, "what you said up there yesterday made a lot of sense. I think you made them think. Plus, everyone knows you support Rob, and having the Karate Man on his side is sure to make a difference."

"Well, I don't know if that's the truth or not, but it does make me feel a little better. Thanks, guys."

The two couples made small talk the rest of the way and soon were pulling up in front of the courthouse. It was still a few minutes before the polls would open, but there was a crowd. Rob was out front with a small army of supporters, and he was pressing flesh and flashing his best smile. Barney was on the other side of the wide sidewalk that led to the entrance doing his best Andy Griffith impression. Mark noticed several uniformed deputies who supported Barnes were there, helping him pass out flyers and greet people. Mark knew many of the deputies supported Rob, but none of them could be seen.

Mark walked up to Rob.

"Morning, Mark!" Rob said loudly. They shook hands, and the new politician smiled.

"Morning. How come none of your friends from the Sheriff's Office are here helping you?"

Rob stepped in closer and lowered his voice. "Seems all of my supporters are on the day shift this week, and somehow all of his have nights."

Mark was pissed. "That's not right. Why don't you call the son of a bitch on it?"

"It's okay, Mark," Rob reassured his friend. "You're not the first person to ask about it. Word will get around, and the rumor mill will do him more harm than me calling him out and letting him fix it or make up some reason."

Mark smiled. "You're getting the hang of the politics game aren't you?"

Rob nodded. "With some help," he added.

Soon the doors opened, and everyone lined up to vote. The line moved faster than Mark had expected. When he got to the front and his voter's registration card was checked, he was given a ballot and sent to a makeshift box. It only took a second since there was only the sheriff's position to vote on. He handed his finished ballot to a man, who made sure there was only one ballot and then deposited it into a locked, metal box.

The Silver Hills foursome met outside and, after wishing Rob good luck, returned to their truck. The drive home went quickly for Mark, as he found himself more optimistic about the election outcome. The briefing with Gunny went quickly, as all three men had done this before. Gunny ran down the information he required. When they had it, or if they hadn't seen anyone by the third morning, they were to come home. Mark hoped the gang was there for two reasons. First, they needed to be dealt with, and second, he hoped they didn't have to stay for three days watching nothing. After the short briefing, Mark went home and got his weapons and gear ready for the two or three day stakeout. He spent the rest of the day with his family.

The late afternoon trip went smoothly. They saw no one on the highways and only noticed a few occupied farmhouses when they got onto the county roads. Others looked as if they'd been abandoned for years. It was hard to believe that in only three and a half months, the world had changed so much. At one of the farms, there were several men working in a field with several others providing security. Even at a distance, Mark could see the men watched their truck carefully until it passed out of sight. He wondered if others were watching that he couldn't see. A chill went down his back.

Mark slowed down even more and watched for trouble, as the other two men continued to talk about the election. Ralph had gone to vote later in the day and reported that there were many more people than he'd expected. Mark pondered if a high turn out would be good for Rob. He hoped so.

Just as the sun was setting, they found a good spot to hide the truck. They removed their gear and covered the truck with some camouflage netting and fallen tree branches. The men put on their packs and struck out for the ranch house. They were about three miles away. Manny took the lead with Ralph behind him and Mark bringing up the rear. They moved silently and spaced apart, as Gunny had drilled into them until it was second nature. Mark looked at the two men in front of him and marveled at the change in them. Manny was thin and wiry. The soft pudge around his middle was gone. Ralph was no longer a lumbering bear. Now, he was a tiger. He was still huge, but now he moved with an effortless stealth that defied his mass. Mark wondered if he'd changed, too. Physically, he hadn't changed much, but he had changed on the inside, he realized. He remembered his first shootout with the MZB's who'd chased them in the truck and how sick he was after he had killed some of them. Saturday night, he'd killed multiple attackers, he didn't remember exactly how many, and had felt nothing but relief when they had fallen. He questioned if that was a change for the better or not.

Sooner than he expected, they were in sight of the house. There were no lights or signs of activity, but the team carefully found a place to watch from and set up their rotations. Mark's watch wasn't until four in the morning, so he ate and sacked out.

When Ralph woke him for his shift, the big lawyer reported that nothing had happened. Mark crawled up to the lookout point and stared at the old white wooden house in the pale moonlight. Nothing moved. Once the sun came up, the only signs of life were a few chickens scratching in the dirt and a squirrel that ran back and forth across the rusty tin roof. A few vehicles were in front, but none of them appeared roadworthy. In its day, the very large house must have been a hub of activity. Now, it was just an empty hull. Mark wondered if anyone had even been living there when The Burst came. He hoped not, as he couldn't imagine what the MZB's would have done to an unprepared family. He speculated as to whether the gang would come back or not. He tried to put himself in their shoes to get some inkling of their philosophy, hoping it would give him some insight. It was impossible, though. His values and beliefs prevented him from seeing things as the hell spawn did.

Mark spent time thinking about the election. One minute, he was sure Rob would win, and the next, he convinced himself Barney was going to be the victor. Mark drove himself crazy and pushed the voting from his mind.

He thought of his family and the neighborhood, how far they'd come in a short time and the twists of fate that had brought them here. If he'd gotten his way, they would have gone to Mr. Davis's ranch and been dead, or maybe worse in Jess's and Sam's case. Without Gunny, who knows where they'd be, he thought. Everyone had pulled together. Silver Hills had become more than a community. They were a family.

Finally, on the third morning, no one had shown up. Mark considered checking out the house and buildings but thought better of altering Gunny's plan. The men trekked out and drove home.

As soon as they drove through the gate, Mark stopped to check on his brother. Mike was still unconscious but was improving. Lisa felt that he might wake up at any time.

Anxious for news on the outcome of the election, Mark was disappointed to learn that the polls were to be open for at least two more days. The turnout had been record-breaking. The election supervisors had only expected about half of the normal turnout, but almost twice as many people as normal had come to vote. They'd run out of ballots by two o'clock on the second day. The committee had printed more using an old, hand-cranked mimeograph machine the Methodist church owned to print their church bulletins. Even with working through the night, they only printed enough ballots to last until noon on the third day. Some of the voters were upset that they had to come back, but most took it in stride and understood the delay.

Mark did feel that the record turnout was a good sign for Rob. That more than offset any angst about the delay. Gunny's debriefing went quickly. The old man speculated that they'd check the place out again in a week or two. Mark returned home in time for lunch. It was much less dreary around the table now that everyone was sure Mike was going to live. Mark didn't want to get his hopes up too much, but he was feeling more optimistic, as well, not just about his brother but about almost everything. He decided he'd go down to the ranch the next morning and help with the disassembly of the cabins. That would take his mind off the election and let him see how things were going.

Early the next morning, he left with a group of men and women who would work at the ranch for two days. They arrived to find the work going well. Two of the cabins were almost totally disassembled, and two more were beginning to be worked on. Mark found Chaparo and got the lowdown. The prisoners were working very hard, hoping their labor might gain them some goodwill.

Mark toiled, loading the trailers and trucks that would return to Silver Hills tonight with a third of the workforce. The work was grueling, but Mark took pleasure in it. It mostly kept his mind off other things, and it felt great to work up a good sweat.

The meal prepared for them that night was simple, but Mark couldn't remember tasting anything so good for a long time. He and the other men he sat with ate like horses. Chaparo laughed that during the first couple of days, the cooks hadn't made enough and had to cook more food at the good-natured demand of the workers.

Mark slept like a baby. With tired muscles, a full belly, and a real hot shower with water pressure, the cot he was on could have been made of barbed wire or cotton candy, and it wouldn't have made a difference. He woke up sore, but refreshed, hardly remembering putting his head on the pillow. This day, he helped to take apart one of the cabins. The work was hard, but not as arduous as the day before. Late in the afternoon, he and the crew he'd brought down returned home.

Mike had woken up. Although he was sleeping over twenty hours a day, he still was able to spend some time with his family. The mood of all the Turners was joyous, as the doctor now gave Mike a better than ninety percent chance for a full recovery. Lisa told Mark that she'd be sure to call him the next time Mike woke up.

The voting had ended, but the election committee had said it might take them two or three days to finish counting the ballots. Mark was again slightly perturbed that he had to wait, but what else could he do?

Early the next morning, Mark got to visit with Mike.

"Hey, Bro," Mark greeted his brother. "You had all of us scared for a while."

"Well, you know me," Mike answered. "I always like to be the center of attention. I heard you upstaged me, though."

"What do you mean?"

"Dad told me about you standing in the middle of the road and shooting biker after biker, so they couldn't get in."

Mark groaned. "Look, I just did what I had to, that's all," he said defensively.

"You don't have to get all huffy about it. I just wanted to tell you what a good job you did."

"Well, if I'd done a better job, you wouldn't be lying here. I'm sorry I sent you out there."

"I appreciate that, Bro, I really do, but it was my own stupidity that got me shot, not anything you did. Now, if you don't mind, let's change the subject."

The two brothers chatted for another fifteen or twenty minutes until Mike announced that he was tired and needed to rest. Mark went back home and spent the rest of the day with his children. The next morning, he returned to the ranch and the mind numbing work. Mark found out Chaparo hadn't been home in over a week. He sent the foreman for this monumental task home that night and told him not to come back for two days. Chaparo protested, but he filled Mark in on what needed to be done and went home with a smile.

Mark noticed that, even though the work was very hard, everyone worked tirelessly. He knew why the prisoners were working so hard, but he wondered why the Silver Hills residents were busting their humps day in and day out. As he checked on the workers to make sure they were staying hydrated, as Chaparo had told him to do, he realized that almost all of the volunteers were people who had moved in with family or friends and didn't have a place of their own. They were all probably hoping that one of the cabins would be theirs. Mark hadn't even considered how they'd have to find a fair way to divvy up the additional housing. There were sure to be more families who didn't have a place of their own than there were cabins. Just what we need, he thought, another problem to solve. He was confident, though, that they would find an equitable solution.

The days passed quickly, and on the third morning, Chaparo returned to find that everything had progressed in his absence. Mark was glad to have the big man back in charge, and he enjoyed a day of work where he was responsible for no one but himself. Friday evening, he returned home to find the election committee had still not announced the outcome. They were being very tight lipped about what was going on and would only say that they were doing a recount to make sure the results were accurate. Most everyone in the neighborhood took this to mean the voting had been very close. Some felt waiting for the outcome was worse than finding out the results, even if they weren't in Rob's favor. Mark couldn't help but be nervous, but he remained optimistic.

Why shouldn't he be optimistic, he wondered. Things had work out fairly well for them. Sure, they'd lost some good people, and some things hadn't gone their way, but compared to how things could be and how they were for many, Silver Hills was in great shape. Mark knew they had many challenges still in front of them, but he knew these people could pull together and do anything they set their minds to. The epiphany was invigorating, and Mark resolved to help meet those challenges head on.

Saturday morning, Mark woke up and looked at his calendar. It had been one hundred seventeen days since The Burst. The world had completely changed in less than four months. Mark still didn't know what had caused The Burst, but he found he was much less concerned with that than he'd been right after it happened. He found it strange that he no longer wanted things to go back to the way they were before it happened. He missed a lot of what civilization provided, but somehow he felt more alive now. It was hard for him to describe, even to himself.

He dressed and made his way to the kitchen and began preparing breakfast. Others began to drift in and help. After a while, Jess appeared, and Mark noticed she was beginning to show that she was pregnant. He kissed her and then bent over and kissed her belly, talking to the growing life inside her with baby talk.

Everyone laughed. Before long, they were sitting around the tables, eating breakfast. Halfway through the meal, Mark heard an unmistakable noise. It was the noisy, six-cylinder diesel of a Dodge truck. A moment later, Greg Hardy's truck pulled around to the back. Greg and Rob got out of the big truck along with Judge Hickman and another man Mark didn't recognize.

"Morning, everyone," Rob said with a big smile.

Mark noticed that all of the men were smiling. His heart leapt. Rob had won.

Greg walked over to the family and friends around the tables. "Everyone, this is Judge Hickman. Judge Hickman, this is Mark Turner and his family."

The judge extended his hand to Mark. "It's nice to meet you, Mr. Turner. It's nice to meet all of you," he said, as Mark shook his hand. "Mr. Turner, this is José Villanueva, the county's election supervisor."

The man reached out to shake Mark's hand. "It's nice to meet the Karate Man," Jose said with a grin. Mark was embarrassed a little but hoped it didn't show.

"Please, just call me Mark. It's nice to meet you both. So, the results are in, huh?" The four men nodded. "What took so long?" Mark asked, since he already knew who had won.

"We had to make sure the winner had at least fifty percent of the vote," José explained. "If he didn't, then there would have to be a runoff election between the top two vote getters."

"But there were only two candidates to begin with," Mark stated, confused at what he was being told.

"That's true, but we had a few write-ins on the ballots."

It made sense now. If the election was close to being split fifty-fifty, then just a few write-ins could cause neither candidate to secure a majority.

"But Rob just squeaked over the fifty percent mark, huh?"

"No, Mark," Rob replied, "I only got about twenty percent of the votes."

Mark's jaw dropped. Barney had won? How could that be? Rob and Greg were smiling like kids on Christmas morning. What could be going on, he wondered. "So, Barnes won?" he asked.

"No. Deputy Barnes came in second," Judge Hickman said.

"Then, then who won?" Mark stuttered.

"You did!" José answered.

Mark wasn't sure what he'd heard. It sounded like José had said he'd won the election, but that wasn't possible. Before he could ask for clarification, Jess did it for him.

"I'm sorry, what did you say?" she asked.

"The Karate Man is our new sheriff," Jose answered.

"How did that happen?" Jim asked, as Mark just stood slack jawed.

José seemed only too happy to tell the story. "We were counting the votes each day as they came in. The first day, the voting was split fairly evenly between Mr. Bowers and Deputy Barnes. We did have a few write-in votes for Mr. Turner that day, but not many. The second day, the number of write-ins increased. They were still only a fraction of the total votes, but the increase was quite noticeable. It seemed like people were talking quietly among themselves about who they were voting for, and more and more people were jumping on your bandwagon. The third day, almost half of the votes were for you, Mr. Turner. It was then I started to believe you might win the election. The next two days, most of the votes were for you, Mark. Then, I had to get Judge Hickman involved."

"Why'd ya have ta get the judge involved?" Gunny asked.

"I was just coming to that," José said. Mark, although still speechless, could tell the man was enjoying himself immensely. "You see, a few of the votes just said 'Karate Man' on them. Normally, we'd have put those in the pile with the Mickey Mouse and George Washington votes, but there were enough that, without them, you wouldn't have a majority. With them, you did. I had to get the judge to make a decision about whether we could count them or not."

Judge Hickman took over. "In normal times, I wouldn't have allowed them, but it was obvious for whom the people were voting, and I felt dragging out the election would do no one any good. I asked José to do a recount, just to make sure you had a majority with the 'Karate Man' votes. When you did, I decided to let them count. If we did a runoff, it was obvious to me that you'd win, as we'd have to put you on the ballot. Barnes has the option to file a lawsuit and force a runoff, but who knows how long that'll take. At least for now, you'll be the sheriff, and everyone won't be left hanging, so to speak."

Mark was flabbergasted. It was too much. Could he do it? There was no way he could fill Curt's shoes. A thousand other thoughts ran through his mind. He couldn't do it, he decided. He was just getting used to the idea that everyone saw him as the leader of Silver Hills. Now they wanted him to lead Wilson County? He needed to refuse. He wondered what would happen if he said no.

"What if I don't want to do it?" he mumbled.

"Then we have to throw out your votes, and Barnes will be the sheriff," Judge Hickman explained.

Mark couldn't let that happen.

"Mark, we know this is probably a big shock to you," Rob said.

'No, shit,' the Karate Man thought.

"You know you'll have all of our support," Greg added. "You can hire whomever you want to help you. We figured you might want to hire Rob as a deputy, and he said he'd be happy to help you. You can also fire whomever you want in the Sheriff's Office. If you don't do this Mark, we're all up a creek without a paddle."

Mark sat down and put his hands over his face. He'd just been thinking that he needed to face whatever came his way with a positive attitude, but he never expected something like this. He pulled his hands to the side of his face, as if he was playing peek-a-boo, and looked at the four men who'd brought the startling news.

"Will you do it?" the judge asked.

Mark simply nodded his head.

A thunderous cheer arose from everyone there. Jess put her arm around Mark and whispered in his ear.

"Can't you say anything?"

He wasn't sure. Only one word formed in his throat. It was the only one that could express the wide range of emotions he was feeling. As it began to travel up across his tongue, he realized it would cost him a dollar, but now that he had a job, he could afford it.

"Damn."

Epilogue

Mark Turner walked into the house.

"Dad, I have a letter for you," the young man called out.

"I'm in here, Marky."

Mark walked into the office. His father sat there, reading by the light of an oil lamp.

"Dad, why do you insist on reading by that old lantern?"

"Habit, I guess," the older man answered.

The younger man smiled. "Lights, on," he said to no one. Energized by the huge photovoltaic system that powered the whole house, the computer-controlled lights illuminated the room. "Isn't that better?"

"I guess," the old man said, as if he were tired of arguing about it. "Where's the letter?"

"Here," the young man said, as he handed it to his father, who might have been just old enough to be his grandfather.

It had an official looking Wilson County Courthouse return address, and the old man saw his name printed in the 'to' section. He fumbled with the envelope, and tore it open. His right arm wouldn't work like he wanted it to, and the frustration showed on his face. Finally, he removed the letter and clumsily unfolded it.

Wilson County Historical Society
Avenue C & 1st Street
Floresville, Texas
Republic of Texas

Mr. David Turner
811 Silver Coin Road
Silver Hills, Texas
Republic of Texas

Re: Dedication of Statue of Mark Allen Turner on April 11th.

Dear Mr. Turner,

As you know, the Historical Society has planned to erect a monument to your father on the Courthouse grounds for some time. What you don't know is that some time ago we commissioned a marble statue of your father's likeness. This work is now complete, and we would like to invite you and your brother, Timothy, to come and speak at the dedication on the 11th of next month. We will be happy to provide transportation if you need it. One of our representatives will be contacting you shortly to make all of the arrangements. We are expecting many dignitaries from the local area, and even a few high-ranking officials from Austin, to help us with the dedication. We look forward to seeing you again and want to thank you for helping us honor your father, a great Texan hero and a favorite son of Wilson County.

God bless,

Neil Villanueva
Chairman, Wilson County Historical Society

David folded the letter, and his hands shook a little more than usual.

"What does it say, Dad?"

He handed the letter to his son. Mark, named after his grandfather, quickly read the letter.

"Dad, Grandpa really was a hero, wasn't he?"

David placed his good hand on his son's shoulder and squeezed it. A small tear formed in his eye. "Yes, he was, son. He never believed it, but he was. I only wish you could have known him."

"Me, too," the young man agreed. He turned and walked out of the room. He knew his father didn't like to get emotional in front of others, and by leaving, he could spare the old man's pride.

David, glad that his son had left before he'd broken down, sat back down in his chair and reread the letter. 'My old man never would have believed this,' he thought. He picked up his book and started reading again. The glare of the white paper hurt his eyes. He looked up and saw that the florescent lights were still on. He really did prefer the soft, yellow flame from the kerosene lamp.

He spoke to the computer. "Lights, out."

Look for
Lost and Found
Coming soon from
David Crawford

...DJ hit the throttle on the big quad as his mind raced between wondering how the rednecks had found him and thinking "Oh Crap." He pushed his goggles up and turned on his headlight. It would have been impossible to stay on the bike at full speed on a bumpy road like this with the night vision goggles. As the bike passed sixty miles per hour, DJ looked behind him. The rednecks were still closing. He could see by their headlights that the potholes in the dirt road were making the truck bounce violently all over the road. However, the driver seemed to have little regard for the damage it might be causing his vehicle.

Even though DJ had the throttle lever pushed fully, he found himself putting more pressure on it. The quad was now starting to pull some air on the bigger bumps, and he could feel the trailer's weight acting as an anchor as it returned to the ground after each aerial event. This was an unsafe speed, he knew, but it was less dangerous than stopping.

He looked for a way out. The fences on each side were barbed wire. They would cut him to ribbons if he tried to drive through them. He could only try to outrun his pursuers. He wanted to look back, but at over seventy miles-per-hour, he had to keep his eyes forward. "Come on, baby. Give me just a little more," he urged his machine.

Find out more at
www.LightsOutTheBook.com

8472462R0

Made in the USA
Lexington, KY
07 February 2011